JAKE

('I'm thinkin'...')

---

* Novel - Preview Edition

978-0-578-00939-1
Fiction
© Neebeeshaabookway

JAKE

(*'I'm thinkin'...'*)

---

* Novel - Preview Edition

Gentle Jen, and...
the double J's that never strayed...

The Smith Ranch twins: Jake and Jade

THE JAKE SMITH RANCH SERIES

- Series of four novels, plus short-story-collections in on-going volumes -

by Neebeeshaabookway

4 - By Neebeeshaabookway - JAKE SMITH RANCH SERIES...

— IN HONOR OF FRIENDSHIP —

<u>DEDICATED TO HIDDEN HEROES</u>

~ AND TO ALL THOSE ~

THAT NAVIGATE THE "SEAS OF THE TALKING"

WITH A DIFFERENT TYPE OF PADDLE...

- AND -

<u>TO TORI IZAGUIRRE</u>

WHO HAD HER FIRST SEIZURE BEFORE SHE WAS ONE YEAR OLD

TO
ROBERT (BOB) FULLER

THE ONLY ACTOR THAT COULD EVER BE
ABLE TO PORTRAY JAKE AND DO HIM
HONOR AND JUSTICE!

THIS BOOK WOULD NOT EXIST IF IT HAD NOT BEEN FOR:

THE WRANGLER TWINS:
KIM & KARI BAKER:

MY BEST "PARDS"

THEY ENCOURAGED ME TO WRITE A STORY:

— **"Seems I never knew I had one... "** —

*plus, a grateful thanks to Barb Taylor!

6 - By Neebeeshaabookway - JAKE SMITH RANCH SERIES...

TABLE OF CONTENTS:

▍TABLE OF CONTENTS CONTINUED:

- GENERAL PRESENTATION -

The way that the JAKE RANCH SERIES shares is through fiction, first. Everyone loves a story, and this story does not pry into anyone's personal life while you learn gain insight. It has a fictional family to learn from—and one that demonstrates LOVE.

All head injuries and seizure cases are NOT ALIKE. This way the character of JAKE SMITH can still share the basic elements—thus—encouraging folks to seek-out further knowledge by their OWN study of head injuries and seizures (epilepsy), secondly.

Also, as all families do NOT SHARE or HANDLE SITUATIONS in the same way—thus—not all families will handle emotions, decisions, and any thing else concerning head injuries and seizures (epilepsy) the way everyone else would.

This novel-series takes you through a traumatic event in this fictional family's life and how it changed a man's way to function—as well as affecting his buddies and family and social life and outreach as to his job and who he was, WHILE, he <u>still</u> seeks to be who he has always been. Something that can not and may not, always turn out the way one wants, after a head injury, or, while living with seizures. And—in this case, tongue-loss and no speech. These are some of the complex hard trails that many folks around us in the world face everyday. Folks that YOU may know—folks that live or work with you.

These folks are not the "world's" heroes that everyone is looking to, for role-models, these days: the ones that must be perfect, first, in all their presentations to the world. No—these folks are those that tackle "hidden hardships" and most folks have no *idea* as to what kind of hard work is involved in their life. A hero-role not desired to be taken.

Yes, for <u>everyone,</u> life can be hard, and being some kind of a hero to one's family or friends is important to most folks—but "hidden heroes" work <u>twice</u> as hard and are usually never seen in the "spotlight" of literature, or TV , which more importantly, leads to <u>*who*</u> is respected and treated cordially in society, in daily conversations, and, to <u>*who*</u> is passed by as unimportant. <u>*Yet*</u>—they are EQUAL victors with every <u>*other*</u> daily hero.

The character (Jake Smith) is seeking new victory in his life, and his gang of buddies and family, are pressing-on to help him succeed with this. <u>They</u> are seeking victory as well, as they are in the battle with him. Someone <u>you</u> know, may be seeking victory as well— let's all lend good cheer whenever we can and wave each other to victory. Learning how others feel and what they have gone through, and what they face for the future, are just a few steps. Let this small fiction story encourage you to learn from real-life stories, now.

Have fun with my JAKE RANCH SERIES which is just now in the new steps of being fully printed and for sale—50%-100% will go to the LOVE INC for the food bank. In the FUTURE if the books sell enough, I HAD FIRST HOPES that money would go to summer camps for kids with head injuries or seizures—perhaps this may still happen. YET— there will still be fund kept for this local food bank first, for those having hard times.

God **bless, and**, treat your "hidden heroes" the SAME as you'd treat every other "hero" - **For more info on the JSRS, go to <u>neebee dream-catchers, web-site, and search.</u>**
*Model pictures, used with kind permission, by said models, for non-profit.

-AUTHOR NOTES-

* I have used various country songs mentioned to show how characters use music to face a situation in life that is too hard to handle, as music soothes the soul, and real folks do this in life, quite often. The song authors are given, as, parts of the verse are mentioned at these times when the character/characters "spouts-off" about how this-or-that song has touched them, or inspired them to do something. These are very well-known and will be obviously recognized. There is also the mention of "good ride cowboy, good ride" and "cowboy-up" and terms that are used commonly these days, in the western and rodeo scene. These are *not* mine, but are used colloquially in the cowboy scene, as well. If there is anything that I have accidentally overlooked in the area of a song, I will gladly acknowledge that, and fix it—as the purpose of this is to get folks to grab onto any readily available thoughts in life to use as inspiration to overcome trauma. There is also a page at the end of the book, listing the songs and the authors, even though these were isolated bits of text. Lastly, not all these songs are in these particular stories.

* Jake's sign language use is not intended to be in perfect ASL style, as he learned thought processes in the English language. This is how one family, in fiction, adopted the use of this wonderful and beautiful language, and try to use it in both ways to suit there unique needs. It is purposely put in a signed frame-set-up, to show the huge change that this man faces to communicate.

* The word mute is used in these stories on occasions, and being that a highly respected man who was truly mute (when without his voice box) had advised me that such a word was truly stating a fact in the use of it—in the case of this character's life—and he stated no wrong in its use, I use it with a clean heart, as I dearly value his work. The words retarded, blind, deaf, Deaf, and "spells", are used according to this advice to me, as well.

* This whole JAKE SMITH RANCH SERIES comes in both small novel form, and it also comes in larger story-book size, and pocketbook-size. And, a story-book size called: The "Series Collector's Edition"—done in an extra fancy partial-color format.

* This whole JAKE SMITH RANCH SERIES, and "INTRODUCING..." is meant to be used for fundraising for those that are sorely in need, due to brain injuries, seizures, tongue loss, or speech loss. If these stories can be of any use to a legitimate fund, for disabled children's camps, or food for Native American children, please let me know.

* **Do you know what to do if you witness a seizure**, whether a complex partial, or grand mal (tonic clonic)? If not, go to: neebee dream-catchers and download a free flyer for your personal use, or call any epilepsy foundation (also found online). There are many different kinds of seizures—Jake's is only ONE example. He was allowed to wean off medication—do not choose to do this yourself, as he is *not* fully seizure-free. This is a FICTION example of one family's choice—this is a hard choice to live by.

* **Thank you for purchasing this book**, it was done on a very limited budget, as a steppingstone for a far-reaching dream to share inspirations for overcoming. There <u>may</u> be some type-errors, not <u>yet</u> caught. God bless, Neebeeshaabookway, (Lizzy Gonzalez).

JAKE

(*'I'm thinkin'...'*)

The Smith Ranch twins: Jake and Jade

12 - By Neebeeshaabookway - JAKE SMITH RANCH SERIES...

CHAPTER ONE

LOOKING BACK, HE FACED THE DAY

HE was home now and oddly—it felt the same—just the same. With all the familiar sights and smells, and the solid, rough wooden walls, all making their own potpourri and meshing into the air, *just* for his benefit. The smell of the old woolen blanket on the bed that he had grown accustomed to all these years, greeted him this morning, as it hugged close to his body, over the sheets. The smell of the leather strips laid out on the shelves, the ones from which he had made belts with many-a-time in the evenings, was richly bathing the room, now as well—and to top it all off with, there was the fresh breeze that came in through the partially open window. Well, it may be tainted a bit with *horse smell* occasionally, but it was fresh *outdoor air* and that's what mattered to him now, hospital air was down-right awful.

He was finally free and back on his ranch, his own place, where he was the boss-man. This was *his* room that he was in now. This was his own special place to come and relax or think, just like when he was a kid. Most truly though, it was his bedding-down place. He had already used it to bed-down late last night after his sister brought him home. He loved her dearly, but the ride home had been in silence, and *not* by his choice. It haunted him now—in ways far beyond his comprehension.

~*~

It was dark and quiet, heavily so, as he rode home in the truck with his sister. He had looked out into the dark and watched the moon; it was off to the side, hanging as a bright, white, sliver in the sky. He had seen such a view countless times and in countless forms and ways, from driving the rodeo circuit that was so-engraved, deep-and-rich (though not always pocket-rich) in his life. Somehow it made him feel good as he watched it dogging them, and felt the easy long-familiar rhythm of the truck on the highway, trying its best to soothe him. But he was at a loss to explain to himself the feeling that had overpowered him when they hit the bumpy old off-shoot road and were finally on the homestretch to their ranch. He knew each bump well, and in the past had loved every minute of it. This feeling of the homestretch and how it would be such a comfort to be home, always added to the pleasure. These feelings that overpowered him now, did not seem to match this time, not in any way.

He had dared to venture a few meek looks at his sister occasionally, along with a slight smile—but that was it. Once they had hit their road though, he lay his head back and lay still as his body remembered all the familiar bumps—alone and in silence. It was so long ago since he had traveled it. It all felt—just the same. Just the same as he had remembered thus-far, just the same as he had once enjoyed. Somehow though, the usual contentment and joy didn't seem to be there this time. It worried him. It worried him to high heaven.

They had finished the ride home together as they had done many times, but this time the silence came between them and hung with a haunt about them, even though it was joined with the usual old slamming of the truck door, and the soft evening air nestled around them—and the same tender hugs. Ending with a pat on the shoulders, they parted for the night in silence.

~*~

As he lay in the bed now, his mind picked up a *scent* and began to wander with it. He looked back—back to some special talking they had about four months ago, just a few days *before*—well—before. He quickly canceled the thoughts as he began to dwell on the "before" and all it entailed. It all led up to something he didn't like, something that had engulfed him and pulled him in, despite his being near-ready for it. Looks like he wasn't as ready as he thought, as when it happened, it was more *on the sly* than he ever could have suspected. A slyness, that exposed itself with terrible power. Never in his wildest thoughts would he have ever expected that it would *end up* this way. Never in his wildest thoughts could he have ever expected that *he* would end up this way.

He took a deep sigh as he lay on the bed pushing away these thoughts, as he pushed his head back into his own pillow and rolled it from side-to-side a bit. *Sure feels good,* he thought, *yep, sure does*, he agreed with himself. The pillow, such a simple thing as it was, was perfectly capable to subject his mind to much more pleasant thoughts than he had been aiming at just a few seconds ago.

Stretched out on the bed, as he now moved to do so, he looked at the ceiling and then towards the window as the sun of the early morning began to stream in, along with another noise that spoke of—sameness.

'Now that's what I do need to hear, I purely do. I missed that ol' rooster near about as much as I missed this ol' bed.' As this beam of morning light now zeroed-in on him, he turned over a bit on the bed to avoid eye contact, as its powerful light filled the room as a streak with sharp edges. He watched the dust particles in the air as the sunlight hit them. The dancing angels, as he always referred to them, had appeared now, with their same dance that he had seen many times for many-a-year—just as to be expected, they were still the same.

Yeah, he thought, *angels.* This was his first morning to wake up here, in his bed, in his home, after quite a long spell. The day was starting late for him actually, so this was now turning into his thinking time. Perhaps even his praying time, as he dwelled on the angels dancing; it sure seemed like a good idea after all he'd come through. *Yep, real angels must have been watching over me, as I was so dad-gummed stupid. More like the good Lord Himself was watching over me, that's for sure. Yeah... yeah... but I never knew. Lookin' back... lookin' back, I-*

He stopped-short and thought on these words, "looking back", and then came to a halt of his *own* choosing. He pushed his head back into the pillow as he stretched out again, it sure felt good, real good. This was all that he really *wanted* to know right now and that's all that mattered, at least maybe for a few *minutes* or so.

He now began to get pulled back into the sameness of it all again, and yielded to it—thanks to his pillow. His routine here on the ranch always started out this way, always leading to another kind of sameness that was never dull or boring, except maybe to city folk.

Yep, after all these month, it's still the same, he acknowledged the fact, pure and simple. *With a pillow this good, a man shouldn't have a care in the world. What the heck am I doing lookin' back for? What good will it do me, it sure ain't gonna' change anything.*

~*~

He hadn't dared to look back yet, not even once through all that time—he took one day at a time in the hospital, as that was all he could manage. All he could do was look forward and get himself through the whole awful unbelievable mess. It seemed so hard to believe then, but for *different* reasons. Now that it was over, it seemed *even harder* to believe.

He didn't even think of a goal the whole time he was hospitalized, as it seemed to keep evading him. The foggy finish line never seemed to manifest clearly in his mind, the goal of going home wasn't real, but drifting in-and-out of the hospital room was. And when he began to near this goal, it turned out that it was only the *heat* for a nightmare race he wanted out of but was now forced to finish—it had come as his unwanted prize, from finishing the *heat.*

He did finally cross that finish line as it arrived one day, but he was just too numb to know whether it felt good or not. One thing he did know, he was as a horse like-to-bolt, and bolt he did, leaving the hospital in the dust of fast hoof beats, hopefully with no looking back. Well, his bolting needed a lot of his sister's help and quite a lot of it at that, as it came in many ways.

Looking back, he had to do though, because *although* everything *felt* just the same, he was *not* the same and he knew it. He was healed and soon would be able to reach his normal physical strength again—with only a few traces of the damage still to be noticed—if he worked for it. If he worked at it in *some ways,* that is, as he was not the same in some regards, and in *these* regards, he would never heal. To look at him none would know, but to move on with his life, all would know.

~*~

He continued there in the stillness, with only a few early morning sing-songs from the field-birds to go with the feisty-fowls, he did some heavy thinking on the word—SAME. There was one thing he knew was *matching-up* to some sameness. The *thoughts* of his mind. They were just the *same* as this *quiet room* that spoke volumes with its unique presence. So full of the richness of a lifetime thus-far lived, for those that would care to stop and listen in a studying sort of way—seeing as it was—that the room had no other way to speak.

A knock on the door out in the kitchen, told him his sister had come for coffee. It was their morning fun, their family breakfast meeting—kind of like playing house, as their folks were long since gone. She had her *own* half of the house just *recently* now, so to speak, as it was linked-on to "his" main house here (where his buddies also stayed) but she always chose the kitchen door to come calling. This—however—*never* felt the same.

She was near ready to marry up—before—but that was over now. He didn't know that, until just about a week ago. The relief in his heart was a hearty welcome at this point in time. Seems they had enough grief lately to muddy-up the back pasture and turn to pig-slopping it. He and his sis seemed to miss the train when it came to courting, or, the right ones were just on some other track. He had a few gals he had *hope* for in the past, but they seemed to take a wrong turn somewhere, and he knew they were not for him. *Something sure seemed wrong about a gal that couldn't love a horse as dear as a friend. Especially, the last gal that had been hangin' around here a ways back... the air sure cleared, dust and all, after I set her straight,* he remembered, but oddly, he couldn't seem to place her name, or who she really *was* toward him—not just yet anyway.

The next knock on the door jolted him back to the fact that his sis was still waiting, but he didn't worry past the knowledge of it. His usual "I'm comin'" was not to be hitting the morning air, and well they both knew. If he didn't open fast enough for her, he knew she would be letting herself in. Their knocking ritual was just for politeness sake. It was time for him to get moving-on to the new day anyway, so this was a good nudge. He stood-up from the bed and its binding covers and stopped his looking back. He stood with a good stretch as the blankets fell off. *Yeah... I slept in my clothes,* he thought, *just like I near-abouts always do if my mind's full-up. And well... after all... it sure was a late, long ride and all. Was near about 2:30 this mornin' when we pulled-up here... leavin' four months and the hospital, behind us.*

With this last thought, he proceeded to approach the door and stopped to grab-up his boots, they sure felt good to the touch. As he neared the half-open door, he could see his sis in the kitchen starting coffee. He was near afraid to go out and face her.

What the heck is wrong with me... she's my sis... if there's anyone in the world that I ain't got to be afraid of now, it's her, he turned with just a bit of a twist and looked back with one last glance of the familiar room. His room of comfort and peace, and now a needed place of solitude—his rein was now loosely slipping free of it.

The sun had now flooded the room and the dancing angels were long-since-gone. After looking back, he faced the day. Well, near abouts, as he first found himself face-to-face with that half-open door and a good bump was now manifesting on the side of his head. A bit shocked, he mocked, '*guess I didn't plan THAT to good, now DID I.*'

He pushed the door a bit out of the way and checked his image in the mirror that hung on it. He always liked that *rugged* wooden frame that the mirror was set into, and had used its reflecting wisdom many a time to push back his hair, as it fell in his face having no mercy on him after he first got up. His thoughts answered back from his reflection's telltale-presentation.

Wavy hair, he thought, *just like a saddle that won't set right, never keeps its place... but it's mine and I like it... hmmm, looks like its turnin' gray a bit.*

As he continued to peer carefully at the image in the mirror, the gray hairs were now the least of his worries, but still, he was for the most-part satisfied. And except for the expected scars: one over his left eye, and a few others down the left side of his face, along his jaw, upper neck and under his chin—scars that he had learned quickly to accept, and was now getting used to—why, he looked down-right fine! Well, all except for the fresh bump on his head, that is. *This sure ain't no way to start my first day home... neither is lookin' back I suppose... best I face it straight-up,* he thought.

Boots in hand, Jake stepped out the bedroom door to *face* his sister and the fresh-made coffee, as well as, the man that he now *was*—or—at least he *hoped* he could. If truth be known, facing the fresh-made coffee was the only thing he felt up to handling, and even *that* was not going to be fun—or easy.

CHAPTER TWO

'*I'VE HAD BETTER MORNINGS AFTER A HANG-OVER*'

THERE she was, smiling. *Smiling, of all things, well what did you expect,* Jake acknowledged and accepted. He looked at her, as she continued smiling, and then shrugging his shoulders a bit, he made a slight face at her and finally smiled in return. He didn't really know what else to do. He approached the table and dropped the boots with a thud near the woodburning stove that was against the wall near his chair, and passed her by. He headed for the coffee as she started to watch him, but she quickly turned away. He expected she'd be watching him, but she wasn't. As he reached the coffee and poured it, he noticed out of habit that he had poured it too full. He felt himself breathing a bit heavy now, his face had a distinct look of disdain on it as he stared at the cup. He sure didn't feel like taking a bath in it, so after fast consideration he poured some down the sink. He wondered if she was watching him, usually she'd be offering cream and sugar by now, same as she'd done for years. It was just part of the fun. He glanced at her finally, as he had to know, and was struck with sorrow as he saw her head was down. Her long dark brown hair was nearly covering her face and her left hand was near the top of her forehead while she leaned over on her other forearm. When he *saw*—he *knew*—and it hit him hard.

I knew it... I knew it... SHE CAN'T HANDLE THIS... and she never let on. She almost had me fooled, he set the half-poured coffee down in haste and ran over to her and lifted her face tenderly. There were the tears, they came slowly, but they were now strongly there. He was right, he was so very right. *Why do I have to be so DAMN RIGHT all the time,* he thought in disgust. *Why, she always said she learned how to handle the rough stuff by watchin' me. Me, the rough tough cowboy, the dirty ol' tough wrangler. She said this would work out for good somehow NO MATTER HOW LONG it has to take, and that she was doing just fine. She said it could have been worse and that her joy now, was just lookin' at me and knowin' each day that I'm alive and not buried out over yonder on the hills out of town, out of sight and out of mind. Where's her joy now?*

He wanted to tell her something—anything—but he couldn't. He let the tears well-up in his own eyes now. Not for himself, no, it surely wasn't. He hadn't thought to cry for himself, though at times with the pain of those past months, he was near tempted to. He had never thought to cry for himself now, either, as to his new way of life—which he had admitted to himself, he sure wasn't fond of. But he was near to cry now—for her.

As he reached-up to his head and rubbed his brow, he was aware that he was sure getting an awful headache, and he shook his head slowly in disgust. He walked over to his bedroom door and leaned against it, and stared down at the floor around the area of the woodburning stove. Maybe he should have stayed in bed and tried some more praying. Seems like this praying-stuff his sis always told him about, was just near to kick-in a few times—during those near-to-sun-up hours just a bit ago, when he had tossed-and-turned trying to chase away his unwanted thoughts. Maybe it would have helped her now, maybe it would have given her some fired-up power of some kind, but it was too late to know.

He walked over to her and slowly lifted her head once more with care and looked into her face as he brushed her hair away. Somehow it struck him a bit funny, the two of them leaking saltwater and all, and the day hadn't even started yet. If this were the case, how would they ever get through this day in one piece? Neither one of them had cried since their pa died. They handled everything together with their face set to mark-out a good trail and not complain until they reached the end—come what may.

As he thought on the past and how they worked so hard to be strong, he made a soft laugh as he felt the tears roll down his own face. He wiped one with his hand and wiped it onto her nose, and he smiled at her. She was so relieved to see some positive emotion from him finally after so long, that she smiled a bit and then laughed as well. She knew what he was thinking, and she stopped him as he tried to think of a way to tell her. She put her hand up, as if to stop a small child, and shook her head. She took his hand and held it for just a minute. He nodded his head a bit, in acknowledgement and smiled at her. Yep—come what may, had snuck up on them—it was *trail-marking* time.

"Go get your coffee, Jet." She said firmly. "I'm fine. Remember... I learned from the best. No, not Pa... from you... and you know it! Best, always comes *after* the good stuff, as the son comes after the father... you're to be the best. Remember?" She looked up at him with her face resting in her palms with her elbows resting on the table, as she sent him on his way.

She took a sip of her coffee and watched him proceed to bring *his* coffee over as he came to sit in his chair. He looked at her, while he handed her a napkin from the table to wipe her face. She took a deep sigh and watched him fix his coffee up just the way he liked it.

"Do you realize how many years we've been doing this?" she mentioned in passing, as she looked out the kitchen window at the light of the day.

The sun hadn't come around to the front yet, but it was still a spectacular view through the front window. There were birds in the bird feeder. They seemed to own the front yard. She stared and soaked this in. No horses were out in the yard to try their luck at it, as yet. It was much too early for them to roam the front yard. This was their pasture time.

"Sure is a wonderful day for your homecoming," she said and continued with, "do you want eggs and toast? I'll smash up the toast for you, you could at least try it."

Jake nodded slightly. She knew he was deep in thought and wondered where this odd morning visit was finally going to lead to. She was almost as afraid as he had been before he stepped through the door, but she wasn't going to admit it. She was determined to see this first morning through for his sake, then, hers.

~*~

He was always there for her, as she was for him. In fact, he had been the hero for her and because he was a hero kind-of-a-guy, his whole life had now changed. She knew not to feel guilty, because it was not her fault, but it had still involved her, and she couldn't forget. The truth had unfolded into a sorry situation and Jake happened to be there at that time. The right time for her, when she screamed for help—but more importantly, the right time for Stoney, as he was in grave danger. Sometimes the right time for some may appear to be the wrong time for others—sadly it was the wrong time for Jake. He wouldn't have had it any other way though and she knew it—well that is, except maybe for *one* thing. One very *stupid* thing. He sure wished he hadn't been drinking and she knew *that* without being told.

The fact is, he rarely ever drank—it was a special occasion thing— and certainly not like he had been doing *that* day. He hadn't even set-out to drink that much the day *before* that day, but he did so none the less, he was only seeking to be alone with some heavy thoughts. He honestly thought he was alone and was drowning his sorrows as to some cold hard facts he had learned about his sister's fiancé. He just couldn't tell her and was seeking a way to find it. Little did she know that Jake had run her fiancé off earlier— to this day she still didn't know, because Jake had not yet been able to tell her. He was in no shape to handle the trouble that had appeared unexpectedly that day. If she had known that, she never would have allowed him to help after he emerged from the barn. They both understood that. But then Stoney would have been dead. They both understood that, as the witness of their souls held firm and honorably to this truth. They both understood that neither of them would have let Stoney die.

~*~

"I'll make some eggs then, and the toast too, right, Jet?"

He nodded again as she stood up and walked past the counter with the coffeepot, and made an abrupt turn to the left (past his door)to face the kitchen stove, it was used more often than the woodburning stove, so breakfast would be fast-in-coming.

~*~

She always called him Jet, just as their ma and pa had learned to do and had done so, as well. It was because of his *jet-black* hair. His name was Jake, but she picked-up on the *hair-phrase* that her pa always spoke of, she called him Jet. She was just a toddler when she chose to do this, but the family soon caught-on as to whom she was always referring to. The nickname had been allowed to take hold into good firm family ground and it took-root and flourished. It was Jet this, and Jet that, in fact Jet was everything to her. If the folks wanted to call him Jake, that was *mighty fine* for them, but if they wanted *any* response out of her, as to fetch him—well, that was a whole other matter. So, in this house, it was Jet. Her name was Jade, as for the jewel stone. They were twins and since she followed him everywhere, their ma teased that Jet was the piece of hardy coal that dusted-up Jade's shine and kept her from being a polished-up shiny-fine gal. The double J's they were, always together, never straying apart no matter *wherever* their little feet sought to wander.

Soon after that, their pa changed the name of the Smith Ranch to the "The Twin J's That Never Stray". 'Try branding THAT on a cow, now... bet you'll pick *ours* out during grazing, right-fast... and without a *spyglass*, to boot!' he was always heard to say—and it was always joined with a Texas-Montana grin that would warm one's heart. Soon after *that* idea though, he had to add, 'course... on second thought, for the cow's sake... best keep it simple,' and with a laugh and some added changes, the SMITH RANCH JJ-NS emerged. 'This will have to do it!' was his final say, followed by a family tradition—a foot-stomp (and—his personal hand-clap, to seal even that). Thus it was, Double J's (Jake & Jade) Never Stray—JJ-NS.

It appeared on the rugged wooded sign that hung over at the far end of the driveway, and also on a plaque over the fireplace, and obviously on their livestock. It was drawn with the *second* J hanging onto the middle of the *first* J, and then a bar, followed by the N, followed by the S beside it—but a bit lower-in which the S's lower-half portrayed a stray-away that had not left. It was to become a *seal* of a living promise.

~*~

Well now, the most natural thing for Jade to do was talk, she loved talking, same with Jake. As she cooked, she went on to tell Jake of the things that had happened at the ranch while he was gone. He sipped at his coffee trying to swallow it as best he could and listened vaguely as she began to relax and ramble easily along with how the neighbors up the road had helped out and all. A few times, though, she stopped and threw in: "well, what do you think, Jet, wasn't that mighty fine?" And these lingered in the air and fell with a dull thud. The thuds were beginning to add up and he didn't like it none.

After about three or four times of this, Jake couldn't take it any more—he couldn't take trying to drink his coffee any more either and slammed the coffee cup down and pushed it across the table. It slid off the opposite edge with a crash, shattering as it hit the floor. With a deep gasp of shock, Jade jumped, dropping the near half-dished-up breakfast *half* over the counter and *half* over the floor. Just as quickly, she turned with one motion to stare in great concern at her brother, quite fully.

He sat there at the table leaning on one forearm, and leaning on the other elbow, while rubbing his hand up-and-down on the spot between his eyes and his forehead. She was afraid to move for a minute and didn't know what to say. She realized it was her questions and the natural response of waiting for an answer that had upset him. Now, she wasn't sure what to do.

Jake's head was aching now. It wasn't from his injuries so many months back, it was from pure frustration, but then because of his injury, frustration seemed to be a side effect, in more ways than one. One injury had now truly made him susceptible to both, as he normally wasn't prone to frustration or headaches. But the other one had made him prone to a more devastating kind of frustration—both were making a powerful impact on his life now—an impact that he was powerless to stop. He had been warned to watch out for headaches if they came too often, or were too severe, no one had yet warned him not to be frustrated. If they had, how was he to stop?

'*Is this how it's going to be from now on? I'm near enough to go nuts now, as it is. Damn it,*' he looked up at her with his jaw clenched tight and breathing heavy. He was feeling helpless. He hated it. It was building up

© 23

too heavy, and he had to open-up and confess it to her somehow, and to himself. The coffee cup sailing into space just seemed to do it for him. He wanted to say he was sorry and he couldn't. He looked over at her, opened his mouth just a bit with a show of concern on his wrinkling brow, cocked his head slightly and tried to form an, *I'm sorry,* and then force it to come out. He shook his head slightly in despair; it had not come. All that came out was some odd sounds—sounds that belonged to *someone else,* someone he heard in the hospital—someone he hadn't heard again, *until now.*

He shut his mouth and bit down, still breathing heavy, as this *sincere sound* of a *longed* for and heart felt, *I'm sorry,* hung in the air, indistinguishable though it was. Jake made a sign for "finished" with a heavy gesture and stood up pushing the chair back with his body as he stood. This *new* sound now hung in the air and was soon followed by his boots, and the echoing slam of the back door just opposite that beautiful front view through the window that Jade has recently commented on. She now stared at the empty hook where his hat had been grabbed up from, the black Stetson was head-warming, instead of hook-warming—it starkly spoke volumes to her. He wouldn't be back soon. As she stood there, her gaze seemed to follow him past the slammed door. He was aware that it was too, as his behavior was uncalled for, but now he was more aware of his *own* thoughts that were trailing along with him.

'I've had better mornings after a hang-over!' he thought into the fresh air of the new day, as he headed for the nearby low-lying hills, off to the left, at the back edge of their ranchland, past the pasture—just along the north, to northwest ridge.

CHAPTER THREE

SOUR APPLES, RED APPLES

$JADE$ was near ready to go out the door and follow him. She knew her brother well—like the back of her hand when it wasn't covered with dirt. Now, when it *was* covered with dirt, that would about explain how *well* she knew him when he was trying to handle being a man. But when he was just her brother, well *hey now*, the back of her hand was *still* her road map, but this was a cleaner hand, and much easier to read. She knew he wouldn't be up *to wanting* her to follow, *but* she also knew he would *be hoping* that she would just the same. They both knew clear-as-a-bright-day, that they would work the issue out once they were face to face. She had no idea what she would say or do once she found him, but by the grace of God she would trust for it and it would come into play. She was stopped just now, by the honking of a truck or car horn, coming from the driveway, just when she finally dared to make her move. Window-viewing had fast-stolen her twin-priority in a usurping way:

Dad-gum! We surely don't need THIS now, Jade started to dig through her mind, I *told everyone to stay away for awhile, to let Jet get used to himself and his new ways. Now who could that be? We sure don't need no help... for now.*

~*~

She knew the heaviest work had been caught-up-on and she knew she could handle most anything else for at least two weeks or so. Even if things didn't improve, they could both go the long haul, just as they had done way back before Matt and Stoney came on and stayed for keeps. Jake was not yet strong enough to do much of anything as he had been laid-up so long, but he was advised he could get back to what he was doing, just warned to start in easy and that was enough for him. Therapy had done wonders for him and all were amazed at how well his body had responded. His left arm was still a bit lame for now, and he had a crooked stride in his left leg that would not be going away. Some times it seemed to be causing him discomfort, as to how much, he sure wasn't about to say, but she saw his face on a few occasions and that was enough to fill her in. With time, he'd be having near to full strength with his arm, if he worked at it—but even so, the leg, due to the severely ripped-up damaged muscle, wouldn't ever quite be the same.

She was the *spy* for his well-being concerning any pushing that he might try too soon. Any pain that may show on his face, she would definitely be keeping track of. She was also the spy, as to other things— things he didn't want to think about. She was to keep an eye on him, backed up with the doctor's orders. If he seemed to take to ailing, from pushing himself too hard or too fast, she was to put a stop to it. She was also told to watch him in a more serious way. This was as to how he was reacting in regards to whether he would choose to adjust to the "fix" he was in—as she called it. This was because if he didn't choose to adjust, she was warned, it could very well affect his future health; she didn't like the ominous way they stated it, either.

Yep, Jade knew Jake. They were a team, very special partners in God's scheme of things in this adventure they shared in life. She knew what to expect from him and how to detour the man in decisions, and as to his injuries, if need be. She had done the same with her pa many a time, after his injuries during his rodeo days. She would like to say she was the "best", but as best usually comes after good, her grandma was good, so Ma was the "best." 'Sure don't know WHAT that makes me... ', Jade always then said—thinking in turn, *but whatever it is, I'll be it, to the utmost!*

~*~

As Jade eyed the truck, she thought, *looks like I got some sharp-shootin' to do.* "Guess I will have to give it my best shot," she spoke-out encouraging herself, as she went to see who had knocked over the *pots and pans* of their expected homecoming-clean-up, which was supposed to be brought to a well-dusted and spruced-up beginning—alone!

She saw a familiar face in the truck outside, and sadly she wondered why this particular face had to pick today to show up.

~*~

It was an old school friend of Jake's that he used to feel close to in their teens. As the girl grew into womanhood Jake lost track of her, as she rarely came back into town, seems she was busy coming-and-going and checking-out the city life seeking a "run-way" career—a far-cry from running a horse ranch. She had come around again just a little more that a year ago, during the 1998 into 1999 New Year, boasting of her successful-enough modeling career. Jake had been still a bit smitten, so when she came back trying to weave into his life, he was quite happy to go along it and get sewed-in again. Trouble was, she had changed. Trouble was, he had realized it too late. Trouble was—she was trouble. She was then working her best and her worse, to change his whole way of life to meld into hers, and he would have none of it. She didn't believe it, and she set-her-face to catch him and reel him in, as a fish on a line, whether he was biting anymore or not. By the time he finally found out what she was up to, and let her know, she didn't take to it much—she had built a whole life for their future in everyone's ears, but his. He had to send her off the hard way, as she just wouldn't let loose of the line. So the day came for a showdown, when he snapped the line hard, in front of her friends, at the SADDLE AND SEED. He left her to owe-up to her own lies, hook stuck in her ego, and fish heading for open waters. Jake sure did love those open waters.

SADDLE AND SEED, was a nice little shop that nearly all the locals had hung-out at when they were kids. Well, it was no kid's game that was played out there that day—that's for sure. But she was just a bit too snooty now, with her city ways, and for some reason she just needed to over-play them in front of the whole town. For the most part, though, everyone in town still took to her, they just couldn't understand how the town "darling" had gotten so mixed-up as to her priorities, but she was one of their little chicks trying to come back home, so they gave her their best.

Jake had tried to be patient and really tried to understand her—opened his heart as far-and-wide as Jake was known to do. As she began to do her weaving though, it became apparent that she had a special pattern, a terrible flawed pattern that appeared each time his friends were around. Not just his local in-town friends, but in dealing with his true and closest buddies, Matt and Stoney.

This was the danger sign that finally marked the cut-off from that trail, as far as he was concerned—the point where her behavior touched his friends' lives. The sights of her trail may have been decorated with some special blooms and sweet smells along the way in the past, but he sure as heck didn't care to see anymore of it now. No matter what promises the lay-of-the-land may lead to, it definitely was not to his liking anymore. He plain and simple didn't care for how she treated his friends, and more recently, that *included* how he himself was treated—so that was the end of it all. He let her know quite *emphatically* too. She received it quite *emphatically* at that, and let everyone *know* it. Had he known that she had this streak in her, he never would have started hanging-out with her in the first place—but he did. And 'now I don't,' he had finally related to Jade, during a night of revelation, back in June 1999. 'Well, how's a man supposed to learn, if he don't study-up,' was his reply to his twin at the time. Jade was sure glad he got an "A+" in learning that the *course* he was studying was *sour apples* and that he gave it up right-fast.

~*~

Well... took him six months, Jade reflected, as she watched the gal pull up and park. *'But on the whole... as to learning from one harvest of sour apples, you do need at least ONE SEASON for the full effect of the crop to be known... good ol' Jet though, at least he recognized by MID SEASON that they weren't settin' in right.*

Jade made a frown, as she now studied her up-close from the front porch while giving the front door a hard pull behind her, *wonder what Miss sour-apples wants snooping around here? Her brother said she's been back east all year with her new boyfriend, so's we needed not to worry about her showing-up here. Thank you dear sweet Lord above,* she sighed, *that my Jet ain't out trying to ease into the ranch just yet. Why, he would have run smack DAB into her, most likely. Why, she ain't set foot here in town since he set her straight at the SADDLE AND SEED shop, and I best be aimin' to do so, too, I reckon.* She stepped up to the drive—near enough to suit her needs:

"I heard-tell you were back east with your new boyfriend this past year, Missy Angie. Sure didn't expect to see you in these-here parts... thought you were long-gone and back to your so called *photo-shoots...*" Jade half rolled her eyes at the notion, and near challenged her, "so... what can I do for you?" She noticed Angie had company in the truck and eagle-eyed the gal beside her.

"Well, when I got back to my East Coast friends, turned-out they had been waiting to *set* me up with Alex. Now, *actually,* Alex was my *true* and *first* desire, no offense to Jake and all. So you see... you heard-tell quite rightly, now *didn't* you, Jade... " she smirked and laughed as she leaned forward happily preening, as she answered her.

Angie continued-on with a bit of a soft sigh, "So how about *that* Jade? Am I *good,* or what? They were always telling me what a catch Alex was, so now I got him. I've been meeting all his family while I caught-up on my career's new enhancement courses... I'm planning on instructing my *own* group of models someday, but we decided to put a stop to the classes for now." She tossed her head back some and showed-off her brand of nobleness for the gal in the truck, but foremost for Jade, "See... I just heard two days ago about Jake's accident so I decided to have Alex bring me back home for a bit. Didn't want the whole town to think I didn't care to offer any help to you all… since our parents were such close friends and all. Besides, it's about time my best guy meets *my* family and friends as well," she powerfully paused, "sure don't know *why* my brother never told me. I was shocked completely to learn that he had gone out of town to help you get ready to bring Jake home from the hospital. Don't know *what* shocked me more, the fact that Jake was in the hospital, or the fact that NO ONE cared to tell me."

She eyed Jade, as she hoped to find some clue as to how Jade was receiving her, "Ray sure had plenty of time to tell me… three-and-a-half months in the hospital, and two weeks in-and-out for therapy, sure was plenty of time all right. Heard all this from the sheriff's office when I got no answer at my brother's home all last week. Four *months* went by and none of you called me. You wouldn't happen to know *why*, now *would* you?"

Angie smiled ominously and shook her black hair back, and ran her fingers through the front layers of its flip as she let her other arm and keys hang out the window a bit. Nobleness had slid-on-off her, like water off a duck's back, sure as ducks love spring waters. The way she jingled her keys now, she was getting rid of every drop of it—Jade was well aware that Angie was rattling the cage. The cage she always seemed to delight in throwing over those that she chose to make sport with.

"So now," Jade presented, as she defied the cage—and the key-jingler, "if you heard-tell all this *just two days ago*, you must have *just* made it into town, you should be mighty wore-out just about now. Don't you need to be getting back and resting-up some? I know *I SURE DO*, as I've been out of town *as well*, you know… not to mention my brother's health. He could do with some resting-up. We sure don't need callers. Didn't your brother tell you that?" Jade noticed the keys stopped jingling and they were quickly shut into her fist with a tight clench. Fun time was obviously over for Angie.

"Ray doesn't know we flew in, only Sheriff Lowrie does. We tended on surprising him, so don't you go and spoil it none. I was just trying to see if you needed some help, is all." She snapped, and quite forcefully.

The gal in the truck was feeling a bit out of place, and tried to apologize, as Angie shushed her. Jade gave her an understanding smile.

"This gal here, Honor, she's a friend of Ray's she's part of the surprise for him. I just happened to pick her up at the drug store. She got in a few days ago as well; she's here to work with kids this summer at our… well… at my brother's ranch. Looks like Alex and I will be taking her out there with us, soon as we check out of the hotel. Soon as I get hold of Ray myself… he sure has been hard to track down."

Angie turned to Honor, patting her on the knee, and said in her sweetest voice, "see, she ain't mad at us," and turned back to Jade. "Since he wasn't home all week and the workers don't tend to answer the phone, she's been holed up in the hotel. It was purely by *accident* that I ran into her, as I needed some magazines... you know... for my classes and all... looks like now, it was meant to be, huh?"

Angie smirked as she went on, "We talked and seems she's in the market for a good horse. Well, I know Jake and his horses... now, with all them hospital bills and all, I was thinking to do you a good turn." Angie looked around the yard as if scouting for any sign of Jake, and Jade began to feel uneasy.

Angie now started to pry a bit more at Jade's seams to see what would unravel. "After what happened, do you think he'll still be working with the horses again? I heard it had something to do with a *crazy bull*, or was it a *crazy horse* from ol' Griff's place? What would Jake be doing with a *crazy bull* like that around here *anyways*, I thought he was a horseman. Must have been a horse then... right? I never liked them nasty snorting beast. I also heard some odd gossip going on as well, nothing *back-handed* now naturally... but heard-tell Jake's got something *mighty* wrong with him and may not be up to having visitors for awhile."

Angie stared point blank at Jade, now, "What's wrong with Jake? Seems he's never been the type to not tackle a bull by the horns, no offense meant as to the *crazy bull*... or *whatever* it was. Never seen him back-down from facing-up to stuff though... sure is what attracted me to him... along with *other* things."

Some of the *other things* were moseying-on-down that lost trail of memory-lane just now, and it shook Angie a lot more than she cared to face-up to. Angie now let her eyes trail-off as she scouted the yard some more; she seemed deep in thought and almost sad.

"Thought it was going work too... " Angie said, as if thinking out loud, "'til that horse-stuff came up between us. Oh, well... He sure put me in my place though... remember?"

They both remembered—as the word hung in the air so long, that they near could pick it apart and put it back together again.

Angie laughed. It wasn't a hearty laugh, it was the type to hide embarrassment and Jade knew it. She also knew it was time for Angie to be moving on.

Angie still had no intention of moving, and she held firm, same as her sprayed, layered flip with its curls, "Didn't he have some bad head injuries or something, can't he think straight now or what... why shy-off from company and all? Friends sure can't cause any trouble if they come calling, if they just want to help, now can they, Jade?" The keys began to jingle again, but there was a heavier melody about to be played, and not by her hand.

"My brother can *think* just fine Angie, even if he *couldn't* he's still loved by all the folks in this town and I don't 'tend to be shying-off from them. They've all helped us more that we can ever repay. Whether Jet chooses to *shy-off* or not, as you call it, is not your business *or* mine! He was told to take it easy for a while... this may be our ranch, but he's the boss-man and he can do what ever he wants here. His injuries are NOT local gossip as far as I'm concerned either, but you sure are making them out to be. They're concerns of all that know him and we don't mind if they need some *talk* to free-up their minds and all, it's their way to get over the reality and harshness of it all. If there is any *more* to be shared though, it will come in *due time*. Due time... as to meaning the FUTURE!"

Jade advanced towards her, Jake-style, as she continued sending her ammunition to its mark, "TIME WHICH YOU DON'T HAVE, as you're DUE to VACATE THE PREMISES!"

Jade looked over at Honor now, with a slow calmness that hushed her harsh features. Sometimes she followed in her twin's footsteps perfectly. Like now. And, just as perfectly she did, in other ways too. She could be protector as well as comforter, just as easily as he could be and always was, to those in need. With the first role accomplished she proceeded to take on the second role.

Jade's former harsh mannerisms had melted into a new stance and she offered up:

"If you need a horse, we'll be happy to help you out, Honor. You'll need to get in touch with Ray first, and then we'll see if there's something we can do. If it's not soon enough for you though, you may need to go elsewhere, but *only* if time is a serious issue. If you'll be here all summer, we're open to help you," she smiled soft and country-humble, "but if you'll be here only this month, or need the horse quickly this month, then most likely we won't be able to. We need to get settled around here and it may be slow in coming." No one saw her pain—no one—but *someone* DID see her kindness.

Angie sulked as to being embarrassed and took one last scan of the yard, she was mighty curious now all right, but her embarrassment was weighing heavily and it fast-showed (seeing as she had worked *hard* to keep her deep-tanning-skin out the sun's rays) she was thus exposed in another way by her flushed face. Sour apples, red apples, it didn't matter which she was to Jade now, Angie was discarded-fruit no matter what. She had left a bad taste in Jade's new day. A day which never had the chance to get seeded, as Jade remembered the plowed-up morning in the kitchen, fertilized with eggs and toast, and then well-watered with a smashed-up coffee. A day that so far had no hope of any soon-coming plants of tender future growth. One thing was about to go well though—and Jade was looking forward to it immediately.

"GIT! Go on, GIT!" she said. "I'm looking forward to seeing your DUST on my drive!" Jade left for the front porch as Angie watched. Jade took a chair and sat on the porch as the sun was now beginning to move around towards the front of the house. It sure felt good to sit there and watch that dust fly—and fly, it surely *DID*!

CHAPTER FOUR

"DO I?"

JADE was still sitting back in the chair—pulled as far to the porch-edge as possible—closing her eyes, the sun was shining PAST straight-on now and was off a tad to the west. It was warming her face and part of the porch, still, none the less, but from a different angle. She didn't realize it but she had fallen asleep. This quiet time, this time spent praying on the porch sure did her wonders of good. Forgiveness was never an issue; she forgave Angie but was not in anyway about to let her stay. She knew this tree had the wrong kind of fruit to partake of in their home. Their home was kept clean and honest; no sly-fox stuff was to be part of their ranch, or their way of life. Their pa learned his ropes the hard way, back in Texas, and he also learned the sure-footed way as well—from their ma. If he married her, it was to rein his horse as near to the good Lord's trail as he was able. He slipped more than her, during his travels on that sure-footed way, quite surely he surely did—and much to his personal regret, he had found. Seems he just didn't pay strict attention to where he put his foot once in awhile. But he never gave up, and always set himself straight, and, made sure his kids knew the straight and narrow—as—someday he would be gone. And gone they both were, now.

Jade sat up and wondered what had become of Jake; he may have wondered why his little shadow had not shown up. She was, as she knew, the younger one—the follower. *It's my duty to show up wherever he goes,* she laughed at her thought, *and always a few minutes later! If I hadn't started right from the start, when our ma pushed us out, I wouldn't be here right now... as a matter of fact!*

A pang of worry came over her as she thought of her brother. She made her second attempt to follow after him, but as she looked up, what she *now* saw, she just couldn't quite believe. It was happening again!

"Dear Lord, why?" She desperately asked, as she searched her soul and looked up to the heavens.

There, coming up the drive was yet *another* truck. This one was not rented though, and as it neared, she knew it was Ray, Angie's brother. She suspected he must have found out his sister had paid them a visit.

He will be relieved to know that no harm was done. Maybe it's good... maybe it's FOR my good, she thought. *I thought I had talked this all out by now... with Ray... back when he came to sit with me those first weeks when Jet was near death. When he helped me to prepare to let Jet go, if it was meant to be. And then again... when I had to prepare to help him face THIS. Something he DIDN'T understand how to deal with, and STILL DOESN'T, even after these last two months. Ray came back-and-forth and continually helped me, even when we had Jet at the hotel. I just thought I was strong enough to handle this first day alone... maybe I'm not. But, who knows my brother Jet better than I do?*

As she pondered these thoughts she felt warm tears stream down her face, she cried out to no one in particular, except maybe herself, "do I... do I? Do I know him? How well?"

She got up slowly as more tears streamed down; she headed for Ray's truck, as if it was a deep-set rock in the midst of her turmoil, one she had hung on to many times. She was going to hang on fast to whatever it could offer. A film of dust in the air from Ray's truck settled like it had a magnetic pull to her damp face. It wasn't some soppy weak woman tears or lost little girl tears. It was a sincere sorrow for being at a loss as to what to do—the same tears she had seen her father shed, when his wife died.

Ray couldn't help but notice as he got out of his truck and came up to her. "Did my sister stir this up?" he said, as he studied her face.

As soon as the words were out of his mouth, he knew better. Jade could handle her own conflicts, especially with another gal, and Angie in particular.

If Angie had caused this, it could *only* be if she had met-up with Jake as well, as seeing Jake hurt in any way would have caused deep sorrow to Jade. *If THAT had happened though, Jade would have been a lot more upset than she was now, she would be fired-up mad, as her protective instincts would have been surcharged,* he began to reason with himself.

Ray thus remembered, Jake had his FIRST confrontation with someone he considered to be an intruder during his much hated therapy and Jade had to leave the room as she couldn't stand to see Jake hurting. It was not something she could face well now, or maybe ever. She had held back her temper though, and admirably, as she knew she was not to blame the poor woman—though she sure didn't TAKE to agreeing with her—she was just doing her job at the time, and Jade had to accept that intrusion. His thoughts still grasped for what was intruding to cause her such troubles, now, seeing as he had ruled out Angie.

"I don't know if I can help him, Ray. Who am I? Do I really know how to help Jet, Ray? Do I?" Jade looked up at her trusted friend with imploring eyes.

Their family had known each other for years as they were all growing up, ever since their family had first moved up here from Texas. Ray's family was originally from these parts, and his folks ran into the Smith newcomers in town, at the SADDLE AND SEED. Ray Emmeric was one of Jake's best friends then-and-now (along with the Lenny the "law") aside-to the other two buddies on the home-front; no one else shared top honors with these four—not a one—except Jade herself. Though fairly it must be said, Jake had a list as long as Main Street of just as near-and-dear friends—they just didn't have the time or opportunities to hang-out as brothers. Thus, honored still, they were—rich milk just under the cream-line of the best.

Ray and Jade sat on the porch now and she shared the JJ-NS's morning news, as reported Jade-style, in the midst of the chickens and the early morning sun.

"He must be wondering where I am by now, he knows I wouldn't let him take-off with out following. I'm the only one that could get away with following him, you know," she turned her gaze around the yard as it to soak-up a clue.

"Look, Jade, you know Jake in *some* ways that I never will, you've known him since birth. I know him in *other* ways... as best pards can know each other, as a big brother, as man to man. He'll come around if he can lasso this proper-like, with his *own* style... but he needs an open door as to insight. If not... I have a grave concern that if he *doesn't* get a firm rope on it soon, now that he's *home*... and even *more* so, if it's not tied *down* right, he could end-up cutting himself right out of the herd. Out and away from everything he's ever known and loved. Oh, he'll stay put here all right, and in *your* foothills, but that's the last we'll see of him... except maybe come sundown and sunup, coming and going. If we're lucky to be hanging around here at them hours."

Ray cracked his knuckles, as he settled into slowly unfolding the make-up of his friend, and continued on, "don't think he'll be happy in the long run, as ol' Jake is such a fun loving person. He tends to be open and always has a way with near everyone in town... helps out at every ranch, any time, night or day. You name it. A more loyal and true friend can't be found... or dedicated mentor.

Pure and simple, he has the best skills and knowledge to share from his early years moving around the rodeo circuits with your pa, from when you guys moved up here. All that wisdom from the saddle bronc riding and team roping work of his, has helped give many a man a new edge on his own skills. Our night campfires each spring and summer, have a quiet hush as he shares what your pa taught him. You know right-well, Jade, when we move around these local and out-of-town ranches and help the young kids learning these skills and *practicing* them, that he out-classes me... he can size it all up, and dish it out proper to each kid... on the trail-rides, we can always count on him to do his share and *more,* yet he's as humble as a new dawn coming-up-slow-and-steady."

He stared off into space a moment to reflect, as he realized the full extent of everything he had just said. His dark gray Stetson seemed to cast a heavy gray cloud over his mind just now, as he was thinking so hard. When he encouraged Jade towards success, as for Jake's new way of life, he had never taken into consideration all *this*. This was tough meat to chew. Ray realized sorrowfully, that the whole expression fit the fix Jake was in, perfectly—too perfectly. If Jake didn't succeed in swallowing this chore set before him, his life would go down hill just as easily as his health would go down hill, from not swallowing enough, or properly—for his physical well being.

Ray walked up and sat on the wooden boards of the porch. He thought of all the times he and Jake sat here at night and talked. Matt and Stoney would always be there too. Matt was usually the night owl with Jake, but during the nights that Ray could stay over, Matt (and later, Stoney) would turn in early. Jake and Ray would continue on into the wee hours—Ray, being freed from his own ranch for awhile, would advise Jake as a good big brother would. They never knew when that might be—they just "went with the flow" as the day finished up around the bend.

As he thought and listened to the words he had spoken to Jade, Ray realized he had been quite ignorant as to his first thoughts. He had only taken the matters of daily living into his concern and although for Jake, this would be hard enough, surely his determination would see him through it. Jake wanted his health and he wanted his horses—they depended on him, he would *never* let them down—he also wanted his *ranch*. Most of all, he wanted his sister to have someone that wouldn't let her down, and only Jake could fill those "boots", if he could ever find some way to get them on straight again. But now, seeing the full picture in such a clear light, Ray was becoming painfully aware that there was much *more* to rope-up and much *more* to rein in here, then *just* dealing with daily living skills, as far as Jake's total participation with life was concerned. And quite rightly, anyone *else's* life, for that matter, he now more fully understood—but *his* concern now *was* Jake.

Jade watched silently, as Ray became lost before her. She knew where he was lost though, and let him roam. She had done it many times, just trying to accept it all. He'd find an answer, some kind of advice for her—if she'd be patient and let him think. Little did she know how far back Ray's mind would go, as he finally was hit by the fullness of the last four months.

~*~

Ray saw it all now. Why, the whole *presentation* of himself, the Jake that they knew and understood, the essence of his inner being, expressed as only Jake could do, was now damned-up at one of the main sources of that "river's spillway". He would *never again* be able to express himself as they had come to know him all these years. The smooth ease and freedom, to speak *whatever* comes to mind at the drop of a hat—as it follows the inspiration of the heart and is quickly passed on to receive feedback and *companionship's* joys of fellowship—which is much *more* than just asking for daily wants and needs; was now *dammed up.* Yep, much *"more"*, was guilty *more-much-so* to make it four-times as hard to face in-flowing issues that could encompass one, when out in the world, *unable* to channel anything out, as before. He was frustrated with this, and they knew it was not going to be an easy chore to get him to use another tributary of this *river*. His river. He was used to the sound of the river's water, *his* water—his *unfailing* water. The other tributaries would be treacherous and not tested. They would have *hidden under currents* and *hostile clashes* against the rocks. All these dangers he had *already* learned and charted in his life, and NOW he must learn to do this all OVER again and in the eyes of friends and others, who would *thus* come to know him as—different. But he wasn't different, not inside, nor in his outward appearance, as the hotel mirror proved to Jake many times, in Ray's own presence before they left the hotel. Aside from some scars that were healing, it was still Jake's likeness that stared back at him.

~*~

"You *do* know him," Ray said with deep sorrow, "and I know him. Any other man would just be thankful to be alive and maybe just *leave* it at that. I know Jake is thankful for that, but there is too much clutter in the way, he is not the kind of man to know how to re-do his whole life while presenting it to *public-view* each step of the way. He likes to set himself aright, in private, so he knows he won't fail to help others when the chips are down, he's then freed-up to be out there doing what he does best. Right now, he feels like he good for nothing and doesn't know how to fix himself.

Whatever he does now, and the way in which he will have to do it, will brand him as someone he doesn't even know yet. But he *has* to face this, to finally be free to be himself again. He looks at himself now as someone he doesn't even know anymore. I could see it in his eyes the first time he *fully realized* what happened to him. After fighting for his life—and succeeding—I think it was too great a shock to him to *even try* to fully understand how this was now part of his life, and how he had no power to change it, at least *not in the way* he wants.

If he tries to *voice* to us that he's the same, as he did try to then... it's quite obvious that he's *not*. He can't handle that constant witness against himself. That confrontation of *what he hears* as being *that witness... THAT ONE PROOF...* that he will never be the same."

Ray stopped now, as he sadly remembered the end of the first month, January, when Jake was finally out of intensive care; he had been in a coma, for the first four weeks—at least technically. As—he finished that last week of January, as alertness surfaced, in all its slowness, still in the ICU, as a precaution. The worst cause for concern had been his skull fracture, and then his badly crushed chest, on the left side. He couldn't breath on his own during his stay in the intensive care unit, and then still needed some assistance when he came out of the coma, he still had to deal with being restrained at times. Even though he was out of intensive care in February, he still was not fully alert or aware and was for the most part minimally conscious and needing serious assistance in many ways. They were still concerned about his left eye, so his eyes were still bandaged, and allowed to rest-up to the end of the first week of February. Although his other injuries were still healing, his face and neck were the ones that caused him the most discomfort—the few times when he did find himself more aware only led him to frustrated confusion. During these time he had seizures, and Jade had to leave the room.

~*~

Jake had nearly bled to death and his lung had collapsed before he made it to the hospital. It was a miracle he lived long enough for the emergency team to give him aid, and a miracle that he survived the helicopter ride to the emergency room of the hospital, and Matt had played a vital part in that miracle before the helicopter emergency service ever arrived. Although it was a cold winter day with light, powdery snow on the ground, those that worked with swift and staunch determination were numb more from the shock of the situation, than from the coldness of the faintly-snowy air. Winter's ruined beauty.

~*~

Ray, setting Jade on hold, still sifted through the past, as he remembered the sparks of recognition he saw in Jake's face during the last week of February, and into the first week of March. By then, Jake had gone through various stages of having cast and bandages removed, along with ongoing therapy, even though he wasn't always sure exactly what was going on. When he began to recognize those around him, his response in these aspects of his healing was met with the needed success. He was still full of tubes, but the trachea tube was not needed any more in February. It was not his luck to be minus a tube, however—it had been replaced with an esophageal feeding tube in his neck. Later, on into March, little did he realize why he should be in need of it. His jaw was still wired shut but ready to be loosened some time during that week or next, from what Jake had heard. He never had a clear understanding as to how much was wrong with him, especially in his mouth, as something felt terribly wrong. He was beginning to become more-and-more agitated and doctors, staff, and friends all were painfully aware that he was full of questions as these questions *waited*—imprisoned in his mind all that time.

As the days drew onward, toward that second week of March, it was his continued desperate wonder as to what was wrong with the inside of his mouth, the pain from it had been subsiding, even though for the most part, he never felt its fullness, because of his medication. This injury had now come to be more of a torment to him than anything else and no one could bring themselves to mention anything in detail to him, not at that time.

Ray, all that time, along with Matt, his wife Galena and Jade, watched, as it soon became worse instead of better, but in a personal way, not a physical way. Jake had fought for the communication that never came, and would never come again—it was during the second week of that third month—that Jake fully realized it. It was at that time that he finally learned what was wrong with him. Once he did, and once he knew, the rest of March was hell, to him and all those that were in tow with him.

Ray remembered how Jake had desperately tried to remember what had happened. Jake had tried to figure how he could have ended-up like this, but couldn't. Jade had told Jake though, so he finally came to know *that* much—taking it all in, by *mutual-twin-trust* at its very best. It was because of a bull. A bull had hit and stomped on him, and he had nearly died—but that was impossible—wasn't it?

~*~

To Jake maybe, but not to anyone else. Ray had no way of knowing, then or now, Jake's racing thoughts OR feelings: *What bull? They didn't HAVE a bull—and their small banded-ones of the past, would never have counted as such.* Yet, as he was THEN functioning with new awareness, and less medication, one night he awoke in anguish as he realized that he *remembered*—at least to some fragmented extent. He remembered that someone had been screaming, and he had run out of the barn, *that damn BULL was in his corral, and it was killing Stoney. How the hell did that bull get here?* He was *running* in his memory—or so he thought.

As the memories came back, and the memories as to whose *fault* it was for the bull being there, Jake had caused so much commotion trying to get up and get out of there, that he fell. He hadn't been up on his feet long enough unaided, as they were still helping him through therapy, and he was not able to stand on his own with such haste and aggression. Ray and Matt had picked him up but he fought with them, he was too weak to do any one any harm—except himself.

They had forced him back to the bed, with his reasons of desperateness locked inside him, and he was sitting there slumped over and breathing hard by the time Jade came back with help from the staff. Jade was the first one into the room, and she had entered it just as Jake went into a seizure. Matt and Ray were not prepared for that, and he fell from the bed to the floor as they stood in shock. Jade weakly fell to her knees onto the floor and let her head sink into her hands as her body heaved sporadically from the dismay of what was happening. Galena knew to stay by her side, Jade was now nearly to the end of her deep reserve of stamina—she broke. Finally courage was gone, and all she had left was the need for comfort.

She had just gotten through the first month with the unforeseen knowledge that her brother would truly live—safely tucked in her brain, was this long awaited fact. Then she had set her face to get through the hard and painful watching-and-waiting of the next phase of his recovery, only to have to face confessing the *full knowledge* of this condition to him. Then that. That out-burst of his—something she was completely unprepared for and couldn't understand. If it was because of what he had learned about himself, it would have manifested with his other desperate cry for assistance for some kind of freedom from his fate. Whatever the reason for it, it had now led to her brother having another seizure. She was so afraid he would end up in the intensive care again. It was *her* brain that was swollen now:

'WHY… WHY DID HE DO THIS, WHY?' Jade had asked herself senselessly over and over.

As the staff did their job, and a doctor was called, Ray and Matt tried to do their job and help Jade, but no one could answer her loud moaning cries of anguish—no one knew why.

~*~

Ray remembered how he was helpless to do any good, as well as Matt—neither of them could settle Jake then. He was sedated after the first seizure because it had led to a second one and the doctors wanted his body to recover from the exertion. Now they would need to determine if there was a new underlying cause or not, since they had hoped *not* to expect them at this point. And, if not, it had possibly been triggered by his emotional stress from this unknown mystery—and most likely by permanent, yet not fully understood, damage. He hadn't had any since back in February, and had not received any more medication for them. His head injuries along with injury and trauma to his brain, had healed with the hoped for success, but they had still left their sorry mark, which he and others were still learning and *yet* to learn in the months to come.

If it was triggered, then perhaps only Jade could help them learn why. The next few days had been extremely hard on Jake; it was all Jade could do to implore him to settle down. She had never seen him so mad before, she finally broke down again and cried. She didn't want to face him dying again, and she was so scared that he would that she broke his heart, and it left a wound in his spirit. He had yielded to her wishes, with what tiny scrap of grace he had left to his name.

Along with that, he didn't want to be strapped down to the bed, and had nodded seriously that he understood he would be, and that his recuperation and therapy would all come to a halt, if he decided to make this a habit. Ray, Matt and Galena witnessed as Jade and Jake lay in each others arms for hours, as she leaned over his bed and calmed him back into sound reasoning—all the while, her hand slipped under his arm socket, her place of safety.

Jake wouldn't let her get hurt anymore. He could only imagine what she had already gone through, she must have seen what happened to him, she was surely the one that screamed when Stoney was under the bull. He finally knew.

Ray and Matt knew that sooner or later, Jake would come to know that Jade had been there and witnessed his injuries. Once this full realization set in, they knew Jake would be ready to face his more difficult task that lay ahead—and he would somehow face it—because he didn't want to see his sister hurt anymore than she had been already. For his twin, he had to accept his new chores.

But the thing that haunted Ray the most as he thought back, was the events of March. He knew Jake and knew exactly how he felt. Now that Jake was aware of what happened to him—due to the trauma of it all—their support to *Jade* was mainly over and was now going to be needed in regards to *Jake's* recovery instead.

It took the last two weeks of March, for the full shock of it to seep in to the depths of Jake's heart, it was all tainted by the sickening knowledge of everything that had led up to his injuries. During this time he continued to slide downhill with all these strangers studying his condition and then trying to explain in full-depth exactly what had happened to him. They were trying to teach him how to take care of himself and how to live with it, when he just wanted to be left alone. It was these last two weeks of March, when he began to withdraw and isolate himself from his surroundings and numbly go with the motions and yield to what ever he was told, while his thoughts were miles away. Miles away, to the years past, wishing he was there— somewhere—anywhere but here. His long stay was nearly at an end, but he was numb as to any thoughts of his future. He was then facing his last two weeks in the hospital, which were the first two of April, he had made successful progress in all areas, even in the area of the one that was to haunt him in different ways—the rest of his life. As—seemed he wasn't a candidate for any options as some folks were. Now his final responses were needed to testing, as to some brain issues, and therapy in other issues, so they would be able to discharge him with all safety precautions covered. Progression through the head injuries was always met with added caution because of the possibility of relapses. Then he had faced two weeks as an outpatient; he had stayed with Ray and Jade at the hotel nearby, numb to receiving any benefits, thus being—more hospital, in his eyes, and more hard times, even so.

He just wanted to get out of that hospital and away from the therapist and nurses and make a bolt for the hills. His hills that he loved, maybe there he could think.

Yep, those last two weeks there as an outpatient, were just about the last straw for Jake. Staying at a cozy-enough hotel, which worked through the hospital, and offered lowered rates for patients and their families, didn't help much. Ray and Jake's buddies, along with people from town, had all chipped in to pay for it, and there was no getting out of it. That last therapy, done on an outpatient basis, was met with every kind of frustration and "deep wanted desire of denial" that he knew he couldn't lay hold of. The witness against him was as plain as a deep gust-of-wind moaning-through-the-rafters at night—it was a vague haunting noise—it seemed to be the only thing that came to mind whenever Jake tired to communicate. Jake was ashamed of it and they knew it.

Matt and Galena had gone back to the ranch at that time and taken-over for Jake. Matt would relieve the neighbors that were looking over the care of the ranch thus far. Ray had stayed; he just hung around as a good buddy for Jake, although he headed home occasional for ranch business of his own.

As to the therapy, Ray had never said anything to Jake except 'come on, buddy', 'let's get going Jake, or we'll be late'. Little common courtesies and such, were all he chose to share, as the three of them set-out to go to therapy for Jake's communication skills, and a whole slue of things Jake was just plain sick of listening to, and, pressed to respond to.

As the memories and knowledge of all that had engulfed the three of them, was now left behind, Ray got up and sat down in one of the chairs. He had never taken the time to think it all through, but now, he had needed to. Having done so, he now felt tired and mentally wasted. But he was desperate even more so, to glean something from this knowledge to offer as assistance to Jade, and Jade now sat near him, eagerly hoping for some kind of advice.

Ray was just about to address the issue at hand, but Jade spoke first:

"It doesn't seem so hard at times, if I think *past* all that we've come through and try to focus on Jet being *here* now. I can picture Jet understanding... he has always settled himself to owe-up and accept what can't be changed. When the chips are down, well, he has always done right-well at finding a way to set things right. I was *ready* to think that once he was home and back in familiar surrounding all would *fall* into place. It seems it's all turning-out wrong." She was now agitated. "I'm going to LOOK for him," she said firmly, as she stood up with determination—her earrings shook as a truth-echo.

Ray grabbed her with an easygoing natural gesture, and addressed her, "Maybe that's what's wrong, Jade... maybe he *shouldn't* be here. That lady, the one that came to try and council him, the one that he threw the pillows at... what was her name?"

"Kaite?" She had turned and was studying him as to catch-his-drift and meet-up with his thoughts.

"Yeah, remember she said she thought it was best for him to go to some kind of school or life skills rehab house, or something... Maybe she was right, you see? Somewhere where no one knows him… then he won't feel he's different. As, who would know *how* he was before he arrived. Right? He could just relax and take it in stride, 'til he found out what way or how best to handle this. Sounds simple enough, don't it? Like a bronc rider with a leg healing-up, and just hanging-out with the young beginners 'til he feels up to par again. No one *knows* he was riding any *other way*, so he's free to relax." *What could possibly be wrong with that,* Ray wondered as he tried to picture *himself* doing it.

"Maybe if Miss Kaite could have explained it *that* way, it might have sounded better. The way she spoke it to Jet, it sounded like she was punishing him because… because… well… because he was different. You get what I'm saying, Ray? Jet don't want to feel like he's being punished. He has his *own* code and tries to live by it. He sure ain't happy if he feels he's in the dog house, not one bit. He's had his share of that when Pa was traveling and Ma, she went with… way up into Canada. The two of us ended-up in boarding school for about two years, when we were nine and ten… wildest orneriest ride Jet ever got through. We were both used to Texas' wide-open spaces… and following them rodeos! To then have to spend some of our early years there in an in-town boarding school was like being sentenced to HELL for him. When we were finally "rescued", as he put it, and heading here to Montana, I swear the sun was rising prettier on his face than it was on them east Montana hills up there."

Ray looked up to those hills as Jade spoke of them. It was now near late afternoon and there was a slight breeze. It should have felt good but it didn't. It made Jade remember that day in January when the whole sorry mess happened. The New Year had started with their usual eve party, followed the next day with a calm comradely and an open-house Texas-style Montana barbecue—in honor of their deceased folks. Hopefully followed by high expectations of reaching new goals for the new up-coming year. It had all been torn apart, just as Jake was—and Stoney, to a lesser degree—under the bull, when January 2nd rolled around.

Here it was May, and they had arrived home for the first day of it. It should be warmer, but the spring showers had led to the coolness of the last few days. The reminder struck her hard. She wanted new memories to come in and tear the other ones down, to lay a firm foundation for something else, but there was none.

Ray recognized her anxiousness, and watched her as she got up to pace the porch. Her boots resounded on the boards; they all knew the sound. It was part of their life, engrained in them, just as each board was, with its

own grain. As, each of them were different, yet placed in harmony—
together. Upholding each other's lives, bearing up, as one unit firmly
joined—just as the porch was.

"*Look*, Jade, *maybe* he's around and he's been watching us all this
time. I'll take-off and let you two be alone... you'll know what to do. You
always do." Ray smiled and squeezed her shoulders, as his dark strong face
and Indian features finally looked peaceful in the morning light, tempting
Jade to accept his nudge for her next steps.

"Do I? Do I?" Her eyes looked up into his, imploring for an answer.
Her long dark braided hair, hanging down over her chest, made her look like
a horse with its reins loose and waiting for guidance.

"Hey now, *don't* start doubting yourself now. You got him through
this. Your prayers and your voice near his bedside."

"Oh no!" She protested, "I had come to a *full loss* of what to do. *You*
were the one that told me I would know deep in my heart what I should do.
I didn't know what to do... whether to believe for him to live, or not. If I
had to give him up, I would *only* do that if I had peace, but then, I *had* no
peace. If I should *fight* for him... you said I would know that too... *so I
fought*. I fought long and hard." Her head hurt with the remembrance of it.

"If you hadn't taken my place by his bedside and talked with him, so's
I could leave him to the Lord while I stayed in the hotel to pray those three
days... I would have had a break down. I trusted you'd call me in time if
any change occurred with him. Being at the hotel was the only way I could
fight for him. I needed to be alone to do that. I didn't see any sign post until
you shook me loose from my shock. I was desperate for one, and then it
came as surely as the crocus bulbs *appear in spring*. It was *due* season, due
season for Jet to wake up, due season for him to fight the good fight. Then I
was strong enough to wait... no matter how hard it was. *God* was with
me... I was able to get through that wait and see whether he'd come out of
the coma, or not... but he did. He woke up, Ray... sure, it was a slow
process, but he woke up... and he *lived*," memories of joy unfolded with an
easy roll before them, and she was newly surprised and pleased.

She smiled as she continued on, "he'll want to see you Ray, I know he
will, please stay."

"No, not yet. He chose to come home, he needs to be here. He needs
YOU Jade. We shouldn't be tempted to listen to Kaite. You know... now
that I've studied my thinking... that would have been a wrong decision. If
Jake threw pillows at her, well then for sure there's something wrong with
her... course, he may still need to co-operate with some of what she says.
Since the doctors still need some missing info and such, which he refused to

co-operate about. But at *least* we will believe this for now... he *wants* to be here, so this is our BEST cornerstone to build on. He hasn't thrown any pillows at *you* has he?"

"Nope, just a coffee cup," she smiled. "And it *wasn't* at me, no sir... it was a sailin' nice and smooth just like I would *imagine*... THAT IS until it HIT the floor! I didn't *actually* see it, understand... but it scared the heck out of me! If he would have thrown a pillow though, I would have been *mighty insulted*, and as scared as a June-bug-stuck-in-a-window-during-a-hot-summer-night-in-Texas, cause then I'd be in the *same league* as Miss Kaite."

Ray folded his arms as he leaned back in thought, and became cautious, and then set forth his words of discernment, "I think before I visit again, it would best to let him get used to his condition. Let him start to find out that, WHO HE IS, *is still inside*. Let him learn he *is* different and let him learn to face up to it. Just make sure he knows he is different *only* in his presentation of himself. If he can get this bridle on the horse-of-it-all, next comes the blanket, and then the saddle. Maybe *then*, it will be *my turn*, okay?"

"But he wants to be the same, he *won't* let go of that," Jade persisted. "He sure can be tenacious when he wants to be, never seen *anything* like it... well, except maybe me, on *occasion*," her voice slowed, but pursued her revelation, "he's afraid he will lose himself Ray. Now how can I get him to *want* to be different, it don't make no sense to me."

"Like I said," Ray pressured her to see, "he must see that the differences are in his *presentation of himself* and yes, it will be quite obvious to others. But doesn't he want to continue on to be the same man he always was as to his CONSCIENCE and INTEGRITY, doesn't he want to *think* the same he always has, accomplish the same goals, share them, and enjoy the same pleasure of this ranch and his long time friendships? I'm sure he does." Ray rested his arm upon her, near as he'd seen Jade's pa do:

"Jade look," he continued, "Jake can still hear, he can still see, he could have lost either or both of those functions as well. He could have had severe brain damage, but he didn't. Ask him how he feels about that? No... on *second* thought... don't... knowing him, he's already asked himself that."

"I *do know* what to do now, Ray... I do. You're right, he *has* gone down the line of all those situations. He's lucky he can still walk, he was lucky his neck didn't get broke, as a matter of fact and he's lucky he has his memory and a good healthy mind after such a bad skull fracture and all. He has to just PLAIN face this. He has to face it head on... what he doesn't want to be true, is forever a part of his life now. I am the only one that can tell him face-to-face, straight up, with any merit… and I will, over-and-over again 'til he *breaks*, then he will *face* it… then he will ACCEPT it!"

She turned, heading out around the right side of the house to the backyard, towards the low hills just before the higher northwest ridge. There she sought her brother out. Ray followed just a bit and watched her as she climbed over the fence and went through the pasture toward their low sculpted hills. Ray was right, he *knew* it now, he saw Jake up on the ridge watching his sister as she neared her destination. Jake didn't try to move out of sight, he took off his hat and gave a small salute to Ray, as he sat down and waited for his sister to climb the path along the hill.

When she came upon him, she sat down in front of him and yelled at him as hard and long as she could. She yelled at him, that he was alive. She yelled at him all the things that were *not* wrong with him.

Jake sat there and watched the power that came out of her inner being and through her mouth, he listened to the loud sounds that this power was changed into as it was pushed and molded through the different shapes of her lips powered by her tongue.

She was now leading-up to what she came to tell him, something that he *didn't want to hear* anymore. He had heard it from Jade first; he had heard it from the doctor, and finally from the therapist, Kaite. Every time he started to look back, he knew. He put it away in his brain and tried not to think about it. Yet he could not rid himself of it, it was still constantly with him; it was tied to every thought that came his way, and even those that hadn't come into being yet. Every time he wanted to say something—he knew. Every time he swallowed—he knew. He knew as he sat there now and studied her face and mannerisms, intently soaking it all in as his eyes moved up-and-down along her face, with full acknowledgement as to what she was presenting him. It seemed surreal, as her facts played-out before him while his ranch seemed diminished behind her, at the scope of her broadcast:

"YOU *CAN'T* TALK, JET! YOU WILL *NEVER* BE ABLE TO TALK AGAIN! The hoofs of that bull kicked-up and smashed-up the side of your face and jaw! Your tongue was ripped-up so severely it's beyond repair… the nerve damage was too severe… whatever slight *ridge* you have left is *COMPLETELY USELESS!* Do you hear me, *IT'S USELESS TO YOU!* It's useless to you except for taking some careful swallows at the base-end… you're LUCKY you've got that… *Do you understand me Jet, DO YOU?* Your voice hasn't got full power left in it now, and it's *not* going to come back EITHER... whatever is left, is all you'll ever have! Foot-stomp it, Jet! FOOT-STOMP IT, and GET OVER IT!

NO ONE CAN UNDERSTAND YOU, EVEN *IF YOU DO* TRY TO TALK! NO ONE! AND IT CAN'T BE FIXED! IT WON'T EVER BE FIXED! *SO WHAT!* SO WHAT! So you can't talk! So *accept* it! There's no way it can ever be changed... your tongue's gone... no *artificial* ones for you either! *IT'S ALL OVER.* You're not the same Jet, you're not the same... but you ARE the same to me. Your *ARE* to me, oh, please, BE THE *SAME* TO ME, JET!"

She was exasperated now and turned around with force, throwing her arms up towards the heavens:

"The way that bull smashed you with its horns and stomped-on you, you're lucky you didn't DIE on the SPOT! Dear God, AIN'T THAT GOOD ENOUGH FOR YOU, JET?" She turned back at him as he sat there staring at her, in a deep pensive heavy state, like a cat studying the best angle of approach when the prey is still far to distant, before it ever would venture to move-in on it.

She opened and threw up her outstretched arms at him as she desperately implored him, "If you have to make noises... I don't CARE what they sound like. If you want to make SIGNS to me, like Kaite said to do... PLEASE JUST DO IT!

If you want to scribble big signs all over the house or paint the walls for your breakfast order, using the barn paint... I don't CARE... JUST do it! IN GOD'S GOOD NAME, JET, PLEASE just *DO* IT! BUT DON'T LOCK ME OUT! JUST DON'T SLOWLY RETREAT, LEAVING ME *SHUT OUT* THAT WAY! TALK TO ME IN *SOME OTHER* WAY JET!"

The awful facts landed at his feet, as, Jade began to run out of steam—she calmed as she slowed down in her speech, "listen to that gut-feeling that you have always listened to before and find some way to be *who* you are. The good Lord KNOWS who you are, Jet... those feelings are there to flow in *any way possible*, but only *you* can do it. He can help you... but you got to step-out and *do* it. You, Jet... *you.*"

With that she broke down and his heart was fully pierced as he saw her cry. With that piercing, a shudder deep within his body shook him free of his intense fixation on her words as his eyes welled-up with moisture. He began to cry and he allowed it freely. He cried with her.

As he did so, she caught her sobs as best she could, dropping down beside him, she looked up at him, saying softly with a faint smile, "You know... you never *could* sing... not even, *Happy Birthday*... so you didn't lose *that*, at least." She lay there quietly and completely still. Then after a few deep sobs, she fell asleep.

He held her close and felt sorry that the day had to be this way. He hadn't intended it to, when he first stepped into the kitchen that morning—something just went wrong. Chute-riding wrong—uncontrolled from the completely unforeseen. He looked down at the ranch below as the nearby grasses blew in the breeze. It was a beautiful sight to behold—he looked at his sister—so was his sister and her loyalty.

She sure knew how to put an old cowboy in his place just now... well, if you could call 40, old. I suppose it's old enough. Old enough for me to have had my big mouth opened long enough. So... now, it's shut up... and there's NOTHING anyone can ever do about it, that INCLUDES me. I always thought I could do somethin' about everything that came my way. Looks like I'm stuck now. Yeah, I'm stuck all right... stuck... TRAPPED INSIDE MYSELF, IS MORE LIKE IT, and I sure don't like it none.'

He swallowed hard. He continued to look at his sister as thoughts moved through his head. If he were blind, he wouldn't be seeing her now, just as in the hospital when his head was wrapped up that month, along with some extra time for his bandaged eyes. If he were deaf, as he near was afraid he was in the hospital during the times when his hearing seemed to come and go... he wouldn't have heard this "phenomenon" he now called "words". Least wise, it seemed like a "phenomenon" to him *now*.

He closed his eyes now and enjoyed the slight breeze that had just teased his face. *So long... it's been so long... sure feels so good.* Jake opened his eyes and looked out over the lay-of-the-land and watched the few wisps of clouds as they moved by. Soft reminders they were, that this was not *the unclouded day* that his ma had always sung of—this was the here and now, yet the thought of Heaven lingered, as he still watched the clouds. They were so high up, he hadn't even notice them earlier as Jade had climbed the hill. After he had waved to Ray, she was all that he had his mind on. He knew why she was following him, and he was glad to see her, she was *still* the *same*. So was the ranch, and in *deeper ways again*, as he know knew, as he took one last full soak—gleaning in each horsetail that twitched and flipped—and not that vastly far-off, out and down below.

Thinking back on his injuries, the split near his eye had been very bad, most of the damage was to the left side of his jaw, face, and upper neck, along with a fracture too, towards the back of his skull. He was lucky he didn't have severe damage to his sight or his hearing, or even his spinal nerves for that matter. He knew right-well, that the vein-of-life in his neck had been spared, or he would have left this world behind, before ever a hand-of-rescue would draw him free of the corral.

As it was, he had nearly stepped into that other world quite a few times. He even faced another world while he yet lived. He had been alone in some dark hidden world it seemed, completely lost in that hospital—at *first* thought. So being, it continually teased him, as to reality. When he was finally conscious off-and-on, one side of his body near hadn't any proper feeling-response, reaction-wise. His body was forced to breathe; he was desperate to move, but couldn't. Then, he had seizures, he was told, but he didn't remember. As his body began to heal, he had continual therapy— along with *unknown* therapy. Yep, somehow he really *wasn't* alone—all because of a *special code*. A special code known only to himself and his sister, since their time spent in their crib as infants—when this tiny hand first discovered him. It was Jade's hand. He felt her hand. He "knew" it was *that hand* because it was nestled under his right arm socket, in the same position it was used to, since they were bundled together during the times that they slept together as babes—even as toddlers. So engrained in his soul, there it was for him—it was *nurturing* that comfort that they both had first felt in the womb, long before they were born—that presence of *life*, very much nearby.

During his stay in intensive care (but not *fully* known to him now) even in the coma, he had been aware of it. Then when he first awoke, during that slow process the ending days of January, he felt it with firm reality. At first he didn't even know *exactly* what it was, as at first he didn't even remember *who* he was, and had no idea *where* he was. But this little hand, this little familiar gesture of comfort that he had known all his life, had brought him to his senses and thus out of death's hands in four week's time. And then later, starting a new week, and into the next month, it brought him to himself, although it was only a weak grasp of himself, he was beginning the journey toward this fog-shrouded knowledge. This little hand had given him a *reason* for his life to *hold on*, as it caused him to feel the *need* to stay. This little hand, while he was lost in darkness, and near unable to hear at times, had shown him he was *not alone*, someone very *special* was near. Seems long-established familiar habits, have a subconscious power all their own, as this FACT took to manifesting its results. Unknown to him, even more-so at that time, was one *other* very important fact, as well. This little hand was praying that a much *larger* Hand would see them through.

Now he knew.

On the whole he was a walking miracle and he knew it. Although there were many that had their hand in it, he knew it was because of Jade's code, the only one that could reach his spirit.

Do I really know her? He wondered. *Do I? She always had been there for me. She was always my special shadow, trailin' me when there seemed to be no sun to make a shadow appear. Yet there she'd be... sun would appear near-abouts the same time. Odd, I thought the sun's supposed to appear first, and then the shadow. DARNED'EST THING I'VE EVER COME TO KNOW! She seemed so strong, always hangin' on to me through thick and thin, and now look at her. Why, she's just fallin' apart inside!*

He never knew that she had looked up to him and he was her delight, the light of her eyes. It was no wonder he saw this shadow seemingly without the sun; he was the sun that made her appear. Brother and sister, twins, side by side. Doing what each did best. He, the big brother showed her the way. She the little sis, followed with admiration and honor. He saw the quiet strength she offered as she shadowed him, learning his kind, strong, bright and sometimes fiery ways. She was strong, when he was strong. She always knew that familiar *need* to shadow, as it was there since before their birth, he was birthed forth—so she just *had* to follow. Thus, that little hand later in the crib, nestled in his right arm socket, something so secure to her—then, and now.

As Jake contemplated deeper because of these thoughts, and the outburst of Jade just a bit ago—he suddenly was aware of the harm he had caused. His burden that he refused to accept, now was falling on *her* shoulders. He had done *her* harm and it tore his heart.

He couldn't help but be drawn into the "well" of it all, *Do I want to live in this misery that I am causin' the both of us? Do I? Do I want to be the cause of her ongoing grief as she is bearin' my burden still? Do I? She had taken on my burden in the hospital for those months, months when I needed her, admittedly. Now, it's expected that I owe-up to my share of this burden... even the whole of it. Do I want to try and let go of it, maybe try to follow those gut-feelings that the good Lord has given me and to press-on?*

He hung his head in shame and held his sister close. *I guess only time will tell,* he thought. He wiped his wet eyes before they moistened his face and shook his head back, cocking it to the side a bit as he did so, hoping to get free of any more that may leak, while trying not to disturb his twin. Jake looked down protectively as his sister began to stir. He had accidentally roused her and she looked at him after acknowledging her surroundings.

She looked up at him with a smile. "Are you well, Jet?"

He smiled back with a gentle nod, as to the affirmative. Taking a deep sigh, bringing the fresh air of the countryside into his healed lungs, he moved to get up. It felt good now, up here on the side of the ridge—he felt good. He helped Jade up, in turn, and they made their way down the hill, through the north pasture, going south, continuing on up to the back porch.

Jade touched his arm, to brush it:

"Shall we take-up where we left-off... with the eggs, Jet?"

Jake nodded at her softly with a smile as he gestured towards the door as to allow her to lead-on.

'Looks like this day may get saved after all,' he thought to her. *'Good thing too, as I'm gettin' mighty hungry after roaming these HILLS most the day.'* He decided to try to yield to some food again.

His spirit told him it would be mighty satisfying right about now, and his stomach did too—but his mind, now full of newer knowledge, just couldn't find meal times anywhere near as special now. It was just some difficult chore to get done now—so he could get on with something else more important. His memories though, were aroused—back to all the past years of morning meals, and the wonderful kick-off it always led to, the sights and sounds of the table-action, the smell of coffee, and someone to share conversation with, in accordance to the new day.

'Yeah, Jade,' he thought at her, *'you beat-up them eggs, gal... show them no mercy. I'm feelin' MIGHTY hungry... sure as HECK am... just maybe hungry enough to wrestle with them eggs... if they're WEAK enough for me to pitch 'em down.'*

CHAPTER FIVE

THIS SIGN MEANS "SHALLOW CROSSING"

AS Jake sat at the table, he watched as Jade took-up where they left-off from this morning. What did he care that it would be supper now? They were back on track at least, just quite a few hours late was all. He looked over at the bedroom door, then out the front window. The evening crew of birds was now taking over the bird feeder. He suddenly realized the horses had been left without their special treats for the day. He had no back-up crew, obviously, he now realized. They had the place all to themselves, with no workers, until Jake gave the go-ahead for Matt and Stoney to come back. He felt ready to take-on at least one step to becoming himself again—his "babies", the horses. Yet, *still*—without his back-up.

Hey what the heck can the horses do, to make me feel WORSE than I do now? Why, what do they know, I'm still the same to them... maybe just a mite quieter than they're used to for the most part. But I've had my quiet times, like when Pa died, so I'm sure we'll get along right-fine. With that thought firmly under his belt, Jake stretched a bit, pushed the chair back with his usual firmness, got up from the table and grabbed his trusty black Stetson from off the nearby wall.

As chair-pushing was a most natural noise to Jade, she didn't think anything of it, she assumed he was heading for the water or possibly to make fresh coffee.

He always did like fresh coffee, she thought, *especially with eggs and toast.* She was wondering if pushing the toast was too much for him, but he had done better than expected so far, in learning how to find a way to eat. She knew he was grateful to get that feeding tube (from his hospital stay) out of the hole in his neck. He would now try anyway he could to learn to eat, as he was desperate to keep free of it. There were worse feeding tubes to deal with, that posed a greater danger to his lungs, and were of more discomfort, than the one in his neck, but he still hated it. He never wanted to see another tube of any sort, unless it was for pouring oil into his truck. He wasn't getting enough protein, so like it or not, he had to use the food syringe. Jade made him soy protein liquids and other kinds of protein drinks, always homemade, to use with it, yet she knew exactly how he felt about eating this way. When he went to feed himself, whether he could speak or not, the look on his face said it all. He felt like a sick horse, being force-fed and he didn't like it one bit.

Jake had now come up behind her though, quite *unexpectedly*, and squeezed her shoulder softly. She turned to look at him as he nodded his head with a slight tilt to the door.

"What is it Jet? Hey, you got your hat on. You want me to go outside with you? What's wrong... the food's ready to serve... see?"

She had stood there and turned with the pan still in her hand, spatula in the other, and was looking at him—and as *sincere* as a twin could a'look.

Realizing she was waiting for some sort of a reply, he softly stretched his hands out before her, with his palms facing her, as he motioned with a "pat" in the air for her to stop. It was nearly as if to *calm* one of his horses with a gentle pat on their side.

She watched his face as she saw the crease in his brows that told her, *'no'*. She knew this part of him, from years of trying to follow when she was tagging along too much, and she stopped any notion of it:

"Well, then... "

He wanted to tell her he'd be right back but he was at a loss as to how. Glancing around the kitchen, he grabbed some plates from the rack, and quickly strode to the table. Dumping them in haste into a noisy pile, he smiled at her:

'See, look sis, all is well... now go on, set up the table... I'll be right back, I promise.' He then walked over to her and made a sign for "little bit", as he knew doggoned-well how to do *that,* and it would plainly get his point across. He then rushed out the door.

She followed after him as the door closed. Peering out through its half-curtained window, she caught the disappearing glimpse of his back. He was heading down the slight hill that was just past the driveway on the left side, and over to the tack-shed, there to his immediate left.

So that's it, she realized, *he finally remembered his babies. After our time up on the hill, I was wondering if we were near-abouts ready to start flowing with some kind of normal home life, so now I know.*

She was a bit amazed with his first show of communicating with her as she turned and looked at the pile of dishes on the dining table. *Yep, a sure sign he's coming back in to eat... a hungry man sure don't want to take any chances on a misunderstanding, leading to a thrown-out and missed meal,* she smiled with a sigh, and these contented thoughts.

As Jade went about her business, Jake took on the business of feeding his babies. The smell of the tack-shed sure smelled good. He loaded up the buckets with the treats and headed to the corral, it was straight ahead and he had full view of the horses—hardly babies—anxiously awaiting their master.

Wonder if they missed me... for sure they remember me, don't they? Four months is a long time. He was now leaning on the fence with horse-noses crowding him, sure felt like heaven, *well, near enough,* he supposed. *It sure don't feel like that hospital or a boarding school THAT'S for sure.*

A well-placed hard nudge personalized his thoughts towards them. *Aww... look, they remember their treats, for sure... they can't help but remember me then, as I'm the one that always brought 'em,* he thought with a smile, as he passed the much-desired treats out with a firm yet gentle stroke to each special nose.

He stood there a bit, completely forgetting about his supper. He watched them as they finished-up within minutes and were back to their fellowshipping and horse-interacting. Content with the fact that he had been remembered, and even more so, content with the fact that not even *ONE* horse had wondered: *...why I hadn't said nothin'*—as Jake put it—with this self-satisfying thought.

Jake felt happy. It sure was a nice evening. It sure felt good to be home. He sure felt the same.

As he felt the same during these cherished moments, he began to do some quick studying as he was always prone to do, especially out by his babies:

Do I want to lock everyone out of my life, do I want to shut myself up and keep others away? Is this my life now? Horses are happier with their buddies, same as most people... sure as shooting-a-well-placed-bull's-eye.

He listened to a few noises of protest that one horse gave another, as they milled around near him. Normally this was a source of pleasure to Jake, a type of fringe benefit, like being part of the herd. Unexpectedly, his wounded self-esteem jumped a bit and in doing so, it was drawing his focus back to himself, and some futile communication attempts of his a few months ago. He now, rightly or wrongly, reflected on the few times he had tried to talk, not believing what he was told—and—how try as he might, the only success was odd foreign noises that made no sense. He felt ashamed at his failure—and helpless.

~*~

He had desperately tried to force success in the hospital, as he tried to implore his sister to get someone to UNDO THIS DAMAGE that he didn't want to accept, but it was in vain. He couldn't get out of the damn hospital bed either and hunt someone down, but he sure tried, and they sure put a stop to it as well. All his sister could do was to tell him that at least he had something back there that was able to allow him to swallow, or he would be in worse trouble. It had been very hard for them to manage doing *that* much for him, with all the serious damage that was done. 'Try to understand, they really did what they could do,' she had said to him as she hid her sorrow.

Matt, who had been with him since he first dragged him from the dead bull and out of the round training corral, had seen Jake go through the worst, but he had trouble with what he witnessed during these times. He couldn't stand watching or hearing Jake's reactions, having to realize and face hard-and-fast, that he had no tongue to talk. Matt had to leave the room.

The more Jake fought it, the worse he sounded, all it got Jake was a lot of emotional pain, and a very awful look of concern on his twin's face, and soon on Ray's, as he tried to keep everyone calm. Ray, Jade, or Galena would finally have to run for the nurse because Matt had seen enough of Jake's pain, both physical or emotional, and would then be no place to be found—leaving Jake with half his safety-net gone.

~*~

Jake was now in need of a subject change. All he could see was the horses and he was getting desperate for an anchor of some sort to stop his wandering mind; he'd have to make do with them.

Horses... suit me up-and-down just fine. I don't need buddies. Why, I got horses. What do the horse care if I succeed in talkin' or not... long as I feed them, they're happy. They can't tell much of a difference in me now, look at them... nothing's different to them. Except, maybe I'm mighty quiet all of the sudden... and WILL BE the REST of my life... Aww, damn it... dear God forgive me, he thought, as he kicked the fence post with his boot. He slipped over the fence and made his way to the old small shed that his best baby, "Gentle Jen", hung-out in. He found her there and stroked her back.

His thoughts hurt his deeply wounded pride as he realized he couldn't even *talk* to his horses anymore, not *even* his own best riding horse, for that matter. There would be no more:

'Hey now... Jake's here to take you off to them hills up yonder, are you ready? If not... well, then I'd advise you to snap to it, gal.' Or, 'you set-a-spell and take-in that nice summer grass, while ol' Jake here does some fishin', okay? And no snorting now, these fish are wise to it... lost two last week 'cause of you... they *know* if *you're* here, I sure ain't much farther-off.' And then there were the late night conversations such as, 'what's a

matter, ol' baby, hey now, don't fret none, ol' Jake's here now, see? What's
wrong? You hear them coyotes out there, huh?'

He knew deep inside that he really didn't want his horse to think he
was "mighty quiet" all of the sudden. But if they did, and it *seemed* to affect
them or *worse yet*, if it affected his relationship's flow and feedback with
them—what could he do about it? Jake sighed out desperately, *'Maybe I
should take up humming, damn it, anything's better than nothin'!'* In one
last forlorn roll-down-the-hill it suddenly dawned on him that he couldn't
even say his own *name*. Correct sounds were now gone, or beyond him.
Jake stared at his horse humbly, taking his hat-to-hand:

"~~Ay m~ih~," he voiced, with great contortions.

'THAT ain't ME... aww, damn it... that AIN'T ME!' he thought
staunchly, as he slammed his Stetson down into the dirt with a forceful half-
spin of his body, and his arm giving a powerful follow-through. He leaned
back against the wall as his emotions welled-up inside him—he slowly slid
down to the ground in the solitude of the old half-broken shed, and wept like
a hurt kid. Yep, Jake didn't rightly know it until now, but twins tend to
break down near-abouts around the same time. They tend to pull themselves
together, in matched-time, even as well. Jake finally quieted and surveyed
his beloved horse, as faint bits of light shone through the shed's boards.
After sobbing, here he was, none the less—still mute. He wiped his face and
stood up. It was time to press on. He WAS Jake Smith, he just had to build
his puzzle to a new picture-box—one he didn't take-to and one that didn't
match. An *impossible* task, if ever he saw one.

'JAKE SMITH, now THAT'S me.' He rolled it over in his mind—
saying what he truly wanted, in the only way he could, followed up with,
*'well, howdy there, I'm Jake Smith, pleased to meet ya'.' Never will I have
the pleasure of sayin' that again.* Jake choked-up and bit down hard, he
realized he was digging into his wounds, and too deeply at that. It seemed
this longed-for moment of happiness had turned sour, and time was fleeting
away too fast, just as the light was now fleeting into a dimness of its own.
He reached down and picked up his dusty hat, not quite exactly the Stetson it
had been, and bid his horse a fond *'see ya' later ol' friend'*.

Frustrated, he headed for the house, dusting his hat off along the way.
As the sun began setting, so did something else. Something unexpected:
*maybe I should take up humming, damn it, ANYTHING'S better than
nothin'!*—it now began to set deep in his mind. It would someday rise-up in
the form of many new revelations. He was soon to realize that this *setting*
would be a *new dawn* for his future, but it would take a rough hard road to
see it. Past the rocky canyons and forsaken areas, and over hills of new

trails, there would be more sun-rises pointing towards a success that would finally be accepted—and last.

Jake entered the kitchen and was greeted with, "Eggs are good *cold* sometimes, but now then, *toast*... well, that don't always *set well* as it gets nasty-hard." Jade sat at the table and smiled over at him as she said this and waited for his response.

The table was set real cute, just as her knack had always been to do so. She always copied from their ma; it was as if she was still in their presence when Jade set a table, and it always felt good even though they knew she was long-since-gone.

Cuteness faded, as glory sometimes can, as, there was that awful reminder—his special cup and spoon. His new tools, so to speak. They just seemed so foreign, the only things that didn't match Jade's artistic well-matched color scheme—but—he *needed* them. Theses new tools bothered him, they just didn't seem to belong there and it didn't set-right with him. Now as for his coffee mugs, though, they *did* belong. For coffee, he would just as soon teach an old cup new tricks, because he needed the feel, comfort, and, inner satisfaction of his coffee mug in his hand. And, as difficult as it may be for him to try and drink from them, he still had the option if he took care—and whatever hard-wrangled sips went down right, were his reward. Truthfully said, *any* swallows going down right, were his reward—whether from his cup, mug, special spoon, or, food syringe. He would set his face to accept it. He still had some taste perception left to him, but not much, sometimes he even wondered it was just his imagination, but he didn't care, at least it was some sort of pleasure to make his determination to eat without artificial aid, worth the struggle. Yep, as long as it was safe for him to do so, he was going to try to accept this struggle, and, as he had already learned during therapy—that's exactly what it was—a struggle.

There were those WORDS again. Accept it, Jake thought. His horses had to accept it, just now—and they would, he'd come to learn. *So, now... I have too, as well,* he admonished himself.

"Seems you were out there near-abouts forty minutes, you must have spoiled your babies something fierce," Jade said, with her smile trying to hold up as she realized something was wrong again. She bit down on the right side of her lower lip, with her upper teeth, watching and waiting, as the smile left, and she paced herself.

Jake wasn't paying attention to his sister now, but *something* was paying attention to him. Something had been hanging around since he was out with the horses, it had followed him in, but Jake couldn't place it—some kind of a dull ache was marking his every move. Jake felt its fullness now; he had a bad headache. He now took one look at the forgotten supper, shook his head, rubbed his eyes hard and nearly fell over. He felt sick and dizzy as she ran to him and fought to hold him up. He stared as though dazed, but he heard Jade's voice, and then knew where he was.

"Go lay down Jet, I'll get the pills, just forget the supper okay? Cold eggs are mighty *shallow* of me to be offering to you. I'm sorry, I'm *really sorry*."

A bit later, as he was lying down in the dark room, thinking and waiting, she came in to help him. She turned on the small table lamp nearby, handed him the crushed-up pills, and watched. He placed a little at a time on his finger and forced it way back, at the base of what was left of his tongue, as he tried to swallow it without gagging himself. He mashed it around with his finger to get some saliva worked-up from his bit of tongue— other cases of tongue loss, pooled saliva, but his mouth didn't make it properly, since his damage. Eventually he swallowed it, and she gave him some water, then waited to see if he swallowed the water and without any trouble. Water being so thin, was harder for him to control—aspiration could prove deadly in the long run. All was well and she now turned to leave. She didn't expect he'd want to try and talk with her at this point, for sure. But she was wrong.

A mighty shocked twin she was, when:

He reached out and took her hand. He let out the only noises he could, as he tried uselessly to use his mouth that had nothing to *partner* it. Noises he was unduly ashamed of, came out. She listened and soaked them in, as the noises broke her heart, and hung in the room until silence did. He then tried to bare the deep heavy thoughts of his heart to her as he searched her face for any hint that she understood them, *'I'm sorry... I'm REALLY sorry... about the supper, about the whole day. I'm so sorry. I'll try, I just can't seem to do it yet... and I just don't know when or how I can... BUT I WILL.'*

He looked at her with pleading eyes as earnest as he could, as he contorted his face in a variety of ways and forced himself to voice again, what he longed to say. He voiced out: "~ah~ ~p~~o~m~~ih~, ~ah~ ~p~~o~m~~ih~."

Jake then hid his face in the palm of his hand. *'I promise... I PROMISE.'* He sat there quietly as this thought began to penetrate through his inner-being, as if a reverse-echo was filling his soul.

He had humbled himself to her and she knew it. This rough, tough, yet kind-hearted-cowboy, her sunshine-of-a-brother—her twin. He always wanted so much to do things by his code, his ways of being honorable. He made mistakes, but he tried to catch-on to what she told him about the good Lord, and fix them. He always prayed, too—but now—he'd pray harder and deeper.

~*~

Their folks taught them well, respect towards God will keep souls on the straight-and-narrow, but it seemed to soak in best with Jade. Jake may have been the sun, for her shadow to be there for him, as if holding him up by her presence, but in the spiritual realm she was the sun, when he was lost in the shadows-of-life that pulled one down, as he sought to care for her.

~*~

She was glad for this moment and she was glad for cold eggs. She had just seen a sign from her brother—she had seen a shallow crossing. Something was getting through. The strong river of inner turmoil and unrest had a place to be crossed safely, it was coming into view. At least this once, anyway. There was a sign here now, a place where brother and sister could still connect—cold eggs.

"'A shallow creek sure ain't no mighty river unless heavy rains come to call... so we can tackle it.' Ain't that what you always said, Jet? Seems like just *maybe* some of them heavy rains are dying-down somewhere, as that mighty river roaring through here, seems a mite tamer now. Mind you... I realize it's got quite a ways to go to become a picnicking-shallow-creek, but least-wise I got something to look *forward* to now... and you do too."

He listened as he lay with his eyes closed now, feeling the pills starting to work, he felt sleep coming-on as they relaxed the pressure in his head. He hadn't had a headache that bad, in at least a month—though there had been others of slightly less degree in Miss Kaite's therapy. He knew he was prone to them now since the accident, and to expect them. It was just another one of the things he would have to accept. When he tried to figure too hard on things, the headaches would come with a vengeance, he would then stop figuring, and walk away to shake-loose of what ever was happening so they would stop. It had been so long since the last one, that he had *gladly forgotten* them. She went up and slipped her hand under his arm, under his shoulder, in that little nook, and prayed to the Lord to give him a good night and quietly left the room—just the same as the warmth of the last ray's sunlight, would slowly slip away, awaiting the dawn.

CHAPTER SIX

- 40 YEARS + ANOTHER NEW DAY = ?

HIS second day home and the light streaming in nearly seemed like a re-ride of yesterday, with the previously shelved-reminder that he just may be in for the same ol' troubles from that same ol' bad ride. The room felt so good though, it surely did, along with the same smells that Jake had met-up with yesterday morning—and after so long, too. Jake sighed deeply, and lay on his bed trying to allow his body to relax. *Sooner or later, this has to get better*—was now a lame floating-thought in the room, trying to *still* match-up to the wonderful smells of being home, and in this room, specifically.

Why, even the same fresh ol' horse-air was coming in loud-and-clear, howbeit, in whiffs, calling-out for the Boss-man to step forth. *Dear God, I'm thankful for being alive, I really am.* He lay there a bit more and figured on doing some prayers, but then maybe a bit of reflecting again toward thankfulness, wouldn't hurt either.

Jake didn't take this renewed gift of life lightly, especially considering how it affected his twin. What *ever* happened to him, she would take-on as personal. If he had died, she would have been lost. If he had been helpless, she would have been helpless as well. They were a team. It was just as clear to others as it was to them.

Why, we're a team even more so than Matt and I were when we took to team-roping. Why, no one team-ropes throwin' a loop over life like Jade, he thought with Texas-Montana-wide respect, as he lay back thinking about his sister—his little twin-gal.

Jake knew to be thankful—it must be said—compared to what kind of shape he could have been in now. If his injuries had run a heavier course, he would have been bed-ridden the rest of his life. This is what made his whole predicament twice as hard, occasionally he felt guilty that he was not seeing that *clearly* enough. But after forty years of who-and-what he *thought* he was, this change was just not an acceptable portrayal in the stage-play of life, as to his knowledge of such who-and-what's. He was just a hard working man, flowing in the main stream of local ranchers and cowboys, being the kind of man that held-up his end, come hell-or-high-water. Doing his share for those in need, for those that he had come to know and love—since both his Texas-days as a young kid, and Montana-teen days—up until rodeo-ranching-adulthood here-and-now. That hellish boarding school sure taught him the value of friendship, and the friends he had, he made sure to honor and keep. Whether they were in Texas, or Montana.

To him, it had all changed now. He just couldn't get a grip on the reins of this way of life. He knew he was in for a long hard road of it and facing this was going to be like plowing through the rocks of some desolate canyons in some forsaken land with no dynamite to blast his way through.

He felt like he had to reinvent himself or play another role. He just wanted to play his starring role on life's stage, the only role he knew and was secure with. The role he knew fulfilled a special place with his circle of friends and his sister.

Part of this role of who he was, was how he got in the accident in the first place. He was laying his life-on-the-line for friend. He knew it. Even though he was drunk at the time—he knew it. Aside from Jade's prayers, the good Lord must have been watching over him, because he laid his life down to save someone else's, and anyone doing *that* sure ain't in a position to *save* himself, as he is now helpless to lay-claim to do so. And thus, he was. He remained helpless, as it was, for about two-and-a-half of the four months.

If he hadn't been half out of his senses from the whiskey, maybe he would have had a better chance—a chance of getting free from that mad bull—but then again, he would never know that now.

How could he have been so stupid, again he had to wonder, *if I hadn't been needin' to tell Jade about Lyle, I wouldn't have been drinking, but I had to tell her, I just had to. Hear-tell, she KNOWS now... and sure as heck, I don't know if I even WANT to know how she came to know.*

Jake was still alive, when his buddy Matt Martinique pulled him from under the dead bull's front legs. He was alive and well now, after months of agony. His face was in fairly well condition considering the internal damage to the inside of his mouth, and around his jaw and parts of his bruised-up neck. His upper left shoulder had been a mess, broken, along with his upper and lower arm, and near all his ribs had been broken-up as well—adding to lung injury, in the process. Who took care of him and how, was a mystery that he only knew *part* of, as yet, although the others all knew in full. It was Matt who had played a major part before the VOLUNTEER EMERGENCY service arrived. How he didn't suffocate or bleed to death, until this emergency help came, Jake never knew. He never did hear the full story of exactly what-all that Matt did, or how Matt came to rescue him after he jumped in to save Stoney.

He did learn what happened to Stoney though, they did tell him Stoney was alive and Jake needed to hear that, even though he wasn't fully aware of why. Stoney had been weighing heavy on his thoughts as he began to recover from his head injury, he needed reassurance for some reason, that Stoney was okay. He just wasn't able to keep it all connected as to why—or even who—Stoney was. Stoney had two broken legs, a bad gash along his side, and a concussion, but he was alive and well. A truer quickly-made friend, Jake had never known—Stoney Holton, holding honors with his buddies now.

All ready to come back to work too, so I heard, Jake smiled with this new thought. Jake caught himself suddenly though, feeling a bit shame-faced at leaving out his other buddies, as he confessed to himself, *aw, what am I thinkin', Matt and Ray are just as ready to come home, too... they're all the same... high-class gold... Stoney just needs to be moving through my unclear memories is all, being that he's a newer part of my life, I reckon... unless... unless it's just all part of the SHOCK of that day that I keep losing-hold of who he is... reckon, I won't rightly know until I lay eyes on him. Or... will I ever rightly know?*

He had not been ready to hear anything more about the accident—not until those two weeks anyway, in the hotel, where Ray guided him through some of it. Yep, learning that he would never speak again had caused him such a set back, the likes-of-which he couldn't fathom. Then the episode of the *remembrance* of how the bull came to be on his property, well—that set him back even more. So for now, the full story had remained on hold and would continue to be held fast, tethered for a bit longer, until someone unfolded the pieces for him or until he got bold enough to seek it out himself. He sure wasn't up to hearing stories of his near-death just yet, as he only recently finished living through those chapters. He *now* had to find a way to live through the chapters of the aftermath that he would face the rest of his life.

He closed his eyes as he tried testing a gateway to his promise in respects to Jade—he would FACE this—yes, he would. Yet—blockages and detours were everywhere, barring his travel toward success. He knew what he faced was not going to be the same trail he had followed these past forty years. He didn't *know* this trail; there were too many slip-ups and landslides that could hit at any unexpected moment. The river that would forever flow from him would be unlike any he had ever known. The sounds of the waters were not to be the familiar ones he'd heard as in the past. As—when he'd call-out to a friend, or joke with his buddies, or order "needs for deeds" for the ranch, all during his *past* visits to town—there was a stream-of-words shared with a *delivery* all his own. The stream was now dammed, and the delivery was useless. Now he didn't even know if he could force himself to ever go to town again.

He remembered how his sister always told him he had a great voice. Sure he couldn't sing, he always proclaimed, but he blended in just fine when his buddies sang country with him, and he could do some Chris Ledoux songs, to no end—especially come rodeo time, being that he was one of his riding-heroes. Memorable to all, Jake's voice was unique as to doing ballads and stories, and he sure knew how to run trail-drives with strong authority, complete with no intimidation, and plenty of encouraging words. He'd do trail-drives and trail-rides with Ray (back and forth, between their ranches, and off to surrounding areas) for spring or summer programs, and occasionally into the fall, for city kids trying-out the cowboy life or local kids that needed to perfect their skills. He had bossed his good buddies Matt and Stoney here on his on spread, with a firm yet equal hand, always held-out in friendship, never over their heads or heavy-handed. As a boss, he was the best. Yet, he wasn't even sure if he could face his best friends again, or anyone, at this point, being that too many memories of who he was *then*, were now in the way. These memories would not match-up with who he was now and he knew it.

HEY, as I'm BOSS-MAN around here, I guess I have the say as to when I want my workers back... so for now... it's best I don't think on it too much, Jake did some right-nice-and-spiffy thought-mulling, as he tried to justify himself. Then he quickly sought to humble himself, as he met-up with something he KNEW he had no say in, '*Well... sure as heck, it's mornin'... whether I got a say on THAT or not. I sure can't deny what's shinin' in through my window, now can I? Now, as to praying harder, Jade says to just throw this all up at You... so, okay... it's all Yours now. Now, let me know when I need to do this again, Sir... and I sure as heck will try. I heard-tell, if we're not careful though, that we tend to catch it all back and carry these burdens that we thought were up high enough... seems somewhere along the line, they must NOT have been, or they would have stuck. Right? Well... this mornin', I hope mine make it... and stick right-tight good.*'

Jake got up and stretched out, dressed and then eyed the door. He decided to work out a bit with the weights that seemed to be staring at him from the floor. He could do some heavy thinking—with some heavy lifting—as heavy as he could manage at least.

He sure wasn't quite feeling like himself physically yet, either. But the hours of therapy in the hospital did wonders as to helping him move about again and use his newly healed muscles. He even toyed with his *own* therapy when he bedded-down at the hotel, along with Ray and his sis, for his last two weeks as an out-patient at the nearby hospital, and—his hated therapy with Miss Kaite. He had then received the unexpected surprise of these small weights, compliments of his sister and her shopping spree. He enjoyed the challenge of the physical therapy at least, because he knew he would receive back long-awaited strength. Miss Kaite's brand of therapy though, no matter how often, or how diligently followed, would never yield him his desired results—to be a healed-up talking man.

What he could achieve was—he seriously needed to put on some more muscle, and his left arm was still weak with lameness from the nerve damage in the neck and shoulder, but there was the knowledge that it would return to fairly good shape in due time. His right arm, which had lost near all coordination while his head injury healed, was weak as well, at first, but was near up-to-par, now.

He had a limp in his left leg, more from the ripped muscle of his leg, than the breaking of his left hip and the shattered break of this same lower leg. If he pushed too hard in the therapy room, he came to learn that there would an onslaught of pain; the limp would even worsen from the abuse. He didn't dare complain though, because to him, the fact that the bull missed his kneecaps gave him something to be thankful for each morning when he stood up out of bed. If all else failed to dislodge a thank you, this could-and-would do it.

Sure-enough then—seems he could deal with his leg problems though, as, his pa had taught him by example:

'Watch and learn, and suck it up', was simple wisdom from his pa. His pa had seen some bad days during his rodeo circuit travels, with the younger Jake lucking-out as to serious hospital-fix-ups. And, time and again, they'd sing-out the ol' Ledoux song at each other, as only a pa and son could. Yep, the ol' "Bare Back Jack" it was—though their bronc-riding days, had fared them well, as to any serious major-threat problems.

"Sure-enough" was getting rubbed into-and-under the skin extra *hard* right-about-now, as it was stinging a mite hard here—seems sure-enough he couldn't deal with his tongue problem—and there'd be no singing-of-songs going on, to wash away the aches and pains:

     Thrown-out before each daily breath, Jake's trouble with accepting this *other* problem, was, that *no one* he knew had seen days like *he* was about to face once again—starting now—as soon as he stepped through his bedroom door, for yet another new day.

     Yeah, these are my days and these are my ways... days where your big mouth is yapping in THOUGHT only... ways you can't change, he reflected, *as you listen to them thoughts stuck in the dark barn-of-your-mind, with the door slammed shut and the door handle ripped clean off. Stuck. Yeah... that's me. STUCK.*

     Starting today again, he was going to try reining himself to a trail, any trail, to try to make some sense of his life again. A great loss—forty year's worth—had just rushed past him, as if lost down-river in the blink of an eye. *- 40 years + another new day* = ?, Jake wondered, as he stepped out of his bedroom door, leading with his best boot forward—leading with a good *right*, the cowboy way.

CHAPTER SEVEN

"WHERE EVER THE SOLES OF YOUR *BOOTS* SHALL TREAD"

IT was now Monday, one week since the Sunday night of Jake's homecoming. Jake and Jade now were facing the end of his first week home and had actually made progress as to feeling in sync at home again. Trouble was, there was a major flaw that had manifested, Jake was GONE all the time—either out with the horses or out with the few cows that they had, or fixing odds-and-ends in the yard. He was able to handle the fences for the most part, but by the end of the day when the strain of this work had mounted, well, he needed help. So—he'd simply find Jade and put her to work on his near *finished* project—even if she had unfinished projects of her own. Sometimes it took some sore hunting on his part, as he couldn't muster-up enough volume in his voice to get her attention by yelling across the yard. She got mad if he used the supper triangle, as "only major issues warrant that!" She had been known to warn many an unsuspecting cowpoke, friend or foe, to "lay off it!" with near enough annoyance to match an angry dog guarding a bone. So then, minus *that* and adding the fact that when he *did* get enough volume from his larynx, the noises that came out of his mouth haunted him all day long, like an off-key donkey-with-a-bellyache would, causing him to pursue the hunt instead, on foot. Once he found her, he'd take her hand, give it a nice gentle pat and then proceed to lead her at top speed, whether she protested or not, right on over to that wonderful near-finished project of his. He'd smile, and then leave her there to go-it-alone, or if he were still *able* in some way, he'd stay and grace her presence with his help.

Projects finished or not, the end of the day was their "quiet time", and it always varied—but only slightly. For the most part, habits *now* tended to flow down this *new* side trail, when evening came: she would read, while he was in his room using the weights. He was purely in dire need of reclaiming what he had lost and he knew it. He was due for a lot more dire-reclaiming as to something else he lost, and he was painfully aware of that too. Communication. But the goat-in-the-garden was, he couldn't reclaim it in any way that he liked much, so he decided to ignore it as much as he could.

Suited *him* just fine, as he most likely would have told her, *if* he could—and she knew *that,* for a fact. She had heard him say it many times, 'suits *me* just fine', when he found his own way of handling things and opted for it. Just doing it by "his code", he always said. Knowing Jake as well as she did, she would look up at him and near read his mind occasionally—well maybe if the winds were drifting just right—and depending on the situation at hand. Yet, when on a "good run", mystifying it was, to ol' twin Jake!

She knew him good enough to know that after that day on the hill, she had better stay in the main house with him, because not to do so, would surely create greater risk of him straying-off like some sick calf from the main herd. Ray was right, if something wasn't done soon; he'd likely become a hermit. She needed some kind of a plan and she knew it. Otherwise, she could see it all played-out in her mind now: *ol' Jet of the high country... heard-tell he's roaming them thar' hills... out back, and up on the north, and northwest ridge! Out into his woods, he disappears... comes in for supper though, PRETTY AS YOU PLEASE, all owing to that gut-need for survival... and a good night's sleep he'll sure roll-on in to... but then he high-tails it off, as the sun seeks to bless a new day.*

She knew him good enough to say to Ray, at least twice on the phone, "Good thing he does his own laundry and keeps up the place, as I'm only guesting-on here in his side of the house for now... holding the fort down you might say. Holding him TO the fort is more like it... and I don't intend to let him go!" Yep, it was more-and-more obvious though—she was back home, roosting where she belonged!

It was near noon, this fine day; resting now, they were out by the barn, sitting on the bales of hay during midday break, and the only barn animal in sight at the moment, was their cat. It was a type of picnic. A simple pleasure and fun for her, though, sadly, not much fun for Jake. Jake loved a quick sandwich in the past, or a fast fire-warmed Tex-Mex taco, as he was always on the go. He couldn't eat them now—if he bit into anything, there was nothing he could do with it, except hopefully open his mouth enough and shake it loose.

~*~

The ever so slight ridge of his tongue that was left to him was mostly anchored to the back lower side of his left jaw area. The tissues here, needed some reinforcement along this area, and this bit of tongue accepted its needed anchoring here, so provided, so that in some way he could at least *hopefully* swallow on that one side. Hopefully, the doctors thought—and hopefully, had come to pass. This was one bit of good fortune that had been left to him. His salvaged bit of damaged tongue edge, now had only a bit of nerve reaction near the base so he could swallow liquid, (the thicker the better) and softly mashed food, once he got it far enough back into his mouth. There was no other way this damaged organ was of use to him. If he opened his mouth wide enough, there was no visible sign of his tongue to the untrained eye. Sometimes he tried to use his finger in the back, to force a bit of saliva near the area and this did help him to swallow smoother. He tried to use his index finger, placed between his broken back teeth, as a chewing-tool to move the soft food around and to keep it in place, which was frustrating, and only rarely did certain types of food work this way— being that food just lodged where it pleased. As if food can have a *pleasure* claimed to itself, as it follows these whims. This having proved too frustrating, was chalked-up as a bad idea on his part. A parting of ways, it was, but not a total loss—he simply used his finger (or his special spoon) to get the mashed bit of food into its proper place so he could swallow it, and bypass any try at chewing, which was now useless to him. He'd turn his head, chin towards his chest, then he'd tilt it a bit to the side, until each movement had added to his success and his goal was ultimately accomplished, then he'd lean his head back, breathe and relax, lean it down some, and take one extra swallow—before starting all over again. It would then be clearly obvious that he had success with each look of relaxation that would appear on his face. He worked very hard for these successes and it was a hard time-consuming, uncomfortable task. The same went for drinking, it was a hard chore of near equal troubles. If he was not careful, liquid or food would enter the wrong area (his lungs), causing aspiration. This could eventually lead to pneumonia and even his death if it went unchecked, especially if his health weakened beforehand from improper nutrition. So now, scores were rising, Jake had chalked-up a whole list of knowledge that he never would have expected to be the added-burdens of this fate, when he first found himself face-to-face with this unbelievable news, as he laid in that hospital bed—unable to whoa the woe. Forever-more, Jade, or a trusted buddy, was to be around when he ate, as much as possible, to see if it all went well.

The bit of taste sensation that he had left, was at first something that gave him some satisfaction, although now, what little joy he was able to get from it was beginning to wear awful thin. The taste for anything savory, just seemed to tease him now, but he would get hungry still—food still had some smell to it—enough to entice him to try. The taste seemed to come and go, and at times seemed to depend on the foods he stuck back in his mouth—on that tiny, rough ridge—his bit of salvaged tongue. A quick sensation of pleasure only, that turned to a near-gagging chore, as he forced a swallow.

~*~

Jade now watched her brother as he stroked the cat. They called her Mama Kitty, and she had now earned that name. She was nursing her babies, in the midst of the hay bales. He was taking sips of warm soup from the thermos she had brought out for him—it was poured into his special cup. He sure looked content today. She wished she could see him happy though, it seemed she never would again. She thought of the past evenings, before the accident, when he came in for supper. They used to have great fun and happy meals with lots of the "you should have seen what I saw or did" kind of talk. Now, he'd come in near supper time, drawn by the wonderful smells that had wrapped around him and pulled him through the door, only to fight with his meal and then resort to her protein drink filling the syringe, instead. She knew he was hungry but his face would soon lose its enthusiasm once he started this process.

He'd hook-hang his hat—caring for this Stetson, same as his pa—and sit down, just like when he was a kid full-up of many pages of heavy homework. Such a simple pleasure had turned into such an awful chore, and she held back her sorrow for him. She had been an anchor for him so far—as to this eating chore. Anchors can't be sad, if they are, she reasoned, they would dissolve and all the substance on board ship—the nutritious cargo—would be lost, floating-off in a sea of gloom. She had helped him through this process when he was finally able to eat without supervision, in the hospital. He was at complete ease for her to join him, where as to let someone else witness and dine with him was highly unlikely as of yet—with the exception of Ray. He was there during the therapy, when Jake learned how to eat. Knowing Jake and the closeness to his buddies, and how they had been near his side all these years, they would soon join the ranks along with Ray, as the "included" accepted—Jade was sure of it.

So—eating was tilled ground now—at least, like it or not, he could do it. There was a small harvest of success and fellowship appearing at the table, or picnic, and just maybe it would bring forth more fruit with future meals—only time would tell. At least this was the one thing that didn't seem to frustrate Jake to the point of *total* despair, he just kept working at it—he took it all in serious stride, in-between the frustrations, as if a man working a rough ol' hiking-trail. Maybe the dreaded feeding tube was keeping his frustrations at bay—he was hopefully leaving it far behind, in the trail-dust of victory.

Well, a man has to eat and will find a way. Maybe when a man HAS to communicate, she thought, *he will find a way.* She decided to add this thought into her repertoire of future plans, but in as *kind* of a way as she could. You see, Jake was a kind man and she would never betray her brother's trust by hurting him, even if it was apparently for his own good.

He looked so handsome in the sun, she thought, *now though, in his condition, I know he won't dare to go near any gals. Now, I guess it's too late for him. Some gal will be missing someone sweet and special, unless the good Lord can surprise us. Sure can't imagine Jet giving anyone any freedom to get within maybe 300 feet of him now.* She looked away with this sad thought, as she hunted for the apple in the bottom of the basket. Her brother used to love chomping on apples just like his horses did—just like *she* did. Jade finally found the apple, and brought it out into the light of the fine day. Suddenly, in light of the fine day, with second thoughts, she put it back. A fine day was much better than a fine apple.

They shared their time as much as they could, and they shared their "looks" everyday. They shared both these things, along with the Smith Ranch JJ-NS.

She looked so much like him, and they both looked t'favor more like their pa, although Jake was taller than Jade, and had black hair and she had dark brown. In color, they favored their ma. People thought they were half Mexican, or perhaps Italian, with their darker olive skin-tones tanning-up right-nice in the sun and their dark hair shining right-fine to frame their faces, yet only the Italian was *truly* correct. Yet, the Italian that they had though, was only on their ma's side, no language of it was ever used, as their ma's family was too far-off, for too long. Sure enough, they were a mystery-mix to all their Tex-Mex childhood pals and any other Texans of any other root-stock round-about them.

She watched her brother again now. Even as he tried to drink the soup, it was obvious something was very wrong with this man. If she didn't know, she herself would have been tempted to wonder—confession so-said.

The left side of his face was repaired with skill on the surface and healed so well, only the scars on his face and upper jaw gave any knowledge away as to the violent damage that was done. His features weren't distorted any, although his jaw was slightly crooked on the left side if someone took a good look, and it was hard for him to smile wide or laugh all the way, but he did manage. *Someone just may still think he is in pain,* she thought, *as the scars still have some fading to do yet.* The scars were thin, not as bad as they thought they would be, but four months ago when he was laying in the dirt, trampled from the bull, who would have believed that he could ever have seen such kindness rendered to his face. They had both seen enough bull and bronc riders from their pa's days, good friends at that, that rode the scar-trail after many a wreck. They knew what to expect, and they would hold-tight to the saddle-horn-of-it-all 'til the scar-ride eased-up and there was peace to be obtained at the end, as the trail turned gentle.

Well now, Mama Kitty had just been nursing her babies. They were just about weaned but still loved this closeness with their mother. Quality family time, Jade smiled with this firmly founded knowledge, "same as for me and Jet."

The cat hadn't had kittens in a long time, as they usually kept her in doors. With coyotes, and even bears out in the woods, cats didn't always make it for the long haul. The babies were starting to scrap now. Jake didn't see, because he had just got up and stretched, and walked over to the nearby corral (walking past the open shed on his left and the tack-shed on his right) to where his babies were—they were beginning to wander over to the fence as nosey horses do.

Just farther-out from *this* corralled-pasture, past its small fence line, straight-out to the next ranch, was the south pasture (veering a tad to the right and bordered by the old road to the highway). Some of Jake's horses had just come from their day-dreams out there, and he was taking-in the lay-of-the-land. His land. There was then, the pump-house pasture, off to the *left* of all of this—plus—another corral to the left of Jake's corral that he was now fence-leaning on, (it ran behind the old small shed, and beyond the open shed's long eastern side) leading farther east, to the Fisher River that bordered the whole side of the ranch, *both* then moving north. That pasture had Jake's other horses, more of his babies, so said, while the cows were off to the north, northeast, and western pastures—behind the barn, boat house and ranch house. Now good ol' Jake, he spent *equal* time with BOTH sets of horses treat-wise, but these *up-front* horses were just used more often to ride, as he had worked with them longer.

He stroked their noses and felt the thrill of being immersed in horse snoots, snorts, and snots, in a snuggling sort of way, as they pushed their heads over to greet him.

She continued to watch the kittens, as the sunlight played in the yard just outside of the barn.

They remind me of all the litter of puppies we've seen in the past, thought Jade, *just like a litter of puppies find a way to communicate by scrapping at times... guess Jet and me are starting all over in some ways... not just him, for dad-gummed-field-plowing-sure... but me, as well. That scrapping during our first meal home must have led us to some new kind of respect, though, I reckon... even though we're just as close as-close-can-be.* This last thought touched her as she thought back to her childhood days and puppy litters, *each litter seemed to have its own gunslinger, the pup that holstered up his paw right under the armpit of his sibling, ready to come out shooting after a dose of security and comfort. I'm the gunslinger and Jet's arm socket is my holster, he always comforted me, if I was scared he'd always have a hug and let me just hold on to him there 'til I felt ready to face my next hurt. I didn't want to take my hand away in the hospital, not for one minute. I was afraid I'd lose him, but I felt comfort as I hid my hand under his arm... I felt like somehow he was still mine. He'll never know how strong he made me feel all these years, or even in the hospital, when all I could do was wait.* With a burst of emotion, she ran across the yard, and up to Jake and threw her arms around him.

"JET I'M SO GLAD YOU'RE STILL ALIVE! I'M SO GLAD JET, DEAR GOD I'M SO GLAD!" She slipped her left hand under his right arm socket and stood there in the sun. "I'm so glad I didn't let go of you."

She was not prepared for what happened next.

Jake slipped her hand away as he gasped and near cried at the same time. He pushed her back firmly, setting both his hands on her shoulders. She stood there in shock—her attention *quite* commanded. It wasn't a rejection, she knew with all her heart—but what WAS this? He had never *done* this before and she looked up at his face in wonder, all too suddenly lost, and unable to know the thoughts racing through his mind that he longed to spill-out to her:

'You don't know, DO you?' Jake stared at her in amazement, *'You don't know what you did. I was dying Jade... but your hand in my arm hollow kept me back. I didn't want to lose it... I didn't want to lose the feel of it.'* He continued to stare at her as he slowly shook his head side-to-side and he sighed softly, *'I wasn't aware of anything... maybe I was still in the coma... I don't rightly know... But I do know that I was aware of it later again, in other ways. There was lot of voices and faces... nothin' that I knew or understood, but I knew that HAND was part of me... and I didn't want to let go... you did that for me, Jade... no-one could have reached me, but YOU did.'*

He leaned towards her now. He lowered his face a bit and strained his brow with a slight gesture of concern as he stared into her face now in depth, fully understanding why she didn't know, *'how COULD you know... dearest Jade, I've never TOLD you... and now I can't!'* Jake implored with his eyes, *'It's all right HERE in my mind, Jade... I wish you could hear it, I WISH with all my heart...'*

He reached over and put his hand on his sister's face as she earnestly questioned what he was trying to tell her, as his thoughts continued, *'That little gesture always helped me, it was security to me, it helped me take charge of who I am. I should have told you all these years, little twin-gal, but it never seemed important...it just seemed natural, was all.'*

His eyes studied her up and down now, *'But it is... It IS important, Jade. It was... and it was when I was dyin'. It was mighty important Jade. As I lay there with my face all wrapped up, out of touch with any of the world I knew, you were my anchor to reality. I could hardly hear, I couldn't see, and near had no feelings on ONE side from along my neck down... but I could FEEL YOUR HAND under my arm... it always found an armpit... seems I never knew for sure which target you could hit, Jade darlin', but it'd be there... clear as a spur nudgin' me back to reality! There it was, little twin-gal... in its place near my chest, YOUR LITTLE HAND told me NOT to pass-on.'*

He smiled with the thought as he relaxed now and held her hands in his, and fondly kissed one, and continued to wish his thoughts to her, *'You always made me strong when you came to me for your strength and you never knew it... I'm just as weak as you sis... I needed you then... and I need you now. Help me Jade... help me get through this.'* He grabbed her up in his arms and hugged her, his eyes had welled-up in tears that were now softly dripping down, but he didn't care.

"Jet," she said, "please, let me help you now. Look, we'll get some paper... write it down for me!"

He pulled back with a start and stared at her.

"Why can't you do that, Jet?" her heart sunk like a pinecone falling to earth, and he knew it. "Please, Jet, Miss Kaite thinks it's just pride. You could have been talking to me all this time, if you'd just write a note. Can't you just humble yourself a bit more and write it out for me, Jet... I'm longing to hear what you want to say to me, Jet... even if it's not with your voice, even if it *ain't* our way... it's still from your heart."

Jake turned and leaned on the fence. He took off his Stetson, and rubbed the back of his head, and then his temples, each in turn. Thinking about writing was beginning to start up a wave of pain somehow. He was getting a headache now and hoped to God it would go away. He leaned a bit on the fence and wondered what the hell she was talking about, seems the words were flying by, or something, although he didn't seem to want to catch them. He felt real sick and the air seemed have an odd presence, maybe it was going to storm, but his mind passed through the essence of it all and it didn't register anymore—not even the warm sun on his face.

"I know it's not the same." She earnestly pressed him. "I know it's a lot of trouble to drop what you're doing every second and to try to communicate that way continually, surely it won't go-over-well in the long run. But times like this Jet, times like this... these are serious," she pleaded vainly. "I want to know what was so very important just now, Jet. You must have wanted me to know, just as truly as diamonds shine... I saw it in your face just seconds ago, Jet."

She went up and reached for his arm, "Jet? How about it? Jet?"

His body went rigid in her hand, as he gasped half-loudly.

"OH MY GOD... please dear God, not now, NOT AGAIN!"

Jake was now shaking as his body was thrown against the fence; he was now laying on the fence half-hanging over the top rail. She couldn't lay him down; he was too tall and heavier than she was. She ran to the house, placed *two* emergency calls—one, being for *her*—and ran back to Jake. All she could do was watch her brother's form as it still thrashed over the fence, from a hidden unwelcomed message that he knew nothing about and was powerless to stop. She kept watch to make sure he wasn't choking against the fence, though the terrible experience was now making her weak. He brother near looked dead as his body suddenly relaxed—during these last few seconds, his hat, Stetson-credits or not, fell from his tightly clenched fist which had now loosely opened, as his body had finally stopped in the near-dead stillness. He was fully collapsed against the fence and starting to slip. She lifted his arms and leaned him against her body and they both fell over, and he landed against her. He was not conscious now, and seemed to be lost in sleep as he lay there. Still shocked, she didn't know what else to do, except to loosen his shirt some, hold his hand and talk to him calmly.

They were so far out of town, she knew it would be a bit of a wait. It brought back memories of the day of the accident, he was bleeding to death and suffocating from his own blood then, if it weren't for Matt, making that necessary cut into the cricoid cartilage, he would have died. Matt had experience, but with cold numb hands, his skills were being sorely tested. Matt was the one able to stop as much bleeding as he could before the VOLUNTEER EMERGENCY service arrived, Galena, his wife, had helped him. They both were familiar with rescues, but she rescued animals. Help came by helicopter that day and took him far away from home, along with Stoney, but he was home to *stay* now, in spite of how it looked at this moment.

She wasn't sure how long it had been, but sirens were in the air. It was the VOLUNTEER EMERGENCY, they could make it to their ranch in half the time, and did, and the ambulance from Libby would have taken nearly an hour at least. She decided to tell them immediately, once they came, that because of Jake's past head injury it would be best for her brother to receive the hospital-trip to Libby. She was so very thankful for the VOLUNTEER EMERGENCY service, and didn't even want to think what would have happened if they had not been available that day of the accident. She had called Ray again this time, even as she had, then, and he would be there for her—waiting at the hospital. He never failed her. She had kept her eyes on Jake for any change in his face and was soon rewarded; he was now appearing to be more alert. Yet, it came in stages. He was just lying there staring, and too long for her anxious mind—perhaps it had been twenty minutes, she'd tell them, she didn't rightly know—but he was moving his head stiffly at odd angles, as if he was listening to something, or *for* something. Something that no one else was aware of—nor himself, fully, it would later prove true. Jade had never seen him this way—he was lost and agitated because of this process, desperate for an anchor of any kind. This being such foreign behavior on his part, Jade was at a complete loss, just a few notches below his tally-mark. Nothing was registering correctly—mind or body—the seizure had struck as a storm, he was laid flat, and needing to rebuild. An anchor was better than nothing—though a firm foundation it was far from being.

She offered him the anchor of her voice and as she grit herself to bear it, her spur-gal nature rose-up, "Hold up there, Jet. Can you hear me... we're fixing to go on a little ride now, lay still. Dad-gum it, lay still, now, Jet," firm, cautious, and as casual as possible, her words came.

He seemed overly anxious all of the sudden and started to push her away, it almost seemed like he was trying to see where the horses were. She let him push at her, and backed-off to watch, and then slowly pulled him down to his side:

"No... not now, Jet... we ain't going by horse-back. This critter's howling its way up the drive, now please lay still." She looked into his eyes, but he was still lost somewhere. She sighed as she sat there and felt the warm sun on her face. As she did, she firmly kept pressing her hand, tapping on Jake's chest to keep him yielding; it was only half-way working. He was restless now and kept trying to get up and wander-off with whatever was going on in his mind—she feared he take-off into the corral. Slowly, she set her mind to face the rest of the day, as she thought, *Dear sweet Lord, of mine... I sure am glad that I took the chance and called Ray too... sure am glad he was there for us, as always. Seems I need his help again, now... I just can't handle seeing this come against Jet... oh dear God... what will we do?* she realized she was crying, all too soon.

They spent the rest of the day in the emergency, while Jake's hat, a sleeping-Stetson, spent the rest of the day in the sun, in the dirt, near the horses, a few feet away from where he had stood so finely enjoying them—in the happy ray's of that warm noon day. It would spend the night there, too—but they would not. They continued on through the night at the hospital in Libby, their local family doctor arrived and decided that Jake should stay, since it was best to make sure there was no serious changes going-on that they may have not noticed before. As it stood now, the doctor had explained, seizures can-and-do follow head injuries, presented at present—or—sometimes years later, due to scar tissue. In their case, it could be become a pattern for Jake, and, if something was causing some built-up stress in his thinking-process from his injury, this would aggravate it. Sorry to say, he had no idea, now, what kind of stresses could be aggravating Jake's seizure condition or why—but they had been told of the areas in his brain that were showing suspicious activity, during his past hospital stay. The seizures started after the accident, in the hospital, and she had heard all this before and feared it, yet, somehow this time it caused her relief instead of distress—meaning, so far as they knew, nothing worse had been found. If he began to have them continually or even more than what they considered usual during his past healing, then they would be needing a trip out of town—back to doctors that saved his life, back to the neurologist and tests, just to make sure it wasn't something else developing, or leftover unseen damages that were *possibly worsening.* Nevertheless, medication would be set up, then, after a series of test—test that the twins had declined, as Jake was too devastated by his tongue-loss, and refused to respond to anyone as to more hospital issues—or communication, in any way.

It was the evening now of the next day and they were home. Jake's hat was in the house, a regal dusted-off Stetson, if ever there was one, and so was he—well, *in the house,* so rightly said, is better said *only,* in regards to *him.* As—his hat was none the worse for wear, but *he* was. He was extremely tired. The sun was near to set, as night would set-foot on the horizon and take its place.

Jake was on the sofa bed, in the family room—the sofa being in bed-form continually for Jade, as she was keeping her sleeping-quarters here for "keeps" since the day she moved back to Jake's half of the house. Perhaps she'd *finally* get back to her *original* bedroom upstairs, but only if their lives found some kind of normal trail once again. So—conveniently, when she came back from the hospital with Jake earlier, she decided she should place him out here in the open. She would sleep on a foldout cot, in the pool-table room (westward from the sofa-bed) and opposite the kitchen's side, moving west. This was the doorway that separated Jade's side of the house from her brother's side (during her courtship fiasco). Upon entering this room, the left side of the wall was of smooth round stone—there was room to sleep here, and still not crowd the pool-table that was in the center, or the walking-area that led to the west room.

This pool-table room connected with their office, and, to another bathroom (both on the left, being the front of the house), and farther west, was the stairwell to the downstairs basement (on the right). If they went further through this room, moving to the complete west side of the house, they came to the west room (naturally—said with a wry smile, by one that knows). This large living room was near about the same size and shape as the family room (as neither were divided-up space). Jade used to sleep in this room, before Jake's accident—she chose the front window-seat-sofa, instead of the other two sofa's at the back of the room. Folding-out fair, they were though, and fairly fetching for fine guest, at that.

Now, back at the family room, its FRONT was joined to a small open-area at the foot of the stairs to the second story, and it *linked* with the front of the kitchen (with no door, and, all at the front south side), but entering the kitchen, was going east. Now, Jake and his ol' sofa bed were in BACK of the family room, in view of the dining area that was in the BACK of the kitchen (all this was on the north side). Besides the staircase wall (walling-off the center of the kitchen) there was no back-wall to separate these rooms, only an open eating-counter. Thus, by peering around walls, it would be easy for her to see Jake from nearly every spot in the nearby rooms, if he slept here tonight, saving her the task of running through the kitchen, into his room to check on him.

She also thought it would be a change for him to wake-up in the main house with a nice fire going in the fireplace—more cheerful than being bedridden alone, she'd bet and win. In the early morning, it was still cool in these-here parts, and Jake liked warming by the fire, when he could, to greet the day. He always told her that when you camp-out in the summer, you have to have a fire too, whether it's hot or not: 'it ain't no camp, without a fire,' he'd staunchly state his say. So, now—Jake was camping-out in May, and his sis was by his side—well, near enough, she'd be.

As Jade thought back to the day before, she knew he must have had one of the bad headaches just before the seizure. He had only had the one headache the other day, the one that caused him to take the pills. She remembered that he had nearly fallen over, but she wasn't sure why. The last seizure he had was witnessed by four of them, in the hospital the night that he was full of anger. He had stopped having them until now, since nearly a month and a half ago. They were warned to watch him carefully because there was still a possibility that stress or complex situations could possibly trigger them. They were warned to guard against any headache progressions, but then still, the seizures could even occur for no apparent reason—headache, or not—and this was due to head injury.

Jade now felt guilty because she was the one that had pressed him to try to write her a note. For some reason, he was completely refusing to have anything to do with writing out his thoughts. They pressed him during therapy, and he would leave the room. Miss Kaite accused him of pride, and Jake who had already had more than his share of her, decided she needed a heavy dose of stable-duty to keep her nose out of other peoples business— especially a *rancher's* business, namely, HIS. He then stopped seeing her— period.

Jake just didn't understand city programs, or that it was Kaite's business to pursue how he was doing and to help him make sure he could function at his best. Jake understood ranching and a whole vast world that she would never know. He knew what he had to do for himself to function in it, and that was all that mattered to him. The doctor's physical therapy was okay if it'd get him back on a horse, but her brand of therapy was making him sick and giving him headaches. Jake had never got sick and never got headaches on any kind of a regular basis, and he wasn't about to do it for her, as since the accident, he found he could get enough headaches on his own.

Jade brought her brother some warm tea, and set it on the table near him. He still seemed dazed somehow and very *very* tired. She pulled up a chair and decided to read to herself, as she kept his company for awhile. About an hour later, she went to turn the light off and came back to check on him before she went to sleep. She was surprised when he grabbed her sleeve.

"What is it Jet? Do you need some water, or do you need to get up?"

As she waited for the reply, he pulled her close and looked at her and then let go. He lifted his hands in a meek way—a bit sheepishly—and made a sign for book as she watched him attentively. She didn't know too many sign's and neither did Jake since he kept leaving the room whenever Miss

Kaite tried to talk to him and teach him. But they both knew a few little signs of general use from ranch work. Times when tractors were too loud, or someone was too far away and they needed a gesture of some-sort to communicate. Ignoring the unused tea, he pointed at her book and pulled her near and touched her lips to show words coming out of it, then he touched his lips and added the same gesture from his own—for good measure, mind you—shaking his head '*no*', in respects himself. He then nudged the air towards her with his face like a horse pushing for a treat, '*read to me, Jade, read to me... please.*'

"Never got a request like *that* from *you* before. Sure, I will, I'll read to you, but you have to go to sleep."

She was reading her own *choice* areas of their ma's Good Book as they called it, but turned to the Psalms for her brother. He didn't know much about it, but he liked and respected the wisdom of the Proverbs, and the moving feelings in those psalms many a times, especially since he could identify with lots of the down-to-earth troubles they dealt with. The main times he listened to them was at night, out by the campfire whenever they'd chose to set it up. His sis's *starlight* reading, was what *he* called it. Fine with him, if it made her happy. After all, it was the *real* Boss-Man's great wide-open, she could do all the reading there she wanted—and the Boss-Man above was smiling for sure. Yep—and she could set to read what *ever* her heart desired. The only other person he ever saw read that book was their ma, and he missed that.

He gave her a hard nudge and she looked over at him as he thought, '*remember Ma used to read to us... said she wanted us to grow-up to be strong trees planted by the waters and be full of fruit in our seasons... remember?*'

He tried pointing to the picture of their ma on the wall, along with making a gesture for something growing. Then he pointed at the trees on another picture, but he could tell she didn't know what the heck he was talking about. She bore witness to this fact, with, "Ma, grew something? Trees? Is THAT what you mean, Jet?"

'*No,*' he sighed softly, with just-as-soft head shakes to match, '*just read, okay, sis... if I fall asleep, I'll see you in the morning.*' Jake closed his eyes as he listened. He remembered hearing her read these fable-like verses just recently, *must have been in the hospital, when my mind was lost to me, off and on. Hmmm, seems while she had one hand in my arm's hollow, she had the other hand in the good Lord's. That's my sis... always ridin' shotgun.*

Jake wanted to sleep now; he tried to move around seeking some comfort, and rolled over. Here he was on the sofa bed. After all these months he'd spent recovering from severe wounds that he couldn't even remember receiving, he was now laying on the sofa bed. He had never used it himself, only company had. Here he was now, *company* he was, in his OWN house. His shirt was pulling his shoulder, annoying his new-found comfort so he rolled-over to his previous position on his back, loosened all the buttons and tried for a re-curl. His shoulders and hip still ached from his seizure. With the shirt still in his mind, along with his fully dressed attire from yesterday, his mind began to roam away from the voice of his sister.

His own thoughts were calling to him now, *seems my thoughts of the accident and all, are like one big useless dress shirt, full of bits and pieces of damages and rips, and good for nothing now. I remember feelin' the pain of the injuries that went with the rips, but I sure don't remember how I got 'em. Don't remember who volunteered to sew these rips up, neither, but the ol' shirt seems well enough to suit everyday purposes... at least... so far... and at times like THIS, that's good enough for me.* With the comforting knowledge that his thoughts were intact, allowing a few *rips*, he tried again for some sleep. Still—he was haunted by something he wasn't ready to confess.

Yesterday's episode touched too near home for him. *What could possibly be wrong with me?* He wondered. *My memories still in tact, kind of, except for some things in the past that relate to dates and times... and some faces don't always match-up real quick... I know the therapist said I can't seem to think on more than one thing at a time now, without blanking-out and havin' to start over... but this... this branding-iron stuff, branding the pages and roundin' them into herds, sure leaves me at a loss. Why should it give me such headaches?* He near got a headache thinking on these "branding irons" just now—his favorite code-name for words—as he tried to recollect them. Even now, he had to shake loose of the thoughts. As his sister went to turn out the light, his eyes caught a quick glimpse of the JJ-NS displayed above the fireplace mantel, just under the horizontal case of his hunting gun. Oddly the glass was gone from the wooden-framed box, but he quickly bypassed this thought, as the imprint of the JJ-NS "iron" seemed to call out to him, as if trying to speak, and he kept it in mind as he rolled over again, and lay in the dark.

If I wait it out... could be, it will sort-out just fine, right? Jake fell asleep with the glow of hot irons seeping through the dark and into his dreams.

Morning had come and it was nice in the house, full of good smells. Jake was up and beat his sister out to the warm morning sun for the first time since he'd been home. There would be no morning campfire indoors from Jade, Jake had a date with the great out-doors, and the huge fired-up sunrise.

Sometimes even May mornings could be foggy and cool, this one wasn't. It was warm and nice out, as Jake sat on the porch that morning with his salvaged Stetson. Jade—with a warm cup of coffee in her hand and a black Stetson of her own on *her* head (punched down flat on top, same as Jake's)—came out to visit with him, in the new morning sun.

"Why, hey there, the cows are out... *you* do that Jet, or did they get loose?"

Jake gestured to himself, with a smile.

"What's the reason?"

Jake patted his heart a bit, softly and gently, as he smiled while leaning to the side a bit as if in happy thought (a near smug look, in Jake's eyes, if ever there was one), *'I just felt like it, is all,'* were his hidden words.

"Oh, so you just wanted to, huh? Well, good for you, it's about time. You need to be feeling like your ol' self again." She took a self-satisfied drink of her coffee. She was a bit too anxious though, and she jumped back, as it dribbled and nearly messed her clothes.

Jake chided her, teasing with an expression that spoke his best: *'watch out for that dancing coffee, little spur-gal!'* as he finished with a finger scold and brow shift, her way.

"Yeah, yeah, I know, Jet... seems I'm never Miss Manners, now am I," she smirked back, near getting set-off-track from her mission—though not realizing they were on the verge of something new and equally important.

She wiped her mouth with the back of her hand and looked at him point-blank, as she slammed him a backhand of another sort, "So when can Matt and Stoney come back? Stoney's legs are healed-up you know." She walked around a bit near the porch, watching the cows. She quietly waited to let the sting set in, as he hadn't served it back yet. She was just doing her job, taking care of his future, she now reckoned, right?

She turned around and studied him, as she took a careful soft sip of her coffee this time, and now tried the soft handed approach, "Matt and Galena stayed with me, as did Ray... right near your side... as much as the hospital staff let us. But Stoney didn't get to see you much.

He was in pretty bad shape, with a gash in his side too... but once he was well enough, he came in to see you too, he was only laid-up for about two weeks and went home with the Daniels, but he came back to see you during February. His adopted family... you know? The ones that took him in before Ray... the Daniels? They know he's a grown man and all, but their whole family loves him dearly and they were so upset and worried about him that Stoney felt he needed to stay with them 'til he was well... the Daniels themselves are getting-on in years, you know. Even though he never felt like it was his home there, through no fault of theirs, it was the best home he'd had, 'til ours... so-says Ray. Stoney *dearly* loves the Daniels and all their kin... they gave him back his self-esteem... he still can't thank them enough," she sighed, as she remembered how he had oddly been confessing all these inner-feelings to them, in the hospital. She zeroed-back-in to her brother, "That's why you didn't see him much, Jet, otherwise he would have been there for you as much as he could have, cast and all. You should have seen him, never seen Stoney hold still in one spot so long... but he had to, with them heavy plaster things on! Why he sure did peter-out just trying to get around and all!" Jade laughed now as she thought fondly on Stoney, and used this to ease her memory of how she saw him fall off the bull, facing death, with none to help, "You were in a coma that first time he saw you," her words hit the unseen slump—but:

Jade sweetened her coffee with some sugar packets from on one of the tables, and continued on, "by February... we assured him you were going to pull through. When he was discharged and left the hospital the first time, to go back to his 'folks', well..." she held onto one of her braids tightly, "you see... none of us knew that... well... none of us knew what was going to become of you, Jet." Jade walked down the porch now, and gazed out over the front yard, and out over the farther-reaching south pasture. It was so good to be home. She turned back to him, and said most solemn:

"You seemed to remember his name and kept grabbing at us, for him... but oddly, Jet... I don't think you *even knew* who he was until you seen him show up for that visit. You bee-lined in on him... do you remember? He sure felt bad about leaving you then... you saved his life, and you were near to losing your own, for your trouble... he's at Ray's now. Matt had to leave town just these last two weeks for a job, but he's back by now though. Galena was with her folks while he was gone."

Jade set what was left of her coffee down on the table closest to Jake, as the mug left a loud thud, she now stood in front of him and presented the same question, but in one simple word, "Well?"

Jake shrugged his shoulders, *'I don't know.'*

"Well, you're the *boss-man,* BOSS... unless you want me to *take-over* for you, if you're figuring you can't make decisions anymore," she said with a wry smile, trying not to be annoyed with him.

Jake made his wry smile right back at her, as she sat down next to him, in this battle of the wits.

He shook his finger at her and without thinking voiced out, "~unh-unh~."

He was shocked as all get-out and sat-up abruptly, just as she did, in unison. It was a sound that ACTUALLY sounded like something—in fact—it *sounded* like what he *wanted* it to sound like. Meaning the *word,* that is. It still sounded like he was a man with a very sore throat and a bad case of laryngitis, even though his throat didn't hurt. He tried it again. It was a habitual response that he had made many times when he could talk. Lots of people use this way of saying no; a lazy man's way, in common society. He didn't try to make *formed* words with his lips this time. Where as before, he was continually trying to do so with each drastically *failed attempt* to talk, because of a lifetime's built-in habits. It was only now that he realized he made the sound in his throat and he didn't need his tongue or its partnership with his mouth to make this noise.

He decided to try 'unh-huh' for yes, but he just couldn't do it, his throat was too dry at the moment. He had to strain his weak vocal area too much and it was hurting slightly. He felt one of his joking moods coming on though, and leaned forward as he set his chin in his hand, as if in heavy thought as to why he couldn't make this sound, and voiced, "~hhmmm~...?" It came from deep in his throat again, and was more of a deep vibration, but it got them both laughing.

He figured he could hold the sound longer with some more efforts, or maybe try it with a slightly different tone from his throat, but AFTER some water. Oddly enough, he really wanted to try again, thus, letting his stoked-up-energies out now, had actually become a priority.

Jade could tell from the distress in his vocal cords that he needed some fluids, so she brought some juice out to the porch, and set it on the little table and after a while he was ready to start up again. He was able to do the "unh-huh" now, but if he preferred, he could shift some of the humming into his nasal and make the "um-humm" noise instead, thus saving strain on his vocal cords, if so desired.

'Well, dad-gum,' he thought, *'I got three nice choice words here, now... with the watered-up 'uh-huh' version, I got four. And the option to choose which ever I want... when ever I want... for what-so-ever*

conversation I choose.' Needless to say, Jake was quite pleased with himself. He got up and stretched out, adjusted his black Stetson as he looked around the yard at the cows, and instigated some fun. He acted out being a vet, and studied one of the cows and proceeded on his with his act:

"~Hmmm~..." he gestured, pointing at its stomach, he pulled his hands far apart as if to show how fat it was, and then voiced, "~unh-unh-unh~", and shook his finger at the cow. He then made his hands come together again, as if to become smaller. Then he hummed out, "~Um-humm~*"* as if to give approval.

His sister was now trying a second cup of coffee, and near choked on it from laughing so hard in the midst of a swallow. This cup of coffee was proving to be a lot more fun than the first one was. One thing for sure, Jake now had his sister's approval, as she was as happy as a kid with a kite! He hadn't seen her happy like this for a long time. Four months, and a week!

"Oh, my Lord, I was just reading something similar to this last night!" Her voice seemed to pierce the sky and strike back with insight, in a lightning-type way.

She stopped in shock. She was now starting to *also* connect this new situation with one of the kinds of "things" that Miss Kaite wanted to try and teach Jake, some kind of therapy. Now it was falling into place—along with what she had read last night. At least this matched-up to Miss Kaite's sharing, and done in Jake's time, Jake's way. Communication with some throat noises. Miss Kaite was trying to get up to this, but Jake wanted no part of her listening to him making noises or evaluating him like he was some sort of an experiment. Plus to him, she was guilty of a worse crime; she was trying to get him to talk about why he was averse to writing notes.

Jake ran up to Jade after hearing her startled voice, "~Humh~?" He nudged his head and shoulder toward her, *'What's wrong sis, what happened?'*

"You're *doing* it Jet, you're finding your way. The whole land is before you, like I just read last night there in the Good Book... *it's the same,* Jet. It's happening. Can you see yourself? You're claiming the land... wherever the *soles* of your *feet* shall tread!" She looked down at his feet as he stood there in the midst of the cows, "Well now, I guess it's safe to say... wherever the soles of your *boots* shall tread." She said as she gave him a hug.

She stepped back from him and breathed-in heavy, as she tried to take hold of the welling-up in her eyes that she had now just become aware of. Wiping it away, she continued, "Well look at you, you're treadin' all over the place with these dad-gummed cows," she sniffled, between her joy.

"And you're getting the feel of something new… it's going to come, can you see it now? It's *communicating* Jet, pure and simple. It's just being who you are, in any *way* you can."

She hugged him with such enthusiasm that he was at a loss as to what to say—if he could have said it. His mind was a complete blank as he let all these words sink in. It dawned on him finally what had just happened. He was goofing around, just like a kid—like what they had together done, for many years. And most of the time, in this very same yard—chickens and all! He realized that he must have just forgot how trapped he'd been feeling, *now how could I forget a thing like that*, he wondered. Oddly now, he realized something *else* while standing in this brief goofing-off moment-of-time that still *lingered-on* during from this thought: he was starting to feel the SAME.

They were now enjoying the same fellowship that they had always enjoyed. So far, only at *rare* moments had they near come close to it—only to see it fraily crumble in their faces. They both had a taste of it now, a taste of things to come, and even Jake had to admit, it sure tasted good. Still, they had a long way to go. *Jake* had a long way to go. They were on the right trail, but there was more untamed wilderness ahead and none of it to his liking.

One of the cows came up to check the porch now, hoping that some of the action it had just seen, may mean someone was moving around looking for apples or something—possibly for IT. Something, anything—even, whatever! All fit the category when it came to a curious cow. Whatever bit of treat one had for it, would be greatly appreciated. Curious cows have a way of bringing you back to your surroundings quite fast, AS THEY ARE QUITE LARGE, and soon Jake and Jade were chasing the cow, plus its buddies, out of the yard and out to pasture. More of the same, matching-up to what they had done for many years together, in unison.

Same—the word that haunted Jake's mind when he first felt the familiar bumps of the old road leading up to their ranch house that first night home. Same—the feelings that haunted him in his room that morning. Same—*that magic word*, that elusive word that Jake was so confused about and seeking to understand how it now could *ever* be applied to him again. Same—it seemed to be parading around in the yard today in plain view— along with the cows.

CHAPTER EIGHT

PLAY - PLAY - PLAY

SHERIFF Lowrie had his coffee mug and donut on the ready-set-go mark, he was just enjoying his late-morning solitude, newspaper and all, when he got a pretty hard-to-deal-with surprise. It came in his front office door, presenting itself with jangling keys—*not* his jail keys, either.

Surprise, surprise, he thought to himself, *everyone has been set-sail by my own hand, for their mid-morning break, and what do I get... a surprise. I would rather have had MY mid-morning break, alone, forsaken, and surprise-less. Sorry, Angie, you're just hard for my comfort-zone at times.*

"Sheriff Lowrie, I heard Ray was in here," she said in an authoritative way, as her authoritative supposed-knowledge was soon found to be wrong, and rightly so—or wrong—at least as to right timing.

"No, Angie... sorry haven't seen him. Maybe he hasn't come in yet, had errands or something... you know... he always does when he gets in to town, and first things first-off... makes sense to me."

"I was driving home about two days ago I think it was. Yes, that's right, just after the weekend. It was Monday. Well did you know there was an ambulance heading-out toward Jake's place? A VOLUNTEER EMERGENCY vehicle? I would have turned around, but Alex was adamant about us getting home in time to catch Ray. Turned-out we missed him anyway. I bet something happened out there and that *she-cat* in spurs, was needing Ray to come a'running again." As she spoke, she came up and sat on the edge of his desk, and peered over into his work.

"Angie, ever since I can remember, you have been the *nosiest* kid I've ever seen!" He pushed his chair back and leaned back and shook his head at her. Not with disgust though, more like as a father would to his child. Yet, they were both forty, as generally as their respective birthdays led to. He just treated her like she was ten most of the time, and had come to learn that this worked just fine in their dealings, as being, it sure *felt* like she was a ten-year-old, and the proof would usually follow. Occasionally though, harsh reminders from her had a way of leaping at his feet and growling when he least expected it. He soon come to terms with this and realized that she was *also playing* in the grown-up world, and on a higher skill-level in those ways, and that he keenly needed to look-out for her teeth. Referring to him, as "Sheriff Lowrie"—was just one of her "*ways*".

"I'm sorry, Lenny", she said as she earnestly got up from his desk and picked out a suitable chair.

"I didn't mean *that*, Angie. I meant it as to the situation out there at Jake's. I didn't realize it at the time, but back when I told you about Jake's accident, I didn't know that Ray hadn't even told you. I had assumed that he had spoken to you by phone at some point in time, so I kind of "stirred the rice" by mistake. You SHOULDN'T have headed out there Angie." He stood up over her like a dad now, with folded arms and a firm look.

Angie stood-up with "now-power" of her own and came near with vigor, "Why all the hush-hush. There's something wrong with him, *right?* The ambulance *did* go out there *didn't* it?"

She continued to press him with what she had gleaned so far, "He was in the hospital a long time, Lenny. I've heard his skull was fractured and his face was split up the side, nearly lost an eye... and a whole lot more. I'm just *concerned* is all. I've known him just as long as everyone else here in town, so what's wrong with me asking?"

She did have her *own* hunches about why no one had told her, but she would much-rather put someone on the spot (as a type of test) just so she could see precisely, and, more-recently, exactly what folks HAD thought of her. First Jade, and now Lenny—she got important feedback this way, and so far, she had added others to her list and chalked-down their reactions for future reference.

She walked over to make a search of the street, by delicately peeking through the window on his office door. She then moved over to the window and tapped at Alex and blew him a cute little kiss to encourage him—he was waiting outside, loyal and true.

Sheriff Lowrie watched her wave, as she then waved Alex off to wherever he wanted to go. Then she turned and faced him as she threw her keys up into the air and caught them with a hard-handed smack, as they landed in her palm, and she wrapped her fingers around them.

"You know," she said, with tones to insinuate pearls of wisdom, "the Bakers, at the SADDLE AND SEED *were saying...* his leg was shattered up really *bad.* Seems they were hoping he'd be able to still enjoy that saddle he got during Christmas, they were hoping he could ride again but hadn't heard anything new about his leg." *Jake and them damn horses,* she thought, as

her mind had picked-up the scent of this rabbit-trail full-up of hoof prints, *what can he POSSIBLY see in those smelly dirty beast?*

She walked across the room now, and stared back over at the sheriff. The echo of her high heels on the wood still played in the air. Lenny couldn't help but think:

Sure sounds hollow compared to Jake's boots, with that deep rich sound he'd make in here. They sure play different music just by walking... sure am glad Jake found out that she was out of tune, before he got smitten all over again.

"They were saying no-one expected him to pull through, *no one*. Just how bad was this accident, Lenny?" She had quizzed him casually this time, as she looked over his bulletin board at all the local town functions that were posted, and then informed him with some info of her own, "I have to go gleaning all kinds of clues from everyone and I don't even know what's *really* true. *You're* always the one with the best info in town, you know," she said almost too subtly, yet not at all worried about it.

She turned back to face him, and walked over softly this time and took his hand into her own as she played the "innocent" and finished-up with, "I used to *date* him, Lenny, you know that. Honest, I am just concerned... that's *all*." She dangled her keys ever so slightly, just like a little kitten wanting to play.

"Angie, that's *great*, just great... now let it be!" Lenny coached, as *he* now sat on his desktop and kept watch over his donut. "Ray will tell you whatever you should know, then you'll just have to wait 'til the twins get back to feeling at home... just like the rest of us got to hold-up-to. We're *just* as concerned as you are, that all's well, believe me." He finished speaking, with a half-stifled sigh, as he hoped she was soon running out of interest with his dull answers, but gave her a pat of reassurance on the shoulder as to him being a fine upstanding lawman. His next sigh was hard to rein in, and she stared, taking note. He was played out.

"Look... this is my first free time all week, Angie... my coffee mug I'm fixin' to fill-up... dunkin' my doughnut then comes next... then lastly my newspaper. Do you think you could just let me be... how about it now, huh?" Lenny eyed his late breakfast that had now become a type of paperweight 'til his office could gladly see this morning's surprise walk back out the door from whence it had come. Keys and all.

Accepting the pat, while ignoring his words, she sauntered around with her jingling keys and came back to face him, head on, "I still say, it's not normal... it's not normal for NO ONE to have gone out there yet. NO ONE. Not even Matt... and not *even* Stoney."

"Matt was out of town, and Stoney's been at his adopted folk's, healing-up. If you would pay attention, you'd learn more gossip *other* then just the SMITH-TWINS' gossip. Now, *please*, go on over and tag-along with Alex, he must be getting tired of waiting on you. Hey, *look*... here comes Ray." Lenny jumped up, so full of new life that it shocked her.

Sheriff Lowrie made his way past her and over to the door and opened it as if greeting a long lost friend, "Ray, a burst of sunshine if I ever saw one... here... take her, she's all yours buddy. I've got work to do."

"I really wanted to talk about something first, Lenny. I guess it could wait. Just make sure that if I don't get back to you, that you give me a call, got it?" He gave him a smack on the shoulder and grabbed-up his sister as she put on the brakes, and near pulled him back on top of her in the process.

"You've been wanting to see me, Angie... and if you stay here, you won't. Now are you coming or ain't ya'?" He was pleased deep inside that his sister's curiosity always got the best of her. He knew how to play-her-along and end-up with the winning hand. He knew how badly she wanted to press him for deeper knowledge of Jake at this moment, so sure enough, she trotted out—just as happy as those horses she hated so.

The day was passing just fine for Ray. He was glad that Angie finally caught-up with him. Maybe now she'll stop prying. Maybe now she will be content to go off and play the perfect hostess with her new boyfriend, as she welcomed him to her hometown. It was about time. The poor guy was getting dragged all around town without much of a chance to meet or enjoy anyone and he was a really nice patient guy, able to blend into this small town with comfort and ease, if given the chance. Being dragged back-and-forth while his fiancée was checking-up on Jake, was a hard ball-and-chain to drag, and to have weighing on one's thoughts. And as to such, Alex surely *did* have some thoughts, but he would wait, and the answers would come: Just who was this Jake anyway? Everyone sure seemed to love him. Did Angie love him too?

Well now... as to Jake? Ray told Angie everything—everything that *everyone else* in town knew. Everyone else in town had kept a vigil as to the details while Jake was in the hospital. Everyone else in town was happy Jake was healed-up and back home. Everyone else in town knew he wasn't ready for company. Everyone else in town knew he had some health issues to still deal with, some sort of *after* effects. Everyone else in town was wondering as politely as they could. Everyone else in town was content to wait. Angie was *not* "everyone else" in town.

He watched her with Alex as they now finally took off. She was still planning to show Alex more of their small town Montana wonders—but naturally—after she took care of business. City-man Alex, actually seemed to love it here.

Wonder what Angie thinks of that? Ray thought.

"Wonder what Angie thinks of that?"

Ray jumped, as he heard his own thoughts crisply moving through the airwave. It was Lenny that had just spoken Ray's thoughts as he had equally witnessed Angie and Alex leaving.

"I said, I wonder what Angie thinks of that?" Lenny was looking over at him, smiling rich and deep, adding, "If her city man turns country, I bet she'll have a fit!"

"Aww, who knows, as long as he don't buy any horses! Angie, she don't mind chickens, ducks or geese, but no horse will ever darken any of her doorways... whether they be of house or coop. Hard to figure... me personally... I think they're messier critters than any ol' horse or cow," Ray laughed back, "or goat, for that matter!"

"How about that talk now, Ray. What's up?" Lenny took in a deep breath of fresh air, as he stretched his arms out to the front in a curve to relieve his shoulder's stiffness and then to the back as a repeat, followed by tucking in his shirt in, as he now gave Ray his full attention.

"I just wanted to make sure Lyle Barlow won't be bothering Jake, concerning Jade OR the accident. Heard he ain't too happy about that dead bull. Heard he's trying to play it to his favor... wants to drag them into court... sure don't know how anyone can stop him if he goes for it."

As the two friends went off to talk, the slight May breeze played a bit along the sidewalk. A few bits of trash floated and danced along with it, and then got caught-up in stirred-up-dust of the gentle cycle. One of the local citizens saw it and picked it up as she continued on her way—there was one piece *left* though. This piece had gotten caught-up in a breeze of *another* sort, trouble was, this breeze was too far away now to carry this piece of trash to its desired spot—a spot of knowledge. Wishing he hadn't arrived on the scene so damn late, Lyle Barlow wondered what Ray was sharing with Sheriff Lowrie as they disappeared from view.

~*~

Dare we say it? Dare we do! Meanwhile, back at the ranch:

A storm was now brewing, perking to the brim, with heavy rumbles, it sure-as-strong-coffee-grounds, was. Dare, we did!

"~Unh-unh~, ~unh-unh~," Jake repeated over-and-over again. *'I ain't letting her in. There's NO WAY that woman is comin' into my house.'*

Jake was pacing the floor in the kitchen, with his hands slipped in his back pockets. This was his usual fare for a good pacing-mode, unless of course, his hands were in his ever-faithful front pockets, instead.

"JET, STOP IT!"

Jake was now near his bedroom door. He turned to face her, hands free, and pointed at his chest, and then threw his right arm out, and off to the side, gesturing as to all that was in front of him. He then pointed with the other outstretched arm, towards the room where the sofa bed was, and even beyond, *'This is MY house Jade... your half's over there. Remember?'*

"~HUMH~!" He voiced, closed-mouthed, to add some kind of authoritative strength to his gesturing. He then pointed at his chest repeatedly with full force and agitation, *'I'm the BOSS-MAN here... I'm the boss-man! Ring a bell? I'm the boss, no one else! Remember? BOSS-MAN JAKE! ME!'*

In frustration he grabbed his ever-ready cowboy hat off his fine groomed hair, and slammed it on the floor, as he tried for a Stetson-status-statement (habitually the same as their Pa always did, costing many an expense, Stetson-wise), *'am I communicatin' enough for you, huh? Am I? Am I? HUH?'*

"~HUH~? ~HUH~?" he added more verbally, with his voice—openly now—as he waited to see if he had succeeded in getting his point across. His chest was heaving, he was plenty mad, and she knew it. He was ready to go another round if need be and started to retrieve his hat, for some back-up-power—and perhaps a second-go-at-it, as to a good throw. But he was not to do so.

He was suddenly aware that ol' Kaite could see him through the window of the kitchen door.

'Awwwww, damn it, she's watchin' me now... '

With large determined steps he strode over, instead, and pulled the curtain shut with force and turned to face his sister. She stood there with his poor ol' hat in her hands, looking up at him with her big doe-eyes, fake lashes and all.

Jake put his left hand to his head and rubbed it, with a deep sigh. Slowly lowering his hand, he then looked into her eyes with a pained look on his hurt face, *'You said when I walked in the position of boss, that you'd always respect and listen. Just like the hired hands, well why ain't ya' listening now, Jade?'* Jake was exasperated, as he held out his hands to her as if to implore her, turning his face now into a question of bewilderment, as he made this same gesture again, with some voice, "~Humh~? ~Humh~? ~Humh~?"

Miss Kaite was out there on *his* property. His *private* property. He had to put-up with her at the hospital, but he didn't have to put-up with her here. He was afraid of getting a headache and calmly walked over and sat at the table. Jade followed and meekly gave him his hard-hit, yet, honorable hat, and he in turn gave it a toss, straight up to the hook on the wall, wishing to high-heaven that he could give Miss Kaite a toss as well. As—it had hit its mark, with marked success—remarkably so.

"Are you done now?" The doe-eyes spoke aloud, aided wholly by well-wishing, speaking lips.

Jake sighed deeply and swallowed hard. He made an awful grimace and pointed at his head and then at his mouth, as if to take a pill. Jade's face turned pale, as she turned to run to the cupboard for to fetch one. On her return, Jake seemed fine. He didn't want to wait for her to smash it. He took it, as he near gagged trying to jab it down his throat—he tried to relax his throat this time—then holding his breath out, for a second, he prepared to swallow, and was thankful he did-so successfully. He was courting danger with his haste to take this pill and he knew it. Finishing-up with some juice after, he now sat leaning over the table with his head in his hands. Jade, in the meantime, went to the door and quietly let Miss Kaite in.

She took her along the side of the kitchen sink-counter (on their left, as she came in their front kitchen door) and along past its large front window, through to the open hallway-of-sorts where the stairway led-up to the second story, and, also joined-up to the family room. They were now in the front of the family room, the opposite end of this room, was where the sofa bed was. This room had a large front window, to match the kitchen window—thus, Jade felt at ease here.

They sat at the smooth wooden bench-and-table set. As they faced the sofa bed's back, the fireplace was on their left side, at mid-wall; the bed was in the middle area, with its right side (if one lay in it) along the right-side wall, but it opened to face the backyard window—another large window that had recently offered a view far-harder to bear.

Course, this right-side wall was actually the stairs, a partition, put to use, to go upward. Matt and his wife, Galena, and Stoney slept upstairs when they were here. Farther-on past the *right* side of this solid partition, was the back-opening into the kitchen, where Jake now sat.

Both these large front windows (being on the south side) had the long porch outside, running alongside them, leading from the front kitchen door, past the family room's front door, and to the office glass-door on the west-end of said porch. This was the porch that the twins used in the morning to greet the day—this is where the invaders-of-peace had been alighting to, lately, by truck and now car.

Miss Kaite and Jade made quiet-talk for quite awhile and proceeded to share how to use signs of communication that substituted for words. Jade soaked it all in as best she could, along with many questions. It was the language that the Deaf community used, it was a lovely expressive language, but Jade seemed overwhelmed by the huge book. Miss Kaite quickly told her the book was *not* to be hurried through, it was a *gift*, and they were to keep it. They worked for awhile with a smaller book as Jade began to relax and now soak it in with a much fuller-sop, savoring each sign to its fullest. True as gravy's-best-when-its-hot, when Jade chose to learn something of great depth, only the *best* sop would do. It was like playing music on the piano to her, she decided. When she tried signing the words or the alphabet, it was the same as using the keys to make music, she reckoned. *Only,* she then thought, *I am playing a tune of emotions instead of sounds.* Up until now, all was going quite well—*surely Jet could handle some of this couldn't he?* she at last ventured to wonder.

"Now then, do you think you can bring Jake in here? I need to talk to him. There is another reason why I am here, you know." Miss Kaite said as gentle as she could, touching Jade's shoulder.

This was what Jade was dreading—seemed she had felt safe, too soon. *Why can't she understand? Jet don't want her treating him like some kind of a case... or worse yet, a tongue-less experiment for her whims!* She was about to protest when Miss Kaite insisted:

"You already know that these newer and artificial ways of trying to replace damaged tongues will NOT be an option for Jake, because of the severe damage done to him. So it's MY job to try to offer other communication options. We need to know if he can understand how to use this ASL alphabet, and you *are* his best bet, as we've *obviously* learned," she tried not to be frustrated by this fact, remembering her previous encounters with Jake. "I'm sure sooner or later, you can teach him the signs, unless something is wrong... as I *do* suspect and he is keeping vital information from us, Jade. If he is, then we need to work with him so we can re-teach him, or if we *can't*, then we can hopefully retrain him in some way. If we can't do either, well... we need to know that too, for his medical records. It is thus-far left as an 'unknown', as to the possibility of any reception damage or such. You know, reading, writing. In-put... out-put. This would go on his disability list, you know," and she spouted-off a few listed things, in scholarly form, much to Jade's heartache.

Try as she might, Kaite could not show any kind of human emotions as to down-home hospitality. *This woman is so business-like and indifferent to feelings,* Jade thought, as she near-to-matched her twin and his sentiments:

"Jet doesn't like it when you start talking about disabilities, Kaite," Jade said firmly, as she made a point to leave out the "Miss". "He's a rancher and horse trainer, one of the best, in both fields. Now that he knows he can still walk, he is perfectly *happy* to continue doing what he's always done, Kaite... course, he can't rodeo anymore... but those years were to wind-down someday, anyway... so ranching and horse-work is all he wants. True... he's NOT handling this business of not being able to talk... it's not at all going well... that *is* a truth we ain't been able to shake-off," she held her head up high, facing their woe, "but all the tests he's been through in therapy so far, have satisfied us that his memory is for the most-part normal, and he still has his wits about him... although sometimes on a slower-grade as to hill-climbing and all, when the *going* is tough..." she paused, remembering back silently, and sadly at that—yet... *if something we haven't reviewed or something NEW pops-up, unexpected, things can go downhill right before our eyes, and right-bad, it seems. And, oddly... he never goes near his desk.*

Jade tossed her braids back over her shoulder, one at a time, announcing as a new-needed matter-of-fact to Miss Kaite, hoping to end the discussion, "But, the doctors even said that as far as they've been able to tell, despite the damage that was done... well, Jake is a walking success story."

The room seemed unusually and uneasily quiet.

She hushed for just a second as she reflected on what she had just said, and then added, "but... because of the damage... they also DID say he would stay prone to seizures, quite possibly the rest of his life," she pushed the books away as if in a trance, "sometimes, though, they don't really know... do they?" She looked up helplessly at Miss Kaite, until she quickly caught herself, and then looked off across the room.

Jade regained her composure and sorely determined to withstand Miss Kaite's request for Jake's presence, and continued, "He may need medication... yes. They told us that if he has the seizures frequently, or if they get worse as to intensity, they will advise us what to do. He has medicine for headaches, his headaches led to seizures in the hospital quite often, and even here... once."

Yep, ol' Jade stared at Kaite with steal eyes—she was done being polite and her spurs were ready to roll-a-rowel a mighty-mite, "I really don't understand what it is that you *still* feel you have to do for him. Isn't this enough information? You've been working with us ever since Jet had to brush-up on how to care for himself, and dress himself... and then when he learned he couldn't talk with his jaw all wired, we all *really* knew why... and *that* made it all the worse, you know. So, what do you mean by you're missing vital information?"

"He's refused to co-operate with giving us any feed back as to reading, writing and comprehending, these are vital parts of communication. If something is wrong here and he is *unable* to, it shows there's some form of brain damage Jade. Doctors can't see everything, some facts are learned by *observing* a patient and seeing what they are able to do or understand as the future unfolds. Every head injury is different, areas may show up as healed in the life threatening aspects... but a *full* healing may be lacking because of many cause-and-affects. Something is wrong, obviously... and it could be one of the things triggering his seizures, if there IS seizure tendencies now."

"They *were* to be possibly expected the doctors said... but... but he's going to get well!" Jade grabbed at this last futile stall.

"Well, all seizures are different... but he's had a serious head injury, Miss Smith... seizure activity can be permanent... yet, even so, occasionally things in the thought-process are stressed due to trying to force his brain to understand something it's not capable of doing anymore... it takes time and patience for new brain-mapping. Until then, this could lead to headaches and those *triggered* seizures... do you understand *now* why I think there is something he is not sharing?"

"Yes, but they told me they could not find any thing DANGEROUS, no more swelling, no bleeding. Obviously, it's because of the skull fracture... but it's healed!" she persisted, slowly adding, " I... I know he does have a hard time if... well... if something is too complicated, or things that happen too fast... or even..." Jade, collecting all these pieces of all that she had learned by watching her brother, both in the hospital and at home, was near Miss Kaite's finish line. Their argument was drawing to a hard close now, Jade could sense it.

Her thoughts were nearly overloading as she tried to figure it all out, *his thinking process... it ain't functioning as it should... oh God, I know this... but... well,then... trying to force it to over-tax itself... it's like making a strapped-bronc chin the moon... a fights going-down... it ain't normal...*

it's some foreign cause... extra unknown extreme pressures... but from
what... headaches? The headaches... that recent seiz-

Jade sat there as the tears ran down her face slowly, she thought back
to the day she had pressed Jake to write her notes, concerning his thoughts.
But dearly needed, she figured they were. She just wanted to know what he
was thinking. Now she began to realize there *had* to be a reason—a *serious*
reason—why he continually walked-out of the therapy, and why he didn't
yield to her that fateful day. And—there had to be a reason for his disdain of
Miss Katie being here today. Jake rarely got mad, and if he did, it was in
defense of his home, or someone being harmed. What was Jake
defending—she HAD to know.

"All right, what do you want me to do… tell me, and I will DO it…
but *not* today." Jade looked-up as she heard Jake's chair move in the
kitchen.

As they watched, Jake came into the room. By-passing Jade, Jake
went up to Miss Kaite slowly, as he watched Jade dry her eyes with her
fingers. Her black eyeliner was smeared along her cheekbones, a pitiful
raccoon, if he ever saw one—and he had seen quite a few.

Jake gestured for Miss Kaite to follow him, and in curiosity, she did.
Jade stood and followed silently at their heels. Jake stopped Jade at the
kitchen sink and lifted the coffeepot for all to see, as he smiled a bit, *'See...*
coffee.'

He led Miss Kaite to the kitchen door and motioned for her to go out.
Jake stepped out the door and motioned in a fine manner—and a most polite
cowboy-style, it was—for Miss Kaite to sit down on the porch. He stretched
a bit as if to enjoy the fresh-air and then walked back into the house and
locked the door. He dumped-out the coffee that Jade had started, letting it
steam-up the sink, as it sunk, and gestured a huge sign for a clearly
understood action—FINISHED!

'I'M THE BOSS... SHOP'S CLOSED... I'M GOING TO BED!' he
thought towards her as he glared at her. He then went in to his room and
went to sleep. Jade smiled as he did, walked over to the sofa herself, and lay
down to sleep, as well. Twinship, it was, at its very best. This time *she* had
the bad headache, and was very glad that the BOSS had taken over. And
Miss Kaite? Recognizing a well-played trick, she sat there a bit, and finally
left—taking the storm clouds with.

~*~

Jade was awakened by the sound of a truck. She was well-rested and
so very glad that she had the chance to escape the heavy thinking that Miss
Kaite had led her into. She let her *last* ones go free as she made her way to

the window. *Maybe Miss Kaite is right... maybe there IS something else wrong with Jet, maybe... but it sure ain't pride. Seems his security in his self-esteem has been taken away though... and that's a powerful blow for any man. His deep-seated concern for his own well-being, as for who he is, had done left... and it sure ain't wrong to want to have that back... leastwise that's what Ma always said... so pride, it SURE just ain't. Whatever else's wrong, though... I need some good keys, somehow... as it's locked inside him and not boxed t'proper order.* Jade was following a right-good scent, just as sweet as any scent in the field could be to a good bloodhound. Jake needed his self-esteem to be anchored again, and as soon as possible. If a person feels well, and this anchor holds somewhere, then somehow they feel that all's well in their little corner of life's trail. Sadly, Jake had been thrown-down off that trail, and it seemed his self-esteem had picked-up and left, in the whole sorry process and—he didn't know how to get it back. But Jade was making it her goal now. *I got to help him find a way... some way to hit the trail again. Yes sir'ee, that ol' trail of who he is. Once he's sittin' that saddle anew... why... he'll be anchored again for sure! Then he can start facing the world again... and oh, sweet, dear Lord, I sure hope it's with some smiles and laughs, again,* she thought with earnest prayer.

Jade studied the window solidly—judging by the amount of light coming through, it was late afternoon, no one would be calling, unless it was Ray. She looked out the window but oddly there was no truck—she moved on through to the kitchen, to peek out, but it was no where to be found. She went to the door just as Ray came walking around the corner of the porch. She went and let him in before he ever had a chance to knock. Truly, something was up.

"I parked in the back, behind the house, hope you don't mind. Where's Jake?" He stared at the empty kitchen table, as she pointed to his room:

"Sleeping, but let me check on him, he wasn't feeling well earlier... Miss Kaite was here."

After checking on her brother, with Ray peeking in, she was content that all was well. She sat at the kitchen table and Ray joined her.

"Why the mystery?" She leaned forward with her chin, on her one elbow, and batted her eyelashes at him, in fun—now repaired from Miss Kaite's visit.

"I'm still thinking Angie will show-up around here again. So I think I've come up with a plan."

"Aww, Ray," she drew back from her "funning" and slapped the table hard. "I thought you settled that for us 'big brother'. We really *haven't* had a very good start... me and ol' twin there." She thumbed over at the door. "First, the coffee, then your sister, now Miss Kaite... and..."

"And me now... as well, right?" He smiled as he tilted his gray Stetson back. Ray always looked so gallant in it, his native-ancestors had come from Canada way back, and he was very dark, like his mother had been, the gray hat framed his big, wise, black eyes, in a most special way. He did not know his full background, even though he had a European last name. His father never ventured to tell them any family history before he passed on, either.

Ray's looks just accidentally seemed to match the tower-of-strength that he always was to them. He was a tower-of-strength to them through this crisis, all the more.

"Oh, no... " Jade defended him from himself—a hero, at heart, she was, though in different ways than Jake. "I *saw* how Jet searched the room for you and Matt, in the hospital. He needed you, and so did I... and we still do. After I talked to him up on the hill... or rather, let him have it with full-force, both barrels, so to speak... I realized I needed to move back in here, like back how it was when our folks were alive. See, look, there's my so-called bed-of-sorts, around the corner."

Jade beamed like a babe with a toy, "I need to keep him in the position of *advancing* and not *retreating*. I think we have had enough alone-time now." She began to relate to Ray everything that happened with Miss Kaite.

"You know, Ray, at first I didn't like her being here, but you know, Jet reacted instead of retreated this time... I know that's because this is his home, but that's what he needs... company to work with, and open-up to. People he knows though, not Kaite's or... Angie's. It's time for Matt and Stoney to come back, Ray, it *really* is."

"Speaking of Angie, listen, how's this sound... " Ray began to present a situation, a kind of presentation, almost a type of play, to Jade. One in which Jake could portray himself in the kitchen, along with Jade by his side, in the presence of prying eyes—Angie's. With some ad-libbing, coming by way of Ray, they could call their production, "ARE YOU HAPPY, NOW?", and send their curious audience, Angie, home.

"Kind of a wild idea, Ray" Jade said, as she tried to picture it. "Well, in a way it's quite likely to work, as Miss Kaite stood out there quite a while and could see and hear all we did until Jake noticed her. I could picture

Angie, hanging out there... after getting no answer to her knocking she certainly would be *hoping* for to look."

"Here listen to this tape, and give it to Jake. Play it for him first and study it. Play it if you see her pull up, and "play-act it out" for all it's worth. Jake and I sounded enough alike that we could get by with this, she's confused us before on occasion. Play some background music, and a little on the *loud* side... that should help. If she comes around, she'll see all is well, and then... chase her off! She'll have no more reason to come back, once her curiosity is settled with the *real* thing. She just wants to see Jake... she's heard so many stories, she's expecting to see a broken-up toy or something.

Jade took the tape, as if taking the first steps to a secret mission, through the sweet sage-brush of the great unknown.

Ray added his last bit of guidance, "Now, she *may* still want to wave her new boyfriend in front of him, but she won't do that here. She'd like to do that in public, so for now... it's safe to say, she'll leave you alone soon once she gets a dose of normal family life."

"Thanks Ray... do you want to stay for supper... you've seen Jake eat during our stay at the hotel, you know he doesn't mind you."

"No, Angie and Alex are expecting me... but you mark my words... she won't give up, not without a good look. What can I say," he spread out his arms, as if at a loss, "I know my sister... but *not near as well* as I wish! Wish I could find a better way to pull her reigns in... thanks for not calling the police, as I don't know who it'd be harder on, Angie, Lenny, or me!" Ray tipped his hat at her, as any good self-respecting rancher would do to a lady.

"Ray, I'd never do that... well, least l hope I wouldn't!" She said with a pretended after thought, as she walked Ray to the door. As his dust hit the road, she hit the pots, and supper was soon on its way. Just as soon, Jake was on *his* way—on his way to the supper table, sitting down before his treasured-twin. Considering how awful he looked earlier, Jade was now amazed.

"What are you so happy about, Jet?" She said, as she sat down near him.

'*Kaite's gone, can't ya' tell*', he smiled wryly, as he had pointed at the kitchen door, then drew all his fingers back, and swatted-out at the door, as if to gesture that she was gone—brushed off—'*and she won't be back, if I reckon rightly.*' Then he opened his hands out in front of him, and gestured the familiar way that most people, use for, *'W-e-l-l...'* –and waited, leaning-back, self-satisfied,

She laughed and gave him a hug, nearly knocking him over backwards, yelling, "You just GOT to stop tilting that *dad-gummed* chair, Jet! If you get me riled, I'll be hollerin', JAKE SMITH! …just like Ma did!"

As they began to eat, she explained Ray's odd idea. Jake listened and thought, and listened some more. *'Angie... huh? Angie? I remember an Angie, don't I?'* He let it soak in a little more, *'Angie, and Ray... yeah, Angie... she left... didn't she... yeah, I made her powerful mad, a ways back... '* The SADDLE AND SEED began to focus clearly in Jake's brain now, he has dad-blamed sure he didn't want her around, not after what he remembered from the SADDLE AND SEED. He set-his-face to piece it all together now, and was mighty glad that Ray was looking-out for him. He was now just starting to marvel at Ray's artistic creation of play-acting. Jade continued to sell the idea, unaware that he tuned-in a bit late. No matter—he was on the right station, and the right song was now playing. She played the tape over-and-over so he could remember it. It wasn't very long, and was just common short household-talk, the type Jade and Jake usually partook of, plus, a small family argument about having company—as in regards to how *soon* to invite folks back to the ranch. She talked more in depth to Jake about the idea, and how she thought it had high possibilities.

He thinks it completely stupid, I can see it all over his face, she thought, *oh well, I guess it is... Actually it's just presenting a lie, is all it is. Dear Lord forgive me, what was I thinking anyways?*

'How the heck does Ray come up with all these creative ideas?' Jake marveled, as he studied this thought and continued to lure-it-in and *wrap-in* the fullness of it all, completely *oblivious* to his sister's dejection.

"Jet… " Jade said, but stopped as she tried to collect her thoughts as to how she could best apologize. She was afraid that she had insulted him in some way.

Jake looked down and played with his odd shaped spoon, twirling it around in circles on the tabletop. *'Anything to be alone right now, suits me just fine Jade... that's the LAST THING I need, is for Angie to show-up and make-sport of me... she sure loves to be the star in everyone else's play but her own. She can have a key role in this one now, and then turn reporter as well. I'll get some free advertisin' as to my health, and some more time to figure out my life... as right now, I feel like I'm trapped in some dark old mineshaft and running-out of any hope to be seein' the daylight any time soon.'*

Jake stood up—supper could wait—as he well-knew, it wasn't fun, anyhow. But this tape was quite palatable and easy to swallow, tempting him to tasting adventure. He continued to mill this over in his mind, trying to think of the best way possible to set it up. He was now fast concerned, concerning this unwanted visitor—*'Who knows when-or-where we could be caught off-guard. If she's due to show up, I sure as heck don't want it to be outside. Seems I've had no concern up to now, as to ol' Angie... hmmm... I never even knew she was back in these parts, did I? Thought when she turned-tail and ran, that was to be the last sighting due us... thought she set-off for richer feeding grounds.'*

Jake turned and faced Jade, and she stood and approached him.

"I'm sorry Jet, I was wrong." She humbled herself. After all, *she* could talk, how did she know how Jake felt? How *dare* her.

Wonder what she's sorry about? He turned his head slightly, lowering himself in a slight hunch and leaned forward a tiny bit, and voiced, "Huh?" But then just as quickly, he chose to shrug it off, and turned from trying to converse body-wise. He was now intrigued and pulled into the hub of this play-acting, as he walked across the room and came back—ready for action. He smiled at her and rubbed his hands together:

'When do we start practicing, little twin!' Jake gestured with his hands out, as if tossing a salad in front of him, but tossing it towards her in repetition, and then gestured with his head as if pushing a nod towards her as well.

Jade smiled back, *Thank God, he's not offended!* She thought.

Jake stood there waiting, with a look of strong questioning on his face, *'don't you understand me Jade, ain't I comin' through, or something... look, I said it's okay... here... listen,'* :

"~Unh hunh~", he voiced-out with a nod. He pointed at the tape recorder. Then he snapped his fingers, a few times to hurry her up:

'There, that ought to do it... you got it now?' Jake thought. He watched her and waited.

"You mean you *like* it... why I thought... "

Jake stopped her, and gestured to her to stop thinking, or at least he tried. He pointed to her first, and then at his *own* temple repeatedly. He wanted to make more-than-sure she got the message, so he then finished by waving his hands back and forth, over each other, as if to put a *stop* to something—he sure hoped it worked:

"~Unh-unh~", he voiced as he shook his finger at her, to end it all, *'NO MORE THINKING... YOU WERE WAY OFF BASE... how the heck*

THAT happened, I'll never know... ' –he sent her a big smile, and grabbed-up
the tape recorder. It was now practice time, being that they had all night to
eat, if hunger set in.

Two hours later, they ate their cold supper in silence. Not that they
didn't *want* to talk this time, or, that they were at a loss to, but Jade was pure
talked-out. Jake was having to deal with his supper—hardly a done-deal.
Jade was trying to be open about what she would cook for him in the future,
and figured she'd try everything he used to like, and let him decide what he
could handle. Setting her eyes and her mind on him now, she just couldn't
help but notice that tonight's supper-chore seemed a mite rougher, but he
didn't seem to be complaining.

~*~

Jake had a terrible time of it the last two weeks in the hospital, as it
was his first time to try feeding himself. Before that, he was just getting his
jaw and face freed up, then, therapy for his mouth and jaw, and there were
test to run, all to see if he could swallow substances, and how well he could
do it, and—if he could continually do it safely. These two weeks were
important, and the doctors didn't want him to go home until they could
witness that he handled it safely, and, also understood all the precautions as
to before-and-after swallowing, and before-and-after eating. If not, he
would have to learn to use a feeding tube, most likely the way he had done
in the hospital, through his neck (although there were *other* feeding-tube
options, but they were very unpleasant and all had potential side effects and
even dangers). She couldn't imagine him trying any of the other
uncomfortable ways, as the one through a hole in his neck, was agitating his
mind-set, as it was.

Then the last two weeks as an outpatient (while they stayed at the
hotel) was just as bad—but for deeper reasons. He was more frustrated with
the long-term facts, being he'd never eat normally again—as opposed to
before, when the frustration was just learning *how* to eat. When in the
hospital, he could then at least pretend it was only a hospital ritual, but once
out in the real world, it was now a rough ride of reality. A reality he just
didn't like, but one that so far, he was accepting.

He would cut up his food and play with it as a little kid smashes-up
his supper when he doesn't want it. Sometimes he would lean-back in the
chair in the room with Ray, and watch TV while Jade slept, and he shot
baskets with the bits of food because he had tired of the whole ordeal.
Sometimes he would stare at the food and then simply throw it away—this
was followed by laying on the bed, doing some long-hard ceiling staring, in
between shutting his eyes and trying not to cry.

They were warned to make sure he was diligent to get sound nutrition and put on weight or he could soon lose his health. Jade was so concerned then—as Jake had become so thin already, as it was—that she disappeared for a few hours to find a solution. She faithfully did well, and showed-up later with a nicely wrapped gift, and presented it to her brother, along with a smile and an energetic bounce—followed lovingly with a nice hug. Unsuspecting twin that he was, upon opening it, Jake was not very happy at all to find himself staring at a plastic feeding-tube with a bright red bow wrapped around it. He tossed the whole thing in the wastebasket with a strong show of disgust on his face. *'Women!'* was about the only thought he had at the time, for *that!* Of course she had got it as a reminder, as, he would have had to go back as an outpatient to get it put in again. It sure did the trick though and worked like a charm, soon he was sitting off in the corner, near the lamp, working at his meal. It was always during the evening, after Jade retired for the night. And, strangely so, somehow it seemed like a good guy-thing to do with Ray, as they watched sports. Ray doing more of the watching though, and Jake setting-attention toward his *own* sporting-challenge, as the roar of the crowds set the ambiance. Although they both loved watching the bull and bronc riding, Ray carefully avoided these stations. He didn't know how Jake felt about viewing it all, or even how much Jake remembered about the accident itself, but the few times of late, that he himself saw the bulls while flipping these stations, all he saw was visions of Jake under each one—and worse yet, he feared Jade would wake to see it played out, from her long-awaited sleep. It didn't set-to-well with him no matter *how* much he tried to reason it to—and he wondered slightly, if it ever would. Yep, it was best buddy Ray, watching over Jake now, while Matt got back to over-seeing the ranch.

Good ol' Ray, why he proved to be a good-sporting cowboy about Jake's eating-trouble, and on some nights would bring in a roasted chicken and have at it, fingers and all—making a most mushy mess—trying to compete for who was the worst eater. Jokes being as rare as they had been in those first back-into-the-world days, Jake felt real at-ease with his buddy Ray, sure enough said, and, for fleeting moments that surfaced without score-card recorders, it dared to dawn on him—they were even starting to have *fun*. A *fleeting glimpse*, into the Jake that was, and hopefully, the Jake that was to be.

~*~

Jade learned a lot watching her brother eat, he was hungry and he was determined in spite of the obstacles. She thought how the alternative, the feeding tube, was worse mentally to her brother's self-esteem, so much more-so than wrestling with the meal he had just finished. He wanted to know he could succeed without it—it was so amazing how it kept him on course. *Men!* was about the only thought she had at the time, as to that! Little did she know that Jake was about to learn, and sooner than she expected, that there are other *worse* alternatives to his self-esteem that would encourage him to chart a course for more nutritious-communication, but at least then, he would finally be feeding this half-starved self-esteem, in an entirely enriching way. But *first* there would be Angie to deal with.

As the evening wore down, and they went their separate ways for the night, Jade called out with a happy, "get ready… we may have an early curtain call… you never know!" instead of her usual "good night."

Two days went by with out anything-unusual happening, but today it turned out that Ray was busy showing Honor the new changes on the property. Alex was intrigued by this since he had never had that much land at his disposal at one time, but bored Angie (having her fill of her brother's property) decided to go exploring—on a trail that she *knew* was off-limits.

Jade saw her coming first, she would have thought it was Ray, if she had not been warned by his initial visit. This time Angie was driving *his* truck. She sure didn't need to waste money on a rented one while staying at her brother's ranch.

Jade and Jake sat at the breakfast table. Jade had the radio on and nice country sounds were in the air as Angie primped herself in her personal pocket-mirror and knocked at the door. It appeared after a few knocks that no one heard her.

Must be the music, she thought, as she peered in through the door to see what she could see. She saw them at the table. *Well, ol' Jake sure ain't in any wheelchair, and I don't see any crutches lying about.*

"She's looking, Jet," Jade said under her breath, as she smiled at her brother and took-up some food to eat, "let's start to play-up now."

As they started their play-acting, Jake pretended to eat, as if he was sopping-up egg yolks on bits of too-hard-to-see toast. In between this, Jake and Jade talked about the usual morning stuff, all in two-to-three word sentences. Jake would mime to Ray's voice, laugh when called for, and gesture most expressly. Fit for the stage, he did it just as pretty-as-you-please. Jade inserted her lines, with perfect grace and skill. It was to be EXPECTED, wasn't it? After all, they were a team, they were born to teamwork, and they played so well off each other, years on end. Who would have ever *guessed* it was a last-minute-take for the premiering "EARLY EARLY SHOW" by an amateur script writer, and acted-out by stand-ins.

True to Ray's prediction, Angie could barely hear their voices over the music. And when the commercial and announcers came on it was even harder. She decided to knock harder, but quickly changed her mind, hindsight told her that Jade would be on her in an instant, and from here she had a front row seat—one she had been most desperate for. Jake was too far away for her to make out the scars on the side of his face, she knew he must have some, but she never could have imagined how bad. To anyone that saw him close up, he would still be his same ol' self, but the pain that he must have felt would strongly haunt a person just by looking at the tracks that were left from whatever had traveled over his intriguingly good-looking features. Yep, these scars were a witness to that. It would be obvious to all for quite a few more months that the side of his face and neck had seen, and come through, very *hard* times. It would be obvious to all, for quite a longer time though, that a man can bear-up under very hard times, without bitterness; it was to be a scarring-type witness of his own—etched into the mind of others who shallowly can become bitter over the most superficial and petty things. As—life is most-rightly said, instead, more *truly* about inner-spirit quality, and NOT the "vase" of one's inner-flowing eternal-values, in the *heavenly* long run of it all. Yep, these scars were a witness to that.

Angie was not very strong, and if she had seen these scars in the past, chances are she would have lost her brilliant city-composure and been at a loss as to how to handle it all, and in all probability it would have made her feel sick. If allowed to dwell on these thoughts long enough, she may have finally found the needed care and compassion for the hurt he had gone through, but then it would require effort on her part to *present* it. This was her main problem. This just wouldn't do. She would much rather present *herself*, along with *her* successes, since her own personal time and agendas in life were her only priorities and values. Thus—effort was for her, and her alone. So—knowing he was healed and back at home, her need for playing the superior would over shadow any good-hearted feelings, and, he was *still* now an old toy, with new possibilities that she could play off of. Empty handed now, she was, though, as she sure didn't see what these new possibilities were yet—he looked and sounded just fine to her.

Angie was suddenly aroused out of her "TV" watching, as it took a dive with a hard spin—it appeared they were now arguing and she stepped back quickly, to remain unseen. Cautiously as possible, she picked up bits and pieces of:

Jade wanting to get the workers back, and how Jake was still tired and needed some time to get back into the full swing-of-things. She would like to get a bit more work done, and he was saying he'd be ready soon. She was saying, I've waited long enough, and he was answering, let it drop.

It had now escalated, and then, just as soon, it now stopped. She was *so* curious as why it was so very quiet, she was intensely moved upon. The shining "lure" of more, easily attracted her. Angie moved-up to the door, she was near ready to peek in the window again when the door opened with a large powerful-strong swing. IT WAS JAKE! He now stood face-to-face with her, if ever his taller presence could—black Stetson topping-him-off in great show. She saw the scars, but she was more shocked by something else. He was giving her his MEANEST stare. Just as quickly, he turned from her presence, and he took-off around the left side of house, continuing through the back and into the north pasture, and up to the ridge and his woods. He was stomping mad, that was for sure. She near fell over and was so completely shocked when he stared at her that she near choked. She was just about to catch her breath, when Jade appeared in the fully opened doorway, as if the wind of his fury:

"We ain't *ready* for company... I thought I TOLD you to git... now GIT GIRL! GIT GONE GOOD!"

Angie's jaw dropped a bit as she tried to swallow, and she backed-up slowly away toward the driveway. She dropped her keys—much to her helpless dismay. There was not a jaunty jingled note to come, from their muffled thud. She bent slowly, still eyeing Jade's mad face, as she moved her fingers in-and-around in the dirt, hoping in earnest for the keys. Upon retrieving them, she took-off with a half-trot toward the truck, and sped-around without another look, pushing for haste—only to have to brake fast. Stunned, she had near forgot to stop to get out and open the gate, making her get-a-way most awkward—but pushing-it once again, she longed for her goal of being long-gone.

Jade watched, savoring the sound of the past-plopped keys-to-dirt. They *had* played something *after* all (if not a full-jingled tune). They had played *satisfaction*, pure and simple—yet, not for Angie, as she was hearing the flat reminder of it, this way:

Yeah, they're twins all right, that's for damn sure! Angie thought, as she finally caught her breath, half-way down the old road—highway soon-to-sight.

Once Jake saw the truck clear the very visible gate to their drive, he came back down and joined his sister. He truly wished Ray was here, he really wanted to thank him. He knew it wasn't ethical, but he thought back to the days when they were kids—Ray could come-up with some *great* tricks back then. They never harmed anyone, and Ray always acknowledged any hurt done, but they had a great time picking-on the girls back then: all of which had included, Angie, Galena, and even Jade! This was the most fun Jake had seen in a long time, well, to tell the truth, four months worth of time. He felt like he had been freed-up to finally do something for himself, even if it *was* just a trick. Oddly, somehow-so, he felt like a man again. He got to be the hero, he took care of his sister and saved the ranch, just like in the movies—and—he liked it. He just needed a white-hat-hero-Stetson, on now instead, cinema-wise, to match his white-hat hero-heart.

He put his arm around his twin sister, his little sister, younger as of three minutes—but every bit his equal.

She looked up at him, with a gleam in her eye and confessed, "It sure is nice to be on the *winning* side with you boys, for a change."

CHAPTER NINE

IRONS IN THE FIRE

JAKE awoke to his sister's voice, it seemed persistent somehow. Grabbing a sheet to cover his boxer-shorts, he ran out to the kitchen but she was no where in sight. It was then that he realized it was the answer machine on the phone, and she was still talking, *obviously* she was repeating his name because she wanted him to pick up.

Well, obviously, I'm, not, he thought.

As he thought some more though, he realized this could go on for a half-an-hour or so, as the machine had a long tape to back it up.

'Aw, dang it sis... just leave me a message, you know I'm here.'

He stood there in the kitchen clutching his sheet, as if he had an audience just waiting for it to drop. Jake in shorts, sure wasn't going to be much of a show, but he was a polite man and a bit on the modest side, no matter if he was home alone or not—so he did this right—by his own personal code! Duck and cover. After all, he lived with his ma and sis in the house all these years. So did his pa, obviously, and like father, like son. Jake senior taught his son well, and Jake's ma, thought it was most swell.

Wishing he had his pajama pants—hanging onto an unruly sheet, and a phone he hated to face—Jake waited and listened as Jade kept on a'calling his name. This time she added clever insights about his morning wardrobe, such as:

"I know you're standing there with the sheet around you, Jet... now *who's* going to see you? Now spit-out a '*huh*' or something... I just want to hear you acknowledge, because I have something important to say to you... aww... come on Jet. Why, I bet you're staring at the phone, hoping I'll hang up, *right* Jet... am I right? Well, I won't give-up and neither will you, huh? But you sure don't want me to worry that something happened to you now, do you Jet... I mean... what if you had a *seizure* and I didn't know it? I *may* have to send someone out to check and make sure you're all right... if I really started to *worry* and all, now, you know... Jet...? Jet...?"

'That does it... that's a DIRTY TRICK sis... real dirty pool, there gal,' Jake picked-up the receiver fast, before she had a chance to hang up.

"Jet... is that you?"

"~~Unh-hunh~," he voiced as loud a he could, hoping it would carry.

"Hey there Jet, you still got your sheet on... or did you drop it fast in order to run to the phone... bet you were afraid I'd hang up... huh, Jet?"

"~~Unh-hunh~," *'aww, now will you cut-it-out, sis,'* Jake was starting to get exasperated with this, *'just tell me what you want and PLEASE hurry up!'*

"Listen Jet... please don't get mad, but... you've given me no choice... I'll be staying in town the rest of the week and... "

"~~UNH-UNH~!" He forced out as loudly as he could. Jake pounded the receiver on the cupboard door a few respectable times, voicing, "~UNH-UNH~! ~UNH-UNH~!" *'DID YOU HEAR ME, JADE!'* Jake was mad now, throwing politeness to the winds of a jaded situation, *'how could you DO THIS to me Jade, there's no food in the house, and the horses are out of treats as well... you said last night you'd run in for it all this mornin' and be BACK by noon!'*

"Now, Jet... I *know* I said I'd be back by noon, but I got to *thinking*... well... are you still there Jet?"

"~~Hehrrrrr~!" He growled in his throat, with displeasure.

"Well, *dad-gum*, Jet... I just figured, if you somehow came out of that coma after near-full four weeks... I just figured there's *some kind of hope* for you getting out of the house, too. Aw, *come on* Jet... I'm still in your corner... say, why I just bet the Cook twin's pa can even come over and keep an eye on you all week, too, why I'd be mighty obliged at that!."

Jade tried to be as sweet as she could—after all, she was high-quality jade, mined from the womb of their ma, and Jake's treasure—not "a jade" off the streets of the world's beaten-down ways.

"I'll be here in town," she continued, "you just come on in and get the stuff you need. If you do, why then, maybe I'll join you at the CORNER&COFFEE café... and I may even *change my mind* and go home with you... as... I might not have to be here all week, if you get my *drift*, darlin' twin-dear." Yep—a treasure she was, but a might on the crafty side, at times.

Jake sighed deeply, in anguish, *this* time he hit his *head* on the cabinet a few respectable times—but very gently—he had enough damage as it was.

"It all depends now, mind you... on just how *fast* you decide to come. I mean, you sure don't want your babies to go hungry, now *do you* Jet? YOU *SPOILED* THEM so, you *KNOW*... didn't I always warn you?" she

laughed gently, and then sassed him with sisterly-sop, "I LOVE YOU JET...
I *lovvvve* you!"

Jake stood there and sighed, *'you do huh...? For real... ...are you
sure? Well good for you, 'cause I'm having some sore-setting DOUBTS
now, myself.'*

"I left a note on the counter there of the things we need... and I left a
note of the room and phone number for my place here in town. Plus, I left
the list for the feed store... you know where to find the money, or even the
checkbook, just in case you need it. I'll be watching for you Jet... Hey,
guess what Jet?" she lingered.

*'I know... you LOVE me... well, I purely don't see how you can say
that to me now Jade. How could you do this to me! Aww dang... this is no
joke, this is MY LIFE you're messin' with!'*

"I love you!" With that, she hung up, and the phone was slammed
down just as fast by Jake, as if it was an echoed onslaught of her spurring-
actions.

Jake looked at all the notes on the counter, his wallet was
mysteriously there in the middle of them. He expected to see three of them,
but there were nine, he sure didn't know why there was such a need for so
many notes, and he sure as heck didn't know what to do with them all. He
grabbed them all up in his fist as he hung-on to his sheet and took-off for the
secure comfort of his room. After lying on the bed for nearly two hours his
conscience finally got the best of him. His babies needed him, and he felt
guilty. They had been out of treats for three days now, and Jade kept saying
she'd go soon. Now he knew why she had been stalling. Now he knew why
there was no food in the house, and now he knew why they had stale bread
and the last two eggs for supper last night. Clearly so, he knew this was all
part of his sister's plan, her cattle-herding skills were crossing into her
home-economics skills. And—one out-smarted cowboy, he was.

Lost on the desolate prairie-of-decision, lone cowboy Jake was tasting
burnt bacon now, and hopelessly black it was, as his life seemed to be
riding-off without him, and down the wrong trail—right into town:

*Well, now... town is usually pretty dead this time of day, don't pick-up
much 'til just near supper when folks are on their way back-and-forth and
needin' last minute stuff... or if they plan on comin' in to socialize a bit after
the day.* Jake thought a bit more and tried to plan.

None-to-happy, Jake got up and dressed, *aww... Pa always said a
man ain't supposed to pout... he ALWAYS said that... well... when I was a
KID, he did. Yeah, and Ma and Jade always said a man ain't supposed to*

pout, too... trouble is... THEY always told me that clear-up 'til Ma died, about six and a half years ago, or so.

Jake was shook-up for just a minute as he dwelled on this remembrance of his ma and her pout-warnings. She sure knew how to deliver them, she warned-away many a pout. He couldn't help but wonder what it would have been like if they were still alive and had actually been here when this *accident* happened. It would have hurt his ma badly, even as tough as she was. She was tough in a wholesome way too, to follow after the man of the house, over miles of rodeo chasing; it had all seasoned her perfectly though, and she had loved it. She was a real tough cookie—a real tough *sweet* cookie, at that—and, a perfect match for an even tougher biscuit. Her man—Jake's pa. And his pa, if he hadn't died five years back, maybe *he* would have gone in to save Stoney—as always, ignoring old age frailties.

Jake was hit hard with that thought last thought, and choked-up slightly, *yeah, and I'd be maybe having to BURY HIM as of RECENT, instead of all them years back. Or, maybe the whole mess never would have happened, as he'd have made sure that DAMN lying-Lyle never came back in the first place!* Jake shook the thoughts loose, he knew he was in no shape to dwell on Lyle. If he started getting his thoughts too confused and mad, he'd risk getting a headache, maybe another seizure, and he was full-up sick of hospitals, now as it was.

He finished dressing, with his topping-off choice of boots being his pa's best pair, since his sentiments were now running high. They had honorably been passed on down, to him. Good thing they fit—both honorably and foot-wise, Jade always said. And, as he knew the entire town would prick-up their ears, or not being *horses* in this case, they'd be perking-up their eyes once he strolled into town, at *least* he'd be a sharp-looking susceptible cowboy-spectacle. Yep, susceptible as to attracting stares—seemed they were mighty contagious at the most awkward, inordinate, inopportune times.

Aw, what am I gonna' do? Jake thought, as he struggled with some cold stale coffee and a mashed-up old piece of roll. Slacking-off as to eating skills, he wasn't paying heed as well as he should have been, and suddenly he held back with his swallow—something was amiss. At least, so he feared. He was worried a slight choke had caused some food to go down wrong. About a few minutes later, he found that all was well and his throat was just dry, a few more correct swallows and a few coughs had set it right, much to his high-soaring relief.

Ingeniously, though fearful as it was, this couldn't have been more well-timed as a counter-move in the Jade-game—Jake's thought picked-up on a yet unseen idea, *I'll cough... that's it, I'll be a bit sick until they get used to me... and I'll smile a lot... I know how to smile, and I can do THAT right-fine.*

'Okay, Jade... I'm callin' your hand, and I'm gonna' try for some more aces. Yeah, I got some aces comin' my way again... they surely got me out of the coma... them aces are gonna' show-up for me here now, too! Yeah... amen to that... well... if you did your fancy praying that is... '

Jake stopped his thoughts and zeroed in on one in particular, *'you DID do your fancy praying... didn't you Jade?'* he wondered as this thought flew through the darkness and hit the stuck barn door that he night-and-daily faced. He quickly realized he couldn't say it, as it was on the tip of his now-gone tongue, and he sat in the stark silence instead, *aww, dad-gum it all... well... Ma always told me I shouldn't go around MUTTERING to myself either...*

He took out the notes and gave them a few futile stares, searching for some last-minute luck, and crammed all the notes back into his pocket as he got up. He grabbed-up his wallet from the counter, leaving the checkbook, and then took-up his every-ready black Stetson and stomped over to the kitchen door. Funny thing was—he couldn't open it. He just couldn't do it. He sat down for about an hour in the family room, picking on the ridging of the chair's stuffing, digging up little wells of self pity, and then he finally got up and paced around the kitchen, eyeing the kitchen door. He couldn't stand it anymore and he finally opened the door and stomped-out and with seriously determined strides, and with no looking back, headed over to his truck, and headed-off toward town. Neither twin yet realized that seizures were *no* respecters of cars, let alone a cowboy's faithful truck.

Thus, Jake pressed on—even pressing buttons—and a tape in the truck was now playing: "Thank God I'm a Country Boy" —leading the way, John Denver style. At any other time, out on the road and out in the country like this, he would have loved it. But now he was going to be a "town boy" and he didn't know if he could handle it, though this town was most beloved. *'Yeah, my life's a riddle, all right... but it sure ain't FUNNY just yet... NOT ONE BIT. Sure wish I could solve it, but it's bull-stomped, for sure.'*

He neared town now and hoped to God he didn't get seizures. He was breathing heavy and his hands were near shaking, *what the hell's wrong with me... come on... suck it up... take it like a man, Jake. These are your friends, you known them most all your life, these ain't strangers waiting to*

shoot you down, like in them boarding-school days. These people are like
family... the best folks in the world... they even sent you cards and flowers,
when they were allowed to... the whole room was filled-up time-and-again
with tons of them! The thought touched him so deeply he had to pull-over
and wipe his eyes. As he did, he sobbed—he broke down and sobbed
deeply.

 'Dear God, this whole town loves me, and they thought I was dyin'...
and I was... and now I ain't... AND NOW I'M HERE. Dear Lord... I don't
know what to say to You. How did I deserve all that special honor? I'm just
Jake... it's just me... a horse rancher... rodeo cowboy from Texas. Why,
Lord, why? Why, dear God... how can this be?' wiping his face, by the
saving-grace of his good ol' cowboy shirt, he confessed-on, *'Not meaning*
disrespect, mind You... it means the world... truly it does... yet... how can I
ever thank them.' He let his face sink into his hands and sighed, *'please, I*
don't want any seizures... I got to get through this day... somehow,
someway... I just GOT to.' He lay his head on the steering wheel as all these
thoughts of all his friends ran through his head, a head he couldn't even trust
himself to, at times like this. He sat there feeling the steering wheel in his
hands now, as he leaned back slipping a bit lower into the truck, and rested
his head on the back of the seat. He just needed to get a grip and relax. He
sucked-up a heavy sigh, let it out just as quick, and took in a few very slow
deep breaths of air—and waited.

 As he calmed himself, he came to realize that he had never felt so
very special in all his life. He made sure he had no more crying left to do.
He didn't want to break down in town, not in front of everyone. He wanted
to make them happy and somehow he was going to do it. He was going to
honor and thank them—the only way he knew. To go into town and be there
with them, to honor them with himself—himself enjoying *them*. For a few
minutes, he forgot all about the fact that he couldn't talk and he almost
didn't much care, in the light of such strong sincere love. Almost.

 Jake was close enough to town that he wouldn't get drowsy, so he
pulled out of his other pocket some other papers. Tissue papers. Inside was
his smashed up pills. He'd have no headache now for sure. He pulled back
onto the road, and went on into town.

 Under past circumstances, this road, his beloved truck, and this
wonderful small rural town, would have been the highlight of his day—but it
was rough churning now:

 He eyed the street up and down, as he took a drive through first. He
knew Jade was there somewhere, and she'd be looking for him. This time

the little shadow went first, and Jake was the follower now—the added awkwardness was an understatement. He finally decided to park. They both knew Angie had gone with Alex to Kalispell, so he was at least safe in this respect.

Yeah, my three-minute little sister, loves me, she really does. He smiled as he remembered how they had chased Angie off, and how Jade had safeguarded the way for him today, in this one respect, as a good scout ought.

Judging as best he could, he knew the worse part was going to be the grocery store, but he had his secret weapon for that. Walking about, soaking in the rustic buildings and good-smelling pine trees, he was shocked how good it felt to be home and back in town. He had that haunting feeling of—sameness.

Same... seems I had forgotten about that nasty old word, he grimaced as that thought *bit* into him hard.

He walked-up to the SADDLE AND SEED. His boots hit loudly with a fine echo on the wooded walkway and porch. He pushed the doors open, as, it had saloon doors that were used during the day, and they creaked down-right loud, both day and night. However, at night, come closing time, it had regular doors for safekeeping, as did all the buildings in this quaint side of town, and then, only night critters were heard creaking. Jake took one last heavy step—a good cowboy boot thud, it was. It was a mite dark in that-there "*saloon*". He'd soon be a well-seen silhouette against the outside light:

I feel just like one of them old gunfighters... coming back after getting' all shot up, and the towns folk are wondering how I could still be alive... and wondering if I'm still even in one piece. Well now... looks like I AIN'T all in one piece. So now... I guess in this case, I'd be minus a piece... but they won't know... not yet anyways. And I sure ain't tellin'... sly ol' fox, that I am. Yep, they all been waitin' for me... wanting to see me well again. Well... dang-it, I sure don't feel too well, now do I... and high-noon is upon me. He had to catch his thoughts again, but this time because he felt like he was driving himself ridiculously nuts!

Jake loomed over the threshold, near fearing he'd fall in, and stepped silently through the saloon doors, but had not yet let go of them. As soon as he had stepped into the calming low light, his sentiments ran too deep for understanding—yep, again. He was just too susceptible and vulnerable to these now-vivid-memories, as he soaked-in the smells and the presence of this old familiar place that he had loved and enjoyed, so many times. This part of his life was real, once again, after being near-lost for far too long. He stood tall in his choice boots, held his shoulders back and smiled his best shot, he let go of the doors and they loudly flapped and creaked the announcement of his presence—he was back.

"JAKE!" Mr. Baker hollered so loud it seemed to echo, and for a short medium-framed man, he packed a lot of power.

It now seemed like the whole store was at attention and expected a show or something. Jake could picture himself twirling a fast-spinning-gun or something, just like the old gunslingers. *Sure wish I HAD one right about now, too, might do me some good. Sure would substitute for good conversation. After some fancy tricks, and some ooo's and ahh's from the townsfolk, why I'd be long-gone... makin' tracks to my next good deed... leavin' a good story behind, without ever needing to open my useless mouth. Yeah... I'd b-.*

"Dear God, son, it's really good to see you! They told us you were too bad-off for visitors, or we all would have been there for you Jake, that's for sure." Mr. Baker was near to tears.

Charlie Baker had known Jake and Jade since they were near-abouts being eleven-and-a-half-year-old kids, and them ol' double J's roamed these streets on the weekends, always ending-up in his store. Well, actually they had always ended-up in the sheriff's jail by the final hours of those days— visiting their pa. Their pa was always just visiting the sheriff, and NOT while being behind bars. That fine old gentleman-sheriff (though strict and strong, as to old ways of honor) had since passed-on, being as that *chore* of all old folks, comes to one-and-all. It was just about a year after Jake's pa had died. Course, this fine old gentleman had a fine young son, as all of Old-Town, knew. It was now this son, Lenny Lowrie that was sheriff in his place—after having *earned* it through years of hard work, from a pa that taught *him* well, too. Seems there were quite a few well-wishers, turned well-doers, by applying themselves, when these youngin's were kids—well beloved pa-folks, they were.

Mr. Baker's wife, Delia had snuck-up behind Jake in a quiet sort of way—though not purposed to catch him off guard—just slowly moving-in to give him a soft hug and a gentle welcome, and thus, it came:

"Welcome home Jake, lets have a look at you! She said. And you *know* what I mean by that, since I been *saying* that to you every time you've come into town after you've been gone a spell," Ma Baker smiled with deep affection, as her words came out into their presence with a gentle love, far from nosey curiosity.

Jake turned and faced her, with tears in his eyes that were ever-so-slight. Maybe none could tell but her—he now reckoned—yet, it remained

to be seen. He gave her a hug back. The tears ran down his face silently
now, his sentiments had instantly betrayed him, but she had always been like
a ma to him, and Jake rested in this. She was such a small tiny lady, that she
nearly got lost in his hug.

~*~

This older couple always thought the world of Jake and Jade. They
had sent Jake a huge carved wooden horse with balloons, during his stay at
the hospital. It was one of the first things that he saw, when his eyes were
freed-up. It was also one of the first things that he had been aware of when
he was coming back to his senses and soaking-in reality. Jade had tried to
tell him who it was from, as his eyes would work their way over all the
deeply engrained curves of the deep rich shades of many tones of browns—
but he didn't understand what she was saying. His eyes just followed the
curves, and soaked-in the richness of the stable firm color, and the smooth,
solid, shape. It was there for him everyday, and gave him some kind of
pleasure in the midst of his on-going distresses—as if it were a valley of
beauty, for him to seek solace in.

He had only been out of the intensive care unit for a week, after being
there all through January, and was at first, still blind to his surroundings.
Then by the second week of February, as he tried to comprehend where he
was, he began to understand Jade better, but he had no idea *who* the Baker's
were and half-way wasn't quite sure if he really knew who he himself was.
He was halfway sure he knew Jade, Matt and Ray, but he wasn't sure *why or
how.* He was full of questions then, but he couldn't talk and didn't know
why. He knew Jade's hand, though, and that was all that mattered to him
then. He trusted her and needed her, but didn't know her name. He was lost
in a lot of confusion during this time, Jade and this wooden horse gave him
some kind of a tangible anchor to hold on to. At times he would nearly
come out of his fog, only to become completely lost again as to who he was,
and what had happened. Everything he grabbed onto seemed to break loose
of his grip and fly back out the window again, but it always came back, and
one day, by the grace of God, nearly every *general* bit had finally *nested* in
the old-familiar-home of his mind.   And—there was that glorious horse at
the core!

By the beginning of March he *knew* that he knew who he was, and he
knew Jade, Matt, Ray, and even Galena, but he was agonizing over *someone*
named Stoney. But he couldn't seem to talk and his mouth was unable to
move, as his facial damage, internal and external were just now reaching a
full healing. It wasn't until March when his mind finally stopped relapsing,
but his mind had still wrestled with— *'Is Stoney alive... Is Stoney alive...?'*

It was a never-ending repetition that kept going through his thoughts, yet his mind never seemed to gain any new understanding to these thoughts—and Stoney had *even* paid him a quick visit, so it was said. Then progressing into the first few weeks of March he finally started to understand that he had been attacked by a bull, although he couldn't remember why. Then as March began to unfold in its fullness, his questions all began to be answered in many ways—and, as to things that he didn't like, and never would. Yet— oddly, the horse *remained* an inexplicable *soothing* balm through all this.

~*~

That beautiful horse cost them a small fortune, he acknowledged, and, he rightly knew where they got it from, at this point. He remembered they had it in this very store and had hoped to sell it during their past holidays. He knew that they sacrificed quite a heavy sum of earnings that it could have brought, and all because they were overjoyed that he was alive. They knew he used to come in and run his hands over the wood, as he shared coffee with them on the weekends. He could near-still feel the wood even now, as of last night, at home.

He snapped back to attention, as Mr. Baker spoke his name.

"So Jake, you finally made it in. We were beginning to get a mite worried, thought your health was still feeling poorly. Sure never seen you this thin, but you look healthy in spite of it. You were always on the lean side, but strong as a good fine horse, surely you'll be back to normal before you know it boy, don't worry. Ma here will have to send some of her good stew over to you soon... or else you just come for supper some night... okay, son?"

Jake wiped his eyes, and let go of Mrs. Baker. He nodded affirmatively, as he turned around to face Mr. Baker. As he turned, he knew it was obvious he had been crying but they were like family so he had no need to feel ashamed in this respect. So next, they all three had a good round of strong serious hugging and didn't let go.

"Okay, then, Jake. We're back in business!" Mr. Baker said with enthusiasm, as he rubbed his hands together. "Now that you're *finally* here, what can I do for you?" Mr. Baker stood there waiting for his reply.

Jake swallowed hard, and looked at him. He was feeling lost all of the sudden, he grimaced a bit, and then coughed. He felt awkward, and a bit like a liar, but his feelings of feeling ashamed, helpless, and downright stupid, soon overpowered him, and he tapped at his throat and hoped for the best.

"You got a cold, Jake, sore throat or something?" Ma Baker asked.

"~Unh-huh~," Jake gave a slight nod yes.

Yep, he'd *done* it now, something he'd never *duly done*—lying through his teeth, he reckoned it was called, yet, he pressed-on—he was a trout heading up-stream now, there was no turning back—that flood of emotion would do-him-in.

He remembered the notes in his pocket and pulled them out. He fumbled through them and stood there a bit as he stared blankly at them. They waited patiently, not suspecting anything—just politely waiting. With that reassurance, Jake could handle this, he was sure he could. He took a deep sigh, and walking up to the counter, he laid out all the notes in a row. He stared some more at them, wondering what to do next—he sure wished he had taken-up acting at some point in his life, as he was grabbing-at-straws now. Jake stepped back from the counter a bit and put his hand up to his mouth and feigned a slight yawn and stretched a bit. Mr. Baker by now had done his duty as the good store clerk and gone up to the row of notes.

"You're feeling tired, huh, Jake. I'll take a look and see what you need here, quite a lot more paper work than normal," he laughed fondly.

Jake smiled and leaned back on the counter, as cool-as-cool could be, (when one near-just *couldn't* quite be) and pretended to take it all in stride, as he tilted his Stetson back to take in a good view of the Bakers' wonderful store.

"I think you can keep the grocery list, and Jade's drug store beauty list," he said as he shoved two of the list Jake's way.

Jake stood to attention fast as he tried to remember which was passed his way first, and shoved them into his left pocket. He gestured with a '*well, what do you know*' and a smirk on his face, and then stood back humbly-so.

Delia Baker had sat down at the counter on the other side now, near her husband Charlie, and took a look at all the six other notes that were left. She picked-up the one that they needed, and with a cheerful smile she gloated as she said, "Oh you men and your messy wallets!" and set-off to fill the order.

Mr. Baker waved Jake over, "Here you go Jake… say… did you know that there was a recipe for chocolate cake here with these two bills receipts? The ingredients are already on the grocery list… I just checked… so it sure is odd that you got that in your pocket… must have got stuck on the back of the other papers, huh? Now, these last two are a list of things we already delivered to her a while back, they're old… I'll throw them out."

Mr. Baker took a quick glance at the receipts before handing them back, *hmmm, must be local receipts… all handwritten,* he thought. He was sure he recognized one of the stores, but quickly stopped being nosey and said, "Looks like Jade's been having fun shopping, don't want to pry as to see what she owes, or what-not... so I'm done, Jake."

He handed them back, all three piled on top of each other, much to Jake's dismay. Jack replied with a "~hmmm~", as he studied the papers, while flipping through them thoughtfully. He then pocketed them, and feigned a larger yawn with the back of his hand over his mouth.

"Hey, I'll get you come coffee Jake, it's fresh... should perk you up some. Sure will be good to enjoy it with you, son... sure will feel good."

Jake tried to grab his sleeve to stop him, but Mr. Baker was already over at the far counter pouring-up two mugs. Jake also heard Charlie's soft mumbles, and it caught him off-guard—it was a near-private hushed-whisper:

"Dear Lord, I remembered when we thought we'd never see this day,"

Mr. Baker returned and sat the coffee down, and Jake stared at it, feeling guilty. He was near-tempted to confess his awful wound—but not near-enough—as "near" up-and-left and down-right-fast, too.

Jake took all the fixings that were on the counter and fixed his coffee up and stirred it, and listened to Mr. Baker talk. Charlie was relating all that happened of-late, and so far, only a few questions had come Jake's way. He answered all with flying-colors thanks to his few magic "~hmmm~'s", and, making sure to fill-in with a few equally powerful coughs. Finally, when a throat tap was needed to get past one of the remarks, Jake was beginning to get restless.

Ma Baker arrived with his list and passed it to her husband, saying, "All done... it's all being loaded-up in your truck for you, Jake."

Jake reached for his wallet and realized he never thought to check if there was any money. Jade said something to him about money—now what was it? She would have left him money somewhere—she knew he would need it since he had been in the hospital and surely hadn't done any wallet-filling, money or otherwise. He had never had the chance to even *use* his wallet yet—maybe *that* was where the money was. He knew he had left it on his nightstand, but he found it in the kitchen immediately after he hung up the phone—it must have been Jade's doing. Sure-enough there was money in it! Jake played with the money, in the fold, flipping it back-and-forth as he wondered what to do next. Time seemed to have stuck in eternity and taken him along for the ride, when:

"How about I just stick it on your bill Jake?" Mr. Baker offered as he reached over and gave him a pat on the shoulder, "you've never been late to pay a bill, and that's a fact," he smiled.

"~Unh-huh~," Jake nodded with a slightly contorted smile as he then resumed staring into his wallet.

"Don't worry, Jake, Jade must have borrowed some."

Ma Baker went up and gave him a sweet pinch on the cheek and played up to him in a soft manner, "Oh, Jake, you're just as cute as ever, and such a gentleman... always worried about not owing a man. Now, you got errands to do, now go-on-then... git with you!" Fixing on his eyes, she smiled, and waved him off.

Jake packed-away his money and with a grateful look, he smiled back at Mrs. Baker. Then with a sincere wave to Mr. Baker, he turned and left.

"Oh... wait... Jake! You must have dropped this paper earlier... it looks like a hotel room number, with a phone number," Ma Baker, called out, as she caught up with him.

Jake smiled and gave her a wink, followed by a hug, and as he turned to leave once again, he stuck that last note into his back blue jean pocket, *So THAT'S what happened to THAT note, I knew I was missing somethin', I counted nine... I'm that smart at least.* An ominous cloud was now hounding Jake though, as he began to wonder just how *smart* he really was.

He now knew he was missing something a *lot* more important than one little note.

So did someone else. As—that ominous bit of cloud left a dab of residue behind:

"Charlie, you know Jake never pays by us from our billing him, he'd have used his bank card if he was short. What was that all about?" she said with a bit of concern.

"I know something's wrong... that's why I set him free to get on his way."

Delia went around to her husband and looked into his eyes. "What is it, Charlie?"

"I'm not sure exactly, Delia. I can't quite put my finger on what we just saw, here. But I do know he was fumbling for help, and I knew that was just the help he needed. I'm sure we'll know when the time is right," he said weakly, and then faced Delia straight on, "man, it sure was *great* to see him back again, though, wasn't it! It's a miracle, a *real* miracle. He looks down-right fine too, after what Matt said that bull did to the side of his face. Remember when ol' Joe had that car accident? His scars pretty-much faded by the end of the year. I know Jake will be quite pleased come next summer.

Jake was now making his way to the drug store. He scoured the streets first for his sister—that traitor to the Smith family name and all that twins hold dear.

'My own twin... splittin' from me and our birthed-up partnership... turning on me...' he just shook his head in quiet exasperation. He was so pleased and deeply touched, though, to see the Bakers, he *had* to admit that. *Women... they sure know how to pull a fast-one,* Jake thought, as he took-off and fast approached the drug store, chalking up fast-ones of his own, but in a man-style-type kind-of-way.

Jake pulled the door open and the first face he saw was Lolly; she must have just finished wiping the glass door, since she still had the spray bottle in her hand. She hastily set it on the counter and turned back to give him her full attention.

"Jake! Oh, Jake, look at you! How are you! You look wonderful," she said, as she studied his face just a little bit too long. She looked down, figuring it was best, and grabbed his hand and pulled it to her face dearly, and grabbed-up the other, and shook them in between both of hers.

She was so happy, just like a little girl—she was beaming like a light house—and with good reason. She had gone to school with them, she was part of the town's history, just like the Smith family, but she was hardly a little girl anymore. Oddly though, she still looked like one. Her hair was in a nice blond pageboy-type cut and matched the fashion-models pictured on the magazines, on the rack near her. *Well, then...* Jake thought, as he compared her to the pictures, *she's as grown-up as she's gonna' get, I guess... but always responsible, and a hard worker, through-and-through... little ol' Lolly.*

Lolly finished shaking his hands, after nearly shaking them clear 'til midnight, and hugged him double-hard, saying happily, "Well... say something!"

All Jake could do was hug her back, as his mind was greatly moved upon, *'Lolly, you've always been such a kind little gal, it sure is good to see you so happy! Aww, Lolly... what I got to say, ain't gonna' sound good at all... fact is, it'll haunt you something-fierce and make no sense to your ears... so... you're gonna' have to trust me from here on out, gal, and grab at my straws here,'* Jake faltered somewhat, as he wondered where *this* trip would lead, and longed to step-off at a depot leading to freedom—a depot that was nowhere to be found.

And Lolly? She waited faithfully for an answer, as if a good little pup.

~*~

Jade had told him how depressed Lolly had been when she heard about the accident. Lolly always had been close to Jake, since *way* back. He helped Lolly when they were kids. Her brother had died one year, fast and unexpectedly, from pneumonia, and Lolly never got over it. Jake had then gone to see her everyday and took her fishing so she could be alone somewhere. He would fish, and she would pick flowers, then he'd take her back home to her family. Her brother had been sick for nearly all his life, he had weak under-developed lungs, and finally he just couldn't go on. Jake and Lolly were forever sealed as to being like-spirits as to being pain-bearers for others.

~*~

"Well then, guess it's MY turn to take you by the hand, and get you moving! You finally made it into town and you got nothing to say? Well, I got stuff to say! This must be the full-end of the miracle, finally seeing you in person! I saw your sister in town... did you know she's here as well? Or did you come together? Well... speak up, or forever hold your peace!"

Jake stepped back some for air as Lolly ran-up to him and gave him one last long-hug-of-relief to seal this fantastic day. He smiled sheepishly and coughed some, and edged around her and over to the cold medicines—spoiling her affections, just a tad.

"Jake, do you hurt or something, I'm sorry. Am I intruding too fast... aww, I'm sorry." She stopped and watched him, checking to make sure all was well with him. She knew how badly he had been injured and was worried that just maybe there were some unknown sore spots. The one he DID have though, she'd never have imagined in *any* respects—not even if she had been invited to do so for a prize.

"~Hmmh-umm~," Jake voiced at a low hum, as he shook his head motioning, trying for negating her fears, with his arms out towards her. He was moving them slightly back-and-forth as if to calm and stop her, both at the same time—good "little pup" gestures, if nothing else. Along with this, he offered her his most sincere look of concern with sincere thoughts to match, *'No, no... don't fret, little gal. Its' okay, Lolly, it's okay, I ain't hurtin'... PLEASE don't worry... honest!'*

"Whew... thanks, Jake. I didn't know what to expect. I mean all this time, and you hadn't come into town yet," she smiled as a salute to their long friendship, and now offered help, "well... what do you need... throat lozenges, right? You got a bad cold, Jake? After being run-down from those months in the hospital, take care... okay? Don't let yourself get sicker Jake, it could turn into trouble, you know," she said with grave concern.

Jake shook his head with an understanding nod of a sorrow, as to this. Once during days long-since-gone, hidden in the years-of-yesterdays, he knew she had lost her brother—he *remembered* this—she was now referring to this lost companion. Memories were even more precious to Jake now, as he watched the power that they worked upon others—and upon him. He thought of his own sister as he watched Lolly's concerns, *aww, I ain't mad at you Jade, wherever you are... you're doing what you think it is best, sure-enough... I'm just feelin' like a wild horse in a boxed canyon... and I hate to be stuck this way... I hate it.*

"Well, spit it out Jake!"

"~Hunh~?" He voiced with a dry whisper as he wrinkled his brow at her. He just now learned he was off-guard with his thoughts and was now completely puzzled.

"What do you need, you want me to help you find something... or do you already know what you want? You hardly ever come in here you know, so I don't expect you'd know where everything is."

Jake reached into his left-side pocket of his shirt; out of the pocket came the two lists, but he couldn't remember which was which, so he nonchalantly handed her both of them as if they were stuck together and—waited. Seemed like he was having to do a lot of that lately.

"Oh, here Jake, looks like your grocery list is stuck to this. So this is for Jade huh? Sure can't figure why she didn't come and get it herself, as I just told you, she's in town. Sheriff Lowrie told me, this morning." She took-off to get the things as Jake stood over by the window watching the streets.

He took all the money from his wallet and stuffed it in his pocket into one big wad. When he saw her at the counter, he went up and fished it all out, spreading it all over the counter. She automatically took out what she needed as Jake stared and watched her hands move, trying desperately to make some sense of it all.

"Don't worry Jake, I can break a fifty for you just fine... were you looking for smaller bills here? I don't see any either... hmmm... that's what you get for cramming it in your pocket, huh?" She took the fifty and gave him change. "How come you got all fifties here? Are you planning on being a big spender here in town, or are you planning to go to the SADDLE AND SEED along with the GENERAL STORE, and more? If you were, you could have gone to anyone of them first and got change from them. It would have been better than having to root through all these fifties just to look for change. But it's okay... I surely don't mind... today, I just happen to have some." She handed him his change as she laughed, and he forced-out a feigned hearty smile as best he could, waved a farewell, and quickly went out the door.

After making his way to the truck, he leaned face-forward his elbows onto its hood and looked a bit off to the side and up into the sky. The sun sure felt perfectly big-sky-wonderful and so did being in town—if it could just be him and his truck, all by their lonesome. Yep, he could sure take to resting in the sun for now, that is, if no one else showed up.

He thought of the GENERAL STORE and wondered if his plan would work, as there would be no one to run around for him there, if he ran into trouble. He was sure getting hungry and wished he could eat, and, he sure wished he could have shared that coffee with the Bakers. He could almost still smell it. Letting morning's minutes move-on-by, Jake leaned there in the warm sun and closed his eyes, it warmed his face and he almost felt he was lost in the past. It could have almost been last summer, if he concentrated on the warmth of face and let his mind wander back in time. As he did so, a flood of memories hit him hard and he stood-up in stabbed shock, as he grimaced at some newfound revelations—one in particular, '*I DID USED TO DO THIS... I know I did... I used to come and do the buyin' all the time... not Jade, not the guys... ME... the boss-man! I did most all of it. I remember, now... I never had BILLS for SADDLE AND SEED. Why, I could swear, I'd pay it all up front... and as ol' Bake gave me change... I'd try to use it to pay for his coffee, as a joke, and he'd say keep it... coffee's on the house. Yeah... I handled money... yeah, I did! Dear Lord! What must he be thinkin' right about now?*'

He leaned back a bit slowly, feeling mighty strange, and eased himself back onto the front-side of his trunk hood and was lost in thought for a few minutes-on-end:

It seems to me like I know all about myself and then again, I keep on discoverin' things that somehow have been hidden somewhere. And... I know from all that rehab therapy stuff... that... well... I ain't too good with time frames in the past, or complicated issues, but Jade said I was right-on-the-mark as to all our family and friends, and my daily needs, and such. I know everyone in the family pictures... my childhood even. How could I have forgot something so important as this? And now there's this money... I can count... I counted my horses... but I don't know what to do with marks on that money... and then, these other symbols and all... this branding-iron stuff... I'm just drawing-a-blank. I seem to get all walled-up somehwheres just lookin' at it... it gives me a headache if I think on it too much. Yeah... I should have been able to use that paper Jade gave me in the hospital... but I couldn't seem to make anything I wanted to say show-up. Nothing showed-up, nothing happened... maybe nothin' was there. Maybe nothin' was SUPPOSED to be there, for all I knew... but... maybe it WAS, and I didn't know it. What did I know? Dad-gum, am I a mess, or what?

Jake's mind was heavy as his heart sunk again. His head was slightly pressuring him, but he continued—trying in a most desperate search through scattered rubble, for any *signs* of trails to lost wealth, *I did try... didn't I? I tried to force myself to think on it, I really did. But I JUMPED! I ditched... I finally couldn't do it anymore. I had to tune it out... I GOT to tune it... or my head feels like my skulls cavin' in. Yeah, maybe that's it... maybe I didn't forget... maybe I just blocked it out or something. But then... what if there's nothin' there to tune out... what if something's missing... maybe I'm tuning THAT out too... but wouldn't I know that... wouldn't someone else know that? Maybe they do... maybe...*

Jake caught himself staring and blinked a few times, *and... maybe... say... where was I...?* He shook his head. He was still there leaning on his truck hood, but as to how long, he had no clue. He tried collecting his thoughts but it was useless.

Aww, dang it... he pushed his head down into his hand, rubbed his face and looked down at the asphalt on the street. *Sometimes I feel like I'm driving on the wrong road, but it looks the same and it feels the same until I hit a bump... then it's all wrong somehow. Just maybe... if I could just pull-over and turn-around somewheres, I'd see the turn-off plain as... plain as that ol' sun up there that's been hittin' me in the face all this time.*

He started seriously wondering if he'd been staring a long time or not, but everything nearby was the same and no one was on the streets. The town on this end, was for the most part, dead. He didn't mind the walk back-and-forth from the truck to the busier store areas. And—in the past, he had always liked this area the best anyway, especially the SADDLE AND SEED. He suddenly felt like running in and apologizing to the Bakers until he just as quickly remembered he couldn't talk. He began to think of the summer months that would be arriving soon. May was nearly over. He wondered if he'd ever see the end of this newest struggle that had been plaguing him. He was going to have to owe-up to it soon—he knew that now. At first he thought maybe this problem was part of his nature, but more-and-more he was realizing this was all something he was *supposed* to know—every one *else* seems to know these things. Obviously, Jade thought he knew what these notes were—these hot fired-up branding-irons were burnt-out onto nearly everything in sight, in all kinds of shape and colors,

and he was now at a loss as to how to handle them. It had not gotten any
better and now he was certain-firm it wouldn't.

This warm sun of the soon-coming summer, would never find him
snuggling-up-cozy to the fired-up-success of these magic symbols, and it
would never allow him success in the area as to where they were birthed
from either, and he was now just beginning to realize this. He knew
something was wrong. No one else knew it though. Jade had given him a
test, half-subconsciously. He was now failing it. He now understood that
this was the reason Miss Kaite was hounding him so. He also understood
why he had felt like fighting her so hard.

Jade didn't know though... did she...? He wondered.

Knowing his sister as he did, Jake was sure that Jade was still open to
the possibility that all he needed was time, and all would be well. She was
thinking possibly that it was just pride, him not wanting to resort to note-
passing, like a little kid having to turn-in homework all the time in order to
show that he had some kind of knowledge to share.

He wasn't sure how to go about telling her, but Miss Kaite must have
told her something. Maybe now it was a ripe-time to finally owe-up to it all.
Well, whether Jade *did* know or not, he had a gnawing feeling in his gut that
soon she would. *Well... looks like she was wrong and Kaite was right after
all,* he thought hopelessly. *Best I get-on with these chores and find Jade,
and get home while my luck is holding. I got too much to deal with now as it
is.*

He took the truck this time and headed down to the GENERAL STORE.
It was actually a small strip-mall-center that had a large supermarket there
and other modern stores as well. It was the one-and-only side of town that
was new and modern. The mall was constructed to "ease" them over into
crossing the border-street into New-Town (a most-recent addition as to
"more new growth" in these here parts). New-Town was nearly added over
night, to Old-Town's border, and became a town, in its own right, as, after
the "ease" mall was added on, Old-Town put a stop to anymore
encroachments. Old-Town's side of this back-to-back city-area, was thus-
now safe-guarded, and would forever remain such a wonderful old
"stomping-grounds of the past" to the local ranching cowboys, and—to
tourist.

Jake parked and went in to try his hand at one of his final
destinations—the huge grocery store—never enjoyed, but yet, never before
feared, as it now was.

First off (after wandering about some, and regaining the feel of the
place), being the boss-man, he picked-up familiar looking stuff in the food

aisles that HE wanted. Then, after walking the aisles in search of a friendly face, any face, he stopped an older woman that seemed to be smiling nice enough as she bid "ado" to a friend, after a friendly conversation. The other woman's "see you later, Esther!" still hung in the air, and Jake ventured forward. The older woman was now reading some labels. He held his list up, and peered with feigned trouble at it, as he moved it back and forth hoping to get her attention. Handsome guy that he was, or, possibly because he appeared as local-color from nearby rural-life presentations—sporting his nice black cowboy hat and boots—he seemed to have gotten her attention. Or—perhaps because he was just *plain* having troubles and she was concerned.

She spoke to him, "Bet you left your glasses at home, right? I've done that before, do you need help?"

Jake coughed a bit, as he did his great sore throat trick—just, in case—and he handed her the note. He set his face to remember as much of it as he could, so he wouldn't have to go through this again. She read the list, and he caught every word. It was actually nothing hard, and he had half the stuff already, so he was mighty relieved. He took her hand and shook it, and tipped his hat.

People can sure be nice, at times, he thought. He then mentally chastised himself as he went on his way, *now why did I think THAT was going to be so bad? I sure have been behaving like a skittish horse, here, I reckon.*

He tried to take a look back at his behavior of the day and wondered if he had been behaving normal or not, when he suddenly heard the loud crash of cans. He realized it was caused by his cart, and quickly bent down to fix-up the mess and was faced by a little girl looking up at him.

"Why did you do that, mister?"

Jake smiled at her and meekly shrugged his shoulders and gave her a pat on the head.

"You're supposed to say, 'excuse me,'" she said, as she watched him turn to leave.

Jake looked back at her and nodded his head in agreement.

"Well... why don't you? I get in trouble if I don't."

Jake was at a loss as to how to graciously step-out of this unexpected situation. He was immediately relieved when he was quickly rescued from the girl's openly displayed etiquette lesson, as her nearby mom finally realized what was going on.

"I'm so sorry... I thought she knocked over the cans and was picking them up. I hope she didn't bother you."

As they left Jake could hear the girl say, "But he didn't say 'excuse me', or even, 'I'm sorry'."

The last words that floated down the aisle as they slipped away, were, "don't worry sweetheart, some people just don't *know* better and they need to learn."

Jake stared there, letting the aisle close-in on him, as he felt stung deep-to-swollen by that— '*I DO KNOW BETTER... and I don't need to learn,*' he thought in useless frantic-haste after them. He could envision it all now, *they'll probably be spreading me out, along with this episode, all across their supper table tonight, as a lesson in manners... and I'll come-out MIGHTY thin. Aww, I'm just takin' this too serious, is all... why should I care.* But he did.

He turned the corner and headed to the check-out counter. He had already learned from Lolly that he had all fifties and change in his other pocket, so he was feeling more self-assured in one way. He knew these new machines could hay-up and throw-out a perfect bale of change. It would then spit-out a printed-approval of its success, for all the world to see, so it was not very likely someone would cheat him. He went to face whatever it was that was going to happen—come what may.

There's the finish line, I just got to step over it, Jake thought with a satisfied smile. Just then, someone grabbed him from the side.

"Excuse me mister... you live around here, right?" Jake tried to head for the line and he did succeed in just getting a foothold with one large cowboy-boot-step, but the lady was following him fast-to-heel. "Didn't you hear me, mister?"

"~Unh-unh~," he regrettably lied as a reply, even though he knew he had heard her, he sure didn't want to make her feel worse, judging by the attitude she was already wielding. She had just caught him unprepared.

"Well, you felt me nearby. I was pulling on your shirt, so you must have... come on now!" She pulled out a map, "Look, I'm in a hurry or I'll be late, can you take a look at this and help me?"

Jake looked at her and shook his head and thumbed over at his groceries, picking out the smaller ones. She was extremely pushy and rude, but he still felt like a heel as he started to put his groceries up on the counter. There weren't many people in the store yet and none seemed to show-up to help.

"Why *not*... a big strong cowboy like you, why *not*? You can't be in *that* big of a hurry, can you? Can't you see I have a function to go to? I'm going to a wedding!" She watched and glared at him as he reached for more groceries and tried to smile politely back at her.

"You think it's funny or something? Just because I'm from out of town?"

Jake looked up at her and shook his head with a slight jerk. He opened his mouth ever so slightly and with a bit of a wrinkled brow and concerned eyes, he gestured at her with his left hand up in the air nearly shoulder high, as if to show a "no". *'Hey ma'am, you got it all wrong! I never poke fun at city-folk or tourist... or anyone... really, I ain't making-sport!'*

"Is that the best you can do? You're just plain thoughtless then, *right?* FINE! THANKS A LOT! I'm sorry I bothered you!" She took-off angered, as she spied another man.

People can sure be nasty, at times, Jake thought with disgust, while making a well-informed about-face as to his last thought on people.

The few people that had now appeared from nearby aisles began peeking a bit to see what he had done to the poor woman, and he tried to brush it off, as he humbly and mutely withstood the judgments. But—he knew he was wounded, and too deep for brushing.

As he went back to what he was doing, the one lady that he had stopped earlier, the one named Esther, came up to him:

"Oh... hey... I knew it was because you didn't have your glasses... it's just bad timing, and it's happened to me, too... so don't worry about it, okay?" She said with a smile and a wink, and, as she left his presence, little did she know that she just made his day.

Jake thought again, just as a fine soldier doing his about-faces continually, *people can be so nice at times.*

He finished the shopping with no more incidents, went out and loaded the stuff into his truck and was ready to go, when he remembered the last two papers. *Now where do I go from here?* he wondered. The one in his back pocket, was Jade's address, he knew that, from the Bakers, but these?

I've had enough of this... Jade can do her own bills, sister or not... this was her trick, she can hit-it-on home now. As for me... I'm done playin'. Sorry sis, game's over. I think I did pretty dang-good. Besides... I'm gettin' hungry and near weak-to-shaking... and most likely, so are my babies. The afternoon's near-gone and the late afternoon-crowd is due to start filterin' in... it's down-the-drain for me, now, I'm out'a here.

Jake got into the truck to leave and there he *saw* it. It was under the wiper. *'NOW WHAT!'*

His patience was gone now, he had to admit it. He could at times be very patient, yep, yep he sure could. He knew it. But when he was done— he was done. Cowboy-pure and cowboy-simple.

Completely worn-out, he stared blankly through the bright glass.

How'd I get a ticket? Aww, maybe it's just a note or something... maybe someone spotted my truck and just left me a message so we can get in touch later.

He got out and studied it, it was printed on paper like a ticket, at least he thought it appeared so, but it had written ink on it, as well. He pulled down hard on his Stetson's front brim, and stared some more:

Hmmm... maybe, if I just leave it with Lenny and some cash, he can sort it for me... he's the only one that could have left it, or Mike... last resort would be Sam. They always check the streets. Or I could wait and give it to Jade... no... I hate to owe.

He took off, parked near the sheriff's office, and forced himself to go in. He and Lenny were great friends—the best, for sure. Jake figured if he had to, maybe now he'd at least try to show Lenny that he couldn't talk. The burden of it weighing-on him today, was near too much, and the trail-through-it-all had near slipped-apart under him, as it was. He didn't have a way to explain all the details, but at least it would be a start—after all, it WAS why Jade had pushed him here for. *I sure ain't afraid of Lenny*, this relief that ran into his soul, as the first comfort of the day, other than warm sun, seemed to settle him.

The secretary greeted him, but the office was empty. Jake at first thought maybe he just stepped off into Hawaii, as he was staring at a medium tanned gal with long dark hair clasped to one side with a tiny trickle of flowers gently flowing down over the hair, accented with nice flowery shell earrings. Just as quick though, he noticed a nice black Stetson sitting upside down on the shelf behind her, next to a beautiful potted Tiger Lily. Nope—this was Montana and he knew it, but he didn't know her—did he? His brain skidded to a halt, at the road-block.

"Are you all right sir?"

Jake looked around the room, no one else was there, that was odd. Jake was now off-course, and forgot where he was. Staring at the gal, was far from helping.

"Sheriff's out for a late lunch and Mike is out on the streets doing a check through town. Can I help you?" The gal's voice rang clear and inviting, and Jake snapped out of it.

Jake, instantly back on course, now wondered where the other gal was, he knew Lenny had a part-time office helper, a secretary, and she was a right-nice gal at that. He would have been at ease around her, and was now wondering what happened and where everyone was. He figured he'd get some answers if he walked over and picked up that metal nametag—at least he hoped that's what it was. It worked.

"Oh, you were expecting Lizzy-Ann, I'm Sofia Chapman... she's gone, she's finally found a ranch job, so I've heard... out in Wyoming. She needs that physical work to keep her refreshed. Can I do anything for you? You're welcome to leave a message."

Jake felt good with that and smiled, giving the "thumbs up" sign.

He went to Lenny's desk, emptying his pocket of the last two papers of Jade's, plus the odd ticket with some money, he folded it all up in a bundle and left. A few seconds later, he came back and peeked in through the door and offered a friendly wave complete with a great Jake smile. In doing so, he got a smile back, along with a wave in return and some oddly flashed gesture she made with her hand, as an added extra type of good-bye. He then left—again.

'Rude, I ain't!' Jake stood on the porch, now agreeing with himself, as he gave his belt a tug to lift-up his slightly sagging jeans and tucked his shirt in, he adjusted his Stetson and stepped down off the porch—feeling a bit like the Jake he once knew.

He continued on to his truck and got in and headed for home, searching for Jade as he passed the CORNER&COFFEE café. He caught a glimpse of Lenny and tried to wave, but it was too late, so he made tracks for home.

It was near supper now. Jake had fed his babies, fed himself, then he cooked a wonderful meal for Jade. It was nothing he could eat well, so he figured if he was full first, it wouldn't set wrong in his spirit. He set the table nice for her, just as she liked it and sat down to rest. Her bed, continually left out, was made up neat for the day. This room looked like a bedroom now, and always startled him when he first came in. In the past it was only this way when they had boarders staying for horse riding, or company visiting for the same. He went over and sat in the chair at the left side of the fireplace and turned it straighter towards the window. Glancing out over the backyard, he looked past the fence and hoped to see deer or elk. Thinking he saw one, he stood and leaned his face along the side of the large picture window. *'Nope'*

He started to sit but he seemed spellbound somehow. There was nothing new out there. All seemed the same. Yet, somehow he was drawn to the fenced-in round corral and its old rodeo chute, there on the western-

side of the backyard. He had passed it (yet, never close-up) many times in
his haste to head through the back door, through the yard, and up to the hills,
moving along the northwest-to-north-ridge, of his woods. He hadn't really
paid any attention to it since he had been home. In the past, he had worked
with the horses many a time in that corral—he knew that—though, today,
something didn't set right with him. His gut-feelings set him into
uneasiness. He sensed something was really *wrong* with the area, though he
drew a blank. He was breathing a bit hard now and was wondering what had
caught and drawn his attention towards it, in the first place.

Jake went to sit again but this time he chose the chair with its back
facing this window-wall (being just off to the right side of the fireplace).
His head didn't hurt, that was a good sign, but he had to admit, he felt funny.
Like he had been there just today, inside that fenced in area, but he knew he
had not. He knew his only problem with memory was occasionally with
past episodes—there was only so much Jade and his buddies could re-
introduce when he was in the hospital. But even as he had just learned today
and in the hospital, when given time—for the most part—it was coming
back into place. It seemed to come back in shifts—near like work—first
shift was done, and even second. Third shift, hadn't needed to kick-in yet,
though he was most likely near on the verge of it. Third shift, being the
hardest, he reckoned, as it was on-going situations that he'd face as the
future unfolded—the roughest brain recalls, not *always* needed. For these,
he just had to rely on others, and trust, if he should confront these blank
walls—or unfinished business, as Jade called it. Then, and only then, could
they all work to fill-in the missing pieces and build a room of recollection—
if possible. And yeah, finished shifts or not, he did catch himself staring a
lot, it went with the head injury territory, but he was aware of things he was
doing and remembered all he did, for the most part, so he was a mighty
grateful man.

Thinking back on his babies that he had just fed, he once again
reflected on how he could still count his horses, but when they were spread
out in groups he couldn't seem to make sense of adding the groups up. He
had to count them through in one take, and sometimes forgot what number
he was at—but this was normal—right?

Content with that, Jake continued to dwell on the thankful aspect of
having his wits about him, he relaxed and nearly fell asleep. It felt so good.
How many times could a man soak in those words, he wondered? How can
a man express how much it means to be home, and, free to go on with one's
life? How can a man describe how good it feels to be home, sitting in his
chair, in his own ranch and being able to be aware of it all? He had no

words to describe it, whether in words, or thoughts. There were just *no words* to describe it—not a one.

"I HAVE NO WORDS TO DESCRIBE IT! THE UNBELIEVABILITY OF WHAT I'VE JUST LEARNED, JET! There are just *no words* to describe it! NOT A ONE!" The door slammed and Jake found himself half-awake and staring at a very riled-up sister.

"~Huh~," Jake voiced a reply, frowning slightly at her, in bewildered astonishment.

"What were you thinking Jet? Are you going to have a bad case of laryngitis the rest of your life? Well... ARE YOU?"

Jade walked across the room and bypassed her bed (as it DID take up a lot of the room), while he pulled himself up straight, and sat at attention.

'What are you talking about?' He cocked his head, and eyed her, trying to be a darn-good cowboy.

"Don't *play dumb* with me, mister!" she threw her Stetson down at his feet—the family's traditional way—howbeit, to the sway of jingling earrings and silent braids.

'Well, yeah... I halfway may know what you're talkin' about,' he confessed, as he pulled himself back into the chair a bit lower and eyed her some more. *'What were you doing, checkin' up on me, like I was a little kid or something? Why didn't you come offer me moral-support or something... wouldn't I have done the same for you... well?'*

"Sometimes I don't know *what* goes *through* your mind, Jet... I thought we respected each other. Instead of playing *games* with this-here chore, this was your chance to see your *friends* again... and break in easy with a few notes or SOMETHING... you have those few expressions you've been using... and a few *politely* shared notes could have done the rest! You could say you'd explain more, later, and for them not to worry."

Jade paced the room, wondering if she had done wrong to force her hand in getting him out. *If a man's hungry enough,* she remembered, *he'll do what ever it takes to get his meal down.*

"Well... so I *did* try to give you a push... and I left you in a hard spot... but you needed it." She turned and faced him. "You *just* had to write a few simple notes in place of *talkin'*...just *simply* letting people know... the Bakers would have understood. They were crying for joy when I went by the SADDLE AND SEED on the way home. They were so happy to see you again, Jet. That's when I began to find out what happened today." She stared at him firmly, "It seems they were worried that something is wrong with you... and it *wasn't* your laryngitis."

It sounded so stupid to her just now, 'your laryngitis,' and then the thought of picturing him pulling this off. She broke down laughing—'til she gasped for control.

She tried to continue, "You *actually* did that everywhere you went?" Then she started to falter in her composure and reached for the other armchair that was in front of his, the one that he had sat in previously.

"Jet... the Bakers said you had no CLUE how to pay them, they also said you laid a bunch of notes on the counter, one of them was a cake recipe. They asked me if you had some troubles left over from your accident, some troubles that maybe I might have wanted to share with them. They asked me as politely as they could, Jet, not to pry, but they were really worried when you left. If you just would have *written* a note telling them that years and dates are a problem, so naturally money might be a little slow in coming, they would have *understood* Jet. Instead, you worried the heck out of them!

Well, after that, naturally my curiosity was *peeked* a step higher, so I went to the see Lolly at the drug store. Well... she thought you were just fine, all *she* noticed was that you gave her the grocery list as well, possibly by mistake, as they were stuck together. She also said you were concerned if she had change for ALL YOUR FIFTIES. You only had to hand her ONE you know.

There was no problem that I know of that surfaced from going to the GENERAL STORE at the strip mall, as we both know that the machines make sure the change is visible, and you'd not expect to be cheated... and surely you had enough cash on you. So apparently that must have turned out *perfect* at least."

Jade got up and walked over to the window and looked out into the backyard. Her eyes traveled slowly over to the fenced in pen, the round corral with its heavy rails. She stared at it for a long time in silence. Jake reached over and touched her hand. She touched it in return, and let him hold her hand. She sighed and swallowed heavy. She wanted to look away from it, as she had been doing ever since they had first come back home to resume their lives. This time she didn't. She forced herself, *if I can force Jet to go into town to face-up to himself, I can set-my-face to face-up to looking at that pen, and facing my thoughts too.*

It soon proved to be too much for her, as her mind began to flash back to the accident—and not to the moment itself, but after. After, when Matt yelled at her to stay away and not try to look at her brother. Her bleeding, broken, brother. Her twin. Her partner. He was dead. She knew it. But Matt had yelled at her: 'He's not dead, Jade... he's not dead, just get out of here and don't look at him! Go find some more clean sheets... and stay with

Stoney until the help arrives. Just GET OUT OF HERE!' The words 'GET OUT OF HERE' were now ringing over-and-over in her mind. She could almost still see the light snowfall, and the near-inch layer of snow, stained as if with berry juice—his blood. She felt weak and leaned on the old-fashioned wooden stereo-encasement (there along the window) and crumpled down onto her knees, now laying her head on it.

Suddenly Jake was by her side, pulling her up and holding her. *'What's wrong?'* his eyes implored over and over. His strong hands held her real gentle like, as if she would crumble. At this time he didn't suspect at all that it had to do with the corral.

She took his hand and took him over to the wooden bench that was across the room, along the front window. The same table and bench that Miss Kaite had sat at during her talk with Jade.

"Jet, why didn't you come and pick me up at the CORNER&COFFEE café, I had to get a ride from Lenny, my car was flat. That bad tire, remember...? Well, it finally gave out. I know you got the note, it was in plain view on your windshield."

He hung-on to the reality of her words as best he could, as he tried not to dwell on a tempting reality of his own: *'Oh... so THAT'S what it was... couldn't figure what I did wrong, when I saw it.'*

"Jet... why did you leave my note on Lenny's desk... and with a fifty-dollar bill folded-up in it? Why did you leave my old bill receipts at Lenny's tucked into my note, as well? They were paid... both had a tally list of all the days and how much I paid. *Why* did you HAVE my old receipts in the *first* place? They were on the counter, so I could file them later with my other paid bills.

You know, Jet... that's the reason I went to the SADDLE AND SEED on the way home... it was because of what I learned at Lenny's. I hadn't planned on checking-up on you, you know. Lenny and I waited for you at the café and when you didn't come, we walked back to his office. Sofia showed him that you left a note, and at first he got a good laugh out of it. He thought you were maybe teasing him and paying him to take me home, to get back at me for making you come into town. I did share with him, you know... at lunch. I explained how I was trying to get you out of the house... and how you've been stubborn as an ornery old mule."

Jade took a long pause. "Well... when he saw my bills stuck in the money and he wondered what that meant. So I had to take a look and it didn't make sense to me either, or the money. If you wanted to get back at me... you would have left a note and you would have written it on MY note... you wouldn't have left old paid bills and money. That's why, on the way home, I had us stop there. I wanted to see if the Bakers happened to notice anything odd... I just had to know. And, Jet... you *knew* the cake recipe was for the Cook twins... you heard them call last night... why on earth would you take it with you?"

Jake sat there in silence as he pictured the fullness of this scene running through his twin's mind. As much as they were different, he knew just how she worked from their constant companionship and close knit relationship. When something was tuned-up wrong, she knew there was a reason, and she'd find out just how to make the strings tighter or looser until the sound not only pleased her, but 'til it brought out a well-played ringing-true kind-of-pleasure to the notes of whatever was being played. He was sure she found her reason now—the twang—as to why he had seemed so out of tune. Now he didn't have to try and explain it—or at least not *all* of it—as she knew exactly what happened today. All except for his awful run-ins in the grocery store that is—Jade did NOT know about that. That wounded him in a different way. It wounded his honor as a gentleman and his sister didn't need an in-depth study of that—not now anyway.

"Jet, your pride may have, or may not have, held you back, as to what I am leading up to. I don't want to pre-judge this... and I haven't been... that's why I've waited and gave you time. We... Miss Kaite and I... encouraged you to try with notes, and her book, hoping maybe you'd pick-up some signs so you wouldn't feel so trapped... so you and I could share-out lives again. Like I said up on the hill, Jet... so I don't lose you... so I don't get locked-out of our life... and so you don't feel isolated. But, this has gone-on since we first tried to find a way for you to communicate with us in the hospital... and it's been saddle-sliding more-and-more, from my view. Something's not synched-up right, Jet."

Jade leaned closer to him. "Jet... I have to finally confess this... Miss Kaite was right and I am *wrong*...."

Jake stared at the floor, suddenly he was tired of the whole damn day, and tired of the whole sorry mess he was in—obviously, he was *sorely* lacking and it wasn't just his missing tongue. Worse yet—his twin was giving-in to Miss Kaite. Yep, something was very, very, wrong, in deed.

She watched her twin's face closely and spoke bluntly, "You don't understand how to use words any more do you... you can't read can you Jet... you don't even know what the letters mean... I mean why else wouldn't you even be able to write them down, at least. You don't understand how to do any of this, do you?"

Jake set his head in the palm of his hand and leaned his weight onto this elbow and sat a minute as her words soaked in, *'I guess that's about the best way to explain it Jade. I don't really KNOW how to explain it... something's gone... it's just gone... or maybe something just ain't workin'... and THAT must be it. I just didn't know if I was SUPPOSED to know that kind of stuff or not... I mean, if I was supposed to know it... I'd be doing it... right? I'm just so glad this makes sense to someone, right now... 'cause it sure don't to me.'*

Jake started to rub his temple with the same hand, and then joined-in with the other, and slowly rubbed his brow all around the bones of his temple. He then rubbed the back of his head and his neck with a lot more force, as Jade just sat there in the following silence and watched. Jade stood up and went around and stood behind the bench he was sitting on and took over. He leaned his head back onto her chest and let himself relax.

"Oh, Jet." She sighed quietly, as the relaxed atmosphere of the now quiet house began to settle over them. His mind was settling now too, just as the coals of a campfire die-down at night and the fire is left still and soft. Before they knew it, they were in lost in the hush, and grateful for such comfort.

The branding irons weren't clanging around in his brain, being up to no-good. A lot of tension seemed to leave his body. It was too hard for him to try and tell her that he wasn't sure how much of this he was supposed to know. He didn't know how to tell her that each day that progressed he became more-and-more aware of her writing things down, such as phone messages, placing orders with their side-business, and *then* he'd even catch her writing notes in her reading books. Little-by-little it just seemed to add-up that maybe *he* should be doing this too, but it just wasn't there if he tried to think about it. The symbols never made sense on the paper, so maybe they shouldn't have in his head, what did he know. So he waited, and sure enough—time exposed what time will—as time always does. Jake decided he liked time. He never thought about it this simple before. He had only thought about time as in: good time, bad time; losing time, making time; wasting time, and appreciating time; private time, and sharing time—but he never thought to just like it for what it was. Time. On-going allotments. Life.

Time was, he could talk. Time was, he was dying. Time was, he couldn't tell his sister about making sense of branded papers or how to get them out of the fire-of-your-mind. Time was, he was cooking his sister supper. Time was, he was ashamed.

Jake thought it was time for supper and got up and dragged his sister along in tow to the kitchen—as he watched her face light up, he served her supper. He made some coffee and then sat with her as she filled him in on how she first came up with her plan. She was having such a good time talking that Jake watched her with wonder. She shared how she watched him through his meals, and how determined he was to do whatever he could to get food in his stomach, no matter the trouble. She shared how she just *knew* he'd get hungry enough to go into town no matter the trouble. She shared how she never—in her wildest dreams—expected he'd show-up with a bad case of laryngitis!

After they sat around the table a bit, Jade got up to clear the table, but Jake stopped her and sent her off to relax—he would do it. As she started for the family room, he caught her hand, and stood fishing something out of his back pocket. He handed her the last note. The one that Ma Baker had found on the floor, the one with the hotel room numbers, and he stood in a half-lean, as he showed it to her. He was grinning at her and had something he wanted to say, locked-up behind that fancy grinning:

'I forgot about this one, Jade... looks like we won't be needing it anymore.'

Jade took it and looked at it, her words weren't locked-up and flowed freely:

"I forgot about this one, Jake... looks like we won't be needing it anymore."

She kissed him on the cheek, and took-off to look for her Good Book. Jake just turned and stared at her in disbelief as she disappeared into the family room, while the sound of her successful "slide" into home-base was still lingering in the air behind her. A twin moment, timely, so.

Jake had his coffee now and was relaxing—the table was cleared and the dishes were washed, and the house was quite. Jade had just turned in for the night—after retrieving her Stetson from its earlier floor-grazing—and having nested it, to hook. Jake was ready to turn in, as the caboose to the day, soon as he finished both the last drop of coffee and last thought of the day:

Time was, he had laryngitis.

CHAPTER TEN

THE ALLURE OF FISHING... FOR THOUGHTS

IT was now June. Jade earnestly studied the book from Miss Kaite. She had never seen the ASL (American Sign Language), until Jake's tongue-loss. She did have Miss Kaite visit her in town on occasions, without telling Jake. She got as much as she could glean each time, and saved it for use with her brother. He wasn't ready for a lot, but he was now open. He hadn't gone back into town yet, but with that door opened once, it was sure to come around and swing again. Jade had sent for Matt and his wife, and Stoney, to come back where they belonged. She knew that once things were back to normal around here at one rung of the ladder, they'd be ready for the next step. First rung was as to their personal family—themselves. Second rung was their add-on family. Being that, Matt had a wife, Galena—she was like a sister to Jade. And—Matt and Stoney were like her brothers. Then this ladder would lead to the ever-changing plateaus of life, more rungs, as new people and situations would come-and-go. She longed for the whole *herd* of them, family, trail-riders, and even the *rung-riders* that used to filter in-and-out of their ranch (mainly during the spring and summer), to return.

Jake had been running the place with her alone, just as they had before Matt and Stoney stayed-on permanent, and, Jade did the family business with their photography and magazine articles. Just as true as in the past, this took away from Jade's time and they were losing money. She needed to run their business with her mind single-set. Jake needed Matt and Stoney's work now, not hers.

This was the end of the week; Matt and his wife were due to show-up for the weekend—sure enough, Jade was instigating the timely nesting. The majority of their things were still upstairs, so they were double-anxious to get home. Stoney was due-in on Sunday. Jake had seen Matt in the hospital—and way-up until his last two weeks staying at the hotel—but the last time he had seen Stoney, was only those few hours before Stoney's adopted family took him home. Stoney still weighed heavily on Jake's mind.

Both Matt and Stoney had been calling and talking to Jake on the phone, and he'd throw-in his few newly learned tongue-less words when the case warranted it, and—they actually had a lot of fun. Cowboy camaraderie—companionship at its best. Complete with added highlights: Jade had told them about Jake and his laryngitis trip. It seemed they all had a special family *joke* going on now, to be used as an ice-breaker that eased any awkward phone-times for Matt or Stoney, in responding to Jake's voiced-responses. Now finally, there was peace in the home as to what Miss Kaite kept pushing for, since the mystery of Jake's aversions to communicate via paper was settled. Matt, Stoney and Jake, could figure the rest out for themselves, as far as any *newer* communication would go. Jade figured that at long-last things were able to be on course without any *worse* frustration for Jake, in this awkward process.

Now that Jake had calmed-down concerning his agitation as to what was wrong with him whenever he stared at paper (even blank papers that teased him to write on them), he was now free to doodle a few things in the way of shapes. He even took to carrying a tiny post-it pad and a tiny pencil. He'd draw chicken or beef, with vegetables or fruit, for supper. He'd draw which area of the property he chose to work on, or set-foot to, and he'd draw which animals were in need of his care, as he took to take-off out the door, come chore time. The notes helped Jade's peace of mind. At least if he didn't show up, she'd know where to look for him. After Jake's fiasco in town, the presence of seizures was always in the back of her head, taunting her usually sturdy, collected, spirit.

The soon-coming arrival of his buddies, was still a surprise for Jake, as Matt and Stoney wanted it that way. 'Hey, he's our buddy, it's okay, don't worry about it,' was all they would say, and each in their own way. Seems they still figured Jake was balking a bit, and a good ol' surprise would force their "mule" out of the shade. What's a gal to do then? She was worried though, that too-sudden an arrival may stir-up memories that were a mite too bright to bask in, and maybe Jake wouldn't take-to-it, at all—she *knew* they were worried *just* as much as she was. Actually, maybe NONE of them were ready for memory-stirring, but it was time for the next open door. Whether it was in town or at home, these doors just seemed to be begging to get opened, some just *sure weren't* polite about it, as Jake had already learned.

~*~

With twin-power churning, Jade had a communication idea of her own, for Jake, one she thought he could handle. Jade had been trying out this idea for her brother since before his in-town chores, and was hoping it would help him in the future, but so far she was not seeing a successful way to get him started. At this point it was in the experimental stage anyway. She never tried to force him into therapy or relearning as Miss Kaite pressed her for, during the visits in town. She had seen Jake have seizures twice now, in the hospital, and here in the home, and she was not going to do anything that would be the cause of anymore anguish.

She had other ideas and ways to help him, some which wouldn't give him headaches or agitate him. She didn't see signing ASL as hard for him, but he was hard on it. He kept dragging her out to the birds, every time she signed words to teach him. She couldn't figure out what the heck he was trying to show her until, one day he sat on the fence and moved his arms around in various positions copying the birds. He smiled back at her, '*You make a right cute-lookin' little bird when you do that stuff Jade, but I ain't a little flapping birdie, I'm a horse man... do you get it now? I just don't feel like me, doing that stuff. That's not how I would say somethin', it just ain't me!'*

She had answered him with, "you look like a big ol' hoot-owl up there, JAKE SMITH!... and what *ever* it is you got to say to me, *sure* ain't going to come out of you, unless you *wise-up* like one!"

Well, if he wasn't ready for full-fledged signs, as he didn't feel like himself when he tried it, she figured her idea was a subtle enough introduction, and hoped to add on more in the future, so:

She baited him with, "aww, come on Jet... humor me... it's fun for me... then I don't have to wonder what's going on in your head. I *miss* you Jet... aww, come on... just do these simple *hand shapes*, then... *please?*" Then she threw in, "who's gonna' see, who's gonna' know?" along with, "it'll be our own code, just like when we were kids... remember the sticks and rocks we used for codes, too... wasn't it just the *best* fun?"

She wanted to give him as many avenues of communications as she could. Growing-up on a ranch, she learned a long time ago, the more work you put into it the better for success. The more you fertilized a tree, along with proper care, the more they produced their best fruit. Their parents made sure their twins grew up just as proper as the fruit trees on their property. Jake was still full of this wonderful fruit, but it was not budding since the accident. It needed to have some new healthy buds, for the years of his fruit to be manifested again, or this tree would be withered and wasted as the years would pass on, and she couldn't bear that. It seemed half of her would wither as well, if she had to witness that. It would now take a new kind of fertilizer but Jade wanted to see that fruit.

'It's all on your own body... you don't have to draw pictures', she had told him. She knew that he had the knowledge for sounds for forming words, because he had tried to make them, she had seen that. He tried to move his mouth to make words when he was in the hospital when he learned what was wrong with him. He didn't want to *believe* it, but being unable to form any words, as he had no tongue to use, he had been shocked into the reality that it was true—he *couldn't* talk. The noises brought him inner *hidden* shame, but they also brought others *wisdom* (though outside of that personal realm). Wisdom that was needed after his head injury—capability type wisdom. He was able to think, and knew how to talk, even if he couldn't. He also knew the sounds in his mind were words and he understood what was happening around him, and had tried to respond. He was flowing with his full capabilities in all those respects.

Thus, Jade devised a system of "pointing" out sounds, to match the signed alphabet. She didn't tell Jet this was to the alphabet, as he couldn't spell with symbols or read, and letters made no sense, so there was no point in explaining this and making it any harder. She was hoping he would be able to show words with sounds, *bypassing* the symbols and go by the *feeling* the reality of it, that first came from out of his mind. Once she got him to know where she wanted him to "point", she pressed him to do it with his fingers in different shapes, shapes that easily matched the feel, or picture, of what he would be doing to make the sounds visible. All these shapes were the proper ASL symbols for these sounds, but would be simpler for him, than trying to learn the ASL as symbols, because he *still* couldn't grasp the multi-task of it all. Maybe in time, once he had a new-formed habit with the way she chose to use these signed letters, maybe he would be able to grasp more. At least he would be ready, and then—only time would tell. For now, she told him, he was to shape his hands, instead of just point—as a "convenience" to HER, she claimed.

She first taught him her idea by pointing out sounds that were in his mind, by using his body as a matched-up-sound-system, so she could see what he was thinking but couldn't say. She hoped and prayed to do a bit more with this later—how much later she didn't know. She didn't want to do anything that confused him or caused him to blank-out or retreat from her. So far, she had success—the next step would be to use it more. He had just recently become comfortable with the points being shapes now, and was practicing them by trying to match them to a word that he would be thinking of. It was a slow process, but it was a good kind of stimulation for his brain, and, as he would just sit back and flow with the sounds (like flowing waters against the bank of a river)—he didn't get headaches.

~*~

Jake was amazed at how his sister could come up with such stuff as this—a way to show sounds. He was off fishing this Friday before his soon-coming surprise-visitors would be arriving. He was enjoying his time alone and was trying to think this all over, and took-to-dwell on the possibilities of how he could use it. It seemed like somehow since her enthusiastic game and her new joy at trying to pry stuff out of his head, that he had stopped thinking on his inability to talk. He was more concerned now to solve what she planned to do with this puzzle. This puzzle didn't give him headaches and he liked that. His sister was happy and he liked that even more. He still wished he could talk, but that was packed-down-dirt now, and he was ready to plow-up some other ground. He started to hunt for just the right patch of dirt right now, as he had it in his mind to fish and needed a "comfy" spot.

~*~

Trying to do pantomiming and charades wasn't his cup of tea either, because he wanted to get to the point and get his thoughts out word-for-word HIS way, not in some round-about way of signed shapes—he was just too frustrated, unable to use his vast past-vocabulary. So THAT went out the window, way back during that last few weeks of rehab therapy. Little did Jake know though, that one day soon, it would climb back in, in an unexpected way, and it would stay as a new-found accepted comfort. It would come from the same *language* that Jade was subtly trying to introduce. This ASL language would have its own signs, even more precise, alongside this alphabet, that was unfortunately so far half-useless to Jake. This new language would some day in the future make his life a lot easier, and happier, and he would have the joy of communicating with those that loved him.

Jade may have been wrong and Miss Kaite may have been right as to suspecting some brain damage in word processing and of its uses. But Jade's way was right and Miss Kaite's was wrong, as how to approach Jake about how he should-or-shouldn't respond in trying to find his freedom from this problem. After all, it was Jade's twin, not hers.

~*~

Jake found his spot, and set his pole up and sat back under the coolness of the trees and listened to the birds. He closed his eyes and thought over Jade's body chart; he could point to any sound he wanted—on himself.

He listened to himself think the word meat, he thought about which part of his body (that she showed him) started with that same sound, as he made it in his mind. He then touched his mouth. If she asked him what he wanted for supper, he could subtly point at the "m" sound (mouth), and use "m" for meat. If she asked him what kind, he could point at:

"ch" (chin) for chicken, or "f" (finger) for fish, or "b" (brow) for beef—giving her something to guess at, success-wise. He had a code to work with now, and they could work it out together for future references as to word-meanings. *Very interesting, who would have ever thought, at least in English, that almost all the sounds are right here on our body.*

~*~

It took him too long to try and stop his thoughts and try to spell-out a whole word this way. He was able to discern what the first sound was of the word he wanted to say, and the sounds in that word, if he stopped and slowly listened to himself, but it took him too long at this point for putting *whole* words together. Analyzing the full future concept was lost to him. So it never dawned on him yet, that it was possible to take all the sounds of the word "meat", and fit it together and show it to her, so she would see that he spelled meat. He suspected it added-up that way somehow, but it didn't for him. If it did for her, well that was wonderful, at least she understood him more now.

Jake had found he remembered this system easy enough, it was all with *phonetical sounds* that matched words that Jade picked for her cues. She didn't use the "c" or "x" for Jake's list, as he couldn't spell in a technical sense. She used the "k". These words were now habitually always in his mind any time he chose to look at his body, and he was **now** forming the shaped fingers to please her, but just the **pointing of his finger,** pointing to a desired spot for the matching sound, would easily do:

"Adam's apple" = a, ah (a point to the Adam's **apple**)
*Ache = ay (a fist twisting at the heart, heart **ache**)
Brow = b (a point to the brow)
Chin = ch (a point at the chin)
Dimple = d (a point to the side of face dimples)
Elbow = eh (a point to the elbow)
Earlobe = ee (a point at the earlobe) *(iih = shown for speech, later, not spelling)
Finger = f (a point touching the other index finger)

Goatee = g (index finger stroking with thumb, along both jaw bones at once, to the goatee point—off face)

Hair = h (a point brushing the top of the hair)

Intestines = ih (a point following the intestines)

Eye = I (a point at the eyeball)

Jaw = j (a point along the jaw or joint on the hand)

Kidney = k (a point to the back for kidneys)

Lip = l (a point at one lip)

Mouth = m (a point circling the mouth)

Nose = n (a point at the nose)

O = o (a point **on** center of top of the hand) ("awh")

O = oh (a point going along **over** the shoulder)

O = ou, ouw (a point twisted at the **outer**-ear canal)

O = oy (a point wiping the back of head, "oily" hair)

Palm = p (a point at the palm)

Rib = r (a point at a rib)(*for Jake's phonetics, w-**rist,** would do, also)

Skin = s (a point rubbed along the skin of the hand)

Shoulder = sh (a point on shoulder)

Teeth = t (a point at the teeth)

Thumb = th (a point at the thumb)

Underarm = uh (a point to underarm)

U = oo = (a point on the curved **moon** of fingernail)

U = eu, as in ould/ood = (a point down at foot)

U = urr (hand on the Adam's apple to feel a purr)

Vein = v (a point along a vein on the top of the hand)

Windpipe = wh/hw (a point down the windpipe/throat)

Yoke = y (a point at, or along the yoke neckline)

Zigzag = z (point a zigzag in air)

Of course, once he knew these by "pointing" and had used them with no problem, clever gal that Jade was, she began to adjust them to suit more specific needs. Needs that he need not know. The formed ASL letters. She coaxed and pleaded with him, to *point* at these spots with the different shaped fingers or hand shapes—yet, in such a way that it felt right and natural, and moved in such a motion shape-wise, to match the object that he touched. Within a week she had taught Jake the ASL sign language alphabet in a molded way, to his brain, although he didn't know it, and it was now becoming part of his life. She even showed him the "k" to make with his hand, as if it was someone "kicking him in the back", in his "kidneys", then he didn't have to point to his back all the time. First letter down, more to go! She didn't want to press her luck, so here it all sat—for now. She could have taught him the alphabet in a much simpler way, and in a matter of minutes, but he just couldn't retain anything without an anchor-system for his "loose-wired brain", as it now was. She also knew that *some* of these shapes were ASL signs for words—words that she hoped he would someday want to learn—along with all the vast signs for words that he kept refusing. But for now, at any rate, what his brain had permanently lost, was in need of a rebuilt-replacement of some sort. A new foundation. She would nurture the new growing structure of a healthy ASL tree later—or at least, a similar off-shoot, for his needs. One able to bear fruit. Communication fruit—a most tasty, choice, highly desired morsel. One that she was aching to taste again—four months had been just too long—and they were now chalking-up more months as it was. This is the situation that Matt, Galena and Stoney were soon to come home to now—it was to be a *lot* easier for them, then it had been for Jade.

~*~

The day wore on and Jake enjoyed his practice and his fishing. He enjoyed the sounds of the river as it splashed in his mind, with words all its own. He knew these words too, they were soothing and relaxing. Jake obeyed them and relaxed and fell asleep, he was awakened about an hour later by a jerking on his fishing pole. Much to his surprise, he had caught a fish, and he wasn't even trying. *Fisher River, name suits it right-fine! Right bait, right lure, right timing... half the battle's won and you haven't even tried,* Jake smiled. *Plus I got me a great hook, with a great barb... once you got that magic system, success is on the way!*

Jake took this meat of his double-success, home, to partake of its nourishment, in body—*and* mind.

CHAPTER ELEVEN

OTHER WAYS - OTHERWISE

JAKE was up early. Since he was unaware of any surprise, he planned to check the fences out in the far northeast hay field. It was one of his *other ways*. He needed them, on account of the *other-wise*. Otherwise, he'd pull up a horse and have a good sit as it traveled the high country, and Jade would have a fit. Yep, a good sit, on a moving horse, right-on-up the nearest trail—off property, as always, and on a farther northwest, and, north ridge, than his. He wanted to go riding so badly, but Jade made him swear to high-heaven that he'd wait.

She was still worried about the seizures, and knew she would never find him up in the hills. She could just picture him being thrown-off his horse and flung down one of the steep inclines of that north or northwest section of the high mountain ridge, lying under some lonesome pine— perhaps for a buzzard. Jake set-his-face that he would not betray her trust. This northeast area of pasture would be the farthest he'd gone back along the property yet. He had spent most of the time catching-up along the house, barn and sheds, and working with the animals. He drew a picture-note of the fences and the nearby landmarks and left it on the table for her, and took-off to his *other ways* for the day, *otherwise*, he'd be none-too-wise.

She found it, sure enough, but it didn't do its delightful duty. Her mind was twisting itself into all kinds of upset thoughts—she needed to go into town, and here was this ol' *I-ain't-here-note*. She wanted to make a special supper for the soon-coming-gang and now she had no way to let him know she was to be store-hopping. Oh, yes she did! She drew a picture of town, and the GENERAL STORE strip-mall, and the groceries. *That will have to do, I reckon,* she thought. She had to get used to him moving around the property, she knew she was wrong to be so overly concerned towards the seizures, but it was just hard for her to find a safe ground for her mind between common sense and fear. This was the best way to deal with it, take life one day at a time, and, sneak-out to follow him when he took t'fishing.

The car was home and completely well now—Jake preferred the truck, so she planned to leave it behind. She knew he wouldn't need it but just seeing it parked there gave her good feelings that he was the same ol' Jake, busy roaming the ranch, but ready to pick-up on a whim and check-out whatever was going-on in his mind at the time. Whether by faithful horse or faithful truck. Typical boy! Typical girl! She was just like him. He had used the truck for the first time, when she had pushed him into chore-duty in town, it had been sorely neglected, sadly so. As she passed the truck now, it dawned on her that she should grab up the insurance papers, they needed to be paid and replaced with the new ones. It was one of the last things left undone since Jake's accident. She was in a hurry and grabbed up all the papers in the glove compartment and figured to sort them in town at the office, as she paid the new bill. She left the ranch.

Jake was halfway finished making his rounds and was enjoying the feel of his body working hard. As his sister had just left, he himself had just left—though in other ways. He had just left his hammer and tools in the tractor, and sat down in the sun. He was dirty and sweating a bit, but he was full-up as a man can be, full-up with the great outdoors. It was hunting him heavy with its heating power, along with breathing down his neck with its hot breath, and teasing him just a bit with a slight touch of cool air and fresh scent of the field. He near-abouts felt like he was in heaven, and he loved it. Well, except for his hip—confession time seemed to manifest with all these outdoor joys, even in the presence of his newfound heaven. The hip was hurting him real bad from crouching on it as he had worked the fences. It ached when he got out of bed, and it hurt when he walked or stood too long in one place, but he was determined to get used to it, and he was gritting-up to it. His crooked gait ached badly in his thigh muscles too and they had tightened-up really bad just now so he could hardly move his leg and his knee was hurting like all get-out. There was no damage to his kneecap, the shattered leg had healed well under it, and never affected it. He knew that— but pressure pulling all around it from his thigh, sure wasn't doing it any good.

He tried leaning back on the tractor now and gazed around the hay field. He remembered many a year his pa worked out here with him. Their pa was near twenty years older than their ma was. He was still eighty and going, and working out here, even the year he died. Pa had gone down-hill a lot, after his wonderful wife died—there was nothing they could do about it—both the twins had witnessed it. He just withdrew and took the hills a lot. Jake had a tendency to do that do, that's why Jade had worried so, and was fighting the best way she knew to stop it.

Yeah, his pa would have been proud of him all right though—a Smith hero, he was. Now, as he hobbled-around trying to stretch out his leg, he was sure glad his pa wasn't around to see him in this sorry-state, because he was *grimacing* a blue streak—minus the cusses—since he couldn't talk. Although he was *not* a cussing man, except for damn Lyle and the DAMN BULL, he wondered if he'd have let these fly. By past habits, he'd pitch a cuss-to-dust by releasing it to God's disposal, before he'd dishonor his folks and spit-it-out to spite—he knew it was a matter of humbling one's heart.

~*~

Jake had a few "dangs" and "damns", but some things just seemed to warrant a strong acknowledgment that they were not acceptable, and they needed a heavy throw down—thus, down they came. He was guilty of exasperation on rare occasions, and a slight bit of frustration, but he never became annoyed with anyone if he could help it. He had been on the other end of the firing-line through many hard-to-face outbursts that had been thrown his way—he never wished that on any. He was known far-and-wide for his patience and tolerance. No hate ever came out of him.

Just before the accident however, there had appeared one person in his life that had tempted him to cross his own line. He was now pulling-in-the-reins-hard so as not to take that step of hate. At that time someone was beginning to pollute the area around his sister's life, and he wasn't going to allow it. He had been at a loss, as to what to do. Now so far, after the accident and since he'd been home, this was pushed back into the far recesses of his mind. He had more pressing issues concerning himself that were heavily weighing on his mind—constant reminders, day in and day out—as he fought to adjust to them. The "pollution" was long gone from their property—at least for now.

Only *situations,* had he *ever* sorted into his "dang" and "damn" category, but never would he allow a person to be personally joined those words, or to fall into that dirty box of those catch–alls of sincere disgust. Course—*lying-Lyle* was now the exception. Maybe in a weak moment, a "dad-gum" would lasso a person, if he were edging toward frustration. He had gleaned the word from his pa. When they were kids in south Texas, Jade and Jake had dad-gummed nearly everything in sight, until their ma put a stop to it. Now, here in Montana, whenever that word came out, even Jade would now still jump up, expecting to see Pa somewhere near. Jake would usually look over at her calmly and say, as casually as he could, 'hey, that was *me*... he AIN'T here now, remember Jade?' He'd give her a tender smile and go on about his business. The air would then be filled with his presence though, and soon they would disperse to some other area and work on some other chore. It was just their *way*—until the bull.

~*~

Jake reached to guzzle down some water, the expectation of looking forward to that experience was just great out here in the fields—until—he remembered he couldn't. That part of his fencing-days was now over. He gingerly took his sips from his canteen as best he good, while his mind agreed with the suffering of that now-lost pleasure, with, *'Aww, nuts...'*

He needed a subject change and tried stretching-out his leg with a walk toward a tree-filled section of fence. As he approached, he near couldn't believe his eyes. It was an owl, a very large Great Horned Owl and he was almost face-to-face with it. It was half-hanging there stuck in some of the branches. He was shocked to realize it was still breathing.

'Well, hey there... you know... if I hadn't had my dad-blamed fill of messing-around with that canteen, why I never would have seen you here. Looks like someone must have tried hard to get some kind of FILL out of you as well, while you came in for a drink or somethin' at this creek. Sure am sorry about that... you don't look like you're gonna' make it.' With an aching heart, Jake thought it over more carefully as he realized the significance of what he had wanted to say to the owl, *'YOU KNOW... there was a time I wasn't gonna' make it EITHER, for that matter.'* Jake knew he should do something, but he was at a loss as to what it was. His mind seemed to be on pause as he continued to run these thoughts through his head, *What is it... I know... I just know... I know how to do this... what is it?*

He walked around in a large circle, as he continued to circle the area and crisscrossed it a few times, he tried to relax and feel at home again. He scanned the grounds and looked up through the trees and off into the clouds and tried to not think. Just maybe, maybe something would drop into his brain. His previously trustworthy brain. Times like this, it really bothered him, as he knew something was just not quite setting-right with him, and he would get desperate for it to set-in-tight with a good, proper shove.

Ramming into his tractor and ramming leg, he realized he was at a forced halt; he backtracked to the fence-line, wondering what he was doing, when he was drawn to the odd shape in trees—it was the owl:

Dang it... there's near nothin' worse than a loose saddle on a tricky ride. He paced a bit more, *'Oh God... this beautiful critter is dying here... it's such a shame...'* Jake looked over at the beautiful creature, and watched its chest heave slowly. *'Mac! It's Mac. That's what I do... I take it to Mac. I got to call in! He'll be ready for it when I get there!'*

Jake got into the tractor and quickly made his way to the house, with the owl—he didn't see the car, but it could have been in the open shed where it was usually parked. Only his truck, stayed outside, he knew that. *I'm sure Jade's around here somewhere... and can call for me... she'll know once she sees the bird...*

He burst into the kitchen and let out as many loud noises as he could, to get her attention, but his voice was just not loud enough to fill the whole house. He reached into the cupboards and threw pots and pans out all over the kitchen floor, but to no response.

She can't be gone... NO! She CAN'T be! He was near ready to run out to the porch and bang the supper triangle, to see if she was in the yard, until he remembered they had planned on leaving picture notes, if one of them took off.

He scanned the kitchen counter near his note, and there was a picture of the GENERAL GROCERY strip mall. He couldn't believe it at first. He looked at the phone. It was now useless to him. It seemed to hang there in space, as his mind was spinning—there was just nothing he could do. No numbers came to mind they were long since gone—lost to him—as he lay under a bull at some past-point in time.

He ran out to the truck, with the owl now in a box that had been used to hold kitchen napkins. He had a long way to go and he didn't even know if he remembered where he was going, but he would have to trust instinct. He found his way into town, didn't he? He was halfway down the old road when he spied their neighbor, Kari—as she was driving up along the road. She was on her way up this same road as it connected to her ranch, which was behind Jake's. Her twin sister wasn't with her, so he wasn't sure if he could get her attention as she approached. He honked heavy on the horn, *'well, that was smart of me... '* he reckoned with a dose of acknowledgement—and some relief.

He lifted up the box and showed her the bird as best he could. He knew she would call for him, they had done it many times when he was out in the fields nearby their place. He wished to God he could ask her to jump in, but she was too quick with her reply, much to his misfortune.

"Is your phone out or something, Jake?"

He shook his head as to the affirmative, and tried to motion for her to get in, but it failed. Miscommunication sure seemed to be running rampant in his life, to no end—as if NO communication wasn't bad enough. He felt like busting the barn door open with his head just about now—as one of his vain, futile thoughts uselessly tormented him to do so, '*get in... I need help... see, it's this OWL!*'

"Get a move on it," Kari yelled over, "I'm on my way, I'll call it in to Mac." With that she sped off, and Jake, staring at the road, was forced to go it alone:

So he did. Moving on blind faith and whatever prompts would presumably pop-up, he left behind all he thus-far securely knew.

He was way out past most of the ranches now, looking for some kind of turn-off he *thought* should be there soon, nearing the last stretch of his destination; Mac lived closer to this larger city that Jake was soon to reach, all in the opposite direction from Jake's nearby local town. Mac was able to get help and donations from many of the leading citizens because of where he was located. His bird rescue mission was really flourishing now. Jake was so desperate to get there now that he had been taking a chance going over the speed limit by near 10-12 miles an hour—or so it *felt* to him, by his new hit-and-miss technique as to speed issues. The view was clear of any dangers, so he took the chance, and so far had not regretted it, as the owl was still breathing. He couldn't tell if it had gone into shock or not, and didn't want it to die on the last stretch. He glanced at the helpless owl as its life was slowly ebbing from it. His mind wandered as he thought of himself. He pictured himself as he lay in the hospital, back during his last month's time (half of March and half of April). Jade had only told him bits and pieces as to that dilemma, mostly just where he was, and how he got there. He now tried to picture himself up in the helicopter, dying while men worked to save him. His injuries must have caused him to go in to shock, they never yet had told him any details; he knew they said he had gone into cardiac arrest, and more times than once. Part of him wanted to know, as he wanted to claim the missing pieces of his life's days and hours—pieces of himself—pieces of what were nearly his last seconds on this earth. It was important to him to understand it all—it was now *equally* a part of who he is. Still, he couldn't ask yet. Part of him wasn't sure if he should know, because maybe he had no right to lay claim of it—maybe it was just for those that were conscious of it—maybe it should be left that way. He didn't know. But—the thoughts pressed him—triggered by the owl.

He was pulled out of this thought-study by a siren. He was ready to pull-over for the emergency vehicle until he realized it was a police vehicle, and it was *him* they were after. He didn't panic until he pulled over, and the knowledge as to who-and-what he was in the *scheme of things*, flooded his

soul. It sunk in real hard, as he sat there stunned. He was mute—
speechless.

The officer approached the car and came up to Jake, and told him to
step out.

Jake got out, leaving the door open, and stood there trying to be as
patient as he could. In his mind was this precious bird, and it was dying.

"Going a little fast there, huh, cowboy? Is there some reason you're
in such a hurry? The speed limit is clearly posted here and we marked you
as going 10 over, back there. Do you have some identification on you, if so,
I'd like to see it right now."

Jake nodded his head as if to answer all the questions at once. He was
just starting to make a move past the officer to try to show him the bird,
when the officer's cautious nature, put Jake in check, and he cut him off:

"Hold-up there cowboy... stay back from that door, I've got a job to
do here, and I got all day. Please just stand there and don't move, sir... just
slowly show me your ID."

Jake was trying hard to curb his desires for the bird and the stalled
rescue, but his thoughts were heading towards being rude now, *'let's get this
done fast... my owl's dying here... come on... get of move on it. Why do you
have to be so DAD-BLAMED SLOW... you were sure in a FIRED-UP-
HURRY a few minutes ago to CATCH-UP with me.'*

Jake slowly reached to his back pocket for his wallet, as the other
officer came and stood nearby. The first officer went and called it in, while
the second watched Jake and eyed him. Jake looked dirty and sweaty, but
more important, nervous. He was now slowly getting agitated, and the
officer didn't like didn't like it. Men like this had given them trouble in the
past and in more ways than one. He took a look casually over his shoulder
towards the truck, and saw the owl.

"Hey, Pete... this guy's got an owl here... come take a look."

Pete looked at Jake, "So this was why you were in such a hurry, huh?"

Innocently, Jake nodded his head, with a sigh of relief. *Now, maybe
my bird here, will get some fast-needed help... and with an escort at that,* he
thought.

"Mister, that's a *Great Horned Owl*. It's against the law for you do
have possession of this bird. We're going to have to take possession of it
and take you in. As of now, you're under arrest for illegal possession of
federally protected wildlife." Pete motioned for his partner to take the bird,
and said, "search the truck then, as well."

Jake couldn't believe his ears and threw his hat down on the street in
disgust, *'You can't do that... you DON'T know... you DON'T understand... '*

"I'm advising you to calm down Mister. This is your fist warning."

Papers! Jake thought, as he tried to move toward the door of the truck—his last hope. *I got to tell him... the papers... yeah, I got papers! I got papers in my glove compartment... I'm LEGAL!'*

"Hold it Mister, I'm advising you to stand still! If there's something you want out of there, we'll be seeing it REAL soon."

Pete took hold of Jake's arm. He readied himself and prepared to reach for the handcuffs as his partner leaned back out of the truck. "Was he going for a gun, in there, Jerry?" Pete asked.

"Nope, didn't find a thing, nothing in the glove compartment, either, it was empty."

Jake was desperate now as he looked at the two of them with his trapped thoughts trying to fly loose, *'The owl is dying you fools, don't you see that... can't you tell it needs help? Damn it... I got papers, I know I do... I know I do... I do have papers!'* His thoughts hit the wall that had come to surround them and fell, just as a flying bird would hit a window and never reach its sighted goal. The thud hurt his head in the heavy disabling way that Jake had come to know all to well.

In just those last seconds as the handcuffs were near to open and ready for use, Jake slammed his fist on the hood of his truck in complete exasperation. Jake's violent outburst shocked Pete to attention and he grabbed hold of Jake, just as Jake vainly tried to make a move towards his pocket, with the innocent thought of, *maybe if I just draw a picture of a bird hospital, or somethin'... maybe then...*

"Help me Jerry's he's resisting arrest!"

"~Unh-unh~!" Jake tried to protest, *'I ain't resistin'... I need my paper... I can't talk... I need to talk to you... wait... I need to show you something!'*

He felt himself thrown down just as the voiced, "~unh-unh~" hoarsely came out of his mouth for a second time. He felt the force of the officers on him, as one pulled his arms keeping them pinned, and the other held his face pressed into the dirt as he lay there just off the road's shoulder, just near his truck. He suddenly realized he was subconsciously trying to get up, and relaxed, as one cuff was closed. The closing of the handcuffs completely, was the final seal to his insulted honor, and he was stuck. His thoughts of rescuing himself and the owl were utterly useless and he knew it, so was his hoarse denial of resisting arrest.

He wouldn't get a re-ride on this wild bronc, not to the arrest, or the *supposed* resist of it. From his desperate desire to try to communicate in the *only way* he could, to save his owl, they had taken it to mean that he was becoming combative. They believed he wasn't going to let them arrest him. His previous violent frustration to the fact that he couldn't talk combined with his emotional pain from his injury, had presented him as a threat. He was in a worse fix now and his bird was left without a hero. He felt like a criminal laying there in the dirt. He watched two cars zooming past him as he lay there off the road and saw them speed by towards the freedom of their destinations as he was grabbed-up by the two officers just in time to see the tail-ends disappear out of sight—far, far, away. He was alone, in the middle of nowhere, being arrested—and rubbing it in worse, his favorite hat was starring back at him from said-same dirt.

He was read his rights, as he looked off into space. His face was dirty and he felt the dirt on his lips. He tried to rub it off by moving his lips. It was futile, as more just smeared over each lip and got in his mouth, and once there, he could do nothing about it.

The officers took good-long-note of this odd behavior, eyeing each other, and one finally had to question him with sternness:

"Mister, do you HEAR me... do you understand me, concerning your rights?"

Jake shook his head slightly in agreement, to avoid more troubles. After the officer finished, Jake added a few thoughts of his own that he thought fit the situation perfectly, *'I'll remain silent all right... that's what us mutes do best... we don't talk. Yeah... I CAN'T TALK... I can't talk to say one dad-blamed word, anyways...'*

He was forced over, and into their vehicle and taken away. He looked back at his truck on the side of the road. He thought of the owl up front with the officers and listened to them call-in about how they were bringing him in. He listened to them talk about wildlife, and how they needed more people to rescue and care for birds such as this. He sat there just shaking his head, as he thought back to how lucky he had felt earlier when he found the bird, and how he near-couldn't *believe* that it was still alive. He couldn't believe now—just as well—that it was all for nothing.

Upon arrival, they pulled him out, as he tried to yield into their momentum as much as he could. His leg was aching so badly now that he could hardly walk. He was worn out and thirsty, and slightly shaking—and—he didn't realize how badly he needed water. He remembered how his favorite hat was left back on the highway, *odd, the things that go through your mind at a time like this... hat sure ain't gonna' to do me no good, no how.'* Jake couldn't relax, and had owl-on-the-brain in a big-time way—aching for the lost rescue and his own freedom. Yep, he was alone and in trouble and had no hero of his own. He had a headache, which had been slightly dormant ever since his outburst, it was seriously progressing now and he wanted to rub his head, but his hands were still cuffed behind him.

They took him in and began to process him. He didn't know this town, he only had been here once with Mac. Mac was very well known in this town because of the fundraising he did for his bird rescue. Jake wondered it the police station had any posters or pictures of the organizations—but no familiar birds appeared from the paper-plastered walls. Lenny's office had lots of that for the locals, but this one didn't seem to.

They frisked him again, more thoroughly here before he was to be placed in a cell. They found the ground-up powder of his medicine this time, in the thin tissue in his upper left shirt pocket, it had been just barely discernable. Jake snapped to attention and made a desperate face at them. He hoped to God that they would ask him about it. He was desperate for it now. When they saw how desperate he became, giving it back was the farthest thing from their minds.

One of the officers, Pete, then leered at Jake, as if to torment him, and said, "Take this as evidence as to possible illegal substance abuse and have it analyzed. He's been behaving oddly, chances are he's been high on something as well... he was making some odd noises when we put the handcuffs on him."

As he saw the others take it away, Jake couldn't take it anymore and his world caved in.

"~Unh-unh, ~unh-hunh," he voiced hoarsely, he tried to get louder, but it wouldn't come out. "~Hey~, ~hey~," he tried vainly instead, as he pulled away from them to get someone's attention. He was quickly subdued, and his cuffed hands were now behind his back instead, once more, and they started pulling his belt off him. Jake couldn't seem to focus on his surrounding now and just stared down the hall at his disappearing medicine, as his useless noises still hung in the air and haunted his mind. He was so weak from lack of enough water during his hard work earlier, that he was beginning to feel faint.

The sergeant in charge came up and intervened after this commotion, looking at Jake and his messed-up dirty condition, his sweaty wrinkled clothes, and his unsteady appearance, thus far—he was not much impressed with him. Jake sounded like he was half-drugged by the sound of his voice and Jake's eyes seemed slightly dazed—his body fought to start its aimless pacing. He was now agitated because of the need for his pills, so after the sergeant had checked Jake out fully, he figured it was time to dish-out some authority.

"We don't get much trouble around here, we're a nice cozy community and we don't need any from the likes of your kind, so why don't you just settle-down and co-operate. We don't take kindly to drug users around here, just in case that *means* anything to you." He continued to eye Jake, as he added, "Put him in a cell by himself, until he calms down, then if he's high on something, it can wear off. Then after that, when he's ready to behave, offer him his phone calls and see if he will co-operates as to questioning about where he got that bird, and what he was planning on doing with it. I've already called the Department of Natural Resources. They'll be showing up to do their full investigation. We've had a lot of trouble lately with people taking them for their feathers, as you both know."

Phone calls? A phone's useless to me now... why ain't this making sense? Jake fought with this thought, as they hustled him down the long hallway, half-pulling him, as he struggled to keep up. His leg hurt and he wished he could let it drag some. But by now he had to co-operate again as best he could. He didn't look forward to being dragged completely like a dead deer, lost of its dignity, as well as its life. Or in his case, dignity and freedom. *Maybe I can find a picture in the phone book or something... of someone I know? Maybe? Jake ol' boy... what kind of a fix are you in now? Looks like you sure got dug into a hole, and more dirt's fallin' in by the minute.*

As they took Jake off, he heard the sergeant's words echo down the hall, "Now, let's see that bird. Owl, was it you said? I think I know just the man that can help us, if it's still alive, that is."

They came to the end of the hall and opened the next door to the cells, they approached the first one, hauled Jake to the floor, pulled off his boots and socks, then uncuffed Jake's hands and gave him hefty slight shove in, slammed the door and left him. He jumped up to the bars and watched them leave as they slammed shut another door. The echo haunted him. He noticed, as he turned the other direction to check out his surroundings, that there was only one other person back there in their area. The guy was in a cell about three doors down, across from his; he looked like another typical rural guy, similar to him, only maybe ten years younger. He must have been resisting too, Jake figured, as he was a guest in this special "visitor's suite", that Jake had just labeled it.

"They get you for speeding too, mister... say, you look familiar... you from around these areas? Or are you just passing-through, huh? Which is it?" The man stared at Jake a bit, "You got a ranch? I think I bought some horses from you awhile back... what's a matter mister... cat got your tongue or something? Or are you too *drunk* to feel like talking?"

Jake let go of the bars, he realized he had been hanging on to them way too hard and his hands were cramping up. He looked over at the guy, and went back and sat down. The remarks stung Jake deep and hard, as a critter a heck of a lot bigger than a cat, just now ran through his mind, bull-dozing-up an awful trail. He sat on the bunk, as if in a trance, staring at the metal bars. He was so weak and his mouth was so dry it was driving him crazy. His head was hurting too much to bear now. He remembered the times in the hospital when he first felt these headaches, and was helpless to tell anyone. He tried to lie down. He stared at the walls and sifted through the unbelievable mess of all that had just happened to him. He sifted and resifted his thoughts as they roamed loose in his mind, missing them by inches, it seemed, as he tried to catch-and-sort them into where they could lead him, but his head hurt so bad he couldn't even think-to-order anymore.

'If you ever heard me dear sweet Lord... let me know... get me some help... how will I call anyone... if they get me an attorney what am I going do with him? I can't talk... aww... sweet Jesus... I'm sendin' up a distress signal... just like that owl must have been doin'... just before I showed up'

Little did he know, that what had happened to him today was leading somewhere toward his future, with a small stopping-off spot here, first. Little did he know that there were a few "someones" following this lonely trail, which had led to his boxed-in canyon. Little did he know that his distress signal was being picked-up in a special way. "Little", lit the way out—but—it'd be *more* than just a little-bit-later.

Jake had not shown up, and Mac had called and gotten no response from Jade. Jade was still in town, but was on her way home now. The sergeant had called Mac, as the owl was amazingly still alive, if it had been dead, the paths for Jake would have led elsewhere. Mac wouldn't have been needed or called. Jake would have passed-through many long paths of thorny brambles, and worse yet—places that would have been darker and much harder for him to travel, in the long run of these systematic system errors. Perhaps even a psychiatric ward—it *had* been known to *happen* to many an unfortunate folk such as Jake.

Mac, whether available or not, had always made sure someone was on duty for emergency calls. But as it turned out Mac *was* there, and he headed-out to the police station, knowing full-well that his staff would help Jake whenever he did arrive. They had always helped him, and knew Jake well.

Going through town now, Mac could have sworn he spied what looked like Jake's truck getting towed, it even had what appeared to be a big black Stetson cowboy hat on the dashboard. *That's odd, could that be Jake's truck... it looks like maybe it's even got a black cowboy hat in it... hmmm... have only seen one other similar truck around any of theses parts... but it's not dented like Jake's... say... that one SURE IS though.* Mac tucked this uneasy thought away and soon pulled into the police station.

As he went in he was greeted by at least three employees that knew him well. He went up and proceeded to talk to the sergeant, and was now in possession of the owl.

Mac stared at the sergeant in disbelief. "John, how did you get this owl?" Mac demanded, in shock.

This was Jake's emergency trip staring him in the face—he was sure of it—and it was near death. Mac continued to talk to his friend, "I just got a word-for-word description of this very bird from a gal I know, and I was expecting its arrival... a good friend of mine, a licensed *volunteer*, he was bringing it in."

The sergeant was shocked, "You're kidding me, right Mac? You won't believe this, but we just processed a guy for being in possession of federally protected wildlife. This is it."

"Well, if that's so, why didn't he say so, or show you his papers? Why didn't he ask to call me right up front? I just can't believe he would have let you arrest him, and never say anything to help this bird, that's not like Jake"

"Jake, you say? Well, one of our officers is waiting for or lab workers to come back from lunch so they can finish-up a report on him. Let's go talk to them, and I'll check out what the report says so far, and let you know who the guy is."

"Listen, this owl is dying, and if I'm going to save it, I'll have to pass on it... if it is Jake, can't you just release him, obviously I can prove he's innocent."

"It's not that simple, Mac." The sergeant looked over at Mac and spoke gravely, "It's best that I let you know straight-up... he sure didn't look like the type of friends you hang around with. He was resisting arrest, wasn't able to talk clearly at all, and *behaving* oddly would be an *understatement*... so *I* heard and partially saw. He'd in our isolation ward in a private cell. Plus, he had some powdered substance in one of his pockets."

"That's not like Jake at all, somehow this must all be a mistake, or something." Mac was now torn between saving the bird, which possibly would be dead before he got back, or try to help his friend. He was going to have to help his friend, "Look, take me to the officers, I have to know what's going on here. I haven't seen Jake for about almost five or six months, but he *couldn't* have changed... not Jake. And... why he'd barely touch an aspirin, if you're hinting at drug behavior."

They moved on down one of the *other* halls to talk to the officers, but the sergeant was very *soon* to be called *back*.

It had been nearly and hour for Jake's wait, so far, but he didn't know that, to him it seemed like eternity. The other guy had been quiet now, and Jake had forgotten he was even there—each cell was separated by brick walls, and hard to see full views. Jake, being trapped here, was wrestling with this headache and was starting to lose. He rolled in agony on the bunk, and tried to sleep—his bare feet kept reminding him as to how his boots were pulled off, and why. Each time it all seemed to pass, he'd think of the owl, and the headache was fed the fire-of-life again—yet—the owl was his only anchor, and sadly even it kept slipping. Now he began to think of Jade. She was sure to be looking for him; it had been an hour's ride just to get near Mac's place. Mac had told him that, in the past. But he wasn't sure how long the ride in the patrol car was, or how long he had been here. She would start to panic if she couldn't find him: *The truck, she'll see I used the truck... maybe she won't panic then... but then what? Maybe... if I don't show-up with the owl... well, ol' Mac will call her... right? And my owl...?* Jake half-crawled off the bunk, not really knowing why, but wondering where his owl was, leaned against the bars and now wondered where his truck was.

Staring at the bars intensely, Jake pulled himself up and started pacing in lost circles—somehow it seemed he was floating—yet stuck. Kind of like a hooked, pulled, fish. Unintentionally he let himself drift into the thought and feel of the pull. Some kind of storm-light seemed to filter though the ceiling somewhere and got his attention drawn, yet it made no sense. He felt sick inside—he was disconnecting without even knowing it.

"Hey... Hey... you all right mister? Hey! Hey!" The man in the other cell waited for a reply, but all he heard now was some kind of dull banging on the jail bars. The loud gasp and thud had *first* aroused him and shocked him, and now the continued violence of the odd banging noise on the bars was now causing him some strict concern. There was no way someone was stupid enough to knock down the wall. The banging continued, and he pressed his face and peered down the cell rows. He was shocked by what he saw; he had never seen anything like it. At first he thought the man was having some kind of fit of anger, but he quickly

realized something was high-set wrong. He couldn't see the man's face
clear, as he was on laying on his right side, but his left leg was banging
violently against the jail bars, and his left arm was thrashing against the bars,
as well. The rest of his body was thrashing to match. Jake was having a
seizure—this one was longer than his past one was. He had fallen sideways,
half on his face and arm, in the process (missing a full-skull hit), and was
now thrashing as he lay twisted on his side. The man lost view of his face,
as it kept grinding into the floor.

"HEY, COME HELP THIS MAN, SOMEBODY! HEYYY! HELP!
DON'T ANY OF YOU COPS HEAR ME? HEYYY! HELP! THIS
MAN'S DYING OR SOMETHING!" the man yelled, feeling like a useless
fool, as he hung on the bars that held him back.

There was no buzzer in this section, being such a small "cozy" town,
and such, so the man kept yelling, and suddenly Jake was still.

Just as suddenly the door burst open. "What's going on in here!"
One look answered his question.

The officer that entered, left just as quickly as he came in, he hadn't
even gone over to check on Jake, he ran to have someone call for an
ambulance, and then came back and opened the cell. He was soon followed
by others. Mac was one of the ones to follow him in, after another officer
had told the sergeant that it was the man that they just arrested because of
the owl.

They turned him over and his head and face were bleeding—it was
obvious that *part* of his head had indeed hit the cement floor, but it *had* been
cushioned by his arm first. He looked dead, but then his chest heaved and
they could tell he was breathing. He had an awful bleeding bruise on his
head, with more on his cheek and chin, and his teeth had cut his lips when he
fell. The officer loosened Jake's shirt.

"That's Jake!" Mac went near to him, "Jake, can you hear me, Jake?"
Mac was now shocked to see how thin Jake was. He was shocked enough
already to see him there laying on the jail floor, *he couldn't be using drugs, I
know him, he'd never do that... but then what's wrong with him? He's so
thin.* Mac couldn't figure how anything could have led to this and was now
extremely concerned, in a host of ways.

The officer that checked him over and had tried to stop the bleeding
from his mouth spoke up, "It looks like he's had a seizure, but I can't be
sure. One of my cousins used to get them... sometimes we'd find him like
this. Go and question that other man, in the cell over there, someone,
please... hurry up."

"Does it look like he's been on drugs, to you?" the sergeant asked.

The officer looked up at Sergeant John, "Don't know, for sure, but we can check for needle marks, at least." The officer, suddenly bewildered, looked up and over at Mac, "Mister, you know this man? Do you know he doesn't have a tongue? Look at the scars on his face, you can still make them out, has he had some kind of an accident... could this have caused a seizure?"

Mac stared in complete disbelief—*he doesn't have a tongue? How can Jake not have a tongue? What could have happened to him?*

The officer got up now and tapped Mac on his shoulder, as he took hold of Mac's arm with his other hand, "Sir? Did you hear me... are you alright, sir."

"Yes... yeah, I'm... I'm fine." Mac looked a bit dazed as he acknowledged the officer, and went on to say, "I guess Jake's NOT though... I haven't seen him for the last five months or so... maybe it's more like six or so... I don't know. Maybe that's why... maybe he had an accident. He'd always come by, even when he wasn't rescuing some bird or some other creature. He'd come by almost once a week... I did wonder why." Mac started to tear-up and was surprised at himself.

"Look, there's nothing we can do for him, an ambulance is on the way, okay? Why don't you go sit down."

Mac stared at the owl in the box; somehow it was still alive. Mac couldn't believe it. He couldn't believe what was going on in the jail cell either. This day had started out so normal and now he was staring at one of best friends, laying on a jail floor as if a criminal, bloody and unconscious. A friend that had apparently had some kind of a very serious accident, and here he never even knew.

"Does he have any family you can call, Mac?" It was John, and he was trying to get his attention. "Did you hear me? We couldn't get anything out of him and with his odd behavior and the agitation and resisting of his arrest, I'm afraid we treated him as a troublemaker. Well, we have the welfare of others in this building to think of and can't risk letting our officers get hurt. We never ran into someone that couldn't talk before. I mean, not many folks don't have a tongue... at least... as far as I know. How were we to know? I'm really sorry." Sergeant John tried to look back at his own actions and now felt bad for Jake, "It's too bad... he had no way to tell us. I have heard of deaf people getting arrested, but they usually have a card or they start signing, and most officers are aware of that more-and-more nowadays."

Mac started to think about Jake's family and got back on track as he finally spoke up, "Yeah, he's got someone, but I tried calling her earlier. It's his sister... he has a twin. I called her when he didn't show up. She must be home by now... if he's had this problem *before*, I can't imagine she'd go too far from home. I'll call her."

He looked up in a forlorn way at John. "Look, are you going to drop the charges against him. Obviously, he was not in illegal possession of this owl... he has papers to certify that he is allowed to bring them in. I can't imagine why they weren't in the truck. He's always had them there, along with his insurance... and as to asking for help and my witness to back him up, you can *clearly* see that was impossible now." Mac remembered seeing the truck now, *so it was Jake's truck and hat after all... seems I made it just in time.*

"Yeah, Mac, we will. The officer's report did say he did have insurance in his wallet, but it was a week old, maybe his sister got into his papers or something. He will still have to answer for resisting arrest, but I'm sure something will be resolved, maybe he was trying to communicate something in some way and it was misunderstood... just like everything else was. I'm really sorry. Seems, like we learn something-new everyday. I'm a big enough man to confess that too, Mac. I'm sorry what happened to your friend."

"Here, you call his sister, would you please, John? Tell her I'll meet her at the hospital, I'm going to still have a go at saving this owl. It's come this far because of Jake." His mind flashed to the joy he had seen in Jake's face many times in the past, after a good rescue. "And if it's still alive..." he continued, "there surely must be a good reason for it... and... and after all Jake's gone through, if I loose it... well... he's going to feel like it was all his fault, and I know that well-and-good."

The ambulance crew arrived and moved past Mac. He hurried out the door, he had a job to do now and Jake was in the hands of someone *else* with a job to do. *The rescue business,* thought Mac as he watched the concerned men go by, *you just never know the rewards it offers.* Mac pictured his friend, as he must have felt, back during his lucky rescue of the owl. Once again, he pictured Jake's smiling face, but all too soon the shock of the arrest and its affect on Jake, hit Mac with a hard blow. *The rescue business... it sure shouldn't have offered a jail cell to ol' Jake as a reward, though... and surely not with such added trauma.*

The rescue of the owl and Jake were both safely underway. Jade was now coming down the drive as she pulled up to open the gate, she was surprised to see that Matt and Galena were already there. Their camper was parked up near the house, and so was their car, but they were no where to be seen.

She pulled-up to the house herself now, and noticed Jake's truck was gone. She got out and started assuming that perhaps Jake took them for a quick spin. She lay that thought aside just a quickly, as she saw them feeding treats to the horses over near the east pasture. Matt started his approach towards her.

"Hey... we both pulled-up about ten minutes ago, hope you don't mind we're a few hours early. So, where's Jake... don't tell me he's gone into town for throat lozenges or something." Matt smiled softly, with a bit of a gleam in his eye. Galena was still over by the horse but sent her friendly wave.

"I just came from town... actually I didn't know he planned to go anywhere. I have no idea. I did leave him a picture note... maybe he left me one as well, let's go check... call Galena..."

Jade opened the house and they followed her in like a lost herd that finally straightened-out and were heading home, home to that wonderful kitchen and the joys of fellowship that they all had come to love—and a room full of noisy cowboy boots. Only this time, it looked a bit of a mess, as there were pots and pans all over the floor. Matt and Galena just looked at each other, made eyes and shrugged shoulders, as it didn't seem to bother Jade one bit.

She pressed the answer machine and played the message. As it played on through it sounded like Mac asking for Jake, but it hung up too quick. She found Jake's note and proceeded to study it. "Bird, and a hospital?" she said, "plus a truck? What does this mean, could this mean he's..." Her sentence had stopped and all eyes were now on the answer machine and then on each other as they stood there hardly able to believe what they were listening to. The rest of the message continued:

'...he was found unconscious on the jail cell floor, and was taken by ambulance to Kalispell. The charges against him have been dropped, except for one. His truck is free for release, as well. Mac Walters from the BIRD&CRITTER VOLUNTEER RESCUE will meet you there as soon as possible. Please call back and ask to talk to Sergeant John West, if you need any more information.'

"Matt... he was here when I left," Jade said, as she side-stepped a pan and pushed another out of the way with her other foot. "How long ago could this have happened? Isn't this ever going to end… it's the seizures… it has to be."

"Come on, Jade, let's go… we'll drive. See, it was meant to be… for us to be here early, that is," Matt said with comfort.

"Maybe he'll be awake and waiting for you then, Jade. Don't worry too much too soon, okay?" Galena took her arm and they headed out the door and off to Kalispell. Jade was tired of that place, it was Jake's home for too long already. And they didn't need to play a one-night-stand *there* either, like the one that they had recently done in Libby after his last seizure.

It was far past late afternoon, and even past supper—Kalispell was a long ride, but they were here. Matt had gone to get some food for Jade and Galena. They were sitting near Jake's bedside, in the emergency room. It was not a one-night-stand they would be playing, they were staying for the weekend or even the rest of the week. Jade was going to need to dig deep into her repertoire of stamina, again. It turned-out that Jake had fallen so hard onto the floor that he had a bad concussion, plus he was severely dehydrated. The doctor that was familiar with him, from his accident, had decided that their original plan for waiting-out the seizures might not an option anymore. He told her that Jake had another seizure as he was being placed on the stretcher at the police station, another one after that on route, and then one even upon arrival. They had to sedate him so his body could recuperate. His seizure-free record since May, was now spoiled quite strongly. Now they wanted to keep him until he was well enough to test out what drugs would be best for him, this was going to take time. She would have to choose. Course, the doctor was just now learning about the day's conditions that led-up to the seizure. Jade didn't know yet, if this was the cause, or if the doctor suspected a progression of an undetected worsening of an unhealed area—he would soon have to clear this up for her.

She was however, aware that she could choose to do the testing after Jake recovered, now, or she could continue on as they had been, and hope this was the last, but the doctor thought it best to do it now since Jake was already here—and he was ready to diagnose this as on-going. Meaning— epilepsy. The mounting pressure towards Jade to make this decision had been building since Jake had first started having the seizures in February. During March they seemed to have stopped, until that one wild night.

Later on that night, after a lengthy talk with the doctor as to the details leading up to his seizure today, it was decided that if nothing else was found to be wrong, then they would continue to wait before turning to medication. They would continue to accept that the stress-related pressures were triggering the brain-damaged areas to go into some kind of distress. It was true that his body had been under stress as well, with not enough fluids. With all these contributing factors, Jade decided she would rather let Jake make his own decision. Jake didn't want the medication, he didn't like *trusting* medication. Jade knew that. He already had to use some for his headaches, and this was enough for him, as he never fully realized how many seizures he had been having during those first months. Being free of them for most of March and April had given them so much hope. Even though it appeared that this hope was waning, and she was starting to fear greatly, she still preferred to talk to him.

No one in their family ever cared for dependence on medications if it was at all possible, and they hoped to keep it that way, as long as they could.

~*~

Complex unexpected situations demanding communication were now becoming noticeable as something Jake could not fully function in without getting strong aversions and then severe headaches. He had never had trouble with any situations before his head injury. Trying to communicate and not being able to be understood was not being received well by him yet either. Who knows, maybe he would have had an easier go at it, if he had not had the head injury in the first place to interfere with his progress, but they would never know that. The head injury also caused a great stress to his ability to function and think at crucial times, this in turn led to headaches as well. Any of this was now possible triggers for future seizures. It was becoming clearer to Jade through these episodes, that this very well may be a part of their life that they must accept. She was going to hope and pray that in the long run, Jake would learn to adjust or avoid the headaches, but only time would tell. Little did she know or understand, that seizure did *not* need obvious triggers of headaches or visible stress, to drop-in-for-a-visit, to fell a man. But she would learn—they all would.

~*~

This was the start of the ongoing weekend and Jake would need a room, and they would repeat some of his past test, checking against inner bleeding and all the etcs. The concussion was what they were watching first; he needed time to rest now. He had not been conscious yet, they were going to keep him under sedation to keep him from the possibility of having more seizures before his body had a chance to recover. Then they would watch his responses, as he was allowed to wake up. They would monitor him and finish-up their duties, and make sure all was well, before they would let him go. Jade had called Ray, and asked him to get and keep

Stoney, as Stoney was due to arrive at the Smith's ranch, tomorrow. The Daniels were near Ray, so this was an easy chore.

Jade sat in the curtained section in the emergency room, and watched Jake.

"So, big brother... you had to get yourself arrested, huh... didn't you? Ma would be turning-over in her grave, if the good Lord didn't have only *good* things for us, up there in the great by-and-by."

She watched him lying there, completely still. His head was bandaged, though not anyways near as solidly as it had been during his accident. His face looked normal and well on *one* side, at least. She smiled at him. His lips were scabbing up. He looked like he had been in a fight, but she knew it was from being thrown down during the seizure. "Your own body picked a fight with you... huh, Jet?"

She reached over and slipped her hand under *into* his arm socket, "What must you have gone through today... I wish to God I understood... oh, Jet." She sighed and lay there near him for quite a long time. It must have been nearly forty minutes, and then she realized someone was there. She turned, expecting that it was Matt, with food for her and Galena. She was pleasantly surprised when she saw Mac.

Galena came from out of the corner chair, where she had been sitting patiently, "I'll go keep a watch for Matt, you two take a visit," came her calm instructions.

Galena already had been filled-in as to the fact that Mac didn't even know anything at all about what happened to Jake. He had just figured all this time that maybe Jake had been on a horse-buying trip or had gone to Texas, as he was prone to do on an occasional bout of homesickness. Thus, Jade filled in Mac, as Mac filled in Jade. He couldn't stay though, and had hoped that Jake would have been awake and was most disappointed, plus, he was really visibly upset as he soaked in the full horrible event that was presented to him. Some of it Jade wasn't even up to relating, and had to causally pass it by, and he sensed this. She made a point to let him know sincerely, that Matt would share *anything* if it would help him in anyway to try and understand what Jake had been though.

"I'll be back, Jade, I promise, I want to see that smile on his face, that I've come to know. I had expected to see it today... " his voice trailed-off as he remembered Jake lying on the floor of the jail, and quickly changed the subject. "I want to keep nursing that owl. It was a miracle that it lived. I swear... who would have ever thought it would have lived that long and through a trip to jail, of all places. I'm sure it will make it now, but I want to be there and see it pull-through personally. At least Jake will get something good out of all this."

Mac turned and put his hand on her shoulder, Jade sensed something important from his touch, and came to attention. She looked up at him and listened to his every word as he said, "I'm going to do a write-up on this for the paper, and a magazine. I won't mention that he lost his tongue, or how this caused him to be arrested. And, I won't do this in such a way as to embarrass him, as there are other ways I can go about it. But the *good publicity* will do him good, otherwise, this could prove to be a personal or even public, set back. Sometimes heroes need some spotlight, even though they don't think so. Besides, if heroes never get some spotlight, how will others see to follow their examples?" The words hit Mac hard, and he added, "What Jake did for Stoney, now that was *real* hero work. The kind that makes a man stand out from the crowd—the deepest kind—that kind that marks a man as quality. A deep running, pure grain, kind of quality— put there by the Man upstairs."

Matt and Galena entered just as Mac was leaving. They had a quick visit, and Mac left.

They ate in silence and Jake lay there in their midst. Their silence was by choice, his silence—was not.

Visiting hours came to an end, but since this was the emergency care, Matt and Galena got up to wait in the chairs lined along the hall, near the waiting area. It would be allowed, as long as they stayed in the waiting area. They were there to take swing shifts with Jade—she'd know where to find them when she needed them.

Jade reached up and stopped them quickly. Her eyes were filled with heavy sorrow, and she looked at them both in turn.

"We've got to find *other ways* for him to communicate, *otherwise*... this kind of misunderstanding will keep on happening... again and again."

CHAPTER TWELVE

"SPEAK!"

THEY were still in the emergency and Jake would be taken to a room soon—after they gradually let him wake and were sure he was responding well. Time was now slowly shifting from Saturday into early Sunday morning. Jake had been unconscious late into the night, but he was finally stirring as the medication was being diminished. The staff was nearby, they were watching to observe Jake to see if he would still be affected by seizures as he awoke. His body was responding to the IV fluids replenishing his dehydrated body, and the doctors were also waiting to see how he was responding in regards to the concussion.

He began rambling on now, half-conscious to his surroundings. Matt went and called the emergency staff, as he had been directed to do. Course, they were at a loss as to what he was trying to say, as it was completely undistinguishable. No one knew but Jake, that it was the *memories* of the arrest that were teasing with his mind and his desires, as he was trapped in an endless dream to catch some lost, wounded, forsaken owl that was flying through the bars—bars that kept turning into locked barn doors. He didn't know where he was now, and this made it worse. He was extremely agitated and was not receptive to anyone, largely because of confused functions distorting his reactions, left over from the seizures, and medication. Sadly Jade knew he was not ready to fully function yet, when his doctor thought it was best to let him sleep through one more night, but with less medication. Again, Jake slept; they sat.

This little group of friends by now had learned their own routine as to the waiting game, and though Ray wasn't here now, he was included just as well in their thoughts. He was busy with a new job this time; it was encouraging Stoney. Ray, Matt, Galena, and Jade had by now learned their way about Kalispell very well.

Matt noticed that Jade was looking so deep-glooming depressed. She was as different as night and day, if he were to compare her to the day he and his wife arrived at the Smith's ranch. Her cheerful day had too soon sunk away into the bowels of the earth, it appeared now, and Jade was lost in the beginnings of a long hard "night" of her own, that was slowly engulfing any leftover colors of its happy start.

"Jade, go out for a walk," Matt whispered as he came up beside her and lay his hand on her shoulder, "get some air, it will clear you mind. We're here, after all we've been through these last months, you surely know that. He won't be fully waking-up until some time tomorrow they said... remember? Go get some breakfast, you didn't eat too well last night... you too Galena, go on!" Matt sent them both away, as Jade tried vainly to protest. Galena helped Matt, as she pulled Jade along with an adventurous smile as she tried very hard to coax her back into the game of life.

Out on the streets, Jade had to admit, the air did feel good. They were all so sick of the hospital. Why, if Jake knew where he was, he'd have a fit for sure and she knew it. Jade stopped as she realized how stupid that sounded but that wasn't what she meant, and the good Lord was her witness—fit was just an expression of emotions, to her.

They picked an outdoor area to sit and Jade went in to purchase food as Galena waited outside. Jade's thoughts were so involved in her brother that she didn't pay much attention to her surroundings at the moment.

"Well... what do you want... didn't you hear me?" Jade was surprised and looked up in alarm, she thought the voice was talking to the other lady, but she was gone. She was just ready to open her mouth when the lady behind the counter spoke to her again, and said, "Look, there's a LINE behind you now... I HAVEN'T GOT all day. Are you going to *tell me* what you want or not?"

Jade was ready to take the bull by the horns as Jake had taught her but she stopped. Jade looked at her and suddenly it dawned on her that her self-respect was being picked apart. She had done nothing wrong and she didn't like it one bit, but a lot of other things started to dawn on her as well, so she proceeded to re-invent herself.

Jade pointed to the picture on the sign, the one with the chicken salad on it, and smiled mute and sweet.

"What are you trying to say... you want THAT one?" The lady studied her, "The chicken salad or the tuna, WHICH is it?"

Jade nudged her hand over a bit more.

"Okay, the tuna, then."

'Oh, wait, you're wrong,' Jade thought. It was too late. There was the order—placed and on it's way.

The lady said, "That will be six bucks."

Jade handed her the money and pointed to the drinks.

"Why didn't you say so all at once?" By the now lady was eyeing her long line and not too happy, "Look HERE'S the list, PICK one!"

Jade was just about to read it when she looked up to the pictures and pointed instead, innocently, yet guilty.

The lady wasn't about to guess through anymore pictures, so she proceeded to read the list herself until Jade stopped her at the right one. After paying, she went outside to join Galena, walking in new light, simply put.

Galena looked at her oddly, "What's wrong with you Jade, are you all right?"

Jade nodded.

Galena then questioned about the food when Jade presented it on the table, "Oh… I thought you wanted chicken salad, what happened?"

Jade looked at her meekly.

"Well Jade, let's have it… what's wrong?"

Jade shrugged her shoulder and shook it off and just smiled, pointed to the food, and started to eat.

Galena continued to watch her oddly, sorting new facts, and then brushed it off—time would tell.

The rest of the afternoon they continued walking through town and Jade would slip into a store or two, while Galena separated and picked stores of her own choice to visit. They would meet-up and Galena would share all kinds of interesting facts she had learned. She was a very fact orientated person, though not in a cold and rigid way. She loved to share new information, especially about animals, and most importantly about dogs and horses. Jade just listened. Galena just watched.

They finally came back to where they had eaten earlier and this time they had their own drinks that Galena had picked up along the way. They were now enjoying the warm sun while sitting on a bench at a picnic-table set.

A young lady, casually dressed, came near their table, and sat with her dog. After a few treats the dog sat by her feet. The lady talked a bit to Jade and Galena. Galena, checking the time, decided to get some food to take back to Matt, and left the two alone.

"You've been so quiet," the lady said, "aren't you feeling well?"

Jade made a so-so motion and admired the dog, which had now come up to her for some affection.

The lady tried talking with Jade, but didn't get far. She finally stopped and just settled for some quiet occasional smiles. Galena came out and the lady started up again with her visit. After some fun chat and laughs,

Galena offered some food for the dog from her bag of sandwiches that she had just bought for Matt.

"Oh, yes... thank you! I reward her when she sits at my feet so nice like this. She does tricks too, see!" After about three or four cute tricks, the lady said, "Watch this, speak Sheba... speak!" The little dog yapped. "Speak Sheba... speak, speak!" The little dog yapped twice.

Galena, being a dog lover as well as a horse lover, was mighty impressed, as the visit continued on.

"As many times as I say the word speak, AFTER her name, she will follow through with the same amount of yaps! But I have only taken her to four... that's enough for the sweet little thing, you know." The lady smiled with Galena as they played some more with the dog, leaving Jade mostly to herself, slipping farther and farther away.

Jade half unnoticed now, got up to leave. Galena watched her with keen interest.

"What's wrong with your friend... I didn't do anything to offend her, did I?" The lady seemed concerned suddenly.

"No," Galena said, standing, as she continued to watch Jade. Jade had stopped at the corner now, and was ready to cross back over to where they had come from—she was working her way back towards the hospital.

"She's awful quiet... can't she speak?"

"She can... but her twin brother can't."

Galena may be a tiny little gal, but she sure had a powerful knack at delivering facts, and this one packed quite a wallop, as it came forth strong, yet with a soft, even, undertone of sorrow. With that, Galena smiled good-bye and walked off to join her friend, as the lady watched and wondered.

CHAPTER THIRTEEN

"BY THE LIGHT OF THE MOON"

BY the time Jade and Galena got back, Matt was waiting with the news that Jake was in a room now. Matt was good and hungry, and Jade and Galena were good and tired. Evening came fast. Jade sat alone in the corner the rest of the night and finally fell asleep. She didn't read; she didn't do anything, she just sat. Oddly enough, Matt and Galena let her be. It didn't seem normal to them, but she wasn't looking depressed. When Matt went to question Galena about it, she made of point of letting him know that when Jade was ready—the answers would manifest loud and clear.

It was now late Monday afternoon when Jake's condition had brought about enough positive results for him to be free of all medication. Jake was still in a slightly dazed condition but Jade was assured it was from the last bits of medication in his system. The doctor was checking on Jake's condition now. Oddly, as Jake was laying there, he kept trying to move his hand around; he was doing something, over and over. Jade watched him and then the doctor, but Jake continued to force his hand in this un-co-operative movement and it was getting in the way of the doctor's work. The doctor tried to calm Jake but he wasn't responding well, so the doctor called the nearby intern over to help him, they had just strapped his arms and one wrist down, when Jade pushed in with an interruption.

"Wait! Wait... he's trying to tell me something, I know it... look!"

They moved back and watched as Jade came to Jake's side. Jade could see he was trying as hard as he could to use her signals on his body but he could not reach any of the spots as his arms and wrist were still strapped down. He finally stopped trying to do any signs on his chest, and was now doing them as his hand lay on the bed. It was now clear to Jade: *j-a ... j-a * -was being signed over-and-over, but he was missing the ending.

"Jet, I hear you, it's me, it's Jade. Do you hear me?"

'Jade... Jade... where are you?' Jake thought to her, *I'm stuck. '* He heard her, but he seemed to be far-off and floating from the medication and

lost her, he wanted to get up but his head was so heavy and he couldn't even keep his eyes open.

THEN—THERE IT WAS AGAIN:

j-a ... j-a -He was stuck as he ground and twisted the fist of the "a" hand, for the long "ay" sound. He couldn't grasp the ending but it finally came to him. Then Jade saw and knew:

j-a-d ... j-a-d ... j-a-d -He made the "d" sound without having to do it as a facial dimple, the way that he had been taught from his sister. He could not reach any of these sign-areas because of the doctor being in the way and preventing him, and his wrists were stuck—well, one was and was *incapacitated*, it seemed—'*why*?' He was thrown off-course, as if in a storm—'*why?*' But, he finally did it any way he could—he had *braved* the high seas and KEPT his course.

She backed-off and let the doctor back in. With a tearful "thank you", she then took-off down the hall to a waiting room to be alone. Galena followed her and waited just outside like a true-blue loyal little pup, that was worried over its companion *now* missing from the litter.

There was more monitoring of Jake while they waited for the results of the previous test, by then it was Wednesday. He was finally slowly coming to his normal senses but was still very tired and only half-alert. He seemed to understand where he was now, but couldn't figure at all how he got out of jail or even if it had even *happened* in the first place. Finally Mac made it back and Jake found himself understanding that it was not a bad dream. He wasn't restrained anymore, there was no more combativeness, and he was relaxed now.

Although he recognized the faces of his friends, he continued to spend his days sleeping. Each time he awoke he was more-and-more refreshed and alert. If he did well the next two days he would be home for the weekend. Jade's surprise weekend was now a week late as Jake's *surprise weekend* had taken its place. All in all, she liked *her* surprise for him, a lot better than the one he had given her. In the long run though, his would prove to be the one of greater long-term benefits, as they all learned something. Although friends are beneficial, as her surprise would have been, so is *communication* with them. Because of Jake's arrest, even he was now aware that in the *long* run he would not only have to adapt to himself but he *now* had to adapt to fit into the world around him—whether he liked it or not.

Jake woke up to his little sister's hand in his arm socket and reached over to her to stroke her hair. He was surprised at the heaviness of his hand, and as he looked over at it he realized it was enclosed in a cast, about halfway up his arm. For the life of him, he couldn't grasp how he had come to do this. His left leg and left arm were aching, because of the bad bruises he received from them banging on the jail bars, and from the seizure itself.

"Hey there, Jet... the cast makes it look worse than it is! It's just a few broken fingers and then two of the bones in your hand are cracked. Only one actually broke... you must have only been grazing the bars... your arm and leg took most the bruises," she smiled at him as she informed him. "It will be off in a few weeks."

Jake was still staring at his hand, when she nudged him; he slowly looked over at her while his brain continued to dwell on his encased hand, as he scouted for the missing pieces in the forlorn, foggy hills of his mind.

"I heard there was an owl and a jail bird needing to be rescued by Mac." She smiled again, "Don't worry none, Jet... Mac fixed it all. It's all over."

She then went on to explain to him that he would have a choice to choose medication for the seizures or wait them out. If he chose to take medication now, and let them test his reactions to the doses, they would be here longer, otherwise he was soon free to leave. All Jake wanted to do was go home and be out of there. No more tests and no waiting to become some kind of an experiment—he just wanted out. He was so ready to prove his point that he made a move to get up-and-out of there, with no further delays.

His sister, on guard duty again, stopped him with a firm hand and, "NOT NOW, silly! Concussions and dehydration just don't add-up to fast-tickets to freedom!"

He looked up at her with a huge grin, voicing, "~Unh-unh-unh~," as he shook his finger at her and then voiced, "~ehhh~!" He pointed at his temple a few times, *'aww, I know it, twin... I was just feather-dustin' your nose with a good tease, is all!'* He sat back now, though, feeling slightly exasperated as the joke moved on, and sighed with a medium-sized huff as he protested with his invisible words, *'but if something DON'T happen soon, I'm jumpin' some fences, Jade, saddled-up proper, or not.'*

"You know, Jet, while you've been here sleeping... well, I've been here in town studying... I was using your *study book*." Her mood, now meandered off towards sullenness.

'You don't say... well, now how's that?' he eyed her with a bit of a concerned brow and motioned for her to proceed.

"I accidentally opened this *study book* of yours when I was getting food with Galena, you see... "

She went on to tell him what happened on her outing and all that she did in the various stores and then zeroed in on the first store where she bought her food.

"I didn't *talk* to her, I didn't speak *one* word when I went to order my food, Jet... and she made me feel like I was a fool or something! Well, perhaps I was... as I could have asked that lady behind the counter for the moon, if I wanted it bad enough... you know me! No one can shut me up, if I really want something!" Jade laughed so hard now, and she pushed herself to go on, "Course she wouldn't have given it to me, that's for dang sure! She was just interested in tangible items, and HERS at that! Not that the moon ain't tangible, but we'd make quite a ruckus in the heavens if we went to *messin'* with it!"

Jake *laughed* with her—he really did—he lover his sister, so very fine and good.

Matt and Galena had caught wind of this family scene and were now moved in closer as Galena had pulled Matt to Jake's bedside, with the firm reminder, "See, I told you we'd know... when Jade was good and ready!" She always knew when Jade was flying with a good story.

Galena wasn't so much a shadow to Jade or an instigator for her, but was always there to frame her whenever Jade needed to add or take things from the picture of her life. And this story had some great add-ins to Jade's life all right. Matt was now going to learn *more* about what Galena had described to him as, the "secret life of Jade Smith" and all it had entailed. Fresh, too, from the streets of their still-ongoing Kalispell visit.

"I did that ALL day, Jet. Everywhere I went, I didn't talk... didn't say a word, not one word! And you know what? No one ever said, 'may I help you', OR, 'if you PLEASE, just show me what you need I will be MOST HAPPY to try and *oblige* you'." Jade stopped suddenly with a light sigh.

She got up and paced the floor just like Jake would do. In fact, she *looked* just like him—as she stared *just* at him—just *for* him. He lay there studying her, as she laid-out her studying:

"I was IN the way, JET! I was an *inconvenience* to everyone I came into contact with, Jet! If I wasn't contributing to them in some financial way somehow, or *even* some personal way... I was IN the way. If they didn't understand me, I WAS STUPID... I WAS DUMB... I WAS IGNORANT... I WAS UNIMPORTANT... that's what I was to them Jet... and once I was even a FOOL!

Well, you know me... I SURE didn't like it none! And I sure didn't enjoy the experience none-to-fine... I take after Pa, you know... if I want or need something, I will get *right* on in there and ask for it... I sure won't keep my mouth shut! BUT I'M POLITE, mind you... " Jade finished with wink as she folded her arms and sent a flashing, dashing smile her *brother's* way, her brother's *way.*

She went over to Galena, "Even that nice lady, she tried talking to me, remember? But after awhile, when she got no response, she JUST STOPPED. Just as *pretty* as you *please*... and didn't even say 'boo' to me again. But, to her credit, she did smile nice to me," Jade thought fondly as she clasped her hands together, lowered them and flipped her hands half-over with a nice stretch of her arms.

Jade quickly disengaged herself from the thought while her hands disengaged from the clasp and flew to her hips as she paraded before them with great gusto, "You know what everyone *wants*, from people? Everyone wants you to SPEAK! They even want their *dogs* to SPEAK! And *more* than ONCE AT THAT! Everyone wants to *know* something... and if you don't say nothin', you don't know nothin'... and if you don't know nothin'... you don't got somethin' for *them*!" Jade finished her parading and looked at Jake real hard.

"I *knew* this was hard for you Jet... ohhh, I knew it. I KNOW the whole thing is terrible, I *know* that too. The accident... OH, GOD! My dear God, I'm sorry..." she hushed in reverence to His faithful honor.

She strolled across the room as she refocused and turned back to face her twin. She then calmly changed the subject, "But I was ONLY seeing by the light of the moon, Jet! I NEEDED to get out into the hot sun and *really* see it. You can only see SO MUCH in the moonlight because everything is softened and easier somehow. Realities are hidden. You can *pretend* in the moonlight. BUT IN THE SUN LIGHT, YOU SEE. You see. You see every harsh detail and every ugly reality." She paused— "Then... it takes the love of God flooding your soul, to keep it all in His perspective."

She went over and sat on his bed and took his hand, "I was only seeing... by the light of the moon. Now I know WHY you never wanted to go into town ever again OR... any *other* town for that matter... now I know why you don't want to draw any attention to yourself. I tried waving my hands up, down, and sideways a few times, to show a lady the sizes I wanted, and some other gal laughed at me. She said I looked like her old *grandma* when she was mad. She didn't know I heard her, but I let her know all right!" Jade laughed as she remembered, "God forgive me, I stuck my *tongue* out at her! Just like a *silly* little girl... yes, I DID!"

Jade was still laughing at the thought and then just as suddenly as the laugh came on—she stopped—her face was devastated:

"Oh... I'm so *sorry*, Jet. I... I wasn't *thinking*... I- "

Jade reckoned *everyone* was thinking mighty hard now, as she sure-enough was, too.

Jake gave her a light punch on the shoulder and she looked up into his eyes, as he smiled at her and then quickly snapped his fingers at her for her full attention, "~Unh-unh~," *'it's GREAT to see you smile, Jade darlin'... don't be sorry... I would have loved to see you do it! Okay?'*

Jade took his hand and kissed it as she shut her eyes hard—and they all waited. She then got up and went on with her sharing—after a good swallow:

"It's obvious you've got a problem and can't be understood... I mean, the noises, about how you sound if you try to talk, Jet." She threw one hand up into the air as she continued on with that thought, "Heck... it's obvious you've got a problem and can't be understood as to how you FEEL about it deep in your heart, either... deep in your inner-most being, where not *another* soul can tread. It's not how you're *supposed* to sound... it ain't the Jet, or Jake, that we all know... or the Jake *you* know. It ain't FAMILIAR to any of us at all! It *ain't familiar*. Familiarity is a mighty strong anchor for people to want to hang on to... and others will think you're dumb or drunk or on drugs. But TO ME... I don't care. I let go of that anchor a *long* time ago... as much as I could, as I got my *own* anchor... with the good Lord. Sometimes it's hard to keep seeing that anchor, but I got it. Lots of others don't have that anchor, and all they GOT is what's familiar to them. What they are *simply* USED to seeing. You know... now I can really understand why they arrested you... you and your condition were out in the sunlight instead of sitting-away all quiet-like, in the moonlight... AND... they didn't know how to DEAL WITH IT!"

CHAPTER FOURTEEN

A LITTLE MATT INSIDE, AND A STONEY ROAD OUTSIDE

JAKE was home now, and was followed into his ranch house by, his sister, Matt and Galena—and the joy of being home. The pots and pans were still all over the kitchen floor. They had been lying there all week. Jade had left them, as they rushed out to the hospital. *This* time, Matt dared to ask her what this meant.

"Oh, it's becau-... no... *wait*... if you want to know, you ask Jake yourself, dad-gum it! Go on Jake, tell him why you make this mess!" Jade demanded, as she spread her hand out in a large swooping gesture.

She then walked up to her twin and stood-up to Jake face-to-face (though gazing-up a mite, on *her* part), "And by the way, you can *pick* it up as well... you need a *whistle* you know... they're NOT just for little kids, as you SEEM to think!" She smirked at him, with her hands on her hips.

Matt had never had a conversation with Jake yet, he talked *to* him at the hospital and was there *for* him, but Jade was the only one that had conversed with him, or actually tried to. The laryngitis-crowd didn't count!

But Matt was game; it was his pard, his buddy. Jake was home now, they all were, and it was time to get down to this business.

"Well, Jake, what are the pots and pans all over the kitchen floor for?" He said, as he adjusted his old brown Stetson, leaned back on the kitchen counter and watched and waited.

Matt was still waiting for an answer as Jake lifted his shoulders and presented his arms out and up, nearly at shoulder length, as if to present something, *'can't you tell?'* He made an accompanying face to go with it.

"What's that supposed to mean? Jade...? Jade...?" Matt turned to go find Jade. She had conveniently, as to Jade-strategy, deserted him, and slipped-out into the family room. But Matt quickly found her, sitting near the pool-room door.

"Jade, what's that supposed to mean when he just *lifts* his arms up like that? It's like he thinks I should know better, or- " Matt stopped-fast and took-off running back to the kitchen as he now heard pans falling all over the floor!

Jake was leaning against the counter, where Matt had been, just as cool-as-cool can be. His black Stetson was already adjusted, and he smiled as he repeated the same gesture, with another bigger smile, *'Now, do you know?'*

"Oh, *I* get it! Say, that's real good Jake... REAL GOOD. Think I will remember that, next time I need Galena!"

"If you do, Matt," Galena warned, "you'll have to pick them up, just like Jake. Right, JADE!" she yelled.

'Well dad-gum... I know when I've been ganged-up on... and in my own house.' Jake looked over at Matt, *'two to two, Matt... you're on my side,'* he gestured with two fingers at them, and two at the girls.

"No, not so, Jake," Matt stated carefully, "Stoney's coming, he would have been here last Sunday but you were sleeping-off your jail-adventure in the hospital. He's been at Ray's." Matt looked carefully at Jake, to see how he was handling it.

Jake stood up—and froze up— *'Stoney... Stoney... well why didn't somebody tell me,'* he looked dumbfounded over at Matt. Jake was a blank now. Then Jake's mind shifted gears suddenly, *'Stoney... dear God... Stoney's goin' to be here... why, he's got to come home to, sure as heck.'* He clearly began to start seeing Stoney—all the fun times came flooding in—along with a flood of confusion.

He hadn't even thought of Stoney showing-up yet. Once he heard Stoney was alive, he let it drop from active conversation desires—kind of like a short-circuit. He kept him on his mind's shelf and studied-on-him some though. Somehow, he knew all was well, but it wasn't really, not for *himself* now, as he soon learned.

Jake's conscience wasn't well now. He felt so bad that he never got back to Stoney:

How could I do that... how could I do that, and not ask about him? I knew Matt and Ray were around in the hospital, off and on... but what about Stoney... he wasn't there all this time... was he really okay? I just been thinkin' about me and my trouble... first in the hospital... and here, too... me and my lousy home-coming woes. Jade told me he was okay, though... she said he was at the Daniels'... yeah, she did, and I heard him on the phone, sure enough. What's wrong with me... why do I keep messin' up here?

Jake was pacing and walked from the kitchen, straight through to the room Jade was still bunking in. He then walked through yet another door, into her past so-called "half" of the house, and stood near the pool-table and began rolling the balls around as Stoney rolled around in his thoughts,

Stoney was going to die under that bull, if I hadn't got there in time. There I was drinking... what if I never heard Jade and had just passed-out or something? Stoney would be dead. He'd be dead... because of Lyle... because of me. He hadn't even thought of Lyle either, except in passing. Not since that night in the hospital when he tried to get up and take-off to *hunt* him down, but it was *him* getting held-down instead. *Well... well, what happened then? Oh, yeah... they said I had a seizure. Damn seizures... well, at least they're over with for now... since I won't be getting' arrested anymore... yeah, since I won't be leavin' the house anymore, if I know what's GOOD for me!* Jake wasn't sure if this logic would work but he sure hoped so, as he rolled the eight ball into the corner pocket with a firm forceful pitch.

Matt followed him in slowly. "You okay, Jake?"

Jake looked at him, still a bit confused as to Stoney. *'Why haven't we been seeing Stoney, Matt?'* His eyes desperately searched Matt's face. *'I'm sorry I didn't call you all back home, Matt... I stalled out... I'm really sorry... is it cause of me... is THAT part of it?'*

"Hey, Jake, it's okay... Stoney's been at his adopted folks, they wanted him home as soon as he was well enough to get out, he needed lots of care, too. He went home broken legs and all, but he first got to see you in the ICU when you were in the coma. He came back towards the middle of February to see you. Remember? He really needed to see that you were going to pull-through. He talked with you quite a bit and held your hand? He held your hand and cried on your shoulder, don't you remember? He wouldn't leave at first, so his *folks* coaxed him and he did, he knew he had to go, he had to get his cast off that day... but he was there to see YOU first. He wanted to stay *longer*, but he couldn't, he just couldn't. Remember?" Matt went up to him and shook him on the shoulder slightly. Jake tried to focus his thoughts, and looked off toward the pool-table where he had been spinning the balls.

'Why do I keep forgettin' this? I only seem to see Stoney and the bull...' Jake stared at the spread out balls in the center of the pool-table and then his eyes slowly glanced around at the other empty pockets.

"You weren't feeling to well, Jake... we're not even sure if you really knew who we were, for that matter... most likely that's why you can't place all this."

"~Un-huh~," Jake agreed with his voice. *'That must be it... yeah, you're right, Matt. It's not 'cause I didn't care about him.'* He started having visions of Stoney under the bull now and it was bothering him, but the usual headaches didn't seem to come. Somehow his mind was keeping things at bay this time and he felt peace in his heart. He took it to mean that all was well—somehow there was a stream of life, ready to bubble-up and flow sweet-healing water here. All he had to do was see Stoney again with his own eyes, and the success of the rescue would be set-to-rest.

Setting things to rest can be serious business at times, and, as there was far-more to set-to-rest, concerning this bull-issue, truly said, *others* in Jake's gang would do their part in helping.

The wrangler twins from next door, Kim and Kari Cook, always could be counted on to look after the ranch, and so could Ray. They had all done so, once again, during this recent week, while the gang was in Kalispell. There was no lack out in the yard, but the house needed to be readied-up with the gang "nesting" back in. While Jade was busy settling her household now, Ray was home, trying his best to settle his. Honor was staying in the bunkhouse. Alex and Angie were in the house, and now, so was Stoney—at least, that last week. Hard times were going on, as Angie wanted to ride along with Ray and Stoney to Jake's. She wanted to bring Alex (was *her* reasoning) so Jake and Alex could meet. After all, why not? Life was moving on—after long-last, Matt, his wife, and Stoney, were now going back home to the procrastinating boss-man. So—why not *her*?

Jake sure looked fit-as-a-fiddle when she saw him. She had *later* found out that he had been into town as well, although she heard he had been sick with a bad cold and laryngitis, he must be over it by now. And now— the magic word, NOW, was finally working. Now, everyone was going, so why not her?

"It's a guy thing, Angie," Ray, explained, "Jake needs some time with Stoney. Jake saved his life, you know... oh... well now... you don't *really* know yet, do you?"

"I just know bits and pieces, Ray, you know that... I was more concerned what happened to Jake, not why he was messing around with that crazy bull... right? ... bull? ...in the first place," she finished.

Stoney was mad now and stood up from sitting on Ray's front room sofa:

"Aww, you don't care, you're just nosey... you're just *plain* NOSEY! You just wanted to see if he was all *busted-up* so you could laugh at him... 'cause he got your friends to laugh at *you*! If you really cared, you would have been asking other kinds of questions. Ray and I heard all that stuff two days ago, when we were in town for supplies." Stoney grabbed-up his suitcase and his cane, threw his slick new Stetson on, pulled down on the brim with a tug and glared hard at her, "You make me SICK, you know that

Angie... you always did!   An' you *ain't* coming with us, that's for HELL-
CERTAIN sure!"

Stoney was walking pretty good now, his one leg just played tricks on
him when he least expected it. Jake's leg looked in worse shape when he
walked, as it went crooked from the muscle, but Jake's was strong enough
not to cave-in. Stoney had a nice pleasant gait to him still, but he slowed it
down now usually, and kept the cane nearby—his leg did cave-in, but he'd
master it, yet. He was done bull riding though, and he rightly knew it.
There was no way he'd be able to hold on now, with a trick leg. Somehow it
didn't bother him at all—and he knew why, above all others. Now, if Jake
hadn't been near killed trying to save him, or if it had just been his *own*
stupid mess during a show, then he would have been *mad* about not getting
on the bulls again—perhaps even to risking his future days. But—while
roping-down some heavy-duty figuring, he came-up with some higher-
reasoning powers as to any future bull decisions—he owed his life to Jake—
and there'd be no bulls. He wasn't about to let Jake face having saved his
life—all for nothing—because he planned on being stupid-careless with that
life, by taking a dumb-bum-step forward. He wasn't about to complain
about that life now, either, or his decision—he was owing-up to each sunny
new day, with a grateful heart.

Stoney stood out in that sun, even so-said, as he soaked in the great
summer day, while waiting for Ray. It was a much more pleasant situation
than soaking-in Angie. But there was something more to soak-in than the
hot summer day. It was a revelation of knowledge, just as strong as that
mighty hot sun beating down. Jade.

"Stoney," he said out loud to himself, "if your leg worked good
enough and you got on a bull and it *killed* you, why ol' Jade would drag your
carcass from here to Texas and back. All for wasting her brother's life after
he *laid* it down for you." Stoney strayed-off with sweet thoughts of Jade,
"Now I sure wouldn't want *that*, now would I?" He smiled again, as he got
a gleam in his eye over her feistiness, "No sir, not with that ol' spur-gal,
Jade! Sure don't want her dragging my carcass around."

"Let's get a move on, Stoney," Ray hollered over, "Alex told Angie
there'd be plenty of time for him to meet Jake *later*, but *not* plenty of time
for them to have the house all to themselves! Romance just saved us... you
see? Honor just left to borrow one of my horses and she'll be gone all day...
they're alone... perfect timing, huh?" Ray laughed as they headed for the
truck.

"You sure ain't like Jake," Stoney looked at Ray, as they drove off.

"Why do you say that, we're all ranchers, we're all best friends, what could I possibly have done to make me fall to the *back* of the line now... and after all this time?"

"Well... here it comes, buddy... you sure *hide* a lot of stuff from your sister. Now, Jake on the other hand, he tells Jade EVERYTHING."

"He has to... have you ever seen that little gal go? Have you ever seen her when she has a hankering to follow someone?"

"Yep... come to think of it... I have. Shucks, sure can't get her to follow me none," he laughed, with a delightful smile.

"Now, look Stoney, you're 30 and she's 40, she probably just never thought about it. Ten years can make a gal feel a mite old you know."

"Aww, I never thought of it like that, Ray"

Stoney glanced over at Ray, "Never should have told her may age... maybe we could start up a rumor, about what a liar I am, huh?"

"Well now... if you keep up that habit of forgetting to shave... you might pass for 35 someday soon!" Ray reached over and gave Stoney a pull on his sandy colored low-growing chin-crop.

They laughed together, as Stoney put on some country music, and they relaxed for the ride. It was barely a half-an-hour ride. Their ranch, along with lots of their friend's ranches, was scattered all around an hour-and-a-half (give or take) drive into Libby. Just Mac, was farther out, and he was going the opposite direction, toward the direction of Kalispell. Jake ended-up a little farther away from Mac's, at the police station from a nearby community. They had sent him to Kalispell hospital instead of Jake's nearby Libby though, first because it was nearer, and second because if he had something seriously wrong with him from his previous accident, the doctors there would have been more familiar with his case. Turned-out they were right to do so, and Ray and Stoney acknowledged this as they readied-up to see Jake, with the ranch in full view.

As Ray and Stoney drove up, the rest of the gang was in the front, on the wooden porch. Matt had the barbecue going. They were all out there *except* Jake.

All the warm social talk started to take place, "Go on... take your stuff in Stoney," Jade said as she gave him a huge hug, complete with tears that came down her face. "Oh my dear God..." she prayed out, "Stoney, it's so good to see you back." She wiped the tears off her face with her arm and then used the other one, just as skillfully—standing there in her boots, blue-jeans and a navy-blue T-shirt—Stetson-topped as always.

"What's Jake doing in the house... getting some more steaks or something?" he took to reasoning.

"I don't know... he just sort of disappeared, maybe he went in for something to drink, he told me was going to, awhile ago... he must still be there."

"Jade... there's plenty to drink out here, now why would he do that? I'll take him a beer and we'll have us a few guzzles!" Stoney reached down into the nearby cooler and took-off.

"Stoney... WAIT!" Jade called to him, "didn't anyone- " It was too late, he had neared the door and was in the house now.

Jade thought Stoney's remarks seemed odd, and she was starting to worry, but then, maybe Stoney was just teasing, like Jake and Matt always did. Jade was soon interrupted from her thoughts, as Ray came up and started to talk about his sister.

As Stoney entered the door, balancing his beers in one hand and suitcase and cane in the other, he nearly ran into Jake, but Jake was too busy to pay much attention. Jake was leaning over the sink-counter in a standing position, leaning just a little on his left elbow, with the cast on his left hand, in plain view. He was twisting his head back around, slowly, down and up, then he'd stop, take a small wait, and he'd start up again. It looked like he was trying to swallow. Stoney could see he was using some kind of a large plastic syringe in his mouth, that he was just removing. Jake grabbed-up a towel and looked up, expecting to see Jade.

'*STONEY!*'/"JAKE!" Simultaneous greetings were echoed, one through the brain and one through the mouth, as Jake hugged Stoney, suitcase, cane and all, and spun around in circles with him, like they were a couple of happy pups.

"So what were you doing there, Jake. You're not sick are you... looks like you're trying to swallow some *horse medicine* there, ain't there an easier way to take care of a cold. Heard-tell from Angie that you had laryngitis real bad. You sure look fine to me. Well now, except for a few scars, I know... I ain't gonna' *play stupid* and pretend they ain't there." He set the beers down in unison with a thud on the counter, and pushed them aside, near the dish rack.

He noticed the syringe was still half-full, but it didn't look like any cold medicine he ever saw before.

"So what's it for Jake, vitamins or something... if it taste that bad that you need to force it down, I'd QUIT if I were you!"

Jake looked at him, puzzled. *Don't he know?* '*Don't you know, Stoney?*'

"Listen... Jake... " Stoney looked down at the floor and looked back up at Jake, as he teared-up, "All this time... I'm sorry... I couldn't be with you." He dropped his suitcase and his cane from his hand. "The Daniels... they were so broke-up, I'm mean, their whole family was just feeling so sick over it. All them little kids that love me, and all... I had to stay put there. Hey... look, I got a scar too," Stoney laughed a little bit nervously and showed Jake his side, "also, a skull fracture... hairline... not any where *near* as bad as yours... real slight. I was dazed off-and-on, but I remember hearing Jade screaming... and I remember hearing Matt yell at her to get away from you. She came over to me, and I don't remember too much then, but I remember hearing a helicopter some time later... yeah... of all things, a *helicopter* just for us. Saw it too, saw them put you in first, Jake... you didn't look too good Jake... I thought maybe-"

Stoney was crying and Jake pulled him close and held him like a dad would to his son, like a big brother would to a little brother—man to man, friend to friend.

Stoney backed-up and wiped his face, "Look at me, I'm crying like a little kid." Stoney laughed nervously, feeling sick, as he tried to brush it away. Then he got really quiet and studied Jake's face.

"How does a man thank another man, Jake? How can I thank you? They done me *dirty*, Jake, but the law can't prove it."

Jake let go and stood back and searched his face for a clue to this mystery that was spilling out of Stoney's mouth, but he didn't see one.

'They?' Jake dug down deep and thought heavy. He was missing some pieces here, obviously, but now wasn't the time.

Stoney wiped his face again and turned to the sink and grabbed-up some snazzy beer glasses from Jade's dish rack and he pulled the beers near. He flashed a big smile, to Jake, "Hey there, buddy... look what I got for us!" He poured the beer into the glasses and gave one to Jake. "Here pal, I been waiting all these months to have this drink with you," he clinked his glass to Jake's and wiped his eyes with his shirt-sleeve one last time, "thanks for saving my life, pard... thanks Jake."

Jake stood there as if in a trance and stared at Stoney.

"What's wrong Jake, ain't you gonna' drink with me? You ain't *mad* at me... are you? Or disappointed with me? I didn't know about the bull... *honest* I didn't. Dear God in heaven, if I did... I NEVER would have got on it."

Stoney was shaking a bit now and his fears that he carried these last months started to flood downhill from his mind and hit him in the pit of his stomach. He felt sick. He set his glass down, and Jake set his down immediately after and gave it a slight push out of the way.

Jake grabbed Stoney up, and held him tight for a long time, his own face was now streaked by fine tears of deep sorrow, *'NO STONEY... I could NEVER be mad at you... that's not it... THAT'S NOT IT AT ALL... there's just something you don't know... '*

Jake calmed him with his hands, by gesturing to him to relax, showing him all was well, and then Jake looked over at him helplessly. Realizing his face was moist, he used his left sleeve, above his cast, to fix it, while he fumbled with his right hand near his right-side belt—slipping it along to his back—and then finally slipped it into his right back pocket. He was trying to collect his emotions and started to slip his left hand into his back pocket just then too—from habit—when he realized it didn't fit because of the cast. Jake fumbled around in place and oddly stared at Stoney. Jake was lost in his own kitchen.

"Something's wrong Jake, right? And if it ain't *me* then... what is it? Jake... Jake... can you hear me?"

Jake snapped out of it, and stared into Stoney's face, but didn't know what to do. Jake started to open his mouth, but he stopped. *'I ain't got a tongue anymore... I can't talk Stoney... and you don't know it, do you.'*

~*~

Jake thought of himself, as he stood there unable to say a thing. He remembered back to the hospital and how he was so desperate to know what was wrong with him. In the ICU, his head and face had been bandaged and he had been lost to any contact with anyone because of the coma. The only memories he had of January, was Jade's hand, during that last week, when he was finally somewhat awake but unable to see and barely able to hear. Even though February was lost to him, except for sketchy recollections of being guided through all kinds of therapeutic help, and faces that were supposed to mean something to him, his mouth was a clear memory. And yet, it felt completely wrong inside, but he wasn't fully conscious or discerning enough to really understand, so he vaguely thought it was severely numbed. No one would tell him—not right away. When he was finally fully aware and realized where he was, and learned how he had been severely injured and had been in such critical condition, he remembered he couldn't *believe* what he was told next. He couldn't believe it was true, and the shock devastated him. He had no tongue. Why, never in his life, had he *heard* of such a thing—not ever. He had to be very careful how he told Stoney now—as—now he understood. Now he understood how Jade and his friends had felt and why they couldn't bring themselves to tell him about this last injury for so long. Some things one's just got to learn easy, a step at a time, or it's too hard to swallow. He knew in more ways than one how it felt to choke-up on something—whether it was food or a truth. He didn't want to see this friend choke-up on this truth that was to come, and feel to blame about what happened because of the bull—and he *knew* Stoney would.

It was hard enough for Stoney to accept how badly Jake was hurt in regards to all else. Stoney blamed himself, and he still did. So at first—no one was able to tell Stoney about how Jake would now be spending the rest of his life, if he lived. Later, during Stoney's visit in February, there was a miscommunication between Jade and Matt and neither one of them told Stoney about Jake, before Stoney left with the Daniels. This last week at Ray's, any talk of Jake had been avoided, as Angie was around. Ray did make it a point to help council Stoney's weak aching conscience though, but that was all. Stoney was about to learn now, what he had missed-out on, and there was no getting around it. It would be a shock for him to handle, heavy as a hard Texas downpour—Stoney had some raw inner wounds still—and near as bad as Jake's.

~*~

Looks like they didn't tell Stoney about my permanent damage... now just HOW did they manage to mess THAT up? Jake wondered, in disbelief. *Stoney must have left before they got a chance, that must be it. Aww Stoney... this is sure gonna' be hard on you... maybe just as hard on you, as it was for me, back when I was told... well... maybe not quite, I reckon... as I'm the one walking-the-walk, here, without talking-my-talk.'*

Stoney sadly set the two beers down on the counter, stinging slightly from pains of supposed rejection—he stared-out, watching the happy group through the kitchen window, "Funny, I planned for so long to have this drink with you, Boss-man... Jake... and here it's a-"

Stoney turned to face him, dead-pan pale— "You're not dying... or something... are you Jake?" He looked worried now. "Why else, wouldn't you drink with me? Unless... maybe you need to tell me you're dying... how can we all be having a homecoming party if you're dying? That ain't it, then... is it. Say... we were dancing around in circles just a minute ago, weren't we? Hey... I'M BACK!" Stoney tried to flash a weak smile, and looked at Jake again. This time his eyes drifted along the counter.

"What's that for, Jake... that thing... that syringe... what were you doing in here alone, using it? Is it for seizures or something? I knew a bull rider once, a buddy of mine... he had a head injury, he took medicine for seizures afterwards. He had a hand tremor… he always used the syringe for his medicine. I never saw him have a seizure though, but I heard-tell it sure weren't a pleasant thing to see. He had to give up the bulls and-."

Jake couldn't stand it any longer, he grabbed-up the two beers, one at a time, and stowed them away, tucked in his upper left arm. Balancing them the best he could, he grabbed-up Stoney's arm, with his right hand and he pulled Stony to the back door. He opened it, and pushed Stoney through it, and resumed pulling him by the arm. They passed the round corral on their way to the back fence, as Stoney's mind zeroed in on the corral. He hadn't seen it all this time and now it seemed to shock him. He really had been lying in there with that bull. Jake was pulling him along too quick now, so that Stoney nearly stumbled as his mind was still locked-in on the corral as he stumbled over visions of Jake being stomped and kicked by the bull. Jake continued to pull Stoney through the back fence and then through the north pasture and up the northwest ridge—dousing their trail with nice cold, ice cold, beer.

"Hey what's the matter Jake… where we going? You could have just said something, you know… you didn't need to drag me… I ain't a lost sheep."

With that last remark, Jake let go and they climbed the ridge.

Instead of staying on the hill, looking down at the house, as he did with Jade, Jake took Stoney back farther, to a clearing in the woods. He sat down on a log and looked at the beer, most of it was still in the glasses, just a little sloshed, and he had lost some on his shirt. He looked over at Stoney and Stoney looked at him.

"Well, looks like our beer made it, huh, Jake? Does this mean I get my drink with you, pal, huh? Nothing like the great outdoors to make a man feel whole and free again after trapped in a hospital. Do I get a glass-tap with you and cheers for our freedom now Jake… huh?" Stoney smiled his flashing smile, "say… if you *wring-out* your shirt… why I just BET we'll have a bit more, for a *second* go at it, too! So… what do you say, Boss-man…? …here's to ya'!"

'I'm gonna' give it my best shot, pal,' Jake smiled back, lifting his glass to his buddy.

"Cheers!"/ *'Salud!'*—they agreed in unison, to the sound of one lone voice, and the chimes of two glasses. Then Stoney drank up, as did Jake, only after Stoney finished his large swallow, he sat staring at Jake.

Jake had his head down a bit, tilted to the side and was still trying to pour the beer out into his mouth without spilling it on himself, he had now succeeded and had turned his head to the side, and back and then up some, and was trying to swallow it, all along the way. When he had succeeded, he then turned the glass sideways and was now trying to work the carbonation out of the beer, with his finger. Jake knew sooner or later that he would be making enough of a spectacle of himself that something was bound to happen—and so it did.

A strong hand reached over and stopped Jake, just as he looked up at the moving form that had finished coming his way. Jake stopped moving, too, and looked-up at Stoney's face.

"Jake. Jake… what's *wrong* with you?" Stoney took hold of Jake's hand a bit harder and stared him in the face. Jake's jaw wasn't quite as even as the other one; he could see that now as he studied Jake's face closer. Somehow he had overlooked that in the kitchen. He could see the scars, but Jake's face seemed fixed-up normal enough.

"I want it straight, Jake. Matt and Jade were acting *really* funny the day I had to leave… and they each wanted to know if I had talked to either of them. *Separately.* I thought it was something to do with the bull and what I did. Now… I know it's not."

Stoney took the beer from Jake, and his own empty glass, and threw them down at a nearby tree and turned to Jake, and half-yelled and half-cried:

"WHY CAN'T YOU DRINK THE DAMN BEER JAKE!"

Jake stood-up and looked into Stoney's face again, *'I want to tell you but I can't.'*

Remembering the shock from the first time he heard himself try to talk, Jake couldn't bare to let Stoney hear him. Remembering his useless noises and the knowledge that it was the only thing that would ever come out of his mouth, Jake took his hands and opened his mouth and let Stoney have a good long look. He had never shown anyone else. Jade was the only one to see, as she helped check to make sure that his mouth stayed clean after eating.

Stoney just stood there becoming more-and-more serious until it dawned on him what he was seeing. Jake had no tongue.

"What happened to you Jake?" Stoney walked over to the tree and leaned on it and stared back at him. He felt so weak inside that he had to fight to compose himself:

"They told me you got stomped on, kicked, and ripped-up real bad. They told me you got your face smashed-up and your skull broke. Yeah… they did," he lifted his eyes up to Jake's, "what happened to your mouth Jake, you don't even got a tongue left, from what I could tell. Stoney shut his eyes and tried to separate from it all, "All this time I thought you were okay and the *worst* was behind us, Jake."

'The stompin', kickin' bull ripped the side of my face... broke-up my jaw and ripped-up my mouth, taking the tongue right along with it... I sure couldn't stop him now, could I? I was out cold, from what I heard,' Jake lamely, gamely, tried to smile, in a lost, awkward, bumbling way.

"What the HELL are you smiling for Jake! Damn it! I did this to you! IT'S ALL MY FAULT."

"~Hey~," voiced Jake seriously, as he put his hand out, like a policeman would do for a "stop", just the same way he always did in the past, when he wanted to ready-up to tell-him-off. It was now boss-man, to kid, and Jake scolded with his finger:

'Jade and I... we don't allow swearing... remember? Although I been sure-as-heck guilty, as of late... dad-gum and dang-it-all. Aww, DAMN it!' Jake pressed his right hand to his pressure-point between his brow-bone, let out a sigh, and dropped his hand to mid-chest, easing his eyes down to Stoney.

"Damn, I'm swearing again… ain't I… I'm sorry, I'll stop." Stoney went over and sat on an old tree stump. "Jake, you can't even talk, can you? That's why you haven't been talking-my-ear-off. I thought it was just tension from all the trauma we been through and us meeting-up again since the accident and all, you know… " Stoney let his face fall down into his hands. "What the he—… " he caught himself, "what have I *done*? What have I done to you, Jake? Look at you. All because of a dang bull… and lying-Lyle."

Jake jumped up, he picked-up on this again, *'lying-Lyle... what's that mean... what are you talkin' about Stoney... I'm gonna' find out, you know,'* Jake had his hands on Stoney's shoulders and shook him once and looked at him hard and long.

Stoney eased back off the stump, as Jake continued forward, straddling over it, and stood face-to-face with him now. Jake began to voice and gesture as he pressed Stoney for answers.

"~Whaa~~?" Jake rounded his lips, and pushed out a voiced noise from deep in his throat, as he stretched his face forward to do it. He turned his head sideways and drew out his lips and pushed out, "~yoo~~," he swallowed hard, twice, trying to moisten his throat, trying again, "~Whaa~~ yoo~~ oh~~?"

Jake waited for an answer as he yelled at him with his thoughts, *'WHAT DO YOU KNOW? COME ON, COME ON, YOU KNOW SOMETHING'* He could make no "n" sound, but with nasal sounds that he vaguely remembered from therapy, he voiced out, "~On~ ~on~, ~on~ ~on." Jake motioned with his hand, coaxing, as he continued brain-wise, *'come on, come on'*, and voiced one last try:

"~Whaa~~ ~~ha~~p'?" he puffed lastly.

Stoney was so upset when he heard Jake trying to talk. He couldn't believe this senseless noise was all Jake would ever be able to do for the rest of his life. He earnestly tried to push it aside—along with his heart-felt guilt for needing to be rescued that awful day. Stoney walked off through some trees and picked another one to lean on as he hid his face in shame. Jake followed him, earnestly voicing noises that were discernable only to himself. Stoney tried not to think how Jake sounded, the man didn't have a tongue, so what was he *supposed* to sound like. He could accept this reasoning, without rejecting his friend. Thus—what he *really* thought-on now, was how could Jake *ever* accept him—it was all *his* fault!

Yep, Stoney was batting in the blame-game, figuring he had the only homer, but there was a curved pitch coming. That being, Stoney's guilt was the farthest thing from Jake's mind now—someone else had the home slide, for now—and Jake kept pitching for it. Jake was hounding Stoney in anyway he could—and—Jake was trying so very hard to talk, that Stoney felt so sorry for him. Stoney finally faced him, and blurted-out what Jake was begging to know:

"Lyle TRICKED me, Jake. He brought a ringer-bull over. I saw a bull-ride back in Kalispell and my buddy rode it and I like it, but I didn't see it except for on a blurred film clip. My buddy said it was a great bull. Well, Lyle said he bought the bull and he brought it here that day of the accident. Then his two wranglers that handled it... some guys from Kalispell... well they said they had the go-ahead to sign me up for a show with a really great sponsor, if I liked the bull and if I handled it good. So we got the bull ready to ride.

Lyle said he was going to move the truck and trailer out of the pasture, and on down the road and turn around somewhere. He wasn't even there when we started, he must have took-off, 'cause none of us saw him again. We knocked out the boards from the old chute on the back-side of the corral and set him up in there, and I rode him out.

Lyle must have paid them wranglers of his, to go along with it... they *knew* it wasn't the same bull or they would have helped me out of there. They were afraid of it! It was *crazy*... or high on DRUGS... or BOTH... I swear it was, Jake! They said they'd bale me out and keep the bull busy if something went wrong... or after the ride, which ever came first. But they

were too afraid of that damn bull... sorry Jake, but it was. It was a damn
bull, is all... it was just a damn crazy bull from hell!

Well, like I said, they had fixed him up in our old practice chute, and I
was on him and they let him out, Jake. I couldn't handle that bull, no way,
no how. They were gonna' be there for me, but they didn't do *nothin'*! I got
hit in the head going down. They left me there to get stomped, and after, my
legs were broke! The bull was twisting around me and *got* me again. And
he was off stomping just a foot away and ready to turn back on me again...
he'd get close... and then back-off. I couldn't get out! Jade was screaming,
and I found out that I had a gash along my side then. Not near as bad as
what you got done to your chest, though Jake... not near as bad.

That's when I saw you come in and stand in front of the bull. If I
wasn't in such a daze, I could have *sworn* you were STONE COLD
DRUNK... and I saw him take you down Jake. It looked like he ripped into
your chest as he threw you, and you were trying to get up... I lost sight of
you because of the bull blocking most of my view then. He stomped and
twisted around and went back at you and he hit you from behind, in the back
of the head with one of his horns. I saw that. It sent you sinking down into
that dirty snow. I couldn't see you any more, that bull was all over you,
Jake. I heard gun shots, over and over, and I saw Matt run in from
somewhere, but I still didn't see you. I saw a mighty dead bull, and Jade
was pulling me out... I was in such pain, I reckon I passed-out some... by
that time Matt must have been pulling you out.... Lyle's wranglers finally
helped when the bull was dead... seems I heard voices. I don't know much
of what happened next. But I did hear Matt later, he was yelling at Jade to
stay away from you. You must have been messed-up pretty bad Jake, to get
all them scars... and... to get your jaw broke-up... and... your mouth
getting ripped-up clear inside... and-." Stoney's heart was wrenched so
greatly as he kept dwelling on it, "-Yeah... you must have been messed-up
pretty bad all over and... *oh God...*" he shook his head. He let his head
hang down in silence as his body slid down the trunk of the tree. A few
seconds later, he stared out into the silence of the woods. A few birds were
singing lightly somewhere off in the trees, seemingly trying to break that
silence with tiny bits of joy. Other than that, there was stillness in the air
around them. Kind of eerie-like, one might say, and easy enough to take
note of—but not for long:

Jake was mad now. The stillness of the woods, and the warm sun on
the small clearing nestled in the trees did not register in the least any more.
He started pacing between the trees and banging his fist on some of them, as
Stoney stood and watched—in shamed silence. Jake knew something

Stoney *didn't know*. That bull, was there *earlier*—a sure *threat* to his horses, critters and family, any day. Lyle was trying to say it was his gift to Jade, it was an early wedding present for the ranch, he had said. Jake had a fit and threatened him with the law, if he didn't get the damn bull off his property. Going a step further—he didn't want to see Lyle anywhere near their land or he'd get him up on trespassing charges and anything else he could throw in. Jake had learned some stuff about Lyle and he was none-to-pleased about it. Jade had been seeing Lyle since the January of 1999 and was engaged during this last Christmas holiday, just before the 2000 New Year, and Jake didn't know how to tell her what he had learned. He had to find some way to tell her—none ever came. Jade had been counting on getting married in April, after the New Year. Jake had to tell her before that, but it kept getting harder-and-harder for him to actually do it.

Jake walked-off his steaming and began to calm down. He remembered the seizures he was told about, but so far nothing had happened other than this headache he was getting. He tried to relax. He pulled out the crushed-up pills from his shirt pocket and leaned against a tree of his own, and wished he had an easier way to get it all down his throat. He was feeling desperate. He was worried he'd spill the powdery stuff because of his one hand being useless, in the cast. After he managed to spread out the tissue, he tried dipping his finger on the powder and jabbing it far back as he could and near gagged a few times—he was sure he got enough on the back of his tongue area, and kept swallowing. He sure needed his throat-spraying water—another hard fact—and it was knocking far too loud. Seemed he had left it in the kitchen. He leaned back against the tree, cradling his head some, and tried to think.

Stoney and Jake were like part of the forest, now—the pine-woods scenery, so still and quiet—but inside, for these two cowboys, there were no rings of aged strength. Inside, there was the weakened-spirits of two previously wounded men, tending to their torn roots.

And—one previously wounded man, had a lot on his mind right about now, *Lyle was trying to ruin Stoney... maybe even kill him, he must have seen how Stoney was so smitten for Jade... Lyle wouldn't have dared to come back here... he knew I'd call the police... but he did, he DID come back. It must have been only an hour later... he must have taken the chance because he knew I was drunk enough to pass-out soon. He just waited 'til he was sure I had enough to drink... enough so I wouldn't be able to function. It ain't Stoney's fault, it's MINE.*

Morally, it's mine. If I had been in my right mind, Lyle would never have been here that second time. I was the one that should have been able to protect my own home. None of this would have happened... if I just hadn't been drinkin'. Legally though, that man was trespassin'. I had the authority to run him off and I did. Trouble is... I have no witness's and he knows it. Legally, he sought to do bodily injury, or even murder to Stoney and me... and the only witnesses are his two wranglers... they'd know if the bull was raging to the tune of drugs, too, so they'd never speak up. Truly, there's nothin' we can do about it. So the bulls, dead, huh? Good. Good riddance! At least some kind of justice has been done... that was one high-priced critter, I'd reckon, and a deep gash in his pocket-book.

Little did Jake know the potential for trouble that the dead bull was still able to cause—as its carcass was still alive-and-kicking, somewhere a far-off, in someone's mind, even now. And:

Stoney was stirring in Jake's mind, as Jake heard a bit of gravel-dust moving, by way of a boot-heeled buddy, stretching out before him—Jake watched solemnly:

"Jake... Can you ever forgive me, can you?" Stoney stood up slowly and walked over to him.

Jake put his arm around Stoney's shoulder and gave him a half-hug, then stood back and shook his head, along with his finger, showing Stoney that Stoney was wrong.

"~Unh-unh~, ~ma~~ ~awl~~", Jake voiced from down deep in his throat, as he stretched his neck out at bit and pointed at himself, *'It's all my fault Stoney and God forgive me... somehow... '* Jake pointed with his finger back-and-forth from Stoney to himself, then he thumbed over toward the direction of the house, down the hill, and voice out, "~~Ehh~ 'oh~." *'Let's go, pal, there's a homecomin' party going-on down there... and it's the BEST way to help you now.*

"You know," Jake, "for a guy that can't talk, you sure talk pretty good," Stoney said sincerely.

"~Huh~?" a weak voiced reply came forth, as Jake set to figure on his buddy.

"You've been talking pretty good, I didn't know a guy in your condition could do that."

'You haven't heard enough of me yet, I sound like a sick donkey braying, I just been tryin' awfully hard to pry this out of you Stoney and I needed every tool available. Looks like I had some I didn't even know about... reckon it was there all the time, too, huh, ' Jake laughed as he gave

Stoney a shove to get him moving. It felt like old times again, somehow, and Jake was very much startled.

As they started down though, Jake wasn't laughing anymore, he was thinking on this:

They had started up on this hill in a hurry, and on the stony side of it. The rocky slip-slides they had traveled had been a bit unsavory, larger rocks all about, without much of a trail. Now, on the way down the hill, this *good* trail, coming out of the woods, was smoother. Lots of small pebbles—but good earth held them down with clumps of well-placed field-grass. When one is on the right trail, things go a lot smoother. When one has a goal and a purpose, one just finds the right clumps to hold-on to. When one's hastily trying to make-do and grabbing at a little-of-this and a little-of-that, one sometimes lets go of the right stuff and grabs onto the wrong stuff, and—it all seems to send one rock-sliding into a mighty hard heap.

You know... he re-routed his thoughts, *I was talkin' up there. I WAS REALLY TALKING. It wasn't real good and it may never be, but some of it can really be understood, if someone knows you well enough. Stoney understood me. I have more than a few 'unh-huhs' at my beck-and-call now. Why, this time, I wasn't mouthin' out my moans and groans that could never be formed into anything. That's how I USED to talk. I can't do that anymore. Every time I try that, in haste, I sound like that awful wailin' wind in some old ghost town. I got to remember to try and talk different... it takes a lot of face muscle, and odd mouthin'. And... seems I got to force it out from my throat somehow... even, my nose, too... yeah...yeah... if I ever get a FOOL-notion to try it again, that is.'*

Jake looked over at Stoney and smiled—he gave Stoney a punch on the shoulder and they both fell over and rolled a bit down the lower half of the hill as they had now just neared the north pasture, behind the backyard.

"Hey, what was that for!" Stoney feigned protest, brushing off the dry grass.

"~I~ ~~whaa~ ~aw'~en!" Jake voiced back, along with some nasal, in flamboyant hand presentation.

"Yeah, right... whatever you said Boss-man... " Stoney just rolled his eyes, as he hadn't a clue, and adjusted his sandy-tan ol' Stetson.

'Well... so much for that one, guess I can't win 'em all.'—Jake shrugged and mugged back.

Stoney jumped up—suddenly the sun sure felt good, "You know... you're getting old Jake, I'm gonna' beat you back to the party, whether my leg gives-out or not!" With that, he took-off half-limping and half-running (to ease any trick that his leg may try to pull on him), with Jake hot on his heels, with an odd limp of his own. Yeah, Jake didn't even know if he could run anymore, but he sure learned fast. He could run all right—just as fast as Stoney. For what it was worth, that's all he needed.

When Jake and Stoney never came back out, Jade knew there could only be one reason—some hard *facts* were going-down, and not the desired guzzled beer. By the time she found Matt, and they both realized what Stoney had been left to face—alone—there was nothing to be done but wait. Then, as these two "horses" came half-hobbling into view, and across the finish line—in a tie—Jade smiled a warm silent victory display at Matt and the rest their gang. A new lap of the race had just been won and this time, there were two winners—and no losers.

200 - By Neebeeshaabookway - JAKE SMITH RANCH SERIES...

CHAPTER FIFTEEN

JADE, GALENA, AND THE THREE BEARS!

BUDDIES are just the best. Jake and buddies—buddies and Jake. No matter how she saw it, Jade never felt out of place or in the way. She did have Galena, just in case some-such girl needs should arrive—sure is always good to have some spare bullets when you're out shooting at the target of life. Galena always added the thoughtful insights and helpful facts that she would always glean from the whole gang. And she was the perfect friend to act as a type of sister because—she was just like Jade—they loved to hang-out with the guys. They had all their gal-stuff to do off-and-on, but there was just nothing like hanging-out with this bunch of mustangs—Ray, Jake, Matt and Stoney. Pretty much in that order—then bringing up the rear was Jade and Galena. Well, good gals just know how to ride herd!

~*~

Although they all were nearly the same age and had all grown-up together since their preteen years (in a type of mixed-age, old-fashioned school-house setting), they seemed to have different places and duties that were apparent in this pecking-order. These had never manifested in their earlier play life, but somehow once adulthood hit, they all gravitated to their niche, and the grout of life continued to set them firmly into place. The pecking-order was not the competitive kind, or the preferred-favorite kind, it was just an off-and-on way of functioning that held them all together. A brilliant work of functional art! They continually varied the roles, as they rolled with the punches, but always, in the end, they fit back into place. Then it all would play a bit *different* next time—when something new came along—except in times of emergencies. In these cases they fell into line and rose to the occasions, as the *ol' professionals* they were.

Ray was a bit of the "older brother type" and kept Jake in check when Jake was worried about serious issues concerning personal problems or his ranching business. Jake had confided in Ray and poured-out his heart about all he had learned about Lyle. Matt was the "equal" brother, in ways, to Jake—they just needed each-other close-by constantly. They, both *naturally*, and with *acute striving*, sought to be in sync—and always checked and made sure that they were. They thought the same, but in a bit different way—Matt was just a little more laid-back and calm. Their hearts felt the same and they knew it, and that was all that mattered. This different way of expressing the same things just blended them into a solid unit—different than the unit of Jake and his twin. Stoney was the newcomer; he did not grow-up with them. He was the baby brother, as he was only thirty! For some odd reason though, as soon as Jake met Stoney and hired him on, they seemed to know each other's thoughts. They just thought the same, right and left, but they were different, Stoney was floating all over like a little puppy and Jake was anchored and strong. The grown show-dog, with the highest awards. True as it was though, Jake was *still* the pup inside, many times—and it could show. Whenever he was with Stoney, it seemed to Jade that some ten-year-olds were on the loose and she didn't know how to stop them. The important thing was—Jake knew how to do the stopping in an anchored and strong way—both for himself and ten-year-old Stoney. To run a ranch, you have to have fixed goals and Jake did. He knew he had to. After all the hard work he had been through with his dad—he learned he had to. Now—he had to.

~*~

"So, Jade," Galena said, "Jake's going to be forty-one in just two days now, right?"

"You're kidding!" Jade stopped drying the dishes and stared at her. "How could I forget my own birthday…? *Our* own birthdays!"

"Well, today *is* the 28th, right?" Galena was now checking herself just to make sure, "Yep, July 28, just two more days and it will be the 30th."

"We nearly were born on the 29th, that was the due date, but when we didn't come after the false labor and all, Ma was SURE we'd be on the 31st… the very last day! We came in-between them both, ha-ha… just like what Pa planned for. He had a 'pot' going for it! It was just *meant* to be."

~*~

It was sure hard to believe that another month had gone by. Since everyone had come back, the place had been keeping a fairly even keel with being normal again. Jake was busy most of the time with the guys and they were learning how to understand him. Jake was already used to Ray, since therapy, so this made a good anchoring for Jake's getting back into sync. Ray, being here every other day or so, forced Jake to toe-the-mark of the harsh reality of it all—just as he had done for Jake during his hospital stay, along with Matt (and, most loyally, again, during the last two weeks of therapy). Jade, had helped him ease back into home life—as to security—

but she could go no further. Jake had then needed the next step—the guys coming home. He had refused, even though Jade tried to harp at him. He just wanted to be alone. He had no hopes for salvaging anything in the way of a future concerning where his life had left off—and—no hopes in how he had expected it to continue-on from this point, in regards to all that he hoped to build with these buddies, his ranch, and his social dealings.

Jade's surprise of bringing them back had done wonders now. The fact that it happened to coincide with Jake's surprise arrests, sure was the icing on the cake though, the attractive layering that made getting back into the swing-of-things look a whole lot better. Better than being alone—or—alone in a sea of people that he may have a run-in with again, someday. People, a sea of them who would never know or understand who he really was—a majority being those who would form wrong opinions and never care.

Matt was the one desperately needed now. Yet—Jake had been stalling and it was because he was fearing something. How could their partnership still be the same now? Matt was so much like Jake. Jake enjoyed this sameness. He wanted to communicate one-on-one with Matt as he always did. He wanted to have their close comradely flow on, and in the ways he *knew*—why, concerning Matt, it was near as-if he was talking to part of *himself*. Now he couldn't, and he was afraid he'd lose the brother that was suited as knit best, to him. He knew they felt the same about life and issues, but he wanted to make sure they kept it that way, even as they always had—through that fine-tuning of earnest fellowship. Through communication.

Stoney, lastly was the most needed of all. For one thing, Jake wasn't sure he even knew who Stoney was anymore and it solved everything when Jake saw him walk into the kitchen that day. For another thing, Jake needed to see, and know first-hand, that this Stoney—the one that he was so desperate to rescue—was still alive. He was so afraid he was dead and feared maybe no one was ever going to tell him that—he needed to *see* him. After all, no one told him that he had no tongue left in his mouth until nearly two weeks after he was first becoming fully aware and conscious. And—it was *nearly* mid-March when they chose to loosen his jaw; they possibly could have done this during the first week of March, as he was capable of following a train of thought then. He didn't know that his family and doctor were worried how he would react, and that they were still dealing with the possibility of any relapses from his recovery of the head injury. He had been having a few bad dreams about Stoney off-and-on since the accident, and would wake up wondering where Stoney was. He couldn't talk—he didn't know what writing was—he couldn't tell Ray or Matt, or even Jade. These people seemed to have all the pieces of his life, why didn't *he* get any pieces? They all seemed to know, for some reason, exactly who this *Stoney* was. They had even reassured him, during the month of February, that Stoney was okay, and one day he was even sure that this Stoney was there talking to him beside his bed. It felt so good that relief moved over his body with waves of emotion. Later, as he became more-and-more aware of his surroundings though, this Stoney was gone. Jake didn't fully understand then. He had no way to ask about it then either. Stoney was just *gone*. Was he dreaming it? Was Stoney still alive? He had to study these unsettling thoughts; *I did save him, didn't I? Or, was I too late?* He had to live with this hidden turmoil all through most of March and April, as he tried to deal with the fact that he had no way to ever talk again. He was having therapy to learn how to eat and was dealing with physical therapy on top of that. The agitation of it all, plus the headaches it caused, had finally forced him to deal with his new awareness of the world, in an emotionally *numbed* state—day after day. He had no way to question Ray or Jade, and they all thought he honestly remembered, and already knew. However, as Matt found out in the pool-table room, Jake did *not* remember Stoney crying on his shoulder, but it was to come back to him now, off and on, during his thoughts at night—in the security of his room. His "same" place. His safe place.

When Jade had questioned her brother, the boss-man, as to these buddies coming back, she never got a definite answer. Jake was then at his first major crossroad—he missed them sorely, but the reminder they gave of his past-self, hurt. The "road closed" sign was up, by his own hand, and this road was not to be passed. That sign had been pushed aside a bit, when he lay in the hospital yet AGAIN, because of the arrest. Seeing Matt and Galena, with Jade again, near his bedside was a real shock. He nearly thought he had never *left* in the first place. Then, lo and behold, they all followed him home! Sign gone, road open. Hmm, and this Stoney was to be expected, as well?

Stoney arrived all right—but "all right" was not up to par. If Jake had not gone into the kitchen to feed himself the day of the homecoming get-together, so the sting of the barbecue-fun wouldn't tear at his hunger pains, he wouldn't have been strategically there to meet Stoney alone in the kitchen. The memories of what he was not to partake of ever again in the way of a meal had been tuned into a precious and most private *meeting* with Stoney, for Stoney's mind to absorb the shock of a new knowledge that was

needed to feed his mind. A meeting—a memory—one to be honored for all
time, between Stoney and Jake.

Stoney needed this private meeting as much as Jake did, not just
because of the miscommunication that failed to inform him of Jake's full
condition, but because Stoney was feeling guilty-as-hell for being the cause
of Jake being critically injured in the first place. Stoney needed to know that
Jake could forgive him, Stoney needed to pledge his deep sorrow, Stoney
needed to get back with the big brother that went through hell for him, as no
other ever had. Stoney needed to be back with Jake. If Jake hadn't been
cautious as to how to reveal the severe damage that had been done to him,
Stoney may not have had the courage to ever face Jake again and Jake *knew*
it.

~*~

Jade finished drying the dishes, as Galena put them away. Jade didn't
take to using the dishwasher much. Jade and Galena went out into the front
yard and sat on the porch. They both spent a lot of free time out there, as it
was the most pleasant place to be any time, day or night. It was pleasant
whether the yard was covered in cows, or covered in horses. It was just as
pleasant if it was covered with chickens or just plain little ol' singing birds.

Jade eyed the sign language book on the table. She was very unsubtle
when it came to keeping to serious duties. She figured this to be her serious
duty, strewing these books all over the house, along with the porch-area
outside, the open shed, and—even the barn. Any place where anyone would
be likely to find one or need one. Jake couldn't read, but his buddies sure
enough *could* and she had made her point very clear: THEY were the ones
to teach him, even though they, for the most part, didn't know a *thing* about
it. She had seen quite a lot of signing from her trips into town when Miss
Kaite came, so Jade told them if they had any problem, 'just come to me and
I'll set it as straight, as I know… and… I *can* and *will* ask Miss Kaite.' And
that, she did! She wasn't about to hear of her brother in some jail again or
who knows *what*—not if she could help it—and that was a Jade-Smith-fact,
now as *spur-gal'ed*, as it could be.

Of course, in the learning process, there was also the deciphering
process. They had to keep figuring-out what Jake was *wanting* first and then
go find a sign to match, and then, make sure that what they *thought* he
wanted, was really *what* he wanted and was *really* what they found. Then
they had to make sure they learned how to sign it the right way. For things
in general, and objects, it became easy after a while. They didn't know how
to make sentences yet, but they only needed to present signs to him for
necessity-use, so if he wanted something, he could ask for it simple and fast.

Building communication would grow, kind of like household framework, they all reckoned—the electric and plumbing would appear, later. *They* were the ones that had to *toe the mark* and learn to understand HIM. Jake threw in Jet's phonetic system to all his ways; so Jade made sure the guys didn't learn ANYTHING ELSE but his way of using the ASL alphabet. They found-out that it was nearly the same (except for vowels), and easily accepted her modifications, and even understood how it helped his mind decipher and retain. Jake was at the point now (since communicating with his buddies) that he could show the words he was thinking of, if he wasn't pressured, or if they were sharing in the quiet of the evenings. He'd sound them out in his head, and form the letters. It made the job of finding signs so much easier than the former "20 questions" game. All in all, Jade was becoming extremely impressed, with not only her twin, but also his best buddies. They truly were—the best.

"Galena... I never knew I could ever feel satisfied again... but I feel so satisfied and content, right about now. We've all been through hell in some kind of a way, but more-so Jet... yet now I can say, I really *do* feel that contentment seeping all through my body. From the top-hat-tip of my head to the soles of my dusty hard-working-boots... and I feel like *to-match*-it-all too. With my *top-half* all fancied-up with the success of thinking it all out, and, my *bottom-half* all dirty from walking it through the plowed-up fields-of-growth." Jade leaned back in the chair and smiled in secret to the good Lord above.

"We're all back where we belong, Jade." Galena said, "you... me... and the three bears!"

Jade sat-up as she heard the three bear's clip-clopping approach, heading their way, by way of horseback.

"Yeah, and one of those three bears is still very much on the *scrawny* side, compared to its brothers." Jade was a bit concerned as she watched them ride past.

The rest of the guys were near the same in height and all were well-built and strong. Men of hard work, that were not near-prone to citified middle-age spread. They were prone to ranch-age spread, instead—the spread of calluses and scars all along their hands. These were men, living life as it was meant to be lived. Stoney was still a bit on the thin side too, but had near-gained all his weight back. He was always on the thin side, anyways, as his gears were shifted just a mite higher.

She watched the three bears, as they were down by the south horse-corral, now hosing their horses off. Jake had—much to his delight—finally been able to ride-off into his favorite hills, now that he had his own "entourage" to pick him up if he fell over. His own personal type of a seizure-patrol, if ever there was one. Maybe with their help now *surfaced*, they could ride shotgun on any headaches that dared to rear-up and hopefully head them off, too.

Although Jake was like a kid stepping into a cowboy book again, he soon found that his love of sitting-a-horse was sorely tested and taught him some new lessons. He first learned that he had to mount from the opposite side, then he learned that he ached to high-heaven from sitting on his horse too long and was constantly readjusting in the saddle. His last lesson he learned, which was the worst of all—was that enduring the ride was actually fun—in comparison to the fact that he could hardly walk once he got off! He took to using Stoney's cane, on these occasions, as Stoney still did just *great* on the horse. Stressing a point, and to tell a tale though, tackling tough-times to take a ride sure t'wasn't to turn to aversion in anyway, for ex-rodeo-cowboy Jake—truth be known—Jake loved it, and Jake was going to do it.

~*~

Jake was five feet and eleven inches and had a very impressive enjoyable-to-look at frame, with well-favored shoulders, arms and hands and a long waist. He was way to thin now. Since the first month with the IV and various supplement tubes and then the feeding tube placed through a hole in his esophagus from February to the second week of March, he sure wasn't dining to his fullest. It didn't get better quickly, either. He was still with a feeding-tube-hole available then, but learning to eat during the second half of March. Then, without the tube's extra aid during April, it was a long serious, and difficult process. Having a strange therapist around to help make sure he was eating correctly had greatly agitated him. He didn't really realize that if it hadn't been for the help of the therapist, introducing earlier therapy during the months of his semi-conscious stages, he wouldn't even be in the cherished position of the freedom to even take care of himself to the extent he was at, now. Yet back then, all he felt was shock and despair. The last two weeks of April, at the hotel, he was finally able to study his new way of eating, in peace, but he still didn't take-to-it well and was discouraged quite often. It seemed like he didn't accomplish getting much down, but he refused to yield to the feeding tube again, so he fought his way to success. He earnestly wanted his mouth to be good for something—not just a sorry empty reminder—that he had no tongue.

~*~

Jade now thought back to the two weeks in the hotel in Kalispell, how she saw him slacking and retreating during mealtime, to an early sleep. Yeah, she was down-right pleased with herself as she had come up with her own special "gift" to use to push him into pursuing his eating—she near laughed thinking about it.

Well, as folks rightly know, *eating* follows a cowboy around wherever he goes, and ol' Jake had always loved to do cookouts with the other bears, and he always loved a good meal. It was so different now, and it was a sad way for a hero to end up. He just wanted to be one of the bears again—just like before—but it was to never be.

"If he ever starts to *hibernate* again, like he did in Kalispell, he won't make it, Galena... he won't," Jade whispered softly, perhaps to be carried on the winds of prayer.

"Hey now, Jade, don't think that way... you know, he's going to be just fine. Remember? That GUT feeling, remember?" Galena gave her a hug, as she dusted the frame of her special friend's stamina with a much-needed reminder. Galena was good at reading animals, and applied this special reading to Jade just now.

"Thanks Galena, and you're right. I had that ol' *gut* feeling after Ray stayed with Jet that *first* time... when I went to the hotel room to pray... when Jet was in intensive care. I just had to go pray. And I DID get that strong anchor that I needed. I was afraid to believe for it, but looking back, it was there... and it came to pass. Well... I got to get his clothes to fit him again... why, look... his pants are *near* ready to slide-off at times, if he didn't a cowboy's best belt! He's got *enough* troubles, without tripping over his pants!"

Jade now sparkled with new rays of hope, yet, the ominous "border" was still too near. Jake's health was no *joke,* once OVER that border—forlornly lost in the dry lands of starvation, perhaps too weak to face such terrain and fight his way back.

"I got me a MAGIC wand, you know, Galena," Jade laughed as she got up, "if he don't get back in shape by fall, why I'll just wave that ol' feeding tube in front of his face, with that nice pretty BOW on it. Ol' Jet, he thinks it's in the garbage, long gone... pretty box and all!" She turned around and smiled at Galena, with a wink of promise, as her many *earring*s sparkled, dangling from her ears, with many *facets* of colors, in the sun. "But I got it... I purely do... just as *surely* as rain-falls-to-the-thirsty-earth-during-a-thunderstorm, do."

CHAPTER SIXTEEN

BIRTHED INTO TOWN

BIRTHDAY-FIXINGS were started and well on the
way. There was some "gnawing" going on around the trees-of-it all though,
there was just too many fixings, all ready to fall over in a heap. Too many
cooks messing with that ol' cooking-kettle out on them-there coals. As this
homecoming year was such a vital marker in their lives, Jade figured there
was plenty of "birthday" days to go around, as Ma was ready for *three*
possible birth dates, during her "fulness"—so why not put these days to full-
use this year? So the very next day, when the 29th of July came, they had the
first of their "birthdays". They all had spent the day riding, and finished the
afternoon off with swimming down by the east river pasture and tubing
along the Fisher River—not fully reasoning in the midst of such joy, that
seizures were still an on-going event, and NOT an odd left-over-drop of past
woes. As night made its rounds, they all spent a quiet thankful night under
the stars, with another family barbecue, Texas style—Jade style. Which
meant some soft country music in the background and a night of sharing a
quiet evening while giving thanks to the good Lord that had made it all
possible—sharing stories about their lives that showed how the *hand of God*
was moving through their midst.

Next, it was the belly-up-to-the-bar Birthday Buddies Beer night, just
the same as Jake and his buddies had always done in years past. Now, Jade
was not about to be left out on her birthday—and Jake would not have it any
other way. But they had their own little ritual to make sport of the situation,
as if Jade really *was* being kept out. So—most naturally, the buddies were
always tailed each year by that little trail-blazer Jade, who would show-up
blazing her own birthday trail as she appeared and joined-in, a few hours
later, with Galena. Then they would all eat together and share kid stories. It
was always a heap of fun and their friends would stop in from all over—as
they were now expecting them yearly, even without the needed *in*vites. This
ritual had gone on many-a-year now and was well-established, yet, Jade
wasn't sure *who* would be stopping by this year, as those that knew of Jake's
accident might think it was too soon to party, since he hadn't been in town

but once. Maybe visitors didn't even plan on *showing* now at all, she just didn't know. The others that *hadn't* heard, would most likely show, she reckoned, so it would prove to be very interesting—especially when explanations of the "new Jake" would be needed.

Trouble had *stewed-over* that original cooking-kettle of the bar night, now, and during the early morning of that traditional eve, when the full savors of tonight's birthday presentation would soon be enjoyed. This steam was *sizzling-up* out of the fire—meaning—Jake wasn't sure he was ready for it *after* all. He certainly couldn't and wouldn't be drinking, as he would most likely end-up being the floor show—unless he found a corner to hide in. But: they were conservative drinkers, having learned the hard way— more or less—in their younger days, so the *main* point was to go to one of their favorite watering-holes and just hang-out and enjoy the sites and sounds with only a few well-placed drinks. So, no way, could he use that, for an excuse—obviously, there was the other aspect of Jake's woe that was bothering him.

"Come on now, Jake... we can *practice* in town first, with some visiting while it's early... you can get used to everyone accepting your new ways, starting with one person at a time." Ray explained to him.

"Yeah, you can have laryngitis again if you want to Jake, it's *your* birthday, you know... you can do whatever you want to!" Stoney threw in.

"Oh, no you don't... it's MY birthday too and I say he's THROUGH with his laryngitis." Jade pushed into the crowd of buddies that were debating in her kitchen. "See here now... do you see what I'm doing here?" She queried them. "I'm putting my foot-stomp on it, see!" She folded her arms and held her head up really proud and stomped her foot down, "There!" She looked around at them all, "WELL NOW... ANYONE GONNA' CHALLENGE ME, HERE, NOW?" Her long dark hair hung down over her shoulders and she looked very dramatically picturesque standing there in the kitchen in the middle of all these tall cowboys—short she was—and stubborn as a mule, with three pairs of long earrings, and one pair of black false-eyelashes. Well, *this* mule wore them, anyways.

Jake made a motion to take the floor, and as he did so, she gave him a little-sister-tug on his shirt and pulled him back. "NO, NOT YOU BUDDY... YOU DON'T GOT NO SAY IN THIS..." She scanned the floor. "ANYONE ELSE...?" Jade stood there tapping her foot, raised her eyebrow at them and smirked, "GOOD!"

"Aw SHUCKS, Jake... she took our fun away," Stoney feigned a sulk.

Stoney motioned for the buddies to go on outside, and they began to filter-out his way:

"OH NO YOU DON'T, I didn't get my present yet!"

Jake turned back from following Stoney and wrinkled-up his brow at his mule-twin and smirked at her, *'well, Jade darlin', it ain't TIME yet... but I do got one for you.'* With that, he signed, *yes-I-have* -and threw his hand up in a gesture, as a wave over his head and behind, *'and you'll NEVERRRRR GUESS what it is,'* he looked at her with a feigned snooty look. He then gave her a fast little foot stomping of his own. "~Hunh~!" he voiced. *'So there!'* he smiled.

"You ain't funny, JAKE SMITH!" She tried not to laugh, during one of the RARE times she'd *dared* to call him such! "YOU... all of you... go on into town and start 'mashing down the long grass' so you can see what kind of scenery we'll be running into tonight. And then according to tradition, me and Galena will be joining you later."

Matt finally ventured his two cents, "Don't you think this is kind of *early*, Jade, what do you expect we'll do all day, until 6:00? We're not shoppers like you all are."

"Well, Matt... " Jade smiled so sweetly, as she gave him a kiss on the cheek. "I expect it will TAKE that long for Jake to *make the rounds* and feel at *ease* with our friends in town that haven't seen him since his *bad laryngitis*. You GOT it now? Now then, are you going to tell me happy birthday? ...this is MY PRESENT from you all, you know."

"Matt, how sweet of you to ride shot-gun for Jake," Galena kissed him, "that's my man."

Jake was ready to protest, as he lifted his hands to try to show Jade in some kind of way, but Ray grabbed him—trapping his *talking*-hands-of-protest, in *mid-voice:*

"That a good idea Jake. After all these years, you don't want a family tradition to go down the drain, just because of some damn old bull, do you? Why heck, what would your pa say? You don't want to be a *quitter,* right, and on your own BIRTHDAY...? What the heck were you birthed for, if it wasn't to be able to conquer any bull, that life has to throw at you? I can just hear ol' Smitty hollering-out loud-and-clear, as to THAT... and I sure don't mean, *Sis Smitty,* here, EITHER."

Ray looked Jake in the eye; "Look how FAR you've come boy," he said sternly. "I know you've been avoiding it... getting into town and facing everyone... and I know why. Yours are hard boots to walk in... but sooner or later, for some reason, you're going to have to go back there, Jake. None of us are going to go into town when supplies are due to be bought next and we all know it, RIGHT STONY?"

"Yeah, if you say so, Ray." Stoney hid his face in his hand. "Sorry Jake," he whispered as he peeked over at him. "I don't know how he knows this stuff."

Jake peeked back with his face bearing the thought, *'don't worry, he knows everything, he hangs around Jade too much, it would appear.'* But he kept solid attention with Ray, and offered every high consideration as to what was being said.

He knew Ray was right, and it all set well with him. Doing it was just another matter; maybe a push out the door might help. But he was sure if they did, he just might end-up as one of those cartoon animals that strategically grab on to all the ends of the door, with all four feet, and refuse to be pushed out—or in—whichever the case may be.

"Jake," Ray continued to explain, "this day is the best way to get it all under your belt and out of your way finally—as conquered ground. Then you can relax and enjoy your birthday tonight as you have always done. You sure don't want forty years, or forty-one years to go down the drain… do you? It's kind of like having to go to the dentist and get rid of a bad tooth, and then you'll be freed-up of a lot of needless pain and grievances."

'Ray, as you know, I don't got much teeth left of recent, as it is… and I didn't lose them from no dentist, but I get your drift.' Jake humbled himself to his older brother—and—to himself. As sincerely as he could, Jake signed, *RIGHT!*

~*~

Signs, a sign of good things to come. Jake—thanks to the camaraderie of his buddies, and the fact that they were running-around showing him all kinds of signs as if it they had discovered gold or something—was finally yielding to using them. He had to admit it sure was much faster and more practical than whatever he had tried to do. He knew they had to strain their minds to understand his severely distorted words— patient and thrilled though they were, to hear him try. Plus, it saved his vocal cords the stress of being overly agitated, by wasting them whenever he *was* brave enough to try his practice-talking. And now—Jake even had PICTURES to use since his victorious paper-breakthrough.

There had been many times when Jake resorted to drawing lengthy pictures of explanation of ideas for his buddies as they worked. Matt, Stoney, and even Ray would all get involved in the process as they all took turns rearranging the pictures into proper order until they all agreed that they all understood what was going on, and THEN—Jake would up-and-change his mind or *forget* what he was doing in the first place. He'd rip the papers up in frustration and throw them up in the air. After each period of snowfall, then they'd have to start all over again. On the rare occasions that this happened once to often, Jake would find these same buddies—his frustrated friends—paper stomping mad. His precious pictures, his FINAL DRAFT, the one that finally explained *exactly* what he was really trying to say-and-do, would then be completely in shreds and stomped on. As—his partners would be claiming that it made NO SENSE WHATSOEVER and that EIGHT papers they had seen the one *truly* worth keeping! After one-such late afternoon incident, Jake was out on the porch, studying the moonlight's effects on the yard. Out of the darkness of the shadows, familiar objects in the yard were being revealed, as the spotlight of the moon, rose upon the yard—out of the shadows of Jake's mind, the facets of his familiar friends and their steadfastness, was being revealed by the light of his admiration towards them through dark situations. Jake had stepped off the porch, as he soaked in his ranch by moonlight, and had become engrossed in these thoughts: *Friends. How wonderful to have them. Friends. How wonderful that they don't up-and-leave you when you decide you need them the most. Friends. How wonderful of them to provide you with more paper... 'specially when you don't know what the HECK you're tryin' to say-or-do in the first place. Friends. How wonderful to have them, even when they TURN on you... tearin' your precious picture-papers to shreds... followed with a display of foot-stomping, and pacing, and hat throwing, and lastly... lingerin' COLD-STARES from their mean-looking, beady ol' dark-brown eyes barreling-in on you... yeah... all three EXASPERATED pairs of them. Friends.*

~*~

"All right then, it's agreed… Boss-man just signed his approval… GOOD for him." Jade plainly stated.

She ran up to Jake and gave him a big hug, which he returned in full.

"This is the best birthday ever!" she happily exclaimed with a sigh.

'This is the worst birthday ever!' he unhappily thought with a sigh.

"Now, shewww!" She kissed him and pushed him on his way.

So off they headed for town in Jake's truck, Ray driving, Jake in front and Matt and Stoney in the back cab-seat. Four cowboy hats and eight black cowboy boots. The "pards" matched-up just as perfect as their boots matched up—they all walked the same trail. Yet, even so—their hats stood for their individuality, as just a *tad* was surely needed—yep, four unique pals, same stewed recipe, but over-lapping spices to be offered from within, to those that knew them.

As they neared town, Ray noticed Jake was awful quiet and rubbing his head, but then, no—he was rubbing his shirt. Just what was he doing? Ray knew he was practicing something. He pulled over just before they hit the older side of town—their side.

"So what's up Jake?" Ray asked

Stoney leaned forward, "Hey, we ain't there yet, you ain't gonna' quit now Jake, right? We're still gonna' go for it, right?"

Matt gave Stoney a nudge to quiet him down, "Yeah, look, Jake's trying to say something to Ray."

~*~

Jake was trying to figure how to use Jade's symbols for use in: "Bakers". He was usually okay at stopping his thoughts at a single *word* that he needed, at this point, in his progression. And—when he looked at something (as an object), it was generally easier to form an ASL alphabet shape for it now, than trying to *pull-apart* a sentence, and do more. If he tried for a whole sentence, he got lost usually, because for-the-most-part only the last word of the sentence would stick in his mind as to hand-shapes matching sounds, and then the first word, as well, would linger. He just seemed to lose the *feel* for the other sounds along the way, and had to backtrack. Trying to use a sign for every sound was like missing a fast train, as his thoughts were long gone. This is where the ASL signs took over; he could sign the ideas instead. Yet, he *could* pick-out one word from all his thoughts and then *zero* in on it, if he sat down and went slowly over his thoughts during conversation-lulls (spelling, is what it was). He desperately wanted to say *specific* things though, and fought to lay-hold of this desire— things that he would have said to a pinpoint, in the past, if—he could talk. He didn't realize it but this determination done in his own time, with his own way of re-channeling his thoughts, was causing him to progress in new ways as he stimulated his brain to work with what resources he had available through other areas of his brain-trails. Yep—some kind of *spelling*, was on the not too distant horizon.

~*~

He was determined to have his say somehow—and now was one of these times:

He wanted to say "Baker" and forming it with Jade's version of the ASL alphabet would have to do.

'The Bakers, Ray, I got to see them first, I got to apologize. It's been eatin' at me, ever since... '

He stopped as he went back to his letter forming.

He formed, **b-**a**-k-ur**   -and signed, **first**   -He had gotten stuck on the "er" sound and until he remembered Jade's "purr of the cat" for that sound—and used the **u** -at his throat. He had some trouble with the noises of the blends of the vowels and consonants, and he had to really think with these, as they blended into so many combinations at times it nearly gave him a headache to form these sounds—eventually he chose his own way, and stuck with it—others would have to learn it. He was getting better all the time, the more he listened to himself think and his confidence was growing. At least this made sense to him, when the reading and writing never *would* again:

~*~

Even though so far, his seizures had stopped and his headaches were not as often and not as severe, he constantly turned his head away from printed material if he dared to try and get involved in it. Occasionally when drawing pictures for Jade or his buddies, a shape similar to an alphabet letter would show up and he'd catch himself staring at it, as if he knew something about the shape that he made. But if he tried specifically to place it, he was met with blank confusion and he turned away or scribbled it out. He'd start over with something else before he couldn't think straight, and was in pain. It was like turning away a fuzzy TV station or a station of complete static. It sure felt good, when it was gone. The only one he never seemed to push aside was the "j". He never knew why, and, it hadn't yet dawned on him that he used that shape almost *constantly* when he formed Jade's name with his finger-shaping alphabet-forms. He would trace it back-and-forth on the paper and felt quite happy with it. Other than that, it made no sense to him what-so-ever since he had first copied this "j" shape from Jade, in the air, and onto his knuckle, by *obedienc*e and never really had *seen* it drawn out. To him it was a sound in his mind that he'd "feel" in the shape: "~~juh~~" and nothing more. It was the "~~juh~~" of his joint, and the "~~juh~~" of his beloved Jade.

~*~

"Bakers it is Jake, it's *your* birthday!" With that said, Ray took-off.

'No it ain't, it's JADE'S birthday... she PULLED it right-out from under me! Mine will hopefully come back tonight... if I ever MAKE-IT through this one, that is... ' he sighed deeply, pout-style. Jake tried to relax—seemed it was the best way to tackle this day, as they continued toward town and the Baker's SADDLE AND SEED.

~*~

Knowing he would have to face Charlie Baker soon, Jake had a lot of things going on in his mind concerning a situation that had followed one of the recent afternoons just after his buddies arrived. It was when the laryngitis episode had come up again in conversation. He had heard Jade and Matt talking about it with Stoney, when they were in another room. Stoney had then shared with them how it came to pass that Jake had showed him the damage done in his mouth, and how he saw the remains of what had been Jake's tongue. The conversation was a good one. Jake had then been relieved to know that he truly *did* handle Stoney's situation the best way possible.

This had even prompted Jade to come in to Jake's room one evening just after that; it was just before he had settled down to sleep. She had come in and revealed to Jake, that even though she had checked-up on his odd town-visit, that she never told anyone that he couldn't talk. She had only assured ol' Bake that her brother was still able to function, except obviously NOT with money! She did say to Mr. Baker, that whatever was wrong, she was sure Jake would be letting him know, when he came *back* into town.

At the time, Jake was wondering what kind of a thing THAT was for her to do to him, but she had softly explained:

'Jake, isn't it better if you come in to town and explain to each person in YOUR own way? In a way that THEY will be able to handle comfortably? They *have* all been so concerned about you, and if *I* tell this to everyone first, not you, then when you *do* come into town, all eyes will be unconsciously watching you and not know what to do next. They will be so afraid to see you hurt anymore in any way, that they will be afraid how to treat you... or how to approach you... or maybe even afraid to talk to you, in the first place! Only YOU can make them comfortable. And the only way YOU will ever be comfortable with how you *think* they feel about you, is for you to present this in a way that *you* know they will channel-back out to you, as free flowing, un-intimidated reactions... as to someone on the same wave-length. Each person MAY react different, but at least you will all know WHERE you're coming from and WHY, as to your pitching-it-out. Take for example, *Stoney*. You *knew* just how to handle that Jet. You're the one that can't talk, this is *your* play. It may be my play, in some ways at times, and I know that too, but on a more personal level, it is YOUR play, Jet. Everyone gets laryngitis at one time or another, Jet... you were allowed your one time... now the rest is up to you.' She had given him a kiss on his forehead as she had brushed his hair back, as if comforting a young child, and let her words soak in while they sat in a thought-provoking silence.

As she had turned to leave that night, she finished with, 'I really do believe that God in his goodness, kept me and Matt from telling Stoney, Jet. God has the right tool for the right job, so as not to ruin the end result. If *we* had told him, I honestly don't think he ever would have come back here. Oh, he's such a doll, he would have sent a letter or something, Jet... but that's the LAST we would have seen of him.'

Within seconds after she left the room, Jake had cried with silent tears that night—and—for quite a drawn-out spell.

~*~

As Jake prepared to enter the SADDLE AND SEED, he hoped to God that he wouldn't cry now. The Bakers knew him and Jade since they were kids and this was his birthday and all. Emotionally, he wasn't sure just what he would be walking into, and he still was touched by that wooden horse they had given him—that wonderful gift of love. It now graced his bedroom on the shelf where he kept the leather and its wonderful, rich smell. He was mighty glad that he remembered these special people that cared enough to give him their best treasure. The last time he was in here, he now knew for a fact, he had been behaving mighty odd. Mighty odd in *deed*. Now *indeed*, it was time to fix that.

His buddies followed him in. They were there through the thick-and-thin of it and they'd be there—or leave there—depending on whatever Jake chose them to do. Whatever it was that they discerned Jake needed, they'd see it through.

Mr. Baker spotted Jake first. He slyly motioned Ma Baker to go to the back, so Jake wouldn't see her.

"Say, where's Jade?" Charlie said, as he welcomed the birthday boy into his store. "I know you got your traditional t'do's with the men-folk-first, and all, but you *both* always come by here the day before... and since we didn't see you yesterday, we kind of expected you and all."

Jake signed, *home* -and then just as quickly swatted his hand down as if he was swatting a fly. *What the heck am I doing?* He thought. He knew Mr. Baker wouldn't have a clue he was doing, so Jake just as quickly used that gesture to pretend he was thinking a bit, as he settled his hand near his chin.

Mr. Baker waved Ma Baker back in.

"Oh, no matter, Jake, don't worry about filling us in on Jade," Charlie stopped him, "if you're not sure... well, she'll show up... she'll be here later. Maybe she's getting herself a present or something."

'No, she's GOT one now... you're LOOKIN' at it... here goes,' Jake thought weakly.

Just then Ma Baker came out from the back with a lit cake and some balloons and cards.

Charlie, spoke up first, "We'll bring your gifts on over to the SLIPPING SADDLE SALOON when Jade shows-up later, sure don't want to leave her out you know. Call your buddies over here, Jake, seems they're more interested in that bag of horse feed than your birthday!"

Jake saw the candles were burning down and the cake was beautiful, and so were the Bakers—and of course, even his buddies, but only to a certain extent. He snapped his fingers loudly a few times and the whole herd of them showed at once. Ray, the appaloosa, with his gray Stetson, Matt, the chestnut quarter-horse with his old brown Stetson, and Stoney, the palomino with his flashy banded, off-white, sandy-tan Stetson.

Jake pointed to the cake. They all admired it quickly and then Jake was urged to blow out the candles. Which he did, to all the hooting-and-hollering of his buddies. He held his head back as he felt the water welling-up in his eyes, *'Dear Lord, I was supposed to be dead now... and here I am standing here blowin' out a cake full of candles... my own birthday cake... yeah... yeah... oh, dear God, help me, please.'*

Matt noticed Jake's eyes first, as the Bakers were too busy cutting the cake and dishing it up. Delia Baker had just as quickly presented a pitcher of refreshing ice water and a pitcher hot of coffee—for to each, their own. Along with glasses, cups, plates, forks and napkins, and—cream and sugar, as usual, were always on the counter.

"Are you okay, Jake?" Matt asked him, with a firm hand on Jake's shoulder. "We'll step aside, okay, pal... you want to take it from here? Am I doing right, by you?" Matt was getting near as choked-up as Jake was. Jake shook his head yes and they all moved back to study the horse feed—along with a pretty gal that just walked past the window, much to their delight. Much too perfect timing as well, as Delia saw this and made a cute comment about it and Jake was free to be alone with the Bakers. He didn't think they'd expect the guys to be hanging-out with horse-feed-bags for too long.

Jake sat down at the counter, where Delia had just pulled up a fancy stool for him.

"Charlie, poke that spoon into the sugar over there, so Jake can start fixing up his coffee. Here you go Jake, and we got you a new mug, here... you always did prefer that to coffee cups!" Delia looked so neat, comfortable, and casual, compared to the elaborate birthday cake on the counter, but her love over-shadowed the cake by much more than any country mile.

Jake looked at them as they started to eat cake and waited for him to join in. His new coffee mug sat in front of him as its wisp of steam invited him to warm his hands and mouth with it.

Jake put his head down and rubbed his forehead for a few minutes in thought, then, he decided to take a tiny piece of the cake—it was his birthday, right? He rinsed his fingers off with some water from the pitcher first, while using one of the napkins. He pulled off a tiny piece of cake and used his finger to smash it and to set it way into the left side of the back of his mouth. He set it up and made ready to swallow it, and went through his head-twisting motions. After the time required for this process, he relaxed as much as he could, knowing he was being studied just a bit by some concerned faces.

He really hadn't had cake yet and it was a surprise to him how easily he took to swallowing it—course, 'til *some* of it stuck on the back-roof of his mouth like all *get-out*, that just *wouldn't* "get out". Yet, it didn't choke him, and was nothing that a hard drawn-out rinse-out, wouldn't fix. Sooner—or most likely—a mite later. And thus, he had-at-it. After his drinking-process and all the trouble it took, he took another mashed piece of cake and he pushed it back, and a tad better this time, and did the process all over again. Sure enough, he was getting the hang of it. Turning his head through his different motions, he finally swallowed this one too, as his buddies all came to attention, adjusted their hats—each in their own way—and watched quietly from the front corner of the store, near the window. The Bakers were concerned all right, he could tell, but they were old-fashioned country folk, and a high class, grade "A" quality, raised with old-fashioned manners—they watched politely. They kept eating with him, but slowed down considerable, so as to stay in sync with him and enjoy his company. Delia talked about how she knew Jade would want the recipe, once she got a taste of it and Charlie made friendly story-time with Jake. Charlie was full of stories and they were the hit of the town.

Mr. Baker did stop once and asked Jake if he needed anything else, and Jake showed him the common gesture of "wait just a sec" as he took another piece of cake. When he stopped, Ma Baker handed him a napkin and Jake smiled with a nice grin at her. She felt a lot more at ease. *Thank God, then, he's not in pain,* she thought, although she couldn't imagine what was wrong. She figured it was bad teeth or something, surely from his accident, as he never had that problem before.

They had noticed he was awful quiet and a few times Mr. Baker was ready to invite Jake to relax and be himself, since he could tell Jake was definitely *not* himself. Granted, he was not in the least bit confused as he had been the *last* time they saw him, so Charlie Baker was so very glad for that! Thus—he let it ride.

He tried this instead, his old "storekeeper" charm, saying, "So what'd you get for your birthday, Jake?" Mr. Baker gave him a friendly nudge as he laughed, hoping for the fun expectation of a Jake-dissertation in regards to anything, or everything, he may have received. And ordinarily, ol' Jake would have discussed a dandy dissertating-dialog, directed right back, and diligently so—with more than a dab of delight!

Jake looked at him, and then at Ma Baker. He shook his head to the side, as if shaking a slight negative.

"Nothing?" Charlie Baker wondered, in reply.

'*No... that ain't it, Charlie... I can't talk... see... I'll try to explain.*' Then, with a deep breath, Jake signed:

Talk -as he showed them that he couldn't, by the shake of the head, for '*no*'.

"Not the laryngitis STILL, is your throat hurting," Ma Baker asked, "I thought maybe your teeth were hurting… I know mine *have* in the past, and they *have* been breaking." She was now worried, she knew that to be sick this long was a bad sign, and so were infections from broken teeth.

Jake quickly showed her, '*no*', with a wave of his index finger, as to the easiest negative. Then—this was the best way he could think of, to show the Bakers:

He stood up, as his buddies eyed the situation in silence, taking care to stay out of Jake's sight now. Jake first signed, *bull* -then showed the formed ASL hand for the horns, out in front of him, as a tool. He carefully showed the horns hitting his body in his chest, throwing him into the dirt, and how he was hit in the thigh, and how he tried to crawl away, but failed. He showed them how the bull came back and how its horn knocked him out and again how he was stomped-on and kicked over his body again. (Of course he knew this full history only from what he was told, but couldn't explain that to them.) Then, he showed them how this happened, more clearly. He signed, *bull* … *hoof* -and showed how the bull stomped and kicked on his thigh, hip, leg, and on his chest, shoulder, arm, and on-up around the now fainter scars on his face, neck, and, in particular up-and-under his jaw. He then signed, *ruined* -which was a fairly universal action, and pointed into where his tongue would have been, and showed and signed, *ripped* -He could clearly understand that they understood now, maybe not in exactly the same words he would have liked, but it was clear enough to know, that Jake was not the same anymore. He would not be talking—ever again.

Ma Baker came up and held him close and said, "One truth takes over though, Jake… thank God you're still able to live and breath… and you're here to share your life with us… and more important, that you're still here joined with Jade. And we're always happy to see you here with us Jake, if you need anything we're always here, just as before." She shyly excused herself, still in shock, and grabbed up some cake and took it to his friends, so her husband could be with Jake.

"Jake, we knew how bad it was, but we never knew there was any permanent damage… please, about the cake and all, we just didn't know." Charlie hung his head shyly.

Jake smiled strong at him, and signed, *I-know-I-understand*   -and voiced, "~I ~~oh~". Jake and Charlie both listened solemnly, to Jake's "new way".

He had introduced his voiced-sound, as he knew Charlie could accept this more than Delia could. She was trying to except all this as a mama-hen would, and later would probably cry. But for *now*, they were having a party and his buddies came back over and had coffee, as Jake set to open his birthday cards. He already knew the Bakers had experienced his note-reading skills. It had given them a huge clue that he had a serious problem—which meant reading in particular—so he gave the cards to his buddies to read. He opened each one and enjoyed the pictures as he passed them on. He figured it'd make for a happier occasion if he explained at a future date to the Bakers, how there was still just a little bit more of Jake Smith missing, than his tongue. Truthfully, he'd rather have his tongue missing, than the past 41 years of brain-learning. And as much as he hated being helpless in this way—fully *dwelt-on* when he lay down at night and when he awoke in the morning—he was very grateful his head injury had not led him to lose those 41 years.

Jake was just about ready to get up and leave, when Charlie stopped him.

"~Huh~?" Jake wondered what was up. Charlie was full of stories and Jake had only heard two. It was during the cake-eating part of his party, and it was more to cover the awkwardness, so the usual gusto was lacking. Maybe now, Jake would get a *good* story. It sure would help make up for the loss of he-himself not having his own usual stories to share in return, with Charlie.

"You're on the HOT-SEAT Jake!" he winked. "Don't you know what you're sitting on? It's not just any old stool, you see, it was made by my pa... he was a *cooper*. He made that stool from one of the barrels he used to make. It's a keg of *cider*. See, stand up and look under the fancy seat-cover... see!"

"Tell him the rest, Charlie!" Delia was almost having more fun at this than her husband was, and by now, the guys suddenly all heard Charlie start-up and were now leaning over Jake, as he sat back down.

'Maybe I shouldn't be sittin' back down now, should I? I just know this is leading-up to something... must be a birthday-boy set-up, I reckon...' Jake's curiosity was now peaked, *'aw... what harm can befall me if I'm sittin' on a cider-keg-barrel... not much worse can happen to me now!'* Jake laughed to himself, as he watched and waited for good ol' Charlie to tell him a birthday story!

"Well... cooper's myth says:
If you're sittin' on cider that's kegged...
Some sparklin' lassie's got you pegged...
Across your path, you'll soon see her tread...
And down the aisle, you'll surely, be led...
Mark my words, 'tis true, thus I've said...

Jake sat there and didn't know what to do. He was a bit taken back. *'Are you trying to get me to marry-up, Charlie...? ...and on my birthday of all things!'* Jake started laughing.

Charlie threw in, "You let us know when she crosses your path Jake, and we'll get out the wedding bells! Copper's myth, you know! My daddy's cider is powerful stuff *too*. In the keg or out of the keg... you'll see! I inherited the recipe! We'll save that stool you're sitting on for your wedding day, then we'll bust it open and celebrate."

Charlie laughed with Jake and gave him a slap on the back, as his buddies threw in more hoots-and-hollering and they all cheered, "Happy birthday Jake! What a fate!" They all left on that cheered note, though Jake had a sorrowful-pain sting his heart all too quick, and he took to scratch a deep added-memo upon the lingering fun of it all—it was *completely* impossible. Powerful cider or not, as, his gal-wooing days were silently done-gone. Buried behind the gravestone of what teeth he had left. So he thought.

They left the birthday-fixings at the Baker's to be picked up later in the evening; the next stop was to see Lolly. She'd be working at the drug store everyday, so they were sure to see her. Then too, there were quite a

few others that Jake *didn't* see on his first trip, but he figured by the time he
ran in to them all, he'd be getting ready to let his buddies speak for him.
This was going to be one long day—one long confession—and one mighty
long, odd, birthday. Now that he made the first step with the Bakers,
seemed his friends could lend a helping hand with such a tall order, and he'd
be sure to press for it. They'd sort it out, as to the who's, how's and why's
of it all, depending on who they'd run into during the course of the day.
Jake was soon to find it easier and easier, though. That is—except for one
case in particular—the case of sour apples. But THAT, was due to bust-out
later.

    Lolly was outside in front, on her break time. She was sitting on top
of a wooden picnic table with benches, near some small tables and chairs, in
the middle of a small patio surrounded by trees. Little birds kept hopping
and jumping in-and-out of the legs of the benches as they found little tid-bits
that fulfilled their search-mission. The table had been provided for the
customers that purchased some small food items from a mini deli-section, at
the back of the drug store. Something else was kind of hopping into their
cowboy view as they drew closer. The nice looking gal that Jake's buddies
had spied earlier, was now plainly before them—a well-placed tid-bit, if ever
they saw one. She had just finished her talk with Lolly and was leaving—
yet, in doing so, she crossed Jake's path, and moved on. She turned abruptly
though and waved back at Jake, offering soft dark eyes and a happy smile—
all of which were warm, sincere, and lingering. He promptly waved back,
and with a mighty happy good-morning grin. It was Sofia.

    'Like I said before... I ain't rude!' Jake congratulated himself and his
good manners, in remembrance of that day at Lenny's door.

    "Say, how do you get-off having *her* wave at you and *not* us... just
what-all have you been up to last time you were here in town, Boss-man?
Did she doctor-you-up with some ol' cold medicine or somethin'? Or is this
a first-time attraction that just hit her from the blue?" Matt worked a good
tease as he started in on Jake, offering medicine for the wounds he knew
were there, as he came over and prodded Jake for answers, with Stoney now
joining in.

    Jake signed, *I'm-special* -twice, and then voiced, "~hey~," in
agreement to himself, as they neared Lolly.

    Lolly had called-out in reply, but no one had heard her, and the gang
of busy cowboys teased on:

    "Oh, no you ain't special, Jake... it's that cider that's so dang special.
Remember? Ol' Bake said it was mighty *powerful* stuff, in the keg or out...

looks like that lassie's got you pegged!" Stoney hooted with delight, as he spun in a circle rubbing his hands in expectation.

Yep, ol' Jake hadn't been paying attention to anything else but Matt, when he signed the answer to him, and then Stoney had jumped in so fast because of Sofia, that Jake never even heard Lolly—but she was determined with joy and responded again:

"*Hey*, what? Didn't you hear me? Are your ears plugged up? You still got some of that nasty cold hanging on, Jake Smith... you sound a bit horse?"

She walked up to him from the table. "Happy birthday Jake!" She gave him a hug and kiss on the cheek. "Did you have fun with your wrecking-crew, at the Bakers'?"

"Say, we haven't wrecked anything lately... what do you got in mind, I'd wreck a good steak, in 8 seconds flat, if you cook it." Stoney came up and leaned on her shoulder.

"Stoney, I'm so glad that you're still walking around after your *last* 8 seconds, that I'd cook you a steak everyday of your life if I could, but I know your heart belongs to another," she smiled, and gave him a shove. "You ol' teaser you!"

Lolly had all kinds of boy friends and liked it that way and Stoney knew it. She was more like a sis to him, and vice-versa. Same as to her and Jake:

"Well Jake," she looked over at him, "since your laryngitis, looks like you finally learned to shut up. Now, if you don't talk within *your* next 8 seconds I'm going think something's wrong with you... and you got three seconds to go."

'Now, I couldn't have walked into any better open doors than this kind of a set-up, and that's for sure-as-shooting-at-unseen-targets and winning... it must be gettin' near MY birthday, now.'

Jake casually gestured to Ray. He was the strongest of his buddies at the moment. Jake wasn't about to dare to put Stoney on the spot, and Matt seen too much hurt already, but Jake needed help now. Jake was too close to Lolly in understanding how Lolly felt when someone was hurt. Jake was going to place these next runs off Ray's pitching, this time, and hope for a successful homer, as Ray guided them all through Jake's mute episode, unfolding before her.

"Actually, Lolly, there is something wrong... that's why we're here, so Jake can fill you in." Ray said calmly, and sat down on the bench that had been previously occupied by her. He adjusted his dark gray Stetson, and avoiding her gaze, reached down and dusted off his boots. He then looked up at her, while he sought approval from Jake. "Right, Jake?"

Jake had walked up to a nearby tree and leaned on it. He seemed to feel at ease around the trees and there was plenty in this area of town. Lolly followed him over and sat on the other bench opposite Ray, as they both waited for an answer.

Ray's words floated around, waiting, as Jake was momentarily distracted when Stoney went into the drug store and Matt followed. They were starting-up a talk with the owner, which led to them to sharing about Jake's problem. The owner was another friend and part of the local Old-Town storytellers, same as Charlie Baker. They'd compete on many a summer night, meeting-up at some of the campfires following the trail-rides. Stoney was quite content there, he didn't want to hear Jake have to do this again, somehow he just didn't think this Lolly-stuff was something he should hear. It wasn't because it was all adding-up to "heavy" in his mind, as he was getting adjusted to it slowly—Jake was alive and by his side—that was the most important thing now. The terrible hospital days and nights were over, too, and that was great plus. Stoney was just making sure the dang *adjusting* didn't slip its gears, so here, he stayed.

Jake, content that Stoney was okay, in agreement to Ray, finally signed, *right* -and waited for Ray to continue, as he trusted in solid rest, that Stoney had plenty to keep his mind busy, with Matt and the storytellers.

Lolly noticed Jake's odd behavior—answering in signs, of all things—but humbly waited. She thought maybe Jake was just being cute and play-acting a bit with his buddy, as they had been known to do so many times, yet in other ways.

Ray began the unfolding, "For the most part, I know everyone in town knows the extent of the injuries Jake went through. For the most part, he's healed-up in one piece... for the most part," Ray said (being slightly evasive as to his main goal) as he tested the waters of her soul.

"Well Ray, go on... go on... as for the most part you've been emphasizing '*for the MOST part*', and you better start getting to the point, please." She drew her breath in and strengthened herself. She had learned a lot about her brother's condition in many ways, and this so-called: "for the most part", had been one of those ways.

"Well, I know you can still make out the scars on Jake's face, right Lolly? I mean, obviously there must have been some kind of damage done there that would be hard to fix and all. There are some important areas around the face and neck, you now. The airway, your throat and... your *mouth*. Things like that. Jake's mouth didn't heal-up right, Lolly. There were some damaged parts that were ripped-up and torn loose, and sadly with not enough left to fix... " Ray looked at Jake to see if this was setting-right so far, or not. One part in particular—the MOST part.

Jake eyed him with a *'go ahead'* type of a look, *'you're doing just fine Ray... I'll be watchin' for her.'*

"Go on now, Ray, such as?" Lolly started watching Jake seriously now, as she saw them eyeing each other.

"Well, you might now be thinking that Jake lost some teeth or something. Jake did lose a few teeth, but there was some worse damage done and along with that damage... and, well... Jake can't talk anymore, Lolly."

Lolly looked at Ray, then at Jake, and waited to see what kind of a joke they were pulling. Ray never messed with a person's feelings though, that was true, and no one started-up laughing, either. Then Lolly, with a slight shake in her voice said, "All right now... this is for real, right? You're telling me Jake can't talk... why would that be... are you trying to say that maybe he can't *remember* how to talk?"

She thought back to the odd situation of Jake laying down all that money on the store counter, but she had seen odder things than that when it came to people trying to deal with money, many times—so, perhaps it was a brain issue.

"Now listen, and think on what I said, Lolly... his mouth was ripped-up inside. That's why he can't talk. But he's learning how to communicate in other ways, it's just taking a bit of time, that's why he hasn't been in town since. He had that laryngitis-thing last time. There was no need to tell anyone yet... so we've been waiting until he came in again, is all." Ray felt better now that it was all out, and he smiled over at Jake.

'You did perfect, Ray... thanks pard.' Jake answered him with an all-knowing look, as he slipped his hands into his pockets, thumbs out, bearing his weight, this time with no cast in the way to stop him, as he hoped to finally relax. But there was still more to come, in dealing with Lolly.

"You're telling me, that Jake can't talk and you're *smiling?* But you're *serious* aren't you?" She looked up at Jake, "Well, hasn't anyone been able to help you try get your mouth to work again? Can you eat, at least?"

She walked over to him, as she still was not really thinking this was something permanent. "My uncle had a stroke and after eight months and lots of hard work, well he's talking just fine now, and just maybe your brain needs a new path an-... "

Jake took her hand gently and shook his head *'no'*. Lolly saw a sad far-away look in his eyes.

"Oh? Oh."

"Lolly, his tongue was ripped up, there's nothing left to use to talk... there was no hope of an artifical one, in his case, for various reasons. What slight bit was left, back near the base is anchored down into the left side of his jaw area, back where he swallows... it helps him *best* that way. There was too much nerve damage to it... it was useless for anything else but that, he's lucky he can even swallow... otherwise... "

Jake quickly tried to catch Ray, on this part, as he voiced out, "~Unh-unh~", suddenly, and shushed him with hand gestures while shaking his head, as to a firm negative. Jake knew Ray was leading to the fact that otherwise he wouldn't be able to eat. This would cause Lolly to picture Jake being fed by a tube, as her brother was—just before he died. He was afraid Lolly would crack under the strain—and even now, she was close.

Lolly answered, "They kept that bit in place to help his swallow? Otherwise he wou-"

Jake reached-out for her and gave her a hug and she leaned on his shoulder and sighed in pain, and then weakly pulled away. She recognized the noise from Jake's voice, as it was similar to her brother's *weaker* noises when he was unable to talk to her, but had exerted himself and tried. This was getting too *real* for her now and far too close to home-feelings. She backed-off from Jake just a bit and wavered like a crushed stem of a bruised flower that still tried to stand with grace:

"I'm so *glad* I got to see you for your birthday, Jake... oh, I so much, am. And I *bet* you'll be getting on fine someday, you'll see... don't worry, somehow it will all work out... you'll see... you'll see. Yes, you will, I know that. Why, just *look* at you now, you're here! You're alive!" She walked around the table once now, and nearly twice, and then put her hand on Ray's shoulder and gave him a pat. "Just look at all these good friends, and the buddies you got, Jake. Why, those fellows in there are right-fine men," she pointed to the store window, watching Matt and Stoney, but hesitated and abruptly said, "well, I got to be going... but do me a favor, will you?"

She walked up fast to Jake, taking his hand and smiled with a hard try, as he kissed her hand real gentle-like and watched her face. "Please... will you?" she finished-up her request, "you guys tell Stoney, I'm so happy he's back too, okay... and then just tell my boss, I had to go. Tell him something... well... just tell him something happened. I need to go now, sure hope to see you both real soon… maybe at the party tonight… maybe… maybe, but I *just* don't know."

Lolly took-off back behind the trees and back on around the drug store, and then crossed over, heading back up towards the Baker's store (yep, over to where the gang had just come from). Their place was just a short bit back up this main road, across the street, and still in view—and— Old-Town's two small hotels (one being on each side) were further down past the drug store (thus ending, the town, except for a used car lot, and various rural lots with scrap iron, old furniture, or what-not for sale—and ranches).

Jake knew Ma would take her home and an odd peace overwhelmed him. Jake took-off walking up town, just to be alone. Yep, he was heading towards the area that led, in the long extra-long-run-of-things, to the newer area of town, but *first*, there'd be by-passing a few small tiny tool stores and such, and the Bakers' SADDLE AND SEED, along with CORNER&COFFEE café (on the drug store side). The rest of the town led to the Sheriff's Office and the SLIPPING SADDLE SALOON (where small tiny gift and flower shops, were nestled in between, off and on). And—farther along the way mainly on the café side of the street, were a few small local clothes shops and more gift stores, and candy stores, and near-lastly a general small-goods shop (back on the Sheriff's and saloon side), both for folks and critters. Then last, came the GENERAL GROCERY strip mall (on the sheriff's and saloon side too)—it being the border into New-Town, and all its modern offices, gas stations, modern convenience stores, and fancy clothes and book stores, and such.

Ray and the gang showed-up a few minutes later with the truck, and they went to sit in the outside-section of the CORNER&COFFEE café, out in the sun—finding Jake, at his favorite table.

After they all took a break, the guys ate. Jake tried some milk with Jade's soy powder that he had brought along. They had the area all to themselves, under more trees and a slight breeze. The lunch crowd would be showing in the next half-hour, so taking advantage of "safe" time, Jake kicked-back with his thoughts and his noon meal, as his buddies took to enjoying a variety of sandwiches. Some were toasted, some were piled high with lettuce and tomatoes, others had cheese, and one was piled high on real homemade French bread, but the one thing these three sandwiches had in common was—they all sure looked good.

The pre-party at the Bakers' had set their time-frame back a bit, but nothing bad. They were getting Jake's message out to his friends, one way or another now. The Bakers would tell their workers. Ray told Jed, the owner of the café, all about Jake—details in full. Matt was explaining Jake's injury to Henry, the café's manager. He was another close-knit friend, along with his wife, Be^. This was another favorite hangout, one of those any-time-of-day type places. Jake had wanted to tell them all personally, but after Lolly, he just wanted to sit and think. Matt, being so much like Jake, tried his hand at telling people just the way that Jake would have done it, seeking to *tailor* the situation to the individual.

They took-off once again (as ever a taking-off gang of cowboys, could) and roamed a bit more and—did a bit more sharing. They ended-up at gift shop and store, owned by long time buddies from the rodeo circuit, the O'Rourkes. This was their gift shop and small-goods store: R's FOR U BRAND.

Their pa had one of the most rip-roaring ranches in Montana, back when he knew Jake's pa. It was Rainy's RIP-ROARING-RESPECTABLE-RANCH, *RR*/RR. Its brand was two tilted R's on top of two firmly founded R's. Their pa only let the rip-roaring go so far—it was good clean respectable fun with lots of country and city folks, continually around. Rainy never traveled the rodeo circuit but he raised the bulls and horses, for many a working, riding, or rodeo cowboy. His two sons used to ride broncs back when Jake was riding broncs, and even though Jake met them *after* high school, their friendship was sealed with long time respect. After Jake's accident, they had *also* come to see Jake once in February, but couldn't see him regularly because of their shop, property and restaurant demands. One of the brothers, Vin, had his leg badly crushed during his rodeo days; he couldn't even walk on it anymore. With bronc riding over for him, he and his brother Carl opened this gift shop and store and took to raising the bulls on the ranch that they had inherited, along with opening a newer and larger restaurant on the said-same grounds, as well—all in honor of their pa. Carl quit the rodeo circuit permanently to help his brother—as his personality was a bit stronger, he held up the business-end right well, but he'd still always give special deals for a friend. Jake knew this was the perfect place to buy his gift for Jade, something special that he had in mind, and Vin's skilled hands could do the job. They would get to meet the new Jake and he would get to enjoy "them ol' boys". Jake sure knew about crushed or shattered legs, even though his old riding buddies didn't know a thing about having no tongue, but Jake knew he'd be just the one to teach them. He sure wished he had something *better* to teach them though, as they had taught him the best of professional bronc riding (both bareback and saddle), aside from Jake's pa, of course.

Jake had a picture of something that he wanted carved and was paying for it in his "drop the money down" and "hope for the best" way. He would be back for it near supper, or would send one of the guys for it. Hardly concerned, though, he was—as his dear buddies would be at the party. Trust was of high honor, here in Old-Town, forever said—somehow it would get there—somehow these cowboys all knew!

Now, they didn't need to go share Jake's news into the modern side of town (New-Town), since they didn't know that many people there. There may have been some acquaintances, plus some nice folk that they knew since school (but never kept in touch with), things like that, but nothing that was a priority. Lenny could always pass-out any news there, if the time ever came. The oddly blended town still didn't make for a big spot on the map, but it was nice-sized, together, and the bit of quaintness against the modern, made it highly unique—two in one, it dearly was. So thus there was New-Town and Old-Town. The tourist, when they *did* come, seemed to prefer both sides of town-phenomenon, and for different reasons. They could find their familiar modern stores and conveniences on one side and much more groceries and finer hotels—but—peace and quiet, and horses and cowboys, on the other.

Course, the quaint side obviously had more crafts for sale, things to do lists, and a home-style restaurant, being Henry's marvelous café. Yep, and the CORNER&COFFFEE also had a large tourist area that could be opened, depending on the time of the year. Then there was the SLIPPING SADDLE SALOON #1, to grace it all, with homemade food just as tempting. Sure, the SLIPPING SADDLE SALOON #2, was in New-Town (and was permitted to pay rent for use of the similar name, if a western theme was kept), and—depending on who the tourist were, both saloons (half restaurant and half bar) were preferred. This held true even for the locals, in some cases, but the #1 was always referred to with the highest regards over the other—and in many ways: the SLIPPING SADDLE SALOON #1, the SLIPPING SADDLE, or even at times, the TRIPLE "S" on rare occasions. For the most part, "#1", would do in a pinch, when folks called-out, on the run—as—it *was* just the best!

The SLIPPING SADDLE SALOON #2, though, was always just that, no matter what: the "#2" saloon—an after thought to locals.

As the day finished up, it would soon be time to get back over to that ol' #1, and anticipations were starting to run high. They took the truck on up to the Mid-Town-Line, a division between sectors. This was where the only small strip mall in town was located—here, where New-Town started. At

the MID-TOWN GAS STATION (opposite that strip mall), they all got out.
Jake filled-up the truck, while Ray sat inside it and coached him. Stoney
and Matt went into the gas station. Just as Jake finished pumping the gas, he
heard some commotion and looked up. Someone from one of the cars that
drove by, was yelling that there was a dog in the street that had nearly got hit
by his car. Jake looked around now and saw it. It was a beautiful purebred
Irish setter and another car had just missed it. Jake ran out after it, he had
taken his shirt off in the process and was flagging cars. The light at this
intersection was nearly as busy as in New-Town itself, so this was a bad
intersection for lost dogs, especially near afternoon's "so-called" rush.

Jake succeeded in stopping some cars and got the dog to come to him,
by clapping, snapping his fingers, and by tapping on his leg to call a dog to
his side. The dog happily came to him—it even jumped up to lick his face.

Cars were honking again now, and one man reasoned Jake didn't have
a lick of sense—despite the warm dog-reward Jake had just received—and
yelled out, "Hey, mister, get your stupid DOG out of here! People like YOU
should get tickets for letting your dogs run loose... you want to cause an
accident or something? You stupid COWBOY!"

Jake, so intent on the dog, just smiled and waved at him to pacify him,
as he dragged the dog back to the gas station.

Jake was really happy and so very pleased that he had been able to
save this lovely dog, he had been in the right place at the right time to do so,
and he sure knew it, *'birthdays have way of birthin' special things... never
knew I'd get to save a dog on my birthday! Looks like Jade knew I needed
my birthday to birth me into town today, and birth me into feeling a bit like
my old self again,'* he thought. He smiled like a happy kid, as he pet this
wonderful dog.

"Wow, mister, you sure handled that well, I thought for sure that dog
was a gonner."

Jake looked over to see an older man and a woman near-abouts forty
or so, in a very nice Mercedes, and they had more to say on the matter:

"It got out of that car over there. Some man seemed to let it loose on
purpose, must be so it could use the bushes over there... sure was a bad
move... sure was stupid. He didn't even seem to care, and then just left the
dog!"

Jake smiled in thanks and took the dog over and put it in the car, the
windows were open just enough to let in good air only, as if they did *indeed*
care for the dog.

Now that sure don't add up, Jake thought as he then went back to Ray.

you–see-that-? -Jake signed to Ray, *dog-almost-accident* - *'How could a man do that to a nice dog like that? Being so careless like that... what kind of fool would do that?'* Jake wondered in disgust.

Ray got out, "Keep your eyes open, Jake, I'll go see if I can find the owner, might as well pay for the gas, if the guys haven't done it yet."

Jake walked over near the road and waved at the folks as they left. After they left, someone else appeared. Someone Jake wouldn't be so well-pleased to wave at. Lyle Barlow had now appeared and was near the outside-back of the store building, with his son. Jake wasn't able to see him at that angle, as the car and the dog were in the way.

~*~

Lyle Barlow had seen Jake and his friends ready to pull-up for gas and had earlier run in to store's side-door. Lyle had quickly sought his son, Hunter, and pulled him out through the same door. Opportunity was finally a weapon in his hand! After doing some fast-talking with his son, Lyle had sent the young man back in. Lyle had one more thing to do then, something he was looking forward to doing for a long time, after that, he then ran back into hiding—and waited.

~*~

Jake had taken one last check on the dog, and was ready to turn and go back to the truck when he heard the loud crash and ducked down covering his head. The air was just as suddenly quiet—but not the dog. Jake stood-up and looked around, nearly at a loss to understand his whereabouts, until spying the dog, anchored his thoughts. There was nothing unusual, except the barking dog—and it was very upset—so Jake went to see what happened. He noticed the whole front windshield was busted in. Jake reached in and pet the dog and tried to calm it. He succeeded and was pleased. He looked over as Ray and the gang came out of the store, Jake had just made a move to get them, to show them what happened—when he stood in shock as he heard someone yelling at him:

"HEY, STOP THAT MAN! HE JUST BROKE MY WINDSHIELD!" Jake left the dog, and looked over to see a young man running up to him. Lyle was there just as fast, along with the gas station's owner, and informed everyone that the police had already been called by a store clerk.

Jake stood there in shock as he was face-to-face with—Lyle.

Ray and Matt were on Jake in a flash and held him back hard, and Stoney joined in, in an instant. They knew full-well that Jake, seeing Lyle like this, here and now, *meant* and *was*—bad news for Jake. They didn't know what he would do and if he started to fight, he'd go to jail for sure. If he beat the man up, that would be even worse, as they knew after what Jake had learned about Lyle and the bull, he just might not think to stop, and could leave serious damage in his wake.

No one knew what had happened to the car, except Lyle and his son. There were no witnesses and Jake was standing only a few feet from the car. Things were bad enough, as they were.

Jake didn't make a move to fight-back his buddies; he just stood there staring at Lyle. *'I know this man... don't I? Yeah... yeah, I'm sure I do... but how?'* Jake looked at his buddies in confusion as his brain started to hurt bad. They were obviously trying to protect him or keep him from this man.

"~Whoo~?" Jake voiced his demand to all of them.

His buddies looked at each other, nearly as shocked as Jake was.

Matt looked at Jake directly and plainly stated, "That's Lyle."

Jake made an effort to advance, more as a way to see study-him-up, hoping his brain would kick-in, but his buddies weren't taking any chances. Jake suddenly felt anger rising-up from inside, his mind had finally pieced his floating puzzled-up-pieces together as he studied the face and joined it to the name. He near burst forth from them in an instant—the bolt they expected, but still weren't fully ready for. They couldn't hold him back now. Lyle and the group near him, backed-off, fast and scared. Ray got in front of Matt and Stoney now, as they still held Jake and desperately tried to drag him back. Ray then grabbed Jake's face with one hand on his forehead and the other hand under his jaw—Jake's greatly wounded jaw—pushing his head back, and he yelled at him in desperation:

"YOU WANT TO GO TO JAIL AGAIN, JAKE! HOW ABOUT PRISON... WOULD YOU LIKE THAT, TOO?"

Jake was breathing heavy and feeling sick, his head was floating, but he heard the *magic* word still ringing in ears—*jail*. Jake relaxed and nearly fell backwards into Matt and Stoney's arms—cops and bars were flashing through his hurting brain. He was still now, and he shook his head repeatedly to mean no—he was near to cry. It was now beyond-clear to his buddies, that Jake's past-injured brain was too just too fragile for this. They released him and he walked back across the parking lot to the gas-pump-area where his truck was still parked and lay his body on the hood, fighting back confused tears that he didn't fully understand, and then stood to as his buddies piled around his side.

~*~

Now Jake had never beaten-up anyone or fought anyone that they *personally* knew of. But Jade had said, during his young adult years when they had gone back for the summer, to Texas, he had seen some bad times and some bad fights and he was *quite* capable. Seems there were some folks that didn't like the Tex-Mex crowd that Jake hung around with down there, and they made a point of causing trouble if-and-when they ran into him. Jake kept his friends though, even if he had to pay a price for his choice, thus he faced the fights—his friends included. Always for self defense, but still, fighting is as an assault, in the eyes of the law—thus—Jake was fast to honor that law, and let-loose for good, one day, of his past youthful ways, as did many of those dear friends. Yep, ol' Jake walked with a white-hat-hero-heart, even more so, then—as truly as he pledged to do so, as a small Texas kid, weaned on old westerns, and his good ma and her *Good Book*.

Now, at this point in time, naturally, with his weakened body, it might be a fairly even fight for a city man like Lyle, but it would be an act of anger on Jake's part, an assault and a crime, as he'd be the attacker. And—Jake was known as a hero through-out Old-Town and all the local ranches, a status firmly marked and well-earned, and cherished and honored in his heart. He was a very well-respected and a well-loved man on the horse-trail and rodeo scenes, too, and he didn't need to ruin himself now, no matter what Lyle had done. With friends like these, he would surely NOT be doing so—and he'd be the *first* to glad-up of it—*if* he'd been readied-up, *first*.

~*~

Jake stood there with his friends, wondering why this kid had accused him, and what the heck lying-Lyle had to do with it, anyways. He didn't know Hunter was Lyle's son. They all stood as if they were in their own corners of a prize-fighting ring—waiting for what—who knew. Hunter stood near his car and tried to comfort his dog. Lyle was near the back hood of the car trying to check out Jake, but Jake was too far away and had moved over near the front door of the store, still surrounded by his friends—a wall of cowboys (well, kind of). The owner was still trying to find out just exactly what happened and was getting information from Hunter. Jake's violent outburst sure fit the story that Hunter was feeding him and Lyle was relishing in it. An officer soon arrived, with a New-Town police vehicle, which could mean more bad news for Jake.

As soon as he pulled up, Jake began to get agitated. He had to get out of there—he was getting a deep heavy headache.

'I ain't gonna' do this again... ' he looked over at Ray and implored with his eyes. Jake's face became dead-serious as his further lodged-thoughts, meant for Ray, were dead to Ray's ears, *'I didn't do nothin'... I'm*

INNOCENT... and I'm high-tailing-it for the high country...soon as I find an open bolting-trail.'

Jake eyed the half-wooded field, and nearby low hills, just behind the gas station as his breathing picked-up a mite.

Matt knew the look and grabbed him just as the officer came up. Jake sat down on the step and rubbed his head and laid it on his folded arms, which were over his knees.

Ray took charge, "Stay with him, Stoney, move over to Matt and don't let Jake run off, no matter what... you hear, *don't* let him run off. I'm really afraid he will."

Ray watched Stoney comply, and set himself to a new chore—the officer.

"So now, what happened here folks?" The officer started to talk to Ray, as Ray motioned him away from Jake. Taking note of this, the other officer went over and watched Jake, as he appeared to be agitated and he feared the situation could turn unstable soon.

Lyle grabbed his son and forcefully pushed him up nearer to the officer, for to speak, and the store-keep followed. Hunter advanced.

"You need to wait your turn sir," the officer replied, firm and cold.

Hunter went back to Lyle.

Then Ray proceeded to tell him about Jake's "problem" and a bit more, and asked him if it was possible to call Sheriff Lowrie, as this was usually his jurisdiction and that his Officer Mike usually patrolled here. The officer agreed and stated that they were actually backup anyway, as Mike was taking care of a speeder and wasn't yet available. The officer called in about Jake and his truck, and was satisfied that he was not wanted for anything. He sternly warned Ray though, that if any trouble happened from Jake, he would have to take over himself—and on his terms only.

Lyle and Hunter proceeded to talk with the officer next, and Hunter made sure to address this complaint as his own personal complaint—independent of his father.

~*~

Lyle purposely stated that he did not see anything, as Lyle was purposing his OWN plan. Lyle was planning on getting back at the Smiths for his bull being killed, but he needed to set Jake up as a troublemaker somehow, first, for his stories to work. He planned to prove Jake was against him, and had been all along, because Jake hated his involvement with Jade. He hoped to get some good money out of this somehow, in court. He knew there was no way that Stoney or Jake would ever have satisfaction in any court, concerning pre-meditated malicious harm he had done them.

He had been very careful, covering all angles. But one can never safeguard themselves from spiritual principles. There was a spiritual principle that was at work here and it had a way of presenting itself with a new beef. If you seek to push any bull against an innocent party, your own bull will fall back on you. Yep, this is a highly honed spiritual principle at that, in effect since before time began. But then Lyle wouldn't have known that, he wasn't a rancher that learned to respect what a man does with livestock—and—he wasn't a reader of the Good Book. He only knew city-stock and was a reader of "which horse was racing at what time"—sometimes called the *bad book*. And—this spiritual principle that he was so unaware of, is better known by its more formal presentation: If you seek to push a stone on the innocent, your own stone will fall back on you—just as true—if you seek to dig a pit for the innocent, you will fall into your own pit. Lyle would never suspect now, that his courting with Jade and his "courting" against Jake would led to all kind of surprises and none he'd like in the end. For a man that lived only for his own pleasure, the end results would be far from the rewards he expected to come his way. An unseen courting of his *own* waited for him—in more ways than one—in the courtyard of a higher, yet unseen, court.

Lyle knew that after what he had done at the Smiths', he had better not get involved in any new confrontations with Jake. His *son* could though, to help his father's cause, and none would blame it on Lyle. His plan was to become the one to be the accuser now, as the victim pointing to a wrong-doer, in a court, and if he planned it careful enough, he would come out the winner—if and only if, he could first set Jake up. Yep—Lyle was going to try to feed a lot of dead-bull to the court, and in any way he could.

Lyle was also in deep trouble because of this bull. He had acquired it in some underhanded ways and greatly needed to get out of the whole mess. He needed money and lots of it. Jake didn't have lots of money, but his ranch was *sure* worth it.

~*~

Ray told Jake that Officer Mike was coming soon to take over and that it was safe to take his crushed pills, there'd be no confiscation to fear. He then went over and listened to what Hunter and Lyle were telling the officer, and then went to listen to what the gas station shop-keep (the legal owner) had to say. Jake tried getting the medicine down, as the other officer watched and learned. This was something he had never seen before, as he carefully watched Jake and his trouble. Matt and Stoney still kept their positions, one on each side of Jake.

Jake wanted to communicate so badly. If he did, he now had three people that could understand him, but he was not going to give Lyle anymore pleasure. Matt and Stoney were flanking him continually and he felt like a prisoner, as he sat in silence, mute to the world, stuck in yet another twisting-spin from it, trying to get up enough nerve to face getting in the squad car. He knew he was eventually going to have to. Yet, over and over, he didn't know if he could, and feared he'd be laying in the dirt again, feeling that firm clasp of metal as it clamped shut—or worse yet—falling into the firm clasp of another seizure and losing a second dose of his dignity. Something he wouldn't feel or know, until after he woke up—only God knows where. He was beginning to wish he could practice lessons for these seizures, so he could take-them-on with some kind of victory, but he knew when a seizure hits, the body does its own thing anyway—he'd just be along for the ride. He knew if a seizure chose to sneak-up on him again, he'd lose this time, as always—sure as the evening moon ain't to be touched by a mere cowboy upon nightly-viewing.

Damn... this is taking forever... Jake lay his head down again in his arms and tried not to feel sick, *there really was a time in my life when my head was well... wasn't there? I wish I knew... I don't know why... but I wish I knew... seems there's a lot of newly built 'damns' roamin' the hills of my mind lately, and not the constructive-type at that... maybe they're keeping me from breakin' loose in a flood of frustration, for all I know, though... damn, I sure don't feel so good...yep, I sure am HOOKED on swearing now, it seems...dear Lord forgive me...seems I'm a mess, all right...*

He knew he was again facing questioning for something he didn't do, and if this Lyle was lying and setting him up, which now he suspected, he greatly feared arrest. He looked up again just to make sure he still knew where he was. The breeze felt good, he remembered it from the café. It was hard for him to place when he was there last, had he just been there today? He mind blanked-out as he sat there, but snapped back to attention when Matt shook him gently and called his name. He was starting to get confused now and wondered where the owl was, until he finally realized he had rescued a dog, but something had gone terrible wrong. Something was wrong now as well, but he couldn't seem to put his finger on it.

'I got to learn to mind my own business... that's what I got to do... my life has gone out the window, in a storm.'

Jake looked up slowly at the nearby officer. The officer had now become worried because of Jake's staring, and had now approached him.

"Mister, are you all right, can you hear me? He looked at Matt, "Is he all right?"

"It must be the medication he just took, he's okay." Although Matt knew it was the stress mixing with Jake's past injury, he didn't want to dare risk the officer trying to call an ambulance—so—no more was said. This was now to be normal for Jake, anyway, whenever a completely new and foreign, complex situation, such as this, chose to hit-up-side his face—they'd just have to accept.

Jake stared at the officer's badge, *'I know the sheriff... yeah, I know the sheriff... he's a good friend of mine. We were just heading-out to see him for some reason... sure don't recollect what it was though.'* The medication was making him tired now and he rubbed his head. He had now completely forgot about his birthday, until:

Ray was beside the officer in charge as they walked-up to Jake and they stared him square in the eyes.

The officer said, "This young man claims that you started a fight with him by *verbally* harassing him. And he claims that you accused him of being in-league with his father and some bull accident. He claims he tried to tell you he was out of town then, and you refused to listen to him. He said you *then* told him you were going to kill his father for what he did to you and someone named Stoney. He also said, you told him you were going to smash him up good with that brick, but he rolled-off the car in time, and you hit his windshield instead. He now wants to press charges, in full, down at the station." The officer looked over at Ray, "Now, from what I just heard from this man Ray, when I first drove up... this whole thing doesn't make any sense. So you will *both* have to go in for further questioning, I am not *arresting* anyone, if you BOTH volunteer to come in."

Jake stared at Ray, as he stood up cautiously. He was afraid that if he moved to sign that someone was going to grab him and he wanted nothing to do with the handcuffs. Jake stared at Matt and then at Stoney in near-disbelief, did they *hear* what he just heard? Surely, they had.

Stoney had been sickened by the whole incident, and had been lost in thought about what Jake must have gone through when he was arrested for the owl. His past guilt was weighing heavy on his shoulder now and he looked completely worn out.

Jake shook his head in sorrow and went up to him and offered his hand for Stoney to stand up. When Stoney did so, Jake gave him a hug and then signed a quickly formed, *o.k.* ... *all-o.k.* -and then gave him a firm pat on the back. Matt got up as well, and stretched out as they listened to Ray mention that the sheriff was driving up.

Well, turned-out it wasn't Lenny, but it *was* Officer Mike. After some quick discussion, they were all to go to Sheriff Lenny Lowrie's office immediately for questioning, voluntarily for all—well—all but Jake. He would have to ride with Officer Mike. Anyone that failed to co-operate now *would* be arrested, or, if anyone failed to show-up to face the charges and questioning soon to be made because of this incident, they would put a warrant out for their arrest. Jake and Ray were frisked for weapons. Jake was put in back, minus the handcuffs, with Ray, as Ray volunteered and was acting as interpreter. Jake's other buddies, took his truck and followed. Hunter's car was left, and he went with his dad. The gas station store-owner went also.

Once in the office, the officers that arrived at the scene presented it all to Sheriff Lowrie; he quickly knew exactly what to do, even as Ray trusted he would. Lenny took them all went into another room for questioning. Lyle was not allowed in the room where the questioning was done. Sheriff Lowrie let the men have their say, the gas station owner first, and then Hunter, while Matt and Stoney were cautioned to remain silent. Hunter went through his statements and stuck to his story. Ray made a few statements, as to the fact that the sheriff did well in sending-out the call for the officers to bring everyone in, as he fully understood that Lenny had been contacted, as well as Officer Mike. This was all arranged so Jake could prove himself and be free of any false charges, and do it in front of as many credible, legitimate witnesses, as this was blatant lying, underway, by Hunter.

Hunter was now angry and said that he was pressing charges and only a court-hearing was allowable to make decisions in these matters and local officers had no right to call him a liar—and—he demanded to see Jake locked up. The sheriff reminded him that no one was arrested yet, and could not be arrested on hearsay, and Lenny set the stage for more:

"Jake, I know that what you have to say, will clear you immediately, at least enough to make the witness completely non-creditable. If it will help... " Lenny, smiled, "I already know more than you think. Jade told me, but I was the *only* one she told. She told me when I drove her home after your *odd* escapades in town here. Do you want to let me to do anything for you, or take over now, as to dealing with this man and his charges... or are you up to it?"

A very confused array of faces now watched Lenny, but Jake's face cleared:

Jake was not confused anymore, it had passed, once he knew he couldn't be arrested—he had hope and it shined upon his grateful heart. Suddenly feeling dad-gummed lame, he realized such good fortune must have been due to Jade's snazzy path-paving praying, once again, for sure—as—never had a birthday gone by *without* it. Here he was, safe at Lenny's, a place that was familiar, and he could think just as clear as he ever could before. The tides of change were by far high-swelling and moving in his favor—his freedom was near at hand, and far easier suddenly, than his last jail injustice.

Yep, just minutes before, in the store's parking lot, he felt completely lost. It was like trying to force open the locked situation solely with a wrong key—and upon finding the right key, everything in the world made sense again, as the door swung open in victory. Here he was going do fine and he knew it.

The officers came to realize they had done the right thing, sure enough, as Jake started to share:

Jake signed, *I-not-smash-car-window* ... *I-not-see-man-before* - He paused as he looked at his friend Ray, and Ray spoke the translation.

Jake continued to sign, *I-not-want* -he stopped, suddenly lost, as he didn't know how to say kill, with signs. He formed Jade's "k" and voiced, "~~iw~" a few times, but felt stupid listening to himself. He had to stop and study the word, and then, this time showing the "k", at his mouth, he forced himself to voice again, from his throat:

"K'~~iw~" and then added the final formed "l", and added, *anyone* ... *NOT* -

Hunter, as he witnessed all this, stood up in disbelief, "HEY, HEY WHAT IS THIS! What's he trying to pull!"

The officers warned him sit, so Jake could continue.

Ray, spoke up for him, "Jake said, 'I don't want to kill anyone.'"

Jake nodded in agreement.

"We need to know why you were standing at the car, Jake," Lenny asked him.

Jake was now annoyed and turned to the officers and Hunter and just stared, *'I SAVED your dog mister... you let it roam the streets and I rescued it... or it would be dead now! That poor dog was scared to death of that brick that YOU most likely THREW yourself. You or Lyle!'* Jake signed, *your-dog-almost-die* ... *I-help-your-dog* ... *you-fool* ... *your-dog-in-street* ... *I-grab-dog* ... *finished* ... *I-put-dog-in-car* ... *finished* ... *I-leave* ... *huge-NOISE* ... *I-turn-back* ... *your-dog-

afraid-in-car* ... *I-see-smash-on-window* ... *I-pet-dog* ... *try-help-
dog-again* ... *who-smash?* ... *I-not-know* ... *maybe-YOU!* ...
right-right-right?   -he formed a large question mark in the air, as he ended
after many firm scary-looking hand-formed, "rights". Then he looked hard-
fixed at Hunter, and voiced, "~WhI~~," and he signed, *why*   -over and
over again, in wild strict action—without a word.

By now Hunter was wondering just WHAT he had gotten himself
into. All because he let his father push him into this, or more truly though,
in his eyes—force him into it. He was getting scared now and Jake was
making strange noises at him and showing him stuff, stuff that he didn't
understand. If it was true—if this guy *couldn't* talk, what was the next step
as to what he had just done? He had lied. He had falsely accused an
innocent man of a violent crime and in front of credible witnesses.

Ray, translated Jake's whole story again for Jake's satisfaction,
although Jake kept INSISTING that Ray say, "smashed the window" and not
"broke the window", each time—as Jake wanted to say smashed, to explain
such a breaking noise, and that was all there was to it! And as far as Jake
was concerned, Ray better say what he *meant*. And as far as Ray was
concerned, he was delighted to!—once he got the proper drift.

Jake had freely interrupted to make this declaration, with "~unh-
unh~," while shaking his finger and signing, *no* ... *no* -and then
followed just as quickly, with the sign for "hit/smash" and showed Jade's
formed ASL shapes for the sounds of: *'s~uh~m~a~sh'*. Oddly, he formed
"sumash" as he drew the word out way too slow in thought, thus, he couldn't
yet fully understand the blended sounds of the "sm" sound of "smash"—but
Ray got his point quickly enough—while others had to *watch* and *wait*.

Now then, when Ray's translation got to the dog, and Jake rescuing
the dog, Hunter stood up in disbelief of *another* kind. Now, *he* was going to
get *technical* about HIS point, and quickly, as well—others were going to
have to watch and wait again—but this time for *his* speech.

"No, that can't be true! My dog was in the car, he never could have
got out! I would never hurt my dog. I LOVE my dog!"

Ray knew that as Jake's friend, it would do no good for him to tell
Hunter that Jake's story was true, as, if he agreed with Jake, Hunter would
think Ray was biased.

After Hunter's out-burst, Jake kept signing, "fool" and "why", every
time Hunter looked at him. He was even ready to stomp his foot at him a
few times for emphases, but Ray headed-him-off-at-the-pass. Ray, needed
to translate what Jake was saying, and stomps *didn't* help the situation one
bit—something was needed now to change the subject, and soon. Ray,

digging-up his own memory, came to found there *was* one more thing to add, he *did* remember something that was true and unbiased—now he could share his own words.

Ray then mentioned the Mercedes and the couple that saw the dog, and how they were witnesses to every detail, that took place. There were not any Mercedes Benz in town, locally, so maybe they could find this one in time, before it moved on, he had reasoned—plus the older man, driving it. But by this time, the gas station owner spoke up—pointing at Jake, and adding more details, he opened up:

"I saw him in the street from the window," the owner said, "I watch the gas pumps all the time and I saw him run out waving his shirt... at first I thought he was crazy or- " The man stopped, "I didn't *mean* nothing by that sir," he finished, and continued anew, "well, at first I thought he was crazy, running out into the street waving his shirt... but a few minutes later, as I got ready to help a customer, I saw him pulling a beautiful setter in from out of the street. I never saw the man anymore after that, until the incident with the brick. Hunter's dad, Lyle came into my store and pulled his son out the side-door. They come in all time and I've never seen them behave that way, so I was afraid something happened... and then a few minutes later, I heard this crash and I ran-out and ran into the dad. That's when we saw the man... him... petting the dog. He was real calm and quite happy with the dog. Lyle said he had already told my store clerks to call the police and we hadn't even seen what exactly happened yet." The man looked over at Ray now, "I can say this too... that Mercedes was heading over to the old O'Rourke Ranch. They were heading-out there to stay for the week. They had reservations for the restaurant tonight and needed directions... if you need to find them... that's where they'll be."

"Then how did my dog get out... how could he? I didn't do it Jake... I'm not fool enough to hurt such a wonderful dog. I got that dog from my mother... I finally was able to pick it up from her house, just a few days ago. My father, he hates that- " Hunter stopped and hung his head down, and then looked up at everyone, "My father *hates* that dog, just like he *hates* my mother... that's why I don't want to stay with him, but I *have* to until I'm 18. He told me if I did this to Jake, then I could legally go stay with her, as he would give up his rights, and see to it. I only had one year left to go... but I don't want to be here with him. My dog didn't like it either... it was worse for him, than for me... it really was. I'm sorry, I'm just so sorry."

"Do you understand how serious this is, or how it could have been? This man could have been arrested and gone to trial. With no witness and no proof, it would have been your word against his and no matter how it turned out... it would have done him harm and possibly a prison term. Why would Lyle risk such a faulty form of an accusation such as this, riding on you, made against Jake?" Unaware obviously of the whole picture, Sheriff Lowrie questioned him again, "Jake's had enough damage...what would be the point of Jake being locked up?"

"I'm really sorry, but I really don't know... all I know, is I wanted to go back home and that was my only way." He looked at Jake, and said, "I'm really sorry. Now what's going to happen to me? Am I going to jail, now?"

"You could have counter-charges brought against you... but that's up to Jake. The only reason this fell apart is because Jake can't talk. You had no intention to back down, or confess the truth."

Jake started weighing-out quite a few issues, needless to keep packed, as they'd be further burdens to his heart. All eyes were on him (and not due to the fact that he was today's birthday boy) as he readied-up to proclaim Hunter's fate:

'It's my birthday and I have better things to do than make this boy's life, or conscience, any worse than it is... and his dog sure needs him,' thought Jake. *'I don't want to ever look back on this birthday with regret, that's for bull's-eye-certain-sure... as it's really turning-out to be somethin' the likes-of-which I've NEVER come across in all my birthday'd-up days.'*

"~'Koh~," Jake voiced and pointed to the door, "~'koh~,"—he sure wished it didn't sound like he was trying for a much-needed throat-clear, but it was the best "go", he could manage.

Hunter gratefully understood and quickly left the room and ran near smack-dab into Lyle in the office, and Lyle followed him out, seeking to hear of their gain. When Lyle found out what happened, he couldn't believe it. It also turned-out that they had a terrible argument in the car on the way back to the gas station, and Hunter took his dog, and went to stay with some friends.

The officers thanked Jake for waiting so patient all that time at the gas station, through such hard questioning, and left. Jake's buddies had now decided that trying to have just *one* day in town with Jake being mute, was a lot harder than they thought.

Right about now, Lenny was so glad to finally see Jake, that he grabbed him up and swung him around the room, saying, "What a way to meet-up with you again... and on *your* birthday of all things! You got anymore trouble you want to get into, now that you're here, Jake? Something that I can get you out of, of course!" Lenny said full of zeal, as he moved over to sit on the corner of his desk. He seemed like a proud bird of prey that had just satisfied himself on vermin for the day. His dark, straight hair—slicked back a mite—and his mustache, added to his regal appearance. "Jail sure ain't where you belong on you birthday," Lenny said, with an added thought, *or after near four months in a hospital, either.*

Jake still couldn't understand why this all had just happened, but he quickly yielded to Lenny's enthusiasm. And well he should, as Lenny was 6'6" and kept himself in great shape—if he chose to swing one around, it was best to yield. Jake's old self was just as prone to bouts of enthusiasm, but his body still wasn't quite up-to-par with Lenny's strength—seems there'd be no more arm wrestling and such, now. However, his joyful heart was up to seeing some *new* action for sure, and through-and-through, and at this rate, clear through 'til party time, as he needed to celebrate a mighty thankful birthday!

Jake pretended like he was holding an imaginary birthday cake, and blew out the candles, and signed, *party-tonight-soon* ... *see-you-later* - With *that*, Jake and his buddies *left* and headed-out to the #1 saloon (presumably), leaving a curious Lenny behind—curious as to signs—but signs of *another* sort. Yep, he had decided to find out *more* about Lyle, and he thought he may *just* know how, too.

CHAPTER SEVENTEEN

HARD-CORE APPLE-CORE

IT was getting close to 4:45 p.m. now, yet they stopped-off at the CORNER&COFFEE café. It was starting to fill-up now, so they just stopped for a quick sit outside again on the patio, for coffee. They soon separated, as Jake and Matt went to get the gift for Jade. Ray and Stoney stayed behind. After what he had seen today, Stoney needed Ray to pick his spirits up.

Stoney had been holding a wealth of anger and hurt in his soul since he realized he was on a ringer bull. He would have lit-out after Lyle, if he had not been needed to protect Jake. He could have ended up in jail, instead of sitting here with Ray. It was still a mystery to him why Lyle would do such a thing. Stoney was just too innocent to understand how there is always money involved somewhere. His "why's" never touched base with that.

~*~

As Stoney was in shock lying there facing the bull with no help, he couldn't understand why this trick had been played on him, that was the only thought that raced through his mind as he was quite possibly meeting his death, *why... why? Why'd he do it... why am I laying here... why ain't no one helping?* When he saw Jake, he knew it was a Godsend. The only way to get the bull off Stoney was for Jake to run up to its field of vision, but Jake was too drunk to move back with any speed or skill. In fact—he didn't move at all. Jake was hit, as soon as he faced the bull.

Once Stoney witnessed the bull hitting Jake in his side and throwing him with the first hit, he didn't care about "why" anymore; he was now full of rage. Jade had been screaming for more help but the Lyle's wranglers didn't seem to want to move. Stoney had slowly pulled himself along the frozen snow-dusted ground until he was closer to the fence, but he wasn't thinking clear anymore. When the bull had hit Jake again, this time in the leg—followed by some stomping on his hip and leg—it had turned around, still thrashing and was heading back into Jake to get him once more. It had caught up with Jake just as he was trying to roll in a ball, to push to stand-up on his one good leg to try and get away—he was unable to do so, and then fell. He was bleeding from his chest, down over his arm, and bleeding from his thigh. Near trying to stand again, he had made one last effort to drag himself and then he was hit in the head, from behind. Neither of Lyle's wranglers ran to help him, either. From a glance to the side, Stoney saw it knock Jake on the back of the head, knocking him out and into the ground. He could hardly see Jake in the dirty snow, but it appeared the bull was stomping and kicking him in the shoulder, arm, and chest.

Stoney couldn't move anymore by then and his brain was starting to spin. He felt some of his own blood as he learned he had a gash on his own side. He was still near the edge of the corral out of danger, since the bull was so busy with Jake. All he could do was watch and wait, he knew it was killing his best friend.

Stoney was ready to kill Lyle, during his last look towards Jake. All he saw was the bull and his last views of what he knew was Jake under the bull's feet. Next thing Stoney knew, he heard gunshot and looked past the fence—Jade was killing the bull. As it fell, Matt showed up out of nowhere, pulling Jake out from the dead bull's feet. Jade was then by Stoney's side, she had to help him and finished pulling him out—light snow was falling in his face. She tried to help him now as best she could, first, though desperate to run to her twin, fearful that he was dead. Little did she know that Stoney was dying inside, emotionally—sick with the knowledge that Jake went down, because of him.

~*~

Stoney needed to rid himself of these feelings now, and thought back as he remembered how much he had already come through, and the thoughts that he had sorted. He had spent a lot of time alone at the Daniels' and Ray and Matt were worried about him. Ray had made lots of phone calls to Stoney and kept him informed on Jake, and held Stoney's spirit up through a phone line. Just recently Stoney finally had a long talk with Ray, about how Lyle had done him dirty, and how he wasn't sure he could hold back if he saw him face-to-face again. It was good that it had happened this way, today, and Stoney knew it. Ray and Stoney were finally settled now, as they finished their talk. Stoney would be able to get over this last wave of guilt, from the waves of comfort that came from a friend.

~*~

Ray was the one who fought this battle with Stoney, striving to heal his conscience. This strong hate in Stoney would have poisoned him greatly, and his guilt would have done him in. While Jake was sleeping and recovering in the hospital from the seizure he had at the jail, Ray took care of Stoney.

Ray was the only one of them all that had not seen the accident, or anything connected with it. Lenny saw the aftermath, but that was all. Ray was the one that was now called on to help all of them. Ray did not witness the active initial trauma, the type that he was dealing with was on a different level—subtle and hidden. His voluntary job was *watching* his friends try to help themselves, together, and go on—and perchance to be their coach.

Ray had no idea how he had been able to hold these frayed threads together, that had once been beautifully rich layered rugs of life. If he wasn't there now for these friends, his special companions, it seemed they would fray into worthless mats of long-gone spender. Too worn and torn, from this bull, to ever be of use in ever sharing their fellowships with anyone again. Today had been a test. Jake had a double test, actually a triple test today: First Lyle, then possible arrest, and lastly having to communicate. It had even worked-out for Stoney's best. This face-to-face encounter with Lyle, was the hardest test either cowboy would ever have to face. Ray knew it was good that Stoney faced Lyle today, as Stoney had been forced to stay in-line, for Jake's safety. Jake had to stay in line out of loyalty to his own name, his honored future as a cowboy of good-standing—a personal account that he never sullied with debts of lawlessness. So far Stoney had only to rein in his hate for Lyle, out of loyalty to Jake as friend and boss-man. It was up to Stoney to owe-up to this emotion of hate, as to revenge, and die to it, just as Jake had chose to be doing. It was time for Stoney to grow-up as well, another notch higher into manhood—and helping his big brother today was the right start.

~*~

Ray and Stoney had finished coffee and were expecting Matt and Jake in less than five minutes, when Ray couldn't believe his eyes. Angie was making her way through the crowed café, and coming out onto the porch. Ray wished they had sat on the front corner, near the street, when they had a chance, then they would have seen her coming but now it was too late.

"Bet you thought you got rid of me, huh, Ray... well, I'm back! Alex is waiting for me inside, we thought we'd have to go on a waiting-list for a table, but we found someone to share a table with instead... one of my friends." Angie laughed, "She was trying to get me to believe that Jake can't talk. She said he's been in town all day, explaining why, and helping people get used to it... like a new pair of boots, I reckon." She tossed her hair back, "Alex likes my hair this way, Ray, what do you think?"

"I think you should have stayed at the bed-and-breakfast with the plans that I set up for you and Alex. They had a whole three days of wonderful scenic-sites that Alex has never seen the likes of, and he even helped pick some of the places out." Ray was really disgusted with her, he honestly didn't think she'd show up, but he now realized that he should have known better. *What's a small-town bed-and-breakfast mean to her anyway,* he thought, *but at least I would have thought Alex meant something to her... sure thought she wanted to be Mrs. Alex Humbolt someday... guess I sure was off-base!*

Ray continued on firmly, "You know, if you SHOW-UP at the Smith's party, Alex is going to think you still have feelings for Jake. Then... Jade is going to have a fit, as she's fed-up with the games you played on Jake's friends, and worse yet, she's fed-up with you messing with Jake's mind, concerning a whole host of issues. Jake himself set you sailing downstream and in none-to-polite of a way. He had no other choice. All in all, you're bad times and bad news, if you show up there, Angie."

"Yeah, Angie... if you show-up tonight, well... someone might just 'pin the tail' on you, by mistake... if you come parading in there, and braying your *city-lingo* at us, and all," Stoney said sharply, and then got up to leave.

"Please, Angie," Ray, took hold of her as he and Stoney got up, "Jake is finally adjusting to being home again. Whatever or however you felt, when it didn't work-out between you and him, set it on the shelf, at least for tonight... huh, okay?"

"I don't know... he made a fool of me... and *twice*," she pouted and swung her car keys, refusing to dare confess the last and *third* time, as she was *snooping* and she knew it—but she planned on fixing *that* now, sure-enough.

"No, Angie... you made a *fool* out of yourself and you needed no help, either... you gave Jake no options. He may have been hooked on you in those early teen years, but you've changed a lot since then and high school, Angie, and not for the good." Ray gave her a kiss on the top of her head, and they left, leaving her to stare after them as she played with her loose fingernail.

They ran into Alex as they were leaving. Oh, they were most glad to have run into him though, but they *did* mention that they were very much surprised. Both were true, and Alex knew best of all. He had to confess this burden, too, he was just as surprised as them, and he sure missed the plans Ray had set up, and the whole issue confused him. It would turn-out, however, that he'd be seeing some sights, all right, local color, but from his fiancée, instead. She'd soon be apple red, this time because of Jake and not Jade. Looks like the twins would be getting an *equal* turn, in facing-off with Angie this Smith-Ranch-apple-season.

With a well-wish for success, Ray left saying, "Good luck with Angie, she can be a handful, you brave man, you!" He was followed by Stoney, as he gave a smart pat on-the-back to Alex. As they came out the door and waited in the early evening air, they were mighty glad that Jake and Matt never made it back in time. They *knew* Jake would be arriving *somewhere*, in time though, and, that was to be the SLIPPING SADDLE SALOON #1.

The saloon was near enough to the café—if one liked to have a little walk. There was parking both up and down the street, or in the saloon parking lot. This whole area had lots of little shops, so most locals chose to walk back-and-forth to various locations, whether they were in town working, or had just dropped-in for the day. They chose to walk everywhere on this side of town, with maybe the exception of getting groceries—as—too much to carry!

Stoney and Ray now recognized Jake and Matt coming down the street and quickly set-out to head them off, no use running any extra risks with Angie and her eagle-eyes hovering near cafe windows.

The four Stetsons now were pointed in the right direction, toward lots of friends. As they neared the swinging saloon doors, Jake was first in, followed by his "wrecking crew", ready to wreck a few steaks. Just as he stepped in, Jake got a surprise roar of happy birthday, and he was down right surprised. And well he should be, as his usual doings was just to mosey-on over to his reserved table, eat with the guys, and get ready for a few social drinks. His friends usually dropped by on their own, along with the gals, Jade and Galena. Like water trickling into a pond, their circle was then filled. There were always a few gifts to open by the evening. He never expected such a waterfall of excitement—seems folks were birthday-party-ready, and that was a fact.

Jake scanned the room, it seemed like everyone was here already, even Lenny, his wife Sara (a box of sunshine, to all), and Mike and Sam (his long-time officers). This was a source of extra pleasure, seeing Lenny here so early in the evening, now Jake didn't have to explain to Jade how he nearly became a jailbird again. Lenny would do it for him! He was glad to be relieved of this burden. Since the first arrest, this was becoming a source of undue stress and impaired his ability to think and function normally. He froze-up one day when a police squad car went up the road to the twin wranglers' spread. He was almost thinking the officers were looking for twin wranglers of a *different* kind, and to narrow it down even more specifically, possibly a lone cow*boy* twin—him. Any time he thought of the police, he started to get headaches and he didn't like it. Yet, time was, cops were regular public servants and accepted in his presence—now he took to hiding from them. He was dreading having to face Jade with this newest squad car ride, even though his buddies rescued him this time.

I wonder if I sign "jail + bird", if that would make sense to anyone, Jake thought, as he practiced it with his hands, completely unaware of his new usual shyness to being watched. He quickly put this aside when he looked up a bit and happened to notice Johnny, out of the corner of his eye, up at the bar. He was holding up a huge sign, with a birthday cake painted on it and tons of candles, and yellow happy-faces. Jake laughed and nudged his buddies, and gave a long point as he reached out his arm in that direction. Jailbird, was now flying free, and lost in clouds of love and down-home companionship.

Johnny Walker was the bar-keep and owner, and yep, that was really his name. He was from Texas' Tip-Of-Tex country, just as Jake's family was. He grew up on a ranch, and as all his folks had passed-away—being the only kid, well, he eventually followed ol' Smitty up to Montana, bringing his wife, Olivia. The locals took to him right-off. He was a fine man. Not too tall, thin, gray hair, and a great conversationalist—though he never wore a cowboy hat or boots, he was still pure south Texas. And, his wife of Mexican heritage was just as fine, whether tagging along behind him, going before him, or just sitting by his side. She was very gracious and good woman, to boot, with thick black shoulder length hair, just a tad on the gray side—and a great *health-walker*, enriching the Walker name, further.

This year's birthday party sure had taken a new turn. Jake's friends just planned this out, on their own determinations, after checking with Jade, of course. No one had seen Jake for so long, true enough. When Jake hadn't been coming into town, they weren't sure whether to go through with it, but it seemed like the best "welcome home" that they could give him—and it now was proving to be true. Seems ol' Jade had more *important* reasons for getting Jake into town today and opening-up about his "new self"—this party was on her mind. None of this would be coming to pass, if he hadn't followed through. Sure pays-off when a twin cowboy buckles down to let his twin-sis have top-shining honors, by having HER way, while he gives up! Seemed her insight, truly was best. Now then, nearly everyone here, in some way now, knew that Jake couldn't talk—thanks to Jade and her quite-capable talking-mouth-of-info, as she took to the phones to pave the way for the guest. And, Jade did inform Johnny Walker to spread the word that Jake couldn't read their cards, so Jake or anyone else, wouldn't get caught in any awkward situations. This was to be a *fun* night and seeing as they halfway pushed him into it, she sure better *ride-herd* on it. Why, it's just the best way to keep things from going astray when one least expects it—keeps it from turning-out wrong, right?

Jake ordered his supper to go, and would have it cooked-up for later, his buddies however, were hungry now though, and that was fine with Jake. He just reckoned it was time to hone-up more on his watching-skills, was all, while they ate to their hard-working cowboy-hearts' content. Yep, as friends, they sure earned some good Johnny Walker steaks, and, they sure earned their *keep*, as well—especially today. Jake wondered if he might have been eating his birthday supper in Lenny's jail, or worse yet—the big jail, over in New-Town's sector, minus Lenny's guardianship.

As time progressed, it was getting harder-and-harder for Jake to get through the evening. He saw the pile of gifts getting higher-and-higher up behind the bar, and his emotions were welling higher-and-higher to match. He near broke-down a couple of times, as he sat through stories that many of his friends came up to share. He felt so good to be in their presence again that a part of himself that had been dormant, had now come back to life. He could feel them water his parched, withered roots. Their words were filling the room with that milling-sound that guest make when a party has filled the room. He was in it, but not of it, but still part of it—a hard feeling to still lay-hold of. He wanted to talk to them and be one of those noises that flowed in unison, but no sorrow tormented him *this* time, he was too happy to be in their presence after being boxed into the walls of that hospital. He was engulfed by the magic of words, right now, and yielding to face it—yep, talking-ambiance, it was—kind of like a good warm fire. Much better than the dark cold coals of refusing to fuel his new way of life, he thought.

~*~

He remembered how he couldn't take the dull silence at the breakfast table that first morning home, when Jade used to leave questions hanging in the air, out of habit. He remembered how she'd wait for an answer that wasn't coming, then continue on. He also remembered the sailing coffee cup, when he just couldn't take it anymore. He now listened to himself, as he added his own versions of "~unh-unh~" and "~unh-huh~" and all the rest of the comments he had since learned to do. In a way, he was stepping into the shallow-end of these warm conversations that were now bathing the room. He had come so far and it moved him deep in his soul.

It was different for him with his buddies, since they had been there with him when he was learning and they had been partaking of this, both in work time issues and projects around the ranch. They had the majority of these hard conversations on a friendly one-to-one basis. Come the end of the day, he'd just hang-back and listen as they all conversed with gusto—including Jade and Galena—while they sipped on coffee around the supper table, after meals. He would join-in on occasion, but he more preferred to watch, study, and listen to them, as he pushed his chair back into the corner near the wall. This was the corner by the woodburning stove, his spot, then he'd just sit and think—and then—think some more. He'd think about how he used to be part of it all in another way. He'd think about all the talks this table had seen after settling down here, after their rodeo road-trips. He'd think further back, to when his folks graced this same table, full of family talk. He'd think of planning for the hard winters, and talks on paying bills—and then, the fun celebrating talks, when they done so successfully. He'd think about all the thoughts still stuck in his mind that he wanted to share right then, right during those minutes, and share in *detail*, just as they did. He'd think of all the different ways a word could be said and the *power* that the speaker had when using them—and, how others would perk-up to attention and listen. He wished he had more to offer than what he could. It still seemed odd to him in those closing hours of the day, that he hadn't said a share of *anything* that was on his mind. He hadn't been able to speak his piece—he had no piece to move. Before, he would have had that simple little chore done and his mind would be free of the day's burden, ready for thoughts of tomorrow to add-up afresh. He still felt like he was locked-out of the gate of a mighty fine pasture and he *longed* to be in it, spouting-out the glories of life, loud and clear.

Then just before turning in, he'd get his evening talks with Ray, if Ray was there that night. He'd be fighting in every way he could to get the details out. Ray in turn, would pass them on, and any new gestures or signs that they came up with, to Matt and Stoney, and then go on home. Jake would then sit out on the porch, watching the stars—thinking. Just thinking, once again.

~*~

Yeah, Jake thought, *just thinking... but now... I'm right here in the ol' swimmin' hole and... I may not be splashing, but at least I'm holdin' my own. The waters were long due, I guess, and I didn't even realize it... but they were on the way. Birthday's have ways of being pond-deep full, with*

many special things swimmin' in them. Looks like Jade knew I needed this
watering-hole here in town, and at THIS time. It was really the right way.

Still thinking on all this and remembering the sailing coffee that went along with all those memories, Jake decided to place his first food order—by himself. He hadn't dared to place an order for anything, since his accident.

Jake raised his hand as the waitress came by, and snapped his fingers at her a few times and flashed her a real smart, handsome, Jake-smile. When he knew he had her attention, he waved her over.

"Hey Jake, what do you want... a date, or something?" Stoney joked at him. "If not... if Jade ain't wantin' t'dance with me tonight, I'll take her."

Jake, with a laughing grin, rolled his eyes a bit at him and gestured as to push or brush him aside.

The waitress came up; she was new since Jake had last been in. She asked Jake what he wanted, although, a bit leery, as by now she knew the flow at this table was a little beyond her. She caught hand signals and heard a few faint odd noises and wasn't sure she knew what to do with Jake. So far, Ray had ordered for everyone tonight—except for some side remarks added by Stoney—he was wanting some side-orders of his own, along with the fun he had ordering them.

Jake signed, *coffee-usual* -and then looked up at her with a big smile again, to see what she would do.

"If it's on the menu I'll gladly get it," she smiled back, "just as long as someone here fills me in on what it is," she smiled again. Stoney seemed the most eager, so he did, and then they all sat back and poked fun at Jake, as she left:

"See now," Stoney presented, "that wasn't too hard... now if you would have just been more at ease, it might have come out 'date' instead of coffee. Now, let's try to get ready and we'll try it again." Stoney made a motion to stand up, as Jake pulled him back down by the belt of his pants!

The coffee put the perfect seal on all of Jake's thoughts. He even decided he'd soon try to drink it—as—hey, why not? The lights would soon to be dim and comforting, and he could remember plenty of drunks that looked much worse than he ever would, while trickling some coffee.

They were having a great time, and many were now sitting at their own tables, waiting for Jade and Galena to show next. Johnny dimmed the lights as usual and got ready for the evening atmosphere as he uncovered the jukebox and lit some oil lamps. It was really cozy. There was a sign outside for this special night, saying: Private Party In Progress. It should have also said, 'NO SHOWDOWNS AT THE JOHNNY WALKER SALOON', as, one was fixing to commence.

The saloon doors pushed open, and in walked Angie, toting her un-pursed six-key-swinger and twirling it to its full-spread splendor a few times. Yep, she had caught their attention. She purely did.

Ray hadn't warned Jake, as he was hoping Stoney's remark was enough to keep Angie away, that, and a good healthy fear of a confrontation with Jade. As—Jade was a lot faster on the draw and could hit her mark without even trying. Angie had to practice-up before she delivered her shots, although, one could get a nasty wound from one of her remarks—and a haunting pain. Jade's on the other had, did a good clean job of finishing-off the guilty—with the cold hard truth.

Angie approached Jake's table while all his buddies closely eyed her.

Most of the town knew about the last confrontation, as news travels fast from the SADDLE AND SEED. Not that the Bakers were gossips, but everyone hung-out there. There were all kinds of needed supplies and even fashions, along with boots and hats in the window. There were magazines and free coffee, and even small, round, tables on the side, for eating food that folks brought over from the nearby café. Why, folks could even stay and keep on visiting as one discussed which saddle one liked best, with one's friends. It was very likely that local news was going to be picked-up and sent traveling to pert-near any ranch or homestead nestled between Kalispell, Idaho, and the Canada-border.

"So Jake, it seems you finally made it into town. Or AGAIN, I should say. Seems I missed your first visit, during your *laryngitis*. I thought that just maybe that crazy bull was too much for you. I *know* it was a bull, now... no thanks to your sister."

"Now that you had your LOOK, why don't you go home to your fiancé, Angie." Matt said coldly. There was a dark heavy shadow hanging-about most-powerful, falling over his face, from his dark brown Stetson—good *showdown* material, if there ever was some.

Angie steered clear of facing him straight-on. She was on a mission.

"Well, I came to clear-up a misunderstanding... it seems I was trying to knock on the door the other day, and well... my plans fell down around me, as ol' Jake came busting-out the door." Angie held her ground just as powerful now, as she pressed-on, "I was *only* coming by to tell Jake in person that I didn't mean to *rile-up* his sister that day I showed up unannounced."

Jake sat and watched her, wishing his black Stetson has some of Matt's shadow-work going for him, wondering when her bullets were going to hit more on target, and he didn't mean as to the target-of-truth, either.

"If that's so Angie, what are you doing here, you know Jade ain't due for at least an hour," Stoney said, and then stood up hard and fast. "You need an ESCORT until then, Angie? I'm *right-good* at escorting… "

"If you try to escort me, I'll holler something awful, Stoney, and you know I will!" She set-her-chin-up and smirked just as hard and fast.

She glanced over at her brother Ray now, and then at Jake, "You going to let *Ray* try to run-me-off next for you, Jake… seems that bull must have *sapped* you an awful lot, as you need other men to stand-up and fight for your space now."

Stoney was tired of hearing about the bull. He'd *seen* enough of it, as well, and was now seeing it all too *clear* again in his mind every time that he looked at Jake—thanks to Angie and her words. He got up to leave.

"I'll be up at the bar, until Jade and Galena get here," he said, as he slid his chair back under the table really nice and quiet, and then banged it hard and heavy on the floor once it was in place. With that gesture, he left. Not *quite* as good showdown material—but good for some high marks.

With planting herself firmer, Angie stayed.

Jake was mad now—Angie had done it again and chased-off a friend. He was hoping that she'd say her piece and leave. He knew she didn't want to really face Jade and he knew she wouldn't risk staying much longer. She had never been to any of their parties, and since he had confronted her *last* year, before the birthday-bash, she never made it to that one, either. Before that, she had a crush on him in school, back when he was smitten for her, but the parties weren't a family tradition until adulthood, and Angie had not been around town much in years. That is—until the New Year's Eve party of 1998 (a year before his accident), when he happened upon her, anew. S0—she had no idea that this was a tight group here—riding hard for the same brand. It was not like *her* group of friends, which were as thin ice and cracking under pressures of adversity and appearing solid when not, as to loyalty.

Jake had hoped to avoid her, in his new condition now, quite *possibly* for the rest of his life, but he supposed that was pushing-it just a bit out of the credibility-range. Obviously it was, as here she stood, and yet again, as an unwanted visitor. He was expecting her to mock him about the bull, and she had, and he was expecting her to mock him as to his silence, but it hadn't yet come. He knew he was still in the firing-line, and by the words she was using she was pushing him to stand-up for himself, so it would soon come. Did she want a showdown, so she could fire-away at his feeble attempts to fire back? He decided he'd take the challenge and fire now, come what may. She couldn't embarrass him here—not tonight—not in *his* place. This was the best he'd get and he knew it. If he could have even a *bit* of success here, he'd hold-his-own in any *future* confrontation. At least her friends were not here to gloat with her, so that was an unexpected-plus he hadn't bargained for.

Jake now stood-up to what appeared to be "snow in July", as he was completely *shocked* by what came to pass, as he signed:

FINISHED ... *YOU-GO* -quite forcefully, with angry eyes glaring.

"Oh, now don't you try THAT with me, Jake, I'm not that *stupid*!" She raised her voice to a medium shout.

Ray got up to try and stop Angie from shouting, as he knew what was coming and chose to have pity on her. Matt stopped him though. He had received many of Angie's bullets as well and wanted to see what was going to happen next. Stoney perked-up and moseyed on over, but not too near. He didn't want her to fire at him, he knew that Jake was the perfect target here now and didn't need any saving—and most definitely it would be very *bad* timing if he was to draw her line of fire, at such a crucial time as this.

"Mute, what a HOOT! You may have fooled all the folks in town into believing that you can't talk, but I know better! I HEARD you all right! I heard you talking and arguing with your sister in the kitchen, *remember*?"

Angie walked around the room like someone bartering for a lower price, as the goods to be bought were found to be faulty. "You may be playing everyone for sympathy and making them to be part of your *game*, but not me... you should be ashamed of yourself, Jake Smith, these folks *cried* when they heard what happened to you." She gripped her keys in his face after a full hard swing—but suddenly her heart smote:

She stopped for a pause, as she realized that no one had even cared to TELL her in the *first* place, so she had to learn it all in the *second* place— mostly from third-person situations, at that—after hanging-out at all four-corners of town, while being a fifth wheel. Seems she had no sixth-sense on the matter. Unable to roll lucky sevens, she was behind her own eight ball.

"Well... so I *heard*." She added softly, as she checked her fingernails, one at a time, and looked up to a sea of faces.

The whole place was watching now, and she knew it, even Jake was letting her have her way with him. Yep, he was mighty curious to hear why he'd pull a *stunt* like that. After all he'd been through, why he would *need* any more sympathy than he had already come to receive, was a mystery to him.

"You just want to win people over to *your* side. So then, when you can *finally* show them how you remembered how to talk again, no one will blame you and Jade for being the cause of Lyle's *bull* being killed, is all… because they will have felt *sooooo* very sorry for you!"

With that remark, Jake put a halt to her. Without thinking, he voiced out, "~~AAWP! ~~AAWP!", as he slammed his hand on the table, and then hit his hand signing, *stop-stop* -and repeating the phrase over again, once more to go with each voiced, "stop". He walked-over in defiance, facing her now, and his buddies began to stand up in sync—though not sure why yet— they still moved to do so.

Angie stood there facing three tall cowboys looking down at her—but she continued:

"I know all about his bull now… I talked to Lyle just the other day, over near the bank. So now, what have you got to say to that… beside all your moaning and groaning and hand threats?"

Jake stared at her really hard as the silence settled over the room as a thick fog. It was thick all right, but not thick enough to keep truth from shining through. Not only did she rip-up his heart before him, as to his own personal dilemma, along with the anguish he went through to try and explain it to others, along with *incorporating* into *this*, his credibility with the whole *town*—but—she even *sided* with Lyle. Lying-Lyle was the same as a murderer now, in Jake's book, and this had all gone too far.

'Angie, you're gonna' wish you never walked in here, and that's a FACT,' Jake readied himself, *'and I ain't settin' you up… and I never did before, either… you just seem to do it to yourself.'*

Jake voiced, "~Hey~," and signed, *light* -repeatedly so, and thumbed-back over his shoulder, pointing to Johnny.

Ray yelled over, "Turn the lights back up, Johnny!"

"Oh, you don't need to give me any lights for what *I'm* looking at now," the fondling of her keys played with her, "I can recognize a has-been cowboy trying to milk a dead bull, when I see one…"

Angie swung her keys with a smile, "And… if you need the lights to show me the door, well, I *know* my way." She started to go, as his buddies blocked her way, "Oh, get OUT of my way, I'm *finished* here now!"

'Yeah… I reckon you are…' came Jake's mute check-mate.

Jake reached over for her upper arm; she turned to him and stared into his eyes. A flood of memories came-and-went in an instant, and she viciously fired-out her last bullet:

"What are you going to say, Jake, that it's all a *lie*, huh? How long do you plan to keep this up, before your BRAIN INJURY suddenly gets better and you remember how to *speak* again?"

Jake took his hands and pulled his mouth open as far and wide as he could, and gave her a good long look, as everyone else watched and waited.

Angie stared hard and as her breath drew in deep. She swallowed in a half-choke, and it was followed by a low gasp as she stood in shock. Her keys hit the floor loudly, as Jake hit his mark, in silence.

Ray softly added, "It was a tape recording of *my* voice that you heard at Jake's house, Angie." He reached down and retrieved her keys and humbly placed them in her small elegant shoulder purse.

She stepped back slowly, shocked and looked around at all the eyes on her, and then ran out the door, setting the doors to flap hard.

She near knocked Jade over on the front boardwalk and sent her spinning, as Jade nearly fell through the still-swinging doors, but caught herself. Looking up, Jade now found herself staring at a room full of silence so thick, she could have sworn she just fell into a butter-churn that just crossed the finish-line. Who the heavy-handed maker was, or the rich occasion, she could only guess—as:

No one was laughing or smirking at Angie, everyone was just dad-gummed quiet. Gummed-up with what had just stuck in their minds, one would reckon. Somehow, what Jake had just done, brought his muteness into a high-gear of reality, and crashed it down really hard into their spirits. This wasn't just some casual thing that Jake was trying to work though, on his way to some kind of personal success, on a few "off" days. This was a full-time hardship, and he had not only suffered through the pain of it as in trying to live with it now, but he had suffered pain when the damage had actually befallen him. Here he was now, in their midst, looking just as happy as could be, having a birthday party, as it nothing ever happened to him. But he had a physical witness, one that stated differently, one that could not be denied. He himself would constantly be aware of it, even though they may not, or *had* not. It was hidden inside, just as any hurts he felt because of it, whether they had been physical or emotional. However, hidden un-ableness, can yet, a hero, make, as he fought to face each day, in ways they could not fully fathom. They all knew in a deeper way now, that he was not the same Jake, even though—he was.

Jade walked in as everyone started to sit down. Galena followed now, as she had offered to park the car.

"Well, now, you all… I see the death of the party just left, now the *life* of the party's just arrived, so let's have at it! Get that music on, Johnny Walker, I'm aiming to turn you into Johnny Dancer, and then set you sailing-off to hoof-it with Olivia! Forget the country music for a few hours or so, I want some fancy drumbeats… some good ol' rock and roll! Once I hit the dance floor and them drums start… you'll be hard-pressed to tell us apart." She meant it too; she had her *own* keys to play with, and they were hanging on her belt loops, set to jingle, and raring to go!

'*Aww, twin gal, we sure need you hootin' and hollerin' right about now… this is another of those shooting-at-the-target, and bull's-eye-hitting that you do so well.*' Jake gathered her up and gave her a huge hug with a twirl.

As the music warmed up, Jade and Galena sat down right-fast, before any dancing and cake or gift celebrating was to be done, her curiosity just had to be settled first about Angie. She had barely gotten filled in, when Angie appeared at the saloon doors, much to everyone's surprise.

The showdown was over—quite plain, it was.

Johnny turned the jukebox down, as the last creaks of the doors faded, and everyone gave her their attention.

Angie came to Jake's table and addressed Ray, Jake, and Jade, as his buddies watched, "Obviously, there must be something greatly *wrong* with me… seeing that you three thought you had to play a trick like that on me. I know I had no business poking my nose where it didn't belong, so I suppose that proves it even more so. Well, I'm not in here to turn the other cheek or change my spots, or what EVER… that only happens in the movies, not in real life, so you better get used to it. I don't know *why* I do what I do, and I don't know how come you *always* can see right through me… but you were *right* to avoid me, because if I had seen right-up that you couldn't talk… I sure would have had a field day, and that's for DAMN sure."

She pushed her black hair out of her face, her loose-layered shoulder-length flip had lost its bounce and was beyond her control, her keys were firmly gripped in her hand—truly humbled, playtime was gone.

"I would have called you a dummy," with an ever-so-slight hesitation, Angie continued "just like that ol' dummy in the Bakers' window, with that nice black Stetson, setting on his head so fine. Yeah… and I would have zeroed-in and told you how your big damn mouth matches your head… it's got *nothing* in it. I would have had my friends enjoying it all too, while I made sport of you," her voice quivered unexpectedly, "yeah, you-all are so right about Angie… she sure has slipped-her-gears when it comes to hometown-proper… well… I just can't change, not now anyway."

She turned to go and looked up to see Alex at the door. She started towards him, but he shooed her back to Jake. He suspected she wasn't finished and wanted her to have her full say. One a mite harder to lay out, it was, but she knew it was owed. She went back and faced Jake:

"What happened to you, Jake, looks mighty awful and it surely doesn't look like fun, and I know getting stomped-on by that bull, had you on your death-bed... but hey... you rolled-off it right-fine. I just want to say... I've been trying to find a way to make a fool of you since the SADDLE AND SEED episode... among one other, as you well *know*. I'd just thought I found a way... but I was wrong... if I had known all this earlier and mocked you, I would have been *twice* as wrong still. With a guy like you Jake, there ain't no way to make a fool of you... but like I said... I don't feel like apologizing... least not until I find what's wrong with me." With that, feeling a mite like a wrung-sponge, ripped near to center, Angie left with Alex. He was the next step she needed in her life, but she had stalled as to taking this next step sincerely. Now she was ready too.

She was hard-core, to the core, and needed some peeling to humble her. It would take quite some time to get through, though, and down to that hard-core heart of hers, but underneath, deep inside, she would some day be surprised that the seeds of new life had been there—just waiting.

CHAPTER EIGHTEEN

TALK AIN'T CHEAP... BUT IT SURE IS SWEET

IT was now July 31st, the last of the three days of celebration. Jade had her day of celebrating with God in the great outdoors on the 29th, Jake's buddies had their way in playing the heroes and keeping the twin's true birthday and family-tradition alive, and now Jake was going to have *his* turn to add to the celebrating. This day would be private. Family and closest friends only, complete with his special gift for Jade, but not the one he bought in town, which had cost him a quite a shiny coin. No, this gift was to top-off the other one, this was the kind of gift that cost him much, much more—the kind of gift that was paid by sheer human spirit.

It was just after the noon hour when folks started to arrive. First the Bakers came, with Lenny and Sara, and then Ray showed up, and then of course there was Matt, Stoney, Galena and Jade. Only simple sandwiches were planned and a picnic on the front porch—their favorite catchall-place. As the day progressed and followed the sun in its passing, it was near-about four o'clock when they went in to share the special family gifts.

~*~

The Bakers had something very special in mind, as they often listened to some of Jade's woes when she came into town. It seemed Jade was near about to go nuts, because Jake was constantly asking her what time it was. No matter where-or-when he got the notion to want to know the time, he'd do his hound-dog hunt (as he had first done during the first weeks home, when he was too tired to do all his previous work) and he'd find Jade. Jade was often times awakened at odd hours of the night, by taps on her shoulder and snapping fingers, and a lot of earnest coaxing. He still had the general idea how long intervals were, but he couldn't retain the numbered time for long, in his brain. And—being the earnest boss-man that he was, he was just used to knowing the time whenever he chose to, and she was now his only option—seems this option didn't take-to-well to his demands, though. Clocks and watches don't talk back, but this *new* way of telling time had some serious drawbacks, as, Jade could be mighty feisty at times. During the day, she become exasperated and would send him off with her favorite catch-phrase ringing in his ears:

"Jet, I don't know... the clock BROKE!" adding, "go make yourself a sundial! Go make some kind of code of your own! Just DO it... and just GET USED TO IT!"

Jake had his own favorite throw-back-phrase—well, for the nighttime hours, at least. If she tried to protest because he was bothering her, the tables were cleverly turned: *no-sun* ... sun-broke!* -

However, in his early days, he would just voice, "~unh-unh~" and point towards to the darkened window of the night hours, out there across from her sofa bed, towards the backyard. Now he was able to add to his communication ways, and would voice with her formed "n" and "s" in front of his mouth, for each respected word, *n*/ "~~oh~" ... *s*/ "~**unn**~", and then slammed-it-on-home, signing, *no-sun!* -while afterwards happily smirking at her, sure to get the elusive time. He'd usually get chased away by a large pillow flung at his face, instead—until he became a more highly-skilled agile dodger.

~*~

Now as to the special gifts, Jade was overjoyed to find a "bird clock" when she opened the first gift; it was given to both Jade and Jake. Understanding immediately, she explained to Jake that all he had to do was remember the song of the bird for each hour and he'd do just fine, she would *teach* him. Simple as reacting to nature, she reckoned—along with some kind of nifty story-line to help.

Everyone was learning that numbers never registered correctly in Jake's reading and writing, but he could still count. His figuring with math was all gone though, and most, but not all of the retaining-number-skills had come to a halt. He understood what hour of the day it was once he was told, but trying to read the clock was just too confusing. She would make sure to set up some kind of teaching system, to match the bird's voices, as well as their pictures, to certain times of the day—he did well with pictures, shapes and images, used as teaching tools to guide his brain onto new paths—repetitive stories would drive it home.

Well, one can imagine the fun now, as the next gift from the buddies, turned out to be cuckoo clock. The guys had their *own* time-telling trials with Jake, and were ready to go a bit cuckoo, same as Jade. They decided this would be best for Jake's room, so he could count the sounds of the cuckoos, in the middle of the night and not have to count on his twin-cuckoo to do the chirping.

Lenny had slipped outside for a bit, during the clock-testing, so there was a hold on the gift giving. Jade got out the dishes and the cake and got it ready for yet another round of candles, but before she could light it, they were interrupted by the honking of a horn out in the driveway. All of them ended-up on the porch looking at Lenny and his gift for Jake. Jake's truck— wearing a new suit.

Jake moved in for a closer look and he signed,
interesting ... *very-interesting* - '*It looks like it's been mighty sick, there Lenny... why, it's all full-up of white bandages. Bandages full of branding iron symbols... and colors, so it seems. What's all this mean now?*'

Jake, with a questioning face, signed, *what's-up?* ... *truck-sick?* -as he voiced, "~Huh~?" not quite sure why his truck needed to stand-out in this way.

Jake folded his right arm up, and rested his left elbow on it, as he rested his chin in his left hand and studied this right-nice, left-side fender-dented truck, left for all to see in the driveway. It left him rightly impressed, from its right side to its left. Thus, as his mind was left to wonder, he knew it would be all right—left as it was—in some *odd* sort of way.

Lenny was starting to wonder if Jake understood what the point was. Was Jake worried about the truck's old paint job, now plastered with new stuck-on clothes? No, Jake wasn't offended in the least, it was done in a very tasteful way and he liked the colorful pictures. He still didn't get the point though, until he moved closer. He was just now starting to recognize the birds on these bumper-sticker "bandages" when Jade moved closer and started to laugh. She grabbed hold of his shoulders from behind, defying her shortness, and shook him.

Ol' Jade was having a hoot, laughing now, as she pushed him closer, "Jet, they're bumper-stickers from the BIRD&CRITTER VOLUNTEER RESCUE center!"

"That's right, Jake. You can transport birds now, and not be afraid of being arrested anymore. You just have to point to the bumper sticker and it has the phone number and your name on it as well. And not only that, but inside I have three copies of your permit and I taped them on in plain view, so any law officer will be sure to see them."

Lenny walked up and gave him an envelope, that Jake proceeded to open. In it was a card that Lenny enclosed in clear plastic, with bright red edges. Jake's puzzled look naturally got him answers.

"It's an emergency card, Jake, it states that you can't talk and you're prone to seizures. If you have this and you are ever stopped, or if you were to be arrested for something else, then the officers are NOT allowed handcuffing your hands behind your back. Now, we are NOT expecting any more arrest, RIGHT COWBOY?" he laughed. "Really though, this is serious stuff Jake, that's why I covered it with this seal, you'll know what this is by the red edges, you don't have to read it. This is protection for you, and on the other side, it has all the phone numbers of every one of us here, in case they're ever needed. There's a second copy... if you want to hang it around your neck as a dog tag, go right ahead! Happy birthday, Jake, you're free to fly now," he rubbed Jake's shoulder, "we're kicking you out of the nest. YOU'RE OWN YOUR OWN... whenever you feel like it."

Jake reached out and shook Lenny's hand and the look in his eyes to this dear buddy, said it all. Jake's mind flashed back to the day that he was arrested. He had never felt so dishonored in his whole life, even trapped in boarding school could not come near the humiliation he felt when the handcuffs snapped shut, as he lay in the dirt, by force. The processing and the jail cell itself had further devastated his spirit. Sitting there stuck, and alone. He'd never forget that experience. But the seizures, those he *did* forget, except for lots of voices that just didn't make sense when he'd begin to awake, and bits and pieces of where he thought he may have been, just before one had hit.

Freedom didn't last long, it appeared, as Jade jumped in with news for Lenny, pushing his good intentions into a full-time parking lot:

"Oh, no! No, he ain't on his own yet," Jade had just interrupted Jake's innocent thoughts of soon-coming plans for his truck. "I still don't trust this seizure-bit that hangs over him like a thunder cloud." Jade said.

"Well, that's true," Lenny turned quiet and serious, "I don't know his *full* medical history, so these precautions may just go unused now... I don't know if he's allowed to drive. We need to see what his doctors say, and then we need it to match-up to what the law says... what have they told you, Jade?" Lenny asked, knowing that situations can very, depending on a variety of things.

"We have a waiting period to go through, or maybe even medication, first." She smiled with relief, "Looks like I took the reins out of your hand, huh, cowboy?" She smiled again, as she shook her finger at him as if to scold him, same as he always loved to do to her.

Jake grabbed the tip of her Stetson, and pulled it down over her face and she gave his a tap and sent it upwards, and took-off running to the kitchen as the gang on the porch moved over to let her barge on through.

Jake gestured, '*after you*' to Lenny, and they followed her trail in, for the next round of gifts.

They sat around the table and Jade gave her gift to her brother—after trying for an unsuccessful stall. She wanted *hers* first, typical as a horse just wanting to dig into the finer points of free-open-pasture, but Jake said he was the boss on *this* birthday, so *she* had to wait.

He opened it up and ran his fingers over a finely carved leather belt, decorated with his name in ASL letters—his first *and* last name, both. On each side of it was carved horses to represent each of his "babies". Since Jake could only make his name out phonetically (by using Jade's formed shapes to pick-out the sounds of his thoughts—learned from key body areas) she had it spelled-out in a way that he could understand. First she had the "j", and then the "a" (but the "a" was twisted a bit to the side, for the long "a" sound, as in "ache" from her "heart ache" symbol) and then the "k"—all being stained *black* on a medium brown belt. Then she had the "e" of his name there, but it was the same color as the belt and not very noticeable. (This was to avoid confusion since he could not hear the silent "e", but it was still being presented lightly—so not to confuse others as to how Jake's name was really spelled). The "Smith" was done in dark letters, and if he took it *slow*, Jake could sound it out okay, thanks to Jade's invented symbol for "th". She had Jake's friend Vin re-invent that symbol, as best he could to make a smooth blend of the "t" with the "h" for the flat belt surface, hoping that Jake might recognize it still.

Jake at first was touched by this gift because of the horses, as the "branding iron" symbols at first hadn't registered with him as being his own name. Jade really wasn't sure if they would, but she had it done just the same—and now watched with intense *alert* eyes. Jake gave her a long thoughtful hug, realizing something was up with his twin, and continued to look at it, seeking for clues—and getting his mind past the horses. It reminded him of something, as he scanned the ASL letters. He felt peace, as it wasn't blocked in his mind, something was flowing fresh here. It was beautiful high quality work, yes, and he recognized Vin's work, and with staunch admiration, but he was recognizing something else. He ran his fingers over it—the shapes looked like hands from the signing book, he knew that now. But theses hand shapes, in such a succession, he had seen before by someone's hand. It dawned on him, that he knew the twisted "a", and the "k"— and then next it dawned on him, that he knew the "s" and the "m" and then even the "i".

'*Hey, I get it now... hey...* ' Jake laughed, as if he was a kid that just solved a riddle. '*I know this Jade, ~s~m~i~th~, Smith. And... ~a~k~ ... that first letter must be the ~j~.'* He traced it with the hand he used for the "j" on his knuckle joint, as he sounded it out, and sure enough it matched. *'Jake Smith'*, he thought, *'why that's my name!' I know my name, Jade!'* Jake turned and looked at her as his eyes teared-up, *'I know it... I know it! I know my name! I know somethin', Jade! I read it!'*

His body started to heave slightly as he was overcome with emotion. Everyone was watching calmly until then, and all began to chip-in with, "Happy birthday!" each in turn, fighting-off the avalanche of emotions sliding in from all sides. Jade went near to her brother and took her twin into her arms as she slid her hand under his arm socket and held him tight.

"Happy birthday, Jet", she whispered. She held tight and wouldn't let go.

'Thank you Jade, thank you.' "~Ay~k' ~oo~," Jake voiced. His thoughts continued as he pried her off of him, to share his joy, as he met her eyes. *'Thank you for your crazy silly system, and thanks for your guts-and-glory and no holds barred, when it comes to wrestling your ol' twin down, when he's a mite stubborn.'* Jake wiped his face with his sleeve, and signed, *she-wonderful* -and shook his head yes, in awe of her.

"Well, now we're ready for some cake and candles, right," Stoney jumped up, fixing to use his lighter, but he saw Jade glaring at him, spur-gal style. "Oops..." he said, as he sat back down with a smile.

"Oops is right, in-door glowworm, it ain't time to spark, until I sparkle with MY present!" and she turned to face Jake again, ready to sparkle to beat-the-stars, "and you sure as hot-coals-keeps-a-fire-warm, better *have* one for me, Mr. Smith!"

'You got your present, remember... when you sent me into town, with a push and a shove, and a "shewww!"' Jake, signed, *you-have-present* ... *finished* ... *remember?* -He made a questioned look at her, and signed, *you-make-me-go-town-yesterday* ... *present-finished* -Jake smirked at her, and added a fancy drawn-out gestured *shewww!* -as he waited to see what she would do.

"Well... that don't count now Jet! So... I want another." She threw one of her braids back, and pouted as she ground her boot heel into the floor, soft and gentle, "Aw, you're just messing with me, right Jet? Come on where is it?" She batted her false eye-lashes at his coyly.

'You're just too dang smart for me, sis!' Jake took her hand and made her sit at the end of the table, in HIS chair.

He motioned to everyone to be quiet. Which sure wasn't needed, as they were all curious, and all lips were sealed. Jake had left the little gift box for her on the table, near the flowers that he had picked for her earlier that morning. The gang could see it all this time, but she couldn't, and if THIS wasn't the gift yet, then… WHAT WAS?

Jake got up for just a few minutes as they waited in suspense. He needed a bit of water, and a lot of courage. Jake bee-lined for the sink, and after about five minutes he came back, shyly, and sat down by her side.

As Jade sat there, she watched her twin go through a variety of head motions and jaw and lip motions (with limits from left-mouth damage making it even *harder* for this chore), all the while, using the sounds of his throat and some from his nasal work, as he spoke forth the fruit of a very hard labor:

"~Hoow~' … ~wuh' … ~whI~ … ~wh~ayr' … ~wh~en~~' … ~how~" He also signed the words as he voiced them. *who* … *what* … *why* … *where* … *when* … *how* -

Jake had a hard-enough time trying to say long "I", but he had a *terrible* time with this *last* part of his gift, soon to come—but he tried hard for Jade. He just couldn't get the long "ee" sound, and in the future he would for the most-part just avoid it as it sounded so strange, but he wanted to include his friends in some way, here, in his speech. He thus voiced another surprise:

"~Hee~" was voiced as Jake pointed at Matt. He then forced breath from deep down inside and out through his teeth, "~Sh~ee~" was voiced the best he could, as he pointed at Galena. "~Iih'~'" was voiced for the word "it" as he pointed at a few objects while he said the word, signing, *it* -He then pointed to the picture of their parents on the wall, "~Pa~" and "~ma~" were voiced by shaping and reshaping his lips, then with a catch in his throat he lastly voiced, "~'k~um~" and motioned for her to come near for a hug, as he voiced, "~~h~~uhk'~", and motioned to hug her.

Jake looked at her, with a look of hoped acceptance on his face, waiting for a smile of approval and joy, but was shocked instead. She was crying as she fell into his arms and wept softly—Spur-gal was falling apart. Jake carefully motioned for the little box. He had just the right touch of magic—his own special medicine. After a few minutes, Jake touched the side of her cheek and jaw, and lifted her face, as he smiled at her. He wiped her face with the best thing a cowboy can find, his shirtsleeve, and this time used it for *her* face, not his. He gave her the box and motioned for all the gang to come near.

Quite, and simple, it worked, as Jade's curiosity was now peaked, "Why, I've just got the best birthday gift in the world, what *else* could I possibly get today?"

She loosened the wrapping paper from little box and after carefully opening it, she took off the top, there was a tiny bit of soft cotton hiding it. She nudged it with her index finger and there was a lovely smooth, white, flat-circled piece of shell, with a thin chain of gold hooked into it. On the shell, engraved in gold, was the ASL "I-L-Y", as it is blended into the sign of "I love you", *i/l/y* -

Jake looked at his twin with admiration and longed to tell her what he felt. *'Matt, he found this sign one night, in the book, out on the porch. I wish I could tell you sis, I wish I could talk to you. We were visitin' and it was just after the moon rose up for the night... like a large white shiny piece of shell... That moon was lighting-up the whole yard... shinin' just the way you love to see it,'* Jake wiped the loose hair back out of her face, *'Matt showed the I~L~Y~ to me and told me what it meant... I knew it was for you.'*

As he looked at her and watched her, his mind *now* took him back yet again, to the remembrance of that first morning home. That morning when he had dropped his boots down and gone to pour his coffee, he had glanced over and seen her sitting at this very table—crying.

I-tell-you-story-later ... *about-how-I-learned-this-sign* ... *o.k.?* -Jake signed to her.

O.k. -Jade signed back, with a smile, and held up her "I-L-Y" hand—as love held-up her heart.

She straightened herself up, with humble country-gal dignity, and stood up to prepare to light the cake.

Stoney stood up and did it for her, and then added, "Well, Jake, I guess it's a good thing you can't talk, *today*, huh? You may have sung well-enough in the past, doing karaoke and cowboy ballads with us, but you SURE AS HECK couldn't sing happy birthday worth a plugged-nickel, and that's a FACT!"

Jake tossed his head back and laughed so hard with Stoney, they near cried, while the others joined it—seems they had some mighty powerful witnesses to back it all up, and right here in this very room!

After a round of happy birthday, and the finished candles, Jake and Jade put their hands on the knife and cut the cake, and got some pictures taken for memories of a newer kind. And—as they smiled at each other with

far-reaching rest, of a day well-done, only the good Lord heard their
thoughts in unison:

Talk ain't cheap... but it sure is sweet.

And only the good Lord above knew how rough-and-rugged the road
had been to this point, and only the good Lord above knew the joys this
same road would bring them through, in the years to come. Years that were
given back to Jake, as he laid his life down for his fellow friend.

It was late in the evening now, and all company had left for home, or
turned in, on the home-front, except for *one* person. Jade. She was near
ready to fall asleep on her sofa-of-guard-duty, when she heard the
undiscernible sounds from her twin, stir her heart. Jake was moaning in his
sleep, although his vocal cords were not as strong as before, the sound still
carried in the stillness of the night. He never slept with his door fully shut,
and as she neared the door and listened, he continued to stop and start with
the noises. It was as if he was talking in his sleep. She went in to him and
was ready to wake him, when she noticed he was smiling. Truly he was, and
most sweet, at that.

'It's a good dream, it is then, Jet?' She thought, *'This time, it's MY
turn to talk to you with thoughts deeply hidden... thoughts from deep within
me. You're not to hear or know what I would say to you now... but there's
no point or need, as you're asleep, I know. But, Jet... dear twin... now I feel
a bit like you must feel... to have no speech...'*

She reached over pulled his covers a bit higher over his chest and
kissed his forehead, *'I remember that horrible look on your face, Jet, when
you realized what the doctor was telling you. I had never seen a more
forlorn, forsaken, look in all my life. Then when you became so desperate
for me to help you, for me to do something, anything... it broke my heart.
But I had to be strong for you Jet... then you lay there day-after-day, trying
to escape the truth... and your thoughts that were trapped within you... but
you couldn't. The room felt was so awkward... we were helping you learn to
eat and all... yet... yet we were near about afraid to talk anymore
ourselves... but we HAD to... we had to coax you to soon face going home!
It was a time when you should have had joy... joy just to be ALIVE! Oh,
dearest Jet! The good Lord is still holding our hands, and here we are...
home! And we're on the road to having joy again, Jet. The trail may be
slow... and it may throw a bit more dust and rocks our way, but the worst is
over now. Some day we'll look back on all this and it will feel like an old
familiar pair of boots. Not a worthless pair, to be discarded, but a pair
that's well broken-in and right-fine for walking the trails up around the
bend!'*

Jade watched him and listened to his noises, noises that he was so ashamed of—but not *now*. Now, unknown to Jade, Jake was dreaming—and *talking*:

~*~

"Hey Matt, look a this mare!" Jake nudged his black Stetson back just a bit, and yelled over his shoulder, half-perching and half-leaning over the top rung. The day was warm, full of cloud-play, and glorious. He was full of excitement as he was watching Stoney ride her, "Ain't she a BEAUTY!"

Matt set his tools down and started making his way near.

Jake then turned around to face Matt as he came closer, "Stoney rides her real fine, don't he, Matt? She's my new 'baby', Matt... Stoney went with me to *pick her up* and I rightly *promised* him the first ride!" Jake spouted-out with a grin full of fun, adjusting his Stetson back even farther on his head and soaked in the full picture—being just as happy as any grown cowboy that felt like a kid could.

He looked around for his twin sis's whereabouts, and then he spied her clear-up near the house:

"Hey you! HEY TWIN-GAL!" Jake yelled, "you *ain't* seen my horse yet... now get-on over here, or Matt's gonna' get the second ride!" He took-in one more view of his wonderful horse, and turned to find that Jade had taken a seat on the porch, of all things, "Aww, come on now, I ain't jokin' none, Jade... we ain't got all day!"

He looked over and she was combing out her long braids, feigning disinterest, so Jake jumped-off from his half-perch on the middle rung of the fence now, and yelled over to her, "All right, twin-gal, I'm coming to get you!" He pulled his Stetson back into place and then called over to Matt and Stoney, "Hey guys, I'll be right back, that twin of mine, she just likes to play the *boss-man* sometimes. But I ain't gonna' let her today, as I got me a new horse!"

Jade took-off running fast for the northwest and north ridge area that led to Jake's woods, laughing for to scare-a-flock-of-Texas-gulf-birds, if there were any to be found—with Jake *hot* on her *heels*.

~*~

Jake tossed and turned a bit more and then was soon quiet—his dream a contented success. Jade left the now silent room, just as *silent* as she had come—full of silent love.

CHAPTER NINETEEN

DOGGING A DEAD BULL

IT was the early morning of a fresh new August, just after dawn, and Jade sat on the porch drinking coffee—she was wrapped in nice fine blanket, waiting for the fast-rising sun (as *she* so-reckoned it) to fully do the chore. She saw the familiar dust-pocket on the old road as Sheriff Lenny's car reached the gate. He stopped and let his car through, and drove on up slowly, and parked next to Jake's truck. Jade waved at him, and poured him some coffee as well. She stretched out her bare feet to reach a spot of sun, farther out on the porch. They always put their cowboy hats on when they came outside, and usually forgot to take them off inside (at least for awhile), but this morning Jade left hers inside on the wall-hook, as she was only half-dressed to meet the day, being in a pajama shirt and her jeans.

"So you made it after all, just as you said!" she welcomed him.

"Yeah, had things to set in order first, and Mike and Sofia can keep it all in line now, until I get back." He walked up and around the wooden split-rail fence that framed the yard in front of the porch. There was no gate there; it was just a fence lining the driveway and encircling some of the front yard, and reaching out then to join-up to the side—and the side joined to the back areas, of the very large ranch house. This was one of the reasons that the cows and horses always sauntered-up to the front porch—it appeared it was one of their favorite places, also.

Lenny went on to say, "I had to find out what Lyle was up to, and I did. I just found out that there is no way it will prosper either, so don't get upset about it, okay, Jade? There is a *key* piece missing and he's soon to learn of it too. When he does, I'm sure he'll be out of here, the very next morning, if not the middle of the night. We've got people that are *looking* for him... we haven't spotted him yet, though. Don't know if he knows he's in trouble with Libby's local law or not, and laying-low ... or maybe he's up to more no-good somewhere else, trying to add to his schemes." After getting his mission, so to speak, out of his system, and a few gulps of coffee into it, Lenny made himself more comfortable, leaning against a wooden post of the porch, as was his habit—and, even more-so, when a good office *desk* was not to found.

Jade sipped coffee, and watched with trust, ready to take each word of his, deep into account.

"A friend of mine named Walter, he runs the bank in New-Town... he over-hears a lot going on from the New-Towner-crowd at their favorite bar and grill, the GRILL&FILL... you've seen it. He always shares things with me just to pass-time after work... we both show-up to visit there... we kind of do a town-swap of info. He was telling me all about the new information he heard from Lyle, about the bull accident... as back when it happened, it was big news all through both sectors of town. Walter had already learned from me four months ago, how I knew all the people involved in it, so he had some interesting stuff to fill me in on. Needed info, at that Jade, as he was concerned about you killing Lyle's bull. He was really afraid for you, he heard Lyle was going to SUE you and Jake for damages. He plans to take you down, for all the ranch is worth."

Jade choked a bit of coffee back, suddenly feeling a bit sick, and sat up more, but let him go on.

"The story goes... Lyle claimed he brought his bull over to Jake, with Jake's full permission and acceptance, as it was a gift for you. Then Lyle claims that Jake wouldn't give it back to him when he decided to *cancel* any and all marriage proposals to you. When he saw how dangerous a 'brother-in-law' Jake was starting to be, he wanted no more of any of you. Lyle also claimed that he was trying to come in with the truck and pick it up, but Jake and Stoney chased him off, saying he couldn't take back his gift. He said Stoney then set his eyes on it... bribed his wranglers with fresh cash so they would help him get up and ride the bull that very day... all for a way to prove he was worth being sponsored... he was trying to hurry before the heavier snow set in. Then Stoney would have a chance to make a big win in the rodeo show coming up, and *plus* make a good name for himself. In the past those wranglers have helped sponsor lots of great riders, but since they hooked-up with Lyle, they've been looking-out after *his* interest instead. They said Stoney even promised them big bucks, saying he could win on a bull like that, and that he even said, if he *didn't* win, he'd pay them up-front anyhow. Now THAT sure doesn't sound like the Stoney that we know, right? He never plans for the long haul, he just hauls-out for the adventure he sees on hand... and he *sure* wouldn't promise money, as he has none to spare."

Jade put her coffee aside and pulled the blanket closer, "I was there when Lyle brought that bull over, Lenny… and he said it was for me and he was presenting it as a pre-wedding gift to our ranch. Well… since he would be living in my half of the house after our marriage, he said he'd be able to take care of the bull for us, in any and all ways. He wanted to offer us something of value, as a gift… it was a great breeder… had papers as well." She stared across the yard at the horse. "I TOLD him, Jet would never take to having a bull of that type around… not with his babies, and all. I wanted to find Jet then, but Lyle promised he'd have it boarded instead… but first he said that the MAIN reason he brought it by, was that he promised Stoney a ride on it, and this might be his only chance, before he took it off to some rancher." Her eyes fell, "Lyle told me that Stoney's buddy had been on it and had passed the word that it was a great challenge, and quite a ride. He said if Stoney could do good on it, he'd sponsor him DOUBLE for the up-coming rodeo, for that bull-riding event Stoney was hoping for. Since near all the money was for charity, riders could even pick their own bulls… but Stoney couldn't find a sponsor with money."

Jade sadly thought back to that day. Stoney had been so excited, and the wranglers had appeared so sincere. Yet, she never could figure why Lyle had took-off down the road as Stoney fixed to ride—supposedly to turn the truck around, but yet took forever to come back. He didn't come back until after the shooting of the bull—when she *herself,* ran him off.

"Well," Lenny went on to say, "he was saying how he had his brother from California out here, and he was in the truck that day and was a *witness*. His brother was seen in town recently, and as far as I was able to hear, he's going along with the story. Then of recent, Lyle and his son tried to set Jake up with that car window incident, to prove Jake was a vindictive bitter man if anyone ever crossed him… bent on the worse kind of revenge and all the etcs. That incident that I told you about yesterday, remember?" he eyed her painfully, "they are prepared to lie in court, and have some really fancy lawyer take the case, as well… he even disowned his son, to keep his own name clean from that failed attempt… he'd swear how Hunter was just a confused kid, mad about his dog, and who knows WHAT."

Poor ol' Spur-gal was meek and humbled as she soaked all this in, seemed she'd have rather filled-up on morning coffee—but this dose was due to come and she accepted it:

"Then it would be *our* word against, against his, and we had no witnesses, and *supposedly* he did. But his brother WASN'T in that truck, Lenny… he PURELY WAS NOT! It was just Lyle and his two wranglers out here. Not Matt or Galena… or Jet…"

She thought back to that day's *aftermath*, and how she was wondering where Jake was. Usually he was paying attention and always up on things when someone was coming-up the drive, but not that day: *He must have been busy in the barn... that's where he had come from, but busy with what though? I found out from the doctors later that his blood, what little he had left of it, had a high alcohol content. What the heck was he doing in the barn? He must have been drinking... he came out with a bottle of whiskey and it was half empty, I know 'cause I found it later in the yard... he must have thrown it down when he started running. Why on EARTH was he drinking? The last time Jet ever drank like that was when Pa died.'*

~*~

Jade didn't know her twin was drinking because he had to tell her about Lyle, and had missed *every* opportunity in the past, and was then getting ready to finally face her. Jade and Stoney had been down in the basement at the time. Jade was working, packing boxes to send out, and Stoney was helping her since some were very heavy. Jake had run Lyle off then and was still disgusted with him. He never expected Lyle would dare to come back. Lyle was *trespassing* the second time he came back. Jake had never *yet* revealed this to anyone, as thus far, he had never talked about the accident with anyone in detail. All Jake knew was the bits and pieces he had gleaned so far, from talk he had heard them participate in, and from what each one of his friends had shared with him, at different times. Even if Jade knew that Lyle was trespassing, there would have been no proof or witnesses to that, so Jake was now holding on to this information as a grumpy dog would with an old bone he's been gnawing on. In this case though, the bone was doing more harm than good to Jake, by his dwelling on each hard gnaw of it.

~*~

Lenny went on hitting Jade with more facts, and moving from post to post, with a small amount of pacing, at times, "Well, unknown to Lyle, his son Hunter ran into me near the bank, just when I was heading over to wait for Walter at the GRILL&FILL. He told me he'd come over and swear in writing how he was manipulated to lie against Jake, and he'd take his witness of that, to court. He said he had been hearing how his father was now getting reading to take Jake to court soon. If Lyle did, when the time came, Hunter said he'd testify against his father and even witness that he knew his uncle was *still* in California at the time. Hunter even filed some paperwork this morning, too, Jade... one of the *very* things I had to *do* early this morning. He has proof of his uncle's whereabouts from his mother, but

Lyle didn't know that. Seems the mother didn't know what was going-down, but now that she does, she will stand up and back-up her son. This woman is a highly respected legal secretary in Los Altos. She divorced Lyle, because he was stealing from their joint account, and had claimed it was for land repair bills, for the homes and property they owned." Lenny whistled that ol' *country signal*, concerning things mighty hard to fathom and continued, "She found-out he was setting-up his own bank account, and that he also lost his past ones all by playing the stock market and race horses. They've had nothing to do with each other since he moved out here to be near his aging parents. It's a damn shame for his parents too, as they are well-respected people over in Libby and they don't need him trying to ruin their lives now. Why, you and Jake, and Ray, have known them for a long time now... you know what good folks they are!"

"Oh my Lord," Jade was shocked. "Why, he's been *flawed* since way before I met him. I never knew... I never saw it. I wonder what kind of a story he must have told his folks about his wife and the divorce, surely he must have lied to them too, right?"

Jade felt crushed to see it all exposed here from Lenny, but that was as far as it went for her now, concerning Lyle—she had no feelings for him. Her feelings in the first place were not a passionate love, but more of an honorable love and respect for what she thought he was and she could live with that in a marriage. She had never had any marriage offers, and she was then thirty-nine, going on forty—she really didn't know what to expect or *want* from a marriage. She had been so very happy with her gang of "mustangs" here, but maybe *this* was to have been her only chance, so she was going to try her hand at it—plus she knew and liked his folks. And—marriage sure worked out good for her ma, surely it would suit her, too, she figured.

~*~

Sure as rotting onions one day bust-out in ooze, Jade learned a lot about Lyle, the day of her brother's accident. What she saw then was enough to free her of any feelings she ever had for him—there would never be any regret to his loss—only regret that she had met him in the first place.

Jade knew his parents well, and so did all their friends, and that was the main reason she had trusted to go out with Lyle. He was a medium built man, with a sports-type look and face, not too tall or heavy, and just seemed like an average man that was succeeding in life. He also looked a bit like one of Lolly's cousins and it made her feel close to him (and quite possibly threw her off-caution). She met Lyle at the New Years Eve party, the same one where Jake had run into Angie again after all those years since school.

It had been Dec 1998, to "see in" the New Year of 1999. It had been near about forty degrees that night, but no snow and none expected, so they all had traveled to Libby for a party given by a friend of Johnny Walker's. It was his planned "special night off" and there'd be no bar-tending for him—not even at the party, rightly said.

Lyle took note of Jade and enjoyed the sparkling warmth she offered, although, if he had known of her spunk, he just might have found it not much to his liking, being quite the cultured city-man that he was. But when he heard she had a ranch, he decided he could-and-would change to rural ways, as—he then enjoyed her even more—but not for the right reason. Little did they know at first that he was a schemer from deep within, although Jake saw some rot in the hay, right-off. Jake was the one to finally find-out one day just WHAT that rot was. He had already learned about Angie, sour apples that she was, but it took him a mite longer to finally see through Lyle—as—Jake hardly ever *saw* him. And—that was actually what finally pulled it all together in Jake's mind, because as to Jake' thinking, it seemed like Lyle was in the process of moving his sister farther-and-farther out of his fellowship range, and to tie the loop before Jake could stop him. He didn't like that—there was some wrangling going-on to separate the herd and this type of wrangling is always done for personal gain—a wolf with an agenda-lasso if he ever saw one—it seemed his sister was in danger.

Jake did some checking-up just by causally visiting Lyle's folks one day and found out that Lyle was in debt and trying to deep-pressure his folks into selling him their land, so he could market it to someone he supposedly knew in California. After presenting *double* the value of it, as his boast, and claiming he could get it, he promised he'd buy them another place. The folks were scared then and had sent Lyle packing, and he had never told Jade. Now, Jake knew that Jade had already accepted an engagement ring during the recent holidays, and the New Year of 2000 was due in less than a week. The whole year of Lyle's courtship with her had been a *lie*. The time spent with Lyle's parent-folks had been very special to Jade and Lyle had always presented himself so well with them—making this a good hook. If she knew then what he was trying to do to them, she would never have become engaged—he'd have seen her spurs for sure. With this incident finally revealed to Jake (just after the Christmas holidays) there was about three days before the New Year. Jake was ready to lay down the law, and had set-his-face to tell his sister *before* the New Year—but the right time *never* came. She was continually with Lyle.

~*~

Lenny now went on explaining all this to Jade, as she listened in near disbelief how Jake had confided in him, and naturally Ray, as well. She felt stunned to know that Jake had been carrying this awful burden and never was even able to tell her.

"Well, why didn't he tell me Lenny... why didn't Jet TELL ME?" Jade sat motionless with eyes pressed shut for awhile, and then took to acknowledging Lenny, "We share everything Lenny, *everything*... well... at least *sooner-or-later* we do. Our folks taught us to be a *team*. Family is family, and we were all they had, and we were their *team*."

"Jade, he wanted to, but he just didn't know how. He had never seen you courting before, and he didn't want to be accused of trying to run your life. He, being your twin didn't want to lose you, but he didn't want to be involved in upsetting your personal relationships. If you were both *girl* twins, like the wrangler twins, he figured then he might have had a better chance." Lenny paced a few steps, trying to guide her, "Girls just know how to share that kind of stuff between them... he was a guy, Jade... we're just 'dad-gummed cowboys' is what he said... so 'what did he know'. He was trying so hard to find the best way, Jade. And he was trying hard to force himself to do it before the New Year... then when Lyle kept you out so late those last few nights, he missed his chance. That's why he was so adamant for you to tell Lyle to stay away during our New Year party we had here this year, remember? Remember how earnestly he pressed you, how it was just *family* as usual... meaning OUR gang... and how it would be our last time for the ol' gang '*as we knew it*', once you got married?"

The sun was fully warming them now, and Jade was out of the blanket, leaning against a porch post of her own, now:

"I remember that, Lenny, I sure-enough, do. I SURE couldn't figure Jet out none, then... he's never been one to do that... to just exclude someone... I thought he would have welcomed my beau to the home with open arms, but it seemed I had seen something new about my twin as of late, then... it was something I'd never seen the likes of, too. And all through New Year's Eve, with our wonderful time set before us... there was something distant about him... but I couldn't place it, Lenny. At first I thought maybe it was Angie... as he was so disappointed that she wasn't what he thought. I thought maybe he feeling bad that it didn't workout with her... she really messed with him, and we all rightly knew it."

Jade's head began to hurt now, as the ol' brain wheels were turning real hard now and she abruptly sat down on the porch-edge to let them roll, throwing the blanket back against the wall:

"Well, now I know... now I *know*... Jet must have been crushed when I left our party just a few hours into it... but Lyle wanted to see me, and so... and so I-"

Jade stopped cold. She gasped and then stood-up fast and grabbed onto the post that was nearest her side now. Lack of color, and trembling-weakness, manifested and Lenny moved toward her in shock:

"Jade...?" Lenny followed her as she moved around the post. "Jade?"

"I *did* this to him, Lenny... I *did* this," she stared around the wooden post at him. "Oh my God, I DID this to Jet." Jade started to shake and to cry.

"Hey, you *stop* that Jade. Stop it you hear! I just got done re-enforcing this into Stoney that night at Johnny's... during your party there... I found Stoney off in a corner, towards the end... he was *still* going over it with Ray and we finally shook him out of it. Do I have to shake you out of it too? Just because you both had stepped into Lyle's circle with your foot, sure doesn't mean you were part of his game. Now STOP it... *please*, Jade!"

"No, you don't understand... *Jet* came out of the barn that day... when I was screaming at Lyle's wranglers for help, JET was the one that came! *He* came to my aid. No one was lifting a finger and I screamed for Matt... then I ran around the side of the house, but he was no where around. THAT'S when I saw Jet come running-out of the barn... I never EVEN KNEW he was home! I thought he took-off *hunting* in the hills. At the time it didn't even register to me how he looked, because help was on the way... it was my Jet and he would know what to do! Soon as I saw him coming I got ready to try and help Stoney if I could, but as I moved in closer there, Jet had jumped in and was face-to-face to the bull... "

Jade had to stop. Flash-backs were hitting hard:

She remembered what she saw and she remembered screaming to Lyle's wranglers that the bull was killing her brother, but STILL no one moved. She remembered the gun! If Jake wasn't hunting, then his gun was up on the rack in the case over the fireplace mantel. She ran into the house and pushed up a chair to fireplace, reaching-up, she smashed the glass casing with the metal stokers for the fire, as she hid her face from harm, and grabbed the gun from the bracket. It was always loaded and she was firing at the bull before she knew it. That's when she saw Matt ride up. She didn't know how many shots she had fired, or how many it took for Matt to hear, but he was there, and he was making his way to her brother.

She wiped her face, "Lenny... I didn't know then what was so
wrong... with what happened to Jet... or with how he did it, or how he
looked, but the doctors later told me about the alcohol in his blood. When I
saw him come running out... it never *dawned* on me then what was wrong...
it never did until later, much later. But, you see... when I saw him... he
didn't have any coat or jacket on at all, he wasn't dressed to suit such a
winter's day. He was just running-out in light *dress-clothes*, and it was 30
degrees out there! There was a soft light snow that was just falling, the
ground was newly snow-dusted and he looked so out of place... like he had
run in, out of another world or something and didn't even know where he
was. He must have bedded-down using his coat and some old blankets out
there... to camp-out and drink and then sleep it off.   That's the only reason
he wouldn't have been dressed in his clothes and coat, proper. He never had
a *chance* with that bull... he was DRINKING because of me, Lenny.
BECAUSE OF ME! Now that's the COLD HARD FACTS! He was getting
ready to try and TELL me about Lyle. If he couldn't have done it when he
planned, he'd do *whatever* it *took* to tell me before it got any later *past* his
goal. He WASN'T going to let me marry Lyle... but he WASN'T going to
let me get hurt by the way he had to *tell* me either."

She sank down onto the wooden porch, "But HE DID GET HURT...
and it was all BECAUSE OF ME!" Lenny tried to take her arm and pull her
up, but she refused and pulled back. "No! LEAVE me be!"

He tired once more, with two hands this time.

"NO, LEAVE ME BE, I SAID!" she *screamed* at him, as she looked-
up at him with wild eyes.

Jake stepped out on the well-warmed front porch, and looked to her
with his good-morning smile, when he was met full-up, as a witness to this
scene. Her face was streaming with tears and black streaks, as she stood up
and equally witnessed-back, his unexpected appearance on the porch. She
took one look at him, and turned and *ran*. She ran around to the far right
side of the house (the west side) and took-off through the backyard, and then
towards the pasture and up towards the hills of the northwest ridge leading to
Jake's woods. She was fast, but she stumbled on the rocks as her bare feet
hit them hard, and Jake was able to catch up with her—he was just no match
for her running, anymore. He held her squarely by the shoulders and
wouldn't let her go.

"~R~onh', ~r~onh'?" he voiced as he witnessed her anguished
turmoil, "~whuh' ~r~onh'?" and he repeatedly signed, *what's wrong?*   -

His face was receiving all her pain, but, more-and-more of it continued to well-up from inside her as she listened to the sounds he was voicing. He couldn't talk—and—it rang too loud, and too clear:

"I did this to you Jet... I DID THIS TO YOU! IT WAS ALL BECAUSE OF ME!" She tried to pull away, but he wouldn't let her. "YES I DID... YES I DID... I DID THIS TO YOU!"

She stopped yelling suddenly, and watched his face blankly, "I just found-out from Lenny that you learned something about Lyle and his plans to try and get his family's home, and how he had been stealing from his ex-wife long before we knew him, and-" She stopped as she heaved in air, "I found out you were drinking Jet... I found out after the accident, and I never told you. But I never could figure out WHY... but *now*... now I know WHY."

She couldn't run-off and she had confessed her heart, and since there was no place to go without him following and nothing more to do, she collapsed on the rough ground of the field, in a shaking heap.

"~Unh-unh~," Jake got her attention, and signed, *NO!* ... *NOT-YOU!* ... *Lyle-come-early-first-time-that-day* ... *I-force-him-go* ... *with-bull-go* ... *I-yell-to-him* ... *go-drive-away* ... *take-bull* ... *go* ... *finished* ... *I-stay-in-barn* ... *yes-drink-long-time* ... *later-hear-screaming* ... *sudden-I-running* ... *see-bull-but-not-understand* ... *how-bull-here?* ... *and-I-see-Stoney* ... *have-time-save-him-maybe* ... *thank-God-I-save-Stoney* -

Jake shook his head. So far that was the most that he could remember, and it had taken him months to even fully know this and place it all in correct order. Jake signed again, *back-months-past* ... *I-remember-some-things-in-hospital* ... *but-I-remember-during-one-night* ... *bull-trailer-and-Lyle* ... *something-happen* ... *I-lost-situation* ... *I-sick?* ... *Matt-told-me-I-had-trouble-that-night* ... *Ray-and-Matt-try-stop-me-Matt-said* ... *finished* ... *but-me-alone-I-know-that-they-not-let-me-go-find-my-goal* ... *Lyle* ... *for-many-days-I-had-much-pain-from-those-thoughts* ... *you-remember-situation-happen?*... *past* -

"Yes, Jet... you had a bad seizure right after that. I couldn't understand why you would try to get up like that... none of us did. Now, I finally understand how and why you were so mad that night." She looked at him as she reflected, "It was terrible, Jet... seeing you fighting to get up, and then falling... and after I finally thought you were getting well."

Some puzzles are down-right hard to do, so Jake had surely learned, and was still learning:

*'Lyle, coming back like that, it still never made sense though, never...
until Stoney talked to me up on the hill out there in the woods.'* He signed,
I-understand-now-Jade ... *later-finally-understand* ... *Stoney-helped-
me-learn* ... *finished* ... *now-I-know-Lyle-come-back-for-second-time*
... *after-I-drink-whiskey-he-come* ... *he-know-I-drunk* ... *he-come-to-
hurt-Stoney-and-me* -

"But it was BECAUSE of me Jet, you know that... why else would he
hurt you both, if it wasn't because of me? I was the one that brought him
here in the first place, when I started seeing him."

*'Jade, how can I get you to see... I was the one that found-out about
him... I was the one that made him mad... I was the one that chased him off
and was going to tell you. He had to come back... it was his only chance to
get me out of your life before I could tell you... and he knew I would once I
was sober... how can I explain all this?'*

Jake was pacing now, but in controlled pacing—he turned and looked
at her, as he gestured emphatically at himself, by pointing his finger at his
own chest. *ME-ME-ME!* ... *only-blame-ME* -he signed. *God-
witness* ... *only-blame-me* -he signed with his highest honor, and wiped
his hands of it, and signed again, *ONLY-BLAME-ME* ... *FINISHED*
-just as emphatically, he stomped his foot to seal it.

*'HE CAME BACK BECAUSE OF ME, and it was MY OWN DAMN
fault I was drinkin'. How would I ever know that DAMN BULL was going
to show-up on my property again? And how would I know that Lyle would
tell you and Stoney a completely different story than he told me?'* Jake
stared at her firmly, trusting his sister to yield to such insightful revelations
as he readied-up to share his last thoughts on his thus-far hidden stupidity,
but was distracted, as he heard Lenny running.

Lenny had given them some time, but then became worried. He
finally joined-up with them now and earnestly pleaded with her to inform
him what had just been said. He was desperate to settle this all for them and
told them he had more to say, but had been interrupted, obviously so. After
Jade did her best to inform Lenny, Jake and Lenny tried to get Jade to relax.
After all, this was *also* part of his mission—clarifying ALL loose ends,
emotional included, for those he loved. Or—their future *healing* was still at
stake, even though the shaky *legal* aspect was pushing ever-nearer to their
favor, and it now favored his aspect towards victory, to make sure they knew
that he was there to see them through BOTH.

"Listen, now... Lyle had so many options no matter how this turned
out, to plan to do Jake harm... or so HE thought, and HE is the only one to
blame." Lenny went on to explain. "His plans to marry Jade had been

nullified... you told him you found out about him, it had all been exposed when you sent him off along with his *proposed* gift. So he turned-up with a new plan, trick Stoney, while still using his plan as presenting this bull to Jade as a gift to the ranch. Jake was in no condition to expose him now, and by the time he was... damage would be done. Stoney would be hurt and Jake as well, as he knew Jake would try to save Stoney. Lyle's wranglers wouldn't help, he knew they were afraid of that bull, plus one of them confessed that Lyle paid them to stay out of it... I know this, because Hunter heard this, one night before he came to me. Lyle saw Jake was drunk earlier that day... and he *knew* to come back just in time so Jake would still be awake enough to try and save Stoney, but still be unable to succeed. Then ol' Lyle would play the hero later, by comforting Jade through her sorrows as she faced the damage done to the two of you. There was no way Jake could live after facing that bull in his condition, and Lyle knew that. Whether Stoney lived through it or not, didn't bother him. Who'd be stupid enough to believe Stoney's ramblings about a 'ringer bull' and a set-up? Why Stoney would just be trying to save face, for being so *stupid* to get on the bull in the *first* place... that's all people would think. Jade would never know how Lyle had been exposed by Jake, as to what he was trying to do to his parents, or how he had been run off by Jake, as Jake would most likely be dead... or in no shape to ever tell anyone... and surely if he was later, it be after a long-enough time for Lyle to fix-up more plans. Lyle knew he'd be free to marry Jade in the future and have the ranch. He could stop all the plans for his folks place... and if Jade ever found out anything, he would just deny it. He'd just tell her, he moved out because they wanted their privacy again and Jake was lying 'cause he was jealous of someone being close to his twin besides him."

Lenny sure had their attention by now, and the three of them sat there under Lenny's guidance, as the rising morning sun, found them here, as well:

"Three things sure went wrong, things that were beyond his control. Things that the power of God took hold of in a way that none can fully understand... and me, being a lawman, I give high regard to God's law being behind justice more than we can ever *truly* get a handle on. You see... all because of your *prayers* Jade, Jake lived. There was no way now that Lyle would ever be able to show his face anywhere near Jade or her ranch again, and he knew that now. He knew sooner or later, Jake would tell her how he ran him off before the accident, and all the rest of his past would be showing, like a trail of pig-slop.

The other thing that went wrong was, Jade *killed* his bull. You don't know all of this Jake, although you did hear that she killed the bull... you don't know that she RAN Lyle off. Jade ran Lyle off at the scene... on her own... he was going to play the hero and show-up after parking the truck all right, but he heard the shots, just as Matt did. He showed-up on the scene and was so shocked and mad that his bull was dead that he lost control. He started yelling to find out who killed his bull. All he cared about was the bull, while you were dying, and Matt was trying to save you... heard-tell Jade couldn't take it anymore. She got up from Stoney's side, and yelled out that she killed it, and she was HIGH PROUD of it... and for him to get off their property! She never wanted to see him come near her or the ranch ever again. From what I heard, Jake, your sister here swung the empty gun at his head and would have smashed his face, if he hadn't ducked and caught-hold of it in time. Jade warned that the cops would be showing-up, and in light of his temper, he took off.

Yeah... Lyle just never would have figured his bull would end up *dead*... there was no one there to kill it. Matt was out on his horse herding in the cows with Galena, it was just that time in the afternoon. And he never knew what kind of a gal Jade was... that she could *do* or even would *think* to do such a thing, never entered his mind. He turned on her, because of it, and his true colors were shown. The woman he was supposed to love and want to marry was secondary to the money he needed immediately from that bull—and everyone witnessed it. Yeah, he left all right, when she chased him off! He was too far exposed... he had arrived to see Jade dealing with a terrible trauma, and he left Jade to DEAL with that terrible trauma... a trauma unknown to her, that he had caused... he did it all, you see... and without a second thought."

Lenny paused as he tried to picture this while taking a good long look at the nearby round corral. Lenny and Ray were the only ones of this close knit group that never saw any of this tragedy. Lenny did get out to the Smiths ranch that day though, and had witnessed the aftermath, and had to do his job as a professional and report all he saw and learned from the scene—and with a hurting heart, he faced it. He had responded to enough of his shared of emergencies that he understood full-well, just how bad it was for Stoney—and Jake—if Jake was still alive. From what he heard, they didn't expect Jake to live long enough to receive the hospital help needed for survival.

They sat there amongst the morning birds that were starting to drop by, and within seconds after Lenny's voice died down, Jade slowly spoke up in a soft voice:

"You were dying right there in front of me, Jet, with Matt doing his best to work on you... he had me bringing him clean sheets, and Matt was then chasing me off and sending me back to Stoney... he didn't want me to see... I trusted, and listened. Lyle's wranglers had finally decide to help Stoney, God only knows why... and Lyle had just pulled-up, he'd come back with his truck, but he parked it right over there," she pointed, "along the side road. He ran out here into the yard, racing over to us, yelling, when he saw his dead bull... he kept yelling-out about how much *money* it was worth, and how it had papers and all... and Jet... you were *bleeding* all over the freezing ground, and the snow was picking up. All them soft-white flurries were falling around us... I felt like we were all trapped in some glass snowball-scene... none of it seemed real... I was just floating through it all."

Jade raised her voice up now, and looked hard-and-long at her twin, "No man can ever *show* his face to me after behaving that way with you dying... no man, ever. Lyle was nothing to me then, Jet. Nothing. I truly ran him off Jet, just as hard as I could! Then later I came to know what he did to Stoney... and now I come to know what he did to his wife, and his folks. And now... now, I come to know what he did to you."

Jake walked up to her and grabbed her up in his arms, as if she was a baby and carried her back.

They sat on the porch and Jake, with gnawing curiosity signed, *what-number-three?* ... *what-other-thing-happen?* -it was racing through his mind while he had carried Jade back, but only now was he finally free to use his hands to ask.

"Well, as you know, Lyle tried to ruin you with Hunter and his car, this was to go along with his court-case plan. This was to be a set-up for him to SUE you and Jade in court for killing his bull... he wanted to prove you were violent... Hunter could be his back-up, see? He also had paid his brother to say that he had left the bull as a gift towards the wedding, and that once it was out in your corral, you had told him there'd be no wedding, that you threatened them and forced them his off your property... with violence, minus said bull. Well... he said he was AFRAID of you, so he left. He claimed he was having problems with the truck, down the road, and that's when he heard shots. He learned his bull was dead when he came to see what the shooting was about. He claims it was your OWN faults that the bull attacked both of you, as you were in possession of STOLEN property. I learned all this from Walter's gleaning of local gossip, seems Lyle's brother drinks too much... but as to this I just learned MORE from California:

The THIRD thing, that went wrong..." Lenny thus leaned closer adding, "and Lyle DOESN'T know, either... is this," he spun his spin on it, "and *wait* till you *hear* it... Lyle was just recently found to be in possession of STOLEN property, the SAME CHARGE he was trying to push on you."

The twins near stared with their jaw's open—they sure weren't rightly sure why, of course, or just *exactly* how this applied them—but it was coming:

"You see, Lyle is expecting to collect big because of the death of this bull. He wants to invest it, from what I just learned, trouble is, the bull was *paid* for with STOLEN money of the exact amount missing from his cousin. A check was shown going out in that amount. Lyle doesn't seem to take the needed time to do full cover-up of his embezzling, until later. He's just in such a hurry to get his way, and then back-track over, after, to settle the dust. That's why he was so mad about the bull. He wanted to take it back after the accident, and resell it, to pay back what he owed... he was going for *buyer* out in California that had bid high. Even if there had been no bull accident, he would have sold it anyway. He just didn't have anywhere to keep the bull, and used this gift story, so he could keep it boarded at your ranch until the buyer came through.

He had *still* planned to set-up Jake and Stoney into some kind of a mess with the bull... he just never expected it would be that very day... but that day Jake chased him off, was his last-and-only chance. You see, the whole mess has been exposed, and I just learned this last part from his two wranglers... I just picked them up for drunk driving near the gas station last night, of all nights... seems one of them had a small-time record and wanted out of Lyle's bigger mess. And the other guy was really busted-up about it all, and not helping Stoney or Jake, and *confessed...*

...How about THAT?" Lenny beamed now, tall and strong, "Seems the geese are getting flushed, huh, Jade... sounds like something your ma would have said, right? Well, now... as to that money... Lyle embezzled a huge amount of money through some kind of connections he had with a cousin's business in California. He doesn't know that they just *found out*. Apparently, they were in Europe, and they had closed up for the year as they had planned to... they were hoping to live there, and were testing it out. No way would they have ever found out that they were missing the money until he put it back, except that his brother found a buyer in Europe for his business, and then brought the man back to see the bank books. It was obvious that something was very wrong, but his brother couldn't tell what it was, and hired someone to find out. They found out it was Lyle that was stealing. We just found out that there is a warrant out for his arrest. Reason being, of course, that they know his parents are in this area, so they passed the word around to us. The cousin claims Lyle plays the stock market and gambles, and has lots of other schemes to try and replace money from wherever he 'borrows'... but it's been piling-up on him... so he came here to try for his parent's ranch. Otherwise, Jade would never have met him."

Letting this sorry note pass, first, Lenny then smiled, "You see, there is NO WAY he can ever take you to court now. So his last alteration to his plan, didn't work either." Lenny moved forwards and gave a little kiss to Jade, "You must have done some powerful praying, little gal. The scales were tilted in your favor, and you never even knew they had been tampered with."

"Maybe if I would have kept to my praying more, and never started seeing Lyle in the first place... none of this would have happened," she solemnly pulled herself closer to her twin.

"Jade, you know as well as I do... this is life, and we work through it. With prayer and wise decisions we succeed, and if we see trouble coming and are able, we make the *adjustments*... but with *other* decisions, no matter how much we pray, we don't have the options of *seeing the results* ahead of time. We have to trust, then. With these hard decisions, we learn to overcome... same as in my law enforcement work... I grew for the best, through it all. Sometimes we don't know the reasoning behind it all, or why we have to face certain decisions that *others* don't have to face... or why we didn't get a chance to fix something sooner, as we sure would have eagerly done so... or why and how our decision had to come to affect others so bad, as we walked through them. Prayer will STILL make a difference... in the end, and you've surely seen that over the years, Jade... you've been well taught by your ma, Filomena. If we had never prayed at all, the end to these decisions could have been worse. Plus we wouldn't have had the option to know that we *gave* it our all, if we hadn't prayed... and we wouldn't have seen others affected with the connection that our prayer had upon them, for good, too, now would we? And," he emphasized, "we would have regretted it for the rest of ours lives in many ways, then." Lenny looked out over the Smith Ranch, JJ-NS, and stared deep into Jade's eyes, "You did all you had to Jade, and so did you Jake... I know there'll be NO REGRETS here." He gave them both hearty long hugs, and set ready to leave, but Jade grabbed his hand in thanks:

"It appears when all is seen in that blazing sunlight of our days, that Someone is bull-doggin' our trail, all right, Lenny. For good or bad, depending on just where we aim to end up, come trails-end," Jade said, as she too looked-out over the Smith Ranch while she leaned on her brother's shoulder with her hand lost in the comfort and safety of his shoulder's underlying arm socket. A mere mortal armpit, it was, she knew, and that of her beloved twin. Yet—her heart was equally lodged, mirroring said-same nook, in the arms and the bosom of the Lord-most-high. The only One, truly, always mighty to save.

288 - By Neebeeshaabookway - JAKE SMITH RANCH SERIES...

CHAPTER TWENTY

SMOOTH COOL JADE

AFTER Lenny left, Jade and Jake seemed to understand that something had seriously shook the foundations of their home. It had even tried to force the shock-waves of its presence, to divide the two of them by something more than just the deep chasms of life. It had tried to usurp that power that had formed these two in the womb. It tried to separate them by death. There is only one power that would ever be able to decide when and how these two would not have the pleasure of the manifestation of the interaction of their thought, presence, and working relationship through life. That same power, and all the love that was present in it, had decided that the time was not to come by the way of that bull. A bull that Jake never in his wildest dreams would have ever dared to face, in ANY condition—if it had not been for the love towards this younger wild-buck of a kid-brother. His so-called "baby brother", that had been *birthed* into the Smith Ranch, one cold windy November, just before thanksgiving.

Jake and Jade were heavy with thought, as they did what they were known to do after any solving of an upheaval. They prepared themselves to take a quiet spell, down on the banks of the Fisher River, near the northeast hay field. This was just down from the fenced pasture where Jake had found the owl. The river ran all along their property, but this was their special spot.

Seems the symbolic manifestations of wisdom, just had to always hang-out there, and that day as well, as they prepared to glean it all in. Seems lots of action just sprang forth from that area, just as the nourishing hay itself did.

Now, if it was problems of the upsetting nature, well then the woods up along the north and northwest ridge did the trick. There were lots of opportunities to see and experience up there. Many different things, that could trigger many feelings, so that with the return of any outgoing thoughts, came the hoped for answers. Or, near enough—at least a trail leading to it would appear, whether well traveled and smooth or partially hidden and rough, it would always be found and always be ready to be tried. Today, after many long trials, it seemed contented reflection was in order, instead. So they headed for the river and its limitless reflections.

They walked down to the river in silence; it was *not* the silence of that awkward night that Jake had arrived home. This was a deep and reflecting silence of unison that the two of them understood—just as clearly they understood how this peace, and deep-laid-firmness of well-being had grown out of a dishevel that they had once been at a loss to understand. They had seen this come to pass in unison, as to how it had affected their bond—thus—in union, they'd savor this healing-time.

They looked at each other now, with a gentle gleam of expectation, *the river!,* they thought. Although the *thought* crossed the finish line for both of them at the same time, what the river *meant* to them was always slightly different, thus they were reaching the finish-line in different ways as to the *approach.*

Jake loved the deep under-working current, and how it affected the surface water, there at its *present* spot, and during its *future* presentations, after moving along its course. He liked the way it played and worked with its surroundings of the banks, plants or rocks and how it left its mark, and how it played on those things that moved through its waters (whether human, critter, or old logs) and its varied ways of moving power.

Jade loved the varied sounds, and the reflections that surfaced from *out* of the strength of the underlying current and would thus sparkled before her eyes. She loved how those that touched or came near to its lively presence, felt the joys and experiences-of-wonder that came from these such-revealed things—even the unexplainable splashy ones—all of which surfaced from such a hidden deeper power. She was always searching out for understanding or deeper knowledge, along her course of daily life.

It was odd, because she was the cool smooth jade, the one that matched what Jake loved about the river, as she was the one that would work new life and pleasures to those around her by her strong diligence to carry-on and her push to get truths to surface for the long haul. He was the various reflections that sparkled out from the strength of heavy currents, and reveled with the shine-of-life moving about him as it spilled out to others. He knew how to face what he had to, no matter how it was revealed, even though he may be doing it for reasons that were somehow hidden too deep from prying eyes. He would then allow all he learned, to play back into life for nourishment to others, and not just his own personal joys. She saw this play come into action so often as she watched him with his precious horse "babies", he'd then turn and relate such wonderful horse-knowledge over to the kids from the trail-rides. But most of all, she learned this through watching him with his buddies—he was a friend of high-shining caliber.

She sat a minute, and wondered if he would ever sparkle the same after coming out of this heaviness that he had been violently thrown down into, and was now moving-along through at such a slow-seeming pace. It seemed to her, that he was near ready to get stuck up along the muddy bank somewhere, and the stagnancy of it all, would haunt her.

Jake watched his sister now, as they sat out on the towels and listened to the sight and sounds of the river. The sun felt warm and relaxing as it seeped into their faces and bodies, and warmed them to their very soul. This was such a contrast in light of how he first met-up with her this morning on their front porch. His twin was content now and at ease. At ease, he was sure now, as he truly discerned she was *able* to understand that SHE was not to blame for what happened to him.

Jake was never one to cast blames. Sure, he understood hidden causes, but good reasoning helped keep blames in check, just as much. He knew Lyle was the cause, by the very nature of the man. If he had not trespassed upon their property and manipulated Stoney with a well-planned lie, their lives would not have been nearly destroyed. In a strange way, Jake, at this point was now near-feeling it was all worth it. Just knowing that his sister's life was out of the clutches of what would have destroyed her (while he and Stoney would have been left to watch and suffer the witness of her *hopefully* trying to survive the long-haul of a marriage like that) was a high-flying freedom. They had already made it through the *long-haul* of living through their injuries and it *sure* wasn't something to be desired in those aspects though, and he knew, above all. Jade had witnessed the flip-side of it all, though, and *she* well-knew now—through much suffering of her own; just as they would have witnessed her suffering, through Lyle, if she had married him. She was already ahead in the race, in that way, so it seemed. Seems they all took a shine to bearing each other's pain, either way.

It was obvious now, that Lyle's presence on the Smith Ranch would have wrecked havoc on the rich harvest that Jake and Jade had come to know and possess in their relationship. It would not have destroyed it, but it would have bruised and marred some of its most tender spots on some of its choicest fruits, just as it had now already done, in some ways, just before the accident.

Casting the name of Lyle aside, Jake set the firmest foundation he could, one needed for his gang to stand strong on—he took the "prize". Jake blamed himself—Jake forgave himself. He was the defender of his ranch—although shared with his sister—it was his to defend. He would not ever make that mistake again. A fool never learns from his mistakes, he reasoned, *well now, I can at least face each day, knowin' I ain't no fool... unless I foolishly think that makes me not susceptible to BEING a fool,* Jake thought with a smile. Seemed they all took a shine at sharing each other's smiles, too, as Jade joined in with a smile back at her brother's, not wanting to be left behind, in his private contentment—whatever it was.

Now then, later in the day, as later always comes (and *after* Stoney and Matt finished doing chores that it *appeared* their boss-man had ignored or neglected), Matt took-off for a ride with his wonderful Galena, and Stoney headed-on-down to the source of his name.

~*~

Stoney was from Texas, and had been adopted when he was a very young toddler and never knew his name. His adopted parents, called him Bobby, then later Bobby-Bob, as he'd weave in-and-out of so many things, and with such gusto. His ma died from pneumonia, and later during his early teens, his pa died from a bull riding accident, thus Stoney rode the rodeo circuits at a loss as what to do without his pa. He had many mentors, but something was missing—a home—a place to call his own. The Daniels took him in, in 1991, and adopted him at the ripe old age of 21, just before he came to know Ray. The Daniels' sons raised horses, and Stoney got to hanging-out with them previously when he'd come through town, the sons naturally invited him home, and home it did become. They lived near Ray's ranch, and Stoney then took to working for Ray, and took to him like butter-to-warm-toast. He'd continue to work for him and loved him as a brother, but neither place was a true home, nothing matched his ache for Texas-style hospitality. These ranches were so large that he felt like he was the little extra morsel that was added on as a condiment, never part of the *real stew* of the place. He needed a down-to-earth little home like the one he knew in the Texas-tip. He found it, that one windy November day at Jake's, 1994—and he found Jade. He sure wished she'd find him, though.

His first day here had been spent at the river, as Ray was giving Jake an introduction to "Bobby" and all his fine points, and, more importantly how he was up from the Texas, by way of the rodeos. As they tried to hunt him down that day, they finally found him at the river—being christened "Stoney", by Jade, as he skipped stones with her. She called him that ever since, and it stuck. By the time Thanksgiving rolled around that year, he was Jake's little brother, never to be turned loose. He still always kept it in the back of his mind though, concerning this one hidden thought—he'd sure make a just as *good* brother-in-law, if the door ever opened!

~*~

As Stoney now approached the river and thought of how he had first met-up with this home—his home—he *too,* was feeling mighty thankful. Thankful to be alive. He was planning on doing some stone-skipping and perhaps some fond reminiscing.

Jade saw him coming and after a hug, she took off to explore the river and all its odd assortment of rocks. She decided twin-sis had *her* turn with Jake, thus now it was time for the guy-talk to start up—by yielding the river bank to Stoney. She had a yield of another sense to accept she deeper reckoned, with each step—her day was now giving her treasures that she enjoyed to no-end. The sorrows of the porch and field were now paved-over with smooth cool rocks. They may not have been rocks of jade, but they were rocks *for* Jade, and here *now*—thus a lovely, fairer, and by farther *better* laid-out treasure, to her than any amount of jade, or any *other* precious stone a gal could think to choose.

Jake felt Stoney had a right to know what Lenny had said, and as best he could, he tried relating it all. Aside from a few miscommunications that Jake was determined to see through until success was reached, it went fairly well.

Stoney actually knew how to pay attention—when it wasn't playtime, this pup could heel. He knew that for his boss-man and close-knit friend, playtime was a thing of the past, as to communication—serious business was now at hand. Stoney earnestly hoped that someday the insurmountable brush of damages would be cleared away, and a whole den of fun would be discovered again—but they would all have to wait, and wait they would.

~*~

Jake was not quite able to get all the complicated issues and time frames signed-out that he desired, and at times was frustrated from it all, as his brain started to lose focus. This muddled lostness and the now-familiar following of a sense of frustration, was due to the old haunting of his head injury, thus at times he would show frustrations that never were his nature. He was lucky though—he didn't like this behavior he saw or felt in himself, he was lucky that he was able to realize it. He would try so very hard to shake loose of it. He wondered how many others in his position, were trampled in this wrestling on-going *battle* of trying to keep one's identity untainted. He wondered if any others were even able to have a *choice* in the matter, or if any others could face the fight-for-it in the *first* place. Being, that it was an upsetting challenge to latch-hold-of *in* that first place—and worse yet—as to having *choices*, he had heard Miss Kaite tell Jade once, that some head injury folks had *no idea* that they were not the same—and this had *scared* him. Was he innocently unaware he was not functioning—other than his reading issue? Would his twin even *tell* him? Would he believe her? Why, he even wondered at times, if Jade would still love and except him if he were never *able* to realize his new weakness towards frustration, and thus try his best to curb it. He would take Matt or Jade aside after any intense time of communication (usually in the late evening) and question them as to whether he was treating them right. He was still worried that he wasn't the same, and not just physically this time—he was a grown man— yet all of the sudden needing reassurance. He wanted to be the same, and yet he knew that somehow he had lots of walls in his mind that refused to let him pass back into the previous rooms of his familiar, capable thoughts—he seemed to get lost in the maze of such. These were walls that would not yield, they would not kick down, or open, and when he tried to go around in the maze, he usually found himself having to start over afresh, without a clue as to what went wrong. Hard-pressed to realize that many of these rooms were unreachable—forever gone. He wanted to be free of this bother that he felt he had become, because of *his* love and sense of duty to those dear to him. Jake, the boss-man, was used to being *their* support, and rightly said.

He tried to keep a mental personal gauge of himself now, ever since the hospital and therapy, because Miss Kaite tried to test him and write out notes about him, as if he was an experiment, and he didn't like it. He had a high disdain for that, as that was HIS job, and no one else's. He didn't fully understand then, that this could be used to help him, or others, that were facing traumatic brain injuries—TBIs. If there was anything that could be learned to help someone somewhere, it was only to be learned from those that had gone through the very things that he now had to face.

His thinking and functioning, and memory was a miracle and he came to understand that, through the talk that Miss Kaite and the doctors had conveyed to him. He had now finally come to accept this as the best miracle one could have, if one could have a choice. Sadly, if the head is sick, as the Good Book says, the whole body is sick. Whether spiritually, or, physically. Meaning if the "engine" is broke down, it is very likely the car will have extreme difficulty trying to get somewhere, no matter how *wonderful* that much loved car is—it wants to go, but it can't. Jade was still continually by his side, telling him his brain-engine was doing just fine—especially since it wasn't *pestering* her for the time every hour.

~*~

Jade was just making her way back downstream to them, when she caught-hold of Jake still trying to relate all that Lenny had said—and she watched. They must have *just* finished up, instead, as she could have *sworn* she saw Jake sign to Stoney, *your-turn* ... *your-turn-be-sweetheart-with-my-sister*   -

Jake had now smiled, and hit Stoney with a light punch on the shoulder, and Stoney was smiling back. Her innocent eyes toward her twin, had seen too much. She stopped cold in her tracks, and moved-off to the side, into the covering of the trees. She felt like an eavesdropper. Jake was smiling and sparkling and so was Stoney.

They must be joking... why, that's it, thought Jade. *It's a miscommunication. Why, I'm much too OLD!*

She watched some more to make sure Jake was done, and then smoothly and coolly made her presence known, all though behind her precious display, she was deep in moving thought.

296 - By Neebeeshaabookway - JAKE SMITH RANCH SERIES...

CHAPTER TWENTY ONE

RAMITA... THE LITTLE BRANCH OF NEW GROWTH

SUMMER was nearly over now; September 1st was just a few days away. Ranch-life pretty much had continued on without anymore incidences since Jake's reassurance to Jade that she was not to blame for his accident. Well, there was one other difference now, since that day—Jade now watched Stoney a bit more closely—although she treated him with all due respects, as the great friend that he was. She still had the thoughts that had been portrayed through her brother's hands, tucked deep in her heart. It was as if they should *be* there for some reason, and not being one to misplace things, this seemed like the best place to guard them.

Jake had not had anymore seizures since his owl rescue, but Matt and Jade had both been aware of Jake's occasional dazes that would hit him when he was trying to think on a project—thus, these were learning times, for all. Matt was keeping it in mind, as he witnessed them more than Jade, but so far, they were minor—passing within a variety of minutes ranging from 1-5. Jake didn't know it, or even realize that he was out of tune with his surroundings—there was no way he would. He would just start over with whatever he was trying to think on, until he succeeded. Jade would always become extremely cautious and make the guys stay near him constantly on those occasions, she was so afraid he'd have a seizure, but he never did—at least as far as she knew. Anything more serious showed only when the issues were more complicated, and Jake could stall-out for up to 20-30 minutes, and just sit on the spot, or even start pacing—which was a lot more dangerous. So far, they had only run into only two such complicated issues. The first was when Jake, Matt and Stoney were figuring-out lumber needed for the open shed. Jake would try to think it out in shaped picture-terms and then lose track and start over, and then, he went on to try to add-up piles of it in length and width sizes, while the guys already *knew* what he needed long before he ever got it figured. The second time was when Jake tried to help figure-out how much new wire he'd need to string in the east pasture, east river pasture, and pump house pasture combined. He was trying to explain it to Stoney when they were out in the east pastures, and finally Jake just ended-up sitting in the field, staring at the fence, and Stoney had to run for help. When he came back with Matt, Jake walking along the fence, trying to start all over again with his figuring. He tried to tell Matt that he just *knew* that he could do this—as he had done it for years. Matt tried to help Jake finish, but Jake's headache finished-him-in instead. Jade had to put Jake to bed with his pills. For now, Matt shelved the information, this was now normal, and considering Jake's injury, Matt knew this was pretty mild stuff. But it wasn't to Jake, not when he was trying to get through it to the other side—the side of success. All in all, though, with only two such serious episodes in the last four months of ranch work, Jake was doing quite admirably in succeeding to run his ranch—for the most part the head injury was "saddle broke", and his life was now taking-to-the-trails with some kind of skill and dignity.

Matt was aware of things like this since he had trained for the emergency rescue service in this area. He wasn't with it anymore, it was so hard for him to make the extra money to travel and keep up with the continual renewing of new skills. The funds brought in for this service were so few, that he couldn't survive on the pay, as he was saving-up for the day that he and Galena would have a family. Galena was one of the youngin's, as Jake called them, just like Stoney—howbeit, she was not quite THAT young. So this had to be the year they would try for their family, as she was thirty-seven already, and couldn't risk to wait any long. Matt had just quit that job for the VOLUNTEER EMERGENCY service during the Christmas holiday, 1999, due to lack of being able to keep-up with all the others in the program. He still worked off-and-on for nearly everyone in town though, as a carpenter, and plumber, aside from his ranch work with Jake.

Today, Matt had been over at the twin wranglers, the next ranch over and behind them. These twins, the Cook twins, used to live at the Smith Ranch before the Smiths came up from Texas.

~*~

The twins, during their pre-teens, as well as the Smiths twins, had spent these years growing-up together with the locals—same school and lots of summer vacations together. Jake had took much better to this small-town schooling than the boarding-school experience, which started when he and Jade were nine years old. This Old-Town school reminded him of his home in Texas. Back in Texas, as soon as school finished, he was soon home and back in the saddle. Here it was just about the same for him, except by now he was working harder for his pa after school and turning into a man. He'd be following the rodeo, with his pa for many a year. Jake and Jade took together in a most excellent way with the twin wranglers—twins plus twins, it was. They took turns paring-off in conversation, depending on how the day was flowing, and sometimes it was even all four mouths going at once. The friendship was cemented after all these years into a nice comfortable "patio", decorated with lots of years of insight into each other's deep-rooted ways. The Cooks didn't come to many functions at the Smith's ranch, as they were a mite shy of a room full-up of people, plus, they enjoyed the company of their pa over anyone else—he was just the best in their book! So they'd just mosey on over, when the gates-of-time were freed-up for a one-on-one visit of two-to-two.

Jake could always trust them to help with any-and-all critter rescues. Kim and Kari were white-hat heroes, as far as he was concerned, and they were A+ top quality kind of gals. Fact is when he was a kid, if there wasn't two of them, he just might have considered courting them when he grew up. He liked them both the same for different reasons and he didn't think he'd ever be able to choose, so this notion quickly passed.

~*~

Now Jade had been washing-up the noon dishes, viewing the yard through her right-nice window, when she noticed Matt was back from the Kim and Kari's ranch. He had finished with his horse but instead of coming in to see Galena as usual, he took-off again, and she took note. *Must be he's looking for Jet, I reckon. I swear... if it wasn't for Matt's brown eyes and dark brown hair, Matt and Jet could near about appear to be brothers!*

Matt was looking for Jake, and he found him in the open shed, just before the pump-house pasture. This pasture was just to the east, but a bit forward (south) of the open shed's back wall. It was also to the east of the huge south pasture, where Jake's babies stayed (their pasture started in front of the tack-shed, but the grassy travel space of the yard, divided them by a good little walk). And, the pump-house was divided from the east river pasture (on its far east), by another larger part of Shriber Creek. The *main east pasture*, that connected the pump-house pasture, and the northeast hay field, was due-east along the side walls of the open shed and the barn. Being, if one would walk out of the open shed's drive in door, they would be heading right towards the barn's front door (by first passing the tack-shed, just to one's left). The south pasture and the pump-house pasture could be seen from the front of the ranch house—more clearly from the porch, but only by a stretch, from the inside window-view.

"Hey Jake... the wranglers next door had a guy come-by doing work for them, he's been up here doing seasonal work for Ray and is due to go back to Texas!" Matt smiled as he patted Jake on the shoulders saying, "How about that... Texas, Jake!"

true? -he signed. *'Aw... Texas... I can feel it now.'* But as he thought on this, Jake just couldn't picture himself ever going back to visit his beloved roots, now. It would just be too awkward—a whole other field to re-plow—awkward work, was more like it, with no guarantee of any predictable successful crops. *'Seems them days are over now, best I be pushin' it aside,'* he reminisced in silent sorrow.

"There's also something of interest they think you might want to know... why don't you come with me and we'll go over?"

"~Unh-unh~," Jake voiced, as he tried to do a subject change to escape the word "Texas". He quickly fumbled for some tools and presented them towards Matt with an anxious smile and a lingering question on his face.

"No thanks, Boss-man," Matt laughed, "you got enough work out of me already today... its break time!"

"~Unh-unh~," Jake just as quickly waved his hand in protest, he only wanted to show Matt what he was going to hurry-off to do, himself. Jake looked at him, *'You don't always get my drift too quick, but when you do, our streams still run the same direction... strong and deep... and today it was lots of extra work! Seems you were right, on that point, Matt, but you just relax now, buddy ol' pal. We both earned our keep with it all, and none to argue the point! Boss-man approves!'*

Jake pointed at himself, showing-off with a boastful satisfied look, voicing, "~I~" -and then added, to clarify, *you-follow-you-watch* ... *visit* -

"You're just trying to throw me, ain't ya, Jake... you know I'll join in, once I get there... naww..." Not wanting to fail in his mission though, Matt tried again, "Hey, remember back during your birthday party at Johnny's? The twins were there, you know... so they know you can't talk now. They were just too shy to come up and say anything, it was all so new to them... plus with all the others around, they thought they'd wait to see you in private, understand? Oh, and they weren't able to bring a gift because they had one coming by mail, its on order... it hasn't come yet. They just wanted you to know, so I'm letting you know... do you hear me?"

Matt studied Jake's face, as Jake appeared to be over-acting at his tool-hunting. "Well... if you want them to fill you in on the gift and when it will arrive, or if you get curious enough to meet this guy and don't feel like *avoiding* the word 'Texas' for too long... go on over. His name is Pedro.

He'll be there today. I think it'd be good for you, as he and you got a lot in common. More than you could imagine."

Jake looked down at his watched and signed, *I-go*
-and hurried off.

"Hey, you can't *tell time*... what are you *trying* to pull?"

Jake turned and laughed, as he signed back, *old-past-habit* - '*and besides... I fixed it... suits me just fine!*' Jake put on a show for Matt, as he gestured putting little stickers on his watch.

"I don't know what the hell you're talking about Jake, and I sure as heck, don't think I'll try to figure it out either, I'm past-due for lunch," Matt said, as he brushed Jake away with a gesture they'd used many-a-time in years past. He watched Jake take-off to the pump-house pasture. Somehow things sure didn't feel the same, though.

Matt headed up to the house and Galena was waiting for him on the porch, and tossed her wide-brim red *cow*gal hat over at him. He caught it and adjusted the black, white and yellow beaded band, as he set it back on her head, along with setting a kiss on her faintly pink cheek.

"So then, what was all *that* about, Matt?" Galena asked, as Matt leaned back on the porch-post and gazed at her.

"Jake is avoiding Texas is all... other than that, not much." Matt smiled as he walked up and pulled her into his arms and gave her a comfortable snuggle and rubbed her nose with his. He had to really lean over to reach it, because Galena was shorter than Jade—tiny as a little alpine meadow-flower, with brown, mossy cascading hair.

"Well, that shouldn't be too hard... seeing as it's so very far away."
She snuggled back. "Hungry?"

"Yep."

They entered the kitchen door and just as quickly Matt caught hold of Jade's attention with a wave, just before she went over to the family room— her room—STILL! But, with no regrets, as she was a great guard dog. And she was enjoying being in the center of things anyway.

"What's all this...?" He then proceeded to put on the same show that Jake just gave him, putting stickers on his watch, only with more emphasis of strength, and seriousness. Matt could be very dramatic at times if he chose, but more in Jake's way, than Stoney's way.

"Oh, that." Jade smirked as she approached them, "Before the cuckoo clocks and all, Jet was driving me nuts about the time. I hadn't yet decided if it's because of his inability to discern the symbols and how they work together... or if it was something deeper, and he *needs* me to keep telling him for the pure-and-simple reason that he just wants to know straight-up."

She paused for a note, "Remember how he was always checking how his day was falling into place with regards to his work-agenda? He made sure things worked out for you guys, too." She leaned-back onto the kitchen counter that was opposite the large window above the sink, and rambled on—seemingly unaware that she was leaning on a wet soapy spot, "Or you see... maybe he just can't retain the time and the concept of how much is actually passing in his mind from when I last told him. Now I'm finally sure it's some of both... I've been trying to study him, and I'm sure of it. And *mind* you, Matt, the good Lord forgive me... but after just so much of that, I was full-up to *here*," she gestured with her hand passing across her lower chin, as it topping-off the fullness that was ready to burst from her. "Whatever the glitch, I just didn't *care* anymore... I just wanted him to go climb a *tree* or something! I mean, in the middle of the night! Sometimes five times a night! My good ol' twin was ready to be let loose and set adrift, by ME! Well, I finally told him to go make a sundial or something... course that's only good for the day... he CAN think you know," she interrupted herself, suddenly realizing her arm was a mite wet as she stood to wipe it, and leaned back in a new spot. "He can count and think, and I TOLD him so! He just can't seem to grasp any functional sense with how to read, use or apply any of these things that we see and read, and count everyday. I see him purposely look away from printed things, as he starts getting very agitated and headaches start to haunt him. And he's *constantly* bringing me stuff from the mail, or books and papers he finds in the office, and asking me to tell him about it. But it was that constant time-telling roller-coaster he was riding that really got to me, Matt... sometimes I just couldn't stand it." Jade stopped, fully ready to slap her own hand for rambling-so before Matt, and added, "Then I started to think how I'd feel, if I knew I couldn't do something anymore and nobody cared to reach-out to help me when I wanted or needed it. Then I stopped to think how much I love him, and what he's come through... you know Matt, I'm thankful that Jet even *realizes* that time *has* intervals at all... truly as a deer looks beautiful, out on the run, with a high-tail to the air!" She turned and fully wiped the wet spot away now—and took a deep breath and turned back around:

Jade laughed as she looked at Matt, who was wondering when she was ready to jump-on-the-saddle of this runaway question and pull-in the reins. Not that he minded. It really helped him too, in understanding Jake. He always came to understand him before, and he sure didn't want to quit now. Matt did know how to spot head trauma and seizures and medical alerts as to the patients he was handling on emergency runs, but he didn't always know about the lasting after-affects that could carry on, or surface, *after* head injuries. There were just so many of them and he had learned only what he needed for his work and that was it. Now he was learning what he needed, for a *friend*.

"He puts tiny stickers on it Matt. He told me he fixed his watch so he could use it. I gave it to him last Christmas, you know... just before... " Jade swallowed hard and walked across the kitchen, past them, and looked out the window, "Well, *you know*. He just looks at the little hand, and doesn't use the big one. He puts a tiny sticker where the little hand is and then later, he will look back at it and depending on how many gaps have elapsed in between the sticker and the little hand, that shows him how many hours have gone by. You know, one, two, or three hours, or whatever. Of course he still doesn't know what time it is, but he can tell how many hours he's been out in the field, or in the barn or what ever. It makes sense to him, and he's perfectly happy with it now. Sometimes he makes a good guess just by judging from the sun, but dad-gum-it... he wants *detail*."

Jade looked out the window, just a second or two, and turned and looked at them, "You know... oddly, just a few day ago, I caught him starting at the license on his truck. He liked the #3, he said it looked like an air view of joined horse stalls showing the *three* sides, so I told him to call it a *three*. He knows it now. He also liked the #1 on the license, as well... well... there is only ONE mark there, so he counts the mark as a '*one*'. Just like if he'd count a horse or a pencil, or something. I just took him over and showed it to him on the watch and we marked them. Now, he does know when it is three o'clock, or one o' clock. Isn't that funny? Maybe that's what he meant by he fixed it... the watch. He can count from the one or the three... maybe he is actually getting more out of it than just the passage of time, only he knows."

Jade pondered this thought, as she watched Matt, while Galena slipped off to set-up a late lunch for him. It was as if she was fixing to feed a youngin', as he sat there waiting for his food.

"You know, Jet looks and behaves exactly the same as the man he was, but when it come to these skills we use for reading-knowledge, he's just like a little kid trying to learn... only thing is... they can learn, and he can't. It's just gone, Matt. It's just *gone* for him... completely gone. You know something ELSE, Matt... I sure am glad he learned a lot before this happened, and I sure am mighty glad that he didn't forget none of it... including us." Jade was so quiet now that she almost looked like a dimmed flashlight, ready to go out. Matt felt it as well, as he saw this and watched it in her face—he never suspected that there was so much connected to little stickers on a watch.

She went around to the refrigerator and poured herself a tall glass of ice tea and sat down at the table and stared out the back kitchen window, toward the field and the northwest ridge. It was definitely time for some refreshments. Matt had something to match the iced tea—juicy Texas limes—well, only in the sense of juicy Texas gossip!

"Hey, guess what, Jade," Matt chewed his lunch as he got ready to "news" her up, "guess what I learned at the wranglers, next door?"

"Never could get the hang of guess-what-ing, so tell me straight-up," she winked.

"They hired a worker from Ray, a guy named Pedro, he's from Texas. I think I've seen him at Ray's before, a few years back. Every time I'd stop by Ray's that year though, it seemed the guy was always too busy with the bales of hay to notice me... and when I passed by him, on other working occasions, he never paid me a mind. Well, it turns out, he never *heard* me... he's deaf. How about that, I just thought he was engrossed in his work. I only saw him about four times. The wranglers said Ray told them that he's up here this year for a few months... his wife just had a baby a few months back, so he came up here to earn some extra money with Ray. Ray learned about him from Johnny, as Johnny's family knew him. It's one of those, 'and so on, and so on's.' The family ranched nearby in Lyford, near where you used to live... but they had most-all of their relatives in Matamoras, Mexico. Pedro lives in Harlingen now, though. Ray says he's the most diligent worker he's ever had, least wise that's what he told me back then, and I saw that myself. See... it just goes to show what happens, when your parents bring you up on a ranch! Well... I got to thinking Jade, that you just might be able to let Jake see how this guy talks... maybe it will help Jake open-up more, or learn something he don't know yet. What do you think?" He shyly stressed this perhaps pivotal-fact, "Jake's never seen anyone *solely* depend on this way of talking before, you know, and now's his chance. Well, Boss-lady?"

"Matt, you know Jet... he don't want anybody else hanging-around... not yet. He still hasn't been back into town since his birthday. You promised to take him in, and I'm expecting you to make good, got it?" Jade suddenly stopped as she realized SHE knew Jake, and better than anyone. And—she *knew* something *else* about him.

"You know... that's a *good* idea... Jet would always help someone in need. This guy needs money for a new baby, and he traveled all the way up from *Texas*. Sure Jet would give him work... at least in the *past* he would have. I think I *will* just hire him on... but as a *surprise*."

"You mean, as in not telling the boss-man that you've usurped-his-authority type-kind-of-surprise?" Matt looked up at Galena, "This will be fun..." Matt smirked at Jade, and then Galena, "yeah, this ought to be LOTS of fun," he finished, as he wiped his mouth with his shirt cuff. A shirt that Galena would soon be washing.

"When will Pedro be done up there?"

"He's done already, Jade, his cousin is there with him, her name is Ramita... she acts as his interpreter. He always writes notes, in Spanish or English, but then he needs to know what his boss' expect of him in the first place, so he needs Ramita there to find out. Sometimes questions can arise if you're just using notes to go on, when you're working... " Matt thought back to all their paperwork-turned-confetti, with Jake, and then continued, "...yeah, notes can end-up as artificial snow at times, if you're not careful."

"Artificial snow, huh?" Jade knew it had something to do with Jake, but let it slide for now.

"Yeah... I seen a dad-burned blizzard once..." Matt commented as he now spied a napkin off to the side of his plate, "well then, back to Ramita... so then, she signs whatever the boss needs done, back to Pedro, and so on. If he has a question later, he can just go to her again, and she goes back to the boss for him. The twins had a very interesting time with him, so did I. He was a real humble down to earth guy and lots of fun. As you-all are always saying, must be 'cause he's *from Texas*!" Matt laughed, "'cause Ramita said he's been like that since he was a kid, just happy to oblige anyone. He already had a son by a first marriage, and that son is deaf, and his new wife is deaf, and so is the new baby. How about that? I never knew that sometimes deafness can run in the family."

Matt looked at Jade, "I didn't mean to get nosy with them, but I had to find out if they go into town and take care of their own shopping and all that. What I mean is, Pedro and his family... and Ramita said of course, why not? But she did make a point of telling me that there were lots of deaf people that she knew that were very shy to be out in public, and they didn't sign as flamboyantly as Pedro. But then no matter what language you speak, or how you speak it, there's always some folks that are shy and others that aren't. You learn this whenever you talk to people, shy folks always hold-back some." Matt reflected as he played with his spoon and spun it around a few times, "My ma was on the shy side when out in public... I remember her stepping-back when she was out among lots of city folks." Matt set his spoon aside, still half-way dwelling on his ma and her private ways:

"Ramita said children learn when they're little to be themselves and go with the flow. They aren't one bit ashamed of signing... they just have-at-it, happy as a little baby bird hungry for the next step. Pedro, why, he's voicing out all kinds of noises and he don't care who hears him! Course, Ramita's aunt, she's hard of hearing and she gets embarrassed by Pedro, but she gets embarrassed easy by lots of things. Maybe Jake can learn not to be so ashamed of himself if he sees how natural this new way of talking is to other people, Jade. Kind of like easing a horse into a trailer, you know, that kind of stuff... you know us mustangs, we ain't never seen *trailers* in the form of this signing-stuff, before."

Matt stood up and walked over to the counter in the kitchen and looked out over the field where he knew Jake was now working. He thought of him out there now, as he remembered how he fought to keep his friend from suffocating in his own blood, and how he desperately tried to keep him from bleeding to death. He turned stoically, looked back at Jade, and then let the memory fade.

"I hate seeing Jake ashamed of himself... I really hate it Jade. He's done nothing to be ashamed of... hell, he can't talk because he's a hero, not a criminal." Matt wiped his eyes, and turned to look out over the field again as he remembered Jake and the watch, *just cause he can't read or write anymore don't make him stupid, either...*

"Then it's time we do something to make Jet feel good about who he is again. You get on back there, Matt, and tell them to come over tonight if they need to, instead of taking that drive back to Rays. I'll call Ray. Say now... why didn't he let me know about Pedro and the signing and all?"

"Pedro's only been here a week, and Ray had to out to Billings, but he's due back any day now." Matt prodded her memory, "You know Ray, he's got lot of workers to keep his place going. Whenever he wants to come by here for a few days, or go out of town, he's free. The twins had called Ray for some workers, anyone that may need a few extra hours was welcomed, and Pedro was the volunteer. So... we just get him a few days earlier than Ray would have sent him, is all." Matt smiled now, as he got ready to go back to the twins, "You know... Ray must have had the same idea, Jade, we all have lots of common ground." Matt tugged his Stetson down at bit snugger, and left, as Jade called Ray's ranch, over at his bunkhouse, and Galena started to get the house in order—starting with the unused napkin.

It was sure a good day for working. First the wranglers, Pedro, and Matt—then—Jade and Galena, down in the basement with the news articles, photos, and all the extras to sell on-line. Then, there was Jake and Stoney, out working different ends of the fields. As eating-time stepped near, Jake was the last to come in for supper and he was met with the feeling that just *maybe* he had walked into the wrong house. Either that or he'd crossed the border into Texas, or possible Mexico. Sometimes you just can't tell in south Texas!

'Looks like ignorin' Texas, just riled Jade up and sent her seeking an occasion against me for my DASTARDLY deed. Now I got Texas in my house of all things! I don't need Texas right now... and hey, now... just who are these folks anyways?' Jake surveyed the situation, as he thought back to the old TV westerns and how the boss-man always seemed to be the last to know when trouble was about, *'do I got squatters on my land now or are they just flying by, with the winds off the prairie?'*

Jake took a look out the window, sarcastically so, *'No wagon train heading down to the border... hhmm.'* He rubbed his chin, deep in thought. Pedro came up and shook his hand with a huge smile, and took-off to the upstairs bathroom to clean up. Now, Jake was left staring at Ramita Gonzalez. She was quite a pretty gal, with lovely black eyes. She sure looked a lot like a school gal that Jake remembered from grade school in Texas, *'Cha-Cha... Santiago's sister... she looks just like Cha-Cha... well, about ten years younger than Cha-Cha would be now, if truth be known.'*

Jake smiled at her shy and sweetly, and winked at her, as he slowly turned and grabbed his usurping sis, *'now just WHAT am I going to do with company???'* He winced at her, *'and just what the heck to you think you're doing? You ain't getting' ready to cut my rope and set me afloat now are ya' twin? What happened to the word team-work, huh?'*

Jade smiled sweetly and batted her eyes at him, fake black lashes and all, as she reached up and tousled her brothers dark-black wavy hair, "Surprise... we got company calling!"

'No we ain't, this is more like an INvite... come at eight and don't be late, or come at nine and we'll still do fine, type of stuff.' Jake signed at her, *what* ... *why* ... *what-you-think-you-doing* -then he drew huge invisible question marks repeatedly in the open space between the two of them. He then brushed the invisible signs out of the way, as he walked past them and faced her, as if they were ready for a showdown.

"Hush up now, Jet, or you'll hurt her feelings."

"~Unh-unh~," he voiced, as he signed, *she-not-know-signs* -

"Oh yes, she does," Jade smiled curtly and leaned forward a bit closer to him, with her hands resting on the back of her hips with her elbows pointed back.

"If we are imposing, Jade, we'll leave, we can just drive over tomorrow so Pedro can work," Ramita said as she watched Jake with curiosity. He had blue colored eyes and most of the folks she knew in Texas had dark brown eyes. It sure seemed different to look at him, as he near-abouts could pass for any Tex-Mex, otherwise. Jade had dark brown eyes to go with her dark brown hair and as a kid she fit into their area of Texas just fine as could be, but Jake's blue eyes always stood out odd, for *their* area of town.

work? -Jake signed this, and then grimaced as he gestured with his hands out in the air, palms up, if saying "now what?"

"Aww Jet... Pedro's wife, in Texas, well... she just had a baby three months ago, and Pedro came up to get a chance to earn some money from Ray, bringing in his hay, and then anything else that comes up. Ray's been a bit late this year with his hay and may run into trouble. His workers were busy with the city kids that showed up for the trail-drives. Then, too, there was the local boys, they had two trail-camps this year, and... since YOU ain't doing it yet, Ray's gotten behind." Jade said her piece well, AND ended with a cute curtsey, as she was right-pleased with herself!

"You may have seen or heard of Pedro, he was up a few years back," Matt threw in, as he tried to relax Jake by reminding him.

baby? -Jake drew a question after his sign, *'Aww Jade, I can't turn him down now... shucks... you all are ganging up on me.'*

They awkwardly prepared for supper and Ramita helped set the table, the atmosphere was happy enough, even though it was missing Jake within seconds. He took his food syringe, a spoon, and Jade's protein mix pack, dumped it all into a plastic bag, and signed for her to bring his supper in to him later. He smiled and waved at Ramita and went to his room. Just as quickly he came back for a pitcher of juice—and his special cup.

Just as he thought he had sneaked around past Ramita, she surprised him, and thanked him. She also introduced herself as Pedro's cousin and went right back to work on the table.

Wishing to avoid any further awkwardness with the newcomers as to how Jake might feel, they had a quick simple meal, and headed-out to the front porch to talk a bit, instead of talking around the supper table. This gave Ramita a chance to ask about Jake. He wasn't deaf, she knew that, and she didn't spot a hearing aid as she introduced herself. As Jade filled her in, Ramita tried to envision all that her host had been through and was amazed how well he looked after all this. She also tried to understand how it must have felt for him to never be able to talk again. Pedro was used to that, he grew up that way and was quite happy. But Jake was doing it the hard way—by waking up after coming to his full senses and facing the fact head-on, with no warning it was to be his fate.

By now, Jake had been able to put a little more weight on, although he had a bit more to go, but at least he looked like a well man now. The whole gang, Matt, Galena, Stoney, and Jade, along with Pedro and Ramita all shared question-time with each other as they gleaned more insight into each other's lives. Ramita was the go-between for Pedro, similar to how Jade and Jake's buddies were for him.

The next morning, Pedro was out early and Jake woke up to homemade tortillas from Ramita, along with huevos rancheros and papas fritas, complete with chile verde. Jade had rolled-out and cooked many tortillas at the ranches of many-a-friend near the Lyford and Harlingen areas in south Texas. But she never learned to make them though, as being a kid, she cared more for following Jake and the horses. All their friend's moms made them, so they knew just where to head for lunchtime. They were always welcomed to stay for supper, but their folks expected them home for supper and that was that. Montana changed all that—Jake knew full-well that he'd never find homemade Mexican food again, unless he went back to the Rio Grande Valley—which he did at least once a year. Yep, twin followed. Unless it was just a fast horse-buying trip and he didn't plan on staying to seek-out old friends. Then twin stayed home—and grumbled.

Jake was now in the kitchen and fondly picked up one of the tortillas. He just got the feel of it in his hand, and even rolled-up-one with the fried potato and some of the eggs and beans that were nearby in the skillet, for its stuffing. He shook his head with a half-cocked crooked smile, with remembrance of how he'd take a good hearty bite of it next, and soon finish the whole thing and be ready for another—chile and all. Jake looked over at Ramita; he then handed it slowly back to her with another soft smile, and then left the house. He just didn't quite feel like feeding himself now—his way, or any other kind of way. He explained to himself, as he tried to justify not eating, *'food can tend to spoil a man, if he ain't careful... same as to having a good cup of coffee... yeah, I sure don't want to spoil myself now do I.'*

Jake by-passed his horses as they were already out in the pasture—eating. It didn't seem the right time for treats just now, either.

Everyone had been gleaning last night, except Jake. So it was after quite a few odd experiences with Pedro, that morning in passing, that Jake began to realize either Pedro was a man of deep heavy thinking, as heavy as his thick black hair, and really lost in his work or—he just didn't have much to say. Or, maybe he was—deaf? Pedro never seemed to notice when Jake came up behind him. And when they did meet up, well, neither man had a word to say. A few smiles were always flashed, but that was about it. Then lastly in the shed, Jake knocked over box of nails, when he was rooting for something in the open shed, and Pedro didn't flinch an inch. Jake was now out sitting on the old stump near the open shed, relaxing in the near-noon sun now. He thinking all this over in his mind, when Pedro came up to him.

Pedro saw how much Jake was enjoying the sun. He came by and pointed up to the sun and then leaned back just a bit and leaned his face up into the sun, so it was now obvious that he was letting it hit his face. He posed there a minute for the full effect to be seen. Then he looked over at Jake and smiled, shaking his head as to the affirmative and voiced eagerly to Jake:

"Hehhhh~ ... ~euuur~", and then Pedro signed, *deaf-mute* -twice, to Jake—as to Pedro, it was a common sign in Mexico, and through-out south Texas. As Pedro began to spell out his name, in ASL, Jake couldn't help but notice that Pedro sounded a lot like himself. Naturally, Jake knew it was because no one ever taught Pedro how to talk or form words, so his tongue had no knowledgeable path to follow. But they did teach him how to communicate and he was doing it now. Jake tried to study the spelling hard but he just couldn't pick up on it fast. Pedro picked up on this very quickly; he slowed to a near halt and did it again. Jake smiled and swallowed hard. Surely, Jade must have squealed on his injured condition, little rat that she was. But then, this was *company*. He couldn't really blame her, they both always made company feel welcomed in every way. But did Jade really get to all the *fine points* of his problems though, he wondered? Obviously Pedro *knew* how to read and write and Jake was missing-the-boat. Jake tried to remember when he *could* read and write, but it seemed like a far-away dream. He studied Pedro's finger spelling again and tried to glean something without getting himself backed into a blank wall, followed by a headache. The "d" and the "r" and the "o" looked familiar, but he pushed the "p" and the "e" aside, even though he was sure he'd seen them too, it was just too much at the moment. He put his face down into his hands and rubbed his eyes and forehead. He remembered pointing for the "d" in dimples and he remembered the "r" when he set it on his rib for the "r-r-r" sound. He just wasn't used to seeing anyone do signs for spelling, or even a continued signed sentence, as there was no need for anyone to use them to *talk* to him. It also tended to look so different when someone ELSE did it! It was an output verses input issue, more than he had seen yet.

~*~

Jake remembered how he had learned his name from his belt. The letters were on his belt and Jade had taught him, but he was used to *feeling* signs while he thought. The only time he had needed to *see* them was when Jade first made him do them to match sounds on his body. But he had been watching himself recently as he would use these "add-ons" of Jade's (alphabet letters)—he used them with the sounds he voiced if he wanted to try to say something bad enough to form a word. He usually did this as a last resort, as it took time to think and time for the others to understand. He was getting better at it now, as time went on. On many occasions, he had actually *spelled* words and was amazed when someone understood this. Jake was *now* after all these months, starting to do Jade's "add-ons" *by habit* just as she had hoped for. He didn't lay them on the matching parts of his body anymore—he did them as Pedro did—with a free moving hand. His mind took to retain this through other channels and Jake's mind now had them available whenever he needed a sound. He would sign them at his mouth, to show the beginning sound or end sound of the word he was thinking, as he voiced whatever vowel sounds he could, in between or wherever needed. He still had trouble voicing certain sounds, but was making his own tricks as he struggled for success. The long "ee" was impossible and thus never really came out well, but Jade recognized it as "iih", so did Matt and Stoney. But it was a higher pitched version of it if he really fought for correctness, done with a noise from his throat that he only had made three or four times, and thus gave up on. He had felt like a whining puppy and it was too upsetting for him to hear. It upset him worse to realize—that this was all he could ever do.

~*~

As he watched Pedro, he was now trying to go through these sounds in his mind, grabbing for some kind of a rational order, without getting frustrated. *This guy is tryin' to talk to me and I sure know how that feels... dang it!* Jake paused, *I did this with my belt, I know I can do this... I just have to relax, is all.*

Pedro came up closer and signed, *sorry* -and, *you-headache* - and Jake gestured for him not to worry, as he continued to think on the "d-r" and by now had added the "o". Jake was thinking on the "dro" sound now and was forming it with his fingers. Pedro then signed, *name* -and then Jake got it, *'Oh, NAME! I know that sign, I know name! You're signin' your name! Why, Matt said Pedro was over at the twins, and that's where Jade got this company from... That's you! So you been trying to show me your name... Pedro... but spelled in Spanish!'*

Jake laughed and smiled up at Pedro, he pointed at Pedro, and as he sounded the name out in his thoughts, Jake finger spelled back, Pedro's way: *p-e-d-r-o * -and then signed, *but-my-brain* ... *say* ... *p-**a**-d-r-**o*** ... *for-SOUNDS-of-your-name* ... *I-confused-when-you-spell-Spanish-way* ... *I-can't-read-Spanish-anymore* ...*I-can't-read-English-anymore* ... *I-only-know-some-word-sounds-to-sign* -'*man, I'm a mess, ain't I?*'

And Pedro voiced back, "~Euuu, ~euuu!" and patted Jake on the back. He flashed a signed, *A+* -at him for getting his name.

Jake signed, *me* ... *j-**a**-k* -He had now taken to signing his name on his heart, with the twisted "a" for the long "ay" sound (taken from "ache"). He signed Jade's name there as well. Somehow, these *heartache* names seemed so appropriate to *Jade*, too, for both of them. Pedro understood right off, even with the twisted "a". Long "ay" meant nothing to Pedro, but the name spoke volumes as to their pain.

It began to dawn on Jake that this guy was quite likely to understand whatever Jake tried to communicate, so he gave it a try. After a few small "how are you's", and all that, Jake had come to know success in expressing himself, and if Pedro went slow, Jake understood him for the most part. Jade had taught him as much ASL signing as possible from Miss Kaite. Jake signed as an English-speaking thinker, because he was so desperate at times to communicate every thing, exactly the way he would have in the past. Sometimes with every detail included, and other times, he signed in broken-English, and even the ASL way, as it was faster and got the idea of what he wanted to say, out into the *world* for someone to try and understand a whole lot *quicker*.

Jake, feeling more relaxed now, signed-out how he was sorry he didn't understand, and how he was slow at some stuff, because of his brain not wanting to behave. Then he explained that he had been hit in the head, by a bull. As he did so, he seemed to really understand for the *first* time that this bull had damaged more than just his tongue.

~*~

It seemed like so long ago that he awoke to find himself stuck in heavy casts and bandages, and didn't have a clue as to what was going on. The pain and the headaches were real enough then, but somehow the damage it had fully done, never quite sunk in. He had not been fully alert, it took time for him to recover from the comatose state and reach full awareness. It wasn't until the first two weeks in March, that he began more-and-more to finally see and understand what had happened. Jade began to unfold it all, along with help from Ray and Matt. After he had come to realize and accept where he was, he was desperately trying to talk and soon learned why he could not—it hit him hard. And—harder yet, it would be.

~*~

Now he really understood that he was different in more ways than he could have understood back then, and it was all because of his head injury. Something he never thought on much—unless he got headaches. Somehow trying to explain it to someone for the first time, set it up on display as a new revelation to him.

Jake sat there a minute trying to reflect on this and wondered how his life used to *really* be. He thought that everything else seemed to be normal for the most part, and it was. His doctors had told him they thought he had progressed so-much-so, that it was a miracle to them. But—no one *knew* at the time, the confusion that was hitting him when he had to deal with written symbols. It was his own fault, he supposed now. How *would* anyone have known—he wasn't cooperating.

~*~

Miss Kaite suspected, but they couldn't force him to face what he wasn't ready for yet. He had full functioning in all others respects and the doctors were pleased. It took diligent therapy through those months to get him to that point, but on the whole he came out of the coma with great success—time to relearn basic functions was an unavoidable part of it all. He was successful in being able to *think* again. Yes, he was.

~*~

Success—he now grabbed hold of this. He was going to have success with communication now too, he had just NOW decided. He hated feeling slow, and stupid, but he had nothing to be ashamed of. Good fortune left him *something*; he didn't want to lose it now. He decided that he had come a long way and was succeeding in running the ranch, in *spite* a head injury, lost processing, and seizures. It was time to move on—a new door was daring him, and it had "Pedro" for its key.

Pedro brought him back to his surroundings, as he waved a note under Jake's face. It was a hand-drawn picture in pencil and Pedro was standing there with the picture.

Pedro signed, *work* -and pointed at the picture, as he voiced some noises. Jake looked at the picture and realized Pedro wanted some information on what to do next.

Jake drew some shelves in on a wall and signed, *loose* -and sent Pedro on his way. As Jake continued sitting and enjoying the sun, he decided he'd go help Pedro and hang around with him. Naturally—after the work—their friendship was sealed. They sat out on the porch gleaning stuff that ol' Jake missed the night before. Jake watched and tired to learn and understand all he could from Pedro. After two days of this, Ray was back and Pedro had to go.

Jake had enjoyed this guy, and not only that, it was finally setting-in-to-roost that there was nothing wrong with communication with these signs. As Pedro was collecting his things to go back, Jake walked over to his horses and leaned on the fence, to distant himself. In the old days, he'd have wished a friend good luck, as to whatever they were off to do, but now he was wishing that he *himself* would have a bit of good luck, and, more specifically, as to those communication skills. It seemed that his luck was driving away.

"Pedro wants me to stay."

Jake turned around in shock, as he didn't hear anyone come up. He was now staring at Ramita.

Without even thinking, Jake voiced, "~Wh~I~?" He was near-ready to sign it, but she caught his hand.

"It's okay, I understood you." She smiled warmly. "He likes you and he thinks I can help you, since I can talk and he can't," she explained to him, as he watched her.

They were both distracted by a honk and looked to see Pedro waving-out-wildly from the truck, as Matt was turning the truck around, to take off with him. Pedro was gesturing his wave with two hands now, and calling out all kinds of noises at Jake, so he could catch Jake's attention. Sure enough, it worked.

Jake waved with a signed, *see-you-later-good-friend* -and turned back to Ramita.

help-me? ... *how?* -Jake signed, as he wondered back at her, suspiciously thinking that she had ideas of turning him into some kind of a flapping bird—a wise ol' owl, perhaps? He was right—and he was ready. He was ready to wise-up and fly—if a hoot-owl could do it, so could he.

"There is so much I can show you with signing that Jade doesn't have time to learn or to show you in the books. Fast tricks and smoother flow, and time frames for the future and the past. Things like that... plus more vocabulary. I know all this and I have time. Pedro has a whole list of stuff to do for Ray, and if there is any communication trouble, then Ray will call me. Pedro's been there before, a few years back... so he is familiar with the place."

he-likes-me ... *right?* ... *appears-I-not-make-him-work-hard-enough!* -Jake signed, topping his "enough" with an explanation mark, as he laughed, and signed, *joke* - *'yeah, we did kind of click at that, he reminds me of Stoney, good humored and raring to go. Talks a lot too, just like Stoney! Well...the good Lord gets my drift as to that,'* he settled into a warm smile.

Ramita laughed back, "Good joke, Jake! Pedro also said he can read your face like you were a cat. Every emotion shows!"

Jake watched her as she talked and noticed she signed also what she was saying—keeping all in sync. She did it again and repeated herself, in words and sign. He sure could learn a lot faster this way, and that was plum-for-certain-sure, in his book.

Jake pointed to the northeast hay field and showed the sign for words coming out of his mouth, as he voiced, "**~Whaa**~/*k*" -The signed "k" was added immediately at his mouth and emphasized as part of the word that he tried to say, (forming the whole word: "walk"). He very well could have signed the word for walk, but after seeing Pedro relate to her with his many noises, somehow he didn't feel awkward to let her hear his voice and he figured he needed the practice anyway. And in all due kindness to his buddies, he wasn't ashamed as strongly with her, as he was at *first* when he had tried to talk to *them*. But—he wanted desperately to feel *the same* when he was with them. The throaty odd noises that he made with them, *still* brought that reality too-close-to-home and it was too hard to bear, at that time, and somewhat, now. However—*maybe someday*, maybe *some* day— was growing. Seemed it was suddenly *someday*, today.

Well, as ranching goes, the rest of the day was shot to pieces now, as far as work was concerned, and Stoney could see that now, as Jade came near and looked over his shoulder while they watched Jake and Ramita take-off. But the *eggs-of-success* were in the basket now, concerning Jake, as the reality of the work that Pedro had accomplished was now being manifested with the teaching of Ramita. With a satisfied handshake, Stoney and Jade were jumping up-and-down, just like a couple of kids. Little did they know that Pedro had helped Jake in a much *greater* way still. Self-esteem. So truly—things that are learned in *great* ways, just "got to manifest" sooner-or-later and shine like the sun. Self-esteem would someday shine in full, no matter how long or rugged the path was, that would lead to this view.

Stoney gave Jade a swing around in his arms after all the jumping, and then dared to brush her hair out of her eyes this time, and did so with a *bit* more tenderness than he dared to try in the past.

"Well, now, cowboy... just what was *that* all about?" she tested his actions.

"Well, I was hoping it was all about something you might have noticed in the past... something you never seemed to see. And I was hoping it *just might* be about something that you *just might* like at *that*." Stoney smiled at her shyly.

"Well, now cowboy, don't you just think I may be accused of robbing the cradle if I yield to any affectations that could grow out of *this-here* garden, set to be sown?" She shyly answered back, as she gently walked her the fingers of her one hand, over her many earrings and stared at him, anew.

"Well, now... I think with all these 'well-nows...' we'll just let the 'well-water' *seep in deep* from all this talk, and see what sprouts-up on *this-here* ranch." Stoney smiled a little more boldly now, as he pushed his light sandy-colored, only *slightly* wavy hair, out of his face and up under his slick new matching Stetson and gave it a secure tug—sealing his confidence, "*Well, now*... just what do you think of THAT?"

"Well!" she sparkled, as she let go of the earrings with a flip of her hand and set her index finger on her chin, in thought, "*well*... now with all this *welling-up* inside my heart, like it is... that just suits me fine, cowboy!"

Two well-meaning happy sighs, came from the two well-diggers, and a sweet lingering silence, until:

"Speaking of '*wells*'", Jade marveled, "well... ol' Jet would have nothing to do with Miss Kaite any time she tried to push signs on him, so I did it myself, in my own way. Now Ramita's taking *her* turn, and danged if we're gonna' have Jet so *full-up* of all this signing, that Miss Kaite will fall right out of her seat, if she ever hears-tell-of-it!"

Stoney and Jade walked over under the tree and stood in the noon shade, as they did so Jade stepped on a branch. Picking it up, she played with it and pulled at the leaves thoughtfully.

"You know, all it took was just a little branch full of tender buds, to start its fresh display... and Jet had a taste of some *fruit* he never knew he could produce. Why, now... with this-here branching-out from the giving-hands of Ramita, Jet will have a full harvest... a good *crop* to see him through what could have been some powerful long-hard-years ahead. Thank you dear Lord... for this little *branch of new growth*... this '*ramita*', that came our way."

CHAPTER TWENTY TWO

FALL... IN OCTOBER

JAKE was on his way into town; Matt and Stoney were with him, and *Jake* was driving. It was a great day for picking flowers, but not in the fields or the woods. Seems Jake, this tough, ranching-cowboy, had recently took to flower-picking. Seems he found a right nice place to do it, as he found a right-nice "flower"—in town. A country flower in town—of all places—would wonders never cease?

~*~

He still hadn't had another seizure episode-so it was innocently chalked-up to the dehydration. Surely he was finally well? Well? Surely, yes, dehydration was an open-door to invite their activity—but—the seizures were already *housed* at Jake's said-brain's residence, and could do as they *pleased*, any time, or place. This, Matt was learning—but being that Jade wasn't handling the subject well, Matt could only occasionally remind her. Matt, Jade, Galena, and Stoney were always eyeing Jake off-and-on though, during some of his heavy "thinking times", which he was now prone to do. He was always a thinker, but these heavy *spells* were usually times after he'd finished certain projects on the ranch and was still making sure that he had tied-up all the loose endings, he'd be giving himself a re-check, but a few too hard and too many. Once in a while—when all was well—when he realized that they were watching him *too* intently, he'd stare-off to the side a bit and over-do a stare, just to see what they'd do. When they discovered that he was playing tricks on them, he usually got hit by a sofa-cushion thrown his way, it was then open-season on him and more would follow. The first pillow always came by way of the local fast-draw of the evening— which varied—depending on who was more alert after a hard day's work. There was lots of ammunition available and plenty of throwers, since by now, Jade had moved upstairs to the room that used to be their folk's room, so the Smith ranchers now had their sofa back!

Her room was now to the left side of the stair, on the second floor. If one made an immediate left again (bypassing her door), the next few feet led to the bathroom (built just behind the stair's railed well) and Stoney's room was just to the slight right of that, and farther down the hall was the a small open room joined to the loft. The left side of the bathroom joined into Matt and Galena's room, which was to the right of the stairs (opposite Jade's). The bathroom had a nice view day-or-night, of the front property from the small window—so did Stoney's. Matt and Galena had two good window-views of the east side, plus a small window on the south, *and,* the north. Pedro and Ramita had stayed in the loft, and it openly (over a rich, dark thick wooden rail) viewed the west room—and—its large downstairs picture window (the ol' glass door).

~*~

Ramita had stayed on two weeks after Pedro and it did wonders for Jake. So much so, that he didn't mind going into town with his buddies now. This was now his third trip with them since his birthday and he was happy to be driving his truck. He'd been driving since after his birthday and was having a great time with it, he felt like a got-loose-hound with a good scent calling his name.

After the last few days in town, Jake was finally beginning to feel that he belonged here now. Lyle was long-gone and no one knew what happened to him, but one thing for sure was, he had high-tailed it out of here with the law on his tail. He was bound to get picked-up sooner or later. Angie had been busy with Alex planning their wedding and trying like heck to get him from turning "too country" on her. So now—Jake's old stomping grounds were feeling real fine under his feet again and it seemed to him that they were getting finer by each visit, as that new flower in town seemed to be blooming so fine—with tendrils that were reaching out towards him by an occasional warm, inviting smile. It was a right-fine flower too, all right, as far as Jake was concerned and he wanted to *study* it a bit more.

He was now sitting on the outside patio of the CORNER&COFFEE café, while his buddies were ordering food inside. Jake already had his coffee and was content. There was no particular reason that the guys didn't want to wait for a waitress, they just happened to run into Henry and were busy chatting with him. Jake was content to sit and listen to the nearby birds in the pine trees. His mind was on other things—the new flower in town.

Where it grew from, he *actually* didn't rightly-know, but he knew it was *potted* in town, for the most part. It was in a nice, comfortable, friendly office and that was how he first came to notice it. Why, he even got a look at this flower's name (didn't know what the heck it was though, until it spoke up) and he was doing important *chores* for his sis at the time, but he was mighty compelled to come back and wave at that nice little flower. *Rude I ain't,* Jake remembered, as he worked at drinking his coffee.

Yeah, it's official... I sure took a fall for that little flower. Never thought I'd ever show my face in town again and now I'm looking at a flower, of all things! Jake thought with a grin. Things had progressed from that one smile she gave him during his birthday trip into town—but only from gazing-distance. Jake wasn't at ease with himself or trying to "talk" with her yet, so the progress he had made so far, was window-peeking and door-waving episodes every time he'd stop by Sheriff Lowrie's office. Today he had stopped by five times and was now, at this cozy little café, acknowledging the fact that he'd finally have to admit that he'd fallen for her—tripped up on tendrils-so-fine, he reckoned, that were leading to blossoms of a lovely heart.

He suspected his buddies knew and he was waiting for the jokes:

Aww, it's all just part of the fun, he happily sighed-out in contentment with a crooked smile, and tilted his head back as he stretched back in the chair, off-setting it some, favoritely so, *I'll find a way to hold my own with them... and it will SURE be worth it.*

When they didn't come back, Jake was wondering what could possibly be keeping them, he had some good come-backs ready and they were going to waste, when suddenly, this *flower* was standing right before his eyes. He was so startled, that he near fell back and out of his chair. The coffee, just as suddenly had presented itself as a small mountain stream over the wooden beams of the table, under the pines, under the clear blue Montana sky. And—worse yet, under his wet hand and sleeve!

"That ought to *teach* you," Sofia smiled in delight, "didn't you mother ever tell you not to tilt your chair back that way?" The medium-dark, olive-colored flower, with a long dark braid down the front and dark doe-eyes, was smiling at him from under the rim of a black Stetson. The flower sure smelled right-fine, even if it *did* take to noticing coffee-messes and falling cowboys of mute-shy-response.

Jake shook his head yes, and continued to do so, as he grabbed up his chair in a hurry and smiled over at the two other customers over on the patio that were now very much amused by him.

He then humbly looked over at the customers, and signed, *excuse-me* -twice, and smiled again at them, with a sparkle in his eye, nodding toward Sofia, and sat down. He didn't even realize it, but he had picked this up from watching Pedro: if someone doesn't understand you, just sign and go on about your business, at least you tried—it would sure give folks something more to think about, wouldn't it? At least Jake made a try at being his same-old self, though little did he know, he *had*. Jake sneaked a look back and it seemed the folks had already forgotten about him and the incident, so he got back to his flower, as he wiped away what was left of the waterfall. A highly *romantic* way to meet, on this Montana, woodsy-type patio, on an October day—though not in *Jake's* embarrassed eye. After clowning around a bit at some final cleaning, he sat down and looked at her—trapped in his silence.

She ain't gonna' understand a thing I got to say... now what? Jake smiled at her again with a tiny salute of the hand, *I reckon she'll understand a smile, all right.*

"So, Jake, your friends said you've been wanting to ask me out to lunch, well, here I am. This is a wonderful place. I loved it since I first came into town. They said you wanted to know all about me, shall I start?" Sofia laughed shyly, "if not, well, then you better let me know... as I'm starting-up now and here I'll stay until the visit's over!" she said in fun.

Jake stood up and took a bow, as he presented a gesture to allow her to proceed, and this time he didn't cause a commotion with his chair. She started by explaining to him that she had been married for twenty-five years and had lived in small Texas town named Harlingen—much to Jake's amazed shock.

~*~

If was an odd marriage that had hidden undertones of unrest that she had never seen until she had moved to the said-same town where her now ex-husband had grown up. When this had happened, the relationship started to deteriorate in the midst of their children's innocent happy childhood. The four children that were her joy, eventual became entwined into the philosophical mess of their father's way of handling life-issues as to respect in the home. As would be expected, trying to teach any *further* respect, honor, and integrity in a home such as this was not to be received well. She was met with many hostilities and assaults on her character, which had left deep wounds. Such things presented in a home to a woman that has been faithful in word-and-deed leaves a home in confusion in the eyes of the children. Thus trying to keep the home together for them, the children for the most-part never saw the full effects of these verbal assaults. It finally came to an end when he threatened her in a store, and she had to leave him. Staying in Texas was no option, as he followed her around town afterwards, for sport. When she left, she left everything she had built-up during the 25 years—children included. Leaving behind her children as her life fell apart was a sorrow she had never got over, but she held tight to the good Lord's hand. They were all young adults at the time and nearly on their own, except for one, but that did not make it any less easy or right in regards to their emotions. Emotions were hurt that would never again be made well. Then, soon there were grandchildren that would never be known—as to go back even now, would be asking for a variety of harsh troubles. Physical trouble, because of the ex-husband. Emotional trouble because of the lies spread all through the small town to all her friends, and the twisting of truth done to the children. The thankful thing, now, was that he had no desire to bother her as long as she was out of sight. He now got to portray himself as the *winner* and the one deserving of pity, and that was feeding his ego and keeping him in his own territory. Trusting a man now, was something she wasn't sure she would ever want to do. So, for the most-part she was alone every day, except for her job.

She had come up here to Montana because she knew the Cook wrangler twins, and after a few hard years she was now finally settled. It had been hard to start over, as the caving-in of all she held dear was so devastating, but Montana was beautiful and she was a country gal. She had just not fit-in all the way yet. She loved living in Texas as she blended in with the Mexican community for twenty-five years, she looked near-enough the same, in features, as all her family and friends—but her Spanish was not fully correct. Her ex-husband never did his part to teach their children his language and she could only do so, so far—thus her children lost that—but at least they were still surrounded by their rich culture in other respects, and it was assured that the grandchildren wouldn't lose these treasures.

Not losing culture was important to her, as somewhere along the line, her dad's ancestors had lost their Ojibwe culture. His relatives, way back, had never let it become known, and generations grew up with no knowledge of the language or culture—it was only known that there were relatives, generations back through a few precious photos, that were Native American. Her mother's relatives came over on Ellis Island, so they *did* have something known to hold on to. This was good enough for the members in her immediate family, and any Native American blood, was for the most part of no interest to anyone else, other than an interesting curiosity of "maybe". She had married into a Mexican family, as she seemed to match them so well, and unintentionally had sought out like-features to match her search of something "missing".

Thus, after her marriage fell, that small bit of Indian was important to her. She came to understand that at one point in time far back, many mothers had paid a dear price to the loss of this ancestry, in the way of lost children and lost homes, by wide-spread damage done their Native

American families. Family damage was something she heavily understood, and she herself had experienced it, but in a far different way. Emotions are seen-and-understood as one shares the heartaches of others that grow along beside one—whether along-side one's paths of life, or, from those of the past and their story—if one cares to listen and learn, even if the trail of inner-tears is somewhat different at the initial point of suffering.

Her folks although originally from Ohio, had moved to San Jose, California, and she had been there ever since she was five until that soon-to-marry teen of eighteen years, she had become. She finished-up her story, with the fact that she had some brothers and a sister in California—one of the brothers being kindly nice enough and keep in contact when he could, and—one or two, gave a good "hey there" on rare occasions. Other than that, it was just her, alone. Here in Montana, now—as "Silicon Valley" had eaten-away the simpler areas of her youth. She was barely getting by, and the winters had been hard, many times with hardly any food or heat, but Sheriff Lenny had learned that she needed help and gave her hope, by helping her learn to work for him, when Lizzy-Ann left to be married.

~*~

As she got up to leave, Jake stopped her.

"~Whay~er~?" he quickly voiced, as he signed, *where* -and pointed with the signed, *go* -followed by a large hand drawn "?" - Confused at her soon-coming exit, his face was clearly puzzled, and he gently pulled her to sit down—afraid to show the disappointment that he'd miss her greatly.

"Oh..." she said, upon sitting. "I thought it best to fill you in with all this... now... as once you knew... you may decide I'm not *really* the special little 'flower' that you'd like to keep viewing everyday," she presented quickly, with a far-off sadness, as she held back the tiny flood-gates to her soul.

Jake was surprised when he heard the word "flower" and peered forward a bit with a curious look on his face, grimacing to voice carefully, "~How~ ... *y*/ ~ooo ... *n*/~oh~" -ending with the signs, *how-know?* ... *about-little-flower* ... *???* -he pointed at the flowered centerpiece, for clarity, and then over to Sofia—and then back-and-forth.

"Oh, your buddies told me... they must be really special... " She lowered her eyes sadly, not meaning to cause him any sad memories towards his accident, "I heard all of what happened to you Jake, and how your buddies went through it all with you... Ray too. I heard about it before I ever *knew* you, as it was my first day on the job when Lenny got the call to

report to your ranch. I had just come in for Officer Mike to help train me.
Later… when Lenny came back from Kalispell, I saw the heartache all over
his face. He had been terribly affected by something. I guess he needed to
get it out, so he told me all he knew… and how close you and Jade were to
him," she dared peek-up to him now, and continued, "he told me how he had
radioed-in from your ranch and left Mike in charge… he then drove out to
the hospital in Kalispell to meet up with Ray, Jade, Matt, and Galena. They
had left for the hospital, and got there first… long before him… because he
was still questioning Lyle's wranglers at the ranch at that time. Then when
he arrived in Kalispell, he could only stay there so long because he had to be
back in the office for morning. I never realized what a long trip it is." She
hushed a bit, saying:

"Lenny said the rescue team told Ray that they lost you due to heart
failure a few times in the helicopter, before they even *reached* the hospital.
Once you came out of emergency surgery, they didn't expect you to make it
'til morning. It was very hard for him to leave, but he had no choice. When
he was back and we were talking, well… he got a phone call. He was just
too scared to pick it up, so Mike did… and me being new here, I was nearly
feeling like I was eavesdropping into someone's private family life."

She drew silent again, as their date-of-sorts had become oddly
detoured, and a mite heavy, but the crisp fall breeze upon them, and Jake's
solemn, awaiting, face, suddenly spurred her on:

"Well… Lenny took the call then, and it was Ray on the phone and
he said he just wanted Lenny to know that they had finally been informed
more on your condition and that you were in a coma. They didn't expect
you'd be waking up, and you could pass-on anytime. Lenny just went and
told us point blank, as any good sheriff should do… then he went out onto
the back porch by the fire-pit and… well… he cried, he just sat there for
nearly two hours and cried. The stalled-out snows were moving again, and
there was a snowstorm expected… and it came down heavy and sudden, so
then I brought him in. It was a very dreary, bad time, Jake… I remember it
well."

Jake was soaking this in deeper and deeper. He had just now heard
more of part of his life—a part that he wished he knew, but wasn't sure he
wanted to go about seeking. He had lived it through once—after all—and
didn't know if he could handle living it through again, even in such new and
different light. Yet, here it was, falling like dew, from the petals of this very
fine flower. One that had nearly walked away, through pain of its own.

Sofia went on, "What I learned from all this, Jake was... you're a mighty fine man... and I wished I could have had the pleasure of meeting you... and being your friend. Little did I know that one day I would."

Well, ol' Jake was double-smitten now, and more than any school-boy crush as his heart stirred him to honor her heart's overflow:

'The last flower I tried to keep in my heart was a skunkweed at that, Sofia, but whatever you've been through hasn't distorted your petals any...' *stay* ... *visit* ... *see-what-happen-next* -Jake had just signed this, when his spying interpreters showed up, boots resounding along the wooden porch.

"He wants you to stay and keep on visiting here," Matt smiled as he tucked his hands in his pockets and leaned forward over the table just a bit, and peered-out from under his old brown Stetson, "so then-"

Stoney cut him off, as he gave his sandy ol' off-white, slick Stetson a tug on the brim, "-so then WE can see what happens next!"

"~Unh-unh~," Jake protested from under his black Stetson as he signed words coming out of his mouth, and grabbed at them, set them on the top of his hand, and sent them sailing with a flick of his other hand. He pointed at Stoney and then voiced a nasal, "~Ronn~!" while signing *wrong* -at the same time. He pointed at Stoney and shook his finger at him with a smirking-laugh, signing, *nosy-you!* -oblivious to the fact that customers on the patio were watching them ALL, now.

Matt, being the matter-of-fact one at the moment, continued to fill her in, "Then, YOU can see what happens next!" He laughed with a small chuckle.

Sofia laughed back at them, "I would love to stay and visit and see what happens! But I think I will be the *wrong* one and the *nosey* one for awhile! I will be nosey and watch and learn all your signs. Then I will be wrong, as I may not catch it all the first time! Oh, I DO sign... I did with my deaf friends in Texas... I don't read it well though, as I have a bit of a problem thinking *new* things into correct format, fast... I have to grasp at straws if things go to fast," she confessed, "but I love the language so very much!"

'So that's what you were doing that day I first saw you at Lenny's!' Jake looked at her, as it dawned on him that he now *knew* the sign she had flashed at him that day that he had presented himself as *un-rude*, in Lenny's office. Jake signed, *remember?* ... **see-you-later** ... *?* ... *remember?* -as he watched for her reaction.

"You remembered... did you? I only did it because of habit, and you were so quiet... like my friends were." Sofia was now lost in thought as she realized her friends were lost to her now, as well as her family, and she missed their sincere camaraderie. She was startled to look up and see three worried faces staring at her, all waiting to be of assistance. It nearly made her cry until she caught herself, again. She had lots of practice catching herself.

"You know... a lady can't help but feel special in the midst of three Stetsons, now can she? Did you all pick your hats to match your hair color on purpose... so you'd keep track of who's hat is who's? Now, didn't your mother ever teach you to label your things?" Sofia laughed with regal joy, as she took her Stetson off, "See? Right here... S-o-f-i-a!"

The lunch came and they all sat down to join in, and—interpret for Sofia if she should stumble, while she in-turn taught them a few signs of her own. The most gracious sign of all, however, was how she reacted to Jake's new eating skills—even though she herself, had some right-proper ones. Just into the meals, much to Matt's delight and surprise, Galena showed-up from scouting around for horse blankets, earlier. Stoney was nearly more happy than Matt, as he was sure Jade was somewhere around, but had to settle for a "no such luck". So then—Jake was now safely out of the tease-game and well, he knew:

Matt teased Stoney with more relish than a good cowboy's sandwich could hold, "Looks like Stoney's more interested in flowers too, than grazing... and we all know what *flower* that is, right?"

Stoney sat down a bit embarrassed until he realized they'd known all along, as he was the one still dropping all the hints—and harder than horseshoes-to-pole. He let the teasing flow, though he had to admit, it just seemed so different now—now that he knew Jade was *approachable*!

Before they knew it they were heading back to the ranch after what was an innocent store buying-trip, turned lunch date. Jake was hoping to pick that flower, sure enough, but he had thought today would just be window-shopping once again, in that respect—this had been a pleasant surprise. So pleasant, that Jake would have been whistling if he could, so he nudged Matt and motioned to him to take-over with some. Stoney joined-in and Jake pantomimed right along with them. To the untrained eye, Jake was just the same as his buddies—and loving it!

Back home and unloading the truck, spirits were happy. Galena drove up from behind, and was still at the gate, locking it back up. She then parked in the open shed, as was her habit. Galena, always cool and practical, made her way into the house. When she had something to say though, she went full speed ahead. She gave Jade a full report. All Jade had been interested in knowing was just how her twin was fairing, and if he was making it over any new obstacles, or if he had any setbacks—such things as that. She never expected that he'd come to be able to let a gal within 300 feet of him, and in a public open-café at that, thus—her jaw kind'a dropped in shock, but spoke-out equally fast upon recovery:

"My, my, my… and well, well, WELL… the new Jet ain't no more to be labeled shy!" Jade was full of joy and near unable to contain herself, "So *who's* the lucky miss?

"That Indian gal that works at Lenny's office, the one that looks so much like YOU, Jade."

"The one with the black Stetson and the tiny flowers down her braid, that took over Lizzy-Ann's place?"

"Yes! She's not near full Indian though… well, she does have some, but only just a bit from far-back on the father's side… she doesn't like to say much, as she doesn't like to present things falsely to anyone. Lenny told me that awhile ago… and she told me more today. Since birth records don't go back far enough, she is very cautious and never mentions it except on rare occasions. She explained to me, that for awhile years back, everyone thought it was the *in-thing* to do, to jump on the Indian 'band wagon.' Sure seemed odd, she said, as there are some that knew for a fact that they had hidden relatives that paid an awful price because they really *were*. To them, it was a treasure, not a thing to flaunt for attention or as a novelty-act of some sort. She didn't judge them badly, she was just extremely curious about it. She's new around here… but from what I've heard, she's known the Cook twins ever since she first came up here a few years *back*."

"Aww, Galena, she don't look like me much," Jade laughed, "I wear enough earrings to drown-a-cow-crossing-the-river-to-pasture!" But deep down inside, Jade was hoping that maybe her brother was *glad* to find someone familiar, someone that looked *just a bit* like his twin. That meant that somehow she was still special, and not to be forgotten in the scheme-of-things, thus she knew she wouldn't be cut-off and set adrift. *Thank the good Lord above that no sour apples were to be part of that scheme now… or… worse yet,* she continued on thinking, *as to me… there could have been a whole web of lies to get free of from lying-Lyle… if the good Lord hadn't freed me from lying-Lyle's web. Freed me… by the pain of another… and nearly… with that other's life.*

With deep remorse, suddenly Jade didn't feel very special anymore—she felt shamefully dirty.

"What's wrong, Jade... you *are* happy for Jake, aren't you... she's a good-gal, a lady... but boots-and-Stetson, down to earth, too. You couldn't be afraid of losing him, are you?"

"I seem to have taken a fall... back into that pit Jet's tried so very hard to keep me out of." Jade's mood turned dark and serious, "I *did* near lose him, and I *was* afraid... and it was all my- "

Galena cut her off at the pass-of-no-return, "Please, Jade... don't start that again, if you do... you may never pull out of it. Jake will see it in your face, you know... and he will blame himself all over again... and then he'll get down on how Stoney was trampled-up and all... and we'll have is a vicious circle into hell." Galena gave her a long hard hug, and for such a little gal, she had to work at it some, "Hey now... we have LIFE here... new life... and look at Jake, why he's even got a gal, and you never thought you'd see the day. By, the way... this one will last, she *loves* horses!"

As the word "horses" hit it all on home, they stared at each other in sealed-approval, knowing full-well as to one *other* fact—a gift from God above had now been dropped in their midst—and hoof-stomped, sure enough. They laughed, doing a joint foot-stomp of their own: Jake had a gal!

With a smile back on her face and Galena by her side, they took-off to the basement to work, followed later by email-checking and supper, they had the rest of the evening filled up.

The guys on the other-hand finished unloading the truck and had gone fishing.

The rest of the week showed itself as a tough one. There was lots of hay to start buying and driving to do to fetch it, and after hauling in back, they were setting it up in the lofts, and replacing other special food, grain, and other supplies for the soon-coming winter. Thanksgiving holiday would be soon-coming and they wanted to be done by then. Snow would be showing-up heavy, unless it stalled-out (as it did on odd occasions), but it would be freezing-up around these parts soon enough.

The workload was becoming hard on Jake, but he wouldn't confess to it. Stoney wasn't doing too well, either. He still carried his cane around, although he really didn't have a need for it—only on *his* rare occasions when he tended to over-favor the leg while he was working, hoping to avoid the strange collapsing-annoyance. He took to leaving it much closer in range now, instead of ditching it in corners, and the guys were tripping over it constantly. His leg gave out three times since they started this work and it was a shock to him. Jake was limping really badly and Matt was getting worried. It was more his hip now, than the muscle damage in his leg, as he would balance oddly and not put much pressure on it, but in doing so his hip took the brunt of it, and when lifting things, this added to the problem. His neck and shoulder were beginning to ache in a terrible way from strain, and his arm was beginning to show signs of serious weakness. He was just plain pushing too hard at his first winter prep-season. Well, shucks—it was his ranch and he loved it! Matt finally had to get up in the night, and do-up as much work in the barn as he could, just so there'd be no work for Jake to do in the morning. With this newfound reassurance that he wasn't needed Jake would limp away somewhere and nurse his wounds and his self-esteem. Either on the sofa, trying to rest, or—in his bed. Trouble was, the soft sofa and his bed *both* had soft holes of discomfort, and he would seep into them and hurt all the more.

Jade finally rolled up towels and propped pillows under him to keep these areas from hurting, as she positioned them to a point of support. The mattress wasn't that old, but it wasn't perfect either, and it would have to do since money was tight. His sleep had been lacking because his neck, shoulder, and hip would bother him most the night and it was wearing him out nearly as much as the work had been, and it was beginning to show. Now he was hoping (with Jade coming to his aid this way every night) that just *maybe* he would have some relief. He still had to be hunted-down and house-jailed as to chores or he'd nullify her towel skills.

One morning, he finally couldn't take this any more and took the tractor off to the northeast hay field. It was now full of broken up field hay. They didn't get much hay from it this year, which is why they were stocking up on supplies. Jake chose this field, as it was farthest from view and always needed more checking. He figured he could handle just checking the fence line. Matt and Stoney were out getting the last load of hay from another ranch and wouldn't be back until a few hours later, and Jade and Galena were in the basement. This was his chance to feel useful again— gung-ho *cowboy* that he felt he was. He drove out along the line and finally parked the tractor.

Dang cows... we just fixed this section and now we're doing a re-ride, Jake spotted the culprits too, and after about twenty minutes he had them heading back where they belonged, and he worked on the fence until he was satisfied with it. Jake turned to go towards the tractor but stopped. He had the feeling that somehow he had forgotten to do something, but he didn't know what it was. He turned and looked, *it can't be the fence... the fence is fixed... well... then what am I doing standing here with these tools?* He stared at the tractor, uselessly wondering, in a daze, as the light from the sun appeared through the clouds oddly and he was lost in it—the air seemed charged and his senses were lost—he was lost. His body had stiffened and arched back, lost to the disturbance in his brain—he fell—unconscious to the world. He began to jerk heavily. Jake now lay in the field, lost somewhere in the unknown, as his body went through a thrashing seizure that he would not remembered. He was left unconscious lying in the field where he fell.

Nearly three minutes later, Jake came to his senses as he stared for while at the blue sky and the whiteness that seemed to be moving across the expanse. His eyes rolled a bit back, as they looked around and then off to the side, as if trying to make a connection with something—anything would do, and all would do. His gaze fell on the grassy field hay and he starred at it for while. His back felt slightly cool against the ground and he smelled field grasses—he knew this smell well. He tilted his head back as if to stretch and turned back to the grasses. It seemed that somewhere far away there were some sounds—something. He had picked-up on the birds, but didn't realize what they were. There was a cool breeze passing over his face now—sure as it was fall, it had picked-up, but his face felt warm from the bits of sunny grace. He began to feel uncomfortable and agitated, but had no clue why. His surrounding were starting to bother him and he desperately tried to find something familiar. Being extremely tired, he gave up. He turned over onto his side, and looked out over the field. It looked liked some place he had been before—didn't it?—his subconscious wavered long. He started to relax a little. He lay his face down on his arm and lay there in a daze, as he began to realize he was hearing birds off in the trees. He began to get lost in the melody as it became sharper and clearer. There were trees along the fence line and he was ready to go take a look to search out the singing, when he suddenly arched violently and was tossed back onto his back. His body thrashed again for about a minute and a half. He awoke about two minutes later and stared at the sky for quite a while watching the clouds, too tired to move once again. He rolled over the other way and lay there awhile and went to sleep. Jake awoke to the sound of birds again. He slowly got up and walked around the field while his brain seemed to float. He was agitated as to why he couldn't remember what he was doing and his body ached bad. Confusion hit him hard and fast and oddly he wanted to cry. He decided to backtrack and walked along the fence. It looked fine. His face was hurting all long his left cheek and jaw, and he realized that his lips were bloody so he wiped them with his shirt. The blood on his old white shirt looked so red that it startled him. His pants were wet, and he wondered what he was doing. The urinated pants had not yet dried—since he slept on his side, they had remained shaded. He looked at his watch to see where his stickers were last set at. It was three spaces back.

Three hours, have I been working three hours? What did I do? Maybe I was down fishin', maybe that's how I got wet... maybe I just came up here? Maybe? I remember fishin', I think. I best be getting back. Jake started to look for a fishing pole but he didn't see one... then he spotted the tools in the tractor's front shovel. *I guess I was working...* he then stared at the tractor for a minute or two, for some reason it looked mighty important, but nothing registered, he had no *idea* what it was for. He turned away from it and walked across the field—leaving the tools as well—and then, on through a gate, into the east pasture, and proceeded across the tiny trickle of water known as Schribber Creek—it was at the edge of the east pasture, just before he reached the next gate. He then climbed through this next gate that opened into the barnyard. He was feeling weak, dizzy and very sick— reaching-out for the gate, he sunk to his knees and tried to vomit but nothing happened. He started again for the house, but instead went into the barn. He was awful tired as he fell into the cool hay. Always after seizures, his past shoulder and hip injuries tormented him, yet he was never able to discern why or what happened—all his body-clues were useless to him, as they slipped from his mind.

About an hour later Stoney and Matt drove up with the hay. Matt, wanting to get some water, went into the house to get it and figured to "place an order" for sandwiches, with his sweetheart. She was not too easy to find. He finally found her with Jade, in the basement, working on some mighty *important* orders that had to be mailed-out later that afternoon. Seems they had lost track of time and were graciously glad he showed-up to get them in-tune with the outside world! Stoney, in the meantime, had entered the barn and found Jake laying near the side of the barn in some hay.

"Hey Jake, did you get tired of waiting for us or something," Stoney gave him a good hearted shove, "come on... rise and shine Boss-man! If you're rested-up enough, well then, just maybe we'll let you help a little."

Jake woke and nearly swung at him, until he realized where he was, and that it was Stoney near his side.

"Hey, what's wrong Jake?" Stoney jerked back, "bad dream, or what?" Stoney looked at him, and noticed his face was bruised, "Did you fall down or something Jake, is that why you were laying down?"

Stoney studied him, and noticed somehow that Jake didn't look very alert. Stoney had never seen anyone have a seizure, and wasn't sure how someone would look if they had one, but he remembered seeing Jake dazed in the parking lot of the gas station and the spacey look on Jake's face reminded him of this. Stoney was slipping into his determined batter-up attitude, and became very serious.

"What were you doing in the barn Jake, did you fall-over in here... were you working? Did you have a seizure, maybe Jake?" Stoney sat near him, as Jake sat up all the way and looked over at Stoney. Jake was awake and knew where he was, but he wasn't quite sure why he came in here.

Jake looked up at the wall where the poles were usually hung. Without thinking, he tried to talk, but his sounds quickly betrayed him as to whatever skill he thought he had, while Stoney just stared at him, trying to figure out what was going on. Jake sat there stunned for a second, hardly believing what he heard, and then started signing:

fishing-pole ... *maybe-I-fishing* ... *finished* ... *yes-I-was-fishing* - '*The poles gone, so I was fishing... I must have left it at the river.*' Jake got up to walk back through the fields to look for the pole until Stoney stopped him, with a firm arm on Jake's shoulder. Jake usually liked to wear a white work shirt, and light-blue jeans, it was obvious that he had bits of dirt and field grass stuck on the white shirt, and in his hair, and his pants were still damp all along the crotch and down the one leg. His hat— faithful Stetson that it was—was *nowhere* to be seen. Something was definitely wrong.

"Where are you going Jake?"

Jake turned back and looked at Stoney, and then looked around the barn. He took a few steps, and then stopped.

"Jake, the poles are over there, remember, we moved them yesterday, after we came back from fishing. You stay right here, okay? I'm going to get Matt."

Jake grabbed his arm, "~Unh-unh~!" He quickly signed, but first messed it up and had to start over. He then signed again, *I-just-fell* ... *not-tell* ... *you-know-Jade* ... *she-will-worry* ... *fine-fine-I-okay* ... *I-very-tired* ... *not-sleep* ... *last-night-not-sleep* -Jake looked at Stoney, with a sorrowful begging look on his face, '*please, Stoney, please... I'm a grown man, allow me some dignity... I don't know what the heck happened. I just don't know. Please... let me try to figure it out... please.*'

Stoney's heart broke and he felt like crying, "Dear God, I wish I knew what's going on in your head right now Jake... I can see most of it on your face though. You're a grown man, Jake... you should be able to make your own decisions. I shouldn't be treating you like a kid, I sure know how that feels," Stoney gave him a pat on the shoulder, as he wondered if he was doing the right thing.

Jake got up and just then Matt neared the barn and hollered, "Stoney! Stoney... we need to look for Jake! The girls just realized they haven't seen him all morning and... oh, HEY... so you *found* him."

Matt looked at Jake, "What happened to your face?"

fall ... *okay-now* -Jake signed a reply.

"Say, where's the tractor? I didn't see it when we pulled-up and turned-around. Did you use it Jake?" Matt slowly took in Jake's appearance; he looked like one of the horses that had just got done rolling in the hay.

Jake suddenly remembered that he had used the tractor to go check the fences. The right key word sent this precious knowledge rushing back through the door from its lost room. It all came back to him now, he remembered he had fixed the fences, but he didn't remember how he got to the barn, or why the tractor wasn't here. He remembered seeing clouds and hearing birds though, but he didn't know why they were so etched in his brain. He couldn't seem to let-loose of this thought now.

Matt came up to Jake, "Jake do you know where the tractor is or don't you, did you fall off it? Jade's told you not to use it unless we're here to go with you. How'd you get all wet, did you slip in the creek?"

creek? ... *tractor?* ... *no-not-fall-off* ... *tractor-northeast-field* ... *I-fixed-fence* ... *yes-yes-I-know* ... *I fix-fence* ... *same-fence-you-know* ... *cows-loose-too* ... *cows-in-now* ... *finish* - '*yeah, that's it...*' Jake signed again, *I'm-tired* ... *need-sleep* -with that Jake smiled and patted Matt on the back and winked at Stoney. Then Jake went to the house and seeing the girls at the kitchen window, waved, as he walked across the porch instead of entering the kitchen, and went over to the office door. He used this door and went into the bathroom on the other side of the office and cleaned up his face, and dusted off his shirt.

'*What did you do to yourself, Jake,*' he wondered to himself as he looked in the mirror, *looks like Stoney was right, I must have had a seizure. Must have been right after I fixed the fence. I remember that now, but I sure don't know why I didn't bring the tractor back... man, oh, man, what was I thinkin'? Don't make no sense to me. Maybe God's watchin' over me in some respects, huh...? ...as it might not have been safe driving it... who knows.* Now he looked down at his damp pants and seemed to finally understand, as he grabbed up a towel, to hide from the gals. At this point, he was feeling *real* glad that he had not been eating lately. Jake left the bathroom and went through the pool-table room, into the family room, and past the kitchen, and on into his room, and went to sleep. He didn't wake up until nearly nine in the evening. Jade was by his side for the last hour reading. When he awoke, she made sure he ate and drank something. She vowed she would not leave the room, if he refused. He chose the eating, giving her freedom to slip-out, and then went back to sleep.

"Looks like he's finally getting some long needed sleep," she addressed the awaiting gang, "these last few days since you guys started all that loading-up on the hay, I've been really worried about him... you know that, don't ya'?" She sat at the kitchen table allowing her presence to stir-up some clues. The guys played cards—and now a bit more intensely. Matt was doing some hunting of his own, as to clues, and Stoney sought to not drop any wrong ones—game-wise or other—while Jake's *old* presence was *sorely* missed. He used to be the *hub* here, this time of night, but seemed he was a discarded rim, now, stashed away in his dark ol' room.

Matt took his play, saying, "Yeah, we caught him waking-up from a nap in the barn, it must have been after he fixed those two patches of fence. He must have done something else though, if you said you hadn't seen him all morning. It would have only taken him an hour to fix the fence there, even if he had to push a cow or two back in." After laying down the facts as bluntly as he could, he eyed Stoney with a long stare—much to Stoney's surprise—then Matt threw down a winning hand, with a hard, unexpected smack, that near made Stoney jump.

"Well, we'll have to ask him in the *morning*," she eyed the cards oddly, pulled into wondering what their private *game* was, between them, and slapped HER hand on the table:

"AS... he's finally getting some *sleep*, and that's all I care about now. I was worried he was going to wear himself out. The doctors said that could cause *stress* and lead to a seizure... just as well as any *hidden* injury triggers, as you all know."

Stoney, after seeing Matt's stare, started to get his conscience in a dire-straight if ever a crooked path could lead to one, and was just a bit stressed himself. Annoyed, he decided to turn in, and was followed by the rest of them as they chose the same decision.

The next few days had gone by without incident and Stoney began to relax. Matt *didn't* though and he stuck close to Jake, not as a guard, but as his best buddy. He took him fishing, and brushed the horses with him, and lastly they even took-off to the twin wrangler's ranch to collect some birds to take to the rescue center. They had some wonderful time with Mac, too, he was so glad to see Jake on his feet again after the way he saw him last. Mac used to play professional baseball, and they always had great visits with him. Not only did his "bat" stories match his bird stories, as to successful entertainment, but his rescue center was highly honored place of refuge far-and-wide. He was tall and on the blond side. He was good with target and skeet shooting, and was an all around outdoorsman. His wife Diane Elaine always loved nature since she was a kid. She was in a sense, one of the "critters" that he had rescued, as she came out of a bad marriage. She finally had a wonderful home with Mac now, and his nature, along with the nature they both loved, would be their continual pleasure, as they rescued other critters and birds along the paths of life. Mac was thinking to rescue Jake at the moment—as if once, had not been enough. He had a private talk with Matt, as Jake was looking a bit run-down. Matt figured by now, that if others noticed, it was time to ask Jade what she wanted to do about it. Jade was already making plans of her own about this and Matt was soon to discover it—and the ride home to this discovery was more like a mission now, than the jaunty truck-romp it had been earlier.

So—being it was the last week of October now and Jade had figured this had gone on long enough. Jake had been refusing to go for any medical check ups, and she made an appointment that had actually been long over due. The soonest she got was November fifteenth. She told Jake though, that if he ended up in the emergency, she would leave him in the hospital, feeding tube and all. If he planned on wearing himself out, she'd sooner care for sick horse—so she claimed—food syringes or what-not. He yielded for an appointment in November.

It was now a beautiful fall morning and Jake was using it (along with Jade) to take pictures of the horses. They were hoping to sell them as calendars. As it neared noon, the rest of the gang joined in. The girls separated and rode the horses down to the river. Matt, Jake and Stoney road the horses up to the off-property northwest ridge, and on up through the dense woods towards the high north trails. Jade would have rather taken the high country and had the guys do the river, since she was still not feeling right about her brother's appearance. But as far as she knew he had been holding his own, and Jake had insisted he was going as he *acted-out* his usual, "I'm the boss-man routine". This "Jake-drama" was now one of his *new* ways to talk. He was becoming quite good at it, with much-added over-emphasized dramatics and flamboyancy—most likely *half-of-which* were unnecessary, but thrown in for the heck of it. Occasionally though, if he ever felt he had intimidated her in any way—he'd end the routine with a bit of his Jake-charm and flashing smile—followed by a tipping of the brim of his Stetson. If he didn't have it on, no matter—he'd go and get it.

Jake wanted some really nice fall pictures for Sofia, as he was making her a calendar of her own for the Thanksgiving holiday. It would be her first time out to the ranch. He had just the spot in mind for some great pictures and assured Jade that he would be fine since Matt and Stoney could take care of him. He and the guys had to do it; they knew what he wanted in the way of scenery, so this was their project. Matt still was not taking his eyes off Jake, but was trying to be as casual as he could about it. Stoney seemed to know something and that bothered him too. But if Stoney wasn't talking, he'd just have to wait it out.

'*This wide Montana land is truly the hand of God,*' Jake thought as he felt his body move with the horse, and took-in the scenery around him and breathed in the mountain air of his delight. They were up in the high Coyote Ridge area and it sure felt great! It was full of fall leaves in wonderful vivid colors. There was a bit of a wind today and the leaves moved in spurts of splashes, and Jake's mind splashed with joy, moving from tree to tree.

He had been out many times on his horse since his buddies came back to roost, but had not anticipated the newest pain-battle that had been added to his "list". He bit down hard on the so-called *bullet*, and endured the haunting pains moving through his hip and leg—it was much better than being haunted by the pain of seeing an unused horse peeking over the fence at him. Those kind of pains weren't to be soaked or rubbed away and ruined a good night's sleep twice as fast as any he'd yet known. Come a good ride, he had no words to express the satisfaction of setting himself to saddle, or the feeling of being in sync with this marvelous creature—the horse. Yep— he was addicted, he'd reckoned, and was not ashamed in the least. The noises of the horse itself as it breathed and snorted was the sound of companionship, and the noise of the creaking saddle and the hoofs on the ground were the noises of wonderful natural movement. Moving along the trail in companionship. Companionship, as it moved along the trail. Either way one said it, it couldn't be better—unless—one was joined by buddies that were in one's life for the long haul. Whether through the fog, or through the bog. Whether through the sun's scorching heat or the storm's fierce furies that beat. Life had a rhyme for every seasonable attribute that it could dish out—when one had the joy of friendship—and a sure-footed horse!

The ride was good, hard, and long, as Jake well knew by now. The air was clean and good. They stopped off-and-on and took some great shots of a variety of things. Jake wanted as much of the property available for his project—whether rocks, hills brimming with trees, graceful flowers, or nooks and crannies being exposed in the sunlight, or even the horses from the rear-view, as they passed-on down the trail through the sunlit edges of the trees.

They were making their way back down now, at a nice pleasant walk, and had come to a slightly rocky part of the path *up* along a steep drop-off. Jake slowly led the way; Matt was next, and then Stoney. The trail was tricky here, and only a thin, single-file access was possible. Matt had just made it past, and now pulled-up near to Jake's left side, as if by some unknown cue. Stoney had just passed through the narrow edge and had joined them. Now they were facing the nearby trees again, and ready to descend once again, to their left, when Matt noticed that Jake had reined-back hard from this simple walk, and the horse struggled within seconds with the odd command, as its front feet came off the ground some, with a slight rearing-up. *That ain't right*, Matt thought. Before Matt fully realized it consciously, he was already grabbing at Jake's reins and yelling:

"STONEY... get over here and grab Jake! HURRY! I can't do this alone, HELP ME!"

Jake's feet—at that time—had pushed out straight, forward, and hard into the stirrups, as he had stiffened back, reins and all, and it had sent the horse into a hard, abrupt stop, with this mid-way rearing and now "dancing". Immediately Jake's body had started thrashing on the confused though well-taught horse, as Stoney had grabbed onto Jake's belt, in back, all the while keeping himself angled, so as not to get hit. Matt didn't even know how he had reached out for him in time. Maybe he had even been expecting it, as Jake hadn't looked right all morning.

Dear Lord, this was stupid of us to do this! Just plain damn stupid! Matt thought, as Stoney was now there, slid *free* of his horse and on Jake's left, trying to grab Jake as his body fell off of the horse and onto him—the fall freeing the reins by his weight. Matt, after moving Jake's horse, was soon dismounted and moved Jake off of Stoney as Stoney crawled out of the way. Stoney had never seen anyone have a seizure, and felt at a loss as he watched Jake. Staring in shock, he quickly moved back and moved the horses all out of the way. Jake's horse was really good about odd things happening, so there was no further incident. Stoney had taken-over with the horses just in time, while Matt was with Jake protecting his head from the trail-rocks.

"Now what do we do?" Stoney blurted-out as he looked down at Matt and Jake.

"There's nothing we can do but wait, Stoney, that's usually all that one can do. Then give them rest. It depends a lot on the seizure history of the person." He sighed, "It'd take you nearly an hour to get back, and then it would take the ambulance maybe near an hour to get out this way, unless we call the VOLUNTEER EMERGENCY... and they may not even be available. We got my jacket under his head now. He didn't hit his head this time either, like in the jail, so he should be all right if we just wait it out now."

"What do you mean there's nothing we can do? What do you mean just wait? Don't you want me to ride down for to call an ambulance ANYWAYS? Matt... look at him, that's terrible... GOD, LOOK AT HIM!" Stoney hollered—and paced along the path, earnestly wanting to see to Jake, but trying twice as hard, not to. He couldn't take it and finally walked off. Matt knew what was going-on in his mind, and sighed deeply as he took care that Jake wouldn't hurt himself on any of rugged ground about him.

"When does it *stop* Matt...?" Stoney asked in sorrow as he glanced over again from a distance. Just then he ran up to Matt, seeking to push him aside, but Matt held him back.

"Let go of me, Matt! He's *dead*... he stopped *breathing*, Matt... look he's DEAD!"

"It's okay, Stoney relax," Matt tried to calm him and quickly checked Jake again.

"He stopped breathing, why don't you *DO* something!"

"No, Stoney, that's what happens when the convulsions are over. Look... see he's breathing. He should be coming around soon. He's not going to be feeling like himself, so be expecting it, okay? If he had another one immediately following and didn't regain consciousness and this continued, yeah, he would be in serious trouble, but from what we know, he has always come out of it... all we can do is hope this pattern is still the same."

Matt began to think back suddenly and added, "He did have three in a row at the jail though, but he was conscious in between... but still that wasn't good, I hope I haven't made a wrong call. But the situation leading to those were extremely upsetting... he was dehydrated... and he did hit his head badly." Matt shivered a bit, being without his jacket, and from lack of full peace now, and looked at Jake again and wished they were not so far away from the help that his buddy could very possibly end-up needing.

"Matt... I got to go for an ambulance... there's something you don't know. He had one a few days ago. I know he did, but he said he just fell... well, that *ain't* true."

"How do you know, Stoney, did you see him?" Matt's words hung in the air as he kept watching Jake. He knew now that his hunches were right as to Jake's general bearing and prepared for the confession that was looming. He had half-way accepted that it was possibly Jake's recent weakened health that was causing his worries, and was having a heap of regrets right about now.

Stoney inched closer, his shadow mingling with Matt's as Matt watched Jake, as Jade twisted and started to stir some and opened his eyes slightly. Matt talked to him quietly and watched for his responses.

"When I found him in the barn, he was sleeping, Matt. So I just thought it was because he's been working too hard, and all. Then I saw his face, and asked him if he had fallen. He looked kind of messed-up and dazed. I asked him what he had been doing... he looked up where the poles used to hang and they were gone, so then he said he was fishing," Stoney shifted his weight, "well, he couldn't have been fishing... the poles were all hung up. I got suspicious when he didn't seem to know what he was doing." Stoney sulked in shame, "I was going to tell you all this, but Jake made me promise. I don't know what was the harder burden... having to make a promise like this to your friend, or having to make it to your boss... and then knowing that he *expects* you not to *break* it. Now look what I did." Stoney sighed heavily, and looked off into the sky as the air cleared and some clouds moved on through. The clouds sure looked pretty against the dark green pines, and the sky was so very blue:

Dang... I sure am feeling blue, to boot, Stoney thought as he stared off along the upper ridge and the spectacular tree-line. Just a few minutes ago they were part of this picture too lovely for words, full of cowboy spunk and having a blast with the horses. Now Jake was laying in the dirt—bruised and soiled. It was all just too much to comprehend right now.

"You didn't do any thing Stoney... you were doing what your heart told you was best at the time. If anyone is at fault, it's me, I had a feelingly he just didn't look right, and I didn't listen. This is new to *all* of us Stoney." Matt threw a stone over towards Stoney's way to get his attention, "Hey, how would we feel, if we felt somehow that we had no say in *our* lives anymore? How would we feel... how do you think Jake feels? He's a grown, man! Blast-it, Stoney... and we're all watching-out for him, like if he's a kid or something." Matt got up and stretched out his legs, and looked off into the trees as the breeze brushed by his face. *God, I love it up here, we all do... what a way for Jake to end up, just because he wanted some pictures... come on Lord, we need some help now*, Matt sighed, as he now looked down towards the Smith Ranch:

It was so far below, and was beckoning strongly to him, with its homey presence. Matt stood there as the sun hit his face through the wispy clouds. The sun sure felt good—it seemed that it was the only thing that felt good, right about now. Matt went back and sat in the dirt at Jake's side.

Though Jake never had excessive saliva drool as a danger, due to his mouth damage, Matt turned him over out of medical habit. Jake luckily never bit his inner lip—and biting his tongue, would never be.

"Stoney, I need help to get him back, we're just going to have to pray that I made the right call. Hopefully he won't have another." Matt noticed Jake move now, trying to roll to his knees and stand, and with more forceful efforts and some agitation.

"Hey there pard, calm down... it's me... Matt... can you hear me, Jake? Let's see if you can relax now, okay buddy?"

Jake yielded to the pressure of Matt nudging him down and stared around at his surroundings, as if in deep concentrated thought. He then started to push at Matt as if to move him out of his way, so he could see what was going on, vainly trying to grasp what was happening. After some time, and a bit of patience on Matt's part, and recovering on Jake's part, they finally reached communication. Matt crouched down near Jake and helped Jake turn over and rest. As Matt explained what had happened to him, Jake stayed on his side with his hand as a pillow and Matt's hand on his shoulder. At this point Jake did not resist any comforting and that was a good sign. Jake was real tired, and now relaxed with the scenery.

Jake noticed Matt's boots, consciously, but from deeper within, and *not* by purpose-driven determined thought: *those boots sure look crisp and clear in the light... looks like some kind of an art picture... with the blue, Levi legs draped over them. The rocks sure add to the feel... kind of a country look.* Jake stared out past Matt's boots and over at his hat that was lying on the ground, and continued, *that looks like my hat layin' in the dirt over there. It sure is black... it sure stands out in the light real crisp-like.* Jake's field of gaze progressed to the grass along the trail, *the grass is movin' soft in the breeze... seems to almost look like its alive... colors are nice. Pretty green... the trees sure look nice... lots of colors, the ranch sure looks nice this time of year, and...*

"~Eueuu~, ~euu~," Jake started to get up, as he voiced out something. Matt helped him sit up. His purposeful consciousness was suddenly aroused:

'*Where am I? What happened?*'—he searched Matt's concerned face. *house?* -Jake was still half-lost as he signed *house,* only, and started looking for it, round about him.

"We're on the outer, far north-ridge trail... Coyote Ridge area, Jake... house ain't here now... it's down the trail, okay... " Matt tried to get his attention, "Can you get it, Jake? Do you understand me? We were taking pictures, remember, now?"

where-my-camera -Jake shook his head, yes, as he signed with slow, fumbling difficulty.

"It's up on the horse, Jake, don't worry about it, it's alright, we were riding, remember?"

where-my-hat? -

"It's over by Stoney, he'll bring it, okay?"

Jake looked up and saw Matt's horse nearby and signed, *where-my-horse?* -

"Let's get up, Jake... we'll go get it, come on, let's go." Having said this, Matt helped Jake up.

The agitation had worn off, but now Jake was uncomfortable in his damp, soiled pants, as well as still half-lost. He lowered his head into his hands, as Matt helped him walk around. As Jake studied the ground, while they walked, it seemed that his mind was as confused as the shadowed patterns of the crisscrossing, multi-tree-branch patterns on the ground. Too many messages trying to be spoken at once, now all jumbled into one message, so all that came out was an over-load, branching out all over an enclosed area, as far as the pattern could spread.

After walking around in the crisp fall mountain-air and sitting in the warm sun-of-contrast for awhile, Matt decided to take the chance that Jake could make it home. Stoney, who had finally calmed down, joked a bit with Jake, as it was his own personal way to lighten his mind of the weighty situation at hand. They covered Jake's nice new saddle with Matt's old jacket and they helped Jake on his horse and Matt mounted up behind him, so they could ride double. Stoney led-on and Matt—helping Jake rein— watched to see that Jake could follow him, as they made their way home. It was a hard enough ride, without them being followed by the stabbing thought that they could have *lost* Jake down the steep cliff of the ridge, just back along that path—depending on which way he may have fallen—if it this episode had happened just *thirty* seconds earlier.

As they neared the house, the girls and their horses were still gone— picnicking, most likely. Jake was glad; otherwise he would have needed to sneak into the house with Matt's *help*. Yep—he was the boss-man, and Matt would *have* to do it—Jake would *see* to that. Now there was something else that Jake was going to *see* to, instead—he made this known the minute they

got him off his horse. Although Jake did not have another *seizure*, he DID
have a serious *protest*. He did not want Jade to know—it was now time to
vow silence. Matt and Stoney were now at a loss, as Jake moved-off to the
side to fetch-up Stoney's cane from its rest against the nearby fence.

"See, Matt... now you've taken a fall into the same bowl-of-trouble as
me. As my adopted Ma always said, we're tainting-the-egg-whites now, and
something just may not whip up right... *now* what are ya' going to do...
huh? Remember, Jake's a grown man... hey, he's *also* our *boss-man*... are
YOU gonna' respect his wishes? Well... what are *you* gonna' do, Matt?"
Stoney stared Matt in the face, as Jake had already grabbed-up Stoney's cane
and moved-on and making his way to the house, dirty pants and all. Half-
way there, half-way dragging his leg—and only half-way on course.

"Were going to take care of the horses, Stoney... we're going to take
care of the horses. If the egg whites don't whip up right... we'll just have to
bail the cook out when the time comes—even if he falls *flat* on his face,"
Matt said, grimacing to match his tone as his eyes followed Jake, and then
quickly looked away, as—Jake *fell* at the porch.

Matt with solemn respects, gave Stoney a nudge, insinuating for him
to follow Jake, just in case, and he took the horses over to rinse them off.
Stoney had near took-off when Matt continued with a few more very
important thoughts—one in particular, that had just finished running through
his head:

"This ranch wouldn't be the kind of special place we've all come to
know-and-love, if we can't even fall-into-line behind the wishes of a
friend... or... *Boss-man*."

Mightily so—a major measure of muteness, was now *theirs*.

CHAPTER TWENTY THREE

WILD-TURKEYS

NOVEMBER was well underway and most of the winter work was done now. Jake's aches and pains had let-up and he was surely enjoying the freedom from his body's usual stronghold on him and was not having to hobble-around as much. They all spent a lot of time in between normal chores, and just enjoying the fire in the family room. They even turned the sofa, which used to be Jade's bed, over to face the fireplace, now. It's back now faced against the wall that encased the family room stairs that led up to the second level. Mama Kitty had made her appearance inside now for the winter. Her kittens all had homes, except one. It was being kept for Sofia. It would be Thanksgiving in two days, Sofia's calendar was ready, and the home was spruced up, as Jade usually had it in an easy-going, casual, appearance. She wanted it special for the holidays, not only if new people arrived, like Sofia, but just for the simple pleasures of it reminding her of her ma.

The evening was nice and peaceful, and the groceries for the holiday were bought. Jade was going to be cooking in the morning so most things would be ready a day early, and she and Galena could relax. The turkey would go into the oven for the Thanksgiving's early morn, and they would eat around four o'clock—so she roughly reckoned.

Jade had been getting "sensitive antennas" lately, which this twin was prone to do. Jake seemed to have been avoiding her, as, every time she came near, Jake made it a clear *point* for her to see the "tons" of projects he was involved in, with his buddies. They all seemed legitimate, so what was she to do? There were the horseshoe crafts, cowboy lampshades, and more, plus there had been the photos to develop and sort, for more calendar designs, and then lastly there was Sofia's card signing and wrapping to do. Jake was a very busy man—so it would seem. Too busy for his twin, so the story seemed to be drifting. And—before that, there was winter's extra household check-up-chores, so at first she didn't pay it much mind when their paths failed-to-cross as often, but now she was suspecting something was wrong. This had been going on since the end of October, during the time that Jake seemed at the end of his rope physically, and now it was November and she still didn't feel at ease. He seemed to have made it though these rough weeks and there he was lying on the sofa, happy as can be, with Mama Kitty.

What am I missing? What is it... dear Lord... what is it? If I don't know, well, YOU surely do. Jade sent up her usual distress signal to the Lord, as she sat down in a chair near the fire, within good staring-range of her brother, much to his dismay.

He smiled at her with fond affection but a bit of added caution. He knew she was ready to close in. As a move for escaping her sisterly or womanly intuitions—he didn't much care which, as they *both* worked, and he needed to hide—he reached for a magazine.

"Jet, you read that *three* times today, and you can't even read," Jade reminded him, as she sent-out her Cheshire-cat smile—and mite TOO bold.

He turned it over and showed her the picture of Texas bluebonnets—there was one page full of them on each side, as a panorama, and not a word in sight. Jake smiled back at her with quickly raised eyebrows, and ducked back to his make-shift hideout.

"I thought Texas was off-limits?" she came up and pulled the magazine away with a skilled abrupt jerk. "Aw, come on twin, I miss you."

She proceeded to tell him about all her plans for the holiday meal, and who would come and when, as she watched him carefully while they took turns stroking the cat—who was loving every minute of this half-hearted beginning, of a heart-to-heart. As, at least *one* heart was stirring, as it approached the familiar starting gate, alone.

Oh my... that's it. It's in his FACE! Jade thought, as she rubbed the cats nose. *Ramita told me how Pedro could read Jet's face so easy. He's just like a cat, you can see all his feeling and emotions. Now I know why, projects or not, there is some reason why I haven't been able to get close and follow my twin. He didn't want me to see his face... he knows there's messages there for me to pick- up- on.* Jade slipped her hand under Jake's arm socket and lay by his side innocently as the fire warmed them. As they sat there in the stillness of the firelight, the noises of the fire became more-and-more apparent, and the warmth in Jake's heart began to stir his soul, as his conscious began to speak with each crackle of the fire.

Jake now knew he was caught, his hideout was in the hands of a sister who knew and loved him well. His hideout was perhaps the very signal-flag that finally got her fullest attention. He realized that he had done-himself-in: *Aw well... us cowboys always face-up... sooner or later... yeah... if our hearts wear a good, fine, clean, white hat that is... even when our Stetson-color may vary on top, it's what's inside that counts,* he half-admired himself, until he realized his guilt. Jake did some fast thought-preparing as he sucked-up and prepared to face his sister—like a good cowboy ought—as she lay there in trust.

~*~

Yep it was firmly packed down, now, Jake had devised a way to use Jade's ASL system, by using it for forming words that were supposed to come out of his mouth. He could only figure-out phonetically sounded thoughts, though. He would start with his left hand first as a signal to show words falling out of his mouth. Then he proceeded to voice, and formed the needed sounds that he couldn't say (consonants and the "ee"), by signing them at his mouth, with the other hand, when he wanted to try to voice a word. This formed a signed/voice word unit. He was surely progressing since his early days of first trying to display words form his thoughts, with his hands. The more often he used a word, the easier it was, as a habit had been formed.

Depending on his mood, or how much trouble it was at the moment, he would decide which sounds to voice. He could sound the "m", and turned the "m" into a "p" if he puffed at it, and if he twisted his jaw and lips he could occasionally get the "b". The "h" and "w" were done from his throat but he had to widen his lips to get the "w" sound, and lastly he could make a catch in his throat for the "k"—and tried to vary it for a "g". He could get very deep low moaning sounds for vowels: ah, eh, oh, uh, and oo. He used the "ih", from his throat. He desperately wanted to perfect them in some way, but they all came out with extreme difficulty, and many were for the most part, undistinguishable, and made *no* sense *without* his *added-on signs*. It was a strenuously hard job for Jake, as he contorted his jaw and mouth, and forced sounds from his throat as he tried to speak—without his tongue. Perhaps with less inner facial damage, he'd have had better luck—but—this he'd never know. Thus, he only resorted to this for heart-to-heart talks, for personal communication. Times when he wished to God that he could talk—why, he'd even overlook how he sounded, because he was so desirous to touch the heart of the one who was in need. His "talk" with Stoney during their "beer" toast was a meager beginning, it had edged Jake to some new thinking all right, but it was Pedro that had led him this far, as to voicing, and Jake humbled himself to walk-on in this way—no matter how much it hurt the wound in his heart. Double-thus and so—this was for Jade, Stoney, Matt and Ray, and very soon—Sofia.

~*~

Jake pushed her back slightly where he could view her more easily, but held her hand just exactly where it lay, and looked deep into her eyes. Jake voiced out the nearest confession he could at the moment, and it started with,

"*f*/~~oh /*r*-*g*/~ih /*v* ... *m*/~~iih" -He followed it up with his signed, *I-not-be-myself-now* ... *I-need-time-think* - *'I can't tell you sis, I've had seizures again, and I just can't confess it... I don't want to see you upset... I just keep thinkin' they will stop. I almost made it three months, I think.'*

"Thank you Jet... thank you. I thought it was me... I thought I've been too much of a mother hen. You may be a grown man, but you're my brother. It seems that now that I almost lost you, somehow I just can't seem to *hold-anchor* for myself anymore. I'm fighting not to drift... not to drift into those deep pockets of the river, where I might not swim-out-of, Jet. If I don't stay stable, or keep trusting us all to my dear Jesus, then we'll all just be drifting... drifting... I have to realize that we're on the trail of this life, and it's heading us all somewhere, but my anchor is on higher ground. I have to trust you to the One who made you... and me, for that matter. My job only goes so far. I have to realize that... or the pressures of life will drown me."

"*s*/~uhm ... h~~ow~ ... ~I~ ... *need* ... h~~eh /*l-p* ... *y*/~~oo" - *'I have to realize too... that you can only take so much... my job maybe has not gone far enough into helping you, sis. I've got some more thinkin' to do.'* Jake held her close and after a strong, long hug, she left to get ready for bed while Jake stayed near the warm fire. Holding the cat, as it purred, Jake felt the rhythm of its soothing "speak" that warmed the heart, and soon fell asleep.

It was the day before Thanksgiving and Jake and Matt were out rounding-up the cows, they then took a ride on the horses, down to get the mail. The day was beautiful, winter-cold and crisply fresh, and the snow's will, still stalled; Jake just couldn't stop the fresh thoughts that drifted back to his last riding adventure—or near-disaster, that it could have been. He trotted-up closer to Matt and swatted out at him. And as Matt turned, Jake gave him a good hearty pat on the back, thumbs up, and a warm smile that said exactly what Jake was thinking, *'Matt... thanks for so much... that's been stuck inside me for too long, lately... it's DUE time'.*

They joined up with Stoney, where he was filling-up water troughs, and checking the heating rods, while he had waited for their return. They all took care of the horses, and sat by the tack-shed for awhile just talking and looking back at last year's Thanksgiving. Matt shared with the guys that Galena was expecting a baby, so in a way there would be one extra in their family this year, but it was a *secret* and she was going to share it on Thanksgiving. Course, it wasn't now, in their inner cowboy-circle, and they all had a hoot-and-holler for Matt, and decided to celebrate. They took-off down to the half-frozen river to fish, and spent the day being lazy men facing the bitter cold, while the gals worked hard to cook the day into a hot array of wonderful scents, scents that they would catch-the-drift of, soon as they neared the house.

As supper rolled near, and then nearly rolled-on past, the guys came up into the barn and were ready to put up the poles, when they were greeted by a shocking, squabbling noise of startled, flustered turkeys that were jumping around in agitation. They were trying to find some way to get out of the corner that they were now blocked into. These wild turkeys had been hanging-around for the bits of winter grain that was spilling some, due to daily use. As it was just a little added treat for the cows to cozy-up to, the guys left it there on the barn floor. It may have only been a minor treat to the cows, but to the turkeys it was a bit of heaven—until this cowboy-episode spoiled their heavenly pleasure. The guys had seen them before off-and-on in the evening just near supper, but this time no one was hanging around, so the flock boldly had entered the barn.

The initial shock had not worn-off yet, and the turkeys were still in a frenzy, jumping around like mad trying to find a way out while going in circles looking for a door that was "men free". When the guys, still in happy surprise, finally moved out of the way, the turkeys took off—it was suddenly over just as quickly as it started. They all had a good laugh as they put up the poles, but all too soon Jake was leaning on the barn door, staring out at the running turkeys, in deep silence, as the heavy winter-air of evening settled its haze, now due, over their trail, and they disappeared from sight.

Seeing that Jake hadn't stirred, someone had to:

"Jake... what is it?" Matt asked softly, as he stood like a firm pillar near his friend's side.

"*th*/~**ih**/*n*/ **k'**~/*ing*" -Jake voiced in replay, as he continued to stare-out past the long-gone wild birds.

"Well, Jake, if you keep on staring long-and-hard like that... that's just what our supper's gonna' be, long gone... and hard to find." Stoney chirped in with a hearty laugh, as he came up behind Jake and rubbed his shoulders with a quick massage.

"So... " Stoney stared at Jake as he had gone around to face him, "So?" he said again.

So-what? -Jake signed at him, as his mind came back to barn-life.

"So, did I massage-out that deep-thinking kink?" Stoney smiled back. "Come on... I'm hungry, and thought we'd make a good entrance if we stampeded the place... like hungry fishermen men back from the fish-hunt."

"This ain't the movies, Stoney," Matt said, "and if it was... I think a director could come-up with directing a better stampede than the three of us could do..." he pointed over his shoulder, "see them COWS over there? How about we just *saunter-up* real nice and friendly-like instead... Jade don't take to stampedes in her kitchen, UNLESS, it's *cows*." Matt gave him a squared shake as he grabbed his shoulders, "Come on boy... come to your SENSES... no matter *how* hungry you are, and no matter *how* much fun a stampede is... you want to be on Jade's GOOD side, remember?"

"Sure do... why, I just thought I could do it if I showed her how *anxious* I was for her good cooking, is all!"

The three buddies took off, as the fabled three of storybook land—the three musketeers, or the three hungry bears, to take a pick—both suited them just fine.

Jake seemed to slip though the supper line, which he had been doing more-and-more since his hurting-days of October. While the gang easily chowed-down in the thick of a hearty meal, Jake's diligent streak for success at his hard eating-chore, was wearing mighty thin. It was just so much easier to skip eating, as it was hard to find fun and fellowship in it anymore. His being tired from over-working himself for so many weeks sure didn't add to the pleasures of it. Unknown to all, he wasn't drinking enough fluids either—though he had been warned at the recent doctor trip, to do so. He was now off on the sofa, by the fire, feeling extremely tired and wore-out from the walk to the river, traveling its bank, and then half-dragging himself back home. Yep, no one seemed to notice tonight as Jake disappeared, and he was glad. It was because Galena was leading up to her surprise and teasing them to hold-out until Thanksgiving, and had all of them in feigned suspense— and Jade more-so, as Matt had shucked-an-ear-of-corn early for Jade too!

Jake watched the fire, and Mama Kitty came up to lay down in his arms. Jake relaxed but his conscience again crackled as if in competition to the fire. He turned over and tried to relax, but his mind kept hauling the wild squawking-turkeys before his closed eyes. The cat had by now, curled up under his chin and he could now feel-and-hear the heavy purrs—her baby came up and joined-in as the purring near-tried to settled his soul. Jake fell asleep dreaming of wild turkeys all delivered up, roasted and stuffed, and lined-up on Jade's supper table. It seems he awoke just as quick, to the smell of them, as well. He turned over and the fire was still there, but it was now morning. The fire, upon closer look, was fresh, and the new day had more than past-dawned.

Jake got-up and saw that pots and pans were out, and biscuits and pies were in the beginning stages, but no one was in the kitchen. *Odd*, Jake thought, as he looked outside. The mystery was thus *fast* solved. Company was heading-up the driveway, with Jade and Galena leading the way, and "fast" was doing its work, once again.

There was Mac and his wife Diane Elaine, Ray and an unknown female, Lenny and his wife Sara, along with Sofia. His flower—with a flower. She had the beautiful Tiger Lily for Jade, as a hostess gift. It looked like Stoney and Matt were off somewhere to care for the horses and pass-out their treats, out-of-sight and out-of-mind, but for just a bit. They planned to ready them up for horseback riding—daring everyone to brave the cold.

True to the obvious, the company hit the kitchen before Jake knew what happened. They all entered with a wonderful atmosphere around them that soon filled the house. It was even better than the wonderful smell of the turkey. The happy sounds of their voices filled the room, and the room gave back its decorated warm comfort, as if in *echo* of this joy.

Jake was overjoyed to see Mac again, and after all the buddy-buddy stuff, he quickly motioned Sofia over and gave her a special hug all her own. Everyone soon found out that Ray and Honor were "together", as he introduced her—she was no more, an unknown. She had been out to Ray's before, for summer trail-rides at his ranch and had helped work with the kids, but no one had paid much attention to her in the past—except Ray. She always seemed to be passed over, or hid in the background. But Ray had noticed her since way back, and what he saw, had stood the test of time, and he figured it was about time he enjoyed her quality company—before time passed him by, as he wasn't getting any younger, though honorably so.

"Don't mind Jet," Jade snickered and made a face at him. "He slept in his clothes... AGAIN!"

"So, cowboy... didn't your mother ever warn you not to sleep in your clothes... in case unexpected company may arrive?" Sofia said with a gracious gentle smile, as she turned her head slightly and peeked up at him with her dark soft eyes.

Jake gestured, his '*well you caught me look*', and slipped-out of their mist to clean-up and change. About twenty minutes later he was leaving his room and into the kitchen and passing through the family room, then the pool-table room. He then joined the gang in the west living room, basking in their presence—in his home. He looked real sharp in his old-west black tie, and a nice white dress shirt, and black vest and matching pants. He looked even more gallant to Sofia, as he caressed the dainty waterfall of flowers that framed one side of her face, entwined in her long dark braid. The sound of country music was soft in the air. The fire was bigger than ever, as it lit the round fire-pit in the center of the room. The warmth touched their bodies and souls and filled the room, yet, not *near* as much as their friendships did.

Jade was in-and-out trying to do last minute baking, and came in serving drinks. She was dressed in a soft, burgundy, two-piece outfit, with tiny added glittered effects in the material, and she used one of Jake's old flannel shirts wrapped around for an apron, and was clomping-around like a horse, in her favorite old boots. Yep—she also had on, three pairs of earrings to match. She really made quite a fashion statement, for ranch-style homemakers—and smart, too—her long braids were safely tied behind her, surely now unable to fall into any bowl of mashed potatoes or gravy. The one day she chose to dress like a fine, fancy gal, she just couldn't do it all the way! Same as for the cooking, seems she just couldn't do it all the way. As much as she tried to prepare early, there was always still something left to do. So—supper was farther down the finish line, becoming a greater prize, but there would be horseback riding and lots to do until then, plus a few simple sandwiches for lunch, and finally that wonderful meal, which was now moved-up to six o'clock.

Jake hadn't eaten the day before or yet today and wasn't quite feeling well because of this. Leaving the *room* behind, he motioned he'd be back, and passed Jade as she was heading toward the west room from the family room, as she left the *kitchen* behind.

"There's grape juice in one of the cupboards, Jet... I bought it just for you... if can't find it let me know, it's a bit hidden in there," she hollered over her shoulder.

Yep, they traded spaces, as he passed through into the family room, and then went on to the kitchen, so he could get a drink—hopefully that wonderful grape juice. About a minute later Jade hear the usual loud sound of pots and pans hitting the floor as it carried through the air, and everyone jumped. Jade didn't think too much of it, though all eyes were in suspense. She quickly finished up what she was saying to Galena, and stood-up as she stated to everyone:

"It's just Jet, you see... Jet has a habit of calling me that way... excuse me, I'll be right back." She went through the family room and into the kitchen—stewing in her juices over such commotion during party-time.

Jade neared the kitchen table, still slightly disturbed at her brother, "Dad-gum-it, Jet, so you couldn't find the juice... did you have to cause such a COMMOTION... we got compa-... " She stopped in mid-sentence as she rounded the refrigerator, turning at the counter, and saw Jake's body thrashing out of control on the floor.

"RAY... HELP ME! IT'S JET!" Jade hollered out. "He's having a seizure!"

Jake was laying on his right side, at an angle to the counter, thrashing, and the back of his upper left arm was starting to hit the lower corner of the cupboards. Jade realized that he never reached the grape juice, or there would have been glass and juice everywhere. She tried to be thankful for this over-and-over, as she looked on in sorrow, unable to do anything for her twin.

Ray ran through the rooms, and the others followed, not out of curiosity, but genuinely hoping to be of help, because Jade had sounded so desperate.

"Jet must have fallen against all the pans, when he was reaching for the cupboard. Ray... we didn't even hear him fall. It's good he hit the pans... or he'd be here alone! Move him away from the cupboards, Ray... look at his arm... and there's *blood* on the floor, his face must be bleeding." They cushioned Jake's head as best they could, with towels.

Jade had moved the pots and pans from her baking, out of the way, and Sofia had helped her. Ray kept an eye on Jake, and noted what stages he was in, and how long Jake was being affected. Honor was back by the doorway to the kitchen, near the stairs, and had asked if they needed to call an ambulance. The phone was right next to her on the wall, where she stood ready. Mac and Diane were by the kitchen table, so were Lenny and Sara. Jade explained that Jake hadn't had one for nearly five months, and that the doctors told her if they refused to accept the medication, they would have to learn to deal with them, unless worse symptoms appeared, or if they become continual. Just then, Matt came in, cold air and all, to tell the guest that the horses were ready to ride, and the first thing he saw was Jake on the floor, as the automations of the seizure were just finishing.

"Not again... call an ambulance," he pointed over to Honor, and she proceeded to do so. Matt continued on, "Jake had two seizures, both near the end October, I'm afraid there could be more... he hasn't been looking well and I've been concerned. You know... I'm beginning to wondering if he's even been eating right."

Jade stood up quickly and darted her shock at his face, she couldn't believe what she was hearing, "Why didn't you TELL me? Oh Matt, how could you do this? *You've* been with him more than I have this week... and you *knew* and you didn't tell me? You're his best friend, you and Stoney, too." Jade's mind was racing now. "Why... you all care more about the *horses*... and fishing... an-"

"Jade that's not true and you know it," Ray stopped her. "Matt called me right after he learned about them... Jake didn't *want* you to know. He was obeying his wishes. What would you have wanted him to do, Jade?"

Ray continued to watch Jake for signs that he was waking up, as his body had completely collapsed now and his presence was lifeless before them for a few brief moments. Jade felt sick and had to turn away. She had witnessed two of them before, and the memories of him hanging on the fence, and being thrown-off the bed in the hospital were just too much, added to this now, was Jake laying there, in the midst of her pans and baking flour. Sofia went up to her, half with caution, and held her close—Jade held her in return.

Jake was staring and seemingly not aware of anything, fifteen minutes later he still was not very alert, and was now trying to push Ray away, as he wanted to do something, but he didn't seem to know what it was. It just seemed that Ray was somehow in his way. He was so tired though that he fell over in Ray's arms and lay there staring at Ray as if he were staring at a blank wall. The right side of Jake's face was banged-up bad—it was bloody near the ear and hairline, near his right cheekbone. Lenny went over to help Ray with Jake, and Sara was just bringing ice and a cold rag for Jake's banged-up face, as Jake's body stiffened back and he had another seizure. Ray laid him back on the floor just in time to avoid getting hit. By now Stoney came in, wondering where everyone was, leaving the door wide-open to more cold air as he hollered:

"Oh no... not *another* one!" he looked over at Matt, "we need to call an ambulance this time, don't we?"   Stifled by shame, Matt had no reply.

Jade left Sofia's arms and walked up slowly to Stoney, near dazed, and just stared at him—she studied him harder, then she opened her mouth, "You too...? You too?" She put her hand up to her head as she leaned her head down into her hand, and then drew it back up to look at him:

"Why... why? If you two had TOLD me, and you too Ray... than maybe this wouldn't be happening now. Don't you REALIZE that!" Jade lowered herself down to the floor in despair as she dared to look at her brother as he continued to have no control over himself. She wished to God that she could just touch him and make it stop, but it was not to be and she knew it.

Stoney stooped down and took her in his arms, just as Jake's body began to stop. Ray and Lenny were quickly with him; he looked dead for a few seconds and gasped suddenly, startling Jade. She looked away and clung onto Stoney, and buried her head in his shoulder.

"I'm sorry Stoney! I'm so sorry, to all of you... I'm sorry... it's that damn head injury! I just want him back like he used to be, he doesn't deserve this... this being thrown-down to the ground... or the dirt... any time or any place. He's *never* thrown anyone down in the dirt or had disregard for anyone's well-being, and look... he has no *well-being* of his own... it just ain't right... it just ain't right."

Jake was real still now and was lying on the kitchen floor, Ray and Lenny had turned him over and Jake was lying there half-asleep and half-dazed. As he lay there Jade ventured up to his side and lay her hand under his arm socket, and stroked his head. She noticed tears fall on his face and realized they had fallen from hers. Sofia came over with a tissue and wiped them for her and sat near Jake's side as well, and held his other hand. Soon, she had discovered, she also, had need of the tissue.

The VOLUNTEER EMERGENCY was out on a run and not available— about one hour later the ambulance finally came from Libby, they were just taking Jake out of the house when he had another seizure. This was too much for Jade and she ran out to the barn to be alone. Matt went with the ambulance and Ray took Sofia out the barn to wait for Jade to calm down so they could drive her to Libby. Sara, Diane and Honor opted to stay and watch her food and, Lenny, Mac and Stoney opted to put the horses away.

They were mighty thankful for clear roads and no snowfall now—no matter how *badly* they had teased of it being missed.

Thankfulness—Thanksgiving—a day to be thankful. This was not at all what most people would be thankful for, but then being thankful, is more that just supper with friends. Being thankful is—knowing that you *have* friends, in the first place. One can always find some kind of scraps tossed-out somewhere and eat garbage if one must, if a supper is hard to find—but one can't find loyal friends just anywhere. A friend does not grow out of bad garbage; a friend grows out of good compost, in the garden of cultivation, with the soil of understanding, from those that have learned that the pollution of defiled garbage poisons the growth of the precious seed of love. Many a seed had been planted in this good compost of life's trials.

Jade *wasn't* thankful she had friends—not now—she was *thankful* that *Jake* had friends. Yes, she truly was.

Leaving their plans for Thanksgiving meal as a discarded after thought, Jade had now arrived at the hospital in Libby, and Jake was in the Emergency, she was informed that they would keep him there, as his body was very dehydrated. Later she learned that he must not have been eating for quite awhile, either. He wasn't in very good physical shape at the moment, and hers nearly caved-in on the spot. The doctor on duty was warning them that after this many episodes, this was *not* going to get better and was giving them future-option of trying drugs for Jake's seizures, and suggesting appointments, but she just had to leave the decision to Jake—whenever it turned out that he would be responsive. So—they would have to wait. He was medicated for now, and would be, until his body could rest without the possibility of more seizures. Besides the IVs, she did give them permission to give him the esophageal feeding tube through a hole in his neck once again, as first priority was to get his strength back through nourishment. Wondering how his recent doctor appointment had not caught this, Jade solemnly vowed to herself that she'd *never* trust anyone again, as to his eating chores—not even Jake himself.

As of now, he would be there possibly up to two weeks. Jade, Matt, and Ray were back playing the hospital circuit, and Jake's well-being was their prize, seemed like it was taking a few re-rides for them to win it, though.

By the next day, Jake was in a room, but it was nearly a week later until he was able to make much sense of anything. His face was healing-up by now, with his body tagging along behind. He was groggy, agitated and not really sure where he was, but he *was* sure that something was wrong, as he was very uncomfortable and seemed—stuck. At first thought, he felt like he was awakening from a dream. He had been injured somehow—from a bull—but he thought he was well now, right? But then he became deeply confused—he wasn't home and he knew it. How long had he been here? Was it all a dream? *Surely* it was, even the *bull*. It was a terrible dream and he couldn't escape it, he had no tongue and it was Thanksgiving—he couldn't talk and he couldn't eat—he was even getting ready to watch everyone else partake. Perhaps it was finally all over.

Jake stirred now, as he tried to call out for Jade—she would know where he was—she always did. She would know what happened. He heard her voice and felt her hand. He had felt it for months, hadn't he? He was all right now, wasn't he? He was soon to learn it wasn't just a bad dream—his mind was clearing. He found himself staring at Jade. She was wearing burgundy clothes--the clothes from "his dream." Except for a few *inside* changes, unseen by them, she had worn the clothes all week. As his face focused on her worried features, yet again, he was now finally waking up, and right *back* where he left-off and he knew it. He had no tongue—he couldn't talk. And—it *was* Thanksgiving. But—*was*—was a mite stronger than he knew.

"Jet, can you hear me?" Jade sat nearby, watching his face. He struggled with the restraints on his wrists, that were keeping all his tube-work safe.

"Euuu~... I~ iih~... ~wha~ hah~~en'," he voiced his reply, half-asleep, followed by the signs, *where?* ... *wrong?* ... *what-happen?* - He signed with his restrained hand.

"You had three seizures... in the kitchen. Well, one was in the doorway, but near-enough. Heard-tell you had *two* others, don't that make FIVE these past months?" Jade smiled wryly. "Is that why you became so *overly* fond of Texas bluebonnets in the family room?" She studied him, highly disappointed in him, while trying so hard to be cheerful. Her twin seemed alert now, and at *least* this relieved her.

'*Kitchen... kitchen? Was I in the kitchen? You were dressed for Thanksgiving... right? Why was I in the kitchen?*' He fought for answers, '*help me sign Jade!... PLEASE! Help my hands...*' he now pleaded while signing without his needed placement: *when-kitchen?* ... *I-think-I-dreaming* ... *what-happened?* -

"Last week Jet, it was Thanksgiving... we never HAD it... the turkey flew the coop, you might say... it was cooped-up in the oven, and it near flew straight through the week, and into the refrigerator. I finally had to *freeze* it for soup. You've been here all week... you've been asleep or agitated, for the most part. The doctor said you haven't been eating. Why haven't you been eating Jet? I swear... don't you *care* about yourself anymore? What happened to you, Jet?"

Jake closed his eyes and tried to think, as he did he fell asleep with Jade's words haunting his dreams. He awoke about an hour later. His head was much clearer now, except for his guilty thoughts. He lay there watching Jade as she very slowly and gently rubbed his forehead, waiting for him to wake. He watched her in silence, as he thought:

'*Jade... I've been sick and tired of it... trying to feed myself... and with that achin' body of mine Jade. I've just been so very tired of it all. I wish I could just sit down to a good meal after a hard day's work, I really do Jade. I really do... October was really bad for me Jade... I did way to* much. Plus... somethin' happened in September, too Jade. I never told anyone... I must have had a seizure... I was sittin' in the barn on a bale of hay, trying to figure-out the fall plannin'... I don't know what happened then, I don't remember... but I woke up in the hay. Ramita saw me later, sitting in the grass, near the horses. I told her I got wet from waterin' the horses, Jade... ain't I a liar? I didn't even know how I got wet... I didn't know that day with Stoney, either, until later... then I realized it. Damn... I wet my PANTS Jade... that's what happened.' Jake closed his eyes now, and held back his tears, 'I messed-up Jade, not you. I'm tired of knowing you're always expectin' you've let me down if I mess up. I'm the only one to let me down Jade... not you... I let me down, didn't I?' He struggled with the restraints, he knew he didn't need them now—he felt so stupid—stuck, like a tethered horse. She couldn't understand his signs this way and his face earnestly implored her, for his freedom, 'Jade... I'm AWAKE now... don't you GET it?'

"Do you want to share with me Jet? I don't have to travel the road that you do... I can't pretend to know. I only have a clue, as I watch you. I didn't have enough clues to help you, did I?" she said, as she freed his wrists, "seems doctors can't even tell from a quick visit, huh?" she sighed as whatever insight she thought she had into this, finally wilted within her.

Jake stared at the white hospital ceiling, and stared at the IV, and reached up to feel the familiar feeding tube. All the memories of the months after the accident were coming to play in the field-of-his-mind as he lay there feeling his now-healed body back in bed—another hospital bed. It had felt so *good* to be free from all the past injuries. It had felt so *good* not to see his friends worried looks. Yet, now he saw them once again, still— though *not* as worried as after the accident. Yep, he had seen these same concerns recently, for these past few weeks at his ranch, and that had been weighing heavy on his mind nearly worse. Every time he had passed Matt and Stoney in the house when Jade was around, he felt like a bad dog that had been sneaking into the garbage, while little "missy homemaker" smiled happily and never knew. There she sat now looking at him—watching and waiting. Like a good sis—like a good twin. And *now* she knew.

'I've been doing some heavy thinkin' Jade... I needed some clues, too. Maybe now that I've corralled all this heavy thinkin', maybe now I'll feel more like eating again... it all started when the seizures started again, and I had so much work to do... work that I always loved, but was now hurtin' me...I just got so dad-blamed depressed... depression is a hard pit to stay out of, sis... you don't see that you're near its pitfalls, as the scenery is still

full of good views, at times... you see? ...you do all you can to ignore the
loose gravel, thinking all will be fine.' He squeezed his eyes shut tight,
really hard, *'I want it all to be fine, Jade,'* he opened his eyes slowly,
breathing easy, *'you think I want to give-up after all that time in the hospital*
and therapy? I don't want to ever lose what I fought for Jade, or what YOU
fought for.' He looked over at Jade with one last desperate plea on his face,
'Please don't let me lose it, Jade... please don't let me, twin-gal.'

Jake made a decision—for now. He only had ONE option for stability
at this point, and he had to *ride* it out, and this he now knew. But, before he
revealed his decision to Jade, he slowly signed out why he had finally
reached it:

wild-turkeys ... *wild-turkeys-flapping* ... *big-commotion* ...
same-example-me ... *you-understand-Jade?*   -Jake looked at her.

"Wild turkeys?" she whispered.

I-need-take-medicine ... *Jade* ... *I-same-example-same-
flapping-turkey* ... *everyone-need-wait-for-me-stop* ... *I-not-know-it*
... *I-never-have-suffer-from-see-it* ... *I-not-know-because-I-not-awake*
... *I-not-see-or-remember* ... *you-see-and-then-remember* ... *for-all-
your-life-you-need-see-my-seizures* ... *heavy-burden* ... *and-Stoney-
will-always-see-too* ... *you-will-never-have-peace* ... *finish* ... *if-I-
am-alone-and-seizure-then-I-never-know-what-happen* ... *I-confess-now-
Jade* ... *I-had-seizure-during-end-of-Sept* ... *alone* ... *Ramita-found-
me* ... *finish* ... *I-can-hurt-myself* ... *if-I-hit-my-head* ... *brain-
get-worse* ... *I-not-know-what-happen* ... *I-not-like-that* -Jake's
conscience felt free now, and he looked-up and studied her face.

"Jet... I... " Jade was cut-off as Jake motioned for her to stop, as his
face changed from heavy introspection, to the lightness of his release of it.

"*w*/~I~/*l-d* ... *t*/~ur/*k*/~~iih/*s*" -Jake voiced and signed,
as he strained hard for the "ee" sound. *My REAL Thanksgiving meal, wild*
turkeys, just like what I saw... just like in my dream, Jake thought, as it all
came to mind suddenly, *all my seizures served-up on the table... to my*
sister... for her Thanksgiving. It's due time.

"Jet... not just for me, or us... " Jade was *also* worried about
medication and side-effects, but now, it seemed Jake was worried about
something more—the seizures and the side-effects that they *threw* at her and
his friends.

o.k. ... *not-for-you* ... *for-ME* ... *I-want-STILL-drive-my-
truck-and-swim-deeper-in-river-AND-ride-my-horse!* -Jake laughed,
NOW-feel-better-you? ... *???* -

"Okay twin, wild turkeys it is... time to tame them. No more seizures. Aww, Jet... this is *better* than any meal I could have cooked-up for Thanksgiving. But, once you get *out* of here... you're still in big trouble mister cowboy! I'm having *every* meal with you again. Every single one... EVEN if I have to cram the food syringe down your throat. I've fed sick horses before, you know... and I sure as HECK can feed a stubborn ornery 41 year old mule, to boot! You just wait and see!"

After another week of replacing nourishment, and drug trials starting, Jake was free of the hospital and ready to face a *new* kind of freedom. And just in time, as the stress of the soon-coming New Year would soon test him, as well as add to him, his last missing pieces of a day-gone-wrong. Pieces to a *story* that he had not yet been ready to hear.

CHAPTER TWENTY FOUR

CHRIST-MUST TIME

"**I** think this is the best Christmas I've ever had in my whole life… not that the day should be seen as anything different as compared to any other day. There are so many wonderful days… like the day I learned that Jet would live… barring any complications. He was in the intensive care for the month of January. He couldn't breathe alone for so long… one of his lungs was collapsed and there was so much damage to that left side… broken ribs, but *nothing* crushed or punctured his heart. It was as if the 'waves of adversity' could 'hit the shore, but thus they could go no farther'… just like my ma always said.

He wouldn't come out of the coma, though… all we could do was wait. They didn't know for sure how bad his head injury would manifest to be, but if he *lived* then they would be able to tell by his progress. They told me he was near death, and to be ready for it. Guess it just wasn't time for him to wake-up until he was ready… guess it just wasn't time for him to *go* until he was ready… guess it wasn't time for him to go until SOMEONE ELSE was ready. Guess I don't have to be guessing no more, if I'm mighty grateful and glad he got through it, truly said.

Oh, I was *purely* grateful when he did wake up… oh YES I WAS! His eyes were bandaged and he wasn't responding though, it was slow waking… but at the end of that week he was out of the ICU. At least that was a good sign. A week later his eyes were freed-up, but this didn't help him to recognize us, as I had hoped for. He may have been awake, but he just wasn't capable of functioning correctly, it was like his mind would come-and-go, and he'd *sleep* so much. It was terrible to see him that way… he was still pretty much *lost* to us. The staff was moving him through many types of therapy though, and he was actually progressing, health-wise. We all got involved and helped. He'd tire so easily and sleep that off, too. Then when he was fully aware in March, after his initial awakening, he recognized us… oh *yes*, he did! Then even later, he KNEW us… and we *really* knew we had him back.

Ray *said* I'd be the one to know whether I would get him back on not... and I knew... and I did. I *did* get him back! But Jesus took me through some mighty powerful praying... alone in my hotel room... as I just couldn't see it at first. So you see, Sofia... I already *had* Christmas. That was MY Christmas, my special Christmas... the *real* kind from God above... I just knew it was. My twin brother was given *back* to me."

Leaving such conversation behind, the kitchen was now empty—so was Jade's heart, of one more piece of the past.

Sofia and Jade had just come out from the kitchen, and now sat among the guest. The same Thanksgiving crowd was now here, to have the meal they missed. The Bakers had stopped by earlier, and so had Johnny and Olivia, and the wrangler twins along with Pa Cook, and even Vin and Carl.

This evening, by the fire, Galena had finally announced her new-one that was on way, for those that *didn't* yet know. There was a lovely fresh Christmas tree in the west living room, that they had all decorated, and it smelled real fine, and it was full of lights—along with the cut-up feeding tube that Jade had kept all these months. Earlier she had strung it as beads, along with other beads on a golden cord, and hung over the branches, as Matt and Stoney brought her blindfolded brother in to see her marvelous creation. After voicing his complaints at such a sight, and taking it off the tree, they had a good chase with it, ending back in the living room. She told him it was her way of proclaiming her faith in him, and that she knew he would press-on for the gold—the golden cord of the un-needed feeding tube, and his continued health. With that speech that she had proclaimed (while standing on a chair in the living room in front of the gang) all Jake could do was give her a kiss on her forehead and hang it back on the tree—being thankful to high-heaven that she had stirred-up this escapade *well-before* company arrived.

The center fire-pit was lit and country music was in the air, just like before. If one looked out this window there was a beautiful view of the west pasture, well-lined with trees that followed the road up to the right, to the wrangler twins' ranch (behind Jake's, to the north). If they cut up into the hills across the road, and to the left of it, it would take them up the off-property northwest ridge without having to go through the back northwest pasture just below *Jake's* northwest ridge, to get there, as Jake had done so many times on past riding trips—treading though a field of huckleberries.

Jake now stood here looking out on the west yard. The snows of winter had been playing tricks these last two years, coming and going in spurts—it was the oddest two winters the whole Montana area had seen.

They didn't pay it much mind, as many states were having weird weather—
Jake just personally hoped it would work towards getting their ranch-life
back on track. Yep, with winter sneaking in slow, they were well-able to
face it. There was no snow worth-speaking-of, but there was a flurry of a
fluffy, furry memory, of two years back that hit Jake just now. He used to
play with his *dogs* here, but they had died of old age, both during that same
year that led to his injuries. He hadn't found any to replace them yet. He
had been too busy testing "sour apples", among other things—things he had
hoped not to dwell on tonight. Jake stood there with his arms folded, and
one hand on his chin, as these thoughts all started begging for his attention,
just as his dogs used to beg for his.

 *Nearly two years ago, I ran into those sour apples... nearly two years
ago... Jade ran into Lyle... nearly one year ago... a bull ran into me. Sure
as heck sounds wrong to call it an accident... but then, that's what it's
called when somethin' unexpectedly goes wrong... but it was intentional...
and intentionally set-up to be much more than an accident. It was more like
a grave mishap... nah... it was a traumatic disaster. Yeah, that's what it
was,* Jake was finally satisfied as to what to name his "accident". *It was a
traumatic disaster... aww heck... it sure wasn't... Stoney lived and I saved
his life and I even lived through it, too. That was no disaster. If they had to
bury us both... that would have been a traumatic disaster... and a cryin'
shame. Yeah... nearly one year ago, I had a tragic accident.*

 Jade walked up and leaned on his arm, "What ya' thinking about Jet?"

 "~Uhh~," *nothin'*   -

 "That's good… sometimes, you can get to introspecting a lot… did
you know that, Jet?" Jade smiled up at him fondly. She loved her
introspecting brother.

 With one thought-chore done, Jake looked out the picture-window
(glass door) and then *at* the picture-window, as the lights of the tree reflected
like magic *dancing* stars, drawing his attention. He then introspected some
more—this time as to how *Sofia* might be at dancing.

 He signed, *dance*   -and pointed to Sofia, she saw him, and shook
her "yes" hand in affirmative, and they danced to the song that happened to
be on: Charlie Pride's "Kiss an Angel Good Morning"—and here, Jake now
had one of his own—a dancing angel!

 "~~**Hey**~ … *we* … ~**ha**~~/*v* … *Texas* … **m**~~oo~ /*s*/~ih
/*k* … *here*"   -After Jake voiced this, he went on to sign, with a smile,
Mexican-music … *horse-music* … *just-for-you!*   -

 "Horse-music?" Sofia looked at him and wondered.

Jade laughed, "Oh, Sofia... he means CUMBIA! He loves the drum beat, he says it's like riding a horse... it's the flow of the beat, see? Horse music! Go on... dance!"

"Oh, well hey now... I'm the Cumbia-Kid... I can go all night... this music is my body's language. The emotions, feelings, and sounds in space, and the sound movements joined in secession. The invisible vibrations that become manifested by instruments played from the heart! Wonderful drums and percussion... the heart-beat of the inspirations and joys of life... all meshed-in the cumbia," she elaborated with happy, inspired gal-gusto, near as well as Jade could.

that-good–enough-for-me! -Jake signed, as he laughed at her way of putting out such enthusiasm for his horse-music.

As they danced, and quite a few at that, Jake threw-in some Tejano Tex-Mex for good measure, and eventually stopped dancing and slid back a few feet just to watch her. The way she presented the music was like seeing the drums in action, like seeing the music and all the other instruments, presenting themselves on display, as if painted on a live canvas. He marveled how she could do that. It was sometimes a bit sensual, but always clean and somehow still pure. It was coy and coquettish, yet happy and full of the pure love of fun. A few times it seemed to reflex deep thought and a bit of melancholy, but would come back out into the flow of life again with strength. Never had he seem so much expressed in so many ways. It was like watching nature in the fields with all the variety of life at hand, appearing in different ways. The steps were simple, and repetitious, and she enhanced them with Middle Eastern belly dance, along with Tahitian and some Hawaiian. This was a dancer, he now knew, and one that he enjoyed. Yep, he was sure of it, now—seemed he found a dancing angel, the kind that wouldn't *disappear* when the sun was out of sight for a season. He took one more glance at the sparkling tree-lights reflecting in the window that had led to this new path of dancing, and left any more "introspections" to fend for themselves—truly vowed—as he was doing right-fine, engrossed in dance-appreciation.

Now it was her turn to enjoy him, as he shared his smooth fluid dancing-ways along the floor as a *river* that sparkled for her heart, and he had a few foot-stomping moves as well, which added to the fun while Sofia clapped and snapped her fingers to the beat. This encouraged Stoney to grab-up Jade, and Matt grabbed Galena. They had moved around the tree, from one side, and back again, and now had a set-pattern to follow—finally even Mac and Diane Elaine joined in, and Lenny and Sara. Sara was always overflowing with fun, once she got started. Lenny had a great time with her and they'd end-up laughing even *more* than dancing. Now, Ray and Honor Wade seemed to have their own private, but respectable dance going-on, *over* near the corner of the tree. Honor never seemed to have a Stetson of her own and was always borrowing, when the need arose. Ray was just now sharing a new Stetson with her, letting her know that she'd never have to be borrowing again. They were quite content with their slow dancing, after *that* remark—it may not have matched the tempo of the music on hand, but it matched the tempo of their hearts as they pondered deeper thoughts. Thus, Honor, was welcomed to the fold, by all.

~*~

Seems like this year, the New Year would ring in with three new couples that would eventually drink from the rivers-of-delight in the years to come—one that flowed as a gift, from the hand of God. Not the spiritual delights that only He can give, as to eternity—those were there as well—but these were the pure delights of the union of hearts-and-spirits becoming one in a most honorable way—marriage. There would be a few years of nurturing, first, for sure, but the new roots would then show that they could hold the upheavals of life and stand firm and strong—together in one soil. There would now be no regrets as to these unions that would come from this year and reach-on into the future years—starting with the New Year that was soon to be.

~*~

Jade and Stoney snuck out from their midst, and climbed the open stairway that was on the side of this west room, opposite the tree (built into the room's east-side wall partition—with a stairwell to the basement, as well). They now stood there along the rich solid-wood railing, on the west-end of the home's upper loft (an enclosed "room" that ran along the southern front of the house, from a small partitioned room, just after Stoney's room, to here, where it now opened freely).

The view of the Christmas gathering, Jade's lovely party, was displayed before them. Stoney took this spur-gal's hand, and she held it dearly, in return. As they held hands and looked down, and as her head was on his shoulder, she watched Jake take Sofia over to the window seat on the south side of the room. Jade had hung up something special above the seat there, so this simple act, from her brother, made her smile. She knew what would soon take place—though not until she had climbed these very stairs, at this most proper time.

"Didn't your mother ever tell you… that if you sat under the mistletoe that you just might get kissed?" Sofia asked Jake coyly, "didn't she...?"

"~Unh-unh~, *n*/~eh/*v*/~urr~" -Jake answered her honestly, and sat there with his chin framed in his palm of his "thinking position" hand, between his index finger and thumb, all braced on his other forearm, as he thought on her presence.

After a few minutes, Jake signed, *well* ... *I-waiting* -and then gestured with his hands thrown-out and palms facing up, as in a gestured, *'well?'*

As Sofia ventured close, and Jake met her half-way, Jade continued to watch—gently, her thoughts found their way to the good Lord above, *Christ-must time... Christ must... Christ must love us... very much.* Jade slipped-off silently from Stoney's side as he let her hand slip free—she went to the back of the loft alone. She never could sing, not *even* Happy Birthday. Yep—same as her twin—but she had a very special "except". Except—when she sang to God. Yep—ever since her ma prayed for her, laying a tender hand upon her head, once upon a tender night, she had this special way to sing. Back in the loft, it came out from within her now, in unknown words that floated through the upper house in playful melodies that seemed to speak her recent thoughts, as if revealing them out loud: "Christ must... Christ must love us... very much."

CHAPTER TWENTY FIVE

SPURS... SPOONS... SPIRITS... AND SAP

JAKE was out in the yard with his babies. He was watching two of them chase each other in play, kicking up their heels and kicking up the dust, into the crisp, cold morning air. Jake was kicking-up some dust of his own—but not in play. Jade had the house smelling of venison-lentil stew. This was their traditional New Year's Eve supper, the smell caught him by surprise this morning and it was just too hard to face. He had to escape the tentacles of its hearty smell, and did-so with a wonderful horse-smell. He tried to keep his mind on the horses and their game, but the bones of his face ached from the cold winter air. So now, winter had brought on a whole new set of aches and pains, to remind him of his past injuries. Tonight was New Year's Eve—memories were stirring again.

In two days, it would be one year. One year since he was gored by the bull in two areas of his body, the left side of his chest, and then just as quickly, his left thigh. He was trampled over his legs, leaving him with a broken left hip, and near shattered left leg. The bull spun in a circle as it returned, knocking him out leaving him with a fractured skull, trampling and kicking him some more. Breaking his left shoulder and upper and lower left arm, crushing his ribs, breaking the jaw and other areas on the left side of his face and ripping it up into his mouth, destroying a most precious part of it.

After screaming in vain for Lyle's two wranglers to help, Jade had suddenly realized that Jake had not been hunting and she had ran off to fetch his gun. She had been the one to kill the bull—only by her hand was he saved. If she had not thought to get the gun, he would not be here right now. He had thus-far only gleaned a few chapters of this part of the story, and this was the story, as he had finally come to know it. He didn't know what happened because he was knocked out. Because of this head injury, he was in a coma for a month (or a few days shy of it, technically), and it was nearly another month before he was aware enough to remember much else. He didn't even remember how he saved Stoney exactly, it was all in bits and pieces, and he wasn't even sure if he even knew who Stoney was, for the longest time.

Now as he reflected on the rescue, he wasn't sure if he really wanted to know, or if he was even ready to know. Yet—it was his life, and he was missing the pieces. He was missing the pieces of Matt's rescue, towards him. No one had yet dared to share it. Matt had not dared to share it—the time was never right. Jake had gleaned a bit from Sofia, during lunch at the café, about: how his heart had stopped those few times en-route in the helicopter, and, how Lenny had cried when he found out Jake was dying. Jake looked at his hands, then down at his boots, and was struck by a wave of emotion:

I'm just a simple man... an ol' rodeo cowboy... well, an EX one, now, after all I been through... and... I'm just a dirty ol' rancher like my pa... a flesh and blood, mortal ol' cowpoke... how did I ever become so dad-gummed special to so many people... how was it? Jake thought, as tears that caught him unaware silently rolled down his dusty cheeks. He wiped them the cowboy way—as he always did—on his dusty old white shirtsleeve.

As Jake tried feebly to shove this escaped emotion back into the deep quiet root-cellar of his private property—his innermost being and all its spiritual wealth—he was suddenly interrupted. A car had come up to the gate, and a young man had opened it and was now driving through. Taking care to stop and shut it up proper-like, he now proceeded up the drive and parked in front of the house. After getting something out of the back seat, he began to head for the house until he saw Jake. Jake recognized him, as he approached with the box. He set it near the fence and approached Jake:

"I hope you don't mind that I came, I never fully apologized, I hope you accepted it. Mr. Smith... Jake... sir. I just got into town to stay at my grandparent's ranch for the New Year's celebration and... a few days more."

'*Hunter... after all this time? I thought you'd be long gone!*' Jake's thoughts jumped in surprise.

Jake motioned Hunter over, to come closer. Jake didn't know how to say anything to him, but he remembered what Pedro always did, he just signed something and let his face do the talking, *fine* -Jake smiled at him, and shook his head, yes.

Hunter tried to copy, and signed, *fine* -back:

"I hope that means everything is okay, by us, I mean... I was desperate to get away from my father, and that was my only way. I was wrong. He tried to kill my dog... I know that for a *fact*. I found the Mercedes, at the O'Rourke Ranch, and the people that owned the car told me what happened. Well, he's gone now, Jake. There's no more Lyle Barlow. He's dead."

Jake stared at him in disbelieve. This man that had tried to tear-up their home by greed, was now dead?

Hunter had no trouble reading Jake's face in this sense. "Yeah, when he heard there was a warrant for his arrest, he took off. He was spotted at a gas station, nearing Idaho, and took-off out into some old road... one that has all kinds of offshoots... these winding roads were all along some river gorge. He must have thought he could lose them and maybe lean-out towards the other main roads and hit the freeway later during the night, or something. Who knows... none of us ever will. They didn't find him then, so it looked like he lost them. Well, it turns out some rancher DID find him, it was a few hours later... that's just a guess really, but something near to that, as it was still daylight. His car was dented up, like it had rolled over a few times, and it was half-hanging backwards over the incline along the river, and he was smashed into his car... he couldn't get out and the rancher went to call for help. By the time he came back, the car had fallen near into the river, perched on a huge rock, and he was still pinned in it. About half-an-hour later, a ranger's rescue truck and even a helicopter crew went down to rescue him, but the car slid in before they could get close, while he was still pinned in it. They couldn't get him out in time. He drowned. It turned out later, he wasn't really pinned in it at all... his lower back was *broken* and he couldn't move to get out of the car. All that time he waited and suffered, he could have been lifted out of the car *long* before it fell farther," he stopped for breath, and clarity, "you see, Jake, he was waiting for someone to come *rescue* him FAST... before he'd fall to his death, and all the time he *knew* he could have been easily pulled-up-and-out with a rope! A rope that all ranchers have. And even if this guy didn't have one... his ranch was close enough he could have brought one and pulled him out, instead of having to wait so long for rescue trucks. My dad... Lyle... died knowing that he was within help, and *could* have been rescued, but he helpless to change the facts. Time's judgment was against him, and he faced each slow minute of it as it ticked by, watching that rancher watch him... while time was laughing at him... he saw it slowly run-out as he slipped out of helps reach, to his death."

Jake studied all this in thought very carefully and then voiced, "~WhI~?" as he shook his head for '*not*', and then gestured, *yell* -Jake then repeated all this, in a sign-talk version: "~whI~," *not* ... *yell* -and then he pointed at his lower back and made a sign for, *back-break* -

Hunter just looked at Jake with a puzzled face.

Jake was now at a standstill, puzzled even more than Hunter was, as he realized that he was not making enough sense to Hunter and was helpless to change the fact. Jake then fumbled for some sounds to try and explain his question better, but it was futile, and he quit after his failed attempts. Jake now started to pace the area—such an earned fate for Lyle, was accepted by Jake, but high beyond his understanding as to why—due to one main issue: *'Why didn't he just yell-out that his back was the reason he couldn't get out... why didn't he just say he wasn't stuck? How could he just let the rancher stand there, if he knew that? Can you understand me at all, Hunter?'* Jake started to walk around in circles with his hand on his forehead and was now taking a few deep sighs.

Hunter, stunned for a minute, finally understood that Jake knew there should be more to this *odd* story. He drew up his courage, and came up to Jake and stopped him, as he took him by the arm. Jake was a bit startled and snapped out of his round-of-figuring, as he watched Hunter carefully for some kind of a sign or a clue as to what was now going on. It seemed he was lost somehow, and not just story-wise, he could have sworn he was just now visiting his horses, but here was Hunter. It slowly dawned on Jake that they were talking about Lyle—a now dead-and-gone, lying-Lyle Barlow. Jake now began to wonder all over again, *'Why didn't he just tell the guy he wasn't stuck? Is it me... or am I missing something here?'*

"His face was a bloody mess," Hunter tried to explain. "It seemed he was holding his shirt on his face to stop the blood... he couldn't open his mouth, he couldn't *talk*... he would start choking on the blood flow, if he tried. At least, that's what the rancher saw clearly. And when they took his body out, there was a deep gash on the side of his face into the side of mouth, if he had let go he would have most likely choked on his own blood. And... whether he drowned or choked... his deeds sure came back on his head... that's for sure. It was really strange, Jake... who would have ever thought it." Hunter fumbled awkwardly, suddenly, and stammered, "I... I never came to tell you, I'm really sorry... I just figured you'd find out through Sheriff Lenny. But I didn't know that the police that arrived on the scene weren't tracing his initial trail. I guess they probably never knew the trouble he caused out here, and since it wasn't anything he was wanted for, according to their law, they didn't pass the word of his death on to Old-Town, or any others, nearby. So then," he finished shyly, "I went back to my mom's... free of him... and sorry to say, I don't miss him, Jake. I just don't."

Hunter stared a bit a Jake, as he thought on the noises that Jake had made in his feeble attempt to talk. In the cold December morning, the sun was moving in-and-out of the clouds and as it did so, its movements highlighted the scars that Jake still wore on the left side of his face. Hunter studied them as causal as he could—his eyes traveled downward from above Jake's left eye, and along his eye down the cheek, back under his ear, and along his jaw and around his neck and jaw. Some were deeper and more noticeable than others were. They only were noticeable more when the light hit them at certain angles. None were enough to distort his appearance—he had enough distorted appearance elsewhere—and he was aware of it every day of his life.

"I'm sorry if I've intruded here... I just... I guess, I just wanted to understand... just a little." Hunter stopped, "I mean, what you went through, and all... I never really knew. Until... well, until Sheriff Lenny did tell me later. I'm really sorry Jake. I was going to help in anyway I could, if my father really would have taken you to court... and so was my mother, she was getting some more lawyers, to jump in."

Hunters held his face down in shame, and Jake reached over and lifted it up. Jake thought on the many times that his own pa had lifted-up his own sorry-little-head in just the same way—times when he *himself* had felt ashamed as well.

"**f*/~~I /*n**" -he voiced, as he signed, *all-fine-now* -

"Oh, this is for you... from my dog and me." Hunter went to fetch the box, and handed it to Jake. "Thank you for saving my dog, Jake. Dog heroes are... well... they're hard to find now-a-days." Hunter smiled in admiration—and—now, anticipation.

Jake opened the box and a beautiful Irish Setter puppy popped out, licking his face before he had any warning. They both had a good laugh.

"Just maybe... some how this little pup can remind you that something good came out of all this. I mean, justice was done concerning my father and his deed toward you... and many others received justice as well. Maybe with this little guy running around, well, maybe he'll *harp* at you a bit to remember that God *vindicates* His heroes... as so my mom is teaching me." Hunter held out an envelope, "Keep this for anyone that wants to know, it's some newspaper clippings, and my letter that *explains* it all. I was going to mail it all, but I made it back here. I just had to try, since I had this pup that I wanted to give you... and I just had to know how you were doing... my mom helped me do it all."

Yep, winter snows were ready to bust loose soon for this soon-coming January, long overdue for a full hit, they were, and it was chilling the air— but—it was a deep warm spring in the heart of these two souls, and well they both knew, as it overpowered them both now, and too strong for words.

Hunter then turned to go, but then turned back and gave Jake a hug and then broke down crying. "I'm so sorry what my father did," he said softly, "I'm so very sorry," and fell to the ground, much to Jake's dismay, as Jake put his arm on Hunter's shoulder.

Jake looked at him, at a loss, *'if a man can't cry, he ain't no man... you hear me son? Don't be ashamed... for God's sake son, don't you dare ever be ashamed. If a man can't feel and understand the pain of someone else's soul... then there's something plenty wrong with him! I wish to God I could tell you, son... I wish to God I could.'* Jake had pulled the young man up off the ground, and was imploring with his face for the kid to understand. He was so desperate to tell him, and then—Matt showed up.

One look from Matt, at Jake's face, and the young man's tears, and Matt knew what to say. Matt and Jake thought so much the same. Jake gestured to Matt to tell him, and Matt said nearly word-for-word what Jake would have said, and in the very same tones.

They walked Hunter to the car, and watched as he left.

"So what you got there Jake... sure don't look like no horse, to me." Matt laughed

"**M~~I~**" ... *reward* -Jake voiced as he beamed, *'my little reminder! A man's deeds come back to haunt him down... and then to hunt him down... whether the bad OR the good!'*

"Wonder what ever happened to Hunter's pa... lying-Lyle," Matt said as he stroked the puppy dog and it stood up in Jake's arm and licked Matt's face. Jake's serious stare caught Matt in mid-dog-play:

"So, you know, do you, huh?" Matt replied.

Jake handed him the envelope, "**~H~~iih~** ... ***t*/~oh~/*l-d*** ... ~m~~ih', ~M~ahh~," he voiced with some added signed letters—yep, more sign-talk, it seed-planting, *was*.

They walked up to the house and Matt started to read the papers. He finished-up on the porch before they went in, and gave Jake a long hard stare of disbelief. Jake and Matt stared at each other for a brief second in silence, and then clasped each other in a long hard hug, little pup in their midst—it seemed it was raining from two pairs of cowboy eyes, both, blue ones and brown ones. After the so-called rain let up, they shook hands with a good, firm handshake and made use of their long sleeves in the cowboy way. They stepped into the kitchen, just as "pretty-as-to-please" and Jake let his little pup out into its new home—hoping to *please*.

"Oh Jet... where'd this little guy come from! Why, he's a real SETTER!" Jade squatted down to watch him and fell in love, quite *pleased* at that.

"No he ain't, he's a real *runner* look at him go! I just *bet* Jake spoiled him already with some kind of treat. Look he's taking-off after him already," Stoney declared loudly, "what a hoot, Jake with a dog again! Oh, his 'babies' got *competition* now, that's for dang sure!"

The pup followed Jake into the living room, where the Christmas tree was still up, and as Jake sat on the window seat, the pup sat with him. Unbeknown to the pup, mistletoe fever must have hit him, because he set into kissing Jake's face to all get-out! Jake spent the rest of the morning in that room, in silent thought, laid-out on its sofa cushions—so silent that at first his buddies thought he was asleep. They lifted his hat, a lame Stetson, it seemed, and just as they proceeded to nudge him, he opened his eyes and *gestured* with his hand, as if he caught them, holding them tight like buzzing flies—but sending out to them, one of his best smiles ever! As the overcast-skies were in plain view now to all, framed in the rich, wooden window-frame next to where Jake lay—Jake's heart was in plain view, displayed as if framed in a window all his own. Framed to his buddies, forever etched this day in their minds, and he was not *overcast* in the least!

"Come on Jake, time for our 'end of the year ride'... this will two years in a row we beat the snows ... sure can't waste such good ridin' fortune... snows are due heavy next week, so I heard though... and they just may not let up! Let's go, cowboy! Ray and Honor will be here later for sandwiches, and then we got to get dressed-up for pictures and all... for tonight... now MOVE IT BOSS-MAN!" Matt pulled Jake off the window seat, by his boots, and Jake fell on the floor, pup and all! Seems little pup was learning Smith-ranch duties fast—up and at it, were the rules of the day!

Jake snatched-up his new baby, and took-off toward the kitchen, and grabbed-up a tote bag out of Jade's kitchen drawer and ran out the door with his buddies.

"You need a *diaper* bag, to go with that baby harness, Jet... " Jade studied him as he latched onto her stuff, on the run. It was just too great to resist the urge, as she chastised him most *properly,* lastly, "Now don't you go forgettin' his bottle... DADDY JAKE!" she yelled out after him.

Jake was going horse-riding with his buddies, he was going to take the same route they took in October. This time he just had a gut feeling that it was going to be a trip that he'd fully *remember* and enjoy. So it was now here—the last of the year. There was a lot to put behind, in the way of memories. Then, tomorrow they would do the "first ride of the year"—

then—there'd be a lot of new memories to start chalking up. None would ever be as terrible as the ones left behind. None would ever match the memories of January 2000, the near four-month hospital stay, and a shattered ripped-up body that wasn't ever to be fully repaired. This ride was well-worth taking memories up to the *high-point* and letting them go. As the snows had not hit, except with minor flurries, this ride was still possible, otherwise, their "end of the year ride" was the *mail-run* if the snows were too deep. And—occasionally, their "first of the year ride" was near-about the same! Yet—never neglected. Yep—traditions give a family anchors. Anchors make for good family-rooting. Rooting holds deep, through the soil of life, keeping families solid for the long haul, truly said.

Ride *over*, and successfully tucked away, it was nearing the evening now, but still hours before the New Year. Jake and Jade were over in the west side of the house. Jade was looking down from the loft, out over the living room and enjoying her now-apparent "ten-year-old" twin. Jake was rolling on the floor with his new critter—dress clothes and all, rolling out the kinks in his leg, and rolling some kinks into his dress clothes. Every time he tried to get up and leave, his pup would head-him-off at the pass, any pass, or trail him to no-end. The pup, true to promise was following Jake and yapping at his heels—a constant reminder that he was there—probably for reasons all his own, as he loved puppy-treats. Plus, Jake was his new daddy, he just *had* to make his presence known!

"Your baby's harping for treats Jet. He's not going to give you a moment's peace, you know. Boy... you sure *done* it now twin!" Jade hollered down at him from the loft, "if Sofia weren't so busy out there checking out the stars, I just bet she'd have some 'didn't your *mother* ever tell you' stuff to say about *that*, that's for dang sure!" She stomped her foot at him, and hollered some more, "Now go get everyone for the pictures! It about *time* we seen you dust-bums put them dress clothes to use!"

Jade came down the open stairs, and stood halfway down the staircase, leaning over the side-rail, and faced the lit-up tree, as the guys came in. They looked really sharp in their black pants, white shirts, black vest and old west ties. They all had black Stetsons on tonight, silver buckles, and silver spurs on black boots. Ray, Jake, Matt, and little brother Stoney—tonight it was the four musketeers, as Ray was here for the night. An array of buddies—north, south, east, and west, all were equal, all the best!

After the guys' pictures were done, it was the gals' turn. This year Honor was included—and Sofia. Honor, Sofia, Galena, and the recent-cradle-robber, Jade. After some mix-matching with each other during the pictures, they were ready to count down the New Year, which was about two hours away. They sat down for conversation, shared some music, and enjoyed the decorated tree, and some gifts and spirits. There was the usual fare, in the bar, along with some fine wine, sent over earlier from Johnny. Matt, Jake and Stoney, got their shiny silver spoons out, and Jade as well, and they played spoons.

It was quite a family show, they played spoons with some foot stomping and hooting and hollering, just as fine-as-fine could be. Jade finally backed-out so the guys and their silver buckles, spurs, and silver spoons could put on a sparkling show, matching together for an in-sync cowboy show like no-other. They even played spoons on the spurs, and on the side-edge of the huge silver buckles. It was a treat such as Sofia had never seen before, nor Honor as well. Everyone was soon relaxed and dividing up in groups, telling and re-telling ranch-stories, with the spirits of each other mix-matching, just as the spirits of the bar were being mixed with perfect shots of success—and *never* an overdose.

Through all this celebrating, Jake now had *two* shadows, his *pup* was at his heels now, and Jade was to be, later, as her brother's heart was calling her. There was now no Lyle to send static to cloud her reception; she'd *keep* this meeting.

Jake, bundled up, had gone to sit out on the back door's wooden step, and was looking out at the stars. Jade, warmly bundled to follow suit, slipped out from the crowd and silently shadowed him, until she sat quietly at his side. Jake looked down at her now, there beside him.

This was the night one year back... This was the night I was going to tell Jade about Lyle, but she wasn't here at the party long enough... she went with him. Then he'd pick her up that next day... New Year's day... they'd go into New-Town to stay, to buy things and plan the wedding, and then at night she came home too late. I kept missin' the right time to talk with her, there was never a way to tell her.

Jake was in deep thought, and true to his usual stress, his head was hurting from it, but he didn't feel sick from it, and that was a good sign. He continued in thought, *then I never saw her again for a month... and when I did see here, I didn't even know if I knew her... but I knew her hand. Then... when I really knew her... I couldn't talk to her... I was never able to talk to her again. I never got to talk and tell her what I learned about Lyle. It happened... some other way.*

He gazed a few times out at the corral as it hauntingly pulled at his thoughts. It wasn't lit too clearly in the backyard, just enough that the corral manifested itself with a near invisible black velvet appearance. It was just past the small yard, a little to the left of the door, and the north pasture fence connected to it. Now, if there had been full snow on the ground—the fence line AND the round corral would be seen in fine display in the winter light—Jake was glad this was *not* so.

As Jade sat near Jake, and slipped her hand under his arm socket, they sat in silence for nearly the whole hour that remained to the year. It was near freezing, but they were bundled, and Jade's blanket that she had brought along, was great for cold feet. Soon the others found their way out to them, bringing glasses for all. Counting-down the New Year, they all walked around to the west side of the house, where the picture window was, and looked in at the decorated tree. They toasted to the New Year, to the sparkling of warm colors, in the blackness of the winter night.

There was a whole "clean sheet" of time laid before them; the old "time-sheet" was to be ripped-up now. They even used real paper. Past woes were written upon it earlier, now to be let loose of. They loved their "paper" ritual and this year there were new members of the *herd* to join in on it. Jake was the first one to take his paper out of his pocket, and they all followed the boss-man's lead, as they ripped their paper of the past year's trials, into quarters, and then, again some, and they threw them in the air, to fall where they may. Tomorrow they would pick them up and throw them away, as: all grief and cares that could be seen lingering-on, would be gone as they symbolically hit the garbage. If any woes dared to remain or surface, they would have no fullness to them, just as the ripped paper upon the ground, had no more fullness—and, would one day be—long-since-gone.

After coming in from the cold, they all warmed-up with lentil stew and venison, and warm talk. Then the girls headed-up for bed, Ray and Honor did the same. Sofia and Honor slept in the loft, and Ray took Stoney's room. Jake camped-out for the rest of the night leaning against the house on the back porch step, flanked by Matt and Stoney (and their version of *tons* of blankets) as he thought on the round corral.

Come sunrise, there were three huddled bundles, covered with the same *tons* of blankets, but—on the family room/kitchen floor instead—all blocking the back kitchen doorway that joined these two rooms, near the open counter. They had come in from the frozen northern air, sure as warm-sleeping-quarters-beats-heavy-frost-on-a-Stetson, and had fallen asleep on the *floor* after deciding to wait for the soon-coming new day of the New Year—in the house. They awoke to the New Year's day, with the smell of bacon and biscuits coming from the kitchen. They looked at each other with riding-gleams in their eyes, and headed out to ready-up the horses and hit the trail—bacon or not. Yet, much to their surprise, home-coming found them face-to-face with—bacon *and* biscuits—it had been *worth* the risk. A new batch was made, as one of the "gal-scouts" saw them coming back down the road that led down from the far northwest ridge. It was a right-nice way to start-off the New Year, with such a win. This was the easy part, though— the *hard* part was soon to come—for Jake and Matt.

New Year's day was always spent in town, come morning—and usually Jake's ranch would have a barbecue, Texas-style, within that very first day, or at least before the end of the week (to salute starting-out on the right foot). Johnny Walker had a get-together for everyone, and everyone was there. Even Angie and Alex. For the most part, Angie was civil, but spent her time with her soon-to-be bride's maids, as they talked wedding talk. Alex was with some of the other ranchers, and was talking about buying some land for after the wedding.

Last year, Jake did *not* come into town and had missed the get-together. Jade and Lyle had been here though—stopping by after their shopping. Jake and his buddies had been home—they had tried to help Jake as he tried to decide when-and-how to tell Jade about Lyle, after Jake's attempt to do so before, had fallen through. They knew he was extremely upset, and they just stuck by his side and stayed in the house. Jake had taken to drink. Drinking into and after New Year's Eve, and they had wanted to make sure he was going to be okay. Another day would pass him by again—until that second day of January.

Jake didn't quite feel at ease now, here at Johnny's, as the memories of where he was last year drifted in-and-out of his head. But these were his friends and Jade wanted new memories of the New Year here with Stoney— to wash out the old one of lying-Lyle.

Jake, Sofia, Matt, and Galena, sat in the corner and talked, as Matt did his *best* to cozy-the-day with new memories. He got Sofia to share how her past New Year holidays were spent. Always a good door-to-conversation, when new friends were joined-in anew.

~*~

Sofia's past holidays had brought her sorrows of her own, very deep ones long-since-gone. Yet, sharing, seemed to warrant the situation, as Jake had his own sorrows that haunted him, so, she shared how since her life fell apart unexpectedly one day, during a day that was as innocent-appearing as any other. She never had holidays of the same importance, ever again. She was never the same again either, deep inside, where no one would ever see-or-know, or thus, reach-out to heal. The good Lord held her hand through it all, she stated, as she walked each day alone, knowing she'd lost her whole way of life, her home and the heart of her children, and all the precious joys she had cultivated and watched grow for 25 years. The upheaval was never to be fixed, and there had never been new memories to heal the deep wounds of her heart, magnified because of children's lives that she would never be able to share again. New years and holidays, her birthday, and everyday— they were for those that had family, not her. She had herself, and God's love, though. God had kept her safe through her marriage and her divorce, and had seen her through times of no food, no companions, and no jobs, and no success no matter where she turned. Finally, her life's path brought her to the Cook twins. She had wanted her final days to be enjoyed under the Texas skies, with family—yet, maybe now instead, *Montana* skies would heal the wounds.

~*~

"Oh my," Sofia said, "now I have a job that pays enough to live on, because of Lenny's faith in me. Remember... I have problems learning new systems some times, but I make a foundation, first, in my mind, and do the repetitions... but after that, I'm fast-to-go! ...he *trusted* me to do good work, when others wouldn't... and he has been very kind and patient. Now he wouldn't get rid of me, if you paid him! No more washing dishes in the restaurants! No more living in a house so cold that I can see my own breath! Why, I can even buy *food* now and take care of my cat! After seven years something has fallen into place." Sofia smiled over at Jake, "And... something has fallen into place, in more ways than *that*... all because a cowboy opened a door, and waved 'bye'... just to be polite. I think his *mother* taught him... and taught him well," she said with tears in her eyes and a gleam in her long-humbled heart.

Well, now, this sure hit the spot for ol' Jake. If ever he needed some new memories, this sure *did* it. On this New Year's Day, he just learned that he had found someone that understood how he felt. Someone that had to build their life all *over* again after they lost something precious in an unexpected way—after they nearly lost *who* they were, *as well*. Oh, his buddies and Jade understood, because they knew him. But this gal was new in town, and he just met her, but he sensed there was an instant camaraderie when she first sat down. There was some connection and he knew it. He never would have thought he could find someone with so much in common in levels of understanding that mirrored his. Something in her heart was sweet, special and genuine. Integrity standing tall against all odds, not to be tarnished by the stains of others that sought to ruin it—the perfect match for his heart. Cider-keg perfect, so it was.

'*My whole life was nearly ended by lying-Lyle... someone that sought to tarnish me, as well, and take away my home... and my twin sis.*' Jake thought about what she had said and applied it to himself, and his new life. '*She knows what that's like, and even a step farther, as her own children don't care to ever acknowledge companionship with her again. I was so afraid I'd lose Jade and her companionship if I dared to tell her about Lyle. If I had told her and hurt her... and if she didn't understand what I was doing... what would have happened to us? The bond of a woman and her children is a bond as strong as a twin for another. It can't be explained... to lose that is like losin' part of ourselves. I never had to face it to THAT end, as my twin came to know the truth. But my whole life changed into somethin' I couldn't face, in the process... only Jade and her prayers helped me stay afloat... just as Sofia's prayers held her afloat. She's finding her a new way... a way she didn't want to face, and I am findin' my new way... a way I didn't want to face.*' Humbled by this stirred brew of feelings:

Jake reached over and took her hand firm and tender. '*Some things are just hard to figure... how they come our way, when we least expect it. Who would have ever guessed that I'd find a flower such as Sofia, in Lenny's office, as I was play-acting out my scene from "laryngitis, Jake-style"? Who'd have ever guessed that this flower came from the same kind of soil as my roots? From knowin' sorrows, to loving horses... and knowin' how to face the wonderful sun with a smile on your face and forgiveness in your heart... even when occasionally situations may be ice-cold hard.*'

New Year's Day came and went, sending everyone to their proper homes, come evening. Jake awoke early to the morning frost, and a tiny bit a sun peeking through the cold dreary clouds that still hadn't busted loose. This time he awoke in HIS room. Today was the second day after the New Year Eve. One year ago from—the day. The day he had no tongue and would never talk again. The day he would have to live with seizures or medication. The day he would never understand how to read or write again. The day he had permanent headaches and staring-spells from certain thought-processes that couldn't function. The day something somewhere in his brain was lost to him. The day he "died" three times in the helicopter, and a nearly a few times in surgery. The day that led-up the morning he went into a coma and was not to awaken for *nearly* four weeks. The months that led-up to him realizing he couldn't talk, and hated the sound of his own wordless voice and would thus live being mute, near-fully. The months that led-up the fact that he'd never be able to EAT the same again, or have the pleasure of enjoying a simple meal, alone *or* with his friends. The day that led-up to the months when he nearly broke his twin sister's heart because he just didn't know if he could toe-that-mark. Yeah, that day—a year ago today.

     'And I STILL ain't the same... as could be expected...' he thought as he looked into the mirror and then made his way to the kitchen. Ray and Honor had stayed in town this time and then gone home to Ray's ranch, and Lenny and his wife Sara had taken Sofia home. It was just the regular guys and gals, ready to face the whole new year—hopefully a great one—once Jake got through, *today*.

     Jade had made sure Jake was eating, and after he had, he moved on in to the family room near the fireplace. There was almost always a fire here in the winter, and in the west living room as well, all though they kept that one smaller, and tended to let it burn-out more, than the one in the fireplace. Today Jake sat in the chair closest to the fireplace, for comfort, and casually looked across to the window and out into the backyard's north pasture—in the back of his mind he thought of the round corral, yet he had not *planned* to so.

     Jake stood up, strangely drawn, grabbed his coat and walked outside through the back door. He looked over at the corral and stared. He didn't really remember anything. Not until, two months later in the hospital when Jade had to re-tell him about the bull, and how he was injured very severely, triggering a dislodgment of some of the memories. He remembered hearing the screaming and he knew he had to help—someone was in trouble. He remembered entering the fenced corral, he even remembered seeing Stoney and the bull's face, but that was all. He wasn't even sure how he got to the corral, until later, when he remembered he was drinking. He knew he had a whiskey bottle in his hand—it seemed he was running—running like he'd never run before.

     Jake turned away from the corral and walked to the barn and sat down where his had hid the bottles of whiskey. One of them was still stashed in the corner, the empty one. The empty one—he had finished what was left of it that day, and was starting on the other, when he heard the screaming. He sat there awhile, almost afraid to come out and re-face it in the same *way*. By the same *path*. Sure—he had come out of the barn many times, but purposely never headed through that side door, or, exactly along this same route and usually tried to *avoid* that direction completely. He had always gone from the barn and traveled to the front yard, or out to northeast pasture. And—when he went up to the north or northwest ridge, through the north

pasture, he always made sure to avoid eye contact with the round corral, as
he climbed over the connecting fence that divided the backyard and the
pasture. He had enough on his mind when he headed-up to the hills on those
occasions—he sure didn't need an extra dose of sorrows then, as he was
seeking solace in his beloved woods.

Matt was on the front porch just now, and he saw Jake enter the barn,
and from the *back* of the yard. Jake didn't have his trusty black Stetson on
and he *always* put it on when he went outdoors. This being an ice-cold
January day, it sure didn't make sense, Matt reckoned. He went in and
asked Jade if she knew what Jake was up-to in the barn, and learned that for
all SHE knew Jake was *still* in the house. Matt grabbed up Jake's neglected
hat and went out the back door—shocked, he was face-to-face with Jake.
Matt slowly handed Jake the black Stetson, in silence, as if he was passing-
on a wealth-of-experience, as if a crown, to a worried successor. Jake knew
he was receiving much more that just his hat—beloved Stetson, though it
was.

Jake looked back at Matt, and then sat on the porch. Matt sat near
him and stared out over the yard. Jake set his hat towards the back of his
head, off his brow, and leaned with his head over, rested in his palms, as his
elbows rested on his knees, as his body rested with a deep sigh. He felt like
he had finished a long race but still had one more to do. Jake's gaze
happened to fall to the side of the steps, and his playing-spoons were there.
He had set them down when Jade had come out on New Year's Eve. He had
been thinking to play them that night, as he sat in there in thought, but the
corral had haunted him instead.

Jake picked them up, and played a bit with them as from habit. He
loved the sound of it; it reminded him of the bucks that skipped up over the
rocks with a secret melody all their own, with hoofs hitting on the rocks, as
loose rocks fell into a follow-through and an echoing *phrase*. He looked at
them, wondering how he could have forgotten them here, as he then
deduced, *'so there is a way I can still use a spoon... sure enough... spoons,
any and all spoons, are for playin' now, and not for eatin' with... except
that spoon from the hospital... that special ODD one that I need now. I'd
sure like to be able to chuck it...* ' Jake looked at them again, and held them
up for Matt to see, as he played them over his fingers and *caught* them to a
halt, into his palm.

Jake stuck the pretty silver spoons in his coat pocket. He lowered his
head into his hands and rubbed it hard, especially around his temples. His
head was hurting real bad. He reached in and took his crushed pills and lay

back and rested, as Matt stayed by his side. Matt knew what Jake was
leading up to—this was the day.

Jake adjusted his Stetson and slowly stood up and walked near to the
corral. He moved closer and reached for the wooden side-rail of the
corral—he suddenly got weak inside. He had no intention to go in, he just
wanted to touch it. His mind soaked-in the feel of the wood. He rubbed
both hands along it, and then firmly placed them solid on the rail, and gazed
into the penned area as if to imagine Stoney—with the bull *over* him.

"*t*/~eh /*l* ... ~m~iih~ ... p~~/*l*/~iiih /*s* ... ~M~~a~ /*t*"
-Jake voiced, as he stared off in shock for a minute—he had never said
anyone else's name, except Jade's, and *that* was an utter failure, at that.

What little he could *say* of Matt's name, lingered in the air—it
sounded just the same as any *number* of words he may try to say, yet, it was:
Matt. It felt odd, he had forgotten what it was like to say his best friend's
name, and he'd forgotten how he *himself* even used to sound, in speaking.
Now Matt's name would forever be etched in his mind, as the "~M~ah~" he
had just heard. Jake stopped and looked down at the ground along the dirt
and collected his thought again and looked back up at Matt.

"Jake... *Jade* was the one that had a good view of what happened to
you, and she was over near the other side of the corral and was trying to
reach for Stoney, when you appeared and jumped in. Later, she said she
could tell there was something wrong with you, as you didn't move away
from the bull, and... you were wearing only that thin dress shirt and dress
jeans... yet oddly, you seemed to have just *crawled* out of bed or something.
She saw the bull hit you and it threw you across the corral. She saw you try
to rise, but you were bleeding real bad from your chest and it was running
down over your arm as you tried to hold it in. You fell before you could get
up all the way, the bull just that quick ran up in to you and hit you in the leg,
and you completely fell. It stomped on your legs... or leg, it really was...
and circled around, as you were trying to stand on the one leg, after curling
up to do so... using your arm. You couldn't... as you weren't even near
halfway up, trying to drag yourself. The bull came back and hit you in the
back of the head and... dear God... " Matt stopped as a weak sick feeling
rushed through his body as a strong wave. "Jade said... you were trying to
balance using your right arm and right leg, to get up... but you couldn't do
it, your other hip and leg were broken up. It was impossible for you to get
up... you never had a chance, Jake... it hit you from behind, and you went
down... it stomped and kicked you in to the dirt and snow. Jade's screams
for your aid, were still unanswered by Lyle's wranglers. Then suddenly, just

before that, Jade said it had dawned on her that you weren't out hunting, so your gun would be on the shelf above the fireplace mantel. She knew it was kept loaded... she ran in, climbed up and smashed the glass case with the fire stoker... took it off the bracket, and ran out and fired away into the bull 'til it fell dead. By that time you were still laying in the dirty snow where the bull had decked you. She never had a chance to run over you to you after... I got there to do that. I heard her shooting, since the first shot. I rode up from herding the cows, and I was in the corral before her. It's a good thing she didn't get to you, Jake... it's a good thing she didn't go in there," Matt said as he looked at Jake. He swallowed hard and just shook his head. "I didn't even see you at first... I just thought she killed the bull... I sure as heck didn't know where the bull came from and I didn't know why she killed it... until I got closer. I didn't even know you were lying there, at first.

   After the first shot, I had rode up fast from the cows, from the lower end of the north pasture... we weren't all that far away, you know. The bull fell just as I arrived and jumped off my horse. Like I said... I didn't even see you at first Jake, so I didn't know what happened. I went to run around to where Jade was fast approaching the fence, and I saw you... then I ran in to get you. Jade was screaming that you were dead and the bull had killed you and she was too late. She kept saying:

   'The gun was there all the time and I never knew... I could have saved him... dear God... I didn't know... I didn't know.' She kept saying it over and over, while I dragged you out from under the bull's front feet."

   Jake stared into the corral as the words he had not wanted to hear in the past settled in. The air was quiet cold and still. He knew that this had been hard on his friends, but he could never fathom to what depth, until now. He himself was unconscious, and he didn't have to see what had happened. Now, even though it was over, some of them still had to and deal with what they saw from the bull during the attack, and some had to deal with the aftermath of the damage from the bull only—any missing pieces of his life would come from them. The burden of sharing was just as hard to bear as the burden of seeing.

   He listened as Matt explained more to him—more on how Matt was the one that was then in charge of the aftermath. He was the one that desperately sought to save a dying man that was bleeding to death from many severe wounds. A man—his friend—that was going into shock. He was the one that would have to make fast decisions as where to apply pressure and where to wrap up the blood flow. He was desperate for help; he could not do it alone. Jade was the one that placed the emergency call and she was the one to run for clean sheets, towels, and blankets, as Matt's one-and-only thought was to try to save his friend, with Galena working by his side, as soft snowflakes started to descend and dance over them with unwanted revelry—numbing their hands.

Jake's mind flashed on the broken gun case, as he pictured Jade going through all this—but he suddenly realized that something was *wrong*—something was mighty out of place. *'Why did she think I was hunting... I wasn't huntin'?'*

why-she-think-I-hunting? -Jake signed. *'You knew I was in the barn, you saw me drinkin', you and Galena... why would she think I was hunting? You wouldn't tell her I was drinking... but you wouldn't tell her a lie, that's for dad-gum-CERTAIN-sure. Stoney wouldn't tell her a lie either, even if he would have known where I was... which he didn't...'* Jake came out of his thoughts and looked up with a cold hard stare—he *knew*. He knew. It was Lyle—it HAD to be.

"Lyle told her, Jake... she told us later that Lyle told her you went hunting. He never said it as in regards to any gun-power, he didn't know that a gun would come into play. He just didn't want her to go and seek your advice about the bull being in the yard, and he didn't want Stoney to seek you out either... least wise, was all I could figure. But if she wouldn't have had that knowledge in her mind, she truly would have run for the gun sooner... when the bull was over on Stoney. And you... Jake... you never would have had to go in there."

Their breath was showing mighty *heavy* in that cold winter air now. Yep—and a lot of other things were showing heavy, too.

Matt looked at Jake now and marveled at how well he looked in spite of his past wounds. He looked like he had seen hard times, but he looked well now. He was a lot stronger and finally getting his weight back after his awful time through October and November.

"I had to yell at Jade to get away... the left side of your face was broken up and bleeding all over... it was kicked-up really bad, near your eye too. You body was covered with blood. She never would have been able to handle what that bull did to you Jake. But she didn't want to leave you Jake, she just kept circling around like a bird in distress, she didn't want you to die without knowing that she was there. I think she was still in shock from what she saw happening *before* I even arrived. She finally went over to Stoney, and those wranglers finally gave-in and helped him once the bull was dead. Right about that time, Lyle showed up. I didn't see Jade's confrontation with him, I learned of it later... I was busy... busy with you." Matt hung his head down as he swallowed, and let his mind sit in the quiet darkness of closed eyes, as he breathed slow-and-deep upon remembrance.

Matt wrapped his jacket closer as the numbing cold air was beginning to affect the both of them, just as the memories were now doing. "I had to cut into your cricoid cartilage, and find a way to breathe for you Jake... I don't know if my hands were shaking from the cold... or because... or because you were my friend." Matt related, as if reading from an inventory list, trying to distance himself, as he did during his emergency rescue days, but his voice choked-up as he nearly broke down, giving himself away.

~*~

Matt went on to share how Galena had been out with him herding the cows, since Jake was in no condition to, as Matt had discovered him in the barn drinking. She arrived just seconds behind Matt. He had just started pulling Jake out, yelling at Jade, and the first thing he realized was that Jake was already starting to *suffocate* in his own blood. Jade was making the emergency call, and was getting sheets, so Matt desperately yelled for Galena to run in for his first aid kit, as Jade had come back out with the sheets. Galena helped by applying pressure and on his wounds with the sheets from Jade, while Matt yelled yet-again at Jade to go away so she wouldn't look at her brother. Matt made the cut into Jake's cartilage with freezing hands, and tried to get Jake breathing, he continued, never giving up.

~*~

"I remember once... I couldn't find a pulse... but I didn't go by that. I just didn't let GO of you Jake," he near laughed and cried. "Galena continued to apply pressure on the wounds and she used her arms and even her leg to reach every spot she could, and by whatever means she could... and I *breathed* for you with that tube. We pulled you up off the frozen ground onto some blankets that Jade had brought out when she grabbed the sheets.

The local VOLUNTEER EMERGENCY rescue team showed up, and shortly after that, Lenny did too. They must have called him, we never did. The emergency staff took care of you and Stoney until the helicopter came, then they took you and Stoney away, Jake... and that was it. The dead bull was lying there, with a trail of your blood leading out of the corral. We were all left there in shock, as to what happened, and as to what we just did. Your blood was all over the frozen ground... it not only stained the fresh snow, but it had permanently stained our minds. Looks like that cold weather was for the best maybe... or maybe you would have lost a lot more blood faster than you did. All we had left of you was your blood, Jake... I'll never forget it." Matt looked up towards the clouded northern mountains, "You know Jake... once we were all out of here, I heard-note that the snows came in heavy... trying to help erase it all, perhaps... who knows... but it's still *shaking* us, huh?"

They rubbed their arms against the power of the cold, as Matt finished bearing his soul, "I did so many emergency runs, and helped so many people, and saved lives and seen some go... as far as I knew, you would have no chance of making it to the hospital in time. Not in the shape you were in, Jake. Jade must have some kind of connections, that's all I can say... with that All-Mighty Boss-Man up stairs, that is. Either that, or plain and simple, it wasn't your time to *go* yet."

Jake watched Matt now. He had rarely seen him like this, he was extremely sullen. Matt became quieter still, and had withdrawn into thought now. He moved over near the backyard fence that divided the backyard and the back north pasture. As he leaned there, Jake joined him; they both leaned against the fence, and looked into the yard and then down along the slope towards the barn. They stood in silence as they watched their breath move about in the cold air.

Matt's eyes scanned the yard again, this time they were drawn to the west side of the yard. "It's hard to believe that we had a helicopter over there in the yard... it seemed so odd when they took you both away... " Matt slowly looked over at this best buddy as he swallowed hard, "I had your life in my hands, Jake. It never hit me, at the moment... I just did what I was trained for. Until, I soon realized you were dying. It seemed that the flakes of snow wouldn't let me be then... it was as if by hitting me in my face they were trying to make light of the situation. They were free to dance around completely indifferent to our struggle, pestering me, while I was fighting for your life." Matt's features turned troubled, and he added, "I felt helpless. I was desperate to do something else, but there was nothing I could do. When I made that cut in your neck, I thought I was too late, then you were breathing... but I still lost you, Jake. Your heart stopped and I lost you," Matt's eyes welled-up as he couldn't quite go on. He held his hand up over his eyes really tight now, and pressed hard on his eyes. He took a deep breath and went on relating, as Jake stood in sealed silenced—though NOT by choice. "I got you back, Jake... I got you back... yeah, and I was talking to *Jesus* every step of the way, all right... just like my *ma* always did... and *He* was in charge." Matt tried to smile feebly, "Well... I got your heart beating again, and Galena kept helping to stop the bleeding."

Matt's face felt like it was freezing as his smeared tears were along his icing-up his upper cheeks. Matt scanned the area where he had fought to save Jake's life. It was calm, crisp and getting colder, but no snow flurries to tease, this time.

"Say... do you realize Jake... if I had not *quit* my volunteer work for the rescue service, I wouldn't have even *been* here to ride-up at just the right time?" Matt stared at the spot again. "You wouldn't be here now, Boss-Man. We wouldn't be celebrating any of the holidays that we just finished sharing. I wouldn't be talking to you right now, Jake. You see? You were passing-over Jake... I don't know *why* you didn't go... I don't know how I could have handled that... having you die in my hands. I know I haven't said it, but it goes *without* saying, I reckon... I sure am GLAD you didn't die, Jake."

Matt's fixed gaze, stayed on the spot, as he now spoke of Jade, "Jade stared at your blood in the yard, it was blatantly reminding us of what had happened... I almost couldn't pry her away from it. She was sure you were dead up in that chopper, and was afraid to leave. She wandered the yard for quite a bit while we got things ready for us to go. She knew what the next step was, and she wasn't sure she could take it... it led to the hospital in Kalispell and what she was afraid would be the proven-facts of your death... and paper work... and your body-" he stopped cold.

Cold bodies, theirs, got them moving, and Matt and Jake warmed up some, walking along the fence-line until it came to the west-side of the house where the helicopter had landed and left from. Matt allowed himself to be lost one more time into those memories, as he stared into that fenced-area with the same intensity that he had just felt as he had stared moments ago on the yard behind the house. The yard did not look the same today, the light layer of snow was gone—but none the less—Matt still felt the same as he did one year ago.

He now watched Jake staring into the yard as if to imagine what he was not capable of knowing, and Matt confessed greatly:

"Jake... I couldn't even reassure her... I just couldn't. I knew what kind of condition you were in, and I knew what kind of obstacles you'd be facing. I had no promises to give her... I'm sorry Jake." Matt held his head back with a sigh, as he fought back the welling of the tears again, and let the cold air fill his lungs, then looked off into the gray sky, as he let his breath mark the air:

"I'm sorry Jake... there was nothing I could do for her after they took you away." Matt shook his head to the side, with a blink to his eyes, and continued bluntly, "I told her we needed to go, that Stoney shouldn't be there alone. He'd be needing us. I also told her that if you *wouldn't* be needing us, well then… we needed to know that, as well."

Jake walked up to Matt—as he was finally done—and rubbed his shoulder, offering support, and they now walked back together to the corral, where they had first started. Here, Jake pulled him aside from the corral and looked him in the eyes with deep concern. Jake was now the one to swallow hard this time, as his choice words were ready to spill-out hard, knowing quite-well that Matt would still never hear them:

'You did MORE for me than any man could have done, Matt… and you never gave-up on me. That was the best kind of help you could have given my sister… That, and by not tellin' her lies and giving her false hopes. You did all a man could do Matt… you did all a friend could do.' Jake simply signed, *fine* … *fine* -and *over/the/head* -meaning, far beyond fathoming, as he shut his eyes and felt the overwhelming gravity of his silent conversation combined with Matt's story.

Matt leaned over the heavy rail of corral as his face fell into the palm of his hand knocking his hat back a bit, a weaken Stetson it appeared to be— he tried in such earnest to relieve his mind of its heaviness. Jake came up and put his arm over the shoulder of this "brother", his dear buddy, and they leaned together, arm and arm, over the corral, until Matt regained his composure. Then they walked along the outside of the fence-line (east instead of west) to where its gate then opened to the north, to where Matt had been with the cows, one year ago. They went to the farthest end of the property, and veered off to the right (south), and doubled back some, through the far end of northeast hay field. Then they moved-on-down towards the Fisher River (on the far east ranch-border), moving still south, as they gave their trusty Stetson's a tug for the brisk walk.

As they hit the banks, Jake reflected on everything as they moved-up stream along the frozen waters, while the waters moved unseen, under the ice, passing them by. *'Some of my life just passed me by, up there in the yard, one year ago… a part that I truly never saw… a part that has been hidden from me. I know of it only because my friends chose to share and reveal it… must be I'm finally ready to hear it now, as it's breakin' loose fast, and flowing my way. So this is what it's like, to be out of the picture. This is what it's like to be the broken toy, no longer able to be salvaged. Yeah… I was a kid once… I had things that were precious to me, and I knew what it was like and how it felt for them to be damaged beyond repair… and even gone. Never to bring that special joy to my heart again. How much more so… to lose a friend… or a loved one in the family, and to lose such joy. We didn't want to lose Stoney that day when I saw the bull attacking him and ran to save him... and they didn't want to lose me either... they saved me.*

As they walked over the smooth rocks that Jade loved so much, Jake thought on her. She had seen the worst of it all. *I wasn't there for her when I should have been... I shouldn't have been drinkin', I should have stepped up to the plate, and grabbed the wedding flowers out of the hands of her heart, and stomped on them. I should have told her right-off and straight-up, but I didn't... I just didn't. At least Jade had Ray and Matt to get her through this... as I was helpless. Helpless to be much of anything at all for months... except nearly... a memory.*

They finished the walk and came up through the south-east river pasture, and then through the pump-house pasture, crawling over fences like a couple of kids that had been off on a lark, and moved-on-past Jake's babies, in their fenced corral. They neared the house, and parted company at the barn. They had to. The mysteries of the cold outdoors were still calling Jake. Matt went to the left, and up to the front door of the house. Jake went to the right, and over to the slight incline that led from the barn (past a tiny shed and the boat house) up to the backyard and the round corral—the same area he traveled that day, the day he was aroused out of his drunken stupor, by Jade's screams.

As Jake now neared the area of the yard where the corral was in sight, he could almost see the bull in his mind, and it began to play back unexpectedly to him. He felt his heart racing now, and his breathing was heavy. He could see Jade off to the side of the corral, and a man getting stomped by a bull. He could hear her, from the past:

~*~

'JET! JET! It's Stoney... they won't even help him!'

~*~

He felt himself in with the bull now, as he ran up to the rail of the corral, and stopped. He was as if part of another world now, as somewhere it seemed he had stepped over into it. He remembered facing the bull, just as he had thus far remembered. Only now though, Jake remembered the force of the bull hitting him, and being on the ground. He remembered through his former haze, how he had tried to get up and was hit again in the left leg as the horn ripped into it, and how the bull stomped on him, and how he had felt his hip and leg breaking. Oddly, he hadn't felt any pain. He remembered his shock that the bull was gone, and he that had a chance to get away. His head had been spinning and he had hardly been able to keep his eyes open. He had tried in vain to get up on his right leg, curling-up for to maneuver, and using his right arm, and how he had seen that he was losing blood all over clothes. It had been running down from over his left arm, from his chest. He hadn't even realized that he was holding it up to his ripped up chest, either, until he saw the blood. He had not been able to get up. He had then felt the pain as he tried to drag himself and light flakes of snow kept hitting him in the eyes. Everything around him had seemed to be getting dark, he was ready to faint, but he had still tried dragging himself— the freedom of the fence seemed miles away—time stood still. After that everything had gone black with a terrible force hitting his head. He had been hit in the head from behind, and never had realized what happened or what it was that hit him.

That's when I was hit in the head from its swingin' horns. That's when I was knocked down into the dirt, and trampled and kicked until Jade killed the bull.

Jake leaned on the fence rail, and stared in the corral, this time alone. The memories sunk to the ground before him. He was told he would never remember—head injury trauma did this to folks. Yet, some do, oddly so, and so he had. There was a strong, odd hush over the yard. He was aching so *bad* for it, and it now come over him. It was as if a hand of compassion was engulfing him now. He had not approached these rails until today with Matt. His first good look inside, though from a distance, had been New Year's Eve, and now he had finally approached it. He was not ready to go inside, he had too many sorrows, for all involved. He still was in shock—in a way that none would *ever* possibly understand. Jake just couldn't believe that he was even seeing a bull that day in his corral, in the first place. He was drunk and couldn't think straight, but he KNEW he had sent it off in a truck, and he had witnessed it leave, with his own eyes. He still couldn't quite even accept it; it was almost like a bad dream. But then—a bad dream doesn't trample a man under foot, or rip apart his tongue.

I didn't even hear the sound of the gun that saved my life. Jake straightened himself, as he moved off-and-away from the corral, ever so slightly. The deep hushed peace moved with him, yet, his gaze drew back, he had nearly missed something. Something glimmered just for him. Something caught his eye. He reached back over, and pulled off a piece of oozed-out, clear, golden sap, from the rail. As he examined it in his hand— he moved a few feet out into the yard, his heart being stirred within:

'*Sap... the lifeblood, so to speak, of the tree... I lost a good portion of my life's sap... my life's blood. Right here, under my feet... but the Lord God was my stay.*'

Greatly humbled, and moved to tears, Jake looked down to the ground on which he stood, and then he looked up into the heavens. There was no light snow flurries today, but something was lightly falling. A warm feeling was falling into Jake's heart; his sap had been precious to Someone. His life's blood had been precious enough, so's not have it be wasted on this ground that he stood on. It wasn't just precious to his twin, and his buddies. It was precious to Someone else. Jake yielded to his body as he let it fall to his knees, down on to the cold winter earth that he nearly died on and gave up quiet thanks, a thanks that only One other, could hear. He gathered his last thoughts as to this matter, and went into his house—his place—the place where he belonged.

390 - By Neebeeshaabookway - JAKE SMITH RANCH SERIES...

CHAPTER TWENTY SIX

HORSE SCENTS

WITH the holiday, family and friends, all firmly rooted back into
Jake's life, he continued to weave himself back into the structured
framework of where he belonged, and who he was. There were still some
vital pieces missing, and just *when* these pieces would fall back into place
was anybody's guess. Winter's late snows were now over, it was mid April
now, the rivers were full, and there had actually been three local trail-drives
come-and-gone (with more planned), all full-up with local kids, and lots of
skill-honing and teaching going on. Jake was not part of it. Added to these,
were trail-rides still going on now. He was not there for last year's spring,
as he was in the hospital, and he was not to be found in the summer
programs that followed his homecoming, either. He was then honing his
own personal skills, which were, just being alive again and back home. Ray
sorely missed him and his wonderful social presence, not to mention his
great cowboy expertise. So did the teens that took part in all spring and
summer projects. Matt, Stoney, and Jake, always had the kids pass-on-
through Jake's place with these rides, and also took turns letting them work
on his place, and setting-up camp. Then, they'd also take turns volunteering
at Ray's with his groups, and at least two of the guys would always stay
behind and keep-up with the ranch duties. There was some sad news,
though—and blatantly seen. The trail-rides were *not* coming through Jake's
place anymore now—he had put a stop to it.

Matt and Stoney were taking turns again helping Ray this year,
starting with spring, as Jake's life had finally settle back into some kind of a
routine that he could handle. He was still taking seizure medication,
although he didn't like doing it, in spite of his new vow. Since their family
was just brought-up to be medicine free, naturally he was leery of the whole
idea. He was less fond of seizures though, and their after-effects on all
involved, and, waking-up in hospitals had finally caved-in this ol' ranch-
camel's back—so what was his stalling, as to this next step? He had more
freedom. He had not had a seizure for nearly five months, and *this* time it
was a fact. Yet, none the less, Jake was just staying put, there would not be

trail-drives or trail-rides for him, here, there, or anywhere. No socializing, no campfires and storytelling—nothing. He couldn't confess to himself or admit it to others, that he *sorely* missed belonging where the action was—it hurt too much. And—the action was—*"talking"*. His functioning-level as to his new self, was for the ranch, close friends, and now Sofia—although surprisingly, it had branched-out into town where "tourist" could-and-did, freely roam. Most of the winter was spent at the ranch though, so there had been no need to branch-out any farther. No need to stretch out and develop new muscles aside the essence of his present capabilities.

If Jake confessed to himself, which in THIS case he did, he didn't particularly have any desires to branch out into nearby Libby, or anywhere else that would cause him to *not* take kindly to trying to function around an even greater onslaught of strangers—and with no place to hide, such as Lenny's or Henry's. Pedro could do it, he reasoned, because Pedro always functioned around everyone with this language all his life. To Jake, well, Jake had functioned as *Jake* all his life, and having himself walled-up in his own personal *jail* was still a deep wound, it pained him if he dared to think on it. Having to try and communicate by waving through the bars, or with muted-noises through the heavy doors that shut the jail off from the main rooms of socializing, was not something he had totally felt comfortable with. Most likely, he never would. He still missed—Jake Smith. He still felt like he had lost him—back in the hospital bed—back in Kalispell, that day he first tried to talk.

Jade had no more solid plans and no new ways to push Jake into any of the social-life that he had before. She was grateful that he had not separated himself from their *personal* herd, as that was an accomplishment in itself. Why, he even had a girl friend, the biggest shock of all! And—Miss Kaite never even *bothered* to try to come around again, and hardly *ever* came to town anymore to see Jade—as—in her opinion, Jake had progressed so well in learning to communicate, compared to his pillow-throwing days, and setting people *adrift* on front porches.

They had finally solved the puzzle of just what kind of brain damage he had, and how much he had been left with, permanently. There were more appointments to set-up and keep (for his blood work) because of the seizure medication, and, his eating and swallowing habits, which had to be checked on, and his general health, would always be on-going issues. Because of the way he had to live now, he couldn't afford to get run down, or undernourished—it was too hard to recover, as he so dramatically had learned before the new coming year.

They were all beginning to learn, too, that if he wasn't to take care with his eating, there was always the danger of aspiration that could lead to pneumonia. He still had bad headaches whenever he was under pressure, or if he ran into something unexpected, or even just too much complex multi-tasking that he sought to do. Usually his pills put a stop to it, but sooner-or-later he'd have to lay down and sleep it off—come to find, he'd lose much of the day, but he had to accept that. They all did. Thus far, these were only caused from his "known" condition, and no other damage had appeared in his brain. Staring-spells would always common, but he always snapped out of them, and got back on track. Although he had to start all *over* at the *beginning* of whatever said-track, by the second or third time, he would actually reach success and felt good about himself.

He continued to leave pictures of the yard, out of respect to his sister whenever he took off, as apparently, they learned, there was no medical guarantee that a seizure could never happen again—even though he keep up with his medication. Confessed staunchly, to all, then, it made Jade's day a lot more relaxing if she could hunt him down for "spying" purposes. She even finally put up a plastic picture map, so Jake could put an "x" for which area he was in. One day, much to Jade's shock and pleasure, Jake started to put "j" instead of "x". Since his birthday belt, and staring at the JJ-NS, and signing the "j" in the air, for his ASL codes, he finally discerned that "j" could be used for his map. If he made a "j" for Jade, he just added a little heart to it—one could just *imagine* how that made his twin-gal, feel.

Yes, Jade was still determined to hound him in the health area—and—he allowed her to hound him, as he was very much not wanting to wake up in anymore hospitals. However—any hounding to get him back into the trail-riding circuit, and working with the kids, whether local or city, was NOT her business. Least wise, not unless she could come up with a plan on the sly. Which, she had not—but she was praying hard for open doors of insight!

Ray had tried a variety of ways to get Jake to come over to his ranch, but Jake would have none of it. He knew he'd get tricked into facing a trail-drive, and felt well protected on his own property. Well now—surprise, surprise—seems he wasn't as protected as he thought. He was protected only by a small flimsy fence on this-here property, as he was soon about to learn.

With no more access to Jake's ranch there was lots of adventure rides sorely missing for the kids, so the wrangler twins—the double-KC-gals—opened up THEIR place. Jake was shocked one day as he was fixing fences along the northeast hay field, down near the Fisher River, and commotion came his peaceful way. A whole group of them went by, and he narrowly had a chance to duck out of sight. This fence and its trusted protection had just nearly failed him! What's a boss-man to do? Hide—turn *tail*, and *hide* his ol' sorry *hide*!

It was later in the day and near supper and Jake was now off fishing. Stoney had gone off with Matt and Ray for a cookout and campfire, plus a real camping-out night, complete with songs, and music over at the Cook wrangler twins. Sofia was due to come out with Lenny and Sara, but that was much later in the evening. She was coming to see her cherished "flower-cultivator", first and foremost, but she had had some other pleasures on her agenda to enjoy and tend to. It seemed that the Cook twin's pa had some mighty fine grandkids there at this time, and they took to Sofia, like hummingbirds to bright red and hot-pink. Sofia now had grandkids to love, and right next door to Jake's! There were four of them, three little girls, and an older boy. The oldest, Nick, was not only loved by his sisters, Sara and Victoria, but joyously by Camri—in a special way—but he had made a doubly-special niche in Sofia's heart, as he reminded her of her sons.

Well now, with his little "flower" and company coming later, this was the boss-man's time to relax with some fishing, and listening to the river and the birds—spring was nice to cozy up, in *these* way. Much nicer than last year as he thought about it, now occupying himself with thought-fishing, added on the side. Tomorrow it would be one year to the day that he got out of the hospital and into the hotel, and then *soon* one-year to the day that he arrived home here, in the dead of night. Jake continued to think on this, as he watched the river. He was startled as he heard the rocks tumble nearby, and looked-up to see Honor. She must have come from the group at the twin wrangler's spread.

"Hey, Jake... so how's it going? You fishing hard, or fishing easy?" She looked at him, slyly, "I caught a glimpse of you earlier... don't know if you knew or not."

"~Unh-unh~," Jake voiced, *not-see* ... *yes-I-see-kids* ... *but-not-you* -

"Oh, I was there... and I was riding with Kim and Kari, just a few minutes ago, and then on our way back I spied you just now... that's the second time today. I kind of thought that I might not get another opportunity, so I thought I'd better stop now," she drew closer, "I've been meaning to *ask* you something." Honor brushed her wispy bit hair out of her face. It was a nice light brown, and seemed to blend in with the spring surroundings, just like a rabbit in the fields would.

Jake motioned for her to sit, and she came to him and sat. "My horse is just over there a bit, see him? Kim and Kari went on to help get the supper ready up there. You should be there Jake, you know... you belong there. But just so you don't chase me off, that's not why I'm here."

~*~

Honor wasn't very good at understanding Jake and his new way of talking, as she had been spending all her time at Ray's. Only during the get-togethers, did she have a chance to learn more about this "mysterious Jake" that Angie just HAD to see when she first arrived into town and ran into her. Oh, Honor had heard of Jake, during her previous work at Ray's, but Honor was just a helper on the trail-drives, and usually did most of the runs with Ray only. She originally came out because of an advertising ad in her local Spokane college newspaper, and she came as a part-time worker through a college that she worked at. She worked for Ray while she gathered information on trail-drives, and things that were in tune with his ranch, because she was doing a project on ranch-life for city kids. In many respects, she decided to stay longer and gathered information from other workers' skills and facts on Old-Town, and on how others chose to run their ranches, so she was a very busy trail-hand. Ray always invited her back, even when the project was done. She still had many friends on the ranch, and this was her third year—it seemed to her that it was becoming a nice habit. She knew Stoney mostly, as in the past Matt worked for the VOLUNTEER EMERGENCY rescue service and was busy with them, quite often. Jake did the rides out of Ray's place, with Stoney, but Stoney would usual head over in the truck and meet up with Ray and his group, by himself, and *then* head out, so she never saw Jake, personally—Jake joined Ray on mid-trail. Matt was always around in the evenings, but by then Honor usually had headed-on-back to Ray's bunkhouse to spend the evening with the wives of the men that worked there. These family holiday times at the Smith Ranch, the JJ-NS, was where she finally learned about Jake, and why he was loved and appreciated by so many. Armed with this knowledge, she felt safe to open her heart to him, about herself.

~*~

"I am wondering about something, Jake. Maybe you could help me. I've known Ray for these three years, since I first came out in the summer of 1998. It seemed to me that there was something special starting to happen with us, as to the way he treated me, but I always backed off. I was, well, for the *first* part trying to be a careful boarder, and let him know that I was there to do my work. Then by the next year, during the spring... and back again in the summer... I was more at ease. But it seemed during the summer that he was spending so much time with Jade, that I was worried that I had been getting the wrong impression, and that maybe Ray was just being polite with me. Then... this year... meaning before the New Year... I almost wasn't going to come out, as I felt a little out of place, but as you can see... I came."

Honor got up and walked over to the other side of Jake, across from him, to see his face straight on.

"Jake... I was worried that I was tempting Ray to go astray from Jade. That maybe... being single, and being in his home so often, even though there *were* other couples there... well... I was worried that I was a distraction to his previous feelings towards her. He always made it a point to treat me extra special, you see. Well, when I left during the summer of 1999, he insisted that I come out again. He had something special to talk to me about, something about us... I thought it was about extra pay for more work. But then I got a call just after *that* New Year, and Ray was very upset... he cancelled all his spring plans, he said he wasn't even sure about summer's, either."

Honor, laughed a very slight uneasy laugh, "Well, summer's come-and-gone, winter too, and spring is here now, and I've been coming-and-going between Spokane many times... I keep finding myself here... as I am now again."

She looked more intently into Jake's face now, as she was fumbling with some sticks that she had picked up. "Obviously when I did arrive and met up with Angie, last year in May... I learned of the accident. Jade needed all the help she could get from all her friends, and I understood that. Ray had asked me to come in May, and things seemed to fall back into place... but it wasn't until after your birthday, that I seemed reach the threshold of a whole new relationship. Somehow I always seemed to be kind of waiting in the wings."

She moved closer to Jake now, and was nearly face-to-face with him, "Jake... I want to make sure that I didn't somehow come between Ray and Jade. Maybe with all the troubles she went through, well, maybe she just wasn't ready to commit to Ray... and maybe somehow, I took her place. If I *did,* in any *way*... I need to know, so I can talk with her. I would *never* do such a thing, Jake. I would never do anything on the sly Jake, never... I'm always up-and-up. She's your twin, Jake, so please help me understand, so I know what to do. I'm not sure how much closer I should allow Ray into my heart. "

Jake smiled at her, and shook his finger, as "no-no", and then gestured that all was fine. He was at a loss as how to explain the fine delicate relationship that Ray and Jade, and really, all of them had. Jade was part of the four of them, as she was so much a part of him. His little shadow. She went to Ray for any-and-all big-brother-stuff, same as Jake, Matt and Stoney did.

~*~

What he wasn't able to explain though, was that during the summer before the accident, Jade had needed advice about her soon-coming marriage, and how she was afraid it might affect Jake. Jake had been starting to act mighty odd about it, and she was worried he didn't want to risk the possibility of her someday *maybe* even leaving. She also got the impression that Jake didn't like Lyle, but she couldn't put her finger on it, and didn't want to approach him, yet. She was afraid he might take it wrong, if she presented it too early. This was before Jake ever took his trouble to Ray during those few days before the New Year. Neither twin had never ever faced the possibility of separating, and weren't sure how much their need for companionship would be tested, and they weren't sure how much they would be willing to yield. Their parents taught them since birth, that they were a team and it became precious to them, but so was the other's desire for happiness in-and-through life's travels. They always kept an open eye and heart to be ready for such a thing, as one of them just might *stop* fence-lighting at any unexpected time, and take to-wing-off to new places.

~*~

Jake new that Ray had too much on his mind for romance of any kind, with his big spread to run, plus the added Smith Ranch troubles that arose. But he also knew that if there was a special gal around, Ray was sure not to let her slip away. They all witnessed this finally, when Ray showed up on Thanksgiving—with Honor—in that place of honor. Jake figured this was a good place to start with, as to explaining things to Honor.

After a short try at charades with Honor and some failed attempts at talking, Jake gave her an understanding hug, followed by some signed "okay's" combined with his voiced, "~Oh~'kay'~". He knew he must have been successful, as there was a smile of comfort on her face.

Hero Jake, rides again, he thought, with a deep feeling of humble contentment in his soul. He thus waved her off, to be on her way.

As she took to leave, she tried walking off the other way, in a new direction. She hoped to avoid her earlier path so she would not have to stumble over the small incline of the rocky slope. She walked over to the one shallow spot of the river, off to Jake's side. She got through the river all right, through the rocks and logs that were scattered along that spot, but once across, she was heading towards a thickly over-grown patch that had hidden deep holes. Everyone on *Jake's* ranch knew to avoid it, even the horses did—but *she* did *not*. She was now too far off for him to call her, although he tried. Jake's habit was pots and pans, or the dinner triangle, and *neither* was handy out here and that was a fact that couldn't be beat. What's a guy to do? Jake picked up some rocks and began throwing them off to the side of where Honor was standing. She covered her head in dismay and turned in amazement, as she couldn't figure-out why it was raining rocks, or where they *possibly* could have come from. She never suspected they would have come from Jake! As she had turned she saw him waving wildly at her—it sure seemed he wanted her to stay put, and with such desperate measures on his part, she did. She watched as he made his way over to her, voicing something at her that she could not understand. His face told it all, something was really wrong. She was getting a definite sense of warning through her eyes, if not her ears, and stood still until he arrived.

"*h*/~oh /*1*" -Jake signed and voiced, and even signed, *hole* - and pointed down through the field grass. He went and broke-off a branch from a nearby tree, and showed her how deep it went. She would have fallen down only to her knees, but it could have left her with a fair amount of damage.

After the recovery of this *double* surprise, and another hug and pats of joy on their backs, Honor and Jake had just turned and separated, when Jake heard a very familiar and *humiliating* phrase, and turned to face Honor. Her words kind of took the wonderful wind out of his fine sail of such a successful rescue, as it now flapped helplessly in his mind. He smiled meekly at her, and wrinkled his brow. He looked almost like a little kid that had done something wrong, but sure didn't mean to and the thud in his heart halted any more joy.

"Well...?" she smiled at him as she began her repetition of it:

"Why don't you just carry a *whistle*? I mean, rocks Jake... you might have hit me if I had dared to move." She smiled, "I carry one on the trail-rides, see? You never know when you will have to get someone's attention far down the trail, right?"

The whistle bit... I can't believe it... I just save her from a hole, poor damsel that nearly had a distress... and me, the hero, gets... the WHISTLE bit! Jake smiled sheepishly, as he slipped his hands into his back pocket, and swayed slightly as he did it. *Aww... the hero is shot down fast... looks like it's just a flesh wound though. Well, maybe I shouldn't have thrown*

rocks at her, she's right... I might have hit her... THEN what kind of hero
would I be?

"You know Jake... speaking of whistles and trail-rides... " she now
made her way back to him, "you belong on them. Both the trail-drives AND
the trail-rides. You may not be able to talk, and it may bother you, but there
are lots of hard-working teens, soon to be young men, and they *miss* you and
need your advice. Since you've recovered and Ray has relaxed, I have heard
constant stories and on-going lessons as to how Jake Smith does things, and
how they succeed! Nearly everyone that's come for the trail-rides has now
heard how you saved Stoney from a bull attack. They see you as a mentor,
friend, and hero, Jake... if you show-up one day and can't talk, I have a very
strong hunch, that it won't make them think any less of you. All they know
is that your health hasn't quite been ready for extra duties... but word is
slowly getting around that you can't talk now, as they hear things from town
during their visits there."

Jake walked over to the tree that he had just taken the branch off of,
and leaned against it as if he was retreating from an enemy, and eyed her
with a hint of suspicion.

Now let's get this straight. She came out here to talk about Jade. Not
whistles and trail-rides, right? Or was this her purpose all along? No, not
Honor... not after the way she felt about Jade. If she was truly tryin' to push
me into trail-drives, she would have said something to any of the guys, and
they would have come to me with her concern, just as I'll take her concern
to Jade. Hmm, am I still tryin' to be a hermit, of some sorts, again?
Hermits can get mighty suspicious, and I SURE seem to be suspicious of this
poor gal.

"Jake... why don't you take a new step?" She stood there like an
innocent little bunny in the grass, as her wispy hair framed her, and her eyes
waited.

Jake turned away from her with the thought being too heavy to bear,
and took off his Stetson and swatted a near by tree with a forceful release of
pressure and let it fall—staring at it.

'You don't understand, I can't function the same, I don't like it... I
just can't handle it yet... I don't know why... maybe I'm afraid. I'm afraid I
lost myself, and I don't know who I am, and I keep seeing somebody else
walking in MY boots and in my life... and even RIDING my own personal
horse. I know who I am on my ranch and with friends, and here the
reminders of me being different are slowly fadin' away... and here, they still
see ME. I know they do. And... I want to still be ME.'

Jake kept staring at his hat as it lay in the field grass. The whole field was now very still and quiet, and he could now hear the river. It seemed to be talking to him, but he quickly sidestepped its gentle comments with, 'I *got to stop doing that... ruins to many good hats,'* he thought with sigh. *'No wonder Ma was always surprising Pa with new cowboy hats all the time... I sure didn't get it... guess I just hadn't lived long enough then,'* he reflected as he lingered over his innocent hat.

A forlorn-looking Stetson, begging to cherished once again.

He reached to pick it up, but Honor had beaten him to it. As she handed it to him, she remembered there *was* one other reason why she had come down, and she spoke it softly to him, "Jake...please, follow the river downstream and join us. The twins *have* something for you up at the ranch... the whole camp will welcome you. Please do." She took his hand in hers and kissed it, slipped her whistle in his pocket, and then she left.

Jake looked at her and desired to follow, he longed for the camp, oh he *truly* did, but he still longed to be alone—he *needed* to be alone. He needed to think, and sometimes the headaches and confusion of it all was more than he was able to handle.

As the river began to remind him of its presence, Jake thought, *'yeah... yeah, I'll follow the river, but UPSTREAM... and through the field, back HOME instead.'* He crossed over and picked up his gear. He *did* follow the river, but did *not* go home through the field.

Jake watched the river. He loved this river, it was always the same, but always different. The main path cut the same crevice in the earth, and it moved to its required and designated goal, even though at times the crevice became hard to recognize as a river in some places—times when it appeared to be just a weak stream. It was *still* the same river though and would flow strong again, at some point in time. It always had something new and something of interest, no matter what. One never knew what one could expect of it up-around the bend, or on its surface-waters and nearby-surroundings.

Always the same, but... different. Different, but always... the same. As Jake thought on this, he decided to take a much longer walk—farther up the river. Jake eventually made his way up through the far-east pasture of the property and over to the pump-house pasture and into the south pasture, with his horses, on into the tack-shed. He came out with treats for his horses, and soaked-up the scent of their afternoon sweat. He imagined the trail-rides of the past, and remembered each horse he had taken, and how they each behaved so differently on the trails. He remembered his delight

watching the stream of horses, as they'd make their way along the trails.
The sound of his buddies and the kids, as they joked and talked, were always
meshed as one with the sounds of nature, and set to linger in the unbridled
outdoor air—air that he longed to ride through, right now.

His own personal horse, his own special baby, came up and nuzzled
him, as if she sensed he was somehow in dire need. '*Gentle Jen,*' Jake
thought, '*you're so wonderful... a truer friend and companion a man could
never find. You've been with me all these years, and know all my trails, and
how I take to them all. The hand of God is truly good... He gives good gifts
to us ol' cowboys.*' He nearly cried as he realized how very lucky he was to
still be able to ride, he could have spent the rest of his life, in a bed,
completely unaware of his surrounding—but he was home. He was on HER
the day he had the seizure on the Coyote Ridge trail, he fell off of her, as
well. She was so in tune with him from years of teamwork that she waited
patiently after the initial struggle, as if by a secret cue, until he was collected
in safety, by the hands of his friends. He stroked her nuzzle now, and gave
her some treats, and calmly reassured her that he was okay, and shushed her
on her way. But:

He wasn't okay. His head was hurting now. When it did in the past,
he never seemed to think of the possibility of a seizure, even though, looking
back in passing, he would remember that he *had*, had one, *most* of the time
(but not always) before a seizure struck him down. Sometimes hours before,
or sometimes just minutes before, it was always different—and the times he
didn't' have a seizure, were unremembered now and unimportant. Yet,
because he had taken his headache pills and slept-off the headaches, perhaps
those times *were* just as important—as—there were a few seizures, unknown
to him, that he had *truly* avoided. Now when it hurt, he thought on the fact
that he didn't *have* to worry about those kinds of seizures—somehow this
was *very* important to him right now—in more ways than he understood.

He went back to the tack-room for more treats for the horses, and
stopped to look at all the saddles, his mind seemed to be getting haunted
with sights, sounds and scents of the horses. Before he knew it he was
saddled-up and taking-off, possibly still lacking horse sense as to his whole
dilemma, but horse scents of another kind had finally had gotten the best of
him. Nope, no trail-rides for Jake—but a personal ride. He was more
interested in how the river was the *same*—yet *different*—and thought he'd
ride along in view of it, and think.

As nature can be a more engrossing-thought-capture than dwelling on
seizures that might possibly choose not to listen to medicine, ol' Jake
moved-out with nature's call. Seemed someone was thinking on seizures,

though, as just out of his view, behind his back, this time it was *Jade* throwing HER Stetson down in exasperation. Being that, after catching a glimpse of him, she had just charged out of the woodshed from behind the house, a few minutes too *late* to stop him—catching an even lesser-glimpse of him taking-off to *who* knows *where*, or—for how long. Yep— occasionally *she* needed new Stetsons as well.

CHAPTER TWENTY SEVEN

MAY BE... MAY JUST BE...

JAKE lay in bed, as he listened to the roosters and chickens and let his thoughts drift back to that first morning home, that morning when he soaked in all his surroundings after finally waking up in his own bed. As he lay there now, he knew Jade would not be knocking on *this* May 1st, and, she was happily back to staying upstairs. Most likely he'd smell her handy work in the kitchen, and quite soon. It was good that she had come back to his side of the house since his homecoming, he had needed it and still did— it was one of those "same" things that he still desperately had to lay hold of. Her presence was the same. There'd never be a trial at split-life again, and in so-stating, their childhood foundation was the best "same" of all.

After a few more rooster crows, he stretched and rolled-over and thought on getting up. His backtracking was done now, and enough dust had been strewn over the trail in his mind, it was now time to face-up to the fact that he had now been home for one year. This was his life as he had now come to know it. One year ago, he never could have imagined himself at this point. He vaguely thought on the river, and his slow thoughtful ride from the other day. It was now cutting a path deep in the back of his mind, and seeking for an out-let as if to spring-up and in *doing* so, bring new things to sparkle in the light.

He took one last nestle into the pillow, and sighed with a slight smile. He always felt like a little kid again at this point. No worries, no cares—lots of comfort—and someone to make *breakfast* for you. The sun had just moved into alignment to shoot its beam into his room. He turned slightly in the bed so not to be face-to-face with its powerful light. It was now *that* time again. As he scrunched up his pillow, he studied the light as it shone in the window hitting the dust particles in the air, *yep, there they are, same each morning... dancing angels... just like my sister,* he thought. *If she hadn't always been here turnin' this mess into somethin' I could see a way out of... I would have lost a whole year of my life, and quite possibly... my friends.*

Now he not only heard the chickens, but the song of the birds in the nearby trees. The chickens seemed to overpower them though, just as the babbles of life can at times overpower simple soothing joys. They never had that many chickens to fuss with, but the few that they did have, just seemed to hold their own. They *did* get eggs from them, occasionally, and Jade had fun with that. Picking up eggs and putting them in a basket—just like her ma, before her. Jake now thought back to the eggs and smashed toast that his sister made him for breakfast on year ago, that one early May morning. He also thought on how he never ate them, but had come really close. Since then, he had eaten eggs at their table quite often with his *magic* spoon, although he preferred to use his finger—though this required more skill. May be that all would go well, and today an egg would do. May be also, that all would go well, and smashed toast and coffee would do. Maybe... may be... may just be.

True to his prediction, Jade did some wonders with eggs and smashed toast in the kitchen. This morning's meal was very quiet, but happy, not *awkward* as it was last year at this time. He even caught her singing—not crying. Jake finished his meal, and as he had taken to eating less than a normal person would, as he went a long-mite slower, he supplemented it with the food syringe—having finished this also, he turned to his sister. She was just making a move to clear the table, when he snuck up and grabbed her and spun her around.

"Well, now... just what are *you* so happy about this morning, JET?" She said in amazement, as she hugged him back.

Jake took her into his room, and faced her to the window. *dancing-angels* -he signed with a laugh, *dancing-angels* -he signed again, and clapped his hands.

Jake walked into the kitchen. He grabbed-up his Stetson, as usual, and took-off to feed his babies, leaving the sound of his heavy boots trailing behind him. One new little baby, that had previously grown some, now shadowed after him, harping at his heels. They had been keeping him close near the property until he learned his boundaries, and he was now ready for the great outdoors.

Jake had finished with the horses, and was now out on the porch playing with his pup with the first day of May warming his face, as he sat on the wooden porch-boards down near the grass. His pup was rolling in the grass and just as happy as a bird taking a bath on a hot summer day—but barking, instead of peeping.

Each time Jake looked at him, he remembered Hunter. He remembered his words, and so true were the words that he had spoken, *this little pup serves as a reminder all right, justice was served at a point in time, concerning me... as proof that Someone was watchin' over me as to vindication... and sure as ma taught us dear-to-heart, I truly know Him richer now. As even so... He was watching, over me before that, as I didn't die in that round corral... under a bull.*

Jade came out into the morning sunlight, "So when are you going to name that little harpin' heeler-nipper? He's trying to take-over my *shadow* duty, Jet... you let him know I got first *say* in it, now, you hear?" She took a seat near her brother, "So... it's May now, twin." She looked over at him, as he looked back in response to her and their eyes met.

Jake shook his head in acknowledgement, *'that thought seems to have been crossin' my mind all morning since I first woke up, little spur-gal.'*

"Everyone's still off on the trail-ride, they'll be back-in tonight though, after supper. Looks like it's just the two of us... same as it was when you first came home, huh, Jet?" She looked at her brother. He looked well and strong, not at all how he looked when he first came home, his deep tanned olive color had returned, causing his scars to show a bit more than usual, in a new way, but he was not bothered by it. This time the scars marked a special healing, and not the awful, tender wounds that were dogging him. He looked the same to her, maybe a near five pounds thinner, but nothing like the frail version of him that had caused her such concern in the hospital.

"Hey, I got something for you Jet, let me go get it and... "

Jake stopped her, as he reached out and grabbed her arm quickly, "~Unh-unh~, 'koh~ ~whaa~k'," he voiced in full, and pointed to the barn, *'I need to talk to you, Jade-gal... that can wait.'* She looked up into his eyes, as they spoke to her.

"All right, Jet, to the barn, right?" She got up and followed her brother, she knew his eyes had more to say.

The smell of the horses was in the air, and the smell of the barn added to the scene. Jake was comfortable and at ease here, and watched his sister as she sat down. There was so much he wished he could say. He longed for the days of the past, where he could just open his mouth and spill-it-all-out and she'd respond, and their bond of understanding grew thicker and deeper, as magic *words* enhanced the companionship that they had since birth, and their simple happy joys would then be their reward.

He sat down beside her and pulled her face towards him, as into full attention. She knew now this was something to do with last May. She was ready to cry, but held firm and waited for these deep, long held-back feelings, to come up from her twin's "river" that had been hidden, yet flowing, since the accident—the release was coming.

Jake signed to her, *I-never-accept-this* ... *not-before* ... *I-accept-this-now* ... *finished* ... *I-not-*like*-live-this-way* ... *I-*never*-will* ... *but-one-year-now-done* ... *finally-I-yes-accept-this* ... *I-must* -Jake took her chin in his hand first, lined her up straight, and then let it go, as he signed, *I-take-full-responsibility-*remember* ... *never-*blame*-yourself* ... *never-again* ... *thank-God-Stoney-alive* ... *thank-God-I-alive* ... *never-think-more* ... *NEVER!* -Jake then got up and gathered his thoughts, and welled-back some tears as he looked back at her. She was busy, doing the same.

Jake laughed as he zeroed in on her mannerisms, *'Jade, even identical twins AIN'T the same, yet lookin' as us, I'd swear we're EXACTLY the same at times,'* he shook his head as he remembered all the things they had been through growing up. She stared up at him, in trust, and waited.

He walked up close now, and signed, as near to his own thoughts as he could, *I-never-make-this-success-alone* ... *I-never-arrive-here-to-this-point-in-my-life* ... *but-*only*-because-of-you* ... *Jade* -he emphasized with hand force and face power, *from-YOUR-help* ... *I-have-SUCCESS-now!* -He signed on, *only-from-you* ... *I–was-really-lost* ... *Jade-you-save-me* ... *true-example* ... *sun-always-find-crack-for-shine-through* ... *same-way-it-shine-on-us* ... *one-little-crack-of-light-can-break-into-darkness* ... *if-we-think-we-not-want-sun* ... *it-*still*-finds-us* ... *you-kept-trying-to-save-me* ... *you-never-failed-me* ... *you-LIGHT-for-me-when-I-was-in-dark-times* -Jake sat down and faced her again, and continued, *I-owe-it-all-to-you* ... *there-not-any-words-for-witness-how-great-your-success-work-for-me* ... that-over/my/head-true* ... *TRUE* ... *but* ... *I-*really*-believe-you-KNOW-how-I-feel* ... *you-KNOW-my-HEART!* -he smiled, gesturing to the full *past* time-frame: *you-led-the-way* ... *you-guided-me* ... *you-never-let-go-of-me* ... *you-did-everything-to-solve-every-puzzle* ... *you-also-let-me-choose-how-to-follow* ... *you-let-me-feel-same* ... *SAME* -he emphasized, and continued, *even-if-I-*not*-same-*now** ... *you-MAKE-me-*feel*-same* -

Jake had tears streaming down his face now, openly and with no shame he let them come stronger, there seemed to be no end of them. He leaned forward and gave her a soft kiss on her forehead and turned away and walked out of the barn, he headed for the river, wiping his face on his shirt's sleeves—first one and then the other. Jade wiped her own tears on the back of her wrist, being that she had no long sleeves today, as she watched him go, somehow she just *couldn't* seem to stop the flow of hers, either. It was a twin-thing, she reckoned.

She sat peaceful, yet poised, now. Her face was smeared black from her eyeliner, and her fake lashes were loose, but she didn't care, she would follow his lead—soon—just as she always did. A few minutes later. They were equal—she belonged by his side.

Well, now—there is something about a river that no words can quite describe. It does something very special to the spirit and soul. As it moves on its journey to places far-off that one may never see, it yet stays *stationary* in the heart as to the first place-and-time that one met up with it. Here was the first place that the twins had met-up-with the Fisher River. They had discovered it on their own, as their folks checked out the property. This spot forever stuck in their minds, as, "the river". Whether it changed or not, according to the snow and rainfall, it was still "the river". It was the *river*, to their close buddies, too, though in a different way. And, through the years they came to learn that it was the *river* to many others, in many other places—in many different shapes, and depths, through happy times or sorrows. But this was the piece of the river that they loved the most. There is a lot that one can learn, just from a small portion of a river—and if so, how much *more* so—from the whole river itself. They had learned a lot about themselves just sitting by this river. Why, they had a *river* of experiences *inside* themselves. They had a *river* of experience to give—and more to learn from future encounters with its *inner* flow. And, their *inner* river reached-out and shared-out, too, to their buddies and others, as this private spot always did for the two of them. Even so, the *larger* portions of their *inner* river even reached-out its sharing to many *unknown* others, some just in passing, and others that would perhaps even one day share their lives—same as the Fisher River boasted of doing, to those that met up with it, rightly said. Moving in *their* unique ways, their *inner* river was subject to changes at times, too, yet it was still "their unique river" that did the sharing. Jake now shared his thoughts of the river with Jade, flowing in signs, until she shared in return:

"You know, Jet… " Jade smiled with joy, "there *is* one other thing rivers are good for besides soul-searching." She walked over and splashed at him.

* Fishing!*   -he signed, with a laugh. *'Do I get an A+, now sis?'* he thought to her.

"No, silly... swimming!" She took off her boots and slipped in. It was too slippery for walking, so she had to just slip-on-in with care, or *slip* in the "hard" way, as she always put it:

"Come on Jet, take a slip!" She smiled from the waters, as she floated down stream a bit, and came crawling-out to do a re-try, beckoning him over. Dwelling only on childhood memories, she was free in such play.

Jake thought, *'aw, sis... come on... you're just like a big kid. Just like me! This ain't play time... it's thinkin' time.'* Jake went up to her, and took off his boots and then took off his shirt to hand it to her as a towel, but she pulled him in to the deeper spot that she had just crawled out of. Naturally, he slipped on in—well, minus the shirt which he luckily was able to toss ashore, to join-up with his land-loving Stetson. The shirt would later be up for grabs, as they would race after it and the chase would be on, with the winner getting to use it as a towel. Jade knowing her brother couldn't run in any way that would catch her speed, would be stopping-and-starting along the way back home, though, as a good twin should.

After such a fine run, as had come to pass, the house was mighty inviting, as they set-about to seek a change of clothes now. The swim and the playtime did them both good. This was a wonderful re-ride as to the ushering-in of May. Jade now believed it was purposely planned this way— no one else was home. She was near cleaned-up and dressed, and it was past noon. Kitchen thoughts, and cooking, were in her mind, when she suddenly froze at the sound of pots and pans crashing to the kitchen floor. Her heart jumped. Seizures had near-been fully forgotten!

"Jet... Jet... I'm COMING!" She was near-set to take her time, but since the November seizures mingled-among-pans, somehow she could *never* be casual again. She ran down in a flash, she was sure he was all right, she really was—wasn't she? Could the medication be failing?

Jade ran into the kitchen and was face-to-face with Jake leaning-back on the edge of the counter with a grin on his face, wearing a fine *new* black Stetson—swinging—a *whistle*.

"So, JAKE SMITH, you finally got tired of having to pick up my pots and pans, huh...? I see you got your *hat* on, Jet."

She waded over to him through the pots and pans, and gave him a friendly little tug on the front brim, "Sure suits you big brother... truly it does, Jet," she said fondly, as she banded-up her one wet braid, and started to fix the rest of her loose wet hair to match.

Jake gently kicked a pot out of the way, and went over to the table, and showed her the box. *twins* ... *why?* ... *?* -he signed with a loopy question mark in the air, and goofy eyes.

"It was your *birthday* present from way *back* in July, but it was back-ordered all this time... seems they had it special-made, but the owner was out of town. The twins' got the size from me, naturally," she smiled, batting her fresh false eye lashes at him. "Guess you could call it an *early* birthday present now, as birthday-time will be here in three months! Or maybe, it just may be a *May-Day* present... and a right-fine one at that!"

She was surprised at the enthusiasm in her voice just now, and reflected on their day and the course that it had taken thus far:

"Kind of like a seal of approval... for your first year back home... " she added, as she finished banding-up her other wet braid, and looked up at him with a soft gentle smile. With a gentle wink back, he reached over and gave both braids a tug, at the same time, as if the cute distraction may help him sneak off. He made his move to sneak away, as she smiled and flipped both braids backward, over her shoulder, with her usual fancy skill, and turned and *caught* him.

"Oh no you don't, Jet! Now... after you finish *picking-up* my pots and pans, I could use them for to fix-up some late lunch, while YOU go figure-out how you want to use that whistle... outside seems best to me, for now anyways... now speed it up, and shewww!"

Jade followed and watched her brother through the backdoor's window, as he and his pup walked out into the yard. She continued there at the door and watched as he sat at the old picnic table near the open woodshed, just to her right (east) of the door. She slipped silently back into the kitchen and spent the next hour cooking.

When she came out to call him in, she was surprised to see him at the round corral, leaning over the rail, and apparently in deep thought.

He turned and showed her "s-o-s" on the whistle, he was surprised how it had come to remembrance, since it had been years since they used it in play, as kids. Jade had tried to teach him some Morris code, recently, from a book a while back. She had hoped he could have used it for drawing out notes, but he couldn't retain it and got bad headaches, but—this "s-o-s" seemed to come out of his past with odd ease—he was so *very* pleased, that it had. At least it was something that perhaps someone *else* could understand.

He also showed Jade "three whistles" for the house, as it was so large, "two whistles" for the barn or horse area—and "one" for her. If these were heard, then anyone near hearing-range was expected to show-up in the said-respected places, he informed her. And, of course, long, over-and-over repetitions were for emergencies.

"So I only get *one*, huh?"

"*y*/~oo ... *special!*" -he laughed, and sealed it with a tap on her nose. *'Besides, sis, what do you think you'd DO to me if I dared to loudly blow this fool whistle more than ONCE in your kitchen? Best we not be finding out!'*

"So... now that our whistle-business is over with... what were you thinking so *heavy* on... just a bit ago, Jet?" She said as she looked off over their pastureland and up into the big blue Montana sky.

Jade's mood had become slightly solemn; she then turned and watched her twin lean back on the corral. It was still hard for her to look at the corral, or to even go into the backyard, and she usually avoided it completely (as Jake did) or ventured as far as the picnic table, only. Then, there she would sit facing the boat shed that was down the incline, just before the barn. So far, their "May 1st" had been blossoming into a far better potential than last year, and she hated to see its fresh bud get frostbit, out of season—or worse yet, clipped off—as a *new* bud possibly may not bloom again until clear-up to their July birthdays.

As no answer came, now she was a mite worried that she had even sought to ask—but she *had*.

'I'm thinkin', Jade... I'm thinkin'... I'm thinkin' that it's a good thing my thoughts have found some kind of ways to slip under that stuck barn door... It ain't the same as talking, and it will never be. I'm thinkin'... and THAT'S all. But it's just as REAL and as IMPORTANT to me as any words that would bust-out through that stuck barn door of my mouth... if they could.'

Jake played with the cold metal whistle and rolled it around in his hand—his newest tool to replace words. He sure wished he had his tongue instead. He was nearly lost in thought again as he was tempted to wonder how it felt to make words—he seemed to have forgotten—and loops of faint recollections were pulling him deeper down the-inner-hallways-of-his-mind, when he heard his sister's voice. She had waited long enough, and had staunchly decided that she had opened a wrong door, a door that led *too* far back—*best be closing it for now*, she reckoned:

"Come on Jet, it can wait... " she said with a determined gentleness in her voice, "your little shadow, 'harper', here, is hungry... see, look at him."

She tried the gentle nudge of big dark pup-eyes this time—as a subject change—as her *new* worry now was that she had waited *too* long, to fix her blunder, and at this point she wasn't sure if his thoughts were best left to play-out indeed, or still opt for the "subject change" and all its cuteness.

'Harper...' Jake thought as he bent down to respond to him, *'harper? Yeah... he's a heck of harper, all right. Harper. Jes' Harper, that's all... suits me jes' fine... as he's a constant reminder as he harps on my memories in a healin' sort of way... every time I think on that day... and that bull. Yeah...'* Jake started to think hard-and-heavy now and slowly stood, as he turned back to the round corral, and then turned farther, and stared-out over the wonderful north pasture and on up to his north and northwest ridge, graced by his crop of woods against the skyline:

Yeah... there's ways set-up for a man to walk in, and if we follow, we'll end-up right where we belong. If someone tries to stomp those goals out of our reach... and stomp on the Stetson-of-our-heart-and-soul, somehow, in the full scheme-of-things, we'll end-up right back on track. I'm back on track... and I'll finish course to the end of my trail. Even if it means facing the trail-drives and the trail-rides again... somehow I'll do it. It may be... that it won't be in May... but it just may be REAL soon. Summer ain't far off... as I can feel it warmin' my face just now.

Jake roped his last thoughts in:

Seems I used to know a man named Jake Smith... seems I thought I LOST-HOLD of him somewheres. Seems now... I do know a man named Jake Smith... seems he's been here all the time. I may be different... but somehow... I'm findin' that my underlying-current is still the same, and it's headin' in the right direction still. Sure ain't easy... sure ain't fun at times either... but I ain't LOST no more... and that, I rightly-know.

Jake let his mind roam the heavens this time, as he smiled up towards the big blue sky of Montana—same patch where his sister had just finished setting *her* mind free-to-run-and-roam. Truly said, he was a mite overwhelmed, *' maybe... maybe someday I'll be settin' my mind to roam Texas skies once again as well... yeah...maybe... just may be.'*

As he felt the sun *warm* upon his face, from between the high-up wispy-clouds—as if a *reply* sent *gentle* from above—he moved to face the round corral again, and he thought with a deep sincere reverence, concerning his desire for his beloved Texas:

'I just need a few more gentle nudges... from a high-up and Gentle Hand.'

A hand on a much *less* grand-a-scale, now slipped itself under Jake's arm socket, and a small face with searching dark-doe-eyes, and long dark braids, gently nudged his.

Jake put his arm around the shoulder that belonged to the small hand and face, of his little nudging twin, as they walked into their house—together—followed by Harper, and the good Lord's warm sun upon their backs.

———

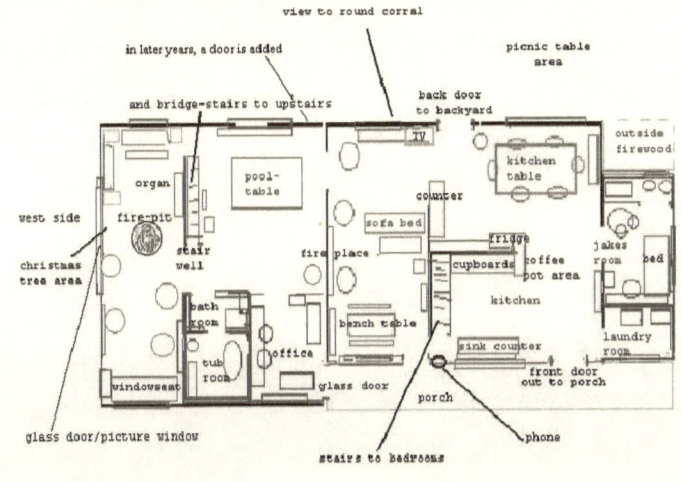

JAKE SMITH'S RANCH HOUSE – MAP FOR ADVENTURES

414 - By Neebeeshaabookway - JAKE SMITH RANCH SERIES...

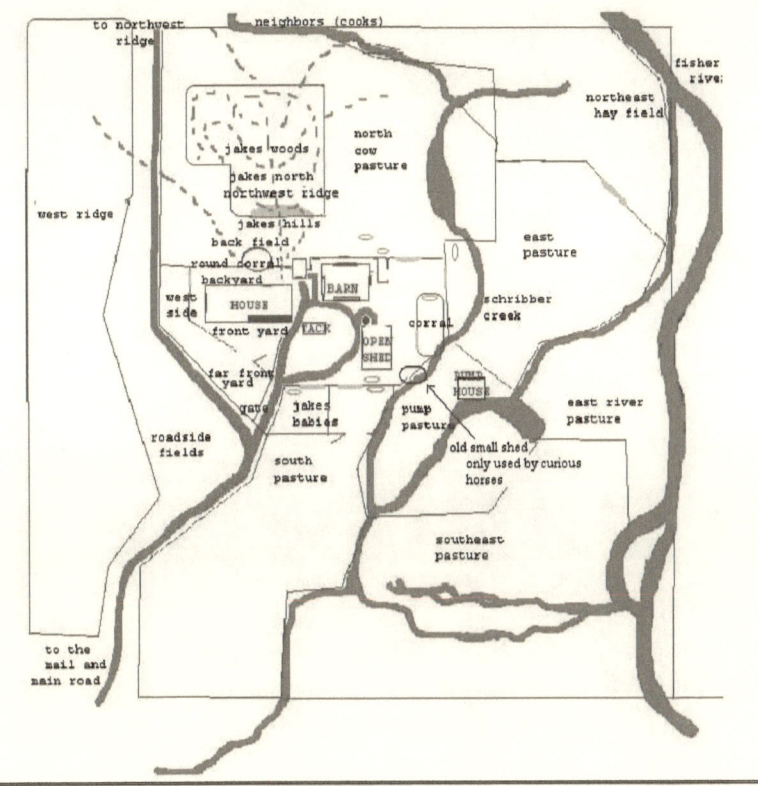

JAKE SMITH RANCH LAND – MAP FOR ADVENTURES

416 - By Neebeeshaabookway - JAKE SMITH RANCH SERIES...

JAKE SMITH'S WRITING CODE - FROM JADE

~	ER -As, a bit of fur.
!	OI -As, a drop of oil.
@	I (long vowel) -As, an eye.
#	A (long vowel) -As, a gate.
$	ING -As, a spring.
%	O (long vowel) -As, two holes.
^	OO (for h<u>oo</u>t, who, etc.) -As, a tunnel to go through.
&	EU, EUE (for c<u>ou</u>ld, b<u>oo</u>k, etc.) -As, the only sound he COULD rope.
*	OW -As, a flower.
+	TH -As, a thorn.
=	EE -As, an even ease-way.
CC	CH -As, chain links.
>	SH -As, shooting arrows.

A, E, I, O, U   (apple, egg, ink, ox, cup) (these sounds never change)
Y   (yes)

T^ M@ FL*~.
S~PR@Z.
@ L~ND # W# T^ R@T T^ Y^.
HAP= B~+D#.
M@ +OTZ O~ N* ON P#P~.
N* @ HAV M%~ W#Z T^ TOK.
@ LUV Y^ S%F=U.

Jake writes and reads using capital letters, but he can recognize some lower case letters.
FROM: JAKE HUGS TEXAS, by Neebeeshaabookway

418 - By Neebeeshaabookway - JAKE SMITH RANCH SERIES...

* Songs that are in some way quoted or referred to, or used to prod the characters in some way, in the JAKE SMITH RANCH SERIES, and "INTRODUCING…"

The Unclouded Day... Josiah K. Alwood
I'm So Lonesone I Could Cry... Hank Williams
Kiss An Angel Good Morning... Charlie Pride
Thank God I'm A Country Boy… John Denver
Forever And Ever, Amen... Randy Travis
Cross My Heart... George Strait
He U'i... (ua kakau 'ia e) Danny Kua'ana
Aloha No Wau I Kou Maka... Hawaiian composition by, Leleiohoku
Stand By Your Man... Tammy Wynette
A Good Hearted Woman... Waylon Jennings
Remember When... Alan Jackson
Deep In The Heart Of Texas... June Hershey
It Must Be Love... Alan Jackson
Tall Tall Trees... Alan Jackson
Let Your Love Flow... Bellamy Brothers
Just To Be Your Man... Josh Turner
God Blessed Texas... Little Texas
Deeper Than The Holler... Randy Travis
I Like It, I Love It... Tim McGraw
Good Ride Cowboy... Garth Brooks
Act Naturally… Buck Owens
I Will Sail My Vessel... Garth Brooks
I Ain't As Good As I Once Was... Toby Keith
The Broken Roads... Rascal Flatts
(What A) Wonderful World... Sam Cooke
That Girl Is A Cowboy... Garth Brooks
Living On Love... Alan Jackson
Louisiana Nights... Mel McDanial
Have You Ever Really Loved A Woman... Bryan Adams
I Don't Know A Thing About Love… Conway Twitty
Building Bridges... Brooks and Dunn
Me And God… Josh Turner and Dr. Ralph Stanley
It Just Comes Natural... George Strait
Friends In Low Places... Garth Brooks
She Don't Like My Kind Of Music… Ray Scott
My Heart Skips A Beat… Buck Owens
The Ride… Sonny Tillis and Sam Weedman, sung by Chris LeDoux
Bareback Jack… Chris LeDoux
Small Town Country Man… Alan Jackson
Thank God I'm a Country Boy… John Denver

420 - By Neebeeshaabookway - JAKE SMITH RANCH SERIES...

THE JAKE SMITH RANCH SERIES PICTURE
-STORY LIST -

JAKE
('I'm thinkin'...')

JAKE AND SOFIA

JAKE HUGS TEXAS

STEPPINGSTONES
THROUGH JAKE'S RANCH
- in volumes -

40 years later-   JAKE'S RANCH AND THE SECOND GATE

The Jake Smith Ranch Series, by Neebeeshaabookway !

THE JAKE SMITH RANCH SERIES CONTINUES NEXT,
WITH:

- JAKE AND SOFIA -

Preview for:

JAKE AND SOFIA

424 - By Neebeeshaabookway - JAKE SMITH RANCH SERIES...

~*~ CHAPTER SIX ~*~

FIREWORKS, SPARKLES AND AMAZING MESSAGES IN THE NIGHT

(Taken from: JAKE AND SOFIA, pages 75-83)

needing to be saved himself. Later, he used his truck again, it had been in October, *about* four months after he had his last seizure (so *he* thought) and *about* five months since he had been home from the hospital. Sadly a few weeks later, right in the middle of this hard, fall season of ranch work, the seizures manifested again, finally leading to Jake's yielded will, and the acceptance of medication. But he was as free as a got-loose hound then, on both truck and horse, with buddies or without, as he was certain his hated seizures were under control. Jade was just as near as free herself, since she was the one that did the most worrying, as she usually had a front row seat of his seizures (so *she* thought).

~*~

As much as Jake and Jade hated medicines from their ma's old-fashioned ways, he wished now that it was working for him again. It had taken a lot of situations for Jake to yield to that medicine, and after finally realizing he needed it, now he was feeling at-a-loss as to what was to become of himself. Those weeks of June, it seemed the new dosage of medication they were using was too strong, or affected him slightly wrong. Maybe he just wasn't eating enough yet, since his bad move playing chess-game-trail-drive. Maybe the doctors would still find the right fixings for him, and he would be able to carry on again—maybe. For now, he was somewhere in between his regular dosage that he started out with in November, and the dosage that was keeping him in an early hibernation of sorts. He was eating much better again—well, as of the last four days. The doctors told him, there was still hope that a happy medium could be reached, but many things effect head injuries, and things can change due to many unknown hidden causes. Still, if he had been free for six months, their hope was that he would see freedom for another six months after some adjusting, and who knows, others have seen success for years, and finally rare freedom. Jake didn't yet know, if he would be one of the *few* fortunate others. For now, though, he did his very best to not forget how very thankful he was that he still had his brain-learning of the past 41 years, and the knowledge of his wonderful twin, buddies, and even something new—a fiancée.

He looked out the backdoor now, at that fiancée. He wondered if he should allow THAT to be taken back too, as he watched her playing in the yard with Harper. A more beautiful sight he had never seen, not yet anyway—deep in his spirit he was hit by a heavy jolt, as he realized he would regret it all his born days, if he let her be taken back. He had a choice in this matter; she wasn't a truck or a horse. But then, a truck or a horse never personally judged him for his seizures, or lack of speech, or full comprehension. A woman-gal, could. He suddenly felt vulnerable, but should he? The fight with his inner confusion was on; the best man would win. Trouble now was—who was the best man? The old talking Jake? The new muted Jake? A combination of Jake from both past and current—or *maybe* it was the Jake of the future. The Jake that was *still* growing off the rootstock of the Jake that the good Lord saw him as—the Jake he always was, always would be, and was meant to be. As he continued to stare out the back door, distressed by the thoughts from the back of his mind, he suddenly realized that he had lost track of Sofia, his little flower must have bent its boughs back into the bushes with the breeze or something. Wondering where she was now, he took a closer look through the windowpane of the door. Startled, he was face-to-face with Sofia, as she smiled through the windowpane and through all the list of possible pains—as fragile as the list of various panes of glass—and saw the love of her life, Jake Smith, for who he was now. Jake now smiled back with joy, it came forth beaming and overflowing from his heart; whatever it was she saw in him just *now*—he loved it. Yep, little did he understand how *simple* it was to fully understand her heart and what she was giving, but, he *fully* knew *this* much—he loved it. Even less, did he understand that Stoney was sneaking up on him—and Stoney loved it! Loving it—triple-hits; revelations of a most fun kind!

"Well get OUT there lover-boy!" Stoney's words shook him, as Jake near hit his head on the glass pane, and Sofia let out a harmless laugh on the other side, watching him.

He grinned back at her, and flashed a few signed "okays" at Stoney, after he first stepped back and dramatically held his ears, as if his eardrums had felt the effects of Stoney's surprise-announcement, clear through his body down to his boot heels! Jake loved to be dramatic at times with his new way of talking—it helped him forget the fix he was in. It helped him forget his old quirky, fun way with words, his clever insights that he often shared, and the goofing around that he had so much loved to do when the mood hit him on occasion. Well, it *had* to be on *occasion*, as he wasn't about to be seen as a goofy cowboy, he was firm, solid, and stable, and honorable as the day and night was long, combined. He just had his fun-loving moments, was all—now he had to have them in a different kind of way—if the mood hit at all. And, to the shock and pleasure of the whole gang at the Smith's place and in town, the fun-loving moods would still hit, and the Jake they knew and loved was starting to walk in his old boots again.

Jake opened the door just as Sofia did, and she fell into his arms and looked up at him with a startled smile, asking, "Didn't your mother ever tell you to open doors cautiously, cowboy?" He kissed her, as proof of his gallantry, and a gentle touch on her forehead it was, and casually he let her slip back onto the porch. He had to, naturally, as he needed to free-up his hands to talk to his beloved. Plus he thought "flowers" looked right pretty sitting on backyard porches, especially when they were looking up at him.

not-that-I-remember -Jake signed in reply, '*hhmmm... my ma told me a LOT about doors, Sofia. Yet, I don't think she ever TOLD me that pretty gals could fall through them. I seen a cow-or-two bust-through barn doors though... and even a few horses... and one even busted-through the tack-shed door on occasions,* Jake thought with a quiet laugh.

"Jake Smith... what's your secret that you're laughing about now? Are you going to share with me?" she asked coyly. "Is it about pretty gals, falling into your arms?" She reached up and pulled him down to her side, as Stoney peeked out and watched the boss-man. Stoney was hit with a whole sack full of memories, stale as old grain, and moseyed off to sit at the kitchen table as he nursed his guilty hurting soul, with a cold cup of coffee.

'*Well, actually, little darlin'... it is about a pretty gal and doors and my arms... only THIS here gal, was gentle Jen's sis... and she was none to gentle... and my arms were full-up of her as I tried my best to push her out of that ol' tack-shed. I reckon it took me about near 25 minutes to do so!*' He laughed again, with the memory. Jake suddenly realized she was watching and waiting as these thoughts flew by, which should have been words, so he caught them for her, as he did a *rerun* of a re-ride, and repeated what he already "would-have if he could-have" presented:

long-time-back-years-back ... *my-horse* ... *her-sister* ... *she-insist-and-push* ... *push-into-shed* ... *to-see-me* -Jake pointed over to the tack-shed, to make sure she knew which place he meant.

~*~

He had never shown her a sign for tack-shed yet, as it had never come up between them. He had his own sign for a lot of stuff on his ranch. They were combinations of the ASL, and his own ideas of what helped him think clear, as his mind at times, got stuck, and he had to do a quick rewind, thus starting again. Everything would be fine, if he remembered any new-learned signs by easy to see shapes, or personal matching thoughts or feelings that he had toward the objects—fast-ball recollections, it was then, as he called it!

~*~

Jake continued his beloved horse thoughts, *if-you-see-me-then* ... *during-that-situation* ... *very-much-fun-and-very-much-funny* ... *she-too-big-for-me-*dance*-with-in-that-little-room* ... *finally-*dance*-finished* ... *I-push-her-outside* ... *only-because-I-stuff-horse-treats-in-my-shirt pocket* ... *she-smell-them-as-I-push-and-she-yield* ...*yield-to-*dance*-out-with-me* -As Jake *acted* his way with some gestures through his whole story, he was satisfied that Sofia understood, and he took a bow, and tipped his Stetson as he then stood tall. Yet afterwards, it seemed his heart was stooping just a bit, and not matching-up to his tall-standing desires. *It sure didn't sound like I planned it to sound... it sure didn't match how I thought of it first... but that's the best way I could get it out, so it will have to do. Sofia sure seemed to understand, and she enjoyed me tellin' her with a bit of dancing fun, to boot,* Jake thought, as he helped her up. He couldn't help but notice Stoney move away from the back kitchen dining-window. Jake peeked in from the outside corner of the window, unseen. Stoney had gone back to his coffee and was sitting with his head in his hands now, and slowly lowered himself onto the table. Sofia saw Jake's face twist in sorrow's grip now, and reached out her arm offering him a solid anchor—herself—by which she had *learned* by watching Jade. Gentleness was good, but more was needed now, to lay-weight to the shifting-thoughts at high-sea. Jake accepted her strength and looked at her—as he looked back, Stoney was gone. Jake looked into her eyes, and spoke words to her that his face was now becoming adept at, and she nodded yes in return—she knew that fun time was now over. A rescue was on-the-spur, and he was now able.

From the midst of their interweaving, Jake was gone, he was off to fish his dear friend out of the sinkhole of despair. As Jake knew, Ray had a pretty good lure to *hook* this stony fish as to *counseling* it, but Jake had the best bait, it was himself—after all, he was the hero that had been damaged trying to save Stoney. He knew full-well what he was doing that day, drunk or not. Stoney needed him now, and Sofia was learning that this was to be an ever-present part of the Jake that was to be her lifelong partner. She had her *own* ever-present things of the past to deal with, and Jake knew that well. Between the two of them, the deep waters of these currents of hurt, passed and intertwined, and as the currents surfaced anew, the waters spread out into strong clean flows of unison, and flowed in the same direction. The direction of a new full life, going in a new direction, to the fullness of an outpouring of compassion towards each other, as living souls—and to their needs—and the needs of those around them. There *were* no selfish currents running on the Smith Ranch. Any such streams would be thoroughly cleaned or routed-off, as only the streams of water that refreshed the good-of-all and healed any-and-all wounds with fresh sparkle, were what was treasured here. Their folks had taught them this, and these waters had always run strong here, they were running extra strong here now, since January 2000, when Jake lay dying in the backyard, leaving *all* terribly wounded from what caused it. Sofia came into the picture late, with her own wounds, and deep they were, although from other hurts, in other ways. Other ways, caused her to fit in right-fine here and now. Otherwise, there would not have been that instant bond, in heart and mind, the day they met. Jake saw it in her eyes, he knew that she could understand the road he'd be taking. Sofia saw it in his eyes, that he would not hurt her petals or take her down that road of hurt that she had finally bend able to turn off of. The "eyes" were the majority, in unison, over the nays that never did appear. The eyes agreed. Nary a nay would appear, in truth. Although the mirrors of the soul knew that there were no nays, the mirror is only a *reflection* of the full knowledge of truth, thus causing Jake and Sofia a few weak moments of self-doubt—as if tests. One is allowed a slight doubt, if one can do their best in the eyes of truth, to pursue and understand it—if truth is accepted and believed as the truth it is. Which for them, it was—and truly so—then one will succeed to live up to it, if one chooses to. As—truth has a way of blatantly spilling out to light, *even* if one has NO IDEA what truth, of any kind, is.

    Jake couldn't figure where Stoney had gone to, he scanned the yard. Then it dawned on him, he must have gone around the side of the house, and made his way up to the hills somehow unseen. *The hills, I know it... he's gone to the northwest ridge, in back... like his first day back, the day of the barbecue.* Jake remembered how he had dragged Stoney up there when they were finally reunited, and he now came back to the backyard as Sofia watched him pass by her and head out, *after* he climbed over the pasture fence. She wished him God's special speed. She went off herself, to look for Jade in the basement. She'd be working, and work seemed to be a good thing to do right about now, surely it would keep her mind off the hard work facing Jake and Stoney. After the fourth of July, Sofia would be back working for Sheriff Lenny, at least for awhile, until Sofia felt secure enough to let it go. Jake didn't mind, although he would love to have her working on the ranch. Money would be only as tight as before, and she would add to his life more with her presence, than with her banking-checks.

It was near supper now, as Jake and Stoney came down out of the hills. Stoney and Jake were just like a couple of frisky pups, and Harper loved this most of all. A bewildered Sofia, wasn't quite sure what to think of this, Stoney and Jake seemed that they hadn't a care in the world, and *sorrows* had seemed to have been non-existent. So, she did what folks do with odds and ends—one put them on the shelf until one understand just *what the heck* to do with them—finally giving them a place of their own. After supper, out on the porch, the whole gang was out enjoying the stars. Matt and Galena turned in early, there was going to be lots to do tomorrow on the fourth. Johnny Walker was going to be having his party going-on in Old-Town, their stomping grounds, and this year the Smiths were past recuperation, and on to restoration, and would be back in the saddle of his party there, gang and all.

Ray was here tonight, he had just dropped in after supper, as was his habit quite often to join with the night talks, catching up on any missed events, and the missed camaraderie. The three-musketeer spirit, in the three bears, was now the four musketeers, as big brother bear had arrived. Big brother was here come evening, more often than not, until Jake's accident. Jade wanted him here, but he had backed-off. He played his role, with care, and stayed behind the scenes until Jake was ready for Matt and Stoney. Ray was an anchor for Jake, but he knew Jake had to untangle his tack, and then ride tall, yet deep, and accept his buddies back home. *This* year was to be *their* time, but it had been hard for Ray to get over for his visits, he had been stretching himself thin, and was just as precious as fine honey to them. Between the Smiths tragedy, and continuing the trail-rides and trial-drives, he had his own ranch to catch up on now. But each time he finally made it over, these four buddies were in the center ring displaying their skills in smooth unison, they worked as brothers would, each knowing their proper function without being told. Juggling all the problems of the day, displaying themselves as the team that they were:

'One for all, and all for one... still including Jade when the day was done.'

Including Jade? Well, that was *their* motto, and Jade made sure they KNEW it. If truth be known, *many* a time, this group was shadowed by her. TWIN for twin and twin for TWIN, equals a highly polished team. Jake and Jade were inseparable, and there would be no challenge to her place in their

group. If Jake or Jade ever chose to add on a mate—or any of the other
bears—fine and dandy, but the motto stayed, and mates were only the
"understoods", yet equally as precious, none the less. They'd just drag the
extra companions right along, fine and dandy-fine. Matt had done so with
Galena, and soon, Jake, Ray, and Stoney would as well. Well, actually, Jade
would be *Stoney's* drag-around companion, from their cowboy standpoint,
when the time came, but she would NOT be yielding her place as Jake's
certified shadow.

Ray, as big brother, was getting down to business now. Seems he
needed some help. "Jake, since Matt will be doing his last day at Lenny's
tomorrow before the party, and ready to tackle kids and cows, how about
you and Stoney helping me get the cows ready for their return trail-drive...
back to where they were dropped-off? Marsh will be out at his buddies'
place. Seems that even though he doesn't have a girl friend, and he keeps
playing the field, there's an old flame of his out that way, with his kid... and
she's been *hoping* to see him. He wants to see the kid too, so I've come to
know. Since he moved back to these parts now, he's been visiting him... I
think he's starting to get a guilty conscious about neglecting him these last
few years. He used to work at the O'Rourke's old ranch, and his buddies
live near there, so does the gal. I think it just might make a change in him
some day... soon I hope... as you know, he can be a real jerk at times, but
he's family and a good worker."

Ray knew Marsh was a sore spot with Jake now, and intended to keep
his best friend safe from any hardship. *Family* was not even allowed to ruin
his relationship with Jake, who was as dear as a brother to Ray—that was
proven many times over, in the dealings of his sister Angie and Jake—Jake
always came out the winner, in Ray's book. The test of their many loyal
years, had been what held the Smith-gang together through Jake's accident.

Jake paced a bit nervously, yet, he knew Ray wasn't going to rope
him into anything he couldn't handle, he had ALREADY DONE THAT.
But, but in full-out truth, he had *let* Jade and Ray rope him into his last
troubles because of Matt needing help. This was just down-home simple
stuff, he didn't see any harm in helping Ray with something so natural as
this. Ray had always gone above and beyond duty for him and Jade. Stoney
quietly watched, as he rolled a pencil back and forth on the kitchen counter,
he didn't like to do anything to influence Jake now, since he felt to blame for
the mess Jake's life was in, as such, he sure didn't want to risk adding to it.
A rolling Stoney, would gather no mess—it was Ray's turn to gamble again.

"Go ahead, Jet, you love working with them cows, and that's a strong-
hoofed fact and you know it." Jade smiled, "Ray will keep a good eye on

you, he promised me. I know you been a bit frustrated since the changes going on with your medication. Go on then, be a wranglin' cowpoke for a few hours, Jet... you know you'll love it... he DID ask me first, you know. You ain't going to hurt me with worries now, Jet." She looked at her twin with the trust he had come to know since their youth, she even sealed it with her heart, as she slipped her hand into the familiar home, under his right arm socket and nudged his shoulder with her chin. He grabbed her braid in return, and twisted it around in his hand, as his wrinkled brow remembered all her fearful looks that followed his many seizures. Looks that he was tired of witnessing from hospital beds.

"Sofia can meet up with you later at Johnny's," she continued, as she left him and moseyed over to the front stairs for to fetch her slippers— comforts of the slipping-in-type were warming her happy mind.

"I'll keep her busy with Galena and the baby, as we cook some potted-up luck, and we'll all meet for the fireworks later. Our cows will be in for the day... and we sure don't need dirty ol' cowboys to help with the cookin'... you know... you wrangle them, we cook 'em!" she laughed as she leaned against the sink, in her very unclean clothes, fumbling around to kick her boots off for the night. "You can rinse off at Rays, he knows how to pad the tub."

Jade had seen her twin's troubles all through June. They were written all over his face, even more clearly than his faded scars and the tale that they told. She hurt for him because of this waiting period, as to the medication, but there was nothing she could do, it was still in the hands of the doctors for now. Maybe this bit of freedom to feel normal again would help. Jake playing hero for Ray, seemed good-right now.

She also had to do this during his first months being home, and it had been hard. She had to learn he was still a grown man, and she had to let him be free to face the risk in his own way. He had faced the bull by choice, for Stoney's life. She had to let him face the life he now had to live, or this new life would be worthless to him, in the long run—and so would he. She would never be able bear it and would join him in the ruin—pulling all down-with, from the powerful wake.

Jake looked off over his shoulder, as Sofia nodded with approval, while then flinging her head back, brushing her now-opened, habitually-one-sided dark braid. She had taken the baby-breath flowers out of it now and loosened it, for brushing. It was a cascading waterfall of rich Texas tea— dark, softly-kinked-up, tresses of hair—which was now distracting him something fierce. He wanted to bury his face in it, and hug her preciously.

Well, one can imagine. After being a gentleman for so many years, in honor of his ma—in honor of the good ol' cowboy ways that he grew up watching on TV—why, he was a mite *surprised* how his gentlemanly ways kept wanting to play rodeo and take a wild shoot-the-moon with his well-fashioned intended. So—he tenaciously, tenderly intended to keep these intentions attended-to, attentively. As her hair danced before him, Jake thought on how he had promised his dancing angel some dances during Johnny Walker's party at the SLIPPING SADDLE #1. They even planted his jukebox with some cumbia music along with special country songs for the occasion, *without* neglecting Jade and her desire for drums! After thinking on this, he was near ready to pick HER over the cows, and stay home—but he didn't. He knew that Ray's birthday was added on to the Fourth of July party, as his birthday was on the fifth, so this would be a nice pre-party time, well spent, helping a good buddy, as a gift of friendship.

    okay … *appears-good-for-me* … *now-Sofia-and-me-we-need-our-nightly-walk-under-those-stars*   -Jake signed, with a smirk, '*if you get my drift... Ray.*'

    Jake signed off, with a final salute to Ray, and nodded towards Sofia, she quickly glided like a soft summer breeze and joined up along side him. He had a wonderful little stroll in mind, a delight for any gal. A romantic stroll, to match any city-slickered-up courting-man's. A stroll along the horse rail, under the stars, listening to the happy grunts and snorts of those horses, one of which stood her ground firm, during one of Jake's seizures and guarded his whereabouts, during another. One, that had even lent her sister out, as it tried to dance Jake over a barrel, toward a ton of treats. One of which, at a time upon Jake's homecoming, had witnessed Jake throwing his hat down in deep turmoil, as he realized it hurt him to high-heaven, to know that he'd never talk to her again—not *here* in the fenced pasture, nor out on the *trail*—not ever.

    I just love a good woman and a good horse... why, heck, I just love a good woman that LOVES a good horse, fact is... I love a good horse, but I love a good woman in a whole different sort of a good way, and I sure do want to let her know, and in a right-good way. Milling on stuff such as *this*, was just great for romantic walks, one would reckon—and walk, they did—with Jake milling-up food for romance.

    Jake stopped his walk, on the homeward stretch and took her in his arms. '*I wish I could say more to you than I feel I can. I always wished I had a woman to say special things to. I had all kinds of little treasures to share. I never seemed to catch the train though, I missed all the gals that I thought I had a feelin' for. Now I got the right one... the right one... and I can't even talk to you. Maybe if I never talked in my whole life, this wouldn't be so hard on me, Sofia, as that would be the real me, the me I know. But I DID used to talk... I REALLY DID... and I did a whole heap of it, and I loved it. I LOVE TALKIN', do you see what I'm tryin' to say Sofia? Aww, heck, darlin', I know you don't. I'll sit and sign it all out to sometime, you know I will, but I want to hold you and whisper this stuff in our ear, and I want to point at things, and shout them out to you, with my voice. I had a right-nice voice, so they all say... but dang it, I sure don't remember it none, it's been only a year... barely over... and I only remember this awful noise that I make now, darlin'... the noise that you know as me... maybe I shouldn't care about how I used to sound, you sure don't care none, now do you, little flower?'*

"Jake, look up there," Sofia said calmly, "the whole host of heaven is up there. It's in the reflection of all those little lights. They may be just

*Thank you for enjoying this preview!

THE JAKE SMITH RANCH SERIES -

Jake's Ranch
And The Second Gate

Jake Hugs Texas

Jake And Sofia

Jake   (*I'm thinkin'...*)

- <u>HELPFUL SCRIPTURE NOTES</u> -

Romans 10:13
For whosoever shall call upon the name of the Lord shall be saved.

Timothy 4:18
And the Lord shall deliver me from every evil work,
and will preserve me unto his heavenly kingdom:
to whom be glory for ever and ever.   Amen.

Philippians 4:13
I can do all things through Christ that strengthens me.

Romans 10:11
For the scripture saith, Whosoever believeth on him shall not be ashamed.

Acts 19:2
He said unto them, Have you received the Holy Ghost since you believed?
And they said unto him, We have not so much as heard
whether there any Holy Ghost.

James 5:16b
The effectual fervent prayer of a righteous man availeth much.

May God bless you – Thank you so very much for reading THE JAKE SMITH RANCH SERIES!

<u>FROM:</u> THE HOLY BIBLE

The King James Version
The World Publishing Company

438 - By Neebeeshaabookway - JAKE SMITH RANCH SERIES...

978-0-578-00939-1
Fiction
© Neebeeshaabookway

440 - By Neebeeshaabookway - JAKE SMITH RANCH SERIES...

www.ingramcontent.com/pod-product-compliance
Lightning Source LLC
Chambersburg PA
CBHW030347030726
47497CB00002B/224